Thomas Kerchever Arnold, George Granville Bradley

A Practical introduction to Latin Prose Composition

Thomas Kerchever Arnold, George Granville Bradley

A Practical Introduction to Latin Prose Composition

ISBN/EAN: 9783337367244

Printed in Europe, USA, Canada, Australia, Japan

Cover: Foto ©Andreas Hilbeck / pixelio.de

More available books at **www.hansebooks.com**

TO

LATIN PROSE COMPOSITION

BY

THOMAS KERCHEVER ARNOLD, M.A.

Edited and Revised

BY

GEORGE GRANVILLE BRADLEY, D.D.

SOMETIME DEAN OF WESTMINSTER

LATE MASTER OF UNIVERSITY COLLEGE, OXFORD
AND FORMERLY MASTER OF MARLBOROUGH COLLEGE

NEW IMPRESSION

LONGMANS, GREEN, AND CO.

39 PATERNOSTER ROW, LONDON

NEW YORK, BOMBAY, AND CALCUTTA

1908

PREFACE

SOME years have passed since I was requested by the Publishers of the late Mr. T. Kerchever Arnold's educational works, to undertake the revision of his *Introduction to Latin Prose Composition.*

The wide and long sustained circulation of the book, both in England and America, was a proof that, whatever might be its defects, its author had provided something which commended itself as a practical aid to an exceedingly large class both of students and teachers of the Latin language.

The task, however, of so revising such a work as to place it on a level with the requirements of the present time I found far more serious than I had expected. The result of much labour, and of more than one unsuccessful attempt to satisfy myself, may be stated broadly as follows :—

In the first place, an Introduction has been prefixed containing three parts, two of which are new, the other much modified.

1. The first of these is an explanation of the traditional terms by which we designate the different "parts of speech" in English or Latin. The exposition is confined to the most simple and elementary points; but it is scarcely necessary to remind any experienced teacher of the extreme vagueness with which the nature of such essential distinctions is often mastered, even by those whose mental training has for years been almost confined to the study of Language.

2. This is followed by a few pages on the Analysis of the Simple and Compound Sentence. Such logical analysis of language is by this time generally accepted as the only basis of intelligent grammatical teaching, whether of our own or of

a 2

any other language. At all events, no teacher, who would care to make trial of the present work, will regret the insertion of a short explanation of the general principle on which all its exposition of syntactical questions is directly founded.

3. I have followed Mr. Arnold's example in prefixing some remarks, retaining so far as possible his own language, on the Order of Words; I have added some also on the Arrangement of Clauses in the Latin Sentence. It is desirable to point out, at the very earliest stage of the learner's progress, not only the great differences between the structure of the two languages in this respect, but also the grounds on which these differences rest, and to indicate the general laws which regulate what may appear to the uninstructed the loose and arbitrary texture of the Latin Sentence.

The matter for translation as comprised in the various Exercises has been almost entirely rewritten. I have not, after full consideration, taken what would have been the easier course, and substituted single continuous passages for a number of separate and unconnected sentences. I found that for the special purpose of the present work, dealing as it does with such manifold and various forms of expression, the employment of these latter was indispensable, and I have by long experience convinced myself of their value in teaching or studying the various turns and forms of a language which differs in such innumerable points from our own as classical Latin.

At the close of the Exercises, I have omitted Mr. Arnold's "List of Differences between English and Latin idioms." As these differences are, or should be, brought home to the reader in almost every line of the present revision of his work, such a list would either convey a false impression of general similarity with occasional disagreement, or would reach a length which would defeat its purpose. It is better that the pupil should learn from the very first, that as a general rule, Latin and English express the same or similar thoughts by a more or less different process, and that a perfectly literal translation of every word in one language by a corresponding word in another will, whether he is translating English into Latin or Latin into English, almost inevitably result in absurdity and solecism.

A few words may be added on the order in which the various subjects treated in the different Exercises are arranged. Some surprise may be caused at its want of scientific method, and apparently of definite principle. It would have been quite possible to have started with exercises on the shortest and most elementary form of the simple sentence; then to have traced its various enlargements through all the manifold uses of the pronouns, oblique cases, uses of adjectives, adverbs, participles, gerunds, and prepositions, and thus to have deferred to the second or rather final portion of the work any notice of the various forms of the compound sentence, of many uses of the infinitive, of even the most ordinary uses of the relative, and of all subordinating conjunctions. I observe that in Seyffert and Busch's last edition of Ellendt's Latin Syntax, the construction of the accusative with the infinitive is not reached till two-thirds of the work have been read, that of the "indirect question" till considerably later. But had I followed this course, the pupil must have been conducted, by the aid of a long series of elaborately constructed specimens of the Simple Sentence, through all the range of usages that could possibly be comprised within its limits. Not till this was done could he have attempted to deal with the very commonest turns of language, such as meet him in every line of natural English, and form the texture of every sentence in Caesar or in Livy. He would have wasted his strength and patience in mounting and descending ladder after ladder of artificial language before he was invited to set foot on the free and natural paths of speech. It is difficult, no doubt, to decide which among the innumerable idioms of a language so unlike our own has the first claim on the attention of the teacher; and the precise order which should be adopted is a matter less of principle than one dictated by various and complex considerations of practical utility. But I have not hesitated to invite the learner, who will follow the guidance of the present work, to leave at a very early period the artificially smoothed waters of such simple sentences as are carefully framed with a view to exclude the most ordinary forms of speech in both English and Latin, and to face as soon as possible the constructions of the Infinitive Mood, of the Relative and Interrogative Pronoun, of the Conjunctional Clause, and some of the main uses of the Subjunctive Mood, and of the Latin, as compared with the English, Tenses. It appears to me that after thus obtaining some firm grasp of the great lines in which the Latin language is modelled under the influence of that great instrument of thought, the Verb, he will be far more likely to notice and retain a permanent impression of the usages and mutual relations of other parts of speech, than if he had followed step by step an opposite system under the guidance of a synthetically arranged Syntax. At the same time, as some amount of systematic arrangement is desirable even on practical grounds, the Exercises have been arranged, as a glance at the Table of Contents will show, in groups of closely related subjects. Such questions as the use of the Cases, and of the various Pronouns, presented considerable difficulty. Placed where they are, they somewhat interrupt the main current of the general teaching on the structure of the Latin sentence, yet I hesitated to relegate them to the end of the book. As it is, I have used them largely, and I hope successfully, not only to elucidate the subject of which they directly treat, but also to renew, impress, and enforce the principles and details laid down in the earlier sections. At the same time there is no reason why the teacher should not postpone their use for a time, and pass on to any of the groups of Exercises which follow.

It only remains that I should express my obligations, not only to the great German Grammarians, including the recently completed *Historische Syntax* of Dr. Draeger, to Schultz's *Synonymik* and Haacke's *Stilistik*, but also to two such English writers on Latin Grammar as Professor Kennedy and Mr. Roby. To the former, eminent alike as a teacher and a writer, I owed, as a comparatively young teacher, my first full perception of the educational value of a systematic study of Latin Syntax as based on the Analysis of the Sentence; to the second volume of Mr. Roby's valuable work I am largely indebted. I may also mention the less obvious but not less real assistance which I have received from the published works and ever ready assistance and guidance of Professor Max Müller; also from Professor Earle's treatise on the Philology of the English tongue, and from some interesting Lectures of Professor Burggraff of Liége.

I must also express my obligations for much help received in an earlier stage of the work from Mr. A. M. Bell of Balliol College; more recently from Mr. F Madan of Brasenose College, and for the great aid given me in shaping the Vocabulary and drawing up the Index, by Mr. T. W. Haddon, late Scholar of my own College.

G. G. BRADLEY.

TABLE OF CONTENTS

[1] See Preface, p. viii.

INTRODUCTION.

THE PARTS OF SPEECH.

1. By Parts of Speech we mean the various classes, or headings, under which all words used in speaking or writing may be arranged.

2. In English Grammars eight are usually enumerated, viz. :—

Noun.	Pronoun.	Adverb.	Conjunction.
Adjective.	Verb.	Preposition.	Interjection.

3. Besides these there is a ninth, the Article, definite and indefinite, *the; an, a.* The former is merely a shortened form of the demonstrative pronoun *that;* the latter two of the numeral adjective *one;* and both may be classed under the adjective.

But in Latin Grammars the list is somewhat different, and it will be more convenient to follow the usual arrangement.

4. There is no Article in Latin, and the Adjective is included under the Noun.

i. Noun { Substantive. Adjective.	iv. Adverb.
ii. Pronoun.	v. Preposition.
iii. Verb.	vi. Conjunction.
	vii. Interjection.

As all these names will be frequently used in the following pages, it is necessary that their meaning and nature should be understood.

The Noun.

5. (i.) The NOUN is the name (*nomen*) which we give to any person, thing, or conception of the mind; for even conceptions we may regard as *things.* We may name such

A

persons or things in two different ways; nouns therefore, or *names*, may be of two kinds.

6. The **Substantive** is a name which we give to a person or thing to distinguish it from other persons and things: Caesar, table, goodness; *Caesar, mensa, virtus.*

It denotes the assemblage, or *sum-total*, of all the qualities by which we recognise such person or thing.

Hence its name (nomen *substantivum*), as a name denoting what was once called the *substantia*, or essential nature of persons and things.

It denotes also something which is looked on as having an existence (*substantia*) by itself.

7. The **Adjective** is a name which we add or apply to a person or thing, to denote some *one quality* which we attribute to it: good, white, small; *bonus, candidus, parvus.*

8. As this one quality may be shared by many persons or things, the adjective is not well fitted to stand by itself as the name for persons or things; many different persons and things might be "good," "white," or "small."

Its proper use, therefore, is either to be attached to the *nomen substantivum*, or general name of an object, so as to define its meaning more closely, as *white* horses, *good* men ; equi *albi*, homines *boni;* or to be *predicated*, that is asserted, of such substantive: the men are *good ;* homines sunt *boni;* in the first case it is called an *attribute*, in the second a *predicate.* Hence its name, nomen *adjectivum;* a name, that is, fitted for adding, or attaching, to another name, from *adjicere*, "to add to."

9. In Latin this *fitness for attachment* or *addition* is even more marked than in English. Latin adjectives have, what the English have not, *inflexions, i.e.* variable terminations of gender, case, and number, which vary with those of the substantive *to* which they are attached, or *of* which they are predicated. Thus *mulier superba; vir est superbus; arbores vidi altas.* In English the adjective has no longer any inflexions: A *proud* lady, the man is *proud*, I saw *lofty* trees. We can attach the same word *proud* to *lady* and to *man;* the same word *lofty* to *tree* and *trees.*

Pronouns.

10. (ii.) PRONOUNS are words substituted for nouns (*pro nomine*) to *indicate* or *point to* a person, thing, or quality, without naming the thing, or its quality: *I, you, he, she, it ; that, such, who,* and many others.

The noun then, and pronoun, *name* or *point to* persons, things, or the qualities of persons or things ; but,

The Verb.

11. (iii.) The VERB *makes a statement* as to them, it joins together *two* such objects of our thought.

> *Vales,* you are well ; *curro,* I run ; *vincuntur,* they are conquered.

In each of these Latin words not one but two separate conceptions are included ; "you" and the "being well," "I" and "running," "they" and "being conquered ;" of these, the first is called the *Subject,* the second the *Predicate.*

12. The Latin verb differs from the English in not requiring the aid of a separate pronoun (*ego, tu,* etc.) to make its statement. The pronoun is contained in, and expressed by, its final syllable.

> *Vivo, I* live ; *vixisti, you* have lived ; *amat, he* loves.

13. The verb then is a *saying* about persons or things (*verbum* = *Gk.* ῥῆμα : a saying, or thing said).

It makes a statement, or, as it is called, a *predication,* as to the state of, or action done either by, or to, some person or thing.

> *Valeo,* I am well ; *vinco,* I conquer ; *vincor,* I am conquered.

14. All these parts of speech have in Latin their *inflexions, i.e.* variable and movable terminations, answering to those in such English words as do*st,* table*s,* come*s,* and admit of other changes in form (cf. *I, me ;* come, came), by the aid of which they express various relations, or notions, of *number, case, gender, degree of comparison, time, person, mood.*

In English, many, if not most, of these relations are expressed by separate words, as pronouns, prepositions, auxiliary verbs, or by the place of the word in the sentence; thus compare,

> *Pater filium videbit.*   The father *will* see his son.
> *Patrem filius viderat.*   The son *had seen* his father.
> *Hunc librum tibi dederam.*   *I had* given this book *to* you.

15. But the other four parts of speech are not inflected, or *declined;* they are all called particles (*particula*), or less important *parts* of *speech*, because they are not so essential to the formation of a sentence as those already described. The first three can form a sentence by themselves, not so the last four.

The Adverb.

16. (iv.) The ADVERB (*adverbium*) is so called, because its main use is to attend upon the *verb*. All verbs make a statement; the adverb qualifies the statement which the verb makes, by adding some particular as to the *manner, amount, time,* or *place* of the state or action asserted.

Fortiter *pugnavit.*	tum *excessit.*	ibi *cecidit.*
He fought *bravely.*	*then,* or *at that time,*	he fell *there,* or
	he went out.	*in that place.*

17. But adverbs, especially those of *amount* or *degree,* may also be joined with *adjectives,* and even with other *adverbs.*

> Satis *sapiens.*   Admŏdum *negligenter.*
> *Sufficiently* wise.   *Very* carelessly.

18. Adverbs when derived from adjectives are capable of one kind of inflexion; that which expresses "more," "most," *sapienter, sapientius, sapientissime.*

19. Observe how often the adverb may be interchanged with an adverbial *phrase; i.e.* two or more words equivalent to an adverb: negligently, *with negligence;* hastily,

in haste; then, *at that time.* The same is the case in Latin : *Tunc = eo tempore.*

Prepositions.

20. (v.) PREPOSITIONS are words which are joined with, and almost invariably *placed before* (*praeposita*), nouns and pronouns, to define their relation to other words in the sentence.

Ad *me vēnit.*	a *Caesare victus est.*	pro *patriā mori.*
He came *to* me.	he was conquered *by* Caesar.	to die *for* one's native land.

21. There are a great many prepositions in Latin, and the same preposition is used in various senses, *e.g.,* a (*ab*), "from" *and* "by." They are rarely used with any but the accusative and ablative cases.

22. But the case-ending alone will often express what in English must be expressed by a preposition.

Ense me percussit.	*Romam Narbone rediit.*
He struck me *with* a sword (instrument).	He returned *to* Rome *from* Narbonne (motion from and to a town).

23. Many words used as prepositions are also used as adverbs, *i.e.* are not joined with nouns but with verbs.

Ante te *natus sum.*	*Hoc nunquam* ante videram.
I was born *before* you (prep.).	I had never *before* seen this (adverb).

24. Many also are prefixed to and compounded with verbs, to modify their meaning. Very often they convert an intransitive into a transitive verb.

Pugno, I fight ; op*pugno,* I assault (a place).

The same was the case in Old English ; we still use *over*come, *with*stand, *gain*say. In later English the preposition is placed after the verb : "He is *sent for*," "I am *laughed at.*"

A list of prepositions, with the cases which they govern, or are joined with, will be found further on. (See Ex. XLIII., XLIV.)

Conjunctions.

25. (vi.) CONJUNCTIONS are indeclinable words which join together (*conjungo*) sentences or clauses,[1] and occasionally even words.

26. Their proper office is to unite two or more sentences or clauses, and to show the relation between the clauses which they unite. "You went, *but* I remained behind," the *but* expresses *opposition;* "you did this, *therefore* I will," *therefore* draws an *inference.*

27. *Obs.*—They often connect *words,* but generally the word connected represents a clause left out, *e.g.* You and I saw this = You saw this, *and* I saw this.

Sometimes however they really connect words, and words only : "This good *but* poor man would often say," or "two *and* two make four."

For the list of conjunctions and their classes see below.

Interjections.

28. (vii.) INTERJECTIONS are so called because they are words inserted (*interjecta*), or *thrown in among* the other words of a sentence to express some feeling or emotion. They are either mere exclamations, as *heu, vae,* alas ! woe ! or abbreviated sentences, such as *Me Dius fidius (juvet).* Compare "good-bye" (God be with you). They do not enter into the construction of a sentence, and their *syntax* therefore presents no difficulty.

FURTHER REMARKS ON THE PARTS OF SPEECH.

29. THE NOUN.—(i.) SUBSTANTIVES are of more than one kind.

(*a.*) The **proper** name (*nomen proprium*), *i.e.* the special name appropriated to and the *property* of a single person or place : *Caius, Roma, Italia.*

(*b.*) The **common** noun or name (*nomen appellativum*), by which we can designate either a whole class, or an individual of the class: *arbor, flumen ;* tree, river. Any tree or river may bear this name. Without the help of

---

[1] See below, Intr. 78.

these words we should require a separate name for every object that we speak of.

(*c.*) **Collective** nouns, or nouns of multitude (*nomina collectiva*) are such as, though singular, yet by their nature denote a number of individuals : *Exercitus, populus, senatus ;* army, people, senate.

(*d.*) **Abstract** nouns (*nomina abstracta*) are words which denote some quality, or state, or action, as *withdrawn* from the person or thing *in which* we see it *embodied* (*concretum*), and looked on as existing *by itself.* Thus *servitium* is the state of " servitude " which we see existing in a number of *servi ; candor,* " whiteness," the quality which is denoted by the adjective *candidus,* wherever that quality is found.

30. (ii.) ADJECTIVES may be divided into—
Adjectives of **quality,** as *bonus, malus, fortis ;* good, bad, brave.

Adjectives of **quantity** and **number** (numeral): *multi, pauci, ducenti ;* many, few, two hundred.

There is also a large number of *pronominal* adjectives formed from or closely connected with pronouns : *meus, tuus, ullus,* etc. ; mine, thine, any, etc. These are more conveniently included under pronouns.

31. Though the adjective is especially fitted for *attaching to* or being *predicated of* substantives, yet where no ambiguity can arise it is capable of being used by itself as a substantive: *boni,* good (men) ; *bona,* good (things), the words *men* and *things* being represented by the masculine and neuter terminations of the Latin adjective ; *-i* and *-a* representing the plural of " he," " it."

32. PRONOUNS.—The personal pronouns answering to the English *I, you,* as also to *he, she, it,* are essential parts of conversation in all languages to represent the person *speaking,* the person *spoken to,* and the person or thing *spoken of.*

We have already seen that they may be expressed in Latin by the termination of the verb. Rules for the insertion of *ego, tu, is, ille,* etc., will be given below.

33. Besides these *personal* pronouns, which indicate, without again naming, the two or three persons before named, there are a large number of words closely connected with them, which are also called pronouns (or in some cases *pronominals, i.e.* words resembling pronouns) Such are—

The Reflexive and Emphatic Pronouns .	*sui, se ; ipse, egomet,* etc.,—himself, myself, etc.
The Demonstrative . .	*hic ; iste, is, ille ; idem,*—this; that; the same, etc.
The Interrogative . . .	*quis, qui* (adjectival), *ecquis ; quot ?* etc.,—who? what? how many?
The Relative	*qui, quicunque,* etc.,—that, who, which, whoever.
The Indefinite	*quidam ; quis ; aliquis,*—a certain one; any; some, etc.
The Possessive	*meus, tuus, suus, noster,* etc.,—mine, thine, his, ours, etc.
The Reciprocal	(No single word in Latin); each other, etc.

The majority of these are used adjectivally; but the personal pronouns of the first and second person, the reflexive *(se), quis* as opposed to *qui, quid* to *quod,* are substantival.

34. There are also certain **correlative** pronouns or pronominals, which are used in corresponding pairs. Such are *is . . . qui ; tantus . . . quantus ; tot . . . quot.* Their use will be explained further on. (See Ex. XII.)

35. VERBS.—The distinction between the different kinds of verbs must be carefully attended to in composition. Verbs are thus classed:—

(i.) **Intransitive** Verbs are so called because any action which they denote does not extend or pass over *(transire)* to any other person or thing besides that which forms the subject or nominative of the verb.

Spiro, I breathe; *curro,* I run; *cado,* I fall; *sum,* I exist.

Any of these verbs can form a complete sentence in Latin, though not in English, in a single word.

36. Some of them, however, hardly give a *clear* sense without the aid of a noun or pronoun to complete the statement which they make; and this is one of the chief uses of the dative case. Thus *noceo*, "I am hurtful," *parco*, "I am obedient," give a vague sense, unless we know *to whom* "I am hurtful" or "obedient"; and these intransitive verbs (which obviously contain an idea resembling that of the adjective) are mostly joined with a *dative* never with an *accusative:* tibi *noceo;* mihi *paret.* They are often represented in English by transitive verbs: "I *hurt* you," "he *obeys* me." There are many such apparently transitive, but really intransitive, verbs in Latin. (See Ex. I. 5.)

37. (ii.) **Transitive** Verbs are those which denote an action which necessarily affects, or *passes over to*, some person or thing other than the *subject* of the verb: *interficio*, I kill; *capio*, I take. Here *I* is the *subject* of the verb, but we ask at once *whom*, or *what*, do *I* kill, or take?

38. This other person or thing, without which the statement is incomplete, is called the *object* of the verb, and is always in the *accusative* case. In English the object follows the verb, in Latin it more often precedes it.

Fratrem tuum *vidi.* I saw *your brother.*

39. (iii.) Both transitive and intransitive verbs are called **Active.** Their inflexions are similar, and both denote *action* of some kind.

For English verbs used both transitively and intransitively, as "I move," etc., see **20, 21.**

40. Many Latin transitive verbs may be used *absolutely* (*i.e.* without an expressed object).

Vinco, I conquer (my enemies), "I win the day"; *scribo,* I am writing (a letter or book).

41. (iv.) By **Passive** Verbs we mean a form or inflexion of the transitive verb which denotes that the action indicated by the verb takes effect, not on another person or thing, but on the *subject* of the verb.

Amor, I am *loved; interficitur,* he *is killed.*

I and *he* are no longer *agents* or actors, but recipients or *sufferers* (*patior*, *passivus*, adj.), and the *agent* is some one else represented in Latin by the ablative with the preposition *a, ab.*

Ab hoste *interfectus est.* He was slain by the enemy.

42. Remember that it is only transitive verbs, *i.e.* verbs which are joined with an accusative, that have a full passive voice. We cannot say *noceor*, or *curror*, or *vivor*.

But there is a very common use of the third person singular of a passive form of intransitive verbs, without any nominative expressed, to denote that the action described by the verb is produced or effected; *Hac* itur, there *is a going, i.e.* men go, in this direction; *tibi* nocetur, *harm is done* to you, *i.e.* you are injured. Owing to the large number of verbs which, like *noceo*, are intransitive in Latin, this construction is of great importance. (See 5.)

43. (v.) Besides these **active** and **passive** verbs, there is a large class of verbs called **Deponent.**

These are verbs which, though having passive *inflexions*, have laid aside (*deponere*) a passive, and assumed an active, *sense.* Of these, some are transitive, some intransitive.

Te sequor, I follow you; *tibi irascor*, I am angry with you.

44. Some are called **Semi-deponents**; they have an active form in the present, a passive in the past, with no change of meaning.

Gaudeo, I rejoice; *gavisus sum. audeo,* I dare; *ausus sum.*

45. It is important to remember that deponent verbs differ from other Latin verbs in furnishing both a past and present participle with an active sense.

Proficiscor, I set out; *proficiscens*, and *profectus*, "setting out," and "having set out."
(See 14.)

46. (vi.) **Impersonal** Verbs are those which are not used in the first or second persons, but only in the third.

Even with the third person of such verbs, the subject or

nominative case is never a person, or even a substantive ; but either (*a*) the vague *it* (or *he*) implied in the termination : or the verb is accompanied and explained by (*b*) an infinitive mood, or (*c*) a whole clause, or (*d*) a neuter pronoun.

> *Pudet. It* shames me.
> Haec fecisse *piget. It* is painful to have done this.
> *Accĭdit* ut abessem. *It* happened that I was absent.
> Hoc *refert.* This is of importance.

(See **123**, and **202**.)

Among these must be classed the very important construction mentioned above (42).

47. (vii.) By **Auxiliary** Verbs we mean verbs used as aids (*auxilia*) to enable other verbs to form moods and tenses which they cannot express within the compass of a single word. Compare "I fell" with "I *have* fallen," where "have" has lost the sense of possession, and only serves as an auxiliary verb to the verb *fall*. Such verbs abound in English, because the English verb often requires the aid of another word—*may, would, should, shall, will, let*, etc.—to express what can be expressed in Latin by a change in the verb itself. Compare "I *was* loving" with *amabam;* "*let* him go" with *eat.*

In Latin, the only auxiliary verb is *esse*, "to be," assisted by the forms, *fore, forem*. This is used largely in the passive voice and future infinitive: *auditus* sum, *audiiturum* fore.

48. But much resembling these auxiliary verbs are certain verbs which are closely united with the infinitive of another verb, and add to that verb various *modes* of expressing its meaning, almost as if they were additional *moods;* hence they are called,

(viii.) **Modal** Verbs. Such are those of *being able, beginning, ceasing, wishing*, etc.

> Possum, nequeo, desĭno, volo, *haec dicere*. I am able, *unable, cease, wish*, to say this.

(See **42**.)

49. (ix.) **Copulative** or **Link** Verbs are those which unite together two nouns or pronouns, one of which, the predicate, is asserted or predicated of the other, the subject.

Caesar est *Dictator.*   Caesar *is* Dictator.

Obs.—The principal of these is the verb *sum*, whose *original* meaning was " I breathe."

When *sum* means " I am," " I exist," it is called a *substantive* verb, because it expresses the idea of existence, *substantia.* (See 6.)

When it merely joins together the subject and predicate of a sentence, as above, it is called a *copulative* verb.

When it supplies the passive voice or infinitive mood with aid to form tenses, it is called an *auxiliary* verb.

50. Besides *sum* there is a large class of other verbs which have in some cases laid aside their original meaning, and are used to connect nouns. Such are *fio* (used as the passive of *facio*), *evado, existo,* and also the passive of verbs of *thinking, naming,* etc. Of course, as link verbs they couple together words which correspond as closely as possible, and the two nouns which they unite will be in the same case.

Caesar fit Dictator.   Caesar becomes Dictator.

For Verbs called **Factitive** Verbs, see **239.**

51. The verb, when its meaning is defined or limited (*finis*) by a nominative case, *i.e.* when used as a true verb, as in the first, second, or third person, is called sometimes a *finite* verb.

But sometimes the verb, to a certain extent, lays aside its true nature as the *instrument of making an assertion by joining together two objects of our thoughts*, and takes that of another part of speech, the noun, both the *substantive* and the *adjective.* The verb is used as a substantive in the *infinitive* mood, in the *gerund,* and in the two *supines.* It is used as an adjective in the *participles*, and in the *gerundive,* or *participle* in *-dus.*

These will all form subjects of Exercises.

52. **Adverbs** have been already classified. The learner must be again reminded that just as in English we use very freely a great number of *adverbial phrases* in place of

adverbs, *e.g. in silence,* for "silently," *to the benefit of,* instead of "beneficially to," the state, so he must not think that every English adverb or adverbial phrase is to be rendered literally into Latin. Full guidance, however, will be given in the following Exercises. (See, for instance, **61, 63, 64.**)

PREPOSITIONS will be classified further on. (See Exercises XLIII, XLIV.)

53. CONJUNCTIONS are divided, both in English and Latin, into two classes; *Co-ordinating* and *Subordinating* conjunctions.

54. **Co-ordinating** conjunctions join together sentences on equal terms; these sentences are of equal grammatical rank, or co-ordinate (*ordo,* rank), *i.e.* each is *grammatically* independent of the other.

You go, *and, but, therefore,* I shall follow.

55. **Subordinating** conjunctions attach to a sentence or clause another clause which holds (grammatically) a lower or subordinate position, qualifying the principal clause just as an adverb qualifies a verb. " I will do this, *if* you do;" the *if*-sentence (or clause) is equivalent to the adverb *conditionally.* (See Intr. 82.)

56. The Co-ordinating conjunctions in Latin and English are—

 a. **Copulative—**
  Et, -que, ac, atque; nec, neque (when used for "and not"); *etiam, praeterea,* etc.
  And, also; nor, and not; moreover, etc.

 b. **Disjunctive,** *i.e.* they join together the sentences, but they *disjoin* or separate from each other the thoughts conveyed : " We must do this, *or* die."
  Aut, vel, -ve ; nec, neque ; sive, seu ; (an, -ně).
  Or, either; neither, nor; whether, or; (or).

 c. **Adversative.** Two statements are opposed to each other—
  Sed, autem, verum, vero, tamen.
  But, nevertheless, notwithstanding, however, etc.

d. **Illative or Inferential.** The statement of one sentence " brings in " (*infert*) or proves the other ;

Ergo, igitur, itaque. Therefore, accordingly, and so, etc.

e. Causal ;

Nam, namque, enim, etenim. For.

57. Observe that Latin has a greater variety of conjunctions than English ; for our " and " it has *et, -que, atque, ac,* for our " or " *aut, vel, -ve,* as well as *an ;* and each of these words has a somewhat different meaning.[1]

58. Very often also the relative pronoun *qui* may take the place of an English co-ordinating conjunction, and be placed at the head of a sentence or clause where we should use " and," " but," " so."

Quae postquam audivit. *And* after he heard *this.*

59. The Subordinating conjunctions are—

a. Final—

LATIN.	ENGLISH.
Ut, quo ; and negative *nē, quominus.*	That (*followed by* may *or* might), in order to, to *with the Infinitive ;* that not, lest, etc.

---

[1] Latin has three Copulative conjunctions to represent our " and,"— *et ; atque, ac ;* and *-que. Et* simply couples words and clauses ; *-que* couples two words as forming one whole, *se suaque,* etc., or connects a closely related clause ; *atque* connects with emphasis, " and also," " and I may say."

Ac, the shorter form of *atque,* must never be used before words that begin with a vowel.

Aut . . . aut, and *vel . . . vel,* both answer to the English *either . . . or,* but *aut* marks a sharp distinction : Hoc *aut* verum est *aut* falsum, This is either true or false, *i.e.* if it is true, it is not false. *Vel* (*ve*) is connected with *velle ;* and treats the difference as unimportant : " whichever you like."

Hoc velim *vel* vi *vel* clam facias.

I would have you do this either by force or secretly (as you prefer).

Hence *vel . . . vel* is often equivalent to *et . . . et,* and both = *alike . . . and.*

Vir *vel* (*et*) ingenio *vel* (*et*) virtute insignis.

A man remarkable *alike* for his ability *and* his goodness.

An is only used for " or " in questions. (See **159.**)

b. Consecutive—

LATIN.	ENGLISH.
Ut; ut non, quin.	So that, so as to; so as not to, etc.

c. Temporal—

Quum, ubi, ut; quamdiu, dum; quoad, donec, priusquam, antequam; postquam.	When, as soon as; while, as long as; until, before that; after that, etc.

d. Causal—

Quod, quia, quoniam, quandoquidem, often *quum; non quo.*	Because, since, inasmuch as, seeing that, whereas; not that, not because, etc.

e. Conditional—

Si; nisi, si non; sive, seu; also *dum, modo; dum ne, modo ne.*	If; unless, if not; whether . . . or; provided that, so long as, on the condition that, etc.

f. Comparative and Proportional—

Quam; quasi, tanquam, sicut, ut, quemadmodum, proinde ac; quo . . . eo, with comparatives.	Than; as, as if, as though, just as, in proportion as; *the* (old abl.) more . . . *the* more, etc.

g. Concessive—

Etsi, tametsi, quamquam, quamvis, licet, ut.	Although, albeit, etc.

h. Defining or Explanatory—

Quod, ut: but their use is limited in Latin, their place being largely taken by the infinitive mood.	That (He says, or knows, etc., *that* I did it. It is true *that* he did it, etc.) Used most widely in English and modern languages.

i. Interrogative (with dependent clauses)—

Cur, utrum, an, num; quemadmodum, ut; cur, quamobrem; ubi, quando.	Whether . . . or, if; how; why, wherefore; where, when.

Observe in how many different senses *ut* and *quum* are used.

60. The relative *qui* is used also very commonly in place of subordinating conjunctions: see Exercises LXIII, LXIV.

ANALYSIS OF THE LATIN SENTENCE.

61. By a **sentence,** whether in Latin or in English, we mean a grammatical combination of words, which either (1) makes a *statement,* or (2) asks a *question,* or (3) conveys a *command* or desire.

Every such sentence, however long or however short, consists of two parts:—

62. First, a **subject**—that of which something is stated, asked, or desired; secondly, a **predicate**—that which is stated, asked, or desired in reference to that subject.

He is well.   Is he well ?   May he be well !
Valet.   *Valetne ?*   *Valeat!*

In each of these sentences *he* (expressed in Latin by the termination, or personal inflexion of the verb: see 12) is the *subject,* the rest is the *predicate.* (See 11.)

63. But such short sentences are rare in all languages. They are shorter in Latin than in English for the reason given in 12.

The following more ordinary form of sentence is one that occurs in Bk. i. c. 1 of Caesar *de Bello Gallico:*—

Hi omnes lingua, institutis, moribus, inter se differunt.
These all (*or* all of these) differ from one another in language, institutions, and habits.

Here in both languages *Hi omnes* (these all) is the *subject;* all the rest is the *predicate.* The main part of the predicate is the verb *differunt,* the rest being *adjuncts* or additions to the verb, explaining and limiting it, telling us *from whom* all of these differ, and *in what points.*

64. A sentence of this kind, whether short (as the examples in 62) or longer (as that in 63), is called a *simple* sentence.

By a **simple sentence** we mean one which consists of a single subject and a single predicate.

65. *Obs.*—Sometimes there is a *single* predicate and *two* or *more* *subjects* united by conjunctions, as

You and I lifted up our hands.
You and I are old.

Sometimes a *single subject* with *two* or *three predicates*, as

> The army *put to flight* and *killed* many of the enemy.

These are sometimes called *contracted* sentences, as they are a shortened form of such sentences as,

> You lifted up your hands, *and* I lifted up my hands.

It may be better to look on them as simple sentences with a subject or predicate consisting of two or more words, united by the conjunction *and*. (See 27.)

66. In both languages the **subject** will always be a substantive of some kind, or its equivalent. The equivalent may be a substantival pronoun (33), or an adjective, participle, or adjectival pronoun used as a substantive (31), or an *infinitive mood* (51), or some combination of words, used as a substantive. (See Examples in 67.)

67. The **predicate** will always consist either of a verb, or else of some adjective,[1] substantive, or combination of words, connected with the subject by a verb expressed or understood (see 49), *e.g.:*—

> *Caesar* vixit.   Caesar *has lived*.
> *Sapientes* sunt beatissimi.   Wise men *are the happiest*.
> *Hic* rex est.   He (this man) *is king*.
> *Agrum colere* mihi delectationi est.   Cultivating the land
> (or farming) *is a delight to me*.

Obs.—Where the link verb is omitted we supply it (at least in English and Latin) in thought.

> Happy the good !   *Quot homines tot sententiae.*
> (There are) as many views as there are men.

68. The subject may, even in a simple sentence, be greatly *enlarged* or prolonged by the addition of *adjectives, adjectival phrases,*[2] *pronouns*, words in *apposition*, etc.

> *Boni reges amantur*.   *Good* kings are loved.
> *Caius, vir* optimus et magnae auctoritatis, *interficitur*.
> Caius, *an excellent man and of great influence*, is slain.

---

[1] The adjective is specially adapted for a predicate ; it may even be said that the substantive when used as a predicate is used adjectivally.

[2] By an adjectival phrase we mean some word or combination of words other than an adjective used in place of an adjective :—

> *vir* summae fortitudinis = *vir* fortissimus.
> *haec res tibi* magnae *erit* delectationi = gratissima.

B

69. So also the **predicate** may be enlarged and made more distinct and intelligible by the addition of oblique cases of substantives to the verb to express its nearer and remoter objects; and these substantives may have in their turn various adjuncts, such as adjectives or other substantives in apposition.

> Pater filio, *puero aetatis tenerae carissimo,* librum *pretiosissimum Romae emptum, dono* dedit.   *The father gave his* much-loved *son* of tender years *a* present of a costly *book* bought at Rome.

"The father" is the subject; all the rest is the predicate.

Obs.—The verb *dedit* says of the father that he *gave* something.   The dative case *dono,* closely combined with the verb, explains (by a special use of that case) that what he gave he gave *as,* or *for, a present.*   The dative case *filio* does the regular work of the dative, *i.e.* specifies the *remoter object* of that gift, the son who benefited by it ; the substantive and adjective in apposition, together with the adjectival phrase *aetatis tenerae,* give some further particulars as to that remoter object.

The accusative case *librum* completes the idea vaguely expressed by *dono dedit.*   It performs the proper function of the accusative case, as it completes the idea only half expressed by a transitive verb, by supplying the (nearer) object of the verb.   (See 38.)

It is in turn made more distinct by its combination with an adjective, *pretiosissimum,* and a participle combined with the local case of a noun, *Romae emptum.*   These tell us its value, and the place where it was purchased.

But the main and essential parts of the predicate are the verb *dedit* with its two accompanying cases *filio* and *librum.*

70. Again, the action described by the verb may be explained and made distinct by the addition of *adverbs,* or of substantives used **adverbially** (especially the ablative and locative cases), *adverbial phrases, participles, gerunds, gerundives,* or *adjectives* used adverbially; *e.g.*

> Diu *vixit.*   He lived *long.*
> *Vixit* nonaginta annos.   He lived *ninety years.*
> Fame *interiit.*   He died *of famine.*
> Summa cum celeritate *venit* (= celerrime *venit*).   He came *with the utmost speed.*

Londini *vixit.*   He lived *at London.*
Pugnans *interficitur.*   He is killed *while fighting.*
Sui liberandi causa *pugnavit.*   He fought *to free himself.*
Invitus *hoc feci.*   I did this *unwillingly.*

In each of these sentences we have adverbs, or their equivalents, fulfilling the proper function of adverbs, *i.e. qualifying and explaining the action described by the verb.*

71. The verb, instead of being, as in the example above, a very important part of the predicate, may serve as little more than a **link to connect together** the subject and predicate.

Ego consul ero.   I *shall be* consul.

Here the verb *ero* is a mere link (adding however the idea of time) between the subject and predicate.

So other verbs in a less degree.

Rex Numa appellatur.   The king *is named* Numa.

(See 50.)

In such cases the predicate and subject will, as already explained, be in the same case, as it is their agreement or identity that the verb asserts.

72. The use of the **adjective**, when it stands in such sentences as the **predicate**, must be distinguished from its use as an **attribute.**   (See 8.)

Hic rex *bonus (predicate)* est.   Reges *boni (attribute)* amantur.

THE COMPOUND SENTENCE.

73. Simple sentences are in English and in Latin rather the exception than the rule.

In Latin, as in English, we can neither converse nor write without using sentences which are either combined with, or contain within themselves as part of their subject or predicate, other sentences or clauses.[1]

I. CO-ORDINATION.

74. Sentences are combined together by **Co-ordination.** That is, two or more sentences are placed side by side in combination with each other; they stand to each other on equal terms; one is grammatically as important as the other.   (See 54.)

75. Such sentences are connected in English and Latin by co-ordinating conjunctions, *and, but, for; et, aut, nam,* etc.

> You do this, *but* I do that;
> I shall go home, *for* I am tired;
> Either you must go, *or* I shall (go).

For a list of English and Latin co-ordinating conjunctions, see 56.

76. It has been stated that even the relative *qui,* among its other uses, is frequently used to connect two co-ordinated sentences.   (See 58.)

In English also this is the case, though more rarely;

I met your son, who told me that you were at home.

Here *who=and he.*

---

[1] The term *clause* is used for the various *sub-sentences* which make up the whole compound sentence.

Notice again how many sentences, and even chapters, in Caesar and other Latin authors begin with a relative.

Obs.—Sometimes co-ordinate sentences are placed side by side without any conjunction.

> *Veni, vidi, vici.* I came, I saw, I conquered.
> *Contempsi Catilinae gladios, non pertimescam tuos.*

77. The syntax of the co-ordinate sentence will cause no special difficulty. The characteristic of a co-ordinate sentence is, that it does not *grammatically depend on another;* it is a sentence combined with another, but on an *independent footing.* The mood and tense of its verb, the case of its noun or nouns, are in no way dependent upon any other sentence.

II. SUBORDINATION.

78. Sentences may be joined together by SUBORDINATION.

A **sentence** may consist of different **clauses**, each containing its own verb, so combined that we have one principal or main clause, containing the principal verb, to which other clauses stand, so far as grammar is concerned, in a *subordinate* or dependent position.

> *Hereupon the commodore,* after he had cast anchor, *sent some of his men to land,* and *ordered them* to ask whether provisions and water could be procured, if the fleet that was yet to come should need them.

Here we have what we may call a *double compound* sentence; *i.e.* two co-ordinate main clauses (in italics) connected by *and,* each with one or more subordinate clauses dependent on it.

79. Such subordinate clauses will answer to the three different parts of speech—the substantive, the adjective, and the adverb,—which form with the verb the chief component parts of a sentence.

i. Substantival.

80. They may be SUBSTANTIVAL. That is, they may stand in the relation of **substantives** to the verb of the principal clause.

The following are three clearly marked instances of different kinds of substantival clauses—

    (*a*) Se regem esse *dixit.*   He said *that he was a king.*
    (*b*) Quid fieret *quaesivit.*   He asked *what was being done.*
    (*c*) Ut sibi ignoscerem *oravit.*   He entreated me *to pardon him.*

In each of these Latin sentences the main clause consists of a single word, the verbs *dixit, quaesivit, oravit;* but each has appended to it a subordinate clause, answering to an accusative case, and containing (*a*) a statement, (*b*) a question, (*c*) an entreaty.

ii. Adjectival.

81. Subordinate clauses may also be ADJECTIVAL. By this we mean that they may stand in the same relation to the principal clause as an **attributive adjective.** (See 8.)

They include all such "clauses" as are introduced by *qui* in its simplest use as the relative; used, that is, to define or specify some previous substantive expressed or understood.

They are called **adjectival** because they define more closely such **antecedent** substantive or pronoun, precisely as an adjective or a substantive used as an adjective, *i.e.* in apposition, would do.

    For "Boni *reges amantur*" we may say "*Reges*, qui boni sunt, *amantur.*"
    For "*Servorum* fidelissimum *misi*" we may say "*Servum misi*, quem fidelissimum habui."
    For "*Cicero* Consul" we may say "*Cicero*, qui Consul est," or "fuit."

iii. Adverbial.

82. There also is a great variety of ADVERBIAL clauses.

By these we mean those which add to the principal clause, grammatically complete without them, some further clause expressing *end in view, result, time, cause, condition, contrast, likeness.*

These clauses play the part of **adverbs** or **adverbial phrases** to the main clause.   Compare—

Hoc consulto *feci,*	with	*Hoc feci* ut tibi placerem ;
I did this *purposely,*	with	I did this *in order that I might please you ;*

where the adverbs *consulto* and *purposely* are replaced by *adverbial clauses.*

Or take an English sentence—

I will do this conditionally.

We have here a simple sentence, in which the predicate is qualified by the adverb *conditionally.*   Substitute—

I will do this, *if* (or *on the condition that*) *you do that.*

Here we have no longer a simple but a compound sentence, the principal clause, *I will do this,* being qualified by a subordinate adverbial clause.

83. These **adverbial** clauses are divided into seven classes—

1. Final, those which denote a *purpose.*
2. Consecutive,   „   *result.*
3. Temporal,   „   *time.*
4. Causal,   „   *reason* or *cause.*
5. Conditional,   „   *supposition.*
6. Concessive or adversative,   *contrast.*
7. Comparative,   „   *comparison* or *proportion.*

84. They are connected with the main clause sometimes by subordinating conjunctions, a list of which has been given above (see 59), sometimes by the relative *qui,* the use of which is in Latin far wider and more varied than in English.

85. The following are instances :—

Final,	.	. Huc veni, *ut te viderem.*
		I came here *in order to see you.*
Consecutive,		. Humi cecidit *ut crus frangeret.*
		He fell on the ground *so as to break his leg.*
Temporal,		. *Quum haec dixisset,* abire voluit.
		When he had spoken thus, he wished to depart.
Causal,	.	. *Quod haec fecisti,* gratias tibi ago.
		I return thanks to you *for acting thus.*
Conditional,		. *Si hoc feceris* poenas dabis.
		If you do this you will be punished.
Concessive,		. *Quanquam festīno,* tamen hic morabor.
		Though I am in haste, yet I will delay here.
Comparative } or Modal, }		*Proinde ac meritus es* te utar.
		I will deal with you *as you have deserved.*

In each case the subordinate clause, or its substitute in English, is in italic letters, the main clause in Roman.

ORDER OF WORDS AND CLAUSES IN A LATIN SENTENCE.

86. The order of words in a Latin sentence differs, in many important respects, from the English order. There are very few sentences in which the natural order of one language corresponds to that of the other. There is much greater freedom and variety in Latin, especially as regards substantives, adjectives, pronouns, and verbs. For these parts of speech are each susceptible of a great variety of changes in their terminations, called *inflexions*. It is these inflexions, and not their place in the sentence, which mark the relations of words to other words. As we have far fewer of these inflexions in English, we are obliged to look for the precise meaning of a word, not to its *form* but to its *position*.

87. If we take the English sentence, "The soldier saw the enemy," we cannot invert the order of the two substantives, and write "The enemy saw the soldier," without entirely changing the meaning; but in Latin we may write *miles vidit hostem, hostem vidit miles,* or *miles hostem vidit,* without any further change than that of shifting the emphasis from one word to another.

But for all this the following rules should be carefully attended to in writing Latin, and variations from them noticed in reading Latin prose authors.

ARRANGEMENT OF WORDS.

88. The subject of the sentence, the **nominative** case, stands, as in English, at the beginning of or early in the sentence.

> Caesar, or *Tum* Caesar *exercitum in Aeduorum fines* ducit.
> Compare—Thereupon Caesar leads his army into the territory of the Aedui.

89. The *verb* (or if not the verb, some important part of the predicate) comes last of all, as *ducit* in the sentence above.

> *Ea res mihi fuit* gratissima.
> That circumstance was most welcome to me.

> *Obs.—Sum,* when used as a link verb, rarely comes last.

90. But if great stress is laid on the verb it is placed at the beginning, and the subject removed to the last place.

> *Tulit* hoc vulnus graviter Cicero.   Cicero *doubtless* felt this wound deeply.
> *Est* caeleste nūmen.   There *really is,* or there exists, a heavenly power.

This position of *sum* often distinguishes its **substantive** from its **copulative** and **auxiliary** uses.   (See 49, *Obs.*)

91. For it must always be remembered that

The degree of **prominence** and **emphasis** to be given to a word is that which mainly determines its position in the sentence.   And,

The two emphatic positions in a Latin sentence are the *beginning* and the *end*.   By the former our attention is raised and suspended, while the full meaning of the sentence is rarely completed till the last word is reached.

Hence, from the habit of placing the most important part of the predicate, which is generally the verb, last of all, we rarely see a Latin sentence from which the last word or words can be removed *without destroying the life*, so to speak, of the whole sentence.

This can easily be illustrated from any chapter of a Latin author.

92. The more **unusual** a position is for any word, the more emphatic it is *for that word*.   Thus

> *Arbores seret diligens agricola, quarum adspiciet baccam ipse* nunquam.—(*Cic.*)

Here the adverb is made emphatic by position; in English we must express the emphasis differently, as by "though the day will never come when he will see their fruit."

A word that generally stands close by another receives emphasis by *separation* from it; especially if it be thus brought near the beginning or end of a sentence.

> *Voluptatem percepi* maximam.   *Propterea quod aliud iter haberent* nullum.   *Aedui equites ad Caesarem* omnes *revertuntur.*

93. As regards the interior arrangement of the sentence, **governed words**, such as (1) the accusative or dative, expressive of the nearer or remoter objects of verbs, or (2) genitive or other cases governed by a noun or adjective or participle, come usually *before*, not as in English *after*, the words which govern them.

> Hunc librum filio *dedi.*
> Compare—I gave this book to my son.
> *Frater tuus* tui *est simillimus.*
> Compare—Your brother is exceedingly like you.

94. Adjectives, when used as attributes, are oftener than not placed *after* the noun with which they agree; but the pronoun *hic*, and monosyllabic pronouns and adjectives of number or quantity, *before*, as in English.

> *Vir* bonus; *civitas* opulentissima; haec *opinio;* permulti *homines.*

When a substantive is combined both with an adjective and a genitive, the usual order is this—

> *Vera animi magnitudo.* True greatness of mind.

95. A word in apposition generally stands, as does the adjective, after the word to which it relates.

> *Q. Mucius* augur; *M. Tullius Cicero* consul; *Pythagoras* philosophus.
> *Luxuria et ignavia,* pessimae artes.

96. Adverbs and their equivalents, such as ablative and other cases, and adverbial phrases, come before the verbs which they qualify.

> *Hic rex* diu *vixit.* This king lived *long.*
> *Agrum* ferro et igni *vastavit.* He laid waste the land *with fire and sword.*
> Libenter *hoc feci.* I did this *cheerfully.*
> Triginta annos *regnavit.* He reigned *thirty years.*

97. But in all these cases the usual order may be reversed to a far greater extent than in English for the sake of emphasis.

98. *Enim, vero, autem, quoque, quidem* (with the enclitics,[1] *-que, -ve, nĕ*), cannot be the first words of a clause; *quoque* and *quidem* follow the words to which they belong.

99. The negative adverbs *non, haud, neque,* are placed always before the words which they qualify; *ne quidem,* "not even," always enclose the word which they emphasise: as, *ne hic quidem,* "not even he."

---

[1] An enclitic is a word which does not stand by itself, but is written at the end of the word which it qualifies: *-nĕ* (interrogative), *-quĕ*=and, *-vĕ*=or, are the commonest Latin enclitics.

Substantival Clauses.

100. Substantival Clauses, whether statements, questions, or commands, usually come before the verb on which they depend. (See 80.)

> Errare se ait. He says *that he is wrong.*
> Quid fiat *dicam.* I will tell *you what is being done.*
> (Ut) hoc facias *oro.* I beg you *to do this.*

English and Latin here differ exactly as they do in the position of the accusative case, which in English *follows,* and in Latin *precedes,* the verb.

101. But if the dependent clause is long and important, and the principal clause short and unemphatic, the order is generally reversed.

> Respondet ille, *si velit secum colloqui,* etc. (introducing a long speech).
> Quaeris *cur hoc homine tanto opere delecter*
> Oro *ut me, sicut antea, attente audiatis.*

Adjectival Clauses.

102. The **relative clause** is placed often where it would stand in an English sentence.

But it may be placed earlier and more in the centre of the sentence than is possible in English.

> *In his,* quae nunc instant, *periculis.*
> In these dangers *which now threaten us.*

This is accounted for by the principle laid down in 91, and the relative clause often, for the same reason, precedes the main clause.

> Quam quisque norit artem, *in hac se exerceat.*
> Let each practise the profession *with which he is acquainted.*

Adverbial Clauses.

103. These, like the adverbs in a simple sentence, usually, unless very emphatic, come *before* the main clause.

They are placed, in fact, much as they would be in an English sentence, but with a greater tendency to place the main and more emphatic clause last. (See 91.)

104. **Temporal clauses** such as, *haec ubi audivit*, etc., together with ablative absolutes (*hoc comperto*, etc.), and participial phrases, *id veritus*, etc., often, like adverbs of time and place, *tum*, *ibi*, *deinde*, etc., form the opening word of a sentence.

So also clauses introduced by *quum* (temporal), *quoniam* (causal), *quanquam* (concessive), *si* (conditional), *sicut* (comparative), usually come before the main clause; as do final clauses (*ut . . . ne . . .*), more frequently than in English.

But **consecutive clauses** (*ut*, so that) usually, as in English, follow the main clause.

105. The following are examples of the *usual* order:—

Quum haec dixisset, *abiit* (temporal).

Having said this, he departed.

Si futurum est, *fiet* (conditional).

If it is to be, it will come to pass.

Ut sementem feceris, *ita metes* (comparative).

You will reap as you have sown.

Quoniam vir es, *congrediamur* (causal).

Since you are a man, let us close in fight.

Romani, quanquam fessi erant, *tamen obviam procedunt* (concessive).

The Romans advanced to meet (them) in spite of their fatigue.

Esse oportet, ut vivas. } (final).

Haec ne facias, *abi*. }

You should eat to live.

To avoid doing this, begone.

Quis fuit tam ferreus, ut mei non misereretur (consecutive).

Who was so hard-hearted as not to pity me?

106. It may be well to add that a repeated word, or a word akin to another in the sentence (such as one pronoun to another), is generally placed as near to that word as possible.

> *Nulla* virtus virtuti *contraria est.* No kind of *virtue* is opposed to *virtue.*
>
> Te-*nĕ* ego *aspicio?* Is it *you* whom *I* see?
>
> Aliis aliunde *est periculum.* Danger threatens *different* men from *different* quarters.
>
> Timor timorem *pellit. Fear* banishes *fear.*

We see that Latin has a great advantage in this respect over English.

107. Of two corresponding *clauses* or *groups* of words of parallel construction, the order of the first is often *reversed* in the second: so that two of the *antithetical* words are as *near* as possible.

> *Fragile* corpus animus *sempiternus movet. Ratio nostra* consentit; pugnat *oratio. Quae me* moverunt, movissent *eadem te profecto.*

To many of these rules exceptions may be found. For the order in Latin is determined, as has been already said, not by any strict rules, but by considerations of **emphasis, clearness, sound, rhythm, variety,** some of which sometimes defy explanation, but which may be easily noticed and understood by any one who reads Latin with observation and intelligence.

As a general rule, **in any but the shortest clause the English order is sure to be ill adapted to a Latin sentence.**

EXERCISES.

ELEMENTARY AND GENERAL RULES.

MOST of the following rules necessarily follow from what has been said in the Introduction. Two or three are added on constructions of exceedingly frequent occurrence.

1. A finite verb (see Intr. 51) agrees with its *subject* (or its nominative case) in *number* and *person*.

> *Avis ca*n*it.*   The bird sings.
> *Aves ca*n*unt.*   The birds sing.

2. An adjective, pronoun, or participle agrees with the substantive to which it is attached, or of which it is predicated, in *gender*, *number*, and *case.* (Intr. 8, 9.)

> *Rex i*ll*e, vir justissimus, pl*u*rima foedera pac*tu*s est.* That just king contracted many treaties.

3. When to a substantive or personal pronoun there is added a substantive explaining or describing it, the latter is said to be placed in *apposition* to the former, and must agree *in case* with the substantive to which it is added.

> Alexander, *tot regum atque populorum* victor. Alexander, the conqueror of so many kings and nations.

Obs.—The substantive when thus used resembles an adjective. Alexander is here described by one *special quality.* (Intr. 7.)

31

4. A **transitive** verb, whether active or deponent, is joined with an **accusative** of the *nearer object;* that is to say, of the *person* or *thing acted upon.*

> *Sacerdos* hostiam *cecīdit.*   The priest struck down the victim.
> *Alius* alium *hortatur.*   One man exhorts another.

This rule is invariable; **every really transitive verb governs an accusative.** (See Intr. 38.)

5. But many verbs that are transitive in English must be translated into Latin by what are really intransitive verbs, and are therefore joined with a **dative** of the person (or thing) *interested in* the action of the verb. *i.e.* the *remoter object.* (Intr. 36.)   Thus—

I favour you,	tibi *faveo,*	(I am favourable *to* you.)
I obey you,	tibi *pareo,*	(I am obedient *to* you.)
I persuade you,	tibi *suadeo,*	(I am persuasive *to* you.)
I please you,	tibi *placeo,*	(I am pleasing *to* you.)
I spare you,	tibi *parco,*	(I am sparing (merciful) *to* you.)

These verbs, in the passive voice cannot be used otherwise than impersonally.

You are favoured,	tibi *favetur,*	(Favour is shown to you.)
You are spared,	tibi *parcitur*	etc.
You are pardoned,	tibi *ignoscitur.*	
You are persuaded,	tibi *persuadetur.*	
You are obeyed,	tibi *paretur.*	

6. The dative of the remoter object is sometimes, but by no means always, marked in English by the preposition *to* or *for.*

But it does not express *to* in the sense of *motion to.*

> I gave this *to* my father.   *Hoc* patri meo *dedi.*

but

> I came *to* my father.   Ad patrem *veni.*

For *to* in the sense of motion to a town, see **9,** *b.*   *For,* when it means "in defence of," "in behalf of," is expressed by *pro.*

> Pro *patria mori.*   To die *for* one's country.

7. The verb *to be,* and such verbs as *to become, to turn out, to continue,* etc., passive verbs of *being named, considered, chosen, found,* and the like, do not govern any case, but act as links between the subject and predicate, and therefore have the same case after as before them. (See Intr. 49, 50.)

> *Caius est justus.* Caius is a just man.
> *Scio Caium justum fieri.* I know that Caius is becoming just.
> *Caius imperator salutatus est.* Caius was saluted as Imperator.

8. (*a.*) With passive verbs and participles, "the thing *by which,*" or "*with which*" (the instrument), stands in the **ablative**; "the person *by whom*" (the agent), in the ablative **with the preposition** *a* or *ab.* (Intr. 41.)

> *Castra vallo fossāque a militibus munita sunt.* The camp has been fortified *by* the *soldiers with* a *rampart* and *ditch.*

(*b.*) But when "with" means "together or in company with" the preposition *cum* must be used.

> Cum telo *rēnit.* He came *with a weapon.*
> Cum Caesare *hoc feci.* I did this *with Caesar.*

Obs.—Cum is written after, and as one word with, the ablatives of the personal and reflexive pronouns (*mecum, tecum, secum, nobiscum, vobiscum*), and sometimes after the relative, as *quicum* (abl.), *quibuscum.*

9. (*a.*) The ablative also expresses the time *at* or *in* which a thing takes place, the accusative the time *during which* it lasts.

> Hoc mense *quindecim* dies *aegrotari.* I have been ill for fifteen days in this month.
> Tres *ibi* dies *commoratus sum,* quarto die *domum redii.* I stayed there three days, I returned home on the fourth day.

(*b.*) With the proper names of **towns** the ablative expresses motion *from,* without a preposition.

> Romā *renit,* "he came from Rome," but ex *or* ab Italiā, "from Italy;" also domo *renit,* "he came from home."

C

Motion *to* a town is expressed by the accusative without a preposition.

> Neapolin *rediit,* "he returned to Naples;" but ad *or* in *Italiam,* "to Italy."

The accusatives *domum,* (to) home, and *rus,* to the country, are used in the same way as towns, without a preposition.

10. One substantive in close connexion with another which it defines is put in the **genitive** case.

> *Horti* patris.   The gardens of my father = my father's gardens.
> *Laus* ducis.   The praise of the general.
> Fortium virorum *facta.*   The deeds of brave men.

This case corresponds often to the English possessive case, the only true *case* retained by English substantives.

11. (*a.*) PRONOUNS.—When a pronoun is the nominative case to a verb, it is not expressed in Latin, except for the sake of *emphasis* or particular *distinction.*

This is because the termination of the verb contains a pronominal element; therefore, to express the pronoun is really to have the person twice repeated.   (See Intr. 12.)

Ama-t is a compound word = Love-he, *i.e.* he loves.   Ille *amat* means, *As for that man,* he loves.   There is a repetition of the pronoun to call special attention to the subject of the verb.

> Ego *hoc volo.   For myself* I wish this

(*b.*) When there is a distinction or contrast between persons to be expressed, the personal pronouns must be used.

> Tu *Tarentum amisisti,* ego *recēpi.   You* lost Tarentum, *I* retook it.

(*c.*) Even the *possessive* pronoun is seldom expressed when there can be no doubt as to *whose* the thing is.

> Tum *ille dextram porrigit.*   Then he (the other) holds out *his* right hand.

But it must be used when emphatic, *i.e.* = *his own,*

or when its omission would cause a doubt as to the meaning.

> Suo *se gladio vulneravit.* He wounded himself with his (own) sword.
>
> *Patrem* meum *vīdi.* I have seen my father.

(*d.*) *He, she, it, they,* and their oblique cases, when they carry no emphasis, but merely *refer* to some person or thing already named, should be translated by *is, ea, id,* not by *ille. Ille* is much more emphatic, and often means "the other" in a story where two persons are spoken of, and sometimes "that distinguished person." *Iste* is "that of yours."

(*e.*) But when *him, her, them* denote the same person as the subject of the verb, *se, sui, sibi* must be used.

> He says he (himself) will do it. *Hoc* se *facturum esse ait.*

The same rule applies to the possessive pronoun *suus.*

12. The relative pronoun *qui* agrees in *gender* and *number* with a substantive or demonstrative pronoun, which is usually expressed in a preceding sentence. Its *case* depends on the construction of its own clause. The substantive to which it thus *refers* (*refero, relati-rum*) is called its **antecedent** (or *fore-going* substantive).

> *Ille est equus,* quem *ēmi.* Yonder is the horse which I have bought.
>
> *Pontem video,* qui *flumen jungit.* I see a bridge which spans the river.

13. The relative is often used in place of the English conjunctions *and, but, so,* etc., combined with the pronoun, *he, she, it,* etc. (See Intr. 58.)

> *Divitias optat,* quas *adepturus est nunquam.* He is praying for riches, *but* is never likely to obtain *them.*

14. PARTICIPLES.—(*a.*) There is no past participle active in Latin except with deponent verbs. (Intr. 45.)

We can say *secutus* for "having followed," from *sequor* (verb dep.) But for "having come," we must say either *quum vēnisset,* or *postquam* (*ubi*) *vēnit.*

(*b*.) With a transitive verb the **ablative absolute** of the passive participle may also be used.

Thus for "*having*," or "*after having*, heard this," we may say either *hoc audito*, or *hoc* quum *audivisset*, or *hoc* postquam (ubi) *audivit*.

(*c*.) The participle in -*rus* is always active, and has various meanings.

> *Hoc* facturus est. He is *going to, likely to, intending to, ready to, destined to,* do this.

15. Where in English two finite verbs are coupled by *and* we may often substitute a Latin participle in the proper case for one, and omit the *and*.

> They marvelled *and* went away.　Admirati *abiere*.
> They heard *and* wondered at him.　Auditum *admirati sunt*.

Vocabulary 1.

Note.—In the vocabularies hyphens (*e.g.* in *contem-no,* etc.) have not been inserted on any etymological principle, but simply to mark clearly the inflexions.

again, rursus.
always, semper.
and, et, -que, atque, ac. (See Intr. 57, *note*.)
arrive (*at*), *I*, per-vĕnio, īre, -vēni, -ventum (*ad* with *acc*.).
begin, *I*, in-cĭpio, ĕre, -cēpi, -ceptum.
blockade, *I*, ob-sĭdeo, ēre, -sēdi, -sessum.
brave, fort-is, -e.
but, sed, vero.
chief, prin-ceps, -cipis, *m.*
city, urbs, urbis,*f.*
consul, cons-ul, -ŭlis.
day, di-es, -ei, *m.*[1]
daybreak, prima lux (lūcis).
despise, *I*, contem-no, ĕre, -psi, -ptum.
district, ag-er, -ri, *m.*
elected, *I am*, fĭ-o, ĕri, factus.
enemy, host-is, -is.

envy, *I*, in-vĭdeo, ēre, -vīdi, -visum (*dat.*).　(See **5.**)
favour, *I*, făveo, ēre, fāvi, fautum (*dat.*).
fire and sword, ferrum et ign-is (*abl.* -i).[2]
fortunate, fel-ix, -īcis.
fourth, quart-us, -a, -um.
friend, amic-us, -i, *m.*
halt, *I*, con-sisto, ĕre, -stiti.
hate, *I*, od-i, isse, -eram.　(Perf. with pres. meaning.)
hear, *I*, aud-io, ire, -īvi, -ītum.
hour, hor-a, -ae, *f.*
human, hūmanus.
I, ego.　(See **11.**)
if, si.
injure, *I*, nŏc-eo, ēre, -ui, -ĭtum (*dat.*).
January, Januarius.
lay waste, *I*, vasto, are.
march (*subst.*), it-er, -inĕris, *n.*
messenger, nunti-us, -i, *m.*

---

[1] Occasionally fem. in sing. only.

[2] Note order.　*Ferrum*, "iron," used for "sword" in metaphorical sense.　(See **17.**)

mid-day, meridi-es, -ei, *m.*
month, mens-is, -is, *m.*
my, meus. (**11**, *c.*)
never, nunquam.
now, jam = *by this time*, can be used of the past ; nunc, *at the present*, at the moment of speaking. (**328**, *b.*)
obey, I, pār-eo, ēre, -ui (*dat.*). (See **5.**)
people, pŏpul-us, -i, *m.*
race, gĕn-us, -ĕris, *n.*
right hand, dextr-a, -ae, *f.*
Roman, Romānus.
send (*to*), *I*, mitto, ĕre, misi, missum (*ad*). (**6.**)
send for, arcess-o, ĕre, -ivi, -itum (*acc.*).

show, I, monstro, are.
sometimes, interdum.
spare, I, parco, ĕre, peperci, (*dat.*). (See **5.**)
speak, I, lŏ-quor, -qui, -cūtus.
stretch forth, I, por-rigo, ĕre, -rexi, -rectum.
take by assault, I, expugno, are.
that (*pron.*), ill-e, -a, -ud.
three, tres, tria.
to (*motion*), ad (*acc.*). (See **6.**)
town, oppid-um, -i, *n.*
you, tu, *pl.* vos. (**11**, *a* and *b.*)
vote, suffragi-um, -i, *n.*
waste. (See *lay.*)
way, vi-a, -ae, *f.*

Exercise 1.

1. I have been elected consul by the votes of the Roman people ; you are favoured by the enemies of the human race. 2. The town had now been blockaded for three days ; it was taken by assault on the fourth day. 3. I sent three messengers to you in the month (of) January.[1] 4. If you are (*fut.*) obeyed I shall be spared. 5. That district had been laid waste by the enemy[2] with fire and sword. 6. I am envied, but you are despised. 7. Fortune favours the brave (*pl.*), but sometimes envies the fortunate. 8. Having arrived at the city at daybreak he sent for the chiefs. 9. I never injured you, but you have always envied me, and you hate my friends. 10. Having heard this he halted for three hours, but at mid-day began his march again. 11. Having spoken thus,[3] and having stretched[4] forth his right hand he showed him the way.

---

[1] *Januarius* is properly an adjective.
[2] Plural ; the singular *hostis* is used sometimes like our "enemy," as a collective noun. (Intr. 29, *c.*)
[3] "These things," *haec.*
[4] Abl. abs., *lit.* his right hand having been stretched out. (**14**, *b.*)

MEANING OF WORDS AND PHRASES.

Though Latin words answering to all the English words in the following Exercises will be found in the Vocabularies, yet some care and thought will be necessary, even with their aid.

16. The same English word is often used in very different senses, some **literal,** some **figurative.** It is most unlikely that a single word in Latin will answer to all the various meanings of a single English word.

(*a.*) Thus we use the word " country" (connected through the French with the Latin *contra,* "opposite to us ") in a great variety of meanings : "rural districts" as opposed to " town ;" " our native land," as opposed to a foreign country ; " the territory," of any nation ; " the state," as opposed to an individual ; even " the inhabitants or citizens of a country." Each of these senses is represented by a different word in Latin. Thus :—

> Rus *abiit.* He went into the *country.*
> *Pro* patria *mori.* To die for one's (native) land or *country.*
> In fines *or* in agros *Helvetiorum exercitum duxit.* He led his army into the *country* of the Helvetii.
> Rei publicae (*or* civitati) *non sibi consuluit.* He consulted the interests of the *country,* not of himself.
> Civibus *omnibus carus fuit.* He was dear to the whole *country* (or *nation*).

No Vocabulary or Dictionary therefore will be of any real use, unless we clearly understand the precise meaning of the English.

(*b.*) Again, we might meet with the word " world " in an English sentence ; but we cannot translate it into Latin till we know whether it means " the whole universe," or "this globe," or "the nations of the world," or "people generally," or "mankind," or "life on earth."

Num casu factus est mundus ? Was the *world* (sun, moon, stars, and earth) made by chance ?

Luna circum tellurem *movetur.* The moon moves round the *world* (this planet).

Orbi terrarum (*or* omnibus gentibus) *imperabant Romani.* The Romans were rulers of the *world.*

Omnes (homines) *insanire eum credunt.* The whole *world* thinks him out of his mind.

Nemo usquam. No one in the *world.*

Multum hominibus *nocuit.* He did *the world* much harm.

In hac vita *nunquam eum sum visurus.* I am never likely to see him in this *world.*

With words therefore used in such different senses we must ask ourselves their precise meaning. Great assistance will be given in the present book ; but the learner cannot too soon learn to dispense with this kind of aid, and to think for himself.

17. There are a great number of **metaphorical expressions** in English which we cannot possibly render literally into Latin. We say, "His son ascended the throne," or "received the crown," or "lost his crown ;" and we might be tempted to translate such phrases literally after finding out the words for "to ascend," for "a throne," for "to receive," for "a crown," and so on.

But the fact is that these words when so combined **mean** something quite different from what they **say**, and to translate the actual words literally would be to say in Latin something quite different from the idea which the English conveys.

Filius solium ascendit, or *conscendit,* would (except in a poem) merely mean that his son "went up," or "climbed up," a throne ; *Filius coronam accepit* that he "received a (festal or other) garland." A Roman would certainly say *regnum excepit,* "received in turn (inherited) the *sovereignty.*"

Obs.—This is only a specimen of the kind of mistakes which we may make by not asking ourselves what words *mean* as well as what they say.

Compare such common expressions as "he held his peace," "he took his departure," answering to *conticuit, abiit*. Mistakes in such phrases as these are more likely to occur in translating longer passages without the aid afforded in these Exercises; but the warning cannot be too early given.

18. There are many English words whose **derivation from Latin words** is obvious. We are apt to think that if we know the parent word in Latin we cannot do better than use it to represent the English descendant, which so much resembles it in sound and appearance; but we can hardly have a worse ground than that of the similarity of *sound* in Latin and English words on which to form our belief that their *meaning* is identical. Most of these words have come to us through the French, *i.e.* through a language spoken by Roman soldiers and settlers, and borrowed from them by the Gauls; the Gauls in turn communicated the dialect of Latin which they spoke to their German conquerors; from these the Normans, a Scandinavian people, learnt, and adopted, what was to them a foreign tongue, with words from which, after conquering England, they enriched the language spoken by our English or Saxon forefathers. It would be strange if the meaning of words had not altered greatly in such a process.

When, therefore, we meet such a word as "office" in an Exercise we must beware of turning it by *officium*, which means "a duty," or an "act of kindness." We shall learn in time, by careful observation, when the English and Latin kindred words correspond in meaning, and when they differ, but we cannot too early learn that they **generally differ.**

19. Thus—

"Acquire" is not *acquirere*, but *adipisci, consequi*.
A man's "acts" are not *acta*, but *facta*.
"Attain to" is not *attinere ad*, or *attingere ad*, but *pervenire ad*, or *consequi*.
"Famous" is not *famosus*, but *praeclarus*.
"Mortal" (wound) is not (*vulnus*) *mortale*, but *mortiferum*.
"Nation" is not *natio*, but *civitas, populus, res publica, cives*.
"Obtain" is not *obtinere*, but *consequi, adipisci*, etc.

"Office" is not *officium*, but *magistratus*.
"Oppress" is not *opprimere*, but *vexare*, etc.
"Perceive" is not *percipere*, but *intellegere*.
"Receive" is not *recipere*, but *accipere*.
"Ruin" (as a metaphor) is not *ruīna*, but *pernicies*, *interītus*, etc.
"Secure" (safe) is not *securus*, but *tutus*.
"Vile" is not *vilis*, but *turpis*.

These are only specimens. The Vocabularies will be a sufficient guide, but the learner cannot too early be on his guard against a fruitful source of blunders, or learn too soon to lay aside, as far as possible, the use of vocabularies and similar aids, and trust to his own knowledge as gained from reading Latin.

Vocabulary 2.

acquire, *I*, ad-ipiscor, i, -eptus. (See **19**.)
admire, *I*, admir-or, āri, -atus.
advantage, emolument-um, -i, *n.*
all (*things*), (*n. pl.*), omnia.
as regards = *from* (*the side of*), a, ab (*abl.*).
attain to = *arrive at*. Voc. 1. (**19**.)
both . . . *and*, et . . . et.
boy, pu-er, -eri.
care. (See *free*.)
country, rus, ruris, *n.*; patri-a, -ae,*f.* (See **16**, *a*.)
crown, regn-um, -i, *n.* (See **17**.)
din, strepit-us, -ūs, *m.*
do, *I*, făc-io, ĕre, fēci, factum.
empire, imperi-um, -i, *n.*
ever = *always*. Voc. 1.
famous, praeclarus.[1] (**19**.)
father, pat-er, -ris.
fight, *I*, pugno, āre.
for (*conj.*), nam, enim. (Intr. 98.)
for (*prep.*), pro (*abl.*). (**6**.)
forefathers, major-es,[2] -um.

foretell, *I*, praedi-co, -ĕre, -xi.
free from care, securus. (**19**.)
from, a, ab (*abl.*).
glory, glori-a, -ae, *f.*
great, magnus.
greatly, maxime.
Hannibal, Hannib-al, -ălis.
highest, summus.
hold, *I*, obtin-eo, ĕre, -ui. (**19**.)
hold my peace, *I*, contic-esco, ĕre, -ui. (See **17**, *Obs.*)
king, rex, rēgis.
last, *at*, tandem.
long (*adv.*), diu.
made, *I am being*, fio. (See *become*, Voc. 1.)
means, *by no*, haudquaquam.
mind, anim-us, -i, *m.*
mortal (*wound*), morti-fer, -fera, -ferum. (**19**.)
much, multus.
native country. (See **16**, *a*.)
nation, civit-as,[3] -atis, *f.* (**19**.)
never, nunquam.
obedient to, *I am*, = *obey*. Voc. 1.

---

[1] *Famosus* means "notorious" in a bad sense, "infamous."

[2] *Patres* is never used in prose for "forefathers." Our use of "fathers" in this sense came into English from Hebrew through the Bible.

[3] *Natio* is rarely used of a civilised and organised nation; it means a people, or tribe, sprung from one race, of the same blood (*nascor*).

office, magistrat-us, -ūs, *m.* **(19.)**
orator, ōrāt-or, -ōris.
pleasing (to), gratus (*dat.*).
ready to, I am, vŏlo, velle, vŏlui.
receive, I, ac-cipio, ĕre, -cēpi, -ceptum. **(19.)**
reign, I, regno, āre.
Rome =: *nation of,* populus Rōmān-us.   (See **319.**)
ruin, interĭt-us, -ūs, *m.* ; clad-es, -is, *f.* **(19.)**
say, I, dī-co, ĕre, -xi, -ctum.
secure = *safe,* tutus. **(19.)**

succeed to, I, (*crown*) = *I inherit* (see **17**), ex-cipio, ĕre, -cepi, -ceptum.
sword (*metaph.*), arm-a, -orum, *n.* ; ferr-um, -i, *n.* **(17.)**
this, hic, haec, hoc.
time, at that, tum. **(64.)**
vile, turp-is, -e. **(19.)**
violence, vis, *abl.* vi, *f.*
whole, totus.
world. **(16,** *b.***)**
wound, vuln-us. -ĕris, *n.*
yet, tămen.

Exercise 2.

1. I was made king by the votes of the whole nation.
2. He attained to the highest offices in (his) native country.
3. I hate the din of cities; the country is always most pleasing to me.   4. Our forefathers acquired this district by the sword.   5. The whole world was at that time obedient to the empire of Rome.   6. He reigned long; the crown which he had acquired by violence he held to[1] the great advantage of the nation.   7. He was a most famous orator, and all the world admired him greatly.
8. He was most dear to the whole nation, for he was ever ready to do all things for the country.   9. He received a mortal wound (while) fighting for his native land.   10. At last he held his peace; he had said much (*neut. pl.*), and (spoken) long.   11. He succeeded to the crown (while) a boy; (as) king he attained to the highest glory.   12. He was now secure from all violence, yet he was by no means free from care as regards Hannibal.
13. He never attained to his father's glory, but all things that were vile he always hated.   14. He foretold the ruin of his country.

---

[1] Use *cum* with abl.

MEANING AND USE OF WORDS—*Continued.*

VERBS.

20. In translating a Verb into Latin, it is most important to be sure of the precise sense in which the verb is used.

We have in English a large number of verbs which are used in two senses, one **transitive**, the other **intransitive** or **reflexive**.

We say " he changed his seat," and " the weather is changing;" " he moved his arm," and "the stars move;" "we dispersed the mob," and "the fog dispersed;" " he turned his eyes," and " he turned to his brother;" " he collected books," and " a crowd collected;" " he joined this to that," "he joined his brother," "the two ends joined."

But in translating such verbs into Latin, we must carefully distinguish between these different senses of the same verb.

If the English transitive verb is used intransitively, or as we should say in Greek in the Middle Voice (as in "the crowd *dispersed*"), we must either (*a*) use the passive of the Latin verb, or (*b*) insert the reflexive pronoun *se*, or (*c*) use a different verb.

43

21. Thus—

(*a.*) He *changed* his seat.   *Sedem* mutavit.

The weather *is changing*,
or *altering.*   Mutatur *tempestas.*

He *broke up* the crowd.   *Multitudinem* dissipavit.
The fog *broke up.*   Dissipata est *nebula.*

The moon *moves* round
the earth.   *Luna circa tellurem* movetur.
He *moved* his arm.   *Brachium* movit.

He *rolled down* stones.   *Lapides* devolvit.
The stones *roll down.*   Devolvuntur *lapides.*

(*b.*) He will *surrender the city.*   *Urbem* dēdet.
The enemy will *surrender.*   Se dēdent *hostes.*

(*c.*) Riches *increase.*   Crescunt *divitiae.*
He *increased* his wealth.   *Opes suas* auxit.
He *collected* books.   *Libros* collēgit.
A crowd was *collecting.*   Conveniebat *multitudo.*

22. Many English verbs, usually intransitive, become transitive by the addition of a preposition: to hope, to hope *for* (trans.); to wait, to wait *for* (trans.); to sigh (intrans.), to sigh *for* (trans.); similarly "to gaze *on*," "to look *at*," "to smile *at*," and many others.

To determine whether the preposition really belongs to the verb, the verb may be turned into the passive; if the preposition *remains attached to the verb*, we may be sure that the two words form one transitive verb.

He *waits for* his brother.   His brother *is waited for.*

To "wait for," therefore, is a compound verb; "to wait" is converted by the addition of a preposition from an intransitive to a transitive verb.

Fratrem expectat.   *Frater* expectatur.

23. Some of the commonest of such words are—

I aim *at* distinctions (high office).   *Honores* peto.
I crave *for* leisure.   *Otium* desidĕro.
I hope *for* peace.   *Pacem* spero.
I listen *to* you.   *Te* audio.
I look or wait *for* you.   *Te* expecto.
I look round *for* you.   *Te* circumspicio.

I look *up at* the sky.   *Caelum* suspicio.
I pray *for* (*i.e.* desire much) this.   *Hoc* opto.

But the number of such English verbs is very large.

24. In Latin (as in older English I *fore*go, I *be*speak) an intransitive verb very often becomes transitive by composition with a preposition prefixed to the verb. (See Intr. 24.)

> *Sedeo*, I sit, obs*ideo*, I blockade (a town); *veh*or, I am ca*rr*ied, *or* I ride, praeter*veh*or, I ride past; *venio*, I come, con*venio*, I have an interview with, as, *ad te* vēni, *Caesar*em convēni.

25. A single Latin verb will often express an English *verbal phrase*, *i.e.* a combination of a verb with a substantive or other words. Thus—

> *Taceo*, I keep silence; *abeo*, I take my departure; *navigo*, I take, *or* have, a voyage; *insanio*, I am out of my senses; *minor*, I utter threats; *colloquor*, I have a conversation; *te libero*, I give you your liberty; *adeo mortem pertimescit*, such is his terror of death.

Vocabulary 3.

absent, I am, ab-sum, esse, etc.
besiege, obsideo.[1] (See *blockade*, Voc. 1.)
bestow (these things on you), I (haec tibi) larg-ior, īri, -ītus.
bloody, cruentus.
carry on, I = I wage, gĕ-ro, ĕre, -ssi, -stum.
country, in the, ruri.
crave for, I, desidero, āre. (22, 23.)
desert, I, deser-o, ĕre, -ui, -tum.
disperse, to (intrans.), di-labi, -lapsus. (20.)
down from, de (*abl.*).
eight, octo (*indec.*).
endeavour, I, cōnor, ari.
exile, an, ex-ul, -ūlis.
fatal,[2] funestus.

flock together, to, congregari.
friend. Voc. 1.
gate, port-a, -ae, *f.*
gather together, to, con-vĕnire, -vēni, -ventum.
Heaven (metaph.), (17), Di Immortales. Caelum would mean "the sky."
leisure, oti-um, -i, *n.*
long (adj. of time), diutīnus.
look for, I, expecto, are. (22, 23.)
look round for, I, circum-spicio, -ĕre, -spexi, -spectum. (22, 23.)
look up at, I, suspicio, ĕre, etc.
many, mult-i, -ae, -a.
mingle with, I (intrans.), im-misceor (20), ēri, -mixtus (*dat.*).
morning, in the, mānĕ (*adv.*).

---

[1] *Obsideo* is "besiege" in the sense of blockading; *oppugno*, in that of assaulting.

[2] *Fatalis* is "destined," "fated," and may be used either in a good or bad sense. (See **18.**)

mountain, mon-s, -tis, *m.*
multitude, multitud-o, -inis, *f.*
noon. See *mid-day*, Voc. 1.
obtain, I, ad-ipiscor, -ipisci, -eptus; conse-quor, i, -cutus. (**19.**)
one (*of*), unus (e, *abl.*).
our, nost-er, -ra, -rum.
peace, pax, pacis, *f.*
pray for, I, (*desire much*), opto, āre (*acc.*).
return (*subst.*), redit-us, -ūs, *m.*
rock, sax-um, -i, *n.*
roll, I (*intrans.*), vol-vor (21, *a*), vi, volutus.
soldier, mil-es, -ĭtis.

struck (*participle*), ictus, (*fr.* ico, icĕre.)
surrender, I, (*trans.*) de-do, ĕre, -didi, -ditum; (*intrans.*) me dedo. (21, *b.*)
swarm out of, I, effundor, i, effus-us (*abl.*).
then, tum, tunc.
towards, ad (*acc.*).
turn, I (*intrans.*), con-vertor, i, -versus. (**20.**)
vain, in, frustrā.
vast,[1] maximus ; ingeñ-s, -tis.
wait for, I, expecto. (**22, 23.**)
war, bell-um, -i, *n.*
world. (**16,** *b.*)

Exercise 3.

Verbs marked in *italics* are to be expressed by participles, the conjunction that follows to be omitted (**15**).

1. We all were craving for peace, for we had carried on a long and bloody war. 2. They at last surrendered the city, which-had-been-besieged (*part.*) for eight months (9,*a*). 3. He prays for peace and leisure, but[2] he is never likely[3]-to-obtain these things. 4. All the world is looking for war, but heaven will bestow upon us the peace for which we pray. 5. Then he *turned* (*part.*) towards his friends, and in vain endeavoured to look up at them. 6. He looked round for his friends, but all for whom he looked round (*imperf.*) had deserted him. 7. The enemy *had swarmed* out of the gates and were mingling with our soldiers. 8. The multitude which had gathered together in the morning dispersed before noon. 9. Many rocks were rolling down from the mountains, and one of our guides *was struck* by a vast mass, and received a mortal wound. 10. On that fatal day I craved for you, but you were absent in the country. 11. A vast multitude had flocked together, and was now waiting for the return of the exiles.

---

[1] *Vastus* does not mean "vast" in size, but either "shapeless," or "waste," "desolate," etc. (See **18**.)
[2] Relative neut. pl. (**13**) = "which things."
[3] "Likely-to," participle in -*rus* of "to obtain." (See **14,** *c.*)

AGREEMENT OF THE SUBJECT, OR NOMINATIVE CASE AND VERB.

26. If one verb is predicated of two or more **subjects** of **different** grammatical **persons**, it will be in the plural number, and agree with the first person rather than the second, and with the second rather than the third.

> *Et ego*[1] *et tu manus* sustulimus. Both you and I raised our hands.
> *Et tu et frater meus manus* sustulistis. Both you and my brother lifted up your hands.

(For the analysis of these sentences see Intr. 65.)

27. But sometimes the verb will be in the **singular** and agree with the subject *nearest itself*.

> *Et tu* ades, *et frater tuus.* Both you and your brother are here.

28. If a single verb is predicated of several subjects of the **third person**, it may either be in the plural number, or it may agree with the substantive nearest itself.

> *Appius et soror ejus et frater meus manus* sustulerunt. Appius and his sister and my brother lifted up their hands.

But "Sustulit *manus Appius et soror ejus et frater meus,*" with the same meaning, would be good Latin.

---

[1] For "Caius and *I*," the Romans, putting "*I*" first, said "*Ego* et *Caius.*" When therefore Cardinal Wolsey said "*Ego* et *Rex meus,*" he was a good grammarian but a bad courtier. Similarly they placed the second person before the third; "Your brother and you" would be, *Et tu et frater tuus.*

29. After **disjunctive** conjunctions (Intr. 56, *b*), *neque (nec) . . . neque ; aut . . . aut,* etc., either construction may be used.

> *Neque tu neque frater tuus* adfuistis.   Or,
> *Neque tu* adfuisti, *neque frater tuus.* Neither you nor your brother were present.

But the latter is much more usual.

Obs.—There is therefore great freedom in all these constructions in Latin ; greater than is usual in English.[1]

30. A singular collective noun (see Intr. 29, *c*) is *occasionally* followed by a plural verb.

> *Magna pars . . . fūgēre.*   A large proportion fled.

But *much oftener,* and always if it denotes a united body which acts as one man, it is followed by a singular verb.

> Vult *populus Romanus.* It is the wish of the Roman
>   people, *or,* of the people of Rome.
> *Exercitus e castris* profectus est.   The army started from
>   the camp.
> *Senatus* decrevit.   The senate decreed.

Obs.—The singular is always used with *Senatus populusque ;* the two words are looked on as forming one idea.

In English there is greater freedom ; we can use the plural if we think rather of the individuals than of the body as a whole.

> The gentry *were* divided in opinion.

Vocabulary 4.

Alexander, Alexand-er, -ri.
army, exercit-us, -ūs, *m.*
before (*prep.*), ante (*acc.*).
brother, frat-er, -ris.
Clitus, Clit-us, -i.
countryman, civ-is, -is.

decree, I, de-cerno, ĕre, -crevi,
  -cretum.
end, fin-is, -is, *m.* (properly, *limit*).
ever, unquam.
exile, I am in, exulo, āre.
flock, gre-x, -gis, *m.*

---

[1] But compare :—
>   "The thought that thou art safe, and he."—COWPER.
>   "For thine *is* the kingdom, the power, and the glory."

Gauls, the, Gall-i, -orum.
great. Voc. 2.
health, I am in good, val-eo, ēre, -ui.
home, domum (*acc.*). (See **9**, *b.*)
honour (*distinction*), hon-os, -ōris, *m.*
kindness, benefici-um, -i, *n.*
kill, I, inter-ficio, ĕre, -feci.
matter, a, res, rei, *f.*
next day, the, postridie.
number (*proportion or part*), par-s, -tis, *f.*
return, I, redeo, redīre, redii.
reward, praemi-um, -i, *n.*

safe (*unharmed*), incolum-is, -e.
senate, senat-us, -ūs, *m.*
settle, I, constit-uo, ĕre, -ui (*trans.*).
spare, I. Voc. 1.
summer, aest-as, -ātis, *f.*
sword, gladi-us, -i, *m.*
third, terti-us, -a, -um.
time, at that, either *tum* (Voc. 2), or use subst., *tempest-as, -ātis, f.*, with *is, ea, id.*
toil, lab-or, -ōris, *m.*
wage, I, gero, ĕre, gessi, gestum.
war. Voc. 3.
well, bĕne (*adv.*).

Exercise 4.

1. If the army and you are in good health, it is well.
2. Both you and I have waged many wars for our country.
3. The Gauls were conquered by Caesar before the end of the summer. 4. The flock returned home safe the next day. 5. Neither you nor your brother have ever done this. 6. A great number of my countrymen were at that time in exile. 7. Both you and I have been made consuls by the votes and by the kindness of the Roman people.
8. I have spared my countrymen, you the Gauls.
9. Having settled[1] these matters, he returned home on the third day. 10. Clitus was killed by Alexander with a sword. 11. The Roman people and senate decreed many honours to you and to your father. 12. Neither you nor I had looked for this reward of all our toil.

---

[1] Abl. abs. (See **14**, *b.*)

D

ACCUSATIVE WITH INFINITIVE.

Oratio Obliqua.

31. The infinitive takes before it (as its *subject*) not the nominative but the *accusative*.

> *Frater cecĭdit.* His brother fell; but—
> *Narrat* fratrem cecidisse. He reports *that* his brother fell.

The accusative with the infinitive is especially used, where in English we use a clause beginning with "that," after (*a*) verbs of *feeling, knowing, thinking, believing, saying* (**verba sentiendi et declarandi**); and (*b*) such expressions as *it is certain, manifest, true*, etc.

In turning such sentences into Latin, *that* must be omitted; the English *nominative* turned into the *accusative;* and the English verb into the *infinitive mood.*[1]

> (*a.*) *Sentimus* calere ignem. We perceive-by-our-senses *that* fire is hot.
>
> Hostes adesse *dixit.* He said *that* the enemy was near.
>
> Fratrem tuum fortem esse *intellego.* I perceive *that* your brother is a brave man.
>
> Rem ita se habere *video.* I see *that* the fact is so.
>
> *Respondit* se esse iturum. He answered *that* he would go.

---

[1] We are not quite without this idiom in English.

"I saw *him to be a knave*" (= "I saw *that* he was a knave").

Such a sentence as "*narravit fratrem suum in praelio cecidisse,*" may be sometimes translated literally, "he declared (*or* reported) his brother *to have fallen* in the battle." At the same time this constant employment of the infinitive, in place of such conjunctions as the English *that*, the French *que*, the German *dass*, and even the very common Greek ὡς or ὅτι, is one of the most characteristic idioms of the Latin language. (See Intr. 59, *h.*)

(*b.*) *Manifestum est* nivem esse albam. It is plain *that* snow is white.

Constat Romam non sine labore conditam fuisse. It is agreed *that* Rome was not built without toil.

The statement made by the verb in the infinitive mood is called *indirect* predication, or **oratio obliqua**; because the statement is not made directly (oratio *recta*), but indirectly, *i.e.* through a verb that is itself dependent on another verb or phrase.

32. Cautions.—(*a.*) Beware of ever using *quod* or *ut* to represent *that* after any verb or phrase *sentiendi vel declarandi.*

Never say "*Scio* quod *erras*," "I know that you are wrong;" but always, "te errare *scio.*"

(*b.*) In English we often express a statement or an opinion as though it were a fact, but with such words as "*he said*," "*he thought*," etc., inserted in a parenthesis.

You were, *he said*, mistaken. You were absent, *he thought*, from Rome. He is, *it is plain*, quite mad.

In Latin this construction must not be used; such expressions as "*he said*," "*he thought*," "*it is plain*," must form the principal verb or clause with the infinitive dependent on it.

We must write—not "tu, *dixit*, errasti," but "te errare *dixit*;" not "Roma, *credidit*, aberas," but "Roma te abesse *credidit.*"

For the use of *inquit* with *oratio recta* see **40**.

33. The English verb *say* when joined to a negative is translated into Latin by the verb of denial, *nego.*

He *says* that he is *not* ready. *Se paratum esse* negat.

He *said* he would *never* do this. *Se hoc unquam esse facturum* negavit.

He *says* he has done *nothing*. *Negat se quidquam fecisse.*

34. The *pronoun*, so often *omitted* in *oratio recta* (*currit*, (*he*) runs), must always be *inserted* in *oratio obliqua*: se currere ait.

He, she, they must be translated by the reflexive pronoun
se (11, *c*), whenever one of these pronouns stands for the
same person as the *subject* of the verb of saying or thinking.

> *Hoc se fecisse negat.* He says that *he* (himself) did not
> do this.

Eum or *illum* would be used if the second *he* denoted
a different person from the first *he*. Latin is therefore
much less ambiguous than English, as it carefully distinguishes the different persons denoted by *he*, etc.

Tenses of the Infinitive.

35. In translating the verb in an English *that*-clause
dependent on a past tense, we must attend carefully to
the following rule :—

An English *past* tense in a *that*-clause will be translated
by the *present* infinitive, if the time denoted by the two
verbs is the same.

> *Se in Asia esse*[1] *dixit.* He said that he *was* in Asia.
> (When ?—at the time of his speaking.)

The perfect infinitive is only used if the verb in the
that-clause denotes a time *prior* to that of the verb
sentiendi vel declarandi.

> *Se in Asia fuisse dixit.* He said that he *had been*, or *was*,
> in Asia. (When ?—at some time earlier than that at
> which he was speaking.)

36. The future infinitive is supplied by the participle
in *-rus* with *esse, fore, fuisse,* and is used thus :—

> Both, He *says* that he
> *will* go ;
> And also, He *said* that } *Se iturum esse or* fore { *dicit.*
> he *would* go. { *dixit.*
>
> He *says* or *said* that he *would have* gone. *Se iturum fuisse*
> *dicit* or *dixit.*

---

[1] Thus the present infinitive represents both the present and
imperfect of the indicative,—the imperfect being the tense which
denotes a past event, not merely as past, but as *contemporaneous with
something else in the past.* (See below, 177, *b.*)

Vocabulary 5.

against, contra (*acc.*).
answer, I, respon-deo, dēre, -di, -sum.
attack, I, oppugno, āre. (24.)
believe, I, cred-o, ĕre, -idi, -itum.
break, I (*met.*), violo, āre.
camp, castr-a, -orum, *n.*
follow, I, sequor, i, secutus sum.
general, dux, dŭcis.
gladly, libenter.
hope for, I, sper-o, āre.
interview, I have an interview with, con-venio, īre, -vēni (*trans.*). (24.)
law, lex, lēgis, *f.*
line (*of battle*), aci-es, -ei, *f.*
man, vir, vĭri.
now. See Voc. 1.
one and all, omnes (*placed last*). (Intr. 92, 97.)
perceive, I, intel-lĕgo, ĕre, -lexi, -lectum. (19.)

place, loc-us, -i, *m.*
plain (*adj.*), manifestus.
please, I, plac-eo, ēre, -ui, -itum (*dat.*). (5.)
Pompey, Pompe-ius, -i.
preceding, proximus.
remember, I, memin-i, isse, (*imperat.*) memento.
reply, I. See *answer.*
repose, oti-um, -i, *n.*
ride past, I, praeter-vehor, i, -vectus (*trans.*). (24.)
say, I. Voc. 2.
sigh for (*I crave for*), desidero, āre (*trans.*). (See 22.)
sin, I, pecco, āre.
soon, mox, brĕvi.
take up, I, sūn-o, ĕre, -psi, -ptum.
to, ad, in (*acc.*).
train, I, exerc-eo, ēre, -ui, -itum.
year, ann-us, -i, *m.*

Exercise 5.

1. He had waged, he answered, many wars, and was now sighing for peace and repose. 2. He says that he has not sinned. 3. Both you and your brother, he replied, were in good health. 4. He perceived that the enemy [1] would soon attack the city. 5. He says that Caesar will not break the laws. 6. It is plain that the place pleases you. 7. It was plain that the place pleased you. 8. It was plain that the place had pleased you. 9. Pompey believed that his countrymen would, one and all, follow him. 10. The soldiers said that they had not taken up arms against their country and the laws. 11. Brave men, remember, are trained by toils. 12. The soldiers answered that they would have gladly attacked the town in the preceding year, but that now they hoped for repose. 13. Having returned to the camp, he said that he had ridden past the enemies' line, and had an interview with their [2] general.   .

---

[1] Sing. (See p. 37, note [2].)
[2] Gen. pl. of *is:* why would *suus* be wrong? (See **11**, *d* and *e.*)

ACCUSATIVE WITH INFINITIVE—*Continued.*

SOME of the *verba sentiendi et declarandi* have **special constructions.**

37. Thus, after the verbs *sperare* (to hope), *promittere* or *pollicēri* (to promise), *recipere* (to engage or undertake), *minari* (to threaten), *jurare* (to swear), and similar verbs referring *to the future*, the *future infinitive* is used in Latin with the *accusative* of the pronoun.

Obs.—In English we generally treat these verbs as *modal* verbs (see Intr. 48) and join them with the *present* infinitive ; in Latin, and sometimes in English, they are used as verbs of thinking or saying something future.

In English we say "he hopes *to* live," and also "he hopes *that* he *will* live ;" in Latin the latter is the regular construction.

> *Sperat plerumque adolescens diu* se victurum (esse).[1]   A young man generally hopes *to live* a long time.
> *Hoc* se facturum esse *minatus est.*   He threatened *to do* this.

N.B.—The verb *posse* is often used in the present infinitive after *spero.*

> *Hoc se facere* posse *sperat.*   He hopes to be able to do this.

38. With active verbs that have no future in -*rus*, and generally with passive verbs, and even as a substitute for the ordinary construction, *fore ut* with a subjunctive is used.

> *Spero* fore ut deleatur *Carthago.*   I hope that Carthage will be annihilated.
> *Speravit* fore ut *id sibi* contingeret.   He hoped that this would fall to his lot.

---

[1] With these *compound* infinitives *esse* is often omitted.

Obs.—The *tense* of the verb after *fore ut* depends upon that of the verb of hoping, etc.; after the present, perfect with *have*, and future, the present subjunctive is used; after a past tense, the imperfect.

39. After *simulare*[1] (to pretend), the *accusative* of the pronoun must be expressed in Latin.

Se *furĕre simulat.* He pretends *to be* mad.

40. The great exception to the construction of *verba declarandi* is *inquam, inquit,*—"say I," "says he."

Inquit always quotes the *exact words used,* and never stands first.

Domum, inquit, *redibo.* "I will," *says he,* "return home."
Domum se rediturum esse dicit *or* ait. He will, *he says,* return home.

Inquit therefore is always used with oratio *recta;* all other words of *saying* with oratio *obliqua.*

41. The accusative with the infinitive is also used after—

(*a.*) Certain verbs of *commanding* and *wishing,* especially *jubeo, volo, cupio, prohibeo.*

(*b.*) Verbs expressing *joy, sorrow, indignation, wonder,* etc.

Milites abire *jussit.* He ordered the soldiers to go away.
Te *incolumem* rediisse *gaudeo.* I rejoice that you have returned in safety.

Vocabulary 6.

assert, I (maintain), vindĭco, āre.
business, the, res, rei, *f.*
country (**16**, *a*), ager, agri, *m.*
crown. Voc. 2, and see **17**.
cruel, crudel-is, -e.
earlier than (= *before*), ante (*acc.*).
fifth, quint-us, -a, -um.
find, I, in-venio, ire, -vēni, -ventum.
finish, I, con-ficio, ĕre, -feci, -fectum.
foe = *enemy.* Voc. 1.
force, vis, *f.* (*abl.* vi).
freedom, libert-as, -atis, *f.*
greatly, vehementer.
highest, summus.
home, at, domi.
husband, vir, viri.

[1] *Simulo* is used of a person who pretends that something exists which does not. *Dissimulo* of some one who tries to conceal something which does exist.

Quae *non* sunt *simulo;* quae *sunt,* ea *dissimulantur.*

land. (See *country*.)
last, at. Voc. 2.
London, Londini-um, -i.   (9, *b*.)
long. (See *so*.)
mad, *I am quite*, fŭro,[1] ĕre.
mind, *I am out of my*, insan-io, ire,
   -ivi, *or* -ii.   (25.)
nation, popul-us, -i, *m*. ; *or* civ-es,
   -ium.   (19, and p. 41, note [3].)
now. Voc. 1.
obtain. Voc. 3.   (19.)
oppress, *I*, vexo, are.   (19.)
presently = *soon*.
pretend, *I*, simulo, āre.
promise, *I*, polli-ceor,[2] ēri, -citus ;
   pro-mitto, ĕre, -misi, -missum.

rejoice, *I*, gaudeo, ēre, gavisus sum.
satisfactory, use adverbial phrase
   ex sententia, "in accordance with
   one's views."
see, *I*, vĭdeo, ēre, vīdi, visum.
shortly, brevi.
sister, sor-or, -oris.
so long, tamdiu.
Solon, Sol-on, -ōnis.
soon. Voc. 5.
swear, *I*, juro, āre.
sword, *by the* (*met*.).   Voc. 2.
threaten, *I*, minor, ari.
voyage, *I have a*, navigo, āre.   (25.)
win, *I = I obtain*.   Voc. 3.
yet, *not*, nondum.

Exercise 6.

1. Solon pretended to be out of his mind.   2. I will pretend, says he, to be out of my mind.   3. He promised to come to London shortly.   4. I hope that you will have a satisfactory voyage.   5. He hopes to obtain the crown presently.   6. He was pretending to be quite mad.   7. Caesar threatened to lay waste our country with fire and sword.   8. He replied that he had had a satisfactory voyage.   9. He swore to finish the business by force.   10. He says that he will not return home earlier than the fifth day.   11. He replied that he had not yet seen his sister, but (that he) hoped to find both her and her husband at home.   12. The army hoped that the land of the enemy would now be laid waste with fire and sword.   13. He hopes soon to attain to the highest honours, but[3] I believe that he will never win them.   14. I rejoice greatly that your nation, (which has been) so long oppressed by a cruel foe, has at last asserted its freedom by the sword.   15. I have not, says she, yet seen my sister, but I hope to find both her and her[4] husband at home.

---

[1] *Furo* is a stronger term than *insanio: furor* often means "frenzy," but it never means "fury" in the sense of mere "anger."

[2] *Promitto*, "I give forth," general word for "I give assurance for the future;" *polliceor*, "I give something *that lies in my own power*."

[3] See **13**.

[4] *Ejus*. Why not *suum?*

NOMINATIVE WITH INFINITIVE, MODAL VERBS, PASSIVE VERBS OF SAYING, Etc.

42. (i.) **A large number of verbs are used in Latin in close combination with an infinitive mood without any intervening accusative.** They are, in fact, a kind of *auxiliary* verb, as they cannot, as a rule, stand by themselves, or make full sense without the infinitive with which they are joined; they are called modal because they give, as it were, a fresh mood (*modus*) to the other verb. (See Intr. 48.)

Compare the English "I can *do*," "must *do*," "ought *to do*," "wish *to do*," etc., where *do* and *to do* are both in the infinitive mood.

Such are verbs of

(*a.*) *Possibility* or the *reverse.*	*Possum, nequeo,* etc.
(*b.*) *Beginning* [1] or *ceasing.*	*Coepi, incipio, desino, desisto,* etc.
(*c.*) *Habit, continuance, hastening.*	*Soleo, assuesco, pergo, festino,* etc.
(*d.*) Many verbs of *wish*, [2] *purpose, aim, endeavour,* etc.	*Volo, nolo, malo, cupio, audeo, statuo,* etc.
(*e.*) *Duty.*	*Debeo.*

(ii.) When a finite verb of this kind is combined with the infinitive, the *nominative*, not the accusative, is used in the predicate.

Civis Romanus fieri, vocari, *cupio.*
I am anxious to become, *or* to be called, a citizen of Rome.

Soleo, or *incipio,* or *festino, otiosus* esse.
I am accustomed, *or* I am beginning, *or* I am making haste, to be at leisure.

Mori malo quam servus esse.
I had rather die than be a slave.

---

[1] This is sometimes expressed by the termination -*sco* of the verb: *senesco,* I begin to grow old. Such verbs are called *inchoative.*

[2] Sometimes expressed by the termination -*urio:* *edo,* I eat; *esurio* I am hungry.

43. With passive verbs *sentiendi et declarandi*, such as *videor*, " I seem," *dicor*, " I am said," and similar verbs, the impersonal construction, "*it* seems," "*it* is said," is not used in Latin.

We must not say for "*It is said*, or *it seems*, that Cicero was consul that year," " *Videtur, dicitur*, Ciceronem *eo anno* consulem *fuisse*," but " *Videtur, dicitur* Cicero *eo anno* consul *fuisse*."

44. But a very common use is *ferunt, dicunt, tradunt*, they *or* men say, etc., followed by the accusative and infinitive. So that for "There is a tradition that Homer was blind," we may either say " *Traditur Homer*us *caecus fuisse*," or " *Tradunt Homer*um *caecum fuisse*," but not " *Traditur Homer*um *caecum fuisse*."

45. Verbs of *purposing, resolving*, and many others, are used with the infinitive and the nominative case, only when *the subject of both verbs is the same.*

> *Constituit Caesar* consul fieri.
> Caesar determined to become consul.

But

> *Constituit Caesar* ut Antonius consul fieret.
> Caesar determined that Antony should be made consul.

(See **118.**)

46.   EXCEPTIONS.

(*a.*) The past tense of such longer phrases as *mihi nuntiatum est, memoriae proditum est*, and others, is used impersonally, and is followed by the accusative and infinitive.

> *Caesari* nuntiatum est *adesse Gallos.*
> *News was brought* to Caesar that the Gauls were at hand.

(*b.*) *Videtur* can be used impersonally, but means, not "it seems," but "it seems *good.*"

> *Hoc mihi facere* visum est.
> It seemed *good* to me (I resolved) to do this.

(*c.*) The impersonal verbs, *apparet* (not "it *seems*," but "it is *clear*") and *constat*, "it is agreed," are very common, and are followed by the accusative and infinitive.

(*d.*) The accusative is sometimes introduced after *volo*, even when the subject of both verbs is the same. We may say either Consul *esse vult*, "He wishes to be consul," or Se consulem *esse vult*, "It is his wish that he himself should be consul."

Vocabulary 7.

accept, *I*, ac-cipio, ĕre, -cepi, -ceptum.

ambassador, legat-us. -i.

ask for, *I*, posco, ĕre, poposci. (22,23.)

become, *I*, fio, ĕri, factus.

begin, *I*. Voc. 1.

blame, culpa, *f.*

break, *I*. (See *word*.)

candidate for, *I am a*, pet-o, ĕre, -ivi, *or* -ii, -itum (*trans.*). (23.)

cease, *I*, de-sino, ĕre, de-sivi, *or* -sii.

chief (*man*). Voc. 1.

clear, *it is*, appār-et, ĕre, -uit. (46, *c.*)

coward, timidus; ignavus.

crown. Voc. 2.

deceive, *I*, de-cipio, ĕre, -cepi, -ceptum.

despair, *I*, despero, āre.

destined, fatāl-is, -e.

die, *I*, morior, i, mortuus[1] sum, moriturus.

either . . . *or*, vel . . . vel; aut . . . aut. (See Intr. 57, *note*.)

free (*adj.*), lib-er, -era, -um.

free from, *I*, libero, āre.

hand, *I am at*, ad-sum, esse, -fui.

jury (*judges*), jud-ex, -ĭcis (*in plur.*).

keep, *I* (*promises*), sto, stare, steti, lit. "I stand on my promises" (*abl.*).

live, *I*, vi-vo, ĕre, -xi, -ctum.

member of the state, civis.

nation. Voc. 6.

offer, *I*, de-fero, ferre, -tuli, -latum.

office. (See **18**, and Voc. 2.)

once, *at*, statim.

patriot, *true patriot*, bonus civis; lit. "a good member of the state."

prefer, *I*. (See *rather*.)

private (*person*), privat-us, -i.

promise (*thing promised*), promissum (*neut. participle*), -si, *n.*

Pyrrhus, Pyrrh-us, -i.

rather, *I had*, *or would*, mălo, malle, malui.

refuse, *I*. (See *unwilling*.)

resolve, *I*, de-cerno, ĕre, -crēvi, -cretum.

rich, div-es, -itis; *comp*. divitior (ditior), *superl*. divitissimus (ditissimus).

seem, *I*, videor, eri, visus.

slave, serv-us, -i; *m.*

surrender, *I*. (Voc. 3, and **21**, *b.*)

than, quam.

townsman, oppidan-us, -i.

tradition, *there is a*, tra-do, ĕre, -didi, -ditum. (**44**.)

troublesome, molestus.

unwilling, *I am*, nŏlo, nolle, nolui.

venture, *I*, audeo, ĕre, ausus sum.

verdict, sententia, *f.* (*plur.*[2])

word, *I break my*, fidem fallo, ĕre, fefelli.

world, *in the* (= *of all men*), omnium hominum. (See **16**, *b.*)

Why not in mundo?

your (*plur.*), vest-er, -ra, -rum.

---

[1] *Mortuus est* is "he is dead;" "he died" is (e) *vita excessit*.

[2] Plur., because each judex gave his own *sententia*, "opinion" or "vote."

Exercise 7.

1. I had rather keep my promises than be the richest man in the world. 2. I begin to be troublesome to you. 3. Cease then to be cowards and begin to become patriots. 4. He resolved to return at once to Rome, and become a good member of the state. 5. It seems that he was unwilling to become king, and preferred to be a private person. 6. It is said that by the verdict of the jury you had been freed from all blame. 7. Having[1] resolved to be a candidate for office, I ventured to return home and ask for your votes. 8. We would rather die free than live (as) slaves. 9. There is a tradition that he refused to accept the crown (when) offered by the nation and (its) chief men. 10. It was clear[2] that the destined day was now at hand; but the townsmen were unwilling either to despair or to surrender. 11. He said that he had neither broken his word nor deceived the nation. 12. The senate[3] and people resolved that ambassadors should be sent to Pyrrhus.

---

[1] See **14**, *a*.   [2] Imperfect tense.   [3] See **30**, *Obs.*

ADJECTIVES.

Agreement of Adjectives.

47. When a single adjective or participle is used as **predicate of several singular substantives,** much variety of construction is allowed.

(*a.*) If several *persons* are spoken of, the adjective is generally in the *plural,* and the masculine gender takes precedence over the feminine.

> *Et pater mihi et mater* mortui *sunt.* Both my father and mother are dead.

(*b.*) But the predicate may also agree both in *gender* and *number* with the substantive nearest to itself. Thus a brother might say for "Both my sister and I had been summoned to the praetor," either "*Et ego et soror mea ad praetorem* vocati *eramus,*" or "*Vocatus eram ad praetorem ego et soror mea,*" or even "*Et ego et soror mea ad praetorem* vocata *erat.*"

The usage therefore greatly resembles that of verbs with more than one subject (**26, 27**).

48. (*a.*) If the substantives are not persons but *things,* the adjective or participle is usually in the plural, and agrees in gender with both substantives if they are of the same gender.

> *Fides tua et pietas* laudandae *sunt.* Your good faith and dutifulness are to be praised.

But *laudanda est* would be also allowable. (See *e.*)

(*b.*) If they are of different genders the adjective is generally in the *neuter*.

> *Gloria, divitiae, honores* incerta ac caduca *sunt.* Glory, riches, and distinctions are uncertain and perishable (things).

(*c.*) Where the substantives are **abstract nouns** (Intr. 29, *d*), the neuter is common in the predicate, even if they are of the same gender.

> *Fides et pietas* laudanda *sunt.* Good faith and a sense of duty are to be praised.

For the neuter *laudanda* means *things* to be praised (as *incerta ac caduca* in *b*); the terminations of the Latin adjective, *us, a, um, i, ae, a,* etc., express the singular and plural of *man, woman, thing,* exactly as the personal terminations of the verb express the personal pronouns. (See Intr. 31.)

(*d.*) Hence *Mors est omnium* extremum, "Death is the last of all things," is as good Latin as *Mors . . .* extrema.

(*c.*) Sometimes, but more rarely, the predicate agrees in gender and number with the substantive nearest itself.

> Spernendae *igitur sunt divitiae et honores.* Riches then, and distinctions, are to be despised.
> *Mihi principatus atque imperium* delatum est. The sovereignty and chief power were offered to me.

49. Where a single adjective is used as the *attribute* of two or more substantives of different genders, it usually agrees with the one nearest itself. Either "*Terras* omnes *et maria perlustravit*," or "*Terras et maria* omnia *perlustravit,*" He travelled over all lands and seas.

It is sometimes repeated with each: *terras* omnes, *maria* omnia, etc.

These rules will cause very little real difficulty, as the freedom which they allow is great. The Exercise will be mainly on what follows.

Adjectives used as Substantives.

50. When the substantive is *"man," "woman,"* or *"thing,"* it is often not expressed in Latin by a separate word, for the reason given above, **48**, *c.*

> Boni[1] sapientes*que* (*ex*)[2] *civitate pelluntur*. The *good* and *wise* are being banished (literally, driven from the state).
>
> *Jam* nostri *aderant*. Our *men*, or *soldiers*, were now at hand.
>
> Hae *ita locutae sunt*. These *women* spoke thus.
>
> Omnia mea *mecum porto*. I am carrying all *my property* with me.

51. Hence many adjectives, pronominal adjectives, and participles, both singular and plural, masculine and neuter, are used precisely as substantives, and may even have other adjectives attached, or *attributed* to them.

(*a.*) Masculine—

> (Singular) *adolescens*,[3] *juvenis* (young man), *amicus*, *inimicus; aequalis* (a contemporary, one of the same age), *candidatus, socius.*
>
> (Plural) *nobiles*,[4] *optimates* (the aristocracy), *majores*[5] (ancestors), *posteri* (posterity), *divites* (the rich), and many others.

---

[1] *Boni* thus used means generally, "the well-affected," "the patriotic party;" opposed to *improbi*, "the disaffected

[2] The ablative may be used here without the Preposition. See Voc. 8 (*banish*).

[3] *Adolescens* denotes a younger age than *juvenis*—it embraces the period from boyhood to the prime of life; *juvenis* is used of all men fit to bear arms.

[4] *Nobiles*, "nobles," *i.e.* men whose ancestors had borne a curule office; opposed to *novi homines*, "self-made men." *Nobilis* never means "noble" in a moral sense. *Optimates*, the aristocracy, as opposed to the popular party, or *populares*.

[5] *Patres, avi*, are never used in prose for "forefathers," but denote "men of the last generation" and "of the last but one." (See p. 41, note [2].) *Minores, nepotes*, etc., are used for "posterity" only in poetry.

(b.) Neuter—

factum, a deed; *dictum*, a saying; *bona*, property; *decretum*, a decree; *promissa*, promises; *edictum*, a proclamation; *senatus-consultum*, a vote or resolution of the senate, etc.

(c.) Also the neuter adjectives *honestum, utile, commodum, verum*, are used in the singular, and still more in the plural, for the English abstract words, "duty," "expediency," "advantage," "truth;" so also

Summum bonum, the highest *good* or happiness.

But the abstract nouns *honestas, utilitas*, are oftener used, and always in oblique cases, and with adjectives.

52. Ambiguous expressions are rarely used in Latin; hence "thing" is generally expressed by *res* (fem.), when the adjective alone would leave it doubtful whether men or things were meant.

Thus "of many things," *multarum rerum;* very seldom, and only when no mistake can occur, *multorum*, which might mean, "of many men;" so—

Futura, the future; but *rerum futurarum*, of the future: *boni*, the good, *or* well-affected; but *bonorum hominum*, of the well-affected.

53. The neuter *plural* of Latin adjectives is constantly used in the nominative and accusative cases where we use the *singular* of an adjective or substantive.

Much, multa.	*Very little*, perpauca.
Very much, permulta.	*Everything*, omnia.
Little (few things), pauca.	*All this*, haec omnia.

So *Vera et falsa.* Truth and falsehood.
   Vera *dicebat.* He was speaking *the truth.*

54. The neuter adjective is used in Latin without a substantive, where we *might* substitute "*things*," but really use some more appropriate nouns, as *property, objects, possessions, performances, thoughts, reflections*, etc.

The learner must look to the *Latin Verb* to guide him to the proper English noun to insert in his translation or to omit in his composition. The Latin adjective in the neuter plural will generally be translated by a substantive kindred in meaning to the verb.

Magna *sperabat.*	His *hopes* were high.
Multa *cogitabat.*	He was revolving many *thoughts.*
Haec *sequebatur.*	He was pursuing these *objects.*
Illa *ausus est.*	He ventured on those *enterprises.*
Multa *mentitus est.*	He told many *falsehoods.*

The singular neuter of the pronoun is used in the same way.

Hoc *secutus est.*	This was his *object.*
Quid *mentitus est?*	What *falsehood* has he told?

These are some of the many instances in which the English substantive cannot be translated literally into Latin.

55. It follows from **51** that we can say *adolescens* optimus, an excellent *young man;* praeclara *facta,* noble *deeds;* even *inimicissimi* tui, your deadliest enemies; the participle or adjective (even a superlative adjective) being treated as a real substantive.

But many of these words retain a double nature, and are treated sometimes as substantives, sometimes as adjectives or participles.

We can say either "Ciceronis *est amicus,*" or "Ciceroni *est amicus,*" either "*Multa fuere* ejus *et* praeclara *facta,*" or "*Multa* ab eo praeclare *facta sunt,*" for "there were many noble deeds of his;" *i.e.* we may treat *facta* as either a substantive or a participle, in which latter case it will be joined with an adverb.

This latter construction is the commoner with participles such as *facta, dicta, responsa,* etc.

Other uses of Adjectives.

56. In English we join the adjective *many* with another adjective, "many excellent men." In Latin we should insert a conjunction, "*homines multi optimi*que, *multi* atque *optimi homines,*" or ". . . *multi,* iique *optimi.*"

Of course we can say "*adolescentes* multi," or "*amici* multi," because these words are used as substantives.

E

So, too, if the second adjective is so constantly united with its substantive as to form a single expression.

Multae *naves longae.* Many ships of war.

57. (*a.*) The superlative degree of adjectives and adverbs is often used in Latin to mark merely a high degree of a quality.

Optimus, excellent; *praeclarissimus,* famous *or* noble.

Sometimes, not always, it should be translated by an English intensive adverb or phrase.

Hoc molestissimum *est.* This is exceedingly, *or* very, *or* most, troublesome.

Hoc saepissime *dixi.* I have said this repeatedly, *or* again and again.

(*b.*) So also the comparative degree is often used, without any direct idea of comparison, to express a *considerable, excessive,* or *too great* amount. It may then be translated by "rather," "somewhat," "too," etc., or by a simple adjective in the positive degree.

Saepius, *somewhat* often; asperius, with *excessive* harshness; *morbus* gravior, a *serious* illness.

Vocabulary 8.

abandon, I, fall off from, de-scisco, ĕre, -scīvi (*abl.*).

accomplish, *I,* ef-ficio, ĕre, -feci, -fectum.

across, trans (*acc.*).

alike (*adv.*), juxta, pariter.

allowed, it is, or *agreed on,* constat (*impers.*).

appear (*seem*), *I,* videor, ēri, visus. **(43.)**

aristocratic party. **(51,** *a, n.*[4]**.)**

attempt, I, conor, ari.

banish, civitate pello, expello; in exilium pello, ĕre, pepuli, pulsum, or ex-igo, ĕre, -egi, -actum.

broad, lātus.

change of purpose, inconstantia, *f.*

contrary, contrarius.

conversation, I have, col-loquor, i, -locutus. **(54.)**

country, fin-es, -ium, *m.* **(16,** *a.*)

courage, virt-ūs, -ūtis, *f.*

cowardice, ignavia, *f.*

deadly. **(55.)**

decree, a, decretum. **(51,** *b.*)

defile, a, salt-us, -ūs, *m.*

deny, I, nego, are.

dictator, dictat-or, -oris.

drive on shore, I, e-jicio, ĕre, -jeci, -jectum.

drive from, I, ex-igo, ĕre, -egi, -actum.

duty, honestum. **(51,** *c.*)

each other, to, inter se.

enemy, hostis, inimicus.[1]

enterprise. **(54.)**

---

[1] *Hostis,* an enemy in war, properly "a foreigner;" *inimicus,* a personal enemy.

everything. (53.)

excellent, optimus. (57.)

faithful, fidel-is, -e.

forefathers = *ancestors.* (51 *a*, *n.*[5])

foretell, *I,* praedi-co, ĕre, -xi, -ctum.

future. (52.)

glorious, praeclarus.

grandfather, av-us, -i.

himself, ipse, a, um.

hopes, *I form* = *I hope.* (Voc. 5, and see 54.)

ignorant of, *I am,* ignoro, āre (*acc.*). (22.)

interest (subst.), utilit-as, -atis, *f.* (51, *c.*)

join you, *I,* me tibi, *or* ad te adjun-go, ĕre, -xi, -ctum.

know, *I,* sc-io, scīre, -ivi, -itum.

last (of time), proximus.

lead, *I,* transdu-co, ĕre, -xi, -ctum.

list of, *I write a,* perscri-bo, ĕre, -psi (*trans.*).

little. (53.)

lofty, praealtus.

marsh, pal-ūs, -ūdis, *f.*

meditate on, *I,* cōgito, āre, de (*abl.*).

merchant vessel, navis oneraria.

mistaken, I am, erro, āre.

much. (53.)

name, good, fama, *f.*

native land. (16, *a.*)

noble, praeclarus. (51, *a*, *n.*[4].)

no one, nemo, nullius.[1]

object. (54.)

oppress, *I.* Voc. 6.

past, the, praeterita, *n.*, *plur.* (52.)

pathless, invius.

persecute, *I,* insector, ari (*dep.*).

poor, paup-er, -ĕris.

popular party, popular-es, -ium.

posterity. (51, *a.*)

praised, to be, laudand-us, -a, -um. (48, *c.*)

praiseworthy, laudabil-is, -e.

proclamation, edictum. (51, *b.*)

promises, I make, polliceor, ēri. (54.)

property. (51, *b.*)

pursue, *I,* sequor, i, secutus (*dep.*).

rashness, temerit-as, -atis, *f.*

resolve, *I,* statu-o, ĕre, -i.

rich, the. (51, *a*, and Voc. 7.)

river, flum-en, -ĭnis, *n.*

saying, a, dictum. (55.)

scarcely, vix.

shatter, *I,* quasso, āre.

sink, *I (trans.*), demer-go, ĕre, -si, -sum.

sometimes. Voc. 1.

spare, *I.* Voc. 1.

speak, *I.* Voc. 1.

storm, tempest-as, -atis, *f.*

strikingly, graviter. (55.)

think, *I (reflect*), cogito, āre.

threats, I make = *I threaten.* Voc. 6.

throne (metaph.). (17.)

traditions, *I hand down,* trad-o, ĕre, -idi, -itum.

transact, ago, ĕre, ēgi, actum.

unhealthy, pestilen-s, -tis.

unjust, iniquus.

variance with, *I am at,* pugno, āre, cum (*abl.*).

venture on (enterprises), *I,* audeo. (54.)

violent (storm), maximus.

vote of the senate, senatus consul-tum. (51, *b.*)

well-affected. (50, *n.*[1].)

winter, hi-ems, -ĕmis, *f.*

youth, a, adolescens. (51, *a*, *n.*[3].)

Exercise 8.

A.

1. He said that he would never[2] banish the good and wise. 2. We are all ignorant of much. 3. He said that courage and cowardice were contrary to each other. 4. It

---

[1] *Nemo* (subst. = *ne homo*) is used in the nom. and acc. (*neminem*). In other cases the adj. (*nullius, nulli, nullo, -ā, -o*) should be substituted.

[2] See 33.

appears that he was banished with you, not by the Dictator himself, but by a praiseworthy vote of the senate.
5. He resolved to abandon the aristocratic and to join the popular party. 6. He said that rashness and change of purpose were not to be praised. 7. He was an excellent youth, and a most faithful friend to me; he had much conversation with me that day about the future. 8. Having returned to Rome he promised to transact everything[1] for his father. 9. The army was led by Hannibal through many pathless defiles, and across many broad rivers, and many lofty mountains and unhealthy[2] marshes, into the country of the enemy. 10. You will scarcely venture to deny that duty was sometimes at variance with interest. 11. I know that your forefathers ventured on many glorious enterprises. 12. He makes many promises, many threats, but I believe that he will accomplish very little.

B.

13. You, said he, were meditating on the past; I was attempting to foretell the future; I now perceive that both you and I were mistaken. 14. He tells (us) that he has been driven by these brothers, his deadly enemies, from his throne and native land; that they are persecuting with unjust[3] proclamations and decrees all the well-affected, all the wise; that no one's property or good name is[4] spared; that rich and poor are alike oppressed. 15. I hope to write a list of the many striking sayings of your grandfather. 16. These objects, said he, did our forefathers pursue; these hopes did they form; these traditions have they handed down to posterity. 17. It is allowed that many noble deeds were done by him. 18. I rejoice that you spoke little and thought much. 19. It is said that many merchant vessels were shattered and sunk, or driven on shore, by many violent storms last winter.

---

[1] See C.   [2] Superl. (See **57**, *a*.)   [3] Superl.   [4] See **5**.

ADJECTIVES—*Continued*, ADVERBS.

58. The adjective and the genitive case of substantives (see **214**) are both used to **define the meaning of the substantive.** So in English, "the *king's* palace," "the *royal* army." Hence the Latin adjective is often used where in English we employ the preposition "of" with a noun. Thus—

Res alienae. The affairs *of others.*
Conditio servilis. The condition or state *of slavery.*
Vir fortis. A man *of courage.*

So often with proper names—

Pugna Cannensis (not *Cannarum*). The battle *of* Cannae.
Populus Romanus (never *Romae*). The people *of* Rome.

Obs. So "*vir* fortissimus," "a man *of* the greatest courage." In Latin this adjectival genitive of quality may be used only where an adjective is added to the substantive. We can say "*vir* summae *fortitudinis;*" not "*vir* fortitudinis." (See **303**.)

59. Sometimes we must use a Latin genitive where the adjective is wanting, or rarely used, in Latin.

Corporis, *or* animi, *dolor.* *Bodily* or *mental* pain.
Omnium *judicio* or *sententiis.* By a *unanimous* verdict, or *unanimously.*
In hoc omnium *luctu.* In this *universal* mourning.
Meâ unius *sententiâ.* By my *single* vote.
Post hominum *memoriam.* Within *human* memory.

60. The Latin adjective is used in agreement with a substantive where we use a partitive substantive express-

ing *whole, end, middle, top,* etc., followed by the preposition
" of."   Thus—

> Summus *mons.*   The top *of* the mountain.
> In mediam *viam.*   Into the middle or centre *of* the road.
> Reliquum *opus.*   The rest *of* the work.
> Ima *vallis.*   The bottom *of* the valley.
> Novissimum *agmen.*   The rear *of* the line of march.
> Tota *Graecia.*   The whole *of* Greece.
> Summa *temeritas.*   The height *of* rashness.

Obs. These adjectives, especially where, as with *summus, medius,*
etc., ambiguity might arise, generally stand before the substantive,
not, as the attribute usually does, after it.

61. The adjective is often used **in close connexion with
a verb,** where in English we should use either an *adverb*
or an *adverbial phrase, i.e.* a preposition and noun.

> Invitus *haec dico.*   I say this *unwillingly,* or *with reluctance,*
>   or *against my will.*
> Tacitus *haec cogitabam.*   I was meditating *silently,* or *in
>   silence,* on these subjects.
> Imprudens *huc veni.*   I came here *unawares.*
> Incolumis *redii.*   I returned *safely,* or *in safety.*
> Adversos, aversos, *aggressus est.*   He attacked them *in
>   front,* or *from behind.*
> So—Absens *condemnatus est.*   He was condemned *in his
>   absence.*
> Totus *dissentio.*   I disagree *wholly,* or *entirely.*
> Frequentes *convenere.*   They came together *in crowds.*
> *Vivus.*   In his lifetime.   *Mortuus.*   After his death.
> Diversi *fugere.*   They fled *in opposite directions.*

62. So the adjectives *solus (unus), primus (prior* if
of two), *ultimus,* are joined *adverbially* with the verb
to express " only," " first," " last," where we should add
a relative clause, or an infinitive mood, and make the adjective the main predicate.

> Primus *haec fecit.*   He *was* the *first* who did this, *or* to do
>   this.
> Solus *mala nostra sensit.*   He *was* the *only* person who
>   perceived our evils.
> Ultimus *venisse dicitur.*   It is said that he *was* the *last* to
>   come.

63. Certain *substantives* also, especially those which relate to *time, age,* and *office,* are used with the verb, where in English we should use an adverbial phrase.

> *Hoc* puer, *or* adolescens, *or* senex, *didici.* I learned this lesson **(54)** *in my boyhood,* or *youth,* or *old age.*
>
> *Hoc* consul *vovit.* He made this vow *in his consulship,* or *as consul.*

So—*Victor.* When victorious; "in the hour of triumph."

64. A single adverb in Latin will often represent a whole adverbial phrase in English; and on the other hand an English adverb will often require a Latin phrase, or whole clause, or combination of words. (Intr. 19 and 52.) Thus—

> *Pie.* With a good conscience.
>
> *Divinitus.* By a supernatural interposition.
>
> *Omnino.* Speaking in general, as a general rule, etc.

So—Easily. *Nullo negotio.*
> Indisputably. *Dubitari non potest quin . . .* (See **133.**)
>
> Fortunately. *Opportune accidit ut . . .* (See **123.**)
>
> Possibly. *Fieri potest ut . . .*
>
> You are *obviously* mistaken. *Errare te* manifestum *est.*
>
> You are *apparently* unwell. *Aegrotare* videris.

It must therefore never be taken for granted that an adverb in one language can be translated by the same part of speech in the other.

Vocabulary 9.

acquit, 1, absol-vo, ĕre, -vi, -utum.	*brought up* (partic. of *I bring up*),
attain to, I = I obtain (Voc. 3),	educatus (edŭco).
or = *arrive at* (Voc. 1).	*change, I,* muto, āre. **(21.)**
beautiful, pul-cher,[1] -chrior, -cher-	*clothing,* vestit-us, -ūs, *m.*
rimus.	*companions, his,* sui, suos, etc.
born (partic. of *I bear*), natus	*conscience, with a good.* **(64.)**
(nascor, *I am born*).	*consent* (*subst.*), consens-us, -ūs, *m.*
boyhood, in his. **(63.)**	*crowds, in.* **(61.)**
break (a law), 1. Voc. 5.	*death, after his.* **(61.)**

---

[1] *Pulcher* is "beautiful" in a general sense; *amoenus,* "lovely *to look on,*" is applied to natural objects such as a landscape or scenery.

distinction, hon-or (-os), -ōris, *m.*
enterprise. (54.)
entrust, *I*, per-mitto, ĕre, -misi, -missum,
eye, ocul-us, -i, *m.*
fair, amoenus. (See p. 71, *n.*[1].)
faith, good, fid-es, -ei, *f.*
farmhouse, villa, *f.*
food, vict-us, -ūs, *m.*
fortune, fortuna, *f.*
funeral, fun-us, -ĕris, *n.*
gather together, to (*intrans.*). Voc. 3.
highest. Voc. 6.
honour, I (*of external marks of honour*), orno, are.
kind of, every, omn-is, -e.
kindness, bonit-as, -atis, *f.*
last, the, ultimus.
late, too (*adv.*), sēro.
lifetime, in his. (61.)
listen to, I, aud-io, ire. (23.)
look down on, I, de-spicio (*trans.*), ĕre, -spexi, -spectum. (23.)
management, procurati-o, -onis, *f.*
marble (*adj.*), marmoreus.
mind, I am out of my. Voc. 6.
miraculous interposition, by a. (64.)
monument, monumentum, *n.*
neglect, I, negle-go, ĕre, -xi, -ctum.
next, the, proximus ; insequen-s, -tis.
office. Voc. 2.

old age, in my. (63.)
other persons, of (*adj.*). (58)
panic, pav-or, -oris, *m.*
plain, camp-us, -i, *m.*
poet, poët-a, -ae, *m.*
point out, I, monstro, āre.
post up, I, fi-go, ĕre, -xi, -xum.
reach, I, pervenio ad . . .
read through, I, per-lĕgo, ĕre, -lēgi, -lectum.
recover myself, I, me re-cipio, -cepi.
relinquish, I, o-mitto, ĕre, -misi, -missum.
safety, in. (61.)
silence, in. (61.)
speech (*to soldiers*, or *multitude*), conti-o, -onis, *f.*
spread beneath, I, sub-jicio (*trans.*), ĕre, -jeci, -jectum ; subjicior (*intrans.*). (20.)
state (*adj.*), publicus.
summit. (60.)
supply you with these things, I, haec tibi suppedito, āre.
tomb, sepulcrum, *n.*
troublesome, molestus.
turn to, I. Voc. 3.
unanimously. (59.)
universal. (59.)
whole of. (60.)
wholly. (61.)
write, I, scri-bo, ĕre, -psi, -ptum.
youth, in my. (63 ; also 51, *n.*[3].)

Exercise 9.

1. He said that the management of other people's affairs was always exceedingly[1] troublesome. 2. In this universal panic your brother was the first to recover himself. 3. I obeyed, said he, the law[2] in my youth : I will not break it in my old age. 4. I was the first to venture on these enterprises ; I will be the last to relinquish them. 5. In his lifetime we neglected this poet; after his death we honour him with a state funeral, a marble tomb with

---

[1] To be expressed by superlative adj. (See 57.)
[2] Plural. *Lex* (sing.) is seldom used in an *abstract* sense ; it means *a law*.

many beautiful[1] monuments, and every kind of distinction.
6. The king having been (14, *a*) the first to reach the
summit of the mountain, looked down in silence on the
fair plains spread beneath his eye (*pl.*).   7. He turned[2]
to his companions and pointed out the farmhouse in which
he had been born and brought up in his boyhood; **too**
late, said he, has fortune changed.   8. He promised to
supply the army of Rome with food and clothing.   9. I
read through the whole of this proclamation in silence; it
seemed to me that he who wrote and posted *it up* (when)
written was out of his mind.   10. He was unanimously
acquitted, and returned home in safety; the next year he
attained with universal consent to the highest office in the
nation.   11. The soldiers, having gathered together in
crowds, listened to his speech in silence.   12. I entrust
myself wholly to your good faith and kindness.   13. No
one can with a good conscience deny that your brother
returned home in safety by a miraculous interposition.

---

[1] Superl. (**57.**)   [2] Participle.   (See **15.**)

THE RELATIVE.

65. In a relative or adjectival *sentence,* each *clause*[1] has its own verb, and its own independent construction. The relative pronoun *qui* is of the same gender, number, and is joined with the same person of the verb, as its *antecedent* substantive, or pronoun, in the other clause. (See **12.**)

> Arbŏres *seret diligens agricŏla,* quarum *adspiciet baccam ipse nunquam.*[2] The careful husbandman will plant *trees,* any fruit *of which* he will himself never behold.
>
> Mulierem *aspicio* quae *pisces vendit.* I see a *woman who* is selling fish.
>
> *Ubi est* puer, cui *librum dedisti?* Where is the *boy to whom* you gave the book?
>
> Adsum *qui* feci. *I, who* did the deed, am here.

For the meaning of the term *adjectival,* as applied to a clause, or to the sentence of which such a clause forms a part, see Intr. 81.

66. Where there is more than one antecedent, the rules for the number and gender of the relative are the same as those for the adjective.

> *Pater ejus et mater* qui *aderant.* His father and mother *who* were present. (**47,** *a.*)
>
> *Divitiae et honores* quae *caduca sunt.* Riches and distinctions, *which* are perishable (things). (**48,** *b.*)

67. Sometimes a *relative* refers not to a single word, but to the *whole statement* made by a clause. When this is the case, we often find *id quod,* for *quod* only. (Here *id* is in *apposition* to the former sentence.) Sometimes *quae res* is found : = "*a circumstance which.*"

> *Timoleon,* id quod *difficilius putatur, sapientius tulit secundam quam adversam fortunam.* Timoleon, *though this (lit. a thing*

---

[1] For meaning of *clause,* see page 20, note.
[2] For place of *nunquam,* see Intr. 92.

which) is thought the more difficult (task), bore prosperity more wisely than adversity.

Multae civitates a Cyro defecerunt; quae res *multorum bellorum causa fuit.* Many states revolted from Cyrus ; *and this* (see **13**) (*circumstance*) was the cause of many wars.

Obs.—"*As*" is often used in English as equivalent to "*a thing which*," or "*which,*" in reference to a whole clause.

"He, *as* you have heard, died at Rome." *Ille,* id quod *audiisti, Romae mortem obiit.*

68. A relative pronoun in the accusative case is frequently omitted in English, but never in Latin.

This is the man *I saw. Hic est* quem *vidi.*
He found the books *he wanted. Libros* quos *voluit reperit.*

69. When in English the antecedent is qualified by a superlative, the superlative is in Latin placed in the relative clause.

Volsci civitatem, quam habebant optimam, *perdiderunt.* The Volsci lost the *best* city they had.

The same place is given to any emphatic adjective, especially those of number or amount.

Equites, quos paucos *secum habuit, dimisit.* He sent away the *few* mounted men whom he had with him.

Use of *qui* with *is.*

70. The demonstrative pronoun which corresponds to *qui,* as *he* to *who,* is not *ille,* but *is. Ille* is only used when great emphasis is laid on the "he;" "that *well known,* or that *other* person." *Is* may be thus used of all three persons.

I am the man I always was. *Is sum* qui *semper fui.*

71. Where the antecedent and relative are in the same case, *qui* without *is* will express " he who ;" where the cases are different, *is* is to be used.

Qui *haec videbant flebant. Those* who saw this (the spectators) wept.
Eis, qui *adstabant,* irascebatur. He was angry with *those* who stood by (the bystanders)

72. *Is, ei* (*ii*), etc., often answer to our " one," " men," " a man," when used to denote a class of persons.

> Eum qui *haec facit odi.*   I hate *one* who, or *a man* who does this.
>
> Eos qui *haec faciunt odi.*   I hate *men* who do this.

Qui alone (**71**) will express the same phrases.

> Qui *haec faciunt, pejora facient.*   *Men* who are doing this will do worse.

73. The oblique cases, especially the genitive and dative, of the participle are often used to represent " him who," " those who."

> Adstantium *clamore perterritus.*   Alarmed by the shouts of *the bystanders, or* of *those who stood by, or* of *those standing by.*
>
> Interrogantibus *respondit.*   To *those who questioned* him, or to *those questioning* him, or to *his interrogators.*

74. But we must never combine *ei, eorum, eis,* etc., with the participle to denote a class. *Eorum adstantium, eos adstantes,* is very bad Latin for " those who stood by," or " those standing by."

75. Sometimes the force of the demonstrative in *is qui,* and similar combinations, *hic qui,* etc., is emphasised by placing the relative clause first, and the demonstrative pronoun, in the other or principal clause, afterwards.

> *Qui tum te defendit,* is *hodie accusat.*   He who (the very man who) then defended you is to-day accusing you. Your former advocate is your present accuser.

This construction is always to be used where a strong contrast is dwelt on.

76. Observe how often the substantive has to be expressed in Latin by a clause beginning with *qui, is qui, ea quae,* etc., *i.e.* by an *adjectival clause.* Thus—

> Qui me ceperunt, my *captors; qui me vicit,* my *conqueror;* (ea) *quae vera sunt,* the *truth.*

(See **175.**)

Is qui, with the subjunctive, will be treated further on.

Vocabulary 10.

again and again, saepe (saepissime). (57.)

agreement (with), I am in, consentio, īre, -si, -sum (cum, *abl.*).

assistance, I come to his, sub-věnio, -vēni (*dat.*).

concerning (prep.), de (*abl.*).

despise, I, de-spicio,[1] ĕre, -spexi, -spectum.

directions, in different. (61.)

disagree with, I, dis-sentio. (See *agreement*.)

dismayed, I am, perterr-eor, ēri, -itus.

dismiss, I, di-mitto, ĕre, -misi, -missum.

entirely. (61.)

first . . . then, primum . . . deinde.

foot-soldier, ped-ĕs, -ĭtis.

gladly, libens (*adj.*) (61), *or* libenter (*adv.*).

halt, I. Voc. 1.

helplessness, in, in-ops, -ŏpis (*adj.*). (61.)

institution, an, institutum. (51, *b.*)

join him, I. (20, and Voc. 8.)

keep my word, I, fidem prae-sto, āre, -stiti.

know, I (a fact), scio (Voc. 8) ; (*a person*) nōvi, nôsse, nōveram (nôram).

man, the, (contemptuous), hom-o, -inis.

meet, I come to, obviam věnio, vēni (*dat.*).

occasion, on that, tum. (Intr. 19.)

one. (72.)

oppose, I, adversor, āri (*dat.*).

order, I, jubeo, ēre, jussi, jussum.

poverty, paupert-as, -ātis, *f.*

present, I am, ad-sum, -esse, -fui.

rather, I would. Voc. 7.

reluctantly. (61.)

repeatedly = again and again.

riches, diviti-ae, -arum.

ruin, exitium, *n.* (18, 19.)

scatter, I (intrans.), dissipor, āri. (20.)

seek for, I, pet-o, ĕre, -ii, *or* -ivi, -ītum.

send back, I, re-mitto, ĕre, -misi, -missum.

set at nought, I, con-temno,[1] ĕre, -tempsi, -temptum.

shout, clam-or, -oris, *m.*

slave, I am a, servio, īre, -ii, -itum.

stand by, I, ad-sto, -stare, -stĭti.

story, I tell a, narro, -are (54.)

suddenly, subĭto.

to-day, hodie.

to-morrow, cras.

treat lightly, I, parvi[2] facio, ĕre, feci, factum.

value highly, I, magni[2] aestimo, āre.

woman, muli-er, -ĕris.

yesterday, heri.

Exercise 10.

1. Those[3] who were in agreement with you yesterday, to-day entirely disagree (with you). 2. Both you and I despise one who[3] would rather be a slave with[4] riches than free with poverty. 3. We know that he, concerning

---

[1] *Despicio, I look down on as beneath myself; contemno, I think lightly of in itself = parvi facio; sperno, I put from me; aspernor, the same, with idea of strong dislike; repudio, I put from me with contempt; neglego, I am indifferent to.*

[2] For this genitive see 305.

[3] The relative clause to come first, *is* to be used in the other clause (See 75.)　　　　　　　　　　　　[4] See 8, *b.*

whom you have told us all this story, expects to attain to the highest offices, the greatest distinctions; but[1] I hope that he will never obtain them, for I know the man. 4. I who[2] repeatedly opposed you in your youth, will gladly come to your assistance in your old age and helplessness. 5. I sent you the best and bravest foot-soldiers that I had with me; and having promised[3] to send them back, you reluctantly kept your word. 6. He ordered those standing by (him) to follow him; but they were dismayed by the shouts of those who were coming to meet (him); first halted, and then suddenly scattered and fled in different directions. 7. The woman for whom you were seeking is present; I will therefore[1] hear and dismiss her. 8. The best institutions and laws you have set at nought, and this[4] will be your ruin to-day. 9. The things[2] which I treated lightly in my boyhood, I value highly in my old age. 10. I who[2] was the last to come to your assistance on that occasion, will be the first to join you to-morrow.

---

[1] The demonstrative and conjunction, *but, therefore*, etc., to be expressed by the relative.

[2] The relative clause to come first, *is* to be used in the other clause. (See **75.**)

[3] See **14.**   [4] See **67.**

For all succeeding Exercises the Student is referred to the General Vocabulary at the end of the Book.

THE RELATIVE—*Continued.*

Qui in Oratio Obliqua.—Co-ordinate and other uses.

77. The verb in an **adjectival clause** is in the *indicative* mood, unless there is some special reason for the *subjunctive*.

For instance, if the verb in the principal clause is in *oratio obliqua, i.e.* is in the infinitive after a verb of *saying* or *thinking*, the verb in the *qui*-clause will be in the *subjunctive*.

Thus—*Mulierem aspicio, quae pisces* vendit. (Oratio recta.) I see a woman who is selling fish.

But—Ait *se mulierem* aspicere, *quae pisces* vendat. (Oratio obliqua.) He *says* that he sees a woman who is selling fish.

Exceptions to this rule will be explained further on.

Obs.—This idiom extends very widely in Latin. It holds good not only with relatives, but with all subordinating conjunctions, and applies not only to indirect statements, but also to indirect commands and questions. (See Exercise LVI.)

78. Besides its use in adjectival clauses, *qui* is also used very largely as a substitute for both kinds of *conjunctions*. (Intr. 53, 54, 55.)

(i.) It is often used as equivalent to the co-ordinating conjunctions *and, but, so, therefore*, etc., and a demonstrative, to connect together co-ordinate sentences and clauses. (See **13**.)

Ad regem veni, quem *cum vidissem*. . . . I came to the king, *and* when I had seen *him*. . . .

Indeed the Latin *relative* is often used where we should use the *demonstrative* only. Thus nothing is commoner than for Latin

79

sentences to begin with—Quibus *auditis*, having heard *this;* Quod *ubi vidit*, when he saw *this;* quam *ob rem*, quocirca, *and therefore,* or, *therefore.*

This is called the *co-ordinating* use of the relative, because it links co-ordinate sentences. (Intr. 74.) The relative so used does not affect the mood of the verb any more than a demonstrative pronoun, or the conjunction *et.*

Thus, if *qui* used for "and" connects (or co-ordinates) a principal verb in *oratio obliqua* with another, it will introduce an infinitive mood.

> *Dixit proditorem esse eum . . . quem brevi periturum esse.* He said that he was a traitor . . . *and that he* would soon perish.

79. (ii.) The Latin relative is also largely used in place of many kinds of *subordinating* conjunctions; *ut*, in order that, or, so that; *quamvis*, although; *quod*, because.

The verb which follows *qui*, when so used, is in the subjunctive.

[The following Exercise will include only its adjectival use as subordinate to *oratio obliqua*, and its *co-ordinating* use as a substitute for a conjunction. Its use in the sense of "in order to," "so that," etc., will be treated further on.]

Other Uses of the Relative.

80. "*But*" after universal negatives, as *nemo, nullus, nihil*, is equivalent to "who not," and should be translated by *qui non*, or by *quin* if the relative is in the *nominative* (or occasionally the *accusative*) case. *Qui non* or *quin* will always be followed by a *subjunctive.*[1]

> Nemo *est* quin *te dementem putet.* There is no one *but* thinks you mad; or *the whole world* thinks, etc.
> Nemo *fuit* quin *viderim.* There was no one whom I did not see (but *quem non* is more usual).

---

[1] The explanation of the subjunctive will be given in its proper place. (See Qui with the Subjunctive, Exercise LXIII.)

81. It has been already said that the English relative with words such as *only, first, last,* as its antecedent, is not usually expressed in Latin by a relative clause, but by an adverbial use of the adjective.

He was the first *who,* or *that* did this. *Primus haec fecit.* (See **62.**)

82. Relative clauses in English, especially such as correspond to a clause beginning with *it,* are often expressed in Latin merely by the emphatic order of the words.

Ab hoc homine *interfectum esse fratrem tuum negat.* He says that *it was not* by this man *that* your brother was killed.

83. When the predicate of a relative clause is a substantive, the relative is often attracted into the gender of the predicate instead of agreeing with its antecedent.

Thebae, quod *Boeotiae caput est.* Thebes which is the capital of Boeotia.

Obs.—The same attraction takes place with demonstrative pronouns. Ea (not *id*) *vera est pietas. That* is true piety.

Exercise 11.

In the following Exercise the italics indicate the use of the co-ordinating relative, **78** (i.).

1. He pretended that he had met the man[1] who had killed the king by poison. 2. There is no one but knows that one who does not till his land will look in vain for a harvest. 3. The exiles believed that they had reached the locality from which (whence) their forefathers were sprung. 4. I hope to avert this ruin from my country *and therefore* I am willing to venture on or endure anything. 5. He promised to lead his troops into the country of the Remi, *and* (said) that he hoped he should[2] soon recall *them* to their allegiance. 6. Having heard *this* he perceived that the ambassadors spoke the truth,[3] and that

---

[1] *Is.* (**71.**) [2] Fore ut. (**38.**) [3] That which (pl.) was true. (**76.**)

the danger was increasing. 7. He said that he had never preferred expediency to duty, *and* (that) *therefore* he would not abandon allies whom he had promised to succour. 8. Having ascertained *this* fact, he promised to break up the crowd which had gathered around the king's[1] palace. 9. He pretended that it was not for the sake of gain but of friendship that he had given me all the books which his brother had left. 10. He said that the friends for whom you were looking round were all safe, *and therefore* that he for his part was free from anxiety. 11. He pretends to reject glory, which is the most honourable reward of true virtue. 12. All the world[2] knows that the moon moves round the earth.

---

[1] Adjective. (**58.**) · [2] See **80.**

THE RELATIVE—*Continued.*

Correlatives.

84. The relative pronouns and pronominal words, *qui* (who), *qualis* (of what *kind*), *quantus* (of what *size*), *quot* (how many), answer respectively to the demonstratives *is* (he), *talis* (of such a *kind*), *tantus* (of such a *size*), *tot* (so many).

When they answer to these demonstratives, all **relatives** except *qui*, and even *qui* with *idem*, **are to be translated by the English "** *as.*"

> Talis *est*, qualis *semper fuit.* He is such *as* (of the same character as) he has ever been.
>
> Tantam[1] *habeo voluptatem*, quantam *tu.* I have as much pleasure *as* you.
>
> Tot *erant milites*, quot *maris fluctus.* The soldiers were as many *as* the waves of the sea.
>
> Idem *est* qui *semper fuit.* He is the same *as* (or *that*) he has always been.
>
> Res peracta *est* eodem *modo* quo *antea.* The thing has been done in the same manner *as* before.

85. When thus used, the two pronouns which correspond with each other are called **correlative**, or corresponding, words.

As with *is* and *qui*, so with the others, the relative or adjectival clause is often placed first, and the other or principal clause last.

---

[1] *Tantus* is sometimes used in a limiting sense. "just as (*only* as) much as;" tantum *faciet* quantum *coactus erit*, he will do *no more* than he is compelled (to do)

83

This is in accordance with the general tendency of Latin to place the most emphatic part of a sentence at or near the end.   (Intr. 91.)

> Quot *adstabant homines*, tot *erant sententiae.*   There were as many opinions as there were men standing by.
> Qualis *fuit domina*, talem *ancillam invenies.*   You will find the maid of the *same character as* her mistress was.

86. "*Such*" in English is often used where *size* or *amount* is meant rather than *kind* or *quality.*   *Such—as* should then be translated into Latin by *tantus—quantus;* not by *talis—qualis.*

We must therefore always ask ourselves whether "such" means " of such a kind " or " so great."   Thus, in "the storm was *such* as I had never seen before," " such " evidently means " so violent " or " so great ;" in "his manners were *such* as I had never seen," " such " evidently means " of such a kind."   In the former case we must use *tantus*, in the latter *talis.*

87. When "such" means "of such a kind," the place of the pronominal adjective *talis* is often taken by the genitive of quality.   (See **58.**)

> *Ejusmodi, hujusmodi, istius modi.*   Of such a kind, of such a kind *as this*, of such a kind *as you speak* of.
> Hujusmodi *homines odi.*   I hate such men (as these).

88. "Such" in English is often combined as an adverb with an adjective,—"*such* good men," "*such* a broad river." *Talis* and *tantus* cannot of course be used as adverbs. We must say—tam *bonus vir*, or talis tamque *bonus vir;* tam *latum flumen*, or tantum tamque *latum flumen,*— not, talis *bonus vir*, tale *latum flumen.*

Obs.—But *tantus* and *talis* are often combined with *hic*, sometimes with *ille;* haec *tanta multitudo*, *this great* number of men, or *so great*, or *such* a, multitude *as this.* . So the adverb *tam.*

Hic tam *bonus vir.*   *So* good a man *as this*, or, this *good* man.

89. The same *correlative* construction is used with relatival or pronominal *adverbs*, as, *e.g.* those of place.

> *Ubi* (where) corresponds to *ibi, illic* (there), *hic* (here).
> *Unde* (whence)   „   *inde* (thence), *hinc* (hence).

Quo (whither)   corresponds to *eo, illuc* (thither), *huc* (hither).
Qua (in the direction in which) ,,   *eā, hāc* (in that or this direction).

> *Inde venisti,* unde *ego.* You have come *from the same place as* I.
> *Eo rediit,* unde *profectus est.* He returned *to the place from which* he had set out.

90. Observe also that with *idem, ac*[1] (*atque*) frequently takes the place of *qui.*

> *Eadem* ac (=quae) *tu sentio,* my views (**54**) are the same as yours.

91. With *alius, contra, aliter,* and words signifying *contrast, ac* (*atque*) is the rule.

> *Aliter* ac *tu sentio.* My views are different from yours.

Sometimes *quam* is used.

> *Res contra* quam (*or* atque) *expectavi evenit.* The matter turned out *contrary to* my expectation.

See Comparative Clauses, Ex. LXII.

92. Where a strong *difference* is pointed out, a repeated *alius* is often used; aliud *est dicere,* aliud *facere,* "there is *all the difference* between speaking and acting;" "speaking is *one thing,* acting *another.*"

93. All that has been said (**77**) as to the mood of the verb in *qui*-clauses applies equally to every kind of relative clause, whether introduced by a relatival or pronominal *adjective,* such as *qualis,* etc., or by a relatival *adverb,* such as *ubi, unde.* Thus—

> *Ubi tu* es, *ibi est frater tuus.* Your brother is in the same place as you. (Dicit) *ubi tu* sis, *ibi esse fratrem tuum.*

So—

> *Qualis* fuerit *frater tuus, talem te esse dicunt.* They say that you are of the same character as your brother was.

---

[1] *Ac* is never used before a vowel : see Intr. p. 14, *note.*

A.

This Exercise (A) contains examples of various *relative* constructions; instances of relative clauses in *Oratio Obliqua* will be
found in B.

1. This is the same as that.   2. You are of the same
character as I have always believed you to be.   3. All the
world knows that the past cannot be changed.   4. The
waves were such as I had never seen before.   5. He died
in the place where he had lived in boyhood.   6. He was
the first who promised to help me.   7. I will send the
most faithful slave I have with me.[1]   8. There is no one
but knows that the Gauls were conquered by Caesar.
9. The island is surrounded by the sea which you (*pl.*)
call ocean.   10. The Gauls are the same to-day as they
have ever been.   11. He was the first to deny the
existence of gods.   12. I was the last to reach Italy.
13. That expediency and honour are sometimes contrary
to each other (is a fact[2] that) all the world knows.   14. I
believe him to have been the first within human memory[3]
to perpetrate such a monstrous crime, and I hope he will
be the last to venture on anything of the kind.

This Exercise may be also varied by placing "he said" before 2, 4,
7, 10, and altering the sentence accordingly; thus:—"he said that
you *were* of the same character, as he *had* always believed you to be."

B.

1. All the world allows that you are of the same
character as your father and grandfather.   2. The scouts
having returned to the camp brought back word that the
enemy, who had flocked together in crowds the-day-before,
were now breaking up and stealing away in different
directions.   3. He said that he would never abandon such
good and kindly men, who had so often come to his aid in
adversity.   4. My objects[4] are different from yours, nor are

---

[1] 8, *Obs.*   [2] Omit in Latin and compare **82.**   [3] See **59.**
[4] Express by neut. pl. of adj. (see **54**); so with "hopes."

my hopes the same as yours. 5. He said that he himself[1] was the same as he had ever[2] been, but that both the state of the nation and the views of his countrymen had gradually changed, and that the king, the nobles, and the whole people were now exposed to dangers such as they had never before experienced. 6. Many ships of war were shattered and sunk by the violence of the storm ; a single merchantman returned in safety to the point from[3] which it had set out.

---

[1] Himself,—*quidem* after "he" (he *at least*, he *on the one hand*).
[2] Ever = always, as in the preceding Exercise, A. 10.
[3] = Whence. (**89.**)

EXERCISE XIII.

THE INFINITIVE AS SUBSTANTIVE.

94. The infinitive[1] mood (see Intr. 51), as doing little more than name the general action or state denoted by the verb, is used as a **verbal substantive of the neuter gender.** Thus—

Sedere *me delectat.* "*To sit,*" or "*sitting,*" delights me.

The English word "sitting" is here a verbal noun,[2] and must be carefully distinguished from the participle, which resembles it in form only. Compare "*sitting* rests me" with "he rested *sitting* on a bank."

95. This infinitive may be thus used as a substantive in two cases only—(1) in the *nominative,* either as subject

---

[1] The infinitive mood is so called because the verb in this form is *not defined* or restricted by inflexions denoting person or number. Were it not for its special use in Latin, already noticed, as marking statements which are made in *oratio obliqua,* it could hardly be called a *mood* at all; for it is only when so used, as answering to what in most languages is represented by a conjunction (*that,* etc.) and a finite verb, that it in any sense acts as a true verb by joining together two conceptions of the mind (see Intr. 11). By a "mood" we mean a special mode (*modus*) or manner in which a verb does this (see **147**). In its other uses, as in that mentioned in the present exercise, the infinitive can hardly be called a mood, but, as explained in **94**, a verbal noun; for it makes no statement, but merely *names* a single idea, that *state* or *action* which the verb not only names, but predicates of its subject. Compare *sedēre* with *sedeo.*

[2] The origin of this English verbal noun in *-ing* does not come within the scope of this work. From its similarity in form to the participle, it has acquired a participial construction, and we no longer say "the seeing *of* you," but "the seeing *you,*" etc. As such, it is synonymous with the ordinary, or prepositional, form of the English infinitive "to see;" but its use is much wider than that of the Latin infinitive, and even than that of the gerund. We can say "he went away without *speaking,*" "instead of *answering,*" where the Latin gerund is inadmissible (see Gerunds); and it also answers to the supine in *-um:* "he sent us out foraging," properly *a* (i.e. *an* or *on*) foraging,—*nos pabulatum emisit.*

88

to *est, fuit*, etc., followed by a neuter adjective, or with an impersonal verb, or verb used impersonally; (2) in the *accusative*, as subject to another infinitive, after a verb *sentiendi* vel *declarandi*.

> Nihil agere *me delectat*. *Doing* nothing is a pleasure to me.
> *Turpe est* mentiri. It is disgraceful *to lie*, or, *lying* is disgraceful.
> *Dixit turpe esse* mentiri. He said that *lying* was disgraceful.

For other cases see 99.

Obs.—The infinitive thus used may be the *antecedent* to a *relative*, which will be in the *neuter gender*.

> *Laudari*, quod, or id quod, *plerisque gratissimum est, mihi molestissimum est.* To be praised, which is very pleasant to most men, is to me most disagreeable.

96. But though the infinitive is thus used as a substantive, it retains some part of its true nature as a verb. For—

(*a.*) It is qualified, not by an adjective, but by an adverb.

> "*Good* writing" is bene *scribere, not* bonum *scribere.*
> Bene *arare est* bene *colere.* *Good* ploughing is *good* farming.

(*b.*) It is joined with or governs an accusative, or other case as its object.

> Haec *perpěti, et* patriā *carere, miserrimum est.* To endure these things, and to be deprived of one's country, is most wretched.

(*c.*) It retains the tenses of a verb.

> *Haec facere, fecisse, facturum esse.* The doing, the having done, the being about to do, this.

97. This infinitive is also joined with a subject, **which is always in the accusative case.**

> Te *hoc dicere mihi est gratissimum.* *Your* saying this is most welcome to me.

Obs.—In English, when an infinitive (or a sentence introduced by "*that*") is the nominative to a verb, it generally *follows the verb*, the pronoun "*it*" being used as its representative before the verb. "*It* is pleasant *to be praised.*" "*It* is strange *that you should say so.*" This "*it*" is not to be translated into Latin. We must write simply, Laudari *jucundum est.* Te *hoc* dicere *mirum est.*

98. This substantival infinitive, with or without other words, will often express the nominative and accusative cases of English *abstract* nouns for which Latin either has no exact equivalent, or for which the infinitive is (often) preferred. Thus—

(*a.*) *Sibi placere,* "self-satisfaction;" *suis rebus contentum esse,* "contentment;" *mentiri,* "falsehood;" *cunctari,* "procrastination" (=cunctatio); *improbos laudare,* "praise of the bad;" *felicem esse,* "success;" *prosperis rebus uti,* "prosperity."

(*b.*) So, too, as Latin has no single word to express "happiness" or "gratitude," the infinitive is mostly used for both. Thus—

Beate vivere, or *beatum esse*=*vita beata,* or happiness.
Gratiam habere=*gratus animus,* or the feeling of gratitude.
Gratias agere, the returning thanks, or expression of gratitude.
Gratiam debere, the being under an obligation.
Gratiam referre, the returning a favour, or the showing gratitude.

These are instances of the general tendency of Latin to prefer direct and simple to more general and abstract modes of expression.

99. But in all such phrases the infinitive is only used in the *nominative* or in the accusative of *oratio obliqua.* In other cases, and with the accusative after a preposition, the *gerund* (or *gerundive*) takes its place.[1] Thus—

Pugnare, to fight, *or* fighting; but, pugnandi *cupidus,* desirous *of* fighting; ad pugnandum *paratus,* prepared *for* fighting; pugnando *vincemus,* we shall win the day *by* fighting.

Obs.—The *gerund* governs the substantive with which it is combined, the *gerundive* agrees with it. See Gerund and Gerundive, XLIX.

Gratias agendo (Gerund).
Ad agendas *gratias* (Gerundive).

---

[1] In Greek the infinitive with the article can be used in all cases,— τὸ, τοῦ, τῷ βασιλεύειν =regnare, regnandi, regnando.

1. It is always delightful[1] to parents that their children should be praised.   2. He said that it was disgraceful to break one's word, but keeping one's promises was always honourable.   3. Both your brother and you[2] have told many falsehoods;[3] falsehood is always vile.   4. It is one thing to be praised, another to have deserved praise. 5. To be praised by the unpatriotic is to me almost the same thing as to be blamed by patriots.   6. Feeling gratitude, says[4] he, is one thing, returning thanks another.   7. Procrastination, which in all things was dangerous, was, he[5] said, fatal in war.   8. Pardoning the wicked is almost the same thing as condemning the innocent.   9. Procrastination in showing gratitude is never praiseworthy; for myself[6] I prefer the returning kindness to being under an obligation.   10. Happiness is one thing; success and prosperity another.   11. Brave fighting, says[4] he, will to-day be the same thing as victory; by victory we shall give freedom to our country.

---

[1] The intensive superlative may be used here and with many of the other adjectives in this exercise. (See **57**, *a*.)

[2] See **26** and *note*.   [3] See **54**.   [4] See **40**.

[5] See **32**, *b*.   [6] See **11**, *a*.

FINAL CLAUSES. *Ut, Ne, Quo.*

100. The English infinitive mood ("to do, to go,"— properly a gerundial use of the infinitive with the preposition *to*) is constantly used **to denote a purpose, or end in view** (*finis*).

But in Latin prose the infinitive mood is **never used** in this *final* sense.[1]

The English final infinitive is expressed in Latin in many ways.

" He sent ambassadors *to sue* for peace " is never expressed in Latin by "*legatos misit pacem* petere," but in various other ways, either by

    a. *legatos misit* ad pacem petendam (Gerundive),
    b.   ,,   pacis petendae causā (Gerundive).
    c.   ,,   pacem petitum (Supine),
    d.   ,,   qui pacem peterent (Relative Clause),

or, especially if the purpose or end in view is strongly dwelt on,

    e. *legatos misit*, ut pacem peterent.

The following rules, therefore, must be carefully attended to.

101. (i.) " That," when equivalent to *in order that*, and followed by *may* or *might;* also " in order to" and " to " in the same sense, followed by an English infinitive, must often be translated in Latin by *ut* with the subjunctive.

    Multi alios laudant, ut *ab illis*[2] laudentur. Many men praise others, *that* they *may be praised* by them, *or, to be praised* by them, *or, in order to be praised* by them.
    Multi alios laudabant, ut *ab illis* laudarentur. Many men were praising others, *in order to be praised* by them.

---

[1] Hence such parenthetic clauses as " not to mention," " so to say," " not to be tedious," must never be translated by the Latin infinitive, but by *ne dicam, ut dicam, ne longus sim.*

[2] *Illis* is here used in place of the less emphatic *is*, as a marked distinction between *themselves* and *others* is intended. (**11,** *d.*)

(ii.) "That"=*in order that*, followed by *not*, or any negative word (the verb having *may* or *might* for its auxiliary), must be translated by *nē* (=*lest*) with the subjunctive. *Ne* expresses a *negative purpose; a purpose of preventing*, and often answers to the English phrase "to prevent," *or* "avoid."

> *Gallinae avesque reliquae pennis fovent pullos*, nē *frigŏre laedantur.* Hens and other birds cherish their young with their feathers, *that* they *may not be* hurt by the cold, or, *to prevent that* they be hurt, etc.
> *Gallinae avesque reliquae pennis fovebant pullos*, nē *frigore laederentur.* Hens and other birds were cherishing their young with their feathers, *that they might not* be hurt by the cold.

Notice the correspondence of tenses *laudant . . . laudentur; laudabant . . . laudarentur; fovent . . . laedantur; fovebant . . . laederentur.* (See **104.**)

102. When the dependent clause expressing purpose *i.e.* the *final* clause, contains an adjective or adverb in the comparative degree, "that" is translated by *quo=by which;* this is equivalent to *ut eo=that by this (means)*, but *quo* must never be used in this sense without a comparative.

> *Medico puto aliquid dandum esse*, quo *sit* studiosior. I think that something should be given to the physician, *that* he may be *the more attentive*, or *to* make him *more attentive.*

103. *Ut* is never used with a negative in *final* clauses; "that no one," when a purpose is expressed, is never *ut nemo*, but *ne quis.* (See **109.**) When a second or third negative final clause is added, *neve* or *neu* is used instead of *neque.*

> *Hoc feci, ne tibi displicerem neve amicis tuis nocerem.* I did this to avoid displeasing you, or injuring your friends.

Sequence of Tenses.

The tense of the verb in a final clause will cause no difficulty. The rule is very simple. (Read the Classification of Tenses, given at 177.)

104. If the verb in the principal clause is in a *primary* tense, *i.e.* present, true perfect, or future, the verb in the *ut-*, *quo-*, or *ne-* clause will be in the present subjunctive.

> *Haec* scribo, scripsi, scribam, scripsero, *ut bono* sis *animo.*
> I *write, have written, shall write, shall have written,* this, in order that you *may* be in good spirits.

If the principal verb is in a *historic* tense, *i.e.* imperfect, aorist perfect, or pluperfect, the subordinate verb will be in the imperfect subjunctive.

> *Haec* scribebam, scripsi, scripseram, *ut bono* esses *animo.*
> I *was writing, wrote, had written,* this, in order that you *might* be in good spirits.

105. The Latin Perfect discharges the part of two English tenses, and has therefore a double construction. (See **187.**)

> Laudavi *te, ut bonus* haberere.   I *praised* you that you *might* be accounted good. (Laudavi is *historical,* an **aorist** *tense.*)
> Laudavi *te, ut bonus* habeare.[1]   I *have praised* you that you *may* be accounted good. (Laudavi is *primary,* a **perfect** *tense.*)

Exercise 14.

1. In order not to be driven into exile, I shall pretend to be mad. 2. That you might not be punished for this crime both your brother and you told many falsehoods. 3. He pardoned, it is said,[2] the wicked, in order to obtain a reputation for clemency. 4. He spared the best patriots when he was[3] victorious, in order that his own crimes might be forgiven. 5. He praised your countrymen again and again in their presence, in order to be praised by them in his absence. 6. The enemy will, they say,[2] be here to-morrow with[4] a vast army in order to[5] besiege

---

[1] But even in the latter case the Romans often wrote *haberere,* looking rather to the past time when the *intention was formed.*

[2] See **32,** *b;* **43.**   [3] See **63.**   [4] **8,** *b.*   [5] Gerundive with *ad.* **100,** *a*

our city. 7. That he might not be condemned in his absence he hastened to go to Rome. 8. It is said that he told many falsehoods to make[1] himself seem younger than he really was. 9. It seems that he wishes to return home in order to[2] stand for the consulship. 10. There is a tradition that he refused to accept the crown to avoid displeasing his brother, or injuring the lawful heir. 11. In order to testify his zeal and loyalty he hastened in his[3] old age to Rome, and was the very first[4] to pay his respects to the new king.

---

[1] See **102**.　　[2] **100, b.**　　[3] See **63.**　　[4] Lit., first *of all.*　See **62.**

Ut, Ut non, IN CONSECUTIVE CLAUSES.

106. *Ut* with the subjunctive is also used in Latin to denote, not a *purpose,* but a *consequence* or *result.*

We see the difference at once in English.

(*a.*) I ran against him *in order to throw* him down (Final) ;

(*b.*) I ran against him with *such* force *that I threw* him down (Consecutive).

In the former sentence, (*a*), nothing is said of the *result,* only the end in view, or *motive,* is mentioned. In the latter, (*b*), nothing is said of the *motive,* only the *result* is named.

It is the peculiarity of Latin that this result, even when stated as an actual fact, is described by *ut* with a verb in the *subjunctive* mood.

> *Tanta vis probitatis est, ut eam vel in hoste* diligamus. Such is the force of honesty, that *we love* it even in an enemy.

"That we love it" is stated as a *fact,* and would be indicative in other languages, but in Latin *diligimus* would never be used after a consecutive *ut.*

107. The Latin *ut,* therefore, is used with the same construction in two different senses, but the context will almost always prevent ambiguity. In such a sentence as *puer humi prolapsus est, ut crus frangeret,* the boy fell down *so that he* broke (*or* so as to break) his leg, *intention* would be absurd. Very often *ut final* will correspond to some such word or phrase as *idcirco, eo consilio, ob eam causam,* etc., in the principal clause ; *ut consecutive* to *adeo,* or *tam,* or *ita,* or *tantus:* and thus the meaning of *ut* is made clear at once.

> *Hoc* eo consilio *dixi ut tibi prodessem.* I said this *to be* of use to you, or *with the intention of being* of use.
>
> *Hoc* ita *dixi, ut tibi prodessem.* I said this *so as to be* of use to you, or *in such a manner that I was of use to you.*

108. The English *as* before the *infinitive,* and after *so, such* (in Latin *tantus, talis, tam, adeo,* etc.), must always be translated by *ut* with the subjunctive.

> *Nemo* tam *potens est, ut omnia efficere* possit. Nobody is so powerful *as to be* able to perform everything.

96

. But *ut*="as," in comparisons, is followed in Latin, as in English, by an indicative.

> Ut *multitudo* solet, *concurrunt.* They are running together, *as* a multitude *is wont* to do.

Here *ut* introduces, not a *consecutive*, but a *comparative* clause (Intr. 85), and the construction may be compared to that of *tantus* followed by *quantus*, as opposed to *tantus* followed by *ut.*

Compare

> Talis *fuit* ut *nemo ei* crederet. He was of *such* a character *that* no one believed him,

with

> Talis *fuit* qualem *nemo antea* viderat. He was of *such* a character *as* no one had seen before,

and note the difference of the moods in Latin.

109. A negative *consequence* is not expressed by *ne*, but by *ut non.*

> Tanta fuit viri moderatio, ut *repugnanti mihi* non *irasceretur.* The self-control of the man was so great, *that* he *was not* angry with me when I opposed him.

The following rule is therefore most important :—

That nobody	) if expressing *purpose*	(ne quis
That nothing	(and followed by *may* or	) ne quid
That no	{ *might* must be translated	) ne ullus
That never	) by	(ne unquam.

But if they express *consequence*, and are followed by a simple English indicative, must be translated in Latin by	{ ut nemo ut nihil ut nullus ut nunquam.

In both cases alike the verb will be in the subjunctive mood. Thus—

> The gates were shut *that no one might* leave the city (or *to prevent any one* from leaving, or *in order to* prevent any one, etc.). *Portae clausae sunt*, ne quis *urbem relinqueret.*
>
> The fear of all men was so great, *that no one left* the city. *Tantus fuit omnium metus*, ut nemo *urbem reliquerit.*

G

110. As *ne quis*="that no one" in final clauses, and *neve*, or *neu* quis="or, and, that no one," so also in indicative clauses,

"and no one" is always *nec quisquam*,
"and nothing"   „   *nec quidquam*,
"and never"   „   *nec unquam*.

Similarly *nec ullus* (adj.), *nec usquam*, "and no where," etc.

111. Closely allied to the *consecutive* is a *limiting* force of *ut*, the negative of which is frequently translated by the English "without."

> *Ita bonus est, ut interdum peccet.* He is good *to this extent* (or he is *only* so far good), that he makes mistakes sometimes.
>
> *Nec perdi potes, ut non alios perdas.* Nor can you be ruined *without ruining* others.

Compare with the first example the limiting use of *tantus*. 84, *note*.

Sequence of Tenses.   Tenses of the Subjunctive.

112. There is no such simple rule for the tense of the verb in the consecutive clause as that given for the final clause, and there is greater variety in the tenses; but in practice there will be little difficulty

Use the tense of the subjunctive mood which you would use if the verb were, as it would be in English, in the indicative.

Thus—

> "He *is* so wicked that nothing *has* ever *called* him away from crime;"

"has ever called" is the "true perfect;" write therefore,

> *Tam improbus est ut nihil eum unquam a scelere revocaverit.*

We have here a *present* tense in the principal, a true *perfect* in the consecutive clause; both are primary tenses.   (See **177**.)

> *Hoc eum adeo terruit ut vix hodie prodire audeat.* This so *terrified* him that he scarcely *ventures* to come forward to-day.

Here one tense is historic, the other primary, but the English is a sufficient guide.

113. The only difficulty is the choice between the perfect and the imperfect subjunctive in the consecutive clause after an historic or *aorist* perfect in the principal clause.

The imperfect subjunctive denotes a *continuous* state, or action ; or one described as *commencing;* or as strictly *contemporaneous with* some point in past time.

The perfect subjunctive represents (*a*) a state or action as simply a fact in the past (aorist) ; or (*b*) a fact still producing a result in the mind of the speaker (perfect).

That the army *was flying*, or *began to fly* (imperfect) ; that the army *fled* (aorist) ; that the army *has fled* (perfect)—will represent the three tenses in English : the two latter would both be expressed in Latin by the words "*ut* fugerit," as opposed to "*ut* fugeret *exercitus.*" (See **184, 185, 186.**)

If the verb in the consecutive clause implies continuance, or contemporaneous time in the past, use the **imperfect subjunctive.** If it denotes a **single fact**, or one looked on as **now completed**, use the perfect subjunctive. Thus—

> *Tanta* fuit *pestis ut permulti quotidie* perirent, *rex ipse morbo* absumptus sit.   The pestilence was so great that many *died* daily, and the king himself *was cut off* by the disease.
>
> *Ducis adventus adeo militum* redintegravit *animos ut impetum* extemplo { facerent. }   The general's arrival so restored the { fecerint. }   soldiers' spirits that they charged at once.

Facerent implies "at once began to ;" *fecerint* may either mean "charged" as a simple fact (aorist), or in vivid language "they *have* charged" (perfect), as though we saw the fact.

With the perfect (aorist), the consequence is looked upon as a single result, at once achieved, and not as spread over a space of time, for which idea the imperfect would be appropriate.

Future Subjunctive.

114. The only future subjunctive is the participle in *-rus* combined with the right tense of the verb *sum*. This must therefore be used where the *result* denoted by the consecutive clause is a future one. Thus—

> *Nunquam posthac* pugnabimus.   We shall never fight again (after this).

But—

> *Adeo* territi sumus *ut nunquam posthac* pugnaturi *simus.*   We have been (*or* were) so frightened that we shall never fight again.

So—

Dixit *se adeo* territos fuisse *ut nunquam postea* pugnaturi essent.
He said that they (himself and his companions) *had been* so
frightened that they *would* never fight again.

115. The pluperfect subjunctive, our "*would have*," is represented
in a consecutive clause by the participle in -*rus* with the *perfect subjunctive of sum*. Thus—

Nemo superfuisset. No one would have survived.

But—

Tanta fuit caedes ut . . . *nemo* superfuturus fuerit. The slaughter
was such *that* no one *would have* survived.

Instances of Sequence of Tenses.

116.

Hoc ita facio, feci, faciam, *ut tibi* displiceam. *I do (am doing),
have done, will do*, this so as to displease you.

Hoc ita feci, faciebam, feceram *ut tibi* displicerem. *I did, was
doing, had done*, this so as *(then)* to displease you.

Hoc ita feci *ut tibi* displiceam (rare). *I did* this so as *now* to displease you.

Hoc ita feci *ut tibi* displicuerim. *I did* this so as to *have* now displeased you, *or* I did this so that (as a matter of fact) *I
displeased* you.

Dixit *se hoc ita* fecisse *ut tibi* displiceret. He said that he did this
so as to displease you.

Hoc ita feci *ut tibi* displiciturus sim. *I have* done this so that *I
shall* displease you (or so as *to be likely to*, etc.).

Exercise 15.

1. I have lived, said[1] he, so virtuously, that I quit life
with resignation. 2. He had lived, he said,[1] so virtuously,
as to quit life with resignation. 3. I will endeavour, said
he, to live so as to be able to quit life with resignation.
4. He said that he had lived so as to be able to quit life
with resignation. 5. The charge of the enemy was so
sudden that no one could find his arms or proper rank.
6. Thereupon the enemy made a sudden[2] charge in order
to prevent any of our men from finding either his arms or
proper rank. 7. Thereupon he[3] began to tell many[4] false-

---

[1] See **40**.   [2] Use adverb, *made suddenly a charge*.
[3] Ille (*the other*), **11**, *d*.   [4] See **54**.

hoods with the intention of preserving his life. 8. He told so many falsehoods that no one believed him then, and that no one has ever put faith in him since. 9. He was so good a king that his subjects loved him in his lifetime, sighed for him after his death, honour his name and memory to-day with grateful[1] hearts, and will never forget his virtues. 10. The waves were such as to dash over the whole of[2] the ship, and the storm was of such a kind as I had never seen before. 11. The cavalry charged so fiercely that had[3] not night interfered with the contest, the enemy would have[4] turned their backs. 12. You cannot, said he, injure your country without[5] bringing loss and ruin upon yourself and your own affairs. 13. I said this with the intention of benefiting you and yours, but the matter has so turned out that I shall injure you whom I wished to benefit, and benefit those whom I wished to injure. 14. So little did he indulge even a just resentment, that he pardoned even those who had slain his father.

---

[1] Superlative. See **57.**   [2] See **60.**
[3] *Nisi* with pluperf. subj.   [4] **115.**   [5] See **111.**

Ut, Ne, INTRODUCING A SUBSTANTIVAL CLAUSE.[1]

117. One of the main difficulties in translating English into Latin is to know when to represent the English infinitive by the same mood in Latin, when to use a conjunction, such as *ut* or *ne* followed by the subjunctive.

We have already seen that the Latin infinitive takes the place of an English conjunctional or *that*-clause after verbs of *saying, thinking,* etc. **(31-32)**.

On the other hand we have seen that the Latin infinitive must never be used to express either a *purpose* or a *result* (**100, 106**).

But besides these clear cases, which need cause no difficulty, many verbs which in English are followed by the infinitive require in Latin an *ut*- or *ne*- clause. These clauses, though originally *adverbial*, are virtually *substantival*.

Thus in *oro te ut hoc facias,* "I entreat you *to do* this," *ut hoc facias* is in the strictest sense an *adverbial* or *final* clause, "I entreat you, *with a view to your doing* this ;" but it may also be regarded as equivalent to an accusative case after *oro;* compare, pacem *oro;* and it is usual to consider those clauses whose final nature is not obvious at first sight as *substantival* clauses, and to class them as such, under the name of indirect *commands* or *entreaties,* with the indirect *statement* and indirect *question.* (See Intr. 80.)

118. The English infinitive after verbs and phrases of **entreating, commanding, decreeing, advising, striving, effecting,** must be translated into Latin by *ut,* or, if a negative is required, by *ne,* followed by the subjunctive mood.

Such verbs are nearly all the *verba* **imperandi vel efficiendi,** such as *oro, peto, precor, opto* (not *volo*), *edico, impero* (not *jubeo*), *hortor, moneo, suadeo, video* (I take care), *permitto*

---

[1] For the meaning of the term *substantival clause* see Intr. 80.

(not *sino* or *patior*), *facio, efficio, impetro* (I obtain by asking), and such phrases as *id ago,* " I make it my aim ;" " *operam do,*" " I take pains."

The Sequence of Tenses, as well as the use of *ne* in negative clauses, will be that of the *final* clause (**104**). Thus—

> *Ut hostem terreret, militibus* imperavit, ut *clipeos hastis* percuterent. In order to terrify the enemy he commanded the soldiers *to strike* their shields with their spears.

Here the first *ut* introduces an *adverbial* (final), the second a (virtually) *substantival* clause.

> *Magno opere te* hortor, ut *hos libros studiose legas.* I earnestly advise you *to read* these books attentively.
>
> *Capram* monet, ut *in pratum* descendat. He advises the she-goat *to come down* into the meadow.
>
> *Hoc te* rogo, ne demittas *animum.* I beg of you *not to be disheartened* (literally, not to let your mind sink).
>
> Effecit ne *ex urbe* exirent. He prevented *their leaving* the city.
>
> *Mihi* ne *quid* facerem imperavit. He ordered me *to do* nothing.

119. We must therefore never say *hoc te* facere, *or* non facere *oro, suadeo, hortor,* for—" I entreat, persuade, exhort you *to do,* or *not to do* this," but always *hoc* ut, or *hoc* ne *facias,* etc. The *ut* is sometimes omitted, especially with the 2nd pers. sing. (See **126**.)

120. But there are exceptions to the rule which must be carefully noticed. The commonest of all is *jubeo* (I bid), which takes an infinitive with the accusative.

Compare

> *Consul* militibus ut (*or* ne) *pedem* referrent imperavit

with

> *Consul* milites *pedem* referre jussit (*or* vetuit).

And the infinitive construction is usual with *volo,* and *cupio* (I wish, desire), also with *veto,* I forbid, *prohibeo,* I prevent, *conor,* I endeavour, *sino, patior,* I allow.

121. It has already been said (**45**) that some verbs of *purposing, resolving,* etc., take the infinitive when the subject of both verbs is the same, but an *ut-* or *ne-* clause when the subject of the second verb is different : *ego ne redirem, curavit, he* took care that *I* should not return ; *nec redire curat,* and he does not care to return. In the second example *curat* is a modal verb (**42**).

122. It is important to observe that the same verb may be used in two senses, and therefore with two constructions.

It may be used as a verb *sentiendi vel declarandi,* in which case it will take the accusative and infinitive (**31**); or it may be used as a verb *imperandi vel efficiendi* (**118**), in which case it will be followed by an *ut-* or *ne-* clause ; thus—

(*a.*) *Moneo* adesse hostem.   I warn you *that* the enemy *is* at hand.
　　 Ne *hoc* facias *moneo.*   I warn you not *to do* this.
(*b.*) *Mihi persuasum est* (**5**) finem adesse.   I was persuaded *that* the end *was* near.
　　 Mihi persuasum est ne *hoc* facerem.   I was persuaded *not to do* this.
(*c.*) *Mihi scripsit* se venturum esse.   He wrote me word *that* he *would* come.
　　 Mihi scripsit ne *ad se* venirem.   He wrote to me (to order or beg me) *not to come* to him.
(*d.*) *Fac* venias.   Be sure *to come.*
　　 Fac te venisse.   Suppose yourself *to have* come.

The same verbs are used in English with a double construction ; but where we use the conjunction "*that*" Latin uses the infinitive, and Latin uses a conjunction where we use the infinitive.

123. Many **impersonal** verbs and phrases are followed by an *ut*-clause containing a verb in the subjunctive. This clause acts in place of a subject to the impersonal verb.

　　 Accidit ut nemo senator adesset.   It happened that no senator was present, *or,* no senator happened to be present.
　　 Ex quo factum est ut *bellum indiceretur.*   The consequence of *this* (**78**) was that war was declared, *or,* the result was a declaration of war.

These *ut-* clauses are properly speaking *consecutive*, as those in 117, 118, are properly *final;* hence *ut nemo*, not *ne quis* in the first example. (See 109.)

The sequence of Tenses will be that of the consecutive clause.

Obs.—Never translate "it happened to him to be absent" by *accidit ei abesse*, always by *ei accidit ut abesset*, or else by *is forte abfuit.*

124. *Tantum abest,* "so far from," is always used impersonally, and is followed by two *ut*-clauses, of which one is *substantival* and subject to *abest*, the other is *adverbial*, being a consecutive clause explaining *tantum.*

Tantum abest ut *nostra miremur* ut *nobis non satisfaciat ipse Demosthenes. So far are we from* admiring our own works, *that* Demosthenes himself does not satisfy us.

Ut nostra miremur; a substantival clause, standing in place of a subject to *abest.*

Ut nobis non satisfaciat ipse Demosthenes; an adverbial clause which, joined with *tantum*, qualifies *abest* like an adverb of degree or quantity.

The same idea might also be expressed by *adeo non . . . ut*, or by *non modo non . . . sed*, as,

Adeo non *nostra miramur* ut *nobis non* satisfaciat, etc. ; or,
Non modo non *nostra miramur*, sed *nobis non* satisfacit.

125. The following verbs and phrases are followed by *ut*, introducing a substantival clause.

(*a.*) It follows ; the next thing is, *sequitur :* or *proximum est.*
(*b.*) It happens by chance, *casu accidit.*
(*c.*) Hence it happens, *ita fit*, lit. thus it happens.
(*d.*) How happens it ? *qui fit ?*
(*e.*) It is possible, *fieri potest ut*, lit. it can happen that.
(*f.*) It is (quite) impossible, *nullo modo fieri potest ut*, lit. it cannot happen that.
(*g.*) It remains, *reliquum est, restat.*
(*h.*) So far from, *tantum abest ut—ut.*
(*i.*) I will not allow myself to, *non committam ut.*
(*j.*) He succeeded (in becoming consul), *effecit (ut consul fieret).*
(*k.*) He contrived (not to be punished), *effecit (ne poenas daret).*

126. *Ut* is generally omitted (especially before the 2nd person singular) when the subjunctive is combined with *oportet, necesse est, velim, nolim, licet.*

Hoc facias *velim.* I would have you do this.
Culpam fateare *necesse est.* You must needs avow your fault.

127. The ordinary construction of the case of the person after words of entreating and commanding, etc., is

(*a.*) Te *oro, obsecro, rogo, moneo, admoneo, hortor, adhortor, jubeo, veto, prohibeo, sino.*

(*b.*) Tibi *impero, praecipio, edico, mando, permitto.*

(*c.*) A, ab (abs) te *peto, postulo, impetro.*

(*d.*) *Posco, flagito, precor,* both with acc. as (*a*), and *a* or *ab* with abl. as (*c*).

128. *Jubeo* expresses our "bid," and may be used in a wide sense, and wherever in *oratio recta* we should use the imperative. *Salvere te jubeo* = salve. It may express the wish of equals, superiors, or inferiors.

> *Impero* implies an order from a higher authority, as from a commanding officer.
>
> *Edico,* a formal order from some one in office, as a Praetor, etc.
>
> *Praecipio,* a direction or instruction from one of superior knowledge.
>
> *Mando,* a charge or commission intrusted by any one.

Permitto differs from *sino,* as meaning rather to give leave *actively;* *sino,* not to prevent. *Permitto* sometimes means "to intrust wholly to," "hand over to."

Exercise 16.

A.

1. I entreated him not to do this,[1] but suggested to him to trust his father.   2. He exhorted the soldiers not to be disheartened on account of the late disaster.   3. He made it his aim to avoid injuring any one of his subjects, but to consult the good of the whole nation.   4. He gave orders to the soldiers to get ready for fighting, and exhorted them to fight bravely.   5. The senate passed a resolution that the consuls should hold a levy.   6. I resolved to warn your brother not to return to Rome before night. 7. And, to prevent him from telling any more falsehoods, I bade him hold his peace.   8. It happened (on) that day[2] that the consuls were about to hold a levy.   9. I prevailed on him to spare the vanquished (*pl.*), and not[3] to allow

---

[1] Co-ordinate relative.   (See **78.**)   [2] See 9, (*a*).
[3] *Neve* or *neu.*   (See **103.**)

his (soldiers) to massacre women and children. 10. I was
the first to warn him not to put faith in the falsest and
most cruel of mankind. 11. You[1] and I happened that
day to be in the country; the consequence[2] of this was
that we have been the last[3] to hear of this disaster. 12.
He said that he would never allow himself to promise to
betray his allies.

B.

1. Thereupon he earnestly implored the bystanders not
to obey men[4] who were ready (subj., **77**) to betray both
their allies and themselves in order to avoid incurring a
trifling loss. 2. He succeeded at last in persuading the
Spaniards that it was quite impossible to leave the city,
(which was[5]) blockaded on all sides by the enemy, unharmed. 3. He says[6] that he never asked you to pardon
the guilty or condemn the innocent. 4. I will not, said
he, allow myself to be the last to greet my king after so
heavy a disaster. 5. The jury were at last persuaded that
my brother was innocent; they could not be persuaded to
acquit him by their verdict, such was their terror[7] of the
mob. 6. News has been brought to me in my absence
that the city has been taken: it remains (for me) to retake
it by the same arts as[8] those by which I have lost it. 7.
So far am I from praising and admiring that king, that it
seems[9] to me that he has greatly injured not only his own
subjects, but the whole human race. 8. So far am I from
having said everything, that I could take up the whole of
the day in speaking; but I do not wish to be tedious.[10] 9.
It never before happened to me to forget a friend in his
absence, and this[11] circumstance is a great consolation to
me to-day.

---

[1] See **26**, note.
[2] See **123**, example 2.
[3] See **62**.
[4] See **72**.
[5] Omit relative and use participle.
[6] See **33**.
[7] See **25**, last example.
[8] See **84**.
[9] See **43**.
[10] See **42**, ii.
[11] See **67**.

Quominus, Quin. VERBS OF *Fearing* WITH *Ut, Ne.*

129. These two compound words are used as conjunctions after verbs and phrases which denote *prevention, hindrance, opposition,* etc.

Quo minus = *ut eo (hoc) minus,* "that by it the less," or "that by this means the less." *Quin* = *qui* (old abl. = *quo*), and *ne,* the old form of the negative, "that by it not."

130. *Quo minus* is generally, *quin* only, used when the verb of *preventing,* etc., is joined with a negative or virtual negative.

By a *virtual negative* we mean *vix, aegre,* "scarcely," "with difficulty," or questions expecting the answer "no," "none," "nothing."

131. *Quo minus* often answers to the English verbal noun in *-ing* combined with a preposition.

> *Naves vento tenebantur* quominus *in portum* redirent. The ships were prevented by the wind *from returning* into harbour.
>
> *Per te stetit* quominus vinceremus. You were the cause *of our not winning* the day.
>
> *Non recusabo* quominus *te in vincula* ducam. I will not object *to taking* you to prison.

In all these instances a negative *result* or *aim* (two notions so often identified in Latin) is expressed by *quominus.*

132. *Quin* is still more common than *quominus*, but is only used after negative words and phrases.

(*a.*) Nec *multum afuit* quin *interficeremur*.   And we were not far *from losing* our lives.

(*b.*) Nec *eum unquam adspexit*, quin *fratricidam compellaret*. And she never beheld him *without calling* him a fratricide.

(*c.*) Vix *inhiberi potuit*, quin *saxa jacĕret*.   He could scarcely be prevented *from throwing* stones.

(*d.*) Nullo modo *fieri potest* quin *errem*.   It is quite impossible *that I am not* mistaken, or *but that I am*, etc.

(*e.*) *Fieri* vix *potuit* quin *te accusarem*.   It was scarcely possible *for me not to* accuse you.

133. *Quin* is also used as equivalent to "*but that*" or "*that*" after verbs or phrases of *doubting*, combined with a negative, or virtual negative.

Quis dubitat quin *hoc feceris?* Who doubts (=no one doubts) *but that* (or that) you did this?

134. *Quin* is also used (see **80**) as containing not a conjunction but a relative pronoun (*qui, quae, quod*, and *ne*).

Nemo est quin [=qui non] *intelligat*.   There is no one *but* (*who* does not) perceives, *or* all the world perceives.

In all these uses *quin* is joined with the subjunctive.

135. But it is also used sometimes as a direct interrogative = *qui non?*

Quin *hoc mihi das?* How (or, why) do you not give me this? *i.e.* give it me ;

and sometimes as a mere emphatic particle = "nay ;" *quinetiam* = "moreover."

In these senses it can be joined with *any mood*.

136. (*a.*) *Recuso* (*quominus*) means properly "I protest against," "give reasons against," (*re* and *causa*) ; hence it is equivalent to our "object." It is sometimes used less emphatically as a modal verb with the infinitive (**42**) ; but the English "I refuse" in the sense "I am reluctant" is generally to be turned by *nolo*, or, if a refusal expressed in words is meant, by *nego* with future in *-rus*.

(*b.*) *Dubito* when negatived (see **130**) is followed by *quin*, but it is also used as a modal verb in the sense of "hesitate," "scruple."

Thus we sometimes find not only

Nec recuso quominus *hoc patiar.*   And I do not protest *against* suffering this.

Nec dubitat quin *hoc facere audeat.*   And he does not hesitate *to venture* on doing this.

but—

Neque hoc pati *recuso, nec hoc* audere *dubitat.*

137. (I.) Words and phrases followed by *quin* with the subjunctive are :—

(*a.*) All the world (believes), *nemo est quin (credat).*
(*b.*) Not to doubt, *non dubitare (quin).*
(*c.*) There is no doubt, *non est dubium* or *dubitandum (quin),* "it is not doubtful."
(*d.*) Who doubts ? *quis dubitat (quin) ?*
(*e.*) It cannot be (it is impossible) but that, *fieri non potest (quin).*
(*f.*) I cannot refrain from, *temperare mihi non possum (quin).* See (*j.*).
(*g.*) It cannot be denied, *negari non potest (quin).*   (Rare : the infinitive is to be preferred.)
(*h.*) To be very near ; to be within a very little, *minimum abesse; haud multum abesse (quin)* ; always used impersonally.
(*i.*) To leave nothing undone to, *nihil praetermittere (quin).*
(*j.*) I cannot but, I cannot help, *.... non possum (quin).*
(*k.*) To restrain, to keep back from, *retinere, tenere* (after negative words, and *aegre,* "with difficulty," *vix,* "scarcely," etc.).
(*l.*) What reason is there against ? *quid causae est (quin) ?*

(II.) Verbs that may be followed by *quominus.*

To frighten from, to deter, *deterrere.*
To hinder, prevent, *obstare* (dat.), *impedire* (acc.).   (So *officere, obsistere, repugnare, intercedere,* etc.)

Prohibeo and *veto* mostly take the infinitive.   (See **120.**)

Verbs of Fearing.

138. The construction used in Latin after verbs of *fearing* is quite different from that which follows verbs of *hoping.*   (See **37.**)

With verbs of **fearing**, *that* as well as *lest* must be translated by *nē*, *that not* by *ut*.[1]

Such verbs are *timeo, metuo, vereor*, etc., and the same construction is used with such phrases as *periculum est (fuit), metus est*, etc.

After such verbs and phrases the English *future* and the *verbal substantive* are translated by the *present* or *imperfect* subjunctive, with *ut* or *nē*.

> *Vereor* ne *veniat.*   I fear *that* he *will* come, *or*, I fear *or* am afraid of his *coming.*
>
> *Vereor* ut *veniat.*   I fear *that* he *will not* come, *or*, I am afraid *of his not coming.*
>
> *Veritus sum* ne *or* ut *veniret.*   I feared that he *would*, or *would not* come.
>
> *Periculum erat* ne *hostes urbem expugnarent.*   There was a danger of the enemy's taking the city.

139. But where stress is laid on the idea of futurity, or the sense of *likelihood* is introduced, the subjunctive future, *i.e.* the future in *-rus* with *sum* (114), is used.

> *Vereor* ut *hoc tibi* profuturum sit.   I am afraid that this *is not likely* to do you good

Obs.—Verbs of fearing are *sometimes* used like *recuso* and *dubito* as modal verbs in close combination with the infinitive.

> *Nec* mori *timet.*   And he is not afraid of dying.

---

[1] The origin of this use of *ne* and *ut* after verbs of fearing is not quite clear. The *ne* is easily explained. "I fear, with a *wish* or *aim* that he may not come"="I fear *lest* he come or be coming" (English subjunctive), compare the French *je crains qu'il* ne *vienne* ; and thus the *ne* introduces a final clause.

On the same principle the *ut* may mean "I *am in fear*, with the desire or aim that *he may* come"="I am afraid of his not coming," in French—je crains qu'il *ne vienne pas.*

The *ut* may also be explained as used in its interrogative sense of "how," "as to how," and thus the *ut veniat* would be a dependent interrogative clause ; "I have fears *as to how* he is coming"="that he is not coming."

This explanation is simple, but involves a totally different origin and construction from that of the *ne*-clause.

1. I never beheld him without imploring him to come to the aid of his oppressed and suffering country; but I fear that he will never listen to my prayers.   2. I cannot refrain from blaming those who were ready to hand over our lives, liberties, rights, and fortunes to our deadliest enemies.   3. All the world believes that you did wrong, and I am afraid that it is quite impossible that all mankind have been of one mind with me in a blunder.   4. He pretends that I was the cause of my countrymen not joining the cause of every patriot.   5. The soldiers could not be restrained from hurling their darts into the midst of the mob.   6. He promises to leave nothing undone to persuade your son not to hurry away from the city to the country.[1]   7. We were within a very little of being all killed, some of us pierced by the enemy's darts, others cut off either by famine or disease.   8. Nothing,[2] he said, had ever prevented him[3] from defending the freedom and privileges of his countrymen.   9. What circumstance prevented you from keeping your word, and coming to my aid with your army, as you[4] had promised to do?   10. I will no longer then protest against your desiring to become a king, but I am afraid you will not be able to obtain your desire.   11. What reason is there why he should not be ready to return in his old[5] age to the scenes which he left unwillingly in his boyhood?[5]   12. Such was his terror[6] of Caesar's victory, that he could scarcely be restrained from committing suicide.   13. He could not, he replied,[7] help waging war by land and sea.   14. News has been brought me, said he, that the general has been struck by a dart, and I fear that he has received a mortal wound.   15. Nor was he afraid, he replied, of our being able to reach Italy in[8] safety; the[9] danger was[10] of our being likely never to return.

---

[1] See **9**, *b*.   [2] See **33**.   [3] *i.e.* himself, **11**, *e*.   [4] See **67**, *Obs.*
[5] **63**.   [6] See **25**.   [7] **32**, *b*.   [8] See **61**.
[9] Lit., that (*ille*) was the danger, etc.
[10] Inf. mood, dependent on "he replied."

EXERCISE XVIII.

COMMANDS AND PROHIBITIONS.

Imperative Mood.

140. The **imperative mood** is used freely in Latin, as in English, in both commands and entreaties, in the second person singular and plural.

Ad me veni. *Come* to me.   Audite[1] *hoc*. *Hear* this.

141. But, especially in the singular, where one person, an equal, is addressed, there are many substitutes for so peremptory a mode of speaking. A short compound sentence containing either a subordinate or a co-ordinate clause is substituted for the simple command.

Thus: for *scribe*, scribas velim, "I would have you write" (126), is often used; or *tu*, quaeso, *ad me scribe*, or *scribe sis* (for si vis): or again, for *ad me veni*, fac, *or* cura ut, *ad me venias*, "be sure to come:" so with the plural, *vos*, oro et obsecro, *attendite*.

Obs.—The subjunctive is used for the imperative in the second person singular; but only where no definite person is addressed, but a general maxim given.

Postremus loquaris: *primus* taceas. Be (*you*, or *a man* should be) the last to speak, the first to be silent.

---

[1] There is also a more emphatic form, *venito, venitote*, which is called the *future* imperative; it is used in both the second and third persons, and is called future from its very common use in *laws* and *wills* which concern the future, and from its often forming the *apodosis* to a future perfect clause; *cum ego dixero, tum vos* respondetote, when I have spoken, then, *and not before*, do you reply. But it is used also for mere emphasis: *nolitote, scitote*, are often met with.

H   113

142. In **negative commands**, or **prohibitions**, the simple imperative is little used. Such phrases as *ne sævi, magna sacerdos* (AEN. vi.) ("be not wroth, mighty priestess"), are almost entirely confined to poetry.

In English also, though in older English, and in poetry, we find constantly "go not," "fear not," etc., yet we generally substitute the infinitive with an auxiliary verb in the imperative : *do* not go, *do* not fear.

In Latin, in addressing a single person familiarly, *ne* is often used with the *perfect* subjunctive.

> *Ne dubitaveris*, do not hesitate ; *lit.* do not (allow yourself to) *have* hesitated, *or* beware against *having* hesitated.

So—*Nihil dederis*, give nothing.

The *present* subjunctive is not used in speaking to a person ; *ne multa* discas, *sed multum* is a general maxim. (See 141, *Obs.*)

143. But by far the more common mode of forbidding or deprecating is by a periphrasis ; using, as we do in '*do* not *do* this,' *two* verbs.

> Noli, nolite, nolitote, *hoc facere*, *or* cave, cavete (ne) *illud facias, faciatis.*

The *ne* is often omitted with the second person. (See **126.**)

144. For the *first* and *third* persons (except in formal documents, see 140, note) Latin employs the subjunctive mood in a *jussive* sense to express *exhortation, wish, or command*, and uses *ne* to prohibit or deprecate.

> *Moriamur, let* us die ; *pereat, may* he perish ; *abeat, let* him go ; ne sim *salvus, may* no good befall me ; ne exeat *urbe, let* him not go out of the city. In older English and in poetry we have "*turn* we to survey," "hallowed *be* thy name."

145. "Nor," "or," "and not," with prohibitions is generally *neve* or *neu*, but *neque* is also used.

> *Hoc facito ; illud ne feceris,* neve *dixeris.* Do this ; do not do *or* say that.
>
> *Sequere,* neque *retrospexeris.* Follow *and* do *not* look behind.

146. There is also a common use of such phrases as *vidĕris*, *viderint*, in the sense of "you, they, must look to it," when the responsibility of giving an opinion is declined or postponed.

> *De hac re tu* videris, *or* viderint *sapientiores.* I leave this to you, *or* to wiser men ; do you, *or* let wiser men, decide.

This is a future perfect indicative, as in the first person *videro* is used.

Exercise 18.

1. Do not then lose (*sing.*) such an opportunity as[1] this, but rather let us, under your leadership, crush the eternal enemies of our country.   2. Do not, my countrymen, count the foes who are threatening you with massacre and slavery; let them rather meet the same lot which they are preparing for us.   3. Pardon (*sing.*) this fault of mine; and be sure you remember that I, who have done wrong to-day, have repeatedly brought you help before.   4. Let us then refuse to be slaves, and have the courage not only to become free ourselves, but to assert our country's freedom also.   5. And therefore[2] do not object to[3] endure everything in behalf of your suffering country and your exiled friends.   6. And therefore,[2] my countrymen, do not believe that I, who have so often led you to the field of battle, am afraid to-day of fortune abandoning me.   7. Let us be the same in the field (of battle) as[4] we have ever been; as[5] to the issue of the battle let the gods decide.

---

[1] See **88**, *Obs.*   [2] See **78**.   [5] See **136**

[4] See **84**.   [5] Prep. *de* with *abl.*

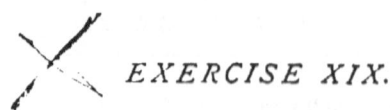

EXERCISE XIX.

REMARKS ON MOODS: THE SUBJUNCTIVE
USED INDEPENDENTLY.

147. By a *Mood*[1] we mean a special form assumed by the Verb in order to mark some special manner (*modus*) in which that connexion between a subject and predicate which every verb implies is viewed by the speaker. (Intr. 11, and see note.)

---

[1] In the words of an old grammarian (Priscian) *modi sunt diversae* inclinationes *animi* (movements, variations, swayings, of the human mind) *quas varia consequitur* declinatio (inflexion, or form). In some languages, especially those which have no written literature, the number of moods is exceedingly large, different modifications of the form of the verb being used to represent many different *moods*, or frames, or attitudes, of the mind of the speaker. Thus, in addition to those forms which denote *time* (tenses), we find separate forms or moods to express *certainty, doubt, inquiry, contingency, negation, command, desire*, etc. But in the languages of highly civilised nations economy is practised in the use of such varied forms; the intelligence of the hearer or reader is relied on, and a single form (as with the case-inflexions of nouns) is used to represent various ideas more or less related to each other. In Greek the two ideas of a command and a wish as applied to a third person are expressed by two moods, ἀπολέσθω, ἀπόλοιτο; Latin is content with one—*pereat*. Both agree with English in having no mood to distinguish a simple question from a simple statement. In modern English prose the subjunctive mood, so exceedingly common in Latin, hardly exists as a true mood, *i.e.* a separate and distinct form of the verb. We retain its use occasionally as a contingent mood after *though* and *if*, "though he *fail*," "if it *be* so;" but as a rule we either disregard those slighter, though real, shades of meaning which call for the subjunctive in Latin (as often in German and French), and are content with the indicative, or, if the difference is too great to be disregarded, we substitute for a true mood a combination of an auxiliary or modal verb with the infinitive mood—"*let* him go," "if he *were* to come," "I *would* not do this,"—exactly as we substitute a preposition with a noun for the case-inflexions of nouns.

As regards therefore the use of the Latin subjunctive, the usage of English will be a most inadequate guide. It would, for instance, never lead us to suspect the necessity of such a mood in such sentences as "he was so injured that he *died*," "it happened that he *was* absent," "I fear that you *are* deceiving me," "tell me why you *did* this," "he said that the man who *did* this should die," "he is one who *will* never fail to do his duty;" yet these are among the most obvious constructions in which the use of the subjunctive is required in Latin.

i. Thus the **Indicative** mood is so called because it simply points out (*indĭcat*) a connexion or agreement between a subject and predicate. In itself it does nothing more than this, and is quite neutral and colourless, so to speak ; but it is capable of being joined with other words which may greatly qualify the meaning which the verb itself conveys. Thus *valet*, " he is well ;" fortasse *valet*, " perhaps he is well" (uncertainty) ; si *valet*, "*if* he is well " (contingency) ; non *valet*, " he is *not* well" (denial) ; and the addition of a particle in Latin, or an inversion of the order in English, or even the mere tone in which the verb is pronounced, may without any alteration of its form (for there is no interrogative mood in either Latin or English) enable it to ask a question, that is, to suggest instead of stating the agreement between the two essential elements of every sentence, the subject and the predicate. (Intr. 61, 62.) *Valet ? valet*ne ? " he is well ?" " is he well ?"

ii. The **Imperative** mood is a form assumed by the verb to mark that the agreement between the subject and predicate is not *stated* or *suggested* but *commanded* or *willed :* aude, audete, " dare thou," " dare ye."

iii. The difference between these two moods is clear ; and it has already (**94**, note 1) been explained that the **Infinitive** mood is hardly in the strict sense a mood at all, being properly the verb used as a substantive, as, *sedere*, "the act of sitting ;" it is however very widely used in Latin as the mood of indirect assertion. (See **31.**)

iv. The **Subjunctive** is the mood which gives rise to the greatest difficulty in the study of Latin. Its use in that language is constant and manifold, while it hardly exists in modern English (see note, p. 116). Nor will its name (*modus* **subjunctivus** or **conjunctivus**) be a sufficient guide, for though so called on account of its being found principally in subordinate clauses, yet such clauses often require the use of the indicative, and the use of the subjunctive, as will be shown shortly, is by no means confined to them.

It perhaps was originally used as a separate form in order to add, to the simple statement made by the indicative, some further idea of *uncertainty* or *contingency.* Hence its use in Latin to express, not a fact which we *indicate*, but something which we regard rather as a mere conception of the mind, as that which we purpose or wish to be a fact, or which we refer to as the result of another fact, or as stated on other authority than our own ; and in this way it is used in Latin in a large number of sentences in which the use of any special mood would never occur to any one who was acquainted only with English.

** These remarks will illustrate the term " modal verb " used above (**42**), and will be of use to those who wish to understand the meaning of the term Mood ; but the following Exercise will be confined to the points stated in **148-153**.

148. The Latin subjunctive is mainly used in certain classes of subordinate or *subjoined* clauses : hence its name (*subjunctivus*). But it is also used both in simple sentences, and in the main clause of a compound sentence, either to make a *statement* (*a.*), or to ask a *question* (*b.*), or to express a *command* or *desire* (*c.*).

149. (*a.*) **The subjunctive makes a statement**: but it does this in a hesitating and uncertain manner; in what is sometimes called the "potential" mood, or *modus dubitativus*, formed in English by the auxiliaries "may," "might," "would," "could," "should."

It is thus used in the present, perfect, and imperfect tenses :—

i. In the first person :—

Hoc dicere ausim. This I *would* venture to say.
Vix crediderim. I *can* scarce believe.
Hoc affirmaverim. This I *would* or *may* assert.

It appears as a polite form (Gk. θέλοιμ' ἄν), in *velim, nolim,* joined, when the wish applies to another person, not with the infinitive, but with another subjunctive without *ut.*

Velim adsis. I wish, or could wish, you *were* here (pres.).
Vellem adesses. I could have wished you *had been* here (used of *continuous* time in the past, or a *vain* wish in the present).
Hoc facias velim. { I wish you would } do this, *or* please do { I would have you } this. (See **141.**)
Vellem adfuisses. I could have wished you had been there (once for all).

ii. In the second person :—

Credas, crederes. You (that is *any one*, no definite person) would believe, would have believed. (This is a common way of expressing "it seems, seemed as though".)

iii. In the third person :—

Dicat (*or* dixerit) *aliquis* or *quispiam.* Some one *may* say, *i.e.* "may perhaps say."

In all these cases we may supply a suppressed condition,—"if I were allowed," "if you should ask me," and the like.

150. (*b.*) The subjunctive also asks a question.

Quis credat? Who would believe? (a virtual negative.)
*Hoc tu dicere aude*as? Would you dare to say this?
(astonishment.)

So when perplexity or hesitation is implied (*modus deliberativus,* probably an interrogative form of the jussive use, **151**).

Quid faciam? What am I to do?
Quid faceret? What was he to do?

Note that these are "rhetorical questions," *i.e.* they are not asked for information; but either imply a negative answer, "no one will believe," and are virtual negatives (see **130**), or are asked in mere doubt or perplexity, implying often, "I have," or "he had, no resource."

If the question were asked for information, the Latin would be *quid mihi* faciendum est? *quid ei* faciendum fuit?

**151. (*c.*) The subjunctive also is largely used in a jussive sense, to express a *wish* or *desire*. It is thus used with or without *utinam;* the negative wish is expressed by *ne.*

Quod Di bene vertant! And may the Gods bring this to a good issue!
Quod utinam ne faciatis! And may you never do this!
Ne hic diutius cunctemur. Let us not linger any longer here.

(See **144.**) (For *ne credideris,* "do not believe;" *abeat,* "let him go," see **142** and **144.**)

152. *Utinam* can be also used, like *vellem,* with the past : *Utinam hoc fecerit!* "May he have done this!" But it generally, as is natural with wishes about the past, expresses a *vain* wish, and is so used with the imperf. and pluperf. subjunctive.

Utinam adesset, "would he *had been* present," contemporaneously with some event in past time ; *or,* continuously and extending (often) up to the present moment, "would he *were* present."
Utinam adfuisset, "would he had been present" (once for all).

153. It is important to remember that Latin often uses the indicative where in English we use the compound potential or subjunctive mood.

Longum est. It *would be* tedious.
Satius, or, *melius* est. fuit. It *would be, would have been,* better.
Quisquis, quicunque es. Whoever thou *be* (subj.).

So also, the indicative is used with modal verbs, *possum, debeo,* etc.

Possum *hoc facere.* I might do this.

Potui *hoc facere.* I might have done this.

Hoc debuisti *facere.* You should (or ought to) have done this.

The possibility or duty is *asserted* by the indicative; though it is implied at the same time that the action expressed by the verb in the infinitive did not take place.

Obs.—In English, in speaking of past time we constantly say, "It would have been better to have done this," where we should more correctly say, "to do this." The present infinitive is used in Latin : *melius* fuit *hoc* facere.

Exercise 19.

1. This at least I would venture to say, that as[1] I was the first to urge you to undertake this work, so[1] I promise to be the last to advise you to abandon the undertaking. 2. What was I to do ? said he, what to say ? who would care to blame me because I refused to listen to such[2] abandoned men ? 3. I would neither deny nor assert that he had looked forward to all this (*pl.*), but he should have provided against the country being overwhelmed by such disasters. 4. On that day my brother was reluctantly absent from the battle at your suggestion; would that he had been[3] there ! For it would have been better to have fallen on the field than to have submitted to such dishonour. 5. In return[4] then for such acts of kindness I would have you not only feel but also show your gratitude. 6. I could have wished that you had sent me the best[5] soldiers that you had with you. 7. The soldiers stood (*imperf.*) drawn up in line, eager for the fight,[6] with[7] eyes fixed on the foe, clamouring for the signal; it seemed as though they were waiting for a banquet. 8. I have consulted, as[8] I ought to have done, your (*pl.*) interests rather than my own; may you not ever impute this to me as a fault !

---

[1] as . . . so, *et . . . et.*   [2] See **88.**   [3] Use *adsum,* **149,** i.
[4] *pro,* abl.   [5] See **69.**   [6] Gerund, **99.**
[7] Abl. abs., "their eyes being fixed."   [8] See **67,** *Obs.*

INTERROGATIVE SENTENCES.

I. Direct (Single and Disjunctive).

154. Interrogative sentences may be divided into two classes, Direct and Indirect.

By the **direct question** we mean a question properly so called, such as is marked by the interrogative sign in English: "Is he gone?" "Are you well?"

These sentences differ from *statements* and *commands*, inasmuch as the connexion between the subject and the predicate is not *stated*, or *desired*, but only *suggested*.

Obs.—As there is no interrogative *mood* in either Latin or English, in direct questions (other than those *rhetorical* questions already (**150**) mentioned) the **indicative** mood is used, unless for some special reason.

155. In English we mark a question by the order of the words, and sometimes by the insertion of an auxiliary verb. Compare "*Saw* ye?" "*Is* he well?" "*Did* you see?" "*Will* he come?" with "Ye *saw*;" "He *is* well;" "You saw;" "He will come;" and in French "*Va-t-il?*" with "Il va."

But in Latin, where the order of the words would have no such effect (Intr. 87), questions are usually asked by the interrogative particles *-ně* (enclitic, Intr. 98, *note*), *num*, *utrum*, *an*, or by interrogative *pronouns* or pronominal *adverbs*.

There is sometimes no definite word which marks that the speaker is putting a question. The tone, manner, and gesture of the speaker supply what in ordinary language is expressed by certain words.

(*a.*) *-ně* is used in questions that ask simply for information, and to which the answer may be either "yes" or "no."

> *Scribitne Caius?* Is Caius writing? (The person who asks the question does not expect one answer more than another.)

121

(*b.*) *Num*[1] expects the answer "no."

 Num putas? Do you fancy?＝Surely you don't fancy?
 (expected answer "no".)

(*c.*) *Nonne* expects the answer "yes."

 Nonnĕ putas? Don't you fancy?＝Surely you do fancy?
 (expected answer "yes".)

156. *Nĕ* is always attached to the emphatic word.

 Praetoremne *accusas?* *Is it a Praetor* whom you are
 accusing?
 Mene *fugis?* *Is it* from *me* that you are flying?

Here, as often, the English expresses emphasis by a separate clause, of which the emphatic word is the predicate, and "it" the subject; the rest of the sentence being thrown into an adjectival clause explanatory of "it."

157. Other interrogative words are either (i.) Pronouns, or (ii.) Interrogative Particles.

Notice that pronouns are used either as substantives or as adjectives, *i.e.* as attached to substantives.

 Quid *fecit?* What has he done?
 Quod *facinus admisit?* What crime has he committed?

Also that for interrogative particles[2] a phrase or combination of words is often substituted: thus *quemadmodum?* "in what manner?" ＝*qui?* "how?"

The following is a list of Interrogative Pronouns and Particles:—

(i.) PRONOUNS—

 Quis? quisnam? quid? quidnam? who? what?
 Quantum? how much? (followed by *genitive,*
  quantum temporis? how much time?)
 Qui? what? *Quot?* how many? *Uter?* which of
  the two?
 Qualis? of what kind?
 Quantus? how great?
 Quot? how many?

---

[1] *Num* is properly "now" (*nunc*): compare *tum* and *tunc.*

[2] These particles are in fact *adverbs,* inasmuch as they qualify the sense in which the verb is used, forming a substitute for an interrogative mood (see **147,** *note* i.); when used to connect a dependent with a principal clause they assume the nature of *conjunctions.* (See Intr. 25, 26.)

> *Quotus?* one of how many? (answer "third," "fourth," etc.)
> *Num quis, qua, quid* (subst.)? *num qui, quae, quod* (adj.)? *ecquis?* any?

(ii.) PARTICLES—

> *Ubi?* where? *Unde?* whence? *Quo?* whither?
> *Cur? quare?* * *quamobrem?* * why? wherefore?
> *Qui?* how? (often in the phrase *qui fit ut?*)
> *Quam?* how? (with adj. and adv.)
> *Quomodo? quemadmodum?* * how? in what manner?
> *Quantum? quantopere?* how much?
> *Quando?* when? (never *quum.*) *Quoties?* how often?
> *Quamdiu? quousque?* how long? how far?
> *Cur non? quin?* why not? how not?

Obs.—The adverb *tandem* (lit. "at last") is often joined with interrogatives in the sense of "tell me," "(who) in the world," "I ask," etc.

> *Quousque* tandem. To what point, I *ask?*
> *Quae* tandem *causa.* What *possible* cause?

Disjunctive Questions.

158. A direct question may be put in another form. In English two or more **alternative** questions may be combined by the disjunctive conjunction *or* (see Intr. 56) so that an affirmative answer to the one negatives the other or others.

> "Are you going to Germany, *or* (are you going) to Italy, *or* to France?"

These are called *alternative,* or *disjunctive,* or *double* questions.

We have here two or more simple sentences joined together by *co-ordination.* (See Intr. 74, 75.)

In English the first question has no interrogative particle (*whether* being obsolete in *direct* questions), the second and any further are introduced by "or," which however is sometimes, where the verb is suppressed, confined to the last.

> "Did you mean me, *or* think of yourself, *or* refer to some one else?"
> "Did you mean me, him, *or* yourself?"

---

* Words with an asterisk are mostly confined to *indirect* questions.

159. In Latin the **interrogative nature** of the first question will be indicated by *utrum,* or the appended "*-ne ;*" in the second, or any further question, the "*or*" will be translated by *an,* never by *aut* or *vel.*

> Utrum *hostem,* an *ducem,* an *vosmet ipsos culpatis ?* Is it the enemy, *or* your general, *or* yourselves that you blame ?
> *Servine estis,* an *liberi ?* Are you slaves *or* freemen ?

But in such questions there is frequently, as in English, no interrogative particle in the first question, and *or* is translated by *an,* or (more rarely by) the enclitic *-ně.*

> *Herum vidisti,* an *ancillam ?* Did you see the master *or* the maid ?
> *Hoc, illudne fecisti ?* Did you do this *or* that ?

"*Or not ?*" in a direct question should be translated by *an non ?*

> *Ivitne,* an non ? Did he go, or not ?

160. The forms for these double questions are :—

1. *utrum,* . . . . *an, an non ?*
2. *-ne,* . . . . . *an ?*
3. ——— . . . . *anne ?*

(The *line* means that the first particle is omitted.)

Num is occasionally used for *utrum* where a negative answer is expected.

161. *An* is sometimes found before a single question. But there is always an *ellipsis,* or suppression of a previous question, so that *an* means "*or is it that ?*" "*can it be that ?*" and hence generally expects the answer "no."

> An *servi esse vultis ?* Or is it that you wish to be slaves ?

Answers to Questions.

162. The affirmative and negative answer is rarely given in Latin so simply as by the English "yes" and "no."

Sometimes "yes" may be turned by *etiam, ita vero;* and "no" by *minime, nequaquam, non.*

But more often some emphatic word is repeated from the interrogative sentence; such a question as *dasne hoc mihi ?* would be answered by *do; do vero, ac libenter quidem*

(= "yes"): or by *minime ego quidem* (= "no"), much
more often than by *etiam*, or *minime* simply.

> *Visne hoc facere?* velle se, nolle se, *respondit.* Are you
> ready to do this? he answered "*yes,*" "*no.*"
> *Num hoc fecisti?* Have you then done this? *Negat.*
> He answers "no." *Feci, inquit.* He answers "yes."

Sometimes *ait* is used as opposed to *negat.*

Exercise 20.

1. Is it possible for a true patriot to refuse to obey the
law[1]? 2. Where, said he, did you come from, and whither
and when do you intend[2] to start hence? 3. Can we help
fearing that your brother will go away into exile with reluctance? 4. What crime, what enormity, has my client[3]
committed, what falsehood has he told, what, in short, has
he either said or done that you, gentlemen of the jury,
should be ready to inflict on him either death or exile by
your verdict? 5. Will any one venture to assert that he
was condemned in his absence in order to prevent his
pleading his cause at home, or impressing the jury by his
eloquence? 6. Was it by force of arms, or by judgment,
courage, and good sense, that Rome was able to dictate
terms to the rest of the world? 7. Does it seem[4] to you
that death is an eternal sleep, or the beginning of another
life? 8. Are you ready to show yourselves men of
courage, such as the country looks for in such a crisis as
this? you answer "yes"; or are you ceasing to wish to be
called Roman soldiers? "no," you all reply. 9. Do you
believe that the character of your countrymen is altering
for the better, or for the worse? 10. Whom am I to
defend? whom am I to accuse? how much longer shall I
pretend to be in doubt? was it (156) by accident or design
that this murder was committed? 11. What am I to
believe? that the enemy or that our men won the day
yesterday? Do not tell more falsehoods on such[5] an
important question. 12. Was he not a prophet of such a
kind that no one ever believed[6] him?

---

[1] Ex. ix. p. 72, *note* 2.　　　　　　[2] Fut. in *-rus.* (**14,** *c.*)
[3] Simply *hic,* this man *by me:* never *cliens.*　[4] See **43.**　　[5] **88.**
[6] Use perf., not imperf. : the *fact* is summed up. (See **113.**)

INTERROGATIVE SENTENCES—*Continued.*

II. Dependent or Indirect.

163. The **dependent question** is a *subordinate clause* introduced by an interrogative word (either a pronoun or conjunction), and connected by that interrogative word with the main clause.

Quis es? who are you? *cur hoc fecisti?* why have you done this? are direct questions, and each is a simple sentence.

But rogo *quis sit, I ask* who he is; dic mihi *cur hoc feceris, tell me* why you did this, are two compound sentences. Neither *taken as a whole* is a question: the first is a *statement,* the second a *command;* but each *contains* an indirect question, *i.e.* a subordinate substantival clause, answering to an accusative case after *rogo* and *dic,* introduced in the one case by the interrogative pronoun *quis,* in the other by the interrogative conjunction *cur.*

164. The Latin verb in such subordinate clauses is invariably in the subjunctive. It is of the utmost importance to remember this, as the subjunctive mood is no longer used in such clauses in English.

Compare the English and Latin moods in—

Quis eum occīdit? Who *killed* him?
Quis eum occīderit, quaero. I ask who *killed* him.

165. The dependent interrogative clause is recognised by an interrogative word introducing it (see list in **157**); but **the principal verb** or clause on which it depends **need not be at all of an interrogative character.**

Quid faciendum sit moneo moneboque. I *warn and will warn* you what you ought to do.
Quando esset rediturus metui. I *had fears* as to when he would return.
Cur haec fecerit miror. I *wonder* why he did this.

The words in the Latin marked in italics are *interrogative* clauses; for they are connected with the main clause by the interrogative pronoun *quid* and by the interrogative adverbs, used here as conjunctions, *quando* and *cur;* but neither *moneo, metuo,* nor *miror* are verbs of *asking.*

126

166. Thus the dependent question may follow not only a wide range of verbs but also many phrases, such as *incertum est; incredibile est; difficile dictu est* (it is hard to say); *magni refert* (it is of great consequence), and many others.

167. A dependent question in English is constantly introduced by the conjunctions "if" and "whether;" but *si* and *sive* are never used in Latin to introduce an interrogative clause.

"If" and "whether" are represented in a single indirect question by -*ne* and *num*, occasionally by *nonne*.

Num in the *indirect* question does not, as in the *direct*, imply the answer "no" (but *nonne* still suggests an affirmative answer).

> *Epaminondas quaesivit salvus*ne esset *clipeus.* Epaminondas asked *whether* his shield *was* safe.
>
> *Dic mihi* num *eadem quae ego* sentias. Tell me *if* you *have* the same opinion as I.
>
> *Quaesieras ex me,* nonne putarem, *etc.* You had inquired of me *whether* I *did not* suppose, etc.

Disjunctive Interrogatives.

168. The form of the *disjunctive* question is very much the same in dependent as in independent questions. The important difference is the substitution of the *subjunctive* for the *indicative* mood.

Thus, utrum *servi* estis an *liberi?* *are* you slaves *or* free men? will be altered into, utrum *servi* sitis an *liberi, nihil refert;* it matters not *whether* you *are* slaves *or* free: and in the dependent clause we may substitute for *utrum* . . . *an* such forms as

> *Servīnĕ sitis,* an *liberi,*
> *Servi sitis,* an *liberi,*
> *Servi sitis, liberi*nĕ,

without any difference of meaning.

Obs.—"Or not," "or no" (*annon* in *direct*), should be turned by *necnĕ* in *indirect* questions.

> *Iturus sit,* necne, *rogabimus.* We will ask *whether or not* he means to go.

169. Notice that *an* is in indirect, as in direct, questions confined to the second place, and answers to "or," which is never to be translated, when used interrogatively, by *aut, vel,* or *seu.*

In the phrases *haud scio* an, *forsitan (fors sit an)*, there is a suppression of a first clause : "I know not," "it is a chance" (*whether something else is the case*), or *whether (rather)* . . . Both are equivalent to "perhaps," and both are followed by the *subjunctive.*

> *Difficile hoc est, tamen* haud[1] scio an *fieri possit.* This is difficult, yet *perhaps (I incline to think that)* it is possible.

But *nescio quis* (subs.), *nescio qui* (adj.), "Some one (or other) ;" *nescio quo modo*, or *quo pacto* (adv.), "Somehow," are taken as single words, and do not affect the mood of the verb ; *accurrit* nescio quis, *some one* runs up. (See Pronouns, **362.**)

170. *Forte* is not "perhaps" but "by accident," and is only used for "perchance" after *si, nisi, ne.*

Forte *cecidit* is "he fell *by chance*," not "*perhaps* he fell."

Forte *abest*, "he is *accidentally* absent" (*indicative*).

Forsitan *absit*, "*perhaps, it may be that*, he is absent" (*subjunctive*).

Nescio, *or* haud scio an, *absit*, "*perhaps* (I incline to think that) he is absent" (*subjunctive*).

Fortasse *abest*, "*perhaps (it is likely that)* he is absent" (*indicative*).

171. The double use in English of "if," "whether." and " or," must be carefully borne in mind.

Si,[2] *sive, seu, aut,*[3] *vel*, must never be used as *interrogatives* in Latin.

(*a.*) You shall die *if* (conditional) you do this. *Moriere* si *haec feceris* (fut. perf. ind.).

(*b.*) I ask *if* (interrogative) you did this. Num *haec feceris* (subj.) *rogo.*

(*c.*) He shall go, *whether* he likes it *or* no (alternative condition). Seu *vult* seu *nonvult, ibit.*

(*d.*) I ask *whether* he likes it *or* no (alternative question). Utrum *velit* an *nolit rogo.*

(*e.*) He is *either* a wise man *or* a fool (disjunctive sentence). Aut *sapiens est* aut *stultus.*

---

[1] *Haud* is mostly used with *scio* and with adjectives and adverbs in the sense of "far from," when a negative idea is substituted for a positive, as *haud difficilis* for *facilis*, etc.

[2] For the special use of *si*, "in hopes that," after *expecto, conor*, and similar verbs, see Conditional Clauses, **474.**

[3] For the difference between *aut* and *vel*, see Intr. 57, note.

(*f.*) I don't know *whether* he is a wise man *or* a fool
Utrum *sapiens sit* an *stultus nescio.*

Obs.—In (*a.*) and (*c.*) " if," " whether," introduce *adverbial* clauses
merely qualifying the main clause by adding a condition (Intr. 82).
In (*e.*) " either," " or," introduce two *co-ordinate* sentences.   In (*b.*),
(*d.*), (*f.*), " whether," " or," introduce *substantival* clauses, equivalent
in Latin to accusative cases after *rogo* and *nescio.*

Exercise 21.

1. Whether Caesar was rightfully put to death, or foully
murdered, is open to question; it[1] is allowed by all that
he was killed on the 15th[2] of March by Brutus and
Cassius and the rest of the conspirators.   2. It is still
uncertain whether our men have won the day or no; but
whether they have won or lost it, I am certain that they
have neither been false to their allies nor to their country.
3. It is hard to say whether he injured the world[3] or
benefited it most; it is unquestionable that he was a man,
alike in his ability (*abl.*) as in his achievements, such as
we are never (Intr. 92) likely to see in this world.   4. It is
scarcely credible how often you and I have advised that
(friend) of yours[4] not[5] to break his word; but it[6] seems
likely that we shall lose our labour to-morrow, as yesterday
and the day before.   5. Be sure you write me word when
the king intends[7] to start for[8] the army; he is perhaps
lingering purposely in order to raise an army and increase
his resources; I am afraid he will not[9] effect this,[10] for
people are either alarmed or disaffected.   6. Some one has
warned me not to forget how much you once injured me
in my boyhood: whether you did so (this) or no matters
little; what[11] is of importance to me is whether you
are ready to be my friend now.   7. As[12] he felt himself
sinking (*inf.*) under a severe wound, he asked first if his
shield was safe; they answered yes; secondly, if the
enemy had been routed; they replied in the affirmative.
8. They asked if it was not better to die than to live dishonourably.   9. He was the dearest to me of my soldiers,
and perhaps the bravest of (them) all.

---

[1] *Illud, i.e.* " the following."   [2] *Idibus Martiis.*   [3] **16**, *b*
[4] See **11**, *d.*   [5] See **118**.   [6] See **43**.   [7] **14**, *c.*   [8] *Ad.*
[9] See **138**.   [10] Relative.   [11] Lit., the following (*illud*).
is of importance.   [12] *Quum* with imperf. subj.

EXERCISE XXII.

Mood and Tense.—Interrogative Clauses for English Nouns.

172. Sometimes the Latin verb in the interrogative clause is already in the subjunctive; in this case no change will take place in the mood, even if we convert the *direct* into the *indirect* question.

> *Quid* facerem? What was I to do? (See 150.)
> *Quid* facerem *dubitavi.*[1] I was at a loss what to do.

In such cases the *subjunctive* answers to the English *infinitive* after an interrogative word.

> *Quid* faciam, *quando* redeam, *dubito.* I am at a loss what *to do*, when *to return*.

173. The use of the *tenses* in (dependent) interrogative clauses will cause little difficulty.

(i.) The *perfect subjunctive* is exceedingly common to express simple past time in such clauses.

> *Quid causae* fuerit *postridie intellexi.* I perceived the day after what *was* the cause (lit. "for a cause").

(ii.) But the *imperfect* must be used if the time denoted by the dependent verb is strictly contemporaneous with that of the principal verb.

> *Quid* facerent *intellexi.* I perceived what they *were* doing. (See 185.)

(iii.) As the only *future subjunctive* in Latin is that formed by the future in *-rus*, "I ask when he *will* return" is, *quando* sit rediturus *rogo;* "I asked when he would return" is, *quando* esset rediturus *rogavi.*

The future in *-rus* expresses also the ideas of *likelihood, intention,* etc. (See 14, *c.*)

The following remarks require careful attention both in writing Latin and in translating from Latin.

---

[1] *Quid faciendum esset* would differ slightly as expressing less perplexity, and somewhat more of deliberation.

174. Dependent interrogative *clauses introduced* by *quis* (*qui*), *qualis, quantus, quot, quando, cur,* etc., are very often used in Latin where in English we use a single word, such as *nature, character, amount, size, number, date, object, origin, motive,* etc.

Latin does not use nearly so many *abstract terms* as English. Thus—

(*a.*) Quot *essent hostes,* cur[1] *advenerint,* quantas *haberent opes, quando domo profecti essent, rogavit* (note carefully the *tenses*). He asked the *number* of the enemy, the *reason* of their having come, the *magnitude* of their resources, the *date* of their departure from home.

(*b.*) Quale *ac* quantum *sit periculum demonstrat.* He explains the *nature* and *extent* of the danger.

(*c.*) Qualis *sit,* quemadmodum *senex vivat, videtis.* You see the *kind* of man he is, his *manner* of life in his old age. (**63.**)

(*d.*) *Haec res* quo *evasura sit, expecto.* I am waiting to see the *issue* of this matter.

(*e.*) Quam *repentinum sit hoc malum intellego,* unde *ortum sit nescio.* I perceive the *suddenness* of this danger, its *source* I know not.

This is only one of the many instances where Latin prefers simple and direct modes of expression to the more abstract and general forms of noun with which we are familiar in English. (See **54.**)

175. For the same reason, as well as from a lack of substantives in Latin to express *classes* of persons, and also of verbal substantives denoting *agents,* such English substantives must often be translated into Latin by a relative or adjectival clause. Thus :—

"Politicians," *qui in republica versantur ;* "students," *qui literis dant operam ;* "my father's murderers," *qui patrem meum occiderunt ;* "my well-wishers," *qui me salvum volunt ;* "the government," *qui reipublicae praesunt ;* "his predecessors on the throne," *qui ante eum regnaverant.*

For the use or omission of *ei* with this use of *qui* see **71.**

176. The difference between these two kinds of dependent clause, the *relative* (or adjectival) and the *interrogative,* will be marked by

---

[1] In indirect clauses *cur* may be used ; but *quare, quamobrem, quam ob causam,* are more common ; and *quemadmodum* almost always takes the place of *quomodo.*

the use of the *indicative* in the one, the *subjunctive* in the other. Thus—

(*a.*) *Hi sunt* qui *patrem tuum occid*erunt.   These are your father's murderers.

Here the relative *qui* introduces an *adjectival* clause, used, as adjectives sometimes are, as a substitute for a substantive.   (See 51.)

(*b.*) Qui *patrem suum occiderint, nescit.*   He knows not who were his father's murderers.

Here the interrogative *qui* (pl. of *quis*) introduces one of the three kinds of substantival clause (Intr. 80), viz., the dependent question ; the mood therefore is the subjunctive.   (See 164.)   So—

(*a.*) Quae *vere* sentio *dicam,* I will *utter* my real sentiments ; here *quae* is a relative :

(*b.*) Quae *vere* sentiam *dicam,* I will *tell you what are* my real sentiments ; here *quae* is interrogative.

The substantival nature of the dependent interrogative will explain why it generally comes before the main clause.   (See Intr. 100.)

Exercise 22.

1. I am waiting to see what is the meaning of this crowd, what will be the issue of the uproar.   2. I wish[1] you would explain to me his manner of life in boyhood ; I know pretty well the kind of man that he is now.   3. We perceived well enough that danger was at hand ; of its source, nature, character, and extent, we were ignorant. 4. Do but reflect on the greatness of your debt to your country and your forefathers ; remember who you are and the position that you occupy.   5. I knew not (*imperf.*) whither to turn, what to do, how to inflict punishment on my brother's murderers.   6. The doer of the deed I know not, but whoever he was,[2] he shall be punished.   7. The reason of politicians not agreeing with the commanders of armies is pretty clear.   8. I wonder who were the bringers of this message, whether (they were) the same as the perpetrators of the crime or no.   9. He was superior to all his predecessors on the throne in ability ; but he did not perceive the character of the man who was destined to be his successor.   10. The government was aware of the suddenness of the danger, but they did not suspect its magnitude and probable[3] duration.

---

[1] 149, i.   [2] Mood ? (See 153.)   [3] 173, iii.

REMARKS ON TENSES.

177. The Latin tenses are generally divided into **Primary** and **Secondary.**

(*a.*) **Primary** tenses are those in which the point of time taken as the standard by which we reckon is the *present,* the moment at which we are speaking :

> (Simultaneous) *scribo,* "I write," "am writing," *at* the present moment.
> (Past) *scripsi,* "I have written," *before* the present moment (true perfect).
> (Future) *scribam,* "I shall write," *after* the present moment.

(*b.*) In **Secondary** tenses (called also **Historic,** from their constant use in history or narrative) the standard of comparison is some point in *past* time :

> (Simultaneous) *scribebam,* "I was writing *contemporaneously with* some time in the past.
> (Past) *scripseram,* "I had written," *before* some point in the past.
> (Indefinite, or aorist) *scripsi,* "I wrote," at some time or other in the past.

Obs.—It will be seen that the Latin *scripsi* belongs to both divisions ; also that it is not easy to fix its place under (*b.*). It is sometimes explained as denoting an event that *follows something else* that happened in the past.

A third division might be introduced by taking as the standard of comparison a point in *future* time :—

> (Simultaneous) *scribam,* "I shall *be writing."*
> (Past) *scripsero,* "I shall *have written."*
> (Future) *scripturus ero,* "I shall be *going to* write."

The Present.

178. The **Latin present tense** corresponds to two forms of the English present ; *scribo* = "I write," and also "I am writing."

179. As in English, but far more commonly in Latin, the *present* tense is often in an animated narrative substituted for the *past.*

This *Historical present* is often in the best Latin writers intermingled with past (aorist) tenses ; and is even followed as a historic tense by the imperfect subjunctive.

> *Subito* edicunt *Consules ut ad suum vestītum Senatores* redirent.
> The Consuls suddenly *publish* (=published) an edict, that the Senators *were to* return to their usual dress.

133

The present, when thus used, may be followed either by the *present subjunctive* (according to the general rule for the sequence of tenses or by the *imperfect subjunctive* (as being itself *virtually* a past tense). (See **104**.) The latter is quite as common as the former. In English we should either say "published," or alter "were to" into "are to."

180. In describing the past, the conjunction *dum*, "while," is constantly used with a *historical present* even when all the surrounding tenses are in past time.

> *Dum Romani tempus terunt, Saguntum* obsidebatur. While the Romans *were wasting* time, Saguntum was being besieged.

This idiom is almost invariable where the *dum*-clause represents, as here, a *longer period within which* the other event is comprised.

181. To express "*I have been doing a thing for* a long time," the Romans said, "*I am doing it* for a long time already." The Greeks and French have the same idiom.[1]

> *Jam pridem* (or *jampridem*) cupio. I *have* long *desired.*
> *Vocat me alio jam dudum* (or *jamdudum*) *tacita vestra expectatio.* Your silent expectation *has* for some time *been calling* me to another point

So also they used the Imperfect for our "had (long) been."

> *Copiae quas diu* comparabant. Forces which they *had* long *been collecting.*

182. The present is used sometimes, but far less widely than in English, in an *anticipative* sense for the future.

> *Hoc ni propere* fit. Unless this *is* done at once.
> *Antequam dicere* incipio. Before I *begin* to speak.

But see below (**190**).

The Imperfect.

183. This tense is used far more widely in Latin than the English compound tense "I was doing," etc.

It denotes a time contemporaneous with some period, or surrounding, as it were, some point, in past time, and hence it has various meanings.

It is the tense of *continuous* or *incomplete*, as opposed to *momentary*, or *completed* action.

---

[1] πάλαι λέγω ; Depuis longtemps je parle.

It is the tense of *description* as opposed to mere *narrative* or *statement*.

Thus it is often used to describe the circumstances, or feelings, which accompany the main fact as stated by the verb in the (aorist) perfect :—

> *Caesar armis rem gerere* constituit, videbat *enim inimicorum in dies majorem fieri exercitum*, reputabatque, etc.

We should use the same tense in all three verbs ; *resolved, saw, reflected ;* but the two last explain the *continued* feeling which accounted for the *single fact* of his decision.

184. For the same reason, the imperfect often expresses ideas equivalent to "*began to*," "*proceeded to*," "*continued to*," "*tried to*," "*were in the habit of*," "*used to*," "*were wont to*," sometimes even to the English "*would*." It must therefore often be used where we loosely use *the* (aorist) *past tense*, and we must always ask ourselves the precise meaning of the English past tense before we translate it.

> *Barbari saxa ingentia* devolvebant. The barbarians *began to* (or *proceeded to*) roll down huge stones.
>
> Stabat *imperator immotus.* The general *continued to* stand motionless (or *was seen to stand*, as if in a picture).
>
> *Haec fere pueri* discebamus. When we were boys we *used to* learn (or *we learned*) something of this kind.
>
> *Hujusmodi homines adolescens* admirabar. These were the men whom I admired (or *would admire*) in my youth.

185. This meaning of the imperfect extends to the subjunctive mood, and must be kept in mind in translating subordinate clauses.

"I asked why he did it" is generally *cur id* fecerit *quaesivi.* (See **173.**) But if we mean "why he *was doing it then*" we must say *cur id* faceret *quaesivi.*

It will also explain the difference between the imperfect and perfect subjunctive after *ut* consecutive. (See **113.**)

These different shades of meaning as regards past time are rarely distinguished in English.

186. What is called the *Historic Infinitive* is often used as a substitute for the imperfect, especially when a *series of actions* is described, and is always joined with the nominative.

> *Interim quotidie Caesar Aeduos frumentum,* . . . flagitare ; . . . *diem ex die* ducere *Aedui* . . . dicere, etc. (Caesar, *de B. G.* i. 16.) Meanwhile Caesar *was* daily *importuning* the Aedui for provisions ; they *kept putting* off day after day, asserting, etc.

The Perfect.

187. The **Latin perfect** represents two English tenses. (See **105, 177.**) *Feci* is both " I did," and " I have done."

"I did" is the *preterite* or *aorist*. It is the ordinary tense used in simply narrating or mentioning a past event.

"I have done" is the true *perfect*, or tense of *completed action*. It represents an act as past in itself; but in *its result* as coming down to the present. "I *have been* young, and now am old." We should say of a recent event, with the result still fresh on the mind, "My friend has been killed ;" we should not say, "Cain has killed Abel."

In Latin the same word *dixi* may mean "I have spoken," *i.e.* "I have finished my speech," or "I spoke." *Vixerunt,* "they lived," or "they have lived," *i.e.* "are *now dead.*"

The context will generally make it quite clear in which sense the Latin tense is used.

Obs.—The English auxiliary *am, are,* etc., with a passive verb, may mislead. "All *are* slain" may be either *occisi sunt,* or *occiduntur,* according to the context.

188. Sometimes the verb *habeo,* "I have," or "possess," is used, especially with verbs of knowledge, etc., in combination with a participle in a use approaching that of the English auxiliary "have."

> *Hoc compertum, cognitum, exploratum* habeo. *I have* found out, ascertained, made sure of this.
>
> *Hunc hominem jamdiu notum* habeo. I *have known* this man long.

Future.

189. Latin differs exceedingly from English in the use of the future. It has **three future tenses :**—*scribam, scripsero, scripturus sum.*

Fut. i. *Scribam* is properly, I shall *be writing* (*at* some time in the future).

Fut. ii. *Scripsero,* I shall *have written* (*before* some time in the future).

Fut. iii. *Scripturus sum,* I am *about* to, or *likely* to, write ; *intending* to, etc. (See **14,** *c.*)

Obs.—Fut. i. and iii. are both represented in the subjunctive mood by the future in -*rus,* Fut. ii. by the perfect subjunctive *scripserim.*

We must carefully distinguish between Fut. i. and ii. in all subordinate clauses where the principal verb is in the future.

190. A **Latin future** is constantly to be substituted for the English loosely-used present.

There was no true future in Old English, and we are obliged to use the auxiliaries *shall* and *will*. We still say, "I *return* home to-morrow," for "*cras domum* redibo," or "rediturus sum."

(i.) An English *present* tense after *relatives*, or "*when*," "*if*," "*as long as*," "*before*," etc., is to be translated by a *future perfect*, when the action expressed by it is still *future*, but *prior to* something still more future.

> *Si te* rogavero *aliquid, nonne respondebis?* If I *put* any question to you, will you not answer?
> *Quum Tullius rure* redierit, *mittam eum ad te.* When Tullius *returns* from the country, I will send him to you.
> *Quodcunque* imperatum erit, *fiet.* Whatever *is* ordered shall be done.

The Latin idiom is correct, as the one action must, though now future, be completed (future *perfect*) before the other begins.

(ii.) When the two actions or states are *simultaneous*, but still future, the Latin Future i. is used for an English present.

> *Dum hic* ero *te amabo.* As long as I *am* here I shall love you.
> *Facito hoc, ubi* voles. Do this when you *please.*
> *Tum, qui* poterunt, *veniant.* Then let those come who *have* the power.

Obs.—Sometimes the English perfect is used for the Latin future perfect.

> *Quae quum* fecero, *Romam ibo.* When I *have* done this, I shall go to Rome.

191. This **future perfect**, though rarely met with in the form "shall have" in ordinary English, is exceedingly common in Latin. It is sometimes found even in the principal clause as a substitute for the first future.

> Respiravero, *si te videro.* If once I *have* seen (*or* see) you, I *shall* breathe freely: lit. *shall have* breathed; implying that the relief will be instantaneous.

For *videro, viderint,* see **146.**

Pluperfect.

192. The pluperfect does not differ materially from the corresponding English tense, " I *had* done, or seen," etc.

But it is used in Latin after relatives and conjunctions to denote *frequency* or *repetition* in past tense.

> *Quum eo* venerat, *loco delectabatur.* *As often as* he came there, he was charmed with the situation.
>
> *Quos* viderat *ad se vocabat.* *Whomever* he saw he summoned to him.

For the use of these *imperfects* see **184.**

Tenses of the Infinitive.

193. (i.) In the infinitive mood the *present* (*laudare,* etc.) answers to both the *present* and *imperfect* of the indicative.

It expresses time *contemporaneous* with that of the verb on which it depends.

> *Dico,* or *dixi, me otiosum* esse. I say, *or* said, that I *am,* or *was*, at leisure. (See **35.**)

(ii.) The *perfect* infinitive (*scripsisse*) answers to the *aorist perfect, true perfect,* and *pluperfect,* of the indicative.

It denotes time *prior* to that of the verb on which it depends.

> *Dico me otiosum* fuisse. I say that I *was, have been, had been* at leisure.

The context must decide between the three meanings.

(iii.) The *future* infinitive is formed by the participle in *-rus.*

> *Dicit, dixit se* venturum esse. He says, said, that he *will* or *would* come.

Where there is no participle in *-rus,* and in the passive voice, the periphrasis of *fore ut* must be used.

> *Spero* fore ut *convalescat,* fore ut *urbs capiatur.* I hope that he *will* get well, that the city *will* be taken.
>
> *Speravi* fore ut *convalesceret,* fore ut *urbs caperetur.* I hoped that he *would* get well, that the city *would be* taken.

(iv.) With *passive* verbs the place of the missing *future infinitive* is often supplied by the supine in -*um*, with the impersonal infinitive *iri*.

> *Credidit urbem* expugnatum iri. He believed (lit. that *there was a going* (Intr. 42) to take the city) that the city *would be* taken.

Urbem is governed by the supine which has an active force, and is itself the accusative of *motion to*, after *iri*.

(v.) A *potential* future infinitive is formed for past time, thus :—

> *Credo hoc te* facturum fuisse. I believe you *would have* done this.
>
> *Credo* futurum fuisse *ut urbs expugnaretur.* I believe the city *would have* been taken.

194. As these remarks are somewhat long, it will be well before doing the exercise to study very carefully the use of the tenses in the following examples on the most important constructions.

1. *Dum haec inter se* loquuntur, advesperascebat.
2. *Jamdiu te* expecto . . . expectabam.
3. Dixi, *judices; vos, cum* consedero, *judicate.*
4. *Signum pugnandi* datum est ; stabant *immoti milites,* respicere, circumspicere ; *hostes quoque parumper* cunctati sunt ; *mox signa* inferre ; *et jam prope intra teli jactum* aderant, *cum subito in conspectum* veniunt *socii.*
5. *Si mihi* pares, *salvus eris.*
6. *Si mihi* parebis, *salvus eris.*
7. *Si mihi* parueris, *salvus eris.*
8. *Si hoc* feceris, *moriere.*
9. *Veniam, si* potero.
10. *Si hostem videro,* vicero.
11. *Tui, dum* vivam, *nunquam obliviscar.*
12. *Quemcunque* ceperat *trucidari* jubebat.
13. *Polliceor me, quum haec* scripserim, *rediturum esse.*
14. *Pollicitus est se, quum haec* scripsisset, *rediturum esse.*

Obs.—In the two last examples the 2d future indicative is represented by the *perfect* and *pluperfect* subjunctive ; these two tenses represent its force in the subjunctive mood after present and past time respectively.

A.

1. I have long been anxious to know the reason of your being so afraid of the nation forgetting[1] you. 2. Both my father and I had for some time been anxious to ascertain your opinion on this question. 3. When you come to Marseilles, I wish[2] you would ask your brother the reason of my having received no letter from him. 4. My speech is over, gentlemen, and I have sat down, as[3] you see of yourselves; do you decide on this question. For myself, I hope, and have long been hoping, that my client will be acquitted by your unanimous[4] verdict. 5. While the Medes were making these preparations, the Greeks had already met at the Isthmus. 6. Up to extreme old age your father would learn something fresh daily. 7. As often as the enemy stormed a town belonging[5] to this ill-starred race, they would spare none; women, children, old men, infants, were butchered, without[6] any distinction being made either of age or sex.

B.

1. He promises to present the man[7] who shall be the first to scale the wall, with a crown of gold.[8] 2. When I have returned from Rome, I will tell you[9] why I sent for you. 3. The Gauls had long been refusing[10] either to go to meet our ambassadors, or to accept the terms which Caesar was offering. 4. Suddenly the enemy came to a halt, but while they[11] were losing time, our men raised[12] a cheer, and charged into the centre of the line of their

---

[1] 138. [2] See 149, i [3] See 67, *Obs.*
[4] See 59. The "your" may either agree with "verdict" or with "all."
[5] Genitive, = "of."
[6] Abl. abs., "no distinction made." [7] See 72.
[8] See 58. In English we may use either the genitive, or "golden," or turn "gold" into an adjective, by placing it before "crown."
[9] Of course dative : "you" is the remoter object of "tell."
[10] See 136, *a*. *Nego* here, because their refusal was expressed in words.
[11] Use *illi*, to distinguish the enemy from our men. (See 70.
[12] Se 186.

infantry. 5. The general had for some time seen that his men were hard pressed by the superior numbers of the enemy, who hurled darts, slingstones, and arrows, and strove to force our men from the hill. 6. I have done my speech, judges : when you[1] have given your verdict it will be clear whether the defendant is going to return home with impunity, or to be punished for his many crimes.

---

[1] *Vos,* to be placed first. (See **11**, *a, b.*)

HOW TO TRANSLATE *Can, Could. May, Might, Shall, Must, etc.*

195. The ideas of **possibility, permission, duty, necessity,** are expressed in English by auxiliary verbs, "can," "may," "ought," "should," "must," etc. (Intr. 47.)

Obs.—These words have, in modern English, owing to their constant use as mere auxiliaries, ceased to be used as independent verbs. In Latin no verb has been reduced to this merely auxiliary state, though the verb *sum* is largely used as an auxiliary. (Intr. 49, *Obs.*)

The same ideas are expressed in Latin, partly (1) by the modal verbs (see **42**) *possum* and *debeo ;* partly (2) by the impersonal verbs *licet, oportet, decet,* and the impersonal phrase *necesse est, fuit,* etc. ; and largely (3) by the so-called participle in *-dus.*

N.B.—In all these cases the difference between the use of the tenses in Latin and English will require great care.

196. Possibility is expressed by the modal verb *possum.*

    (*a.*) *Hoc facere* possum, potero. I *can* do this (*now, or in the future*).

    (*b.*) *Hoc facere* poteram, potui, I *might have done* this (*past*).

Obs.—*Fecisse,* the literal translation of our "have done," would be quite wrong, for it would mean "*have finished* doing."

197. Permission is expressed by the impersonal verb *licet* with the *dative* and *infinitive.*

    (*a.*) *Hoc* mihi *facere* licet, *or* licebit. I *may* do this (*now or hereafter*).

    (*b.*) *Hoc* mihi *facere* licebat, licuit. I *might have done* this (*past*).

Here again notice *facere* in (*b.*).

Licet is also used occasionally with the subjunctive.

    Hoc facias *licet.* You may do this. (See **126.**)

142

Obs. 1.—"*May*," "*might*," must be translated by *possum* or *licet* according as they mean "I have the *power*," or "have *permission*."

Obs. 2.—A very common construction is :

Hoc tibi per me *facere* licuit.   You might have done this, so far as I was concerned, or, I should have allowed you to do this.

Hoc per me *facias* licebit.   I shall *leave you free* to do this.

198. To express **duty, obligation,** "ought," "should," etc., three constructions may be used :—

(i.) The personal verb *debeo*.

  (*a.*) *Hoc facere* debes, debebis.   You *ought* to do this, you *should* do this (*present* and *future*).

  (*b.*) *Hoc facere* debuisti, debebas.   You ought to, *or* should, *have done,* this (*past*).

(ii.) The impersonal verb *oportet*[1] with the accusative and infinitive.

  (*a.*) *Hoc te facere* oport-et, -ebit.

· (*b.*) *Hoc te facere* oport-ebat, -uit.

Obs.—*Oportet* is also used with the subjunctive.

  Hoc faceres oportuit.   You should have done this.

(iii.) (Commonest of all.) The *participle in -dus;* used either impersonally (*gerund*) with intransitive, or as an adjective (*gerundive*) with transitive verbs. (See Exercises XLIX. and L. on Gerund and Gerundive.)

The **person on whom the duty lies** is in the dative.

Gerundive—

  (*a.*) *Haec tibi* facienda *sunt, erunt.*   You ought *to do* this, (*present* and *future*).

  (*b.*) *Haec tibi* facienda *erant, fuerunt.*   You ought *to have done* this (*past*).

Gerund—

  (*a.*) *Tibi* currendum *est.*   You must run.

  (*b.*) *Tibi* currendum *fuit.*   You ought *to have* run.

---

[1] *Oportet* expresses a duty as binding *on oneself*; *debeo* the same duty, but rather as owed *to others,* "I am bound to," "under an obligation to." The participle in *-dus* includes both *duty* and *necessity*, and is far commoner than either *oportet* or *necesse est*.

199. To express **necessity**, use either, as above, the participle in -*dus*, which implies both *duty* and *necessity*—

(*a.*) *Tibi* moriendum est, erit, You *must* die, you will *have* to die ;

(*b.*) *Tibi* moriendum fuit, erat, You *had* to die ;

Or, more rarely and to imply *absolute* (properly *logical*) necessity.

(*a.*) *Tibi mori* (sometimes *moriare*) necesse[1] *est, erit.*

(*b.*) *Tibi mori* (sometimes *morerere*) necesse *erat, fuit.*

200. There are no words in Latin answering to the words "possible," "impossible," "possibility," "impossibility." They must be translated by substantival *clauses* subordinate to the impersonal phrase *fieri potest* with *ut* or *quin.* (See **125,** *e*; **132,** *d.*)

There was *no possibility* of our escaping. Non fieri potuit *ut effugeremus.*

·It is *impossible* for us not to believe this. Non fieri potest *quin hoc credamus.*

Or by a personal use of *possum,*

Non *effugere* poteramus. Non possumus *hoc non credere.*

Obs.—*Potest* can be only used impersonally with passive and impersonal verbs. "It is possible to perceive this" is not "*hoc* intellegere *potest*," but "*hoc* intellegi potest."

201. The case of the predicate after *licet* and *necesse est* should be carefully noticed.

Aliis licet ignavis *esse, vobis necesse est* viris fortibus *esse.* Others may be cowards, you must needs (*or* perforce) be brave men.

This is in accordance with the natural construction of link verbs. (See Intr. 71.)

202. The use of the infinitive mood with such impersonal verbs as *constat, apparet,* "it is evident" (not "it seems"), etc., has been pointed out (**46,** *c*).

It is also used with impersonals, denoting a *feeling* or *emotion.* Me *piget, pudet, taedet, delectat, poenitet,* mihi *libet.* Thus, *haec* me fecisse *pudet, poenitet, taedet,* I am ashamed, I repent, am weary, *of having done* this.

---

[1] *Necesse est* expresses either a purely logical necessity concerning things or ideas, in which case it takes the *accusative* and infinitive, *bis bina quattuor esse necesse est,* "twice two *must needs* be four ;" or the same idea of the inevitable as applied to a person, when it takes *dative* and infinitive, or subjunctive, *haec tibi pati,* (or *haec patiare*) *necesse est.*

Also with *pertinet ad, interest* and *refert,* " it is of importance," and with (*mihi*) *placet, videtur,* " it seems *good* that," (not *it seems that*). With the last two the *ut*-clause is also used.

Mitti *legatos,*	*senatui placuit, visum est.* It was resolved by, *or* it seemed good to, the
Ut mitterentur *legati,*	Senate that ambassadors should be sent. (See **46**, *b.*)

Exercise 24.

1. We ought long ago to have listened to the teaching of so great a philosopher[1] as this.   2. Was it not your duty to sacrifice your own life and your own interests to the welfare of the nation ?   3. The conquered and the coward (*pl.*) may be slaves, the asserters of their country's freedom must needs be free.   4. I blush at having persuaded you to abandon this noble undertaking.   5. You had my leave to warn your friends and relations not to run headlong into such danger and ruin. 6. It was impossible for a citizen of Rome[2] to consent to obey a despot of this kind. 7. You might have seen what the enemy was doing, but perhaps you preferred to be improvident and blind.   8. This (is what) you ought to have done ; you might have fallen fighting in battle ; and you were bound to die a thousand deaths rather than sacrifice the nation to your own interests.   9. Are you not ashamed of having in your old age, in order to please your worst enemies, been false to your friends, and betrayed your country ?   10. Do[3] not be afraid ; I shall leave you to come to Rome as often as you please ; and when you come[4] there[5] be sure you stay in my house if you can.   11. Twice two must needs be four ; it does not follow[6] that we must all consult always our own interest.

---

[1] 88, *Obs.*   [2] 58.   [3] 143.   [4] Tense ? (See 190, i.
[5] For " and there " use " whither," *quo.*   (See 78.)
[6] *Non idcirco,* lit. " we must not for that reason."

K

CASES.

General Remarks.

203. There is nothing in which Latin differs more from English than in what are called its *cases.*

By **Case** we mean such a change in the form of a noun (substantive, adjective, pronoun, or participle) as marks its relation to other words in a sentence.

204. These changes consist in the substitution of one *movable* and *variable termination* for another. Thus *Petrus Petro carus est*, Peter is dear *to* Peter ; *Petrus dominum secutus est*, Peter followed *his* master. We have here three different cases, *Petrus, Petro, dominum*, but the same change of meaning, which Latin represents by different terminations, *Petro, dominum*, we express in English,[1] not by a change in the termination of the word, but by introducing the preposition *to* in the one case, and by the order of the words in the other ; instead of saying *Petrus dominum secutus est*, we place Peter *before*, master *after*, the verb. (See Intr. 14.)

205. In Latin the order of the words will tell us little or nothing of the relation of a noun to the rest of the sentence ; the exact relation of the noun is marked by its case ; but as there are only six or at most seven cases, and the number of relations which language has to express is far greater than six or seven, the case-system is largely assisted by a great number of *prepositions*, which help to give precision and clearness to the meaning of the case.

206. The word "case" is an English form of a Latin word, *casus* (Gk. πτῶσις), used by grammarians to denote a *falling*, or deviation, from what they held to be the true or proper form of the word. The nominative was called, fancifully enough, the *casus rectus*, as that form of the word which stood *upright*, or in its natural position. The other cases were called *casus obliqui*, as *slanting* or falling over from this position ; and by *declinatio*, or " declension," was meant the whole system of these deviations, or, as we call them, *inflexions.*

---

[1] The English language once possessed, as German does still, a case-system ; but this only survives in the strictly *possessive* case, " Queen's speech," etc., and in certain pronouns *he, him ; who, whose, whom*, etc.

146

207. The Latin cases are six in number; the **Nominative, Accusative, Dative, Ablative, Genitive, Vocative.** Besides these there is a case, nearly obsolete in the classical period of Latin, the **Locative.**

208. (i.) The **Nominative** indicates the subject of the verb.

Without such subject, expressed or understood, a verb is meaningless. The nearest approach to the absence of a nominative is in such impersonal forms of intransitive verbs as *curritur*, "there is a running," *pugnatum est*, "there was fighting." (See Intr. 42.)

It was called the *casus nominativus*, as denoting the *name* of a person or thing—*Caesar, Roma, domus.*

209. (ii.) The **Accusative** completes the meaning of a transitive verb by denoting the immediate object of its action. Te *video*, I see *you.* (Intr. 37, 38.)

It was called the *casus accusativus*, interpreted as being that which we use to name a person whom we blame. But the original name (αἰτιατική) was probably given to it as denoting the αἰτία, or cause of the action of the transitive verb.

In English it is usually marked by following the verb, as the nominative by preceding it. "The sun illuminates the world;" "the world feels the sunlight."

In Latin it more often precedes the verb.

Its sense, possibly its earliest, of *motion towards* is still marked by its use after prepositions, implying this idea, *ad, in, sub,* and by its use with the names of towns to denote the same idea without a preposition: *Romam ibo,* I shall go *to* Rome.

It is used also as the subject of verbs in the infinitive mood, te *hoc dicere,* "*that you* should say this."

210. (iii.) The **Dative** is mainly used to represent the remoter object, or the person or thing *interested in* the action of the verb.

It was called the *casus dativus* (πτῶσις δοτική) as that used when we name a person *to whom* anything is *given.*

For the great importance and wide use of the Dative with intransitive verbs which are represented in English by verbs really or apparently transitive, see Intr. 36.

These three cases then, the *nominative, accusative,* and *dative,* are most intimately connected with the *verb,* as representing the one its *subject*, the other two the *objects* to which its action is *primarily* and *secondarily* directed.

211. (iv.) The **Ablative** is also closely connected with the verb, but in a different manner; it is an *adverbial* case, *i.e.* it is, like the adverb, an attendant on, or *satellite* of, the verb. It gives further particulars as to the mode of action of the verb in addition to those supplied by its nearer and remoter object. (See Intr. 16.) Its functions are very wide, for it can express the *source, cause, instrument, time, place, manner, circumstances,* of the action of the verb, as well as the point *from* which *motion* takes place.

> Horā *eum* septimā *vidi.*   I saw him *at* the seventh hour.
> Ense *eum interfeci.*   I slew him *with* a sword.
> Romā *profectus* est.   He set out *from* Rome.

These are only three examples of the many and various senses in which this case is used. ·

It was called the *casus ablativus* (πτῶσις ἀφαιρετική) as indicating, among its other meanings, the person *from* whom anything is *taken;* or the place *from* which it is removed.

212. (v.) The **Locative** case (*locus*), answering to the question, *where? at what place?* remains, as distinct from the ablative, only in certain words.

> *Romae* (-ai), *at* Rome ; *Londini, at* London.

(Compare *ibi, ubi,* there, where?) It also is therefore an *adverbial* case.

213. All these cases then are closely connected with the verb. The nominative sets, so to speak, the verb in motion : its movement is completed and directed by the other cases.

214. (vi.) The **Genitive**, on the other hand, is an attendant on *nouns* rather than on *verbs*. The main use of a noun in the genitive is to define or qualify another noun (substantive, pronoun, adjective, or participle), to which it is closely attached, or of which it is predicated.

Compare " Gallos *vicit* " with " Gallorum *victor,*" " te *amat* " with " tui *est amantissimus.*"

Hence its extremely common use as a substitute for the adjective.

Vir summae virtutis = *vir* optimus.

Its use in combination with verbs (*memini, obliviscor, indigeo*) is quite exceptional. (See **228**, *Obs.*)

It was called the casus *genitivus* as representing descent or race, regis *filius;* but the Greek πτῶσις γενική probably meant the *defining* case, that which added the γένος or class to which a word belonged. It was also sometimes called *possessivus*, sometimes *patricius:* Philippi *filius.*

215. (vii.) The **Vocative** case, *vocativus* (κλητική), is the form used in addressing a person: fili, *my son.* As a mere *interjection* (Intr. 28) it does not affect the syntax of the sentence.

The Nominative.

216. There is no special difficulty in the syntax of the nominative.

The accusative after the active verb (the *object*) becomes the nominative (the *subject*) to the passive verb.

Brutus Caesarem *interfecit.* Brutus killed Caesar. But, Caesar *a Bruto interfectus est.* Caesar was killed by Brutus. Urbem *obsidere coeperunt;* urbs *obsideri coepta est.*

(With passive verbs the passive of the verb *coepi* is used.)

Obs.—It is often advisable in translating from Latin into English, and *vice versa*, to substitute one voice for the other. Thus, to prevent ambiguity, "I know that Brutus killed Caesar" should be translated by *scio Caesarem a Bruto interfectum esse*, not by *Caesarem Brutum interfecisse. Aio te, Acacida, Romanos vincere posse* is an instance of oracular ambiguity, which should be carefully avoided in writing Latin.

217. It has been already explained that many English *transitive* verbs are represented in Latin by *intransitive* verbs, *i.e.* verbs which complete their sense, not by the aid of the *accusative*, but by that of the *dative*. (See Intr. 36.)

The passive voice of such verbs can only be used *impersonally* (see 5); hence the *nominative* of an English sentence is often represented in Latin by the *dative*, combined with a passive verb used impersonally.

Nemini *a nobis nocetur.* *No one* is hurt by us.

Puero *imperatum est ut regem excitaret.* *The servant* was ordered to wake the king.

Tibi *a nullo creditur.*[1] *You* are believed by no one.

Gloriae tuae *invidētur.* *Your glory* is envied.

Obs.—The same impersonal construction is used in the passive with those intransitive verbs which complete their sense by a preposition and substantive.

Ad *urbem pervenimus.* We reached the city.

Jam ad urbem perventum est. The city was now reached.

218. This impersonal construction constantly represents the nominative of an English abstract or verbal noun.[2]

In urbe maxime trepidatum est. The *greatest confusion* reigned in the city.

Ad arma subito concursum est. There was *a sudden rush* to arms.

Acriter pugnatum est. The *fighting* was *fierce.*

Satis ambulatum est. We have had enough of *walking.*

Obs.—In such phrases the English *adjective* will be represented by a Latin *adverb*.

219. With this impersonal construction of the passive when used in the infinitive, *potest, potuit,* etc., are used impersonally (never otherwise, see **200,** *Obs.*); as also an impersonal passive form of some modal verbs, as *coeptum est, desitum est.*

Huic culpae ignosci potest. It is possible to pardon this fault.

Resisti non potuit. Resistance was impossible.

Jam pugnari coeptum (desitum) est. The fighting has now begun (ceased).

220. The use of the nominative with the infinitive when combined with a modal verb has been pointed out: *otiosus esse cupio, debeo, incipio,* etc. (see **42**), I desire, am bound, begin, etc., to be at leisure. So also its use with *videor, credor, narror,* etc.: *videor, credor, dicor servus fuisse, it* seems, is believed, said, etc., *that I* was a slave. (See **43**.)

These points, as well as the indefinite and unexpressed nominative with impersonal verbs and such phrases as *credunt, dicunt,* etc. (**44**) have been already mentioned; so that the following exercises will be mainly recapitulatory.

---

[1] *i.e.* "You are believed *in*, or *trusted*, by no one." *Credo* in this sense is intransitive and governs a dative; in the sense of "I believe" or "think," it follows the usual construction of *verba sentiendi.* "You are believed by no one to have done this" would be *a nullo hoc fecisse crederis.* (See **43**.) [2] See Intr. 42.

A.

1. Your goodness will be envied.   2. Liars are never believed.   3. But for you[1] (*pl.*), do you not want to be free?   4. Do not become slaves; slaves will be no more pardoned than freemen.   5. It seemed that you made no answer to his[2] question.   6. So far from being hated by us, you are even favoured.   7. For myself,[3] it seems to me that I have acted rightly; but you possibly take a different view.   8. I will ask which of the two is favoured by the king.   9. The fighting has been fierce to-day; the contest will be longer and more desperate to-morrow.

B.

1. Thereupon a sudden[4] cry arose in the rear, and a strange[4] confusion reigned along[5] the whole line of march. 2. When I said "yes" you believed me; I cannot understand why you refuse to trust my word when I say "no." 3. When[6] a boy I was with difficulty persuaded not to become a sailor, and face the violence of the sea, the winds, and storms: as an old man I prefer sitting at leisure at home to either sailing or travelling: you perhaps have the same views.[7]   4. You ought to have been content with such good fortune as this, and never (110) to have made it your aim to endanger everything by making excessive demands.[7]   5. So far from cruelty having been shown in our case, a revolt and rebellion on the part of our forefathers has been twice over pardoned by England.   6. It seems that your brother was a brave man, but it is pretty well allowed[8] that he showed himself rash and improvident in this matter.   7. It seems that he was the first of[9] that nation to wish to become our fellow-subject, and it is said that he was the last who preserved in old age the memory of (their) ancient liberties.

---

[1] "But for you," *Vos vero;* "for" = "as for," and is simply emphatic. The emphasis is given in Latin by the *use* and place of *vos.* (11, *a.*)
[2] To him questioning.   [3] *Equidem.*
[4] Adjectives will become adverbs. (See 218, *Obs.*)
[5] "Along" may be expressed by the ablative of place.
[6] See 63.   [8] =agreed on.
[7] "Views," etc., not to be expressed. see 54: cf. 91.   [9] *ex.*

APPOSITION.

Apposition is not confined to the nominative; but it is more often used with the nominative and accusative than with other cases.

The general rule was given in **3**; see also **227**.

221. The substantive in apposition stands in the relation of an adjective to the substantive with which it is combined; in *Thebae,* Boeotiae caput, the words in apposition define *Thebes* by adding the special quality of its being *the capital of Boeotia.*

> *Te* ducem *sequimur.* We follow you as,[1] or *in the capacity of,* our leader.

Hence if the substantive be *feminine,* use the *feminine form,* whenever it exists, of the substantive *in apposition.*

> *Usus,* magister *egregius.* Experience, an admirable teacher.
> But—*Philosophia,* magistra *morum.* Philosophy, the teacher of morals.

222. Where a geographical expression, such as "city," "island," "promontory," is defined in English by *of,* with a proper name, apposition is used in Latin. Thus—

> *Urbs* Veii, the city *of* Veii; *insula* Cyprus, the island *of* Cyprus; *Athenas,* urbem *inclytam,* the renowned city *of* Athens.

Obs.—A similar explanatory "of" may be represented in Latin by the word *res* in apposition to another substantive.

> *Libertas,* res *pretiosissima.* The precious possession *of* freedom.

---

[1] We must always ask what *as* means. "We follow you as (=*as though*) a God" is, *te* quasi *Deum sequimur.*

223. Certain substantives are regularly used in apposition as adjectives.

> *Cum filio* adolescentulo. With a son *in early youth.*
> *Cum exercitu* tirone. With a *newly levied* army.
> Nemo [1] *pictor*, no painter ; always nemo (never *nullus*) *Romanus*, no Roman.

224. The Romans did not combine, as we do, an adjective of praise or blame with a proper name (rarely with a word denoting a person) unless by way of *cognomen* or *title*, as *C. Laelius Sapiens.*

They substituted *vir* (or *homo*) with an adjective, in apposition.

> "The learned Cato " is " *Cato*, vir *doctissimus.*"
> "Your gallant *or* excellent brother" is " *Frater tuus*, vir *fortissimus, optimus.*"
> "The abandoned Catiline" is " *Catilina*, homo *perditissimus.*" (See 57, *a.*)

Obs. 1.—This appositional use of *vir* or *homo* with an adjective often supplies the place of the absent participle of *esse.*

> *Haec ille*, homo [2] *innocentissimus, perpessus est.* This is what he, *being (i.e. in spite of being)* a perfectly innocent man, endured.

Obs. 2.—Sometimes it represents our "*so* good, bad, etc., *as.*"

> *Te* hominem [3] levissimum, *or*, *te*, virum optimum *odit.* He hates so trifling a person, so good a man, as you ; *or* one so good, etc., as you.

225. The substantive or adjective is often used in apposition with an unexpressed personal pronoun.

> *Mater te appello.* I your mother call you ; *or* it is your mother who calls you.
> *Omnes adsumus.* All *of us* are here.
> *Quot estis ?* How many *of you* are there ? Trecenti *adsumus.* "There are three hundred *of us* here." (See **297**.)
> *Hoc facitis* Romani. This is what *you* Romans do.

---

[1] *Nemo* is a substantive : *nullus*, which supplies *nemo* with genitive, ablative, and often dative, an adjective.

[2] The word in apposition generally follows, unless unusual emphasis is to be conveyed. *Rex* comes before the proper name as applied to hereditary kings, *pro rege Deiotaro.*

[3] *Homo* is "a human being " as opposed to an animal or a God : *vir*, "a man " as opposed to a woman or child. Hence *homo* is joined with adjectives of either praise or blame ; *vir* with adjectives of strong praise, *fortissimus, optimus*, etc.

226. The predicate agrees with the principal substantive unless that be the name of a town in the plural, when it naturally agrees with the singular word *urbs* or *oppidum*, etc., in apposition. Thus—

> Brutus et Cassius, *spes nostra*, occiderunt. Brutus and Cassius, our (only) hope, have fallen.
> But—Thebae, *Boeotiae caput, paene* deletum est. Thebes, the capital of Boeotia, was nearly annihilated.

227. **Single words** are used appositionally in all cases; **phrases**, *i.e.* combinations of words, only in the nominative and accusative; in other cases, and with prepositions, a *qui*-clause is substituted.

> *Extincto Pompeio*, quod *hujus reipublicae lumen fuit.*
> *Ad Leucopetram*, quod *agri Rhegini promontorium est.*

Notice in each case the attraction of the relative to the gender of the predicate. (See **83**.)

Exercise 26.

1. Philosophy, he says, was (32) the inventor of law,[1] the teacher of morals and discipline. 2. There is a tradition that Apiolae, a city of extreme[2] antiquity, was taken in this campaign. 3. It is said that your gallant father Flaminius founded in his consulship the flourishing colony of Placentia. 4. Do not, says he, I earnestly implore you, my countrymen, throw away the precious jewels of freedom and honour, to humour a tyrant's caprice. 5. The soldier, in spite of his entire innocence, was thrown into prison; the gallant centurion was butchered then and there. 6. There is a story that this ill-starred king was the first of his race to visit the island of Sicily, and the first to have beheld from a distance the beautiful city of Syracuse. 7. I should scarcely believe that so shrewd a man as your father would have put confidence in these[3] promises of his.

---

[1] See p. 72, n. 2.

[2] Use adjective "most ancient" for adjectival phrase (p. 17, *n.* 2, and see **214**).

[3] "In him making (*participle*) these promises." (54.)

ACCUSATIVE.

228. The accusative has been already defined as **the case of the direct** or **nearer object of the transitive verb.**

It may be said that the direct object of every such verb, including deponents and impersonals, is a word in this case, and in this only.

Te *video*, te *sequimur*, te *piget*, or *poenitet*.

Obs.—The apparent exceptions are not really exceptions. When we say that in Latin the words *pareo*, I obey, *utor*, I use, *memini*, I remember, govern a *dative*, *ablative*, and *genitive* respectively, we really mean that the Romans put the ideas which we express by these three verbs into a different shape to that which we employ ; and that in neither of the three they made use of a transitive verb, combined with its nearer object. In the first case we say, " I obey *you*;" they said, tibi *pareo*, " I am obedient *to* you." In the second we say, " I use *you*;" they said, *utor* vobis, " I serve *myself with* you." In the third we say, "I remember *you*;" they said, tui *memini*, " I am mindful *of* you." In a precisely similar way, where the Romans said te *sequimur*, the Greeks said σοὶ ἑπόμεθα, "we are followers *to you*." They looked, that is, on the person followed as *nearly interested in*, but not, as the Romans did, as the *direct object of*, the action described by the verb (ἑπόμεθα).

229. Many intransitive verbs in Latin, as in English, become transitive, when compounded with a preposition. (See Intr. 24, and also **24.**)

This is especially the case with verbs that express some bodily movement or action ; often the compound verb has a special meaning.[1]

> *Urbem* oppugno, expugno, obsideo, circumsedeo. I assault, storm, blockade, invest, a city.
> *Caesarem* convenio, circumvenio. I have an interview with, overreach *or* defraud, Caesar.

---

[1] *Praestare*, when it means "to excel," is generally used with a dat., though sometimes with an acc. ; but with *se*, *praestare* is common as a factitive verb. (See **239.**) *Invictum se a laboribus* praestitit, he *showed* himself invincible by (*or* on the side of) toils.

Compare "I *outran* him," "I *overcame* him," etc.
Most of these verbs are used freely in the passive. *A te circum-ventus sum.* I was defrauded by you.

Obs.—Transducere, transjicere (trajicere) are used with a double accusative.

> Copias Hellespontum *transduxit.*
> Copiae Rhenum *trajectae sunt.*

So also—*Transjecto Rheno,* abl. abs.

230. Certain verbs of **teaching** (*doceo*), **concealing** (*celo*) **demanding** (*posco, flagito*), **asking questions** (*rogo, interrogo*), may be joined with two accusatives, one of the *person*, another of the *thing*.

> *Quis mūsicam* docuit *Epaminondam?* Who taught Epaminondas music ?
> *Nihil nos* cēlat. He conceals nothing *from* us.
> *Verres pārentes pretium pro sepulturā līberûm* poscebat. Verres used to demand *of* parents a payment for the burial of their children.
> *Meliora deos* flagito. I implore better things *of* the gods (127).
> *Racilius me primum* rogavit *sententiam.*[1] I was the first whom Racilius asked for his opinion.

231. But this construction is commonest with the neuter pronouns *hoc, illud, nihil;* otherwise *very frequently* (and with some verbs *always*) either the *person* or the *thing* is governed by a *preposition.*

Thus, though *doceo* always takes the accusative of the *person*, unlike *dico, narro,* etc. (tibi *hoc* dico, te *hoc* doceo), yet *doceo,* to give information, prefers the ablative with *de* for the *thing* told. After *peto* and *postulo, sometimes* after the other verbs of *begging,* the *person* is put in the *abl.* with *a:* and after *rogo, interrŏgo,* etc., the *thing* often stands in the *abl.* with *de.*

> *Haec abs te poposci.* I have made this request of you.
> *De his rebus Caesarem docet.* He informs Caesar of these facts.
> *De hac re te celatum volo.* I wish you kept in the dark about this.

---

[1] *Sententiam rogare* is a technical expression "to ask a senator for his opinion and vote," and the acc. is preserved in the passive : *primus sententiam rogatus sum,* "I was asked *my opinion* first."

But—*Hoc te celatum nolim.*   I should be sorry for you to be kept
   etc.

Aliud te *precamur.*   We pray you for something else.

But—*Haec omnia* a te *precamur.*   We pray for all these things from
   you.

Hoc *te rogo.*[1]   I ask you this question.

But—De hac re *te rogo.*   I ask you about this.   (See **127**.)

Haec a vobis *postulamus atque petimus.*   We demand and
   claim this of you.

232. Some verbs really intransitive are used occasionally in a
transitive sense; such are *horreo* (oftener *perhorresco*), "I shudder," used
for "I fear," and such figurative expressions as *sitio*, "I am thirsty,"
used as "I thirst *for*," with accusative.   But these constructions are
far commoner in poetry than in prose.   Compare—

   Pars stupet *innuptae* donum exitiale *Minervae.*—VIRG.

233. The accusative after passive verbs of *the thing put on*, or of
the *part affected*, is originally an accusative of the object combined
with what is called in Greek a *middle* verb.

   Longam *indutus* vestem.   Having *put on himself* a long garment.

   Trajectus femur *tragula.*   Having his thigh *pierced* with a dart.

It is exceedingly common in poetry, both with participles and even
with adjectives :—

   Os *impressa toro*, with her face pressed upon the couch ;

   Os humeros*que Deo similis*, like a God in face and shoulders ;

and is extended, with the aid of the *cognate accusative* (see **236**), into
a general accusative of reference : as caetera *fulvus*, tawny *elsewhere.*
But it is a rare construction in classical prose.

234. The accusative of the person is used after the
impersonal verbs

> *Decet* atque *dedecet,*
>
> *piget, pudet, poenitet,*
>
> *taedet* atque *miseret.*

The last five are joined with a genitive of the cause or
object of the feeling denoted.

   Eum facti sui neque pudet neque poenitet.   He feels neither
   shame nor remorse for his deed.

---

[1] The verb "I ask" (a question), may be turned either by *rogo,*
interrogo, with the accusative of the person, or by *quaero* with the
prep. *ab, a : ex, e.*   "I asked him why," etc., may be turned either by
tum eum *interrogavi cur* . . ., or by *tum* ab, *or* ex, eo *quaesivi cur.*

235. The accusative of *motion towards* is found mostly with prepositions, *ad*, *in*, *sub*, etc. ; it is also found as expressing the purpose of motion with the supine in -*um*, a verbal noun preserving its active force (see **402**) :—

> *Me has injurias* questum *mittunt*, they send me to complain of these wrongs ;
>
> *Sperat rem* confectum iri (see **193**, iv.), he hopes that the affair will be finished ;

also with certain phrases, as Venum *dare*, to sell ; infitias *eo*, I deny ; and with the accusative of motion to a *town*, *small island*, and the words *domum* (home), *rus*, *foras* (out of doors), etc. (See below, **313**.)

Exercise 27.

1. As the army mounted up the highest part of the ridge, the barbarians attacked its flanks with undiminished vigour. 2. I have repeatedly warned your brother not to conceal anything from your excellent father. 3. You ought to have been the first to have encountered death, and to have shown yourself the brave son of a gallant father, not to have been the first to have been horrified at a trifling danger. 4. If Caesar leads (190, i.) his troops across the Rhine there will be the greatest agitation throughout the whole of Germany. 5. Our spies have given us much information as to the situation and size of the citadel; it seems that they wish to keep us in the dark as to[1] the amount and character of the garrison. 6. Having[2] perceived that all was lost, the general rode in headlong flight past the fatal marsh (*pl.*), and reached the citadel in safety. 7. In order to avoid the heavy burden of administering the government he pleaded his age and bodily[3] weakness. 8. Many have coasted along distant lands; it is believed that he[4] was the first to sail round the globe. 9. I should be sorry for you to be kept in the dark about my journey, but this request I make of you, not to forget me in my absence. 10. About part of his project he told me everything; the rest he kept secret even from his brother.

---

[1] "What is the amount," etc. (See **174**.)
[2] See **14**, *a*.   [3] See **59**.
[4] "He" is emphatic = "this man" (*hic*).

ACCUSATIVE II.

Cognate and Predicative.

236. Another use of the accusative is called the **Cognate** accusative.

Even intransitive verbs such as "I run," "I live," denote some *action*. The result, or range, of this action, added to define the meaning more clearly, is sometimes treated as a *direct object* to the verb, and placed in the accusative case.

> *Hunc* cursum *cucurri.*   I ran this race.
> *Multa* proelia *pugnavi.*   I have fought many battles.

Thus we say in English, "I struck him *a blow.*"

It is called the cognate accusative because the substantive is either in form or meaning kindred (*cognatus*) to the verb.

237. The substantive when so used has generally, not always, an adjective or its equivalent attached to it.

> Longam vitam *vixi.*   Long is the life I have led.
> Has *notavi* notas.   I set down these marks.

But its commonest use in prose is with neuter pronouns, *hoc, illud, idem,* and with neuter plural adjectives, as *pauca, multa,* etc., and the word *nihil*. Hoc *laetor,* illud *glorior* (instead of, hac re *laetor,* de illa re *glorior*), "this is the meaning of my joy;" "this is my boast." So—

> Illud *tibi assentior,* in this I agree with you.   Nihil *mihi succenset,* he is in no way angry with me.   Idem *gloriatur,* he makes the same boast.   Multa *peccat,* he commits many sins.   (See **54.**)

With these verbs the accusative of a substantive could not be used.

238. This accusative is the origin of many constructions :—

(i.) The adverbial use of *multum, minimum, nescio quid, quantum.*

(ii.) The *poetical* use of the neuter singular and plural of many adjectives : dulce *ridentem,* sweetly smiling ; and even in prose : majus *exclamat,* he raises a louder cry.

(iii.) Such adverbial expressions as id *temporis,* at that time ; *cum* id aetatis *puero,* with a boy of that age ; tuam vicem *doleo,* I grieve for your sake.

(iv.) It is no doubt the origin of the accusative of *space,* of *time,* and of *distance.* Tres annos *absum,* I have been away *for* three years ; tria millia (*passuum*) *processi,* I advanced three miles.

239. The **Predicative**[1] accusative is quite different from the cognate. It is an additional accusative necessary to complete the meaning of a large class of transitive verbs, which in the passive are little more than link verbs, and have therefore the same case before and after them. (See Intr. 49.)

Ego mater tua *appellor.*   I am called your mother.
Me matrem tuam *appellant.*   They call me your mother.

These verbs, as " containing the idea of *making* by deed, word, or thought,"[2] are called *factitive* verbs.

Me consulem creant.   They make me consul.
Se virum bonum praestitit.   He proved himself a good man.

240. To this belong such phrases as

Haec res me sollicitum habuit.   This made me anxious.
Mare infestum habuit.   He infested, *or* beset, the sea.
Haec missa facio.   I dismiss these matters.

And even such uses as—

Hoc cognitum, compertum, *mihi* persuasum, *habeo.*   I am certain, assured, convinced of this. (See **188.**)

Obs. 1. We may compare the accusative after *volo* in such phrases as *te* salvum *volo,* I wish for your safety ; *tibi* consultum *volo,* I wish your good consulted, where the link verb *esse* is rarely found.

---

[1] The *exclamatory* use of the accusative may be classed under the head of the predicative,—*miserum hominem! O spem vanissimam!* "wretched that he is !" "how vain the hope !"   It may be compared with a similar use of the infinitive,—*te,* sometimes *te-ne, hoc* dicere !

[2] Dr. Kennedy's Latin Grammar.

Obs. 2.—In place of this accusative other phrases are common. [Verbs of *thinking*, etc., are rarely treated as factitive verbs.]

I consider you *as my friend*. *Te amicorum in numero habeo.*
I look on this *as certain*. *Hoc* pro certo *habeo*.
I behaved *as a citizen*. *Me* pro cive *gessi.* (See **221** and *note*.)

241. The English verb " I show " is used in a sense which cannot be expressed in Latin by *monstro* or *ostendo*.

" He *showed* himself a man of courage," or " he *showed* courage " is *virum fortem se praestitit,* or *praebuit;* or *fortissime se gessit;* or *fortissimus extitit.*

Exercise 28.

Before doing this Exercise read carefully **54**; also, for the different senses of "such," **86**.

1. And perhaps he is himself going to commit the same fault as his ancestors have repeatedly committed. 2. He makes many complaints, many lamentations; at this one thing he rejoices, that[1] you are ready to make him your friend. 3. For myself, I fear he will keep the whole army anxious for his[2] safety, such is his want of caution and prudence. 4. England had long covered the sea with her fleets; she now ventured at last to carry her soldiers across the Channel and land them on the continent. 5. The rest of her allies Rome left alone; the interests of Hiero, the most loyal of them all, she steadily consulted. 6. Whether he showed himself wise or foolish I know not, but a boy of that age will not be allowed to become a soldier; this at least I hold as certain. 7. This is the life that I have led, judges; you possibly feel pity for such a life; for myself I would[3] venture to make this boast, that I feel neither shame,[4] nor weariness, nor remorse for it. 8. He behaved so well at this trying crisis that I hardly know whether to admire his courage most or his prudence.

---

[1] See **41**, *b*.   [2] **11**, *e*.   [3] See **149**, i.   [4] **234**.

L

DATIVE.

I. Dative with Verbs.

242. The general meaning of the **Dative** has been explained above (210). It expresses the person or thing *interested in,* or *affected by,* the state or action described by the verb, otherwise than as the direct object.

As the accusative answers the question, *whom? what?* so the dative answers the question, *to* or *for* whom or what?

243. In English the difference is often obliterated. "He built *me* a house ;" "he saddled *him* the horse ;" "I paid *them* their debt ;" "I told *him* my story"—are equally correct sentences with "He built a house *for* me ;" "I told my story *to* Caesar," etc. **In translating therefore into Latin we must look to the meaning rather than to the form of the word,** and use the dative of the *recipient,* or *person affected,* with verbs of *giving, telling* (except *doceo*), and even with those of *taking away.*

Multa ei *pollicitus sum.* I have made *him* many promises.
Poenas mihi *persolvet.* He shall pay *me* the penalty.
Omnia nobis *ademisti.*[1] You have taken *from us* everything.

244. A very large number of verbs which in English are, or appear to be, transitive, are in Latin intransitive, and complete their meaning not by an accusative but by a dative. (See **228**, *Obs.*) Such are—

(*a.*) Verbs of **aiding, favouring, obeying, pleasing, profiting,** etc.

Opitulor, subvenio, faveo, studeo, pareo, obedio, placeo, prosum.

---

[1] Compare the French *arracher à,* "to tear *from.*"

(*b.*) Verbs of **injuring, opposing, displeasing.**

Noceo, adversor, obsto, repugno, displiceo, etc.

(*c.*) Verbs of **commanding, persuading, trusting, distrusting, sparing, envying, being angry.**

> *Impero, praecipio, suadeo, fido, diffido, parco, ignosco, invideo, irascor, succenseo,* etc.

(*Confido* takes dative of *person,* ablative of *thing* relied on.)

> *Fortibus* favet *fortuna.*   It is the brave whom[1] fortune *favours.*
> *Haec res omnibus hominibus* nocet.   This fact *injures* the whole world.
> *Legibus* paruit *consul.*   He *obeyed* the law in his consulship.
> *Victis victor* pepercit.   He *spared* the vanquished in the hour of victory.
> *Non tibi sed exercitu meo* confisus sum.   It was not on you but on my army that *I relied.*

Obs.—It has already been said that these verbs must be used impersonally in the passive.

> *Mihi repugnatur.*   I am resisted.
> *Tibi diffiditur.*   You are distrusted.   (See **217.**)

245. But certain verbs of this class are transitive in Latin also.

> *Juvo, adjuvo; delecto; laedo, offendo:*
> *Jubeo, hortor; veto, prohibeo; rego, guberno.*

Libris me delecto.   I amuse myself with books.
Offendit *neminem.*   He offends nobody.
Haec laedunt *oculos.*   These things hurt the eye.
Fortuna fortes adjŭvat.   Fortune helps the bold.

246. The impersonal verbs *accidit, contingit, expedit, libet, licet, placet,* are joined with a dative, not, as *oportet,* and those enumerated in **234,** with an accusative.

> *Hoc tibi dicere libet.*   It is your pleasure, suits your fancy, to say this.

---

[1] See **156,** *Obs.*

247. Many Latin verbs require, to complete their sense, both an accusative and a dative, arranged however in a way quite different to that of nouns joined with the corresponding verb in English.

Mortem mihi *minatus est.*   He threatened me *with* death.

Pecuniam nobis *imperavit.*   He ordered us *to supply,* or exacted from us, money.

Frumentum iis *suppeditarit.*   He supplied them *with* corn.

Vitam vobis *adimunt.*   They are robbing you *of* life.

Facta sua nulli *probavit.*   He won no one's approval *for* his acts.

Hanc rem tibi *permisi* or *mandavi.*   I intrusted you *with* this.

Haec peccata mihi *condonavit.*   He pardoned me *for* these offences.

248. Many transitive Latin verbs, as *metuo, consulo, caveo, prospicio, credo,* etc., are also used intransitively with a dative in a different sense to that which they bear with the accusative.

Compare, to *metuo, timeo,* with *nihil tibi metuo,* etc., I have no fears for you. Te *consulo,* I ask *your opinion;* tibi *consulo,*[1] I attend to, consult, *your interests.* Te (or *a te*) *caveo,* I am on my guard *against* you; tibi *caveo,* I am taking care *for your interests.* Tempestatem *prospicio,* I *foresee* a storm; saluti tuae *provideo,* I provide *for your safety.* Te *credo hoc fecisse,* I believe you to have done this; tibi *hoc facienti credo,* I believe you (trust you) while you do this. Culpâ *vacat,* he is *free from* crime; philosophiae *vacat,* he *has time for* (he studies) philosophy.

249. *Tempero* and *moderor* in the sense of "to govern" or "direct" have the *accusative;* when they mean "to set limits to" they have the *dative. Temperare ab* aliquâ re is "to *abstain* from," and hence (also with the dative), "to *spare.*"

Hanc civitatem *leges moderantur.*   This state is *governed* by law. (**216,** *Obs.*)

Fac animo *modereris.*   Be sure you *restrain* your feelings, or temper.

Ab inermibus *or* inermibus (dative) *temperatum est.*   The unarmed were spared. (The past participle of *parco* is rare.)

---

[1] A very common phrase is *tibi consultum* or *cautum volo.* (See **240,** *Obs.* 1.)

250. *Dono, circumdo,* and some other verbs, take either a *dative* of the *person* and an *accusative* of the *thing*, or an *accusative* of the *person* and an *ablative* of the *thing*.

> *Circumdat* urbem muro ; or, *circumdat* murum urbi.   He surrounds the city with a wall.
>
> Ciceroni immortalitatem *donavit;* or, Ciceronem immortalitate *donavit.*   (The Roman people) conferred immortality on Cicero.

So *induit* se veste, *or* vestem sibi *induit* (*exuit*), he puts on (*or* off) his dress.

Exercise 29.

A.

1. I have long been warning you whom it is your duty to guard against, whom to fear.   2. I know that one so good as[1] your father will always provide for his children's safety.   3. It is impossible[2] to get any one's approval for such[3] a crime as this.   4. On my asking[4] what I was to do, whether and how and when[5] I had offended him, he made no reply (25).   5. Is it[6] your country's interest, or your own that you (*pl.*) wish consulted ?   6. I pardoned him for many offences; he ought not to have shown such cruelty toward you.   7. In his[7] youth I was his opponent; in his age and weakness I am ready to assist him.   8. I foresee many political storms, but I fear neither for the nation's safety nor for my own.

B.

1. It is said that he wrenched the bloody dagger from the assassin, raised[8] it aloft, and flung it away on the ground.   2. Do not (*pl.*) taunt with his lowly birth one who has done such good service to his country.   3. It matters not whether[9] you cherish anger against me or not; I have no fears for my own safety; you may[10] henceforth threaten me with death daily, if you please.[11]   4. You

---

[1] See **224,** *Obs.* 2.   [2] See **125,** *e, f.*   [3] **88,** *Obs.*
[4] "To me asking," *participle.*   [5] Why not *quum ?* (See **157,** ii.)
[6] See **156.**   [7] **63.**   [8] Participle passive. (**15.**)
[9] See **168.**   [10] Future of *licet.* (See **197.**)   [11] See **190,** ii.

were believed, and must have[1] been believed, for all were agreed (*imperf.*) that you had never broken your word. 5. He complained that the office with which the nation had just intrusted[2] him had not only been shared with others, but would be entirely taken away from him, by this law. 6. You have deprived us of our liberties and rights in our absence (61), and perhaps to-morrow you intend[3] to wrench from us our lives and fortunes. 7. The soldiers were all slain to a man, but the unarmed were spared.[4] 8. We are all of us[5] ignorant of the reason[6] for so gentle a prince as ours exacting from his subjects such enormous quantities of corn and money. 9. He never spared any one[7] who had withstood him, or pardoned any who had injured him. 10. I have always wished your interests protected; but I did not wish one so incautious[8] and rash as you consulted on (*de*) this matter.

---

[1] Use participle in -*dus*. (**199.**)   [2] Mood? (See **77.**)
[3] **14,** *c.*   [4] See **249.**   [5] See **225.**
[6] See **174,** *a.*   [7] Use *nemo unquam.*   (See **110.**)
[8] Use *incautus* (**224,** *Obs.* 2).

DATIVE—*Continued.*

II. Dative with Verbs.

251. The verb *sum* can of course never be transitive, and therefore its sense is naturally completed by the dative; we can say,

> Erat ei *domi filia, he had* a daughter at home; '

and most of its compounds, ad*sum*, de*sum*, inter*sum*, ob*sum*, prae*sum*, pro*sum*, super*sum*, are joined with a dative.

> Mihi *adfuit*, his rebus *non interfuit.* He gave me the benefit[1] of his presence, he took no part in these matters.

Obs.—Insum is oftener than not followed by the preposition *in*, *absum* by *a, ab.*

252. The dative is used with a very large number of verbs compounded with prepositions, such as—

> ad, ante, cum (con-),
> in, inter, ob,
> post, sub, and prae.

Also with the adverbs *bene, satis, male.* These verbs may be divided into four classes.

253. (i.) Many are intransitive and take the dative alone. As, among many others—

> Assentari, to flatter; im*minere*, to hang over, threaten (*intrans.*); confidere (see **282**, *Obs.*), to trust in; in*stare*, in*sistere* (sometimes with *acc.*), to press on, urge; inter*cedere*, to put a veto on; ob*stare*, re*pugnare*, to resist; occurrere, obviam ire, to meet; obsequi, to comply with; satis*facere*, to satisfy; male-dicere, to abuse. (See **244.**)

---

[1] A very common meaning of *adsum* with dative, "I am at hand to aid."

(ii.) Others are transitive, and complete their meaning with both the accusative and the dative.

Te illi *posthabeo*. I place you behind him (=illum tibi *antepono*), I prefer him to you.

Se periculis *objecit*. He exposed himself to dangers.

Mortem sibi *conscivit*. } He committed suicide, "laid violent
Vim sibi *intulit*.   } hands on himself."

Te exercitui *praefecerunt*. They have placed you at the head of the army.

Bellum nobis *indixit, intulit*. He declared, he made, war against us.

(iii.) Some are simply transitive verbs and take the accusative.   (See **229**.)

Ad*ŭlari*, to fawn upon ; *aversari*, to loathe ; att*ingĕre*, to touch lightly ; al*loqui*, to speak (kindly) to ; ir*ridēre*, to deride (sometimes dat., as also *adŭlari*).

(iv.) Others require a preposition, in place of the dative.

Haec res ad me (*never* mihi) *pertinet*, or *attinet*. This concerns *me*.

Hoc mecum *communicavit*. He imparted this *to me*.

Ad scelus *nos impellit*. He is urging us *to crime*.

Ad urbem *pervenit*. He reached *the city*.

In rempublicam *incumbere*. To devote one's-self *to the nation*, *or* the national cause.

No universal rule can be given, and the usage of Latin authors must be carefully watched.

Exercise 30.

1. Possibly one so base as you[1] will not hesitate to prefer slavery to honour.   2. He says[2] that as a young man he took no part in that contest.   3. He promises never to fail his friends.   4. To my question who was at the head of the army he made no reply.   5. All of us know well the baseness of failing[3] our friends in a trying crisis.   6. I pledge myself not to be wanting either[4] to the time, or to the general, or to the opportunity; but possibly fortune is opposing our designs.   7. It is said that Marcellus wept over the fair city of Syracuse.[5]

---

[1] **224**, *Obs.* 2 ; *tu* should be expressed.   (See **334**, ii.)
[2] See **33**.   [3] See **94**, **95**.
[4] "Either," "or," after *not* will be *neque*.   [5] See **222**.

8. For myself, I can scarcely believe[1] that so gentle a prince as ours could have acted so sternly. 9. In the face of these dangers which are threatening the country, let all of us devote ourselves to the national cause. 10. It concerns his reputation immensely for us to be assured whether he fell in battle or laid violent hands on himself. 11. You ought to have gone out to meet your gallant brother; you preferred to sit safely at home. 12. I would fain know whether he is going to declare and make war on his country, or to sacrifice his own interests to the nation. 13. To prevent his urging others to a like crime I reluctantly laid the matter before the magistrates. 14. He never consented either to fawn upon the powerful, or to flatter the mob; he always relied on himself, and would[2] expose himself to any danger. 15. Famine is threatening us daily; the townsmen are urging the governor to surrender the city to the enemy; he refuses[3] to impart his resolution to me, and I am at a loss what to do.

---

[1] **149,** i.   [2] Imperfect. (See **184.**)   [3] See **136,** *a.*

DATIVE—*Continued.*

III. The Dative with Adjectives and Adverbs.

254. The dative is used not only with *verbs*, but also with **adjectives** (and even **adverbs**), to mark the person or thing *affected by the quality* which the adjective denotes.

Such are adjectives which signify *advantage, likeness, agreeableness, usefulness, fitness, facility,* etc. (with their *opposites*). So—

> *Res* populo[1] *grata.* A circumstance pleasing to the people.
> *Puer* patri *similis.* A child like his father.
> *Consilium* omnibus *utile.* A policy useful to all.
> *Tempora* virtutibus *infesta.* A time fatal to virtues.
> Convenienter naturae *vivendum est.* We should live agreeably to nature.

In all these cases the dative answers the question, *to* or *for* whom, or what? and the English will be a sufficient guide.

255. But the construction is not invariable.

Thus, *similis* takes the genitive of a *pronoun*, and usually of a *person* ("the counterpart," or "in the likeness," *of*). So—

> Pompeii, tui, *similis.* Resembling Pompey, *or* you.
> Veri *simile.* Probable.
> *Nulla res similis* sui *manet.* Nothing remains like itself.
So also—*Hoc quidem vitium non proprium senectutis est.* This vice is not the special property of old age.

Obs.—Many of these take different constructions: *utilis, aptus, idoneus,* ad *rem*; *benevolus* erga, or in, *aliquem*; *alienus* ab *aliquā re*: *assuetus, assuefactus,* "accustomed to," are joined with the ablative, *insuetus* with the genitive.

256. *Aequalis, affinis, vicinus, finitimus, propinquus, amicus, inimicus,* when used as *substantives*, are joined with the genitive, or a possessive pronoun (*meus, tuus,* etc.).

---

[1] Or *in vulgus*; the form *vulgo* is only used as an adverb.

Propior, nearer, *proximus*, nearest, take the *dative*, but sometimes the *accusative*, especially in their literal sense. Their adverbs *prope, propius, proxime*, take the accusative.

> *Hi homines* prope te *sedebant.* These men were sitting near you.

Thus, nobis *vicini*, "near us," but, *vicini* nostri, "*our* neighbours;" *Ciceron-is* or *-i inimicissimi*, Cicero's worst foes.

The construction therefore varies according as they are regarded as adjectives or substantives. (See **55.**)

Exercise 31.

1. I could not doubt that falsehood was most inconsistent with your brother's character. 2. All of us are apt to love those[1] like ourselves. 3. I fear that in so trying a time as[2] this so trifling a person[3] as your friend will not be likely to[4] turn out like his illustrious father. 4. This[5] circumstance was most acceptable to the mass of the people, but at the same time[6] most distasteful to the king. 5. He had long been an opponent of his father's policy, whom in (*abl.*) almost every point he himself most closely resembled. 6. He was both a relation of my father and his close friend from boyhood; he was also[6] extremely well disposed to myself. 7. For happiness, said he, which[7] all of us value above every blessing, is common to kings and herdsmen, rich and poor. 8. To others he was, it seemed,[8] most kindly disposed, but he was, I suspect,[8] his own worst enemy. 9. He is a man far removed from all suspicion of bribery, but I fear that he will not be acquitted by such an unprincipled judge as this. 10. It was, he used to say,[9] the special peculiarity of kings to envy men[10] who had done[11] them[12] the best service.

---

[1] See 346.   [2] 88, *Obs.*   [3] 224, *Obs.* 2.   [4] 139.
[9] Relative. (See 78.)   [6] *Idem.*   [7] 95, *Obs.*   [8] 32, *b*, and 43.
Tense? (184.)   [10] 72.   [11] Mood? (See 77.)   [12] *se.* (See 349.)

DATIVE—*Continued.*

IV. Special Uses of the Dative.

257. The following idiomatic uses of the dative should be carefully noticed.

The dative is used where we should use a *possessive pronoun* or the *genitive.*

It thus gives *greater prominence* to the person mentioned.

> *Tum* Pompeio *ad pedes se projecere.* Then they threw themselves at *Pompey's* feet.
>
> *Hoc* mihi *spem minuit.* This lowered *my* hopes.
>
> *Gladium* ei *e manibus extorsit.* He forced the sword out of *his* hands.
>
> *Hoc* omnibus *est in ore.* This is on *every one's* lips.

258. The dative of the person interested is sometimes used where we should use the preposition "by," answering to the ablative of the agent

(i.) It is joined with the participle in -*dus*, when used to imply duty or necessity. The person on whom the duty lies is in the dative. (See **198,** iii.)

> *Hoc* tibi *faciendum fuit.* "This ought to have been done *by* you."

(ii.) The dative is used with other passive participles where the agent is looked on rather as the *person interested* than as the actual *agent;* especially with verbs of *seeing, thinking, hearing, planning,* etc.

> *Haec omnia* mihi perspecta *et* considerata *sunt.* All these points have been studied and weighed *by* me, lit. *for me, in my eyes.*
>
> *Hoc mihi* probatum *ac* laudatum *est.* This has won my approval and praise = been approved of and praised *by* me.

259. The last idiomatic use of the dative is that in which it is used to express a *result* or *aim;* two ideas often blended in Latin. (See **106.**)

> *Receptui canere.* To sound the trumpet *for* retreat.
> *Hunc locum* domicilio *eligo.* I choose this place *for* my habitation.[1]

It is much used with *sum, do, duco, verto, eligo;* and (especially with military terms, as *auxilio, subsidio*) with verbs of motion; and is generally combined with the ordinary dative. Thus—

> *Haec res* ei magno *fuit* dedecori. This was (*or* proved) a great disgrace to him.
> *Ipse* sibi odio *erit.* He will be odious (*or,* an object of dislike) to himself = be *hated by* himself.
> *Noli hanc rem* mihi vitio *vertere.* Do not impute this to me *as a fault.*
> *Quae res* saluti nobis *fuit.* And this fact saved us, *proved* our *safety.*
> *Caesarem oravit, ut* sibi auxilio *copias adduceret.* He begged Caesar to bring up troops *to his aid.*

Obs. Hence such verbs as "*proves,*" "*serves,*" etc., may often be translated by *sum* with the *dative;* and an adjective after "*to be*" may often be translated into Latin by the *dative* of a substantive.

260. The following phrases are very commonly used with an additional dative of the *person interested.*

(1.) With *auxilio* (to the assistance);

> *Come,* vĕnire, vēni, ventum.
> *Send,* mittere, mīsi, missum.
> *Set out,* prŏficisci, profectus.

(2.) With *culpae, vitio, crimini;*

> *To impute as a fault,* culpae dăre : *with* acc. of thing; *or* vitio vertĕre, *with* acc. of thing.

(3.) *To give as a present,* dono, *or* muneri, dare, *with* acc. of thing.
> *To consider a source of gain,* habere quaestui.
> *To be very dishonourable or discreditable to,* magno esse dedecori. (*Obs.* 1.)
> *To be hated by; to be hateful,* odio esse. (*Obs.* 2.)
> *To be a hindrance,* impedimento esse.
> *To be creditable, or honourable,* honori esse.

---

[1] *Te* ducem eligamus, apposition with a *person,* "as or *for* our leader," see **239** : *hunc locum* domicilio *eligo,* dative with a *thing,* "as or *for* our habitation."

To be hurtful; to be detrimental, detrīmento, *or* damno esse.
To be painful to, dolori esse.
To be a proof, argumento, documento esse.
To profit, to be profitable to, bono esse.
To bring punishment, fraudi esse.
To be a reproach; to be disgraceful, opprobrio esse.

Obs. 1.—The English adverb *very* will be represented in Latin by the adjective *magno* or *summo;* "how" by *quanto.*

Quanto *hoc tibi sit* dedecori *vides.* You see *how* disgraceful this is to you.

Obs. 2.—The phrase "*odio esse*" forms a passive voice to *odi.* Thus Hannibal, when at the close of his life he expresses to Antiochus his hatred to the Romans, says (Livy xxxv. 19) :—

Odi odioque *sum* Romanis. I hate the Romans and am *hated by them.*

261. The dative in the predicate with *licet,* etc., has been noticed (**201**).

Liceat nobis *quietis* esse. Let us be allowed to be at rest.

So *sometimes* after *nomen est,* etc.

Puero cognomen *Iulo* additur. The surname of Iulus is added to the boy.

But *Iulus* would be equally good Latin.

Exercise 32.

In these Exercises words and phrases marked * will be found in **260.**

A.

1. He promises to come shortly to the assistance * of your countrymen. 2. Thereupon he forced the bloody dagger out of the assassin's[1] hand. 3. I fear that these things will not prove very creditable * to you. 4. I don't quite understand what your friends[2] mean (by it). 5. It is very honourable * to you to have been engaged in such (86) a battle. 6. Such (87) superstition is undoubtedly a reproach * to a man. 7. I fear that this will prove both detrimental * and dishonourable * to the government. 8. Cassius was wont to ask[3] who had gained by the result.

---

[1] Genitive not to be used. (See **257.**)   [2] **338,** *Obs.* 2.
[3] Frequentative form, *rogito.* Tense? (See **184.**)

9. It is vile to consider politics a source * of gain. 10. I would fain inquire what place you have chosen for your dwelling. 11. I am afraid that this will be very painful * and disgraceful * to you. 12. I will warn the boy what (*quantus*) a reproach * it is to break one's word. 13. He promised to give them the island of Cyprus as a present. 14. I hope that he will perceive how odious * cruelty is to all men. 15. Then the ambassadors of the Gauls threw themselves at Caesar's feet. 16. It seems that he hates * our nation and is hated * by us. 17. I hope soon to come to your aid with three legions.

B.

1. He gives his word to take care that the ambassadors shall be allowed to depart home in safety. 2. To this prince, owing to a temperament (which was) almost intolerable to the rest of the world, (men) had given the name of the Proud. 3. And this circumstance is a proof * that no[1] Roman took part in that contest. 4. So many and so great are your illustrious brother's (224) achievements that they have by this time been heard of, praised and read of by the whole world. 5. We know that the name of deserters is hated * and considered execrable by all the world; but we earnestly implore that this our change of sides may bring us neither punishment * nor credit.* 6. Not even (Intr. 99) in a time of universal[2] repose were we allowed to enjoy repose. 7. I can scarcely believe that so monstrous a design as this has been heard of and approved by you. 8. This circumstance, which is now in every one's mouth, he communicated to me yesterday ; I suspect it concerns you more than me. 9. When my colleague comes[3] to my assistance * I can[4] supply you with provisions and arms.

---

[1] See **223**.   [2] See **59**.   [3] See **190**.   [4] Tense ? (**190**, ii.)

THE ABLATIVE.

262. The **Ablative** is more than any other an **adverbial** case; (read carefully **211**). It answers the questions *whence? by what means? how? from what cause? in what manner? when?* and *where?*

Its various meanings may be thus classified :—

> (i.) Removal, or departure; *from (casus* ablativus). (Answers the question *whence.*)
> (ii.) Instrumentality; *by, with.*
> (iii.) Accompaniment; *with*, etc.
> (iv.) Locality; *at* or *in* a *place* or *time.* (Answers the question *where* or *when.*)

Obs.—It therefore represents four distinct cases, the last of which certainly, others in all probability, once existed as separate forms.

263. (i.) Ablative of **removal** or **departure** from.

In most instances, either by itself, or with the prepositions *a, ab; ex, e; de*, it corresponds to the English *from.*

It is so used with verbs expressing literal motion.

> Troja *profecti sunt.* They set out *from* Troy. (Name of *town*, see 9.)
> A *Pyrrho*, ex *Africa, legati veniunt.* Ambassadors come *from* Pyrrhus *from* Africa.

264. It is thus used also with **many** other verbs without, as well as with, a preposition. The preposition is mostly omitted where no merely bodily motion is implied.

> *Abstinere* injuria, to abstain *from* wrong; *abire* magistratu, go *out of* office; *desistĕre* conatu, to abandon or cease *from* an attempt; *cedĕre* patria, to leave his native land; *pellĕre* civitate, to banish.

So also with verbs implying " freeing from," and " depriving."

> *Solvit te his* legibus *Senatus.* The Senate exempts you *from* those laws.
> *Liberat te* aere alieno. He sets you free *from* debt.

But very often the preposition is used.

> *Discedant* ab *armis.* Let them depart *from* arms.
> *Abhorret* ab *ejusmodi culpā.* He is far removed *from* such blame.

176

265. Not only verbs but **adjectives**[1] signifying *want* or *freedom from* are joined with the *ablative,* or sometimes the *ablative* with *a* or *ab.*

> Metu *vacuus.* Free *from* fear. (Compare culpā *vacat,* he is free *from* fault.)
> *Loca sunt* ab arbitris *libera.* The locality is free *from* witnesses.
> Ab *ejusmodi* scelere *alienissimus.* Quite incapable *of* (removed *from*) such a crime.

266. (ii.) The ablative of **source** or **origin**, a very similar sense to that of *departure* from, is used mostly, though not always, without the preposition.

> Consulari familiā *ortus.* Sprung *from* a consular family.
> *Homo* optimis parentibus *natus.* A man *of* excellent parentage.

Obs.—Ortus, oriundus, when used of *remote* ancestors, are joined with the preposition *ab.*

267. (iii.) The ablative of **instrument**, and also that of (iv.) **cause,** may be considered as nearly related to that of *origin.*

> Cornibus *tauri se tutantur.* Bulls protect themselves *with* their horns.
> *Jam vires* lassitudine *deficiebant.* Their strength was now beginning to fail *through* (or *from*) weariness.

(v.) With the **agent,** *i.e.* a *person* as opposed to a *thing,* the preposition is necessary.

> *Clitus* ab Alexandro gladio *interfectus est.* (See 8, *a.*)

*Obs.—*A secondary agent, *i.e.* a *person* used as an instrument, is expressed by *per* (or *operā* with the genitive or the possessive pronoun).

> *Haec* per exploratores *cognita sunt.* These facts were ascertained by means of reconnoiterers.
> *Tuā* operā. By your instrumentality.

So *propter* and *ob* are still more often used than the ablative to express the *cause.* The ablative is mostly confined to a bodily, or mental, or other property of the *subject of the verb.* Tuā fortitudine *hoc meruisti;* but, propter tuam fortitudinem *hoc decrevit senatus.*

---

[1] In the same way *adverbs* are constantly joined with adjectives. (Intr. 17.) Compare also the use of the dative, **254.**

268. (vi.) The ablative of **manner** is nearly related to that of *instrument* and *cause*, and is very widely used.

Hac ratione, hoc modo, by this means, *in* this manner; *summo opere,* earnestly; *casu, by* chance; *nullo modo, by* no means; *consilio, by* design; *jure,* rightly; *injuriā,* unjustly; *nescio quo pacto, in* some way or other; and many others.

Obs.—Many of these are used exactly as adverbs; they only differ from adverbs as being more obviously, what other adverbs were originally, *oblique cases* of substantives.

The preposition *in* is never used in Latin before words signifying *manner :* thus, never "in *hoc modo.*"

269. (vii.) The ablative of **accompaniment**[1] when applied to *things* can hardly be distinguished from that of *manner.* The rule is to use the preposition *cum* unless an emphatic adjective is added.

We can say, Summā *haec diligentiā feci,* "I have done this with the *greatest* care," and we *may,* but need not, insert *cum.* But we cannot say, *Haec* diligentiā *feci,* "I have done this with care;" nor *lacrimis,* for "with tears."

Cum *dignitate mori satius est quam* cum *ignominia vivere.* It is better to die *with* honour than to live *under* disgrace.

Obs.—With the following phrases *cum* is never used.

Hoc consilio, with this intention; *aequo animo, with* calmness, or resignation; *jussu tuo, by* your command; *injussu Caesaris, without* Caesar's permission; *bonā tuā veniā, with* your kind permission; *nullo negotio,* without trouble. But cum *emolumento,* or cum *damno, meo, to* my advantage, or loss.

270. Where however the English *with* is used in the literal sense of (viii.) "**in company with**," the preposition is required[2] both with persons and things.

Cum *fratre meo veni.* I came *with* my brother.
Cum *telo venit.* He came *with* a weapon.
Tecum, mecum, nobiscum, vobiscum, ibit. He will go with you, me, us, you. (8, *Obs.*)

---

[1] The English preposition *with* marks the connexion between the different senses of *instrument, manner,* and *accompaniment.* "I killed him *with* a sword," "I did it *with* ease," "I spoke *with* sorrow," "I came *with* you."

[2] In military language, an army is sometimes looked on as standing in an *instrumental* relation to its general : *Dux* reliquo exercitu *contra hostem proficiscitur;* but even here the *cum* is mostly inserted.

271. Under this head of *accompaniment* is to be classed (ix.) the *ablative* of **quality**.

> Eximiā *fuit corporis* pulchritudine. He was a man of great personal beauty.

Obs.—Here again the adjective is necessary. See below, Gen. of Quality, **303.**

We have thus far had instances of the ablative used to denote *removal from, origin, instrument, cause, agent, manner,* and *accompaniment* of circumstances, things, persons, and qualities.

Exercise 33

A.

1. He replied that nearly the whole of the army was annihilated, and[1] that it made no difference whether it had been overwhelmed by famine, or by pestilence, or by the enemy. 2. Having been chosen king not only by his own soldiers, but also by the popular[2] vote,[3] he aimed at establishing and securing by the arts of peace a throne gained by the sword[4] and violence. 3. Sprung as he was from an illustrious family, he entered public life as[5] a young man, and retired at last from office as an old one. 4. Freed from the fear of foreign war, the nation was now[6] able to drive traitors from its territory, and show its gratitude to patriots. 5. Whether[7] your unprincipled relation has abandoned this attempt, or intends (14, *c*) to persevere in it, I know not; but whether[7] he means to take one course[8] or the other, it seems to me that he is not yet willing to abstain from wrong. 6. So far is my unfortunate brother from having been freed from debt, that he is even now leaving his country for[9] no other cause.

---

[1] Why not *et nihil?* (See 110.)
[2] "Of the people." (See **59.**)
[3] Plural. Compare p. 72, *n.* 2.
[4] Why not *gladio?* (See 17.)
[5] "As" not to be expressed; why would *velut, quasi,* be wrong?
[6] *Jam ; nunc* is "at *this present* moment."
[7] "Whether." (See **171.**)
[8] = to do this, or that.
[9] *Propter* (acc.).

B.

1. I would fain ask, with your kind permission, whether it [1] was by accident, or by design that you acted [2] thus. 2. We set forth from home with tears, with wailing, and with the deepest anxiety; we reached the end of our journey relieved of a load of cares, free from fear, and amidst great and universal rejoicing. 3. He is a man of the most spotless character, and so far removed from such a crime that for my part, I wonder [3] how he can have been suspected of such monstrous impiety. 4. We had rather die with honour than live as slaves (42, ii.); but we refuse to perish in this manner for the sake of such [4] a person as this. 5. I might have [5] faced death itself without trouble, but I cannot endure such a heavy disaster as this [6] with resignation. 6. He was so transported with passion that he threatened not only his brother, but all the bystanders, with death.

---

[1] See **156**.

[2] =did this ; avoid using *agere* for "to act," and notice the real meanings of *agere*.   [3] Mood ? (See **106**.)

[4] See **87**. *Talis* is rarely used contemptuously.

[5] See **196**.   [6] **88**, *Obs.*

ABLATIVE—*Continued.*

272. Other senses of the ablative belong to it as having taken the place in a great degree of the nearly obsolete **locative** case, answering, not the question *whence?*, but *where?*

Obs.—This case, which ended in *i*, so often resembled *in form* the ablative after the latter had lost its final letter *d*, that at last the ablative added to its many other meanings those which properly belonged to the locative, and the same case came to represent *whence* and *where*.

Local uses of the ablative may include those which denote *at a place*, and *at a time*. (See **9**, *a*, and below, **311** and **320**.)

Pericles Athenis *vixit*. Die septimo *venit*.

273. Such too are the phrases, *terrā marique*, by sea and land; *dextrā,* (or *a dextrā*), *sinistrā*, on the right, left, hand; *bello et pace*, in war and peace; *nocte, hieme, primā luce*, etc.; so also *aeger* pedibus, suffering in the feet; altero *saucius* brachio, wounded in one arm.

Obs.—The preposition *in* sometimes makes a slight difference in the meaning; *tali tempore*, simply, *at* such a time, or moment; *in tali tempore, considering the circumstances of* such a time, or emergency, *in spite of*, or *in the face of*, such a crisis.

For the Ablative Absolute, which includes the ideas both of *time* and *accompanying circumstances*, see Exercise LIII.

274. With the *local* ablative may be compared the ablative of **respect** or **limitation**; the English *in*, in the sense of "in so far as concerns," etc.

Specie, in appearance; *re, re ipsā*, in reality; *nomine*, in name.
Lingua, moribus, *armorum* genere *inter se discrepabant*. They differed from one another *in* language, habits, and *in* the nature of their arms.

Obs.—To this use of the ablative belongs the supine in *-u*.
Horrendum dictu. Dreadful *in the telling*. (See **404**.)

181

275. The ablative of **comparison** (or *difference from*) belongs (probably) to the ablative of *departure from.*

In English, a comparative adjective or adverb is connected by the conjunction *than* (originally *then*) with the clause or word with which the comparison is made : He is older *than* he was ; He is more *than* twenty years old.

In Latin also, *quam* is the regular particle of comparison. As it is a *conjunction,* and not a *preposition,* things compared by *quam* will be in the same case.

> *Europa minor est,* quam *Asiă.*   Europe is smaller than Asia.
> *Dixit Europam minorem esse* quam *Asiam.*   He said that Europe was smaller than Asia.
> *A nullo libentius* quam *a te litteras accipio.*   I receive a letter from no one with more pleasure than from you.

276. But in Latin, where two nouns are closely compared with one another, the ablative of comparison, or thing *differed from,* is widely used ; an idiom quite unlike English.

> Hoc homine *nihil contemptius esse potest.*   Nothing can be more despicable *than* this man.
> *Haec nonne* luce *clariora sunt ?*   Are not these things clearer *than* the daylight ?

We should probably say "*so* despicable *as,*" "*as* clear *as.*"

Obs.—This construction however is only used when the comparative adjective is in the nominative, or the accusative after a verb *sentiendi vel declarandi.* It is exceedingly common in *negative* and *interrogative* sentences, as above.

277. The ablative of comparison is largely used after comparative adjectives and adverbs, with such words as *spes, opinio, fama, expectatio,* even *justum* and *aequum.*

> Spe *omnium* celerius *venit.*   He came sooner than any one had hoped.
> *Ne* plus justo *dolueris.*   Do not feel *undue* pain.

278. "Superior *to,*" "inferior *to,*" may be expressed in Latin by this ablative.

> *Omnia* virtute inferiora *ducit.*   He counts everything *inferior to* (of lower rank than) goodness.
> *Negant quenquam* te fortiorem *esse.*   They say that no one is *your superior* in courage.

Nemo tibi virtute praestat would be also good Latin for "no one is, *etc.*"

279. Another ablative often joined with comparatives is that of the **measure of difference**, and is clearly *instrumental.*

> *Multo me doctior.*   *Greatly* my superior in learning.
> *Homo* paulo *sapientior.*   A man of *somewhat* more wisdom than is common; "of fair, *or* average, wisdom."
> *Senatus* paulo *frequentior.*   A *somewhat* crowded senate.

Caution.—These ablative forms, *paulo, multo, eo, tanto,* etc., must never be used with adjectives or adverbs in the positive degree.   Compare the use of *quo* (**102**).

But they may be used with words which, though not comparative in form, imply comparison.

> *Paulo* ante.   A little before, *or* earlier.
> *Multo tibi* praestat.   He is much superior to you.

280. The ablative of **price**, "for," "at such a rate," may be either local (*at*), or instrumental (*by means of*).

It is used with verbs of **buying** and **selling**, etc., *emere, vendere,* etc.

> *Viginti* talentis *unam orationem Isocrates* vendidit.   Isocrates sold one oration *for* twenty talents.

So with verbs of exchanging.

> *Pacem* bello *mutavit.*   He exchanged peace *for* war.

Obs.—The adjectives *magno, parvo, nimio, quanto,* etc., are generally used by themselves, the substantive *pretio* being understood.

> *Venditori expĕdit rem* vēnire *quam* plurimo.   It is for the interest of the seller that the thing should be sold for, *or* at, as high a price as possible.
> *Multo* sanguine *victoria nobis stetit,* or, *constitit.*   The victory cost us much blood.

Verbs of *valuing, esteeming,* etc., as distinct from actual *buying,* take the genitive.   (See **305**.)

Exercise 34.

1. It is pretty well agreed on by all of you that the sun is many times[1] larger than the moon. 2. I have known this man from boyhood; I believe him to be greatly your superior both in courage and learning. 3. The king himself, while he was[2] fighting in front of the foremost line of battle, was wounded in the head. In spite of this[3] great confusion and universal panic, he refused to withdraw from the contest. 4. By this means he became rightly dear to the nation,[4] and reached the extremity of old age in name a private citizen, in reality almost the parent of his country. 5. And[5] this crime must be at once atoned for by your blood, for your[6] guilty deeds are clear and plain as[7] this sun-light, and[8] it is quite impossible that any member of the nation can wish you pardoned. 6. It seems[9] to me, said he, that all of you are soldiers in name, deserters and brigands in reality. 7. The battle[10] was now much more desperate; on the left our men were beginning to fail through weariness; the general, himself wounded in one arm, was the first to become aware of this. 8. You might[11] but lately have exchanged war for peace; too late (*adv.*) to-day are you repenting of your blunder. 9. I was anxious yesterday for your safety; but the matter has turned out much better than I had looked for. 10. How much better would[12] it have been in the presence of such a crisis to have held all considerations inferior to the national safety.

---

[1] " *Parts.*" For case, see **279**.   [2] See **180**.   [3] **88**, *Obs.*
[4] Or country. (See **16**, *a.*)   [5] Intr. **58**.   [6] Iste. (See **338**.)
[7] See **276**.   [8] =nor is it possible. (See **110**, and **125**, *f.*)
[9] **43**.   [10] **218**   [11] **196, 197**.   [12] **153**.

ABLATIVE—*Continued.*

281. The ablative is also used to complete the sense of certain **deponent** verbs.

Fungor, fruor, ūtor (with their compounds), *pŏtior, vescor, dignor, glorior,* take the *ablative.*

> *Hannibal, cum* victoriā *posset* uti, frui *maluit.* Hannibal at a time when [1] (although) he might have used his victory preferred enjoying it.
>
> *Mortis* periculo defuncti *sumus.* We have got over the danger of death.
>
> *Nostri* victoriā potiti *sunt.* Our soldiers gained the victory.

Obs.—This ablative is of course not that of the *nearer object;* but these deponent verbs resemble in their use Greek verbs of the *middle voice. Utor,* I serve myself *with; fruor,* I enjoy myself *with; vescor,* I feed myself *on; potior,* I make myself powerful *with; fungor,* I discharge myself *from; dignor,* I hold myself worthy *at such a price; glorior,* I glorify myself *with:* so that the ablative is in each case used in one or other of its regular *adverbial* uses. (See **228,** *Obs.*)

282. Of these verbs, *potior* sometimes takes the genitive, "I am master *of.*" *Utor* is freely used with adverbs ; *male, perverse, immoderate, utor,* "I make a bad, or immoderate use of," = "I abuse." The Latin adverb must be substituted for the English adjective.

> *Te* familiariter, *te* amico usus sum. I was on intimate terms with you, I found a friend in you.

Obs.—*Gloriari* is used also with *in* and *de; niti,* "to lean, or rely on," with and without *in. Confido* with dat. of person (always dat. of personal pronoun), ablative of thing. Tibi *confisus sum; exercitūs* virtute *confido.* (**244,** c.)

---

[1] Or, "*instead of* using his victory preferred to enjoy it."

283. Compare also with the English idiom the use of the ablative to complete the sense of certain transitive verbs.

> Honore, praemio, *te affeci.*   I conferred on you a distinction, a reward.
> Poenā, supplicio, *eum afficiam.*   I will inflict punishment on him (= *poenas de eo sumam*).
> Honoribus *te cumulavimus.*   We have heaped or showered honours on you.
> Omni observantia *eum prosecutus sum.*   I have paid him every kind of respect.   (Cf. **247.**)

284. Verbs of *abounding, filling, loading,* etc., and their opposites, such as verbs of *being without, depriving of, emptying of,* are joined with the *ablative.*

> Such verbs are *circumfluere* (divitiis), *complēre, onerare, refercire, cumulare* (honoribus), *carēre, egēre, vacare* (cuipâ) *orbare, privare, fraudare.*

> > *Flumen piscibus* abundat.   The river is *full of* fish.
> > *Mortui cura et dolore* carent.   The dead are *free from* anxiety and pain.

> But of these *egeo* and *indigeo* (especially the latter) govern the *genitive* also ; as also *complēre, replēre.*

> > *Res maxime necessariae non tam* artis *indigent quam* labōris. The most necessary things do not require skill so much as labour.

Obs.—In verbs of *abounding,* etc., the ablative is no doubt *instrumental.* Its original sense with verbs of *want* is more doubtful ; probably that of *separation,* freedom *from.*

285. The ablative is joined also with adjectives, in many of its various senses.   (See **265.**)
Dignus, indignus, contentus, praeditus, frētus are followed by an ablative without a preposition.

> *Vir omni honore* dignus.   A man worthy of every distinction.
> *Divitiis opibusque* fretus.   Relying on his wealth and resources.

Be careful not to use a genitive after *dignus.*

286. The ablative of the noun, and occasionally of the participle, is also used with *opus* (and *usus*) when they bear the sense of *need of.*

> *Ubi res adsunt, quid mihi* verbis *opus est ?* When facts are here, what need have I of *words ?*
>
> *Ait sibi* consulto *opus esse.* He says he has need of *deliberation.*

Sometimes the thing needed is the subject to *opus est.*

> Dux *nobis et* auctor *opus est.* We need a leader and adviser.

This indeed is the rule with neuter pronouns and adjectives :—
Quae *nobis opus sunt;* pauca *tibi opus sunt;* omnia, quae *ad vitam opus sunt,* "all the necessaries of life." The infinitive is also used :—

> *Quid haec* scribere *opus est ?* What need is there to write this ?

Obs.—Opus properly means "work (to be done)," and the ablative is the ablative of respect,—"there is work to be done for me *in consultation.*"

Exercise 35.

A.

1. I have now lived long on most intimate terms with your son; it seems to me that he resembles his father in ability and character, rather than in either features or personal appearance. 2. Do[1] not deprive (*pl.*) of well-earned distinction and praise one who has made so good,[2] so sensible, a use of the favours of heaven. 3. I cannot[3] but believe that it is[4] by your instrumentality that I have got over this great danger. 4. All of us, your well-wishers, make this one prayer, that you may be permitted to discharge the duties of your office with[5] honour and advantage to yourself; we all rely on your honesty and self-control, and are all proud of your friendship. 5. Relying on your support, I have ventured to inflict severe punishment on the rebels. 6. He always put confidence in himself, and in[6] spite of humble means and scanty fare preferred contentment (**98,** *a*) to resting[7] on other men's resources. 7. He preferred dispensing with all the necessaries of life (as) a free man, to abounding in riches in the condition of a slave.

---

[1] **143.**   [2] **282.**   [3] **137,** *j.*
[4] See **82.** The periphrasis *factum esse ut* may be used for emphasis.
[5] **269.**   [6] **273,** *Obs.*   [7] See **94.**

B.

1. He promises to supply us with everything that is [1] necessary.   2. We have need of deliberation rather than haste, for I fear that this victory has already cost us too much.   3. In my youth I enjoyed the friendship of your illustrious father; he was a man of remarkable abilities, and of the highest character.   4. He hopes to visit with condign punishment the murderers of his father and the conspirators against their sovereign.   5. I fear that he seems far from worthy of all [2] the compassion and indulgence of which he stands in need to-day.   6. Nothing can ever be imagined more happy than my father's lot in life; he discharged the duties of the highest office without [3] failing to enjoy the charms of family life. 7. Relying on your good-will, I have not hesitated [4] to avail myself of the letter which you sent me by [5] my son. 8. Can any one be more worthy of honour, more unworthy of punishment, than this man ?

---

[1] Mood, see **77**.   [2] Tantus . . . quantus.
[3] See **111**, "so discharged as to enjoy."   [4] See **136**, *b*.   [5] **267**, *Obs.*

GENITIVE.

Two of the main uses of the Genitive, or *defining* case, are—·

The **Possessive**; where the genitive denotes the person or thing to which some other person or thing belongs.

The **Partitive**; where the genitive denotes the relation of a whole to a part.

I. Possessive Genitive.

287. The **Genitive** differs from all other cases (including the obsolete **Locative**) in being **rarely used with verbs**. The proper office of a noun in the genitive is to define, or give the *genus* of, another noun. (See **214.**)

288. It does this in various ways; and the relation between one noun and another, as denoted in the Latin genitive, may be very variously expressed in English : by the *possessive case*, by various *prepositions*, and by the *adjective.* Thus—

> *Libri* Ciceronis, Cicero's books; hominum *optimus*, the best *of* men; mortis *fuga*, flight *from* death; Helvetiorum *injuriae* populi Romani, the wrongs done *by* the Helvetii *to* the people of Rome; mortis *remedium*, a remedy *against* death ; *fossa* quindecim pedum, a bridge fifteen feet *wide;* legum *obedientia*, obedience *to* law; corporis *robur, bodily* strength ; amissi filii *dolor*, pain *for* the loss of his son.

In these instances the genitives express a close connexion between two substantives; but a connexion of very different kinds; in all **the word in the genitive explains and defines the other word.**

289. As being most properly that case in which one noun is attached, or annexed, to another, which it explains, it may be called the **adjectival case**, and in fact often corresponds exactly to the adjective. (See 58.)

> Caesaris *causā*, meā *causā*, on behalf of Caesar, on my behalf; tuā *operā*, illius *operā*, with your, *or* his, aid ; so Sullani *milites=*Sullae *milites.*

290. Of these, the strictly **possessive** use will cause no difficulty ; it answers to the English possessive case in *s* (the only real *case* remaining in the English substantive), to the preposition *of*, to the *possessive pronoun*, and to the *adjective.*

> Pompeii *aequalis ac* meus.   *Pompey's* contemporary and *my own.*
> Noster *atque* omnium *parens*.   *Our own*, and the *universal* parent.
> *Sceptrum* regis (*or* regium).   The *king's* sceptre.
> *Illud* Platonis.   That saying *of* Plato.

Obs.—Under this may be classed such expressions as tui *similis*, Ciceronis *inimicissimi* (see **256**); also Pompeii *causā, gratiā*, in the interest *of*, for the sake *of*, Pompey (meā, tuā, not mei, tui) ; and even sui juris, suae ditionis *facere*, to *bring under* his own jurisdiction, *or* power.

291. To this possessive and adjectival genitive belongs also the following construction :—

The **genitive singular** of a *substantive*, especially when it can denote a class (as *puer*, *rex*) or of an *adjective* used as a substantive (*stultus, sapiens*), or of an *abstract noun* (*levitas, stultitia*) or of a *pronoun*, is often used as a predicate with a copulative verb to denote such English ideas as " property," " duty," " part," " mark," etc.

Obs. 1.—This construction takes the place of the neuter adjective, especially in adjectives of one termination.
" It is foolish" *may* be translated *stultum est ;* but *stulti* is much more usual ; " it is wise" is always *sapientis*, or *sapientiae*, *est*, never *sapiens*, which might mean "a wise *man.*" **Latin is rarely ambiguous.**

Obs. 2.—In the place of the personal pronouns the neuter of the possessive is used.

> *Meum* (*not* mei) *est*, it is *my part*, or *duty*, or it is *for me to*. etc.

Obs. 3.—The same construction is used after verbs *sentiendi* et *declarandi.*

> *Hoc* sapientis esse *dixit.* This, he said, was the wise course, (lit. *the part* of a wise man).

Obs. 4.—This genitive may be translated into English in various ways : and therefore there are various English phrases that may be reduced to this construction.

Such phrases are: *it is characteristic of; it is incumbent on; it is for* (the rich, etc.) ; *it is not every one* who ; *any man* may ; *it demands or requires; it betrays, shows,* etc. ; *it belongs to ; it depends upon ; it tends to,* etc.

292. Examples—

1. Imbecilli animi *est superstitio.* Superstition is a *mark* of (or *betrays*) a weak mind.
2. Judicis *est legibus parere.* It is the *part* (or *duty*) of a judge to obey the law.
3. Ingenii *hoc* magni *est.* This *requires* great abilities.
4. Cujusvis hominis *est errare.* Any man *may* err.
5. Meum *est.* It is my *business,* or *duty.*
6. Summae *est* dementiae. *It is* the height of madness.
7. *Tempori cedere semper* sapientis *est habitum.* It has always been held *a wise thing* to yield to circumstances, *or* to temporise.
8. *Hoc* dementiae *esse* summae *dixit.* He said that this *showed* the height of madness.
9. *Hoc* sui *esse* arbitrii *negavit.* He said that this did not *depend upon* his own decision.

Obs.—To this belongs a phrase common in Livy—

> *Hoc* evertendae *esse* reipublicae,[1] *dixit.* He said that this *tended to* the destruction of the constitution.

Exercise 36.

1. Whether you (*pl.*) will be[2] slaves or free, depends upon your own decision. 2. We know that any man may err, but it is foolish to forget that error is one thing, persistency (98, *a*) in error another. 3. He brought under his own jurisdiction, sooner than he had hoped, the privileges and liberty of all his countrymen. 4. Living[3]

---

[1] The various meanings of this phrase *res publica* (often written as one word) should be carefully noticed. It should never be translated by "republic," but by "the constitution," "the nation," "politics," "public life," etc., according to the context, and should never be used in the plural unless when it means more than one "state" or "nation."

[2] **173,** iii.   [3] See **94.**

for the day only, (and) making no provision for the future was, he said,[1] rather the characteristic of barbarians than of a free nation.   5. Your father's contemporaries were,[2] he said, his own, and none (110) of them had[2] been dearer to him than your uncle.   6. In my absence I did not cease to do everything in your interest and (that) of your excellent brother.   7. A sensible man will[3] yield, says he, to circumstances, but it is the height of folly to pay attention to threats of this kind.   8. Whether we have won the day or no (168, *Obs.*) I hardly dare[4] say; it is, I know,[5] a soldier's duty to wait for his general's orders.   9. It will be[6] for others to draw up and bring forward laws, it is our part to obey the law.   10. You were, he said, evading the law which you had[7] yourself got enacted; a course which, he believed, tended to[8] the overthrow of the constitution.

---

[1] **32**, *b.*   [2] "Were." For tenses, see **193**, i., ii.
[3] =it is the part of a, etc.   [4] Subjunctive.   (**149**, i.)
[5] See **32**, *b.*   [6] **291**, *Obs.* 4.
[7] Mood?   (See **77**.)   [8] **292**, *Obs.*

GENITIVE—*Continued.*

The Partitive Genitive.

293. A word in the genitive often stands to another word in the relation, not of a possessor, but of a **whole** to a **part**. This is called the **partitive genitive**, and is very widely used.

This genitive answers to the English "*of*," after substantives denoting a part, in such phrases as *magna pars* exercitūs, and is used, like that preposition, with *superlative adjectives* and *adverbs*, with interrogative and other *pronouns*, with *numerals*, and with any word which can denote in any way *a part of a larger whole*, such as *nemo, quisquam, multi, pauci, uterque, quisque,* etc.   Thus—

> *Unus*[1] *omnium* infelicissimus, the most unfortunate *of* all mankind ; *tu* maxime *omnium*, you most *of* all ; uter *vestrum*, which *of* you two ; multi *horum*, many *of* these ; duo horum, two *of* these ; quotusquisque *philosophorum*, how few (*of*) philosophers.

294. A more idiomatic use of this genitive is with the **neuter singular** of adjectives and pronouns expressing *quantity* or *degree*, and with *nihil, satis, parum.* These are used as **quasi-substantives**, and are joined with the genitive of substantives and adjectives, an idiom not unknown in English, but exceedingly common in Latin.

Compare Latin and English in—

> Quantum *voluptatis,* how much pleasure ; plus *detrimenti,* greater loss ; nihil *praemii,* no reward ; satis, *or* parum, *virium,* sufficient, *or* insufficient strength ; quid *novi?* what news ? nimium *temporis,* too much time ; hoc *emolumenti,* this (*of*) gain.

Obs.—This genitive is even used with **adverbs**: tum *temporis,* at that time ; eo *audaciae,* to such a pitch of boldness ; ubi *gentium,* where in the world ? and in such adverbial phrases as cum *id* aetatis *puero, ad id* locorum, up to that point (of time).   (See **238,** iii.)

---

[1] Note this **intensive** use of *unus* with the superlative.

295. Cautions in the use of the partitive genitive.

(*a*) It is not used with adjectives where the genitive has no separate form for the neuter gender : write *nihil humile*, not *nihil humilis*, for " nothing degrading."

(*b*) It is not used with adjectives expressing the *whole, middle*, etc. : *tota, media*, urbs, not urbis *totum, medium*, for " the whole," " middle of the city " (**60**).

(*c*) It is not used with words joined with *prepositions*, or with other cases than the *nominative* and *accusative*.

> *Ad multam noctem.*   To a late hour, not *ad multum noctis*.
> *Tanto sanguine*, not *tanto sanguinis*.   At the cost of (**280**) so much blood.

296. With **numerals**, and words expressing *number*, as *nemo, multi, unus, pauci*, etc., and even with superlatives, the ablative with *ex, e, de*, or *inter* with the accusative, is often substituted ; *multi, nemo, unus* e vobis, for *unus*, etc. vestrum.

Obs.—Where *the whole* is a numeral, or contains a numeral or adjective expressing number or quantity, the preposition is always used.

> De tot millibus *vix pauci superfuere*.   Of so many thousands scarcely a few survived.

297. Further Cautions.—The *partitive genitive* is only used to denote a larger amount than the word with which it is joined.

If the two words denote the **same persons**, or the **same amount**, *apposition* is used.   (Nos) *omnes*, " all *of* us " (*i.e.* " we all").   *Equites*, qui *pauci aderant*, the cavalry, few *of* whom were there (lit. who were there *in small numbers*).   (See **225** and **69**.)

298. (*a*) *Uterque* is used as a substantive with pronouns ; but with substantives it is treated as an adjective.

> *Uterque* vestrum ; but frater *uterque*.

(*b*) To the partitive genitive belong the phrases :—

> *Nihil* reliqui fecit.   He left nothing remaining.
> *Nihil* pensi habuit.   He cared not at all.
> *Quid hoc* rei *est ?*   What is the meaning of this ?

1. There was[1] nothing mean in this sovereign, nothing
base, nothing degrading; little learning (but[2]) fair ability,
some experience of life and a dash of eloquence, much
good sense, abundance of honesty and strength of mind.
2. Of the many[3] contemporaries of your father and myself,
I incline to think that no one was more deserving than
he of universal praise and respect. 3. Which of you two
has entailed greater loss and[4] injury on the nation it is
hard to say; I hope and trust that you will[5] both before
long repent your crimes. 4. Fate has left us nothing
except either to die[6] with honour or to live under disgrace.
5. The battle[7] has been most disastrous; very few of us
out of so many thousands survive, the rest are[8] either slain
or taken prisoners, so that I greatly fear that (138) all is
lost.   6. Where in the world are we to[9] find a man like
him[10]; it would[11] be tedious to enumerate, or express in
words his many[12] good qualities; and[13] would that he had
been[14] here to-day!   7. So much blood has this victory
cost us that for myself I doubt whether the conquerors
or the conquered have sustained[15] most loss.

---

[1] Either *sum* or *insum.*   [2] Express by order of words. (Intr. 107.)
[3] Use *tot.* (Compare the use of *tantus*, 88, *Obs.*)
[4] Repeat "greater;" this repetition of a word already used is very
common in Latin in place of a conjunction.
[5] The fut. in *-rus* of *poenitet* rare.   What is the substitute? (193, iii.)
[6] *Ut* with subj., compare 125, *g.*   [7] See 218.
[8] See 187, *Obs.*   [9] See 150.
[10] Use *ille*, why? (339, iii.)   [11] Mood. (153.)
[12] *Tot.*   [13] *Qui.* (78.)
[14] See 152.   [15] *Accipio.*

GENITIVE—*Continued.*

Subjective and Objective Genitive.

299. The Genitive case always implies a **close relation** between the noun in that case and another noun.

(i.) Sometimes that relation is such that, if the other noun were converted into a **verb**, the word in the genitive would become the *subject* to the verb.

Thus *post fugam* Pompeii might be expressed by *postquam fugit* Pompeius.

This is called the **subjective genitive**.

(ii.) Sometimes the genitive as clearly represents the *object* of a verb.

Thus, *propter* mortis *timorem=quod* mortem *timuit.* This is called the **objective genitive**.

> *Obs.*—Both of these genitives may be combined in a single phrase.
>
>> Helvetiorum *injuriae* populi Romani. The wrongs inflicted *by* the Helvetii *on* Rome.
>
> In such phrases the *subjective* genitive is placed first.
>
> We may compare the English, "a *criminal's* fear *of* death," or the French, "le danger *de la mer,*" "le danger *du vaisseau,*" the danger *of* the sea, the ship's danger.

300. The **objective genitive** is very common in Latin. It represents not only the *accusative,* as the nearer object to a transitive verb, but also the *dative* as completing the sense of intransitive verbs; and even such combinations of a *preposition* with an *accusative,* or *ablative,* case, as are used to complete the sense of many verbs. It represents therefore many English phrases besides the possessive case and the preposition *of.*

> Instances are—Litterarum *studium* (*studere* litteris), devotion *to* literature ; doloris *remedium* (dolori *mederi*), a remedy *against* pain ; rei publicae *dissensio* (de r. p. *dissentire*), a disagreement *on* political matters, *or* a political disagreement; Pyrrhi regis *bellum* (cum Pyrrho *bellum gerere*), the war *with,* or *against,* King Pyrrhus ; sui *fiducia* (sibi *confidere*), confidence *in* one's-self. So also, legum *oboedientia,* submission *to* law ; Deorum *opinio,* an impression *about* the gods, and many others.

301. This objective genitive is combined not only as above with substantives, but also with many **adjectives**.

(i.) Thus, adjectives which signify *desire, knowledge, recollection, fear, participation,* and their *opposites; certain verbals* in -*ax,* and many adjectives that express *fulness* or *emptiness,* are followed by a genitive.

Rerum novarum cupidus, desirous *of* change ; *militiae* ignarus, ignorant *of* warfare ; *imperii* capax, with a capacity *for* rule.

These adjectives have an *incomplete meaning,* and may be compared with transitive verbs, as they require a noun to define and complete their meaning.

(ii.) Many of them, such as *cupidus, ignarus, memor,* etc., answer to English adjectives which are followed by the preposition *of,* and will cause no difficulty ; with others the Latin genitive represents (as with substantives) various English prepositions and constructions.

Rei publicae *peritus, imperitissimus, rudis.* Skilled, most unskilled, unversed, *in* the management of the state.
Pugnandi *insuetus.* Unaccustomed *to* fighting.
Litterarum *studiosissimus.* Most devoted *to* literature.
Hujus sceleris *particeps, expers, affinis.* With part *in,* free *from,* connected *with,* this guilt.
Beneficii *immemor.* Apt *to forget* a favour.

Obs.—*Plenus* takes both ablative and genitive, oftener the former ; *prudens* and *rudis,* sometimes *in* with ablative.
Certiorem facere = to inform, has a double construction.

(English) He has informed me *of* his plan.
(Latin) *Certiorem me* sui consilii *fecit;* or, *Certiorem me* de suo consilio *fecit.*

302. The objective genitive is combined with the **present participle** of transitive verbs, when the latter is used as an adjective, *i.e.* to denote a *permanent quality,* not a *single act.*

Thus regnum *appetens* = "*while* aspiring to the crown," but—
regni *appetens* = aspiring to kingly power (*habitually,* or by character).
Such participles are, *amans, patiens, diligens,* etc. (cf. also juris *consultus,* one consulted *on* law).
These present participles, when thus used, admit, as adjectives, of degrees of comparison, *tui amantissimus,* etc.

1. He was always most devoted to literature, at the same time **(366)** most uncomplaining under toil, cold, heat, want of food and of sleep ; for myself, my fear[1] is that he consents to allow himself too little repose and rest. 2. Such was the soldiers' ardour for the fight,[2] such the universal enthusiasm, that they refused to obey the orders of their general, (though) thoroughly versed in warfare of the kind, and as,[3] full of self-confidence and contempt for the enemy, and cheering each other on, they advanced as [3] to certain victory, they fell unawares into an ambuscade. 3. In spite of the greatest disagreement on politics, the friendship[4] which existed[5] between your gallant father and myself remained firm longer[6] than either (*et*) he or I had hoped. 4. He had[7] enough and to spare of wealth, but he was at the same[8] time most inexperienced in political life, with but little desire for fame, praise, influence, or power, and very averse to **(265)** all competition for office[9] or distinction.[9] 5. But these[10] men (though) they-have-borne[11] no part in all these toils, craving only for pleasure and repose, most indifferent to the public interest, devoted to feasting and gluttony, have reached such a pitch of shamelessness, that they have ventured in my hearing to taunt with luxury an army that-has-borne-uncomplainingly[12] all the hardships of a prolonged warfare.

---

[1] *Illud vereor.* (See **341**.)   [2] Gerund, **99**.

[3] Note carefully the different meanings of "as." *As* he does this (time), dum *haec facit. As* (though) to victory (comparison), *tanquam . . .* I did this *as* a boy, puer *hoc faciebam.* (**63**.)

[4] Insert *tamen*, "yet."

[5] "Which *was* to me *with* your," etc. (Intr. **49**, *Obs.*)

[6] See **277**.   [7] See **251**.   [8] *Idem.* (See **366**, ii.)

[9] Plural. Latin would not represent either word here by an *abstract term* in the singular.   [10] *Isti.* (See **338**, *Obs.* 2.)

[11] Use adjective *expers* (**301**, ii.) in apposition with "these men."

[12] Use a single word, "most uncomplaining under."

GENITIVE—*Continued.*

Quality and Definition.

303. The resemblance of the Latin genitive to the adjective is to be further noticed in its next use, the **genitive** of **quality**.

(i.) A Latin substantive in the genitive is often added to another substantive, in the same manner as in English a substantive with "of" prefixed, to denote some quality, either *predicated* of, or attached as an *attribute* to, that substantive. (Intr. 7, 8.)

> *Vir est* priscae severitatis. He is a man *of* old-fashioned austerity.
> *Vir* summae fortitudinis. A man *of* the greatest courage.

(ii.) But this Latin substantive in the genitive has invariably an **adjective** attached to it. "A man of courage" is not *homo* fortitudinis, but *homo* fortis ; a man of good sense, *homo* prudens, *not* prudentiae.

This use of the genitive resembles that of the ablative of quality (**271**), but—

Obs. 1.—If the qualifying substantive denotes *number, amount, precise dimensions, age,* or *time,* the **genitive** is always used.

> Septuaginta navium *classis,* a fleet of seventy ships ; viginti pedum *erat agger,* the embankment was twenty feet high ; *puer* tredecim annorum, a boy thirteen years old ; provectae, exactae, aetatis *homo,* a man advanced, far advanced, in years ; tot annorum *felicitas,* so many *years of* good fortune ; quindecim dierum *supplicatio,* a thanksgiving of fifteen days' duration.

Obs. 2.—The **Genitive** is used mainly to express *permanent* and *inherent* qualities : optimae spei *adolescens,* a youth of the highest promise ; the **Ablative** both these and *external* characteristics of dress or appearance : *canis capillis, veste sordida ;* not *canorum capillorum,* etc. So also the ablative is used for any state or feeling of the moment : *fac* bono *sis* animo, " Be of good cheer."

304. A word in the genitive is sometimes added to another substantive to *explain,* or *define,* or *restrict* its sense: *Virtus* justitiae, the virtue *of* justice; gloriae *praemium,* a reward *consisting in* glory. This is called the **genitive** of **definition.**

Cautions.—The resemblance of these uses of the Latin genitive to those of the English preposition *of* is obvious, but it must be remembered that—

(i.) After such words as *urbs, insula,* etc., apposition is used, not the **defining** genitive, to express the English *of* with the proper name.

> *Urbs* Saguntum, the city *of* Saguntum: *insula* Britannia, the island *of* Britain. (See **222.**)

(ii.) With the names of **towns** or **countries** the Latin **adjective** is used in place of the **possessive** genitive where we use "of."

> *Res* Romanae, the affairs *of* Rome; *civis* Thebanus, a citizen *of* Thebes. (See **98.**)

(iii.) Remember also: *media* urbs, the middle *of* the city (**295,** *b*), *quot estis?* how many *of* you are there? (**297**), and avoid here the **partitive** genitive.

Exercise 39.

1. It is said that serpents of vast size are found in the island of Lemnos. 2. No one denies that he was a man of courage;[1] the real question is, whether he was (one) of good sense,[1] and experience.[1] 3. It seems that your son is a boy of the highest promise, and of great influence with[2] those of his own age. 4. After three days'[3] procrastination he at last set out with a fleet of thirty ships; but being[4] far advanced in life was scarcely competent to carry out so toilsome a task. 5. I would have[5] you therefore be of good cheer, and do not on account of a short-lived panic throw away the result of so many years of toil. 6. He is a person[6] of old-world, as all of us know, and perhaps of excessive, rigour: but at the same time a man[6]

---

[1] What part of speech? (**303,** ii.)   [2] Apud (*acc.*).
[3] 303, *Obs.* 1.   [4] Turn by *homo* in app. (See **224,** *Obs.* 1.)
[5] *Fac* or *velim.* (**141.**)
[6] *Homo,* in a neutral sense, with either good or bad qualities; *Vir,* with marked social virtues. (See **224,** *Obs.* 2, *note*).

of justice and honesty, and of the most spotless life.
7. Gallant fighting[1] and an honourable death in the field
becomes citizens of Rome; let the few therefore of us[2]
who survive show ourselves worthy alike of our ancestors
and of the nation of Rome. 8. It seemed that there
stood by him in his sleep an old man far advanced in
years, with white hair, and kindly countenance, who bade
him be of good cheer and hope for the best,[3] for (that) he
would reach in safety the island of Corcyra after a voyage
of some[4] days.

---

[1] **96**, *a.* [2] **297.** [3] Neut. plur. [4] *aliquot.*

GENITIVE—*Continued.*

Genitive with Verbs.

THE genitive is also used to complete or define the sense not only of nouns but of certain **verbs.**

305. (i.) The **genitive** of **price**[1] is thus used with verbs of **valuing** and **buying,** etc., especially the former.

Magni, maximi, pluris ; parvi, minoris, minimi ; tanti, quanti, nihili, are used with *factitive* verbs such as *facio, habeo, aestimo,* etc., sometimes with *emo* and *vendo.*

> *Te quotidie* pluris facio. I *value* you *more highly* every day.
> *Rempublicam* nihili habet, *salutem suam* maximi. *He sets no value* on the national cause, *the highest on* his own safety.
> Emit *hortos* tanti quanti *Pythius voluit.* He bought the pleasure-grounds *at the full* (or, *exactly at the*) *price* that Pythius wished for.

Obs.—This genitive of value is also used as a predicate with **link** verbs, such as *sum, fio.*

> *Tua mihi amicitia* pluris est *quam ceterorum omnium plausus.* Your friendship is of more value to me than the applause of all the world besides.

306. (ii.) Verbs of **accusing, condemning, acquitting,** such as *accusare, arguere, reum facere, condemnare, absolvere,* take a genitive defining the **charge.**

> *Proditionis accusare, reum facere.* To accuse, to prosecute, *for* treachery.
> Furti *ac* repetundarum *condemnatus est.* He was condemned *for,* found guilty *of,* theft and extortion.
> *Parricidii eum incusat.* He taxes him *with* parricide.
> *Sacrilegii absolutus est.* He was acquitted *of* sacrilege.

---

[1] The origin of this genitive is doubtful ; it may possibly have originated with the locative in -*i* (*at* a price), and in course of time been transferred to other genitives ; but is more probably adjectival.

This construction may be explained by the omission of *crimine,* "on the charge," or *nomine,* "under the title," which are sometimes expressed.

Obs.—Instead of the *genitive,* the *ablative* with *de* is very common.

De *pecuniis repetundis damnari.* To be condemned *for* extortion.

Aliquem de ambĭtu *reum facere.* To bring an action against a man *for* bribery.

So—De *vi,* de *sacrilegio,* de *caede,* de *veneficiis,* etc., *se purgare.* To clear one's-self *of* assault, sacrilege, murder, poisoning.

But—Inter sicarios *accusatus est.* He was accused *of assassination.*

307. The **punishment** stands sometimes in the *genitive ;* far oftener in the *ablative.*

Capitis, *or* capite, *damnatus est.* He was capitally condemned, *i.e. to* death or exile.

Octupli *condemnatus est.* He was condemned to pay eightfold.

But—Morte, exilio *condemnatus (multatus) est.* He was condemned *to* (punished with) death, exile.

308. The genitive is also used to complete the sense of verbs of **compassionating, remembering, reminding, forgetting.**

Such are *misereor, memini, commonefacere, oblivisci.*

But—(*a*) Verbs of reminding, *admoneo,* etc., take an accusative of the thing as well as of the person, with *neuter pronouns ;* hoc, illud,[1] te *admoneo.*

(*b*) *Memini,* an accusative with a person, in the sense of " I still remember him ;" rarely otherwise in *prose. Recordor,* "I recall to my thoughts," is almost invariably used with the accusative.

(*c*) *Miserari,* "to express pity for," "to bemoan the lot of," an accusative.

Thus—

Ciceronem *memini ;* rerum praeteritarum (the past) *memini.*

Nostri *miserere,* take pity on us ; casum nostrum *miserabatur,* he bemoaned our disaster.

But—Illud *nos admonuit,* he reminded us of that ; *nos* officii nostri *commonefecit,* he reminded us of our duty.

Obs.—Even an impersonal phrase equivalent to a verb of remembering is followed by a similar genitive.

Venit mihi in mentem *ejus diei.* I have a recollection of that day.

---

[1] This may be looked on as a cognate accusative (**236, 237**).

The Genitive with Impersonal Verbs.

309. The impersonals, *pudet, piget, poenitet, taedet, miseret,* take an **accusative** of the *person feeling,* a **genitive** of what *causes* the feeling.

> Ignavum *poenitebit aliquando* ignaviae. The slothful man will one day repent of his sloth.
>
> Me *non solum piget* stultitiae meae, *sed etiam pudet.* I am not only sorry for my folly, but also ashamed of it.
>
> *Taedet* me vitae. I am weary of my life.
>
> Tui me *miseret;* mei *piget.* I pity you; I am vexed with myself.

What causes the feeling may also be a *verb* (in the *infinitive,* or in an *indicative* clause with *quod*).

> *Taedet* eadem audire *milites.* The soldiers are tired of hearing the same thing.
>
> *Poenitet nos* $\begin{cases} \textit{haec fecisse.} \\ \textit{quod haec fecimus.} \end{cases}$ *We are sorry that we acted so.*

Obs. 1.—The neuter pronouns *hoc, illud, quod,* are used in place of the genitive with these verbs. Hoc *pudet,* illud *poenitet.* (Cf. **308,** *a.*)

Obs. 2.—The genitive with *pudet* is also used for the person *before whom* the shame is felt.

> *Pudet me* veteranorum militum. I blush *before* the veterans.

310. The construction of the impersonals *interest* and *refert* requires attention.

(i.) The *person* to whom it is of importance is put in the *genitive* with *interest;* but *possessive pronouns, meus, tuus, suus, noster, vester,* etc., are used in the *ablative feminine.*

> *Interest* omnium *recte facere.* It is the interest *of all* to do right.
>
> *Quid* nostrā *interest?* Of what importance is it *to us?* (or, What does it signify to us?)

(ii.) The *thing* that is of importance may be either (*a*) an *infinitive* (*with* or *without* accusative) or (*b*) a *neuter pronoun* (hoc, id, illud, quod), or a *clause* introduced either (*c*) by an *interrogative* pronoun or particle, followed by the subjunctive mood, or (*d*) by *ut, ne.*

(iii.) The *degree of importance* is expressed either by the *genitive* of price (*magni, tanti, pluris*), or by an *adverb* or *neuter adjective* (*magnopere, vehementer, magis, parum: multum, plus, nihil, nimium, quantum,* etc.)

(iv.) The *thing* with reference to which it is of importance is sometimes indicated by *ad.*

Examples.—The following examples should therefore be well studied and analysed :—

    a. Magni *interest* ad *laudem civitatis haec vos* facere. *Your doing* this is of *great* importance *to the credit* of the state.

    b. Multum *interest* quos *quisque* audiat *quotidie.* It is of *great* consequence whom a man listens to every day.

    c. Illud[1] *mea* pluris *interest* te ut videam. It is of more consequence *to me* that I should see you.

    d. Vestrā *interest, commilitones,* ne *imperatorem pessimi* faciant. It is of importance *to you,* my comrades, *that* the worst sort should *not* elect your commander.

    f. Hoc et tuā et rei publicae *interest.* This concerns both *yourself* and the *nation.*

    e. Nihil mea *interest* quanti me facias. *Your estimate* of me is of no concern to me.

The constructions of *refert, it concerns,* are similar to those of *interest,* except that *refert* is rarely used with a genitive of the person concerned, but with the feminine possessive, or *ad.*

Exercise 40.

1. He was a man of moderate abilities, but of the highest character, and in the greatest crisis of a perilous war he was valued more highly in his old age than any[2] of (his) juniors. 2. He was a man of long-tried honour and rare incorruptibility, yet at that time he was taxed with avarice, suspected of bribery, and prosecuted for extortion; you all know that he was unanimously acquitted of that charge; but who[3] is there of you but remembers the (that) day on which he refused to deprecate the undeserved disgrace of condemnation, and not only cleared himself of that indictment, but exposed the malice and falsehoods of his accusers? None[4] of those who were present in the court that day will easily forget his magnificent address; nothing ever made a deeper impression on his audience.[5] 3. The whole nation has long[6] been weary of the war, regrets its own rashness, and blushes for the

---

[1] The substantival *ut*-clause is especially common after *illud* or *hoc* at the beginning of the sentence.

[2] *Quisquam.* (See **358, ii.**)

[3] To whom of you does not, etc., **308,** *Obs.*   [4] *Nemo.*

[5] " The mind (*pl.*) of his audience." Either genitive participle of, or relative clause with, *audio.* (**73, 76.**)

[6] Tense ? (See **181.**)

folly and incompetence of its general.   4. I remember
well the man [1] whom you mention; he was a person of
very low origin, of advanced age, with white hair, mean
dress, of uncultivated and rustic demeanour; but no one
was ever more skilled in (**301,** ii.) the science of war, and
his being made general[2] at such an emergency was of
the utmost importance to the welfare of the state.   5. It
makes no difference to us, who are waiting for your verdict,
whether the defendant be acquitted or condemned; but
it is of general interest that he should not in his absence
and unheard be sentenced to either exile or death.

---

[1] *Ille.* (**339,** iii.)   [2] **310,** ii. *a.*

PLACE, SPACE.
Locative Case.

In answer to the questions, *where? whither? whence?* we employ in English the prepositions *at* or *in*, *to*, *from*, etc.

In Latin all these questions can sometimes be answered merely by **case-endings**; but a **preposition** is often necessary.

311. Place at which; answer to "**where?**"

This is generally expressed by the *local* **ablative** (272, 273) with or even without a **preposition**. Thus, in *Italia*, in *urbe*; and so generally where an adjective is attached; but *media urbe*, *tota Italia*.

Obs.—Of course other prepositions of place are used with their proper cases. Thus—

> Ad[1] *urbem est*. He is *in the neighbourhood* of (outside) the city.
> Ad (*sometimes* apud) *Cannas pugnatum est*. There was a battle *at (near)* Cannae.

312. But with **towns** and **small islands** as opposed to countries, the old rule is as follows:—

If the name of a town, *at which* anything is or happens, is a *singular* noun of the *first* or *second* declension, it is put in the **genitive**; if not, in the **ablative**.

> *Vixi Romae, Tarenti, Athenis, Rhodi, Tiburĕ* (or *Tiburi*). I have lived at Rome, Tarentum, Athens, Rhodes, Tibur.

The explanation of this is that *Romae* (for older form *Romai*) *Tarenti, Rhodi*, are remains of the locative case in *i*, which in other declensions was supplanted by the ablative. (*Tiburi, Carthagini* are perhaps old ablatives.) In the plural the two cases coincide.

Other instances of this case are *domi*, at home; *humi* on the ground; *belli, militiae*, in war (only used in contrast with *domi*). *Ruri*, in the country, *vesperi*, in the evening, may be old ablatives.

Obs.—*Pendēre* animi, "to be in suspense," as also the genitive of *value* (**305**), may be locative cases.

---

[1] This is often used of Roman generals, who could not enter the city without laying down their *imperium*.

313. Place to which—whither?

As a rule the **prepositions** *ad, in,* etc., are used with the accusative; but

With the names of **towns**, etc., as above, the **accusative** is used without a preposition: thus, In *or* ad *Italiam, Africam, urbem, navem,* but, Syracusas, Romam, etc., *rediit.*

Obs.—The same construction is used with *domus* and *rus:* domum *rediit;* rus *fugii.*

314. Place from which—whence?

As a rule the **ablative** is used, joined with the **prepositions** *e, ex, a (ab):* a *Pyrrho,* ex *Italia,* ab *Africa,* e *nave,* ab *urbe.*

But with *towns*, etc., the **ablative** alone is generally used, as also with *domus* and *rus.*

> Romā *scribit,* he writes *from* Rome; *Tarquinios* Corintho *fugit,* he fled, *or* went into exile, *to* Tarquinii *from* Corinth: so, rure, *or* ruri *rediit.*

These rules are quite simple, but the following idiom must be carefully observed.

315.
We cannot, in Latin, say, as in English, "He came to his father *at* Rome," or "from Carthage *in* Africa." With verbs of motion, all such phrases must follow the rules for motion *to* or *from,* given above. Thus—

> He returned home from his friends *at* Corinth. *Corintho ab amicis domum rediit.*
> He sent a despatch to the Senate *at* Rome. *Romam ad Senatum literas misit.*
> He returned to his friends *in* Africa. In *Africam ad amicos rediit.*

In such sentences Latin connects both nouns closely with the verb of motion.

316.
None of the rules given above apply to the names of towns when joined with adjectives.

(i.) We cannot say *totius,* or *toti,*[1] *Corinthi,* for "*in* the whole of Corinth," but must use with both words the **local ablative,** *tota* Corintho. (**311.**)

---

[1] This is because the old locative case no longer exists in any but certain words.

(ii.) When *urbs*, or *oppidum*, comes before the proper name, the preposition must be used.

In *urbe Londino*, in the city *of* London ; ad *urbem Athenas*, ex *urbe Roma*. (See **222.**)

(iii.) With *domus* the **locative** construction is extended to *possessive pronouns*. With other adjectives the preposition is used.

Domi meae (or *apud me*) *commoratus est.* He stayed at *my* house. But—In *veteri domo*, ad *veterem domum*. In, or to, his *old* home.

317. When an adjective is joined with the name of a town, the construction resembles that used with the names of persons. (See **224.**)

The name of the town is placed first, in either the *locative*, *accusative*, or *ablative*, according to the meaning ; then follows the word *urbs* or *oppidum* combined with the adjective, with or without a preposition according to the rules already given. Thus—

Archias Antiochiae natus est, celebri *quondam* urbe (local ablative). Archias was born in the once famous city of Antioch.

Athenas, in urbem praeclarissimam *veni*. I reached the illustrious city of Athens.

Syracusis, ex urbe opulentissima, *profectus est.* He set out from the flourishing city of Syracuse.

318. (i.) **Space covered** (answer to the question **how far?**) is generally expressed by the **accusative**.

Tridui iter *processit.* He advanced a three days' march.

Ab officio cave transversum, *ut aiunt*, digitum *discedas*. Do not swerve "a finger's breadth" from your duty.

(ii.) For **distance from** (question, **how far off?**) either the **accusative** or **ablative** is used. (**238, iv.**, and **279.**)

Ariovistus vix plus duo milia *passuum* (or duobus milibus) *aberat*. Ariovistus was at a distance of scarcely more than two miles.

Obs.—After *plus, amplius, minus, quam* is rarely used with numerals, but the case of the numeral is unaffected by the comparative.

(iii.) **Dimension** is generally in the **accusative**.

Milites aggerem latum pedes trecentos *exstruxerunt*. The soldiers threw up a mound three hundred feet broad (*or* in breadth).

Occasionally the **genitive** of quality, or description, is used and the adjective omitted : *fossa* quindecim pedum, a ditch fifteen feet *deep*. (See **303,** *Obs.* 1.)

319. In English the name of a town or country is often personified and used for the nation or people: "Spain," "France," "England," etc. This is much rarer in Latin prose. (Cf. **17**, and end of **174.**)

"The war between *Rome* and *Carthage*" is *Bellum,
quod* populus Romanus *cum* Carthaginiensibus *gessit.*

For "Rome" in this sense we may use *Populus Romanus, res
publica Romana,* or *Romani,* but rarely *Roma.*

Exercise 41.

1. After living[1] many[2] years at Veii, a town at that
period of great population[3] and vast resources, he removed
thence late in life to the city[4] of Rome, which was at a
distance of about fourteen miles from his old home.
2. His parents, sprung originally from Syracuse, had
been[5] long resident at Carthage; he himself was sent[6] in
boyhood to his uncle at Utica, and was absent from home
for full three years; but after his[7] return to his mother,
now[8] a widow, at Carthage, he passed the rest of his youth
at his own home.　　3. The enemy (*pl.*) was now[8] scarcely
a single day's march off; the walls of the fortress, scarcely
twenty feet high, surrounded by a ditch of (a depth of)
less than six feet, were falling into ruin from age; Doria,
after waiting[1] six days in vain for reinforcements, sent a
despatch by[9] a spy to the governor at Pisa, earnestly imploring[10] him not to waste time any longer, but to bring
up troops to[11] his aid without delay.　　4. Born and brought
up in the vast and populous city of London, I have never
before had permission to exchange the din and throng of the
city even[12] for the repose and peace and solitude of rural
life; but now I hope shortly to travel to my son at Rome,

---

[1] "After living," *i.e.* "having lived." (**14**, *a.*)
[2] Case? (See **321**.)
[3] May be turned either by "flourishing (superlative of *florens*) with
a multitude of citizens and vast resources," or "most populous and
wealthy."
[4] *Urbs* may be removed into the relative clause, "which city."
[5] Tense? (See **181**.)
[6] Participle, and omit "and." (**15**.)
[7] Use verb and *postquam.* (**14**, *a.*)
[8] Why not *nunc?* (See **328**, *b.*)
[9] Why not *ab?* (See **267**, *Obs.*)
[10] "(in) which he implored." Why not participle? (See **411**.)
[11] For construction see **259**. Is "his" *ei* or *sibi?* (See **353**.)
[12] = not even. (Intr. 99.)

and from Italy to sail, before the middle of winter, to the city of Constantinople, which I have long been eager to visit; you, I fancy,[1] will winter at Malta, an island[2] which I am not likely ever to see. In the beginning of spring I have decided to stay in the lovely city of Naples, and to betake myself to my old home at London in the month of May or June. 5. Caesar shows himself, I fancy, scarcely less tenacious of his purpose at home than in the field; it is said[3] that he is outside the city waiting for his triumph, and wishes to address the people. 6. Exasperated and provoked by the wrongs and insults of Napoleon, Spain turned at last to England her ancient foe.

----

[1] See **32**, *b*.   [2] "Which island."   [3] See **43, 44.**

EXPRESSIONS OF TIME.

320. In answer to the question **when? at what time?** the **local ablative (272)** is used with words which in themselves denote *time*.

> *Vere, auctumno, nocte, solis occasu, primâ luce,* etc.

With words which do not *in themselves* denote time, the preposition *in* is mostly inserted, unless an adjective is attached : in *bello,* in time of war ; but *bello Punico secundo,* in the second Punic war. (Cf. **311.**) But the rule is not universal.

Obs.—In tempore means at the *right* moment, but *Alcibiadis temporibus,* at the *time* (in the *days*) of Alcibiades.

For the difference made by the preposition *in,* see **273,** *Obs.*

321. In answer to the question **how long?** the **accusative** is used. (See **238, iv.**)

> *Multos jam* annos *hic domicilium habeo.* I have now been living (181) here *for* many years.

Obs. 1.—Sometimes the idea of duration is emphasised by the addition of *per.*

> Per *totam noctem,* per *hiemem.*

Obs. 2.—The answer to **for how long past?** is often expressed by an *ordinal* adjective (of course in the singular).

> *Annum jam* (or, *hunc*) *vicesimum regnat.* He has been king *for* the *last* twenty years.

322. In answer to **how long before? how long after?** two constructions may be used.

(*a*) The word, or words, expressing the length of time may be in the ablative of *measure of difference* (**279**), and *post* or *ante* may be used as **adverbs.** Or

(*b*) *Post* and *ante* may be used as **prepositions** with the accusative of the amount of time.

For example, for the phrase "the fleet returned after three years," we may write either, tribus *post* annis (tertio *post* anno) *classis rediit,* or *post* tres annos, etc. There is the same variety in English : "Three years *after,* the fleet returned" is English, though "After three years" is less ambiguous.

Obs.—Even when joined with this ablative, *post, ante,* may still govern a case. We may say for "a few days before his death," either "*paucis diebus* ante *ejus* mortem," or "*paucis* ante *diebus,* quam *e vita excessit.*"

212

323. The following examples may be noticed:—

(*a*) " Three hundred and two years after the foundation of Rome."

    1. Anno trecentesimo altero *quam Roma condita est.* Or,

    2. Post trecentesimum alterum annum *quam Roma condita est.*

(*b*) *Pridie quam excessit e vitâ.* The day before his death.

    Postridie quam a vobis discessi. The day after I left you.

    Postero anno quam, etc. The year after, etc.

    Priore anno quam, etc. The year before, etc.

(*c*) (He did it) *three years* after *he* (had) *returned.*

    1. *Post* tres annos (*or* tertium annum) ⎫
    2. Tertio anno[1]   ⎬ *quam* redierat.

    3. Tribus *post* annis (*or* tertio anno) *quam* redierat.

    4. Tertio anno, *quo* redierat. (Rare.)

324. How long ago?, reckoning from the present time, is answered by *abhinc* with the **accusative**; the *abhinc* always coming first.

    Abhinc annos *quatuor Virgilium vidi.* I saw Virgil four years ago.

325. Within, or **in, what time?** is answered by the **ablative**, or the preposition *intra* with the accusative.

The singular of the *Ordinal* ("second," "third," etc.) often takes the place of the plural of the *Cardinal* ("two," "three").

    Vix decem annis, *or* decimo anno, *or* intra decimum annum, *urbem capiemus.* We shall scarcely take the city *in,* or *for,* or *within,* ten years.

Obs.—*His tribus diebus, in* or *for* the last three days (from the *present* time); *illis, etc.,* from a *past* time; *hoc biennio,* within two years from this time.

326. *In* with the **accusative** denotes a time *for* which provision or arrangement or calculations are made.

    In diem *vivere,* to live *for* the day (only); in sex dies *indutiae,* a truce *for* six days; *ad caenam me* in posterum diem *invitavit,* he invited me to supper *for* the next day: (*ad,* an exact date in the future); *ad calendas solvam,* I will pay *on,* or *by,* the 1st; *ad tempus,* at the appointed time, punctually.

    Ex, ab, starting from the time at which a period begins. Ex *eo die* ad *extremum usque vitae diem.*

---

[1] It might be supposed that "*tertio anno quam* (or *quo*) *redierat*" would mean "after two completed years from his return, and before the completion of the third." This however does not appear to be so. "*Octavo mense, quam coeptum oppugnari, captum Saguntum,*" etc. (Liv.); ἐν ὀκτὼ μησί (Polyb.); " *Tyrus septimo 'mense capta est*" (Curt.); πολιορκῶν ἑπτὰ μῆνας (Plut.).

327. In answer to the question **how old**? the usual construction is *natus* with the accusative.

> Annos *quinque et octoginta* natus *excessit e vita.* He died at the age of eighty-five.

But *quum* annos *quinque et octoginta* haberet, or *quum* annum octogesimum quintum *ageret,* would be equally good Latin.

The adjectival genitive (**303,** *Obs.* 1) may also be used : *puer quindecim annorum.*

"Under, over, twenty years," may be expressed by *minor (major) viginti* annis, or annos *natus minor (major) viginti,* and by several other curious variations, such as—

> *Minor viginti* annis *natu.*—Cic.
> *Minor* decem annorum.—Livy.

" When under," etc., by *quum nondum viginti haberet annos.*

Notes on Adverbs of Time.

328. The correct use of certain adverbs of time is important.

(*a*) "**No longer**" is only *non diutius* when a long time has already passed, otherwise *non jam*; "no one any longer" is *nemo jam,* or (with *and*) *nec quisquam jam.*

(*b*) **Now.** *Nunc* is "at the present moment," or "as things are now." It cannot be used of the past. "Caesar *was now* tired of war" is, jam *Caesarem belli taedebat.* Occasionally, if the "now" of the past is very precise, *tum.* *Jam* can be used also of the future : *quid hoc rei sit,* jam *intelleges,* "you will *soon* be aware of the meaning of this."

(*c*) "**Daily.**" *Quotidie* as a rule ; *in dies* only with comparatives, or verbs of *increasing* or the reverse ; *in singulos dies* is more emphatic : *Diem de die,* day after day ; *de nocte,* after night has begun. *Diurnus* (adj.) is "daily" as opposed to *nocturnus*; *quotidianus* is "daily" in the sense of "every-day."

(*d*) "**Not yet**" is *nondum, necdum*; "no one yet" *nemo unquam,* or, where the present is opposed to the future, *adhuc nemo.*
" **Still** " (=even now) is *etiam nunc.*

(*e*) *Jam diu* is " now for a long while " simply ; *jam pridem* looks back rather to the *beginning* of the time that is past ; *jam dudum* " for *some,* or a considerable, time."

(*f*) **Again.** *Rursus,* "once more ;" *iterum,* "a second time," opposed to *semel* or *primum*; *de integro,* "afresh" as though the former action had not taken place ; "again and again," *saepe, saepissime.* (**57,** *a.*)

1. Mithridates, who in a single day had butchered so many citizens of Rome, had now been on the throne two-and-twenty years from that date.   2. It seems that here too the swallows are absent in the winter months; I at least have seen not a single [1] one for the last three weeks. 3. He died at the age of three-and-thirty; when less than thirty years old he had already performed achievements unequalled [2] by any either of his predecessors or successors. 4. The famine is becoming sorer daily; exhausted by daily toil (*pl.*) we shall soon be compelled [3] to discontinue the sallies which up to this day we have made both by night [4] and by day.   Day after day we look in vain for the arrival of our troops.   5. He promised to be by my side by the first of June; for the last ten years I have never so much as once known [5] him to be present in good time.   6. Nearly three years ago I said that I had never yet seen any one [6] who surpassed [7] your brother in character or ability, but in the last two years he seems to be growing daily sterner and harsher, and I no longer estimate him so highly as I did before.   7. I saw your father about three weeks after [8] his return from India.   Years [9] had not yet dulled the keenness of his intellect or the vigour of his spirit; in spite of his advancing years he had commanded an army within the last six months, and was just preparing to be a candidate for office.   8. Misled by a mistake in the date, [10] I thought you had stayed at Athens more than six months.   9. I have spoken enough on this question, and will detain you no longer; six months ago I might [11] have spoken longer. [12]

---

[1] "= not even one." (Intr. 99.)
[2] "Such as (86) not even one (had performed)."
[3] "The sallies must be," etc., part. in *-dus*. (See 199.)
[4] Use adjectives. (328, *c*.)
[5] *Cognosco*, "I find or ascertain."   [6] 328, *d*.
[7] Mood? (77.)   [8] See 323, *c*.
[9] *i.e.* age.   [10] Genitive. (300.)
[11] See 196, *b*.   [12] "Said more." (53.)

PREPOSITIONS.

Prepositions with Accusative.

329. With the use of **Cases** is closely connected that of *Prepositions.*

(i.) **Prepositions** are indeclinable words which, besides other uses, are placed before substantives and pronouns to define their relation to other words. (Intr. 20-24.)

(ii.) Their use therefore is precisely the same as that of the *case-endings* (see **203**), but as the number of cases is not nearly sufficient to mark all the different relations of a noun to other words, prepositions[1] are used to aid the cases in making their meaning more definite and clear. Thus, to take the simplest instance, the use of the preposition distinguishes the relation of the *agent* from that of the *instrument* (**267**).

(iii.) In Latin, as in modern languages, they come, as a rule, before[2] the noun, and are used almost exclusively with the *accusative* and *ablative* cases.

Obs.—The ablatives *gratiâ, causâ,* are used as *quasi-prepositions* with the *genitive,* and resemble such English *prepositional phrases* as " in consequence of," " in spite of," etc.

330. The following prepositions are used with the *accusative :—*

(Those marked with an asterisk are used also as *adverbs, i.e.* without being attached to a noun, but as qualifying a *verb* or *adjective.*)

ante*, apud, ad, adversus*,
circum*, circa*, citra*, cis,
erga, contra*, inter, extra*,
infra*, intra*, juxta*, ob,

---

[1] Prepositions were doubtless originally adverbs formed from nouns and pronouns; in some languages, as occasionally in Latin, they follow the noun ; the case-endings may have had their origin in prepositional words added to the noun, cf. where*of,* where*by,* there*fore,* etc.

[2] For the position of *cum* in *tecum,* etc., see **8,** *Obs.; tenus* also follows its noun (*Alpibus* tenus, *as far as* the Alps), as does *versus,* and occasionally *propter* and others.

pencs, *ponc**, *post** and *praeter*,
prope*, *propter**, *per*, *secundum*,
supra*, *versus*, *ultra**, *trans*.

The following are joined with the *accusative* when they express *motion towards;* otherwise with the *ablative :—*

sub and *subter**, *super**, *in*.

The following are followed by the *ablative :—*

a (ab, abs), with *cum* and *de*,
coram*, *pro* with *ex* or *e*,
tenus, *sine*, also *prae ;*

and where *place at*, not *motion towards* is denoted—

sub and *subter**, *super**, *in*.

331. Their meanings are so various that no attempt will be made to illustrate more than some of the most important.

The *local* meaning is the earliest, but from this many others are deduced.

1. **Ad,** "towards," "to," used after verbs of motion, and transferred to various other senses.

> (*a*) Ad *te scripsi* (to) ; (*b*) ad *haec respondit*, "in answer to ;" (*c*) ad *Cannas*, "in the neighbourhood of," "near ;" (*d*) *hoc* ad *nos conservandos pertinet*, "this tends to our preservation ;" (*e*) *dies* ad *urbis interitum fatalis*, "the day destined to the ruin of the city" (*final*) ; (*f*) ad *unum*, "to a man" = all.

2. **Adversus,** "opposite to."

> (*a*) Adversus *castra nostra;* (*b*) "against," "with," adversus *te contendam* = *contra te* or *tecum;* (*c*) "in answer to" (a speech), adversus *haec respondit*.

3. **Ante,** "before" (*place*), ante *aciem :* but mostly "*time*," ante *me*, "before my time ;" often used adverbially ; see **322.**

4. **Apud,** "close by ;" apud *Cannas*, "near, *or* at, Cannae," but mostly in such phrases as :

> (*a*) Apud *me*, "in my house ;" (*b*) apud *Xenophontem*, "in (the *writings* of) Xenophon ;" (*c*) apud *vos concionatus est*, "he made a speech *in your hearing ;*" (*d*) apud *me*, "in my judgment ;" apud *me plus valet*, "has more influence *with* me."

5. **Circum, circa,** "round :" circa *tellurem*, "round the earth ;" circa *viam*, "*on both sides* of, *along*, the road ;" often used adverbially ; *circa* and *circiter*, "about," with numerals.

6. **Cis, citra ; trans,** " this side," " the other side :" cis, citra, trans, *flumen Rhenum.*

7. **Contra,** "facing :" contra *urbem;* oftener "against," contra *rempublicam facere,* "to act unconstitutionally ;" contra *nos bellum gerit =nobiscum,* contra (praeter) *spem, opinionem,* etc.

8. **Erga** (local sense obsolete): erga *me benevolentissimus,* "full of kindness *towards* me."

9. **Extra,** "outside of :" extra *urbem;* extra *culpam,* "*free from* blame ;" extra *ordinem,* "out of his proper order ;" "extraordinarily."

10. **Inter,** "amongst :" inter *hostium tela :* "between," inter *me ac vos hoc* (or *illud*) *interest;* "this difference between ;" inter *se diligunt* (reciprocal), "they love *each other.*"

11. **Infra,** "below :" infra *montes.*

12. **Intra,** "within:" intra *teli jactum,* "within the cast of a javelin ;" intra *diem decimum* (**325**).

13. **Juxta,** "close to," "near :" juxta *murum;* often adverbially, juxta *constiti;* sometimes=*pariter,* and joined with *ac.*

14. **Ob,** "before, opposite to :" ob *oculos;* "on account of," ob *delictum, quam ob rem=*"wherefore (therefore)."

15. **Penes,** "in the power of :" penes *te hoc est,* "this *depends on* you."

16. **Per,** " through,".(place and time).

  (*a*) Per *provinciam;* (*b*) per *hos dies,* "during the last few days" (**325,** *Obs.*) ; (*c*) "(causal)," per *me licet,* "you have my leave, you may (do it) as far as I am concerned ;" (*d*) (instrument *or* secondary agent), per *speculatores,* "by means of spies ;" (*e*) (manner), per *vim,* "by violence, *violently.*"

17. **Post,** "behind," "after,"=**pone.**

  (*a*) Post *tergum;* (*b*) (time), post *hominum memoriam,* "since the dawn of history," "*within* human memory ;" often adverbial (see **322**).

18. **Praeter,** " past."

  (*a*) Praeter *castra ;* (*b*) "beyond," "more than," praeter *ceteros ;* (*c*) "contrary to"=*contra,* praeter *spem ;* (*d*) "except," praeter *te unum omnes.*

19. **Prope** (**propius, proxime**), "near to :" prope *me,* propius *urbem,* (often adverbial).

20. **Propter,** "close to."

  (*a*) Propter *murum ;* (*b*) "on account of," propter *se,* "for its own sake ;" "thanks to," propter *te salvus sum=tua opera.*

21. **Secundum**, "along" (following).

(*a*) Secundum *flumen;* (*b*) secundum *naturam*, "in accordance with;" (*c*) secundum *pugnam*, "next to, *immediately after*, the fight" (time); (*d*) secundum *Deos*, "next to the Gods."

22. **Versus**, only with *domum* and *towns;* placed *after* the substantive : *Romam* versus, "in the direction of Rome."

23. **Ultra**, "beyond."

(*a*) Ultra *flumen;* (*b*) ultra *vires*, "beyond his strength."

In, sub, super, *with accusative.*

24. **In**, "into," "to."

(*a*) *Athenas* in *Graeciam exulatum abiit*, "went into exile at Athens in Greece" (**315**); *exercitum* in *naves imponere*, in *terram exponere*, "to embark," "disembark," an army ; in *orbem se colligunt*, "form a circle (for defence) ;" (*b*) (*time*), in *quartum diem* in *hortos ad caenam invitavit*, (**326**) "*to* supper *in* his grounds *four days* from that time ;" in *praesens*, "for the present ;" in *dies*, "daily ;" in *posterum*, "for the future ;" (*c*) "against," in *me invectus* est, "inveighed *against* me ;" (*d*) "towards," in *rempublicam merita*, "services *to* the nation" (but *de r. p.* mereri); (*e*) (*manner*), "after ;" in hunc modum *locutus est*.

25. **Sub** ("motion"), "up to."

(*a*) Sub *ipsos muros adequitant*, "they ride *close up* to the walls ;" (*b*) (*time*), "just *before*;" sub *lucem;* sub *haec*, "just *after* this."

26. **Super**, "above."

(*a*) Super *ipsum*, "(next) above *the host* at table ;" (*b*) *alii* super *alios*, "one *after* another."

Exercise 43.

1. Next to heaven,[1] I ascribed this[2] great favour mainly to you and your children. 2. I hope that when once[3] he has reached Rome he will stay in my house. 3. It seems that this year is destined for the ruin of the nation. 4. He is generally believed to be free from blame, and no one supposes that such[4] a good patriot would have[5] done

---

[1] Why not *caelum?* (See **17**.)
[3] Express "once" by the right tense. (**190**, ii., *Obs.*)
[4] **88**.
[2] **88**, *Obs.*
[5] **193**, v.

anything unconstitutionally.   5. He drew up his line on
the other side the Danube; our men, who had now for
some time been[1] marching along the river, halted close to
the other bank opposite the enemies' camp.   6. You had
my leave to return home to your friends in London.
Whether you have gone[2] away or no depends on yourself.
7. There is this difference between you and others: with
them (**339,** iv.) my client has, thanks to his many[3] services
to the nation, great weight; with you, for the same reason,
he has absolutely none.   8. It seems that he invited your
son to supper with him three days from that time at
his house; since that date none of his friends have
seen him anywhere.   9. The enemy had now disem-
barked, and had come within the reach of missiles; our
men hurled[4] their javelins and tried to pass by between
them and the river.   10. Such was their joy for the
present, such their hopes[5] for the future, that no one
suspected the real state of the case.[6]   11. Having inveighed against me with the utmost fury, he sat down;
in answer to his long speech I made a very few[7] remarks.
12. Having ridden past the many[8] tall trees which stood
along the road, I halted at last close to the gate.

---

[1] **181.**   [2] See **171.**   [3] *So* many, *tot.*   (Cf. **88,** *Obs.*)
[4] Historic infinitive.   (See **186.**)
[5] Singular.   In Latin prose *spes* is very rarely used in the plural.
[6] "What was really happening" *(fio),* see **174** ; or "*that* which
etc.)" see **176.**
[7] "Said very little."   (See **53, 54.**)
[8] See **56,** also **69.**

PREPOSITIONS WITH THE ABLATIVE.

332. Here also the **local** meaning is the earliest.

1. **A** (before consonants and *j*, otherwise) **ab**.

   (*a*) " From," ab *Africa;* (*b*) (*time*), a *puero,* "from boyhood ; "ab *urbe condita,* "from (*after*) the foundation of the city ;" (*c*) "from the side of"="on," a *dextro cornu ;* a *fronte,* "in front ;" so, (*d*) a *senatu stare,* "to take the *side of* the senate ;" (*e*) *securus* ab *hoste,* "free from care *as to* the enemy ;" a *re frumentaria laborare,* "to be in distress *for* provisions ;" (*f*) a te *incipiam,* "I will begin *with* you ;" (*g*) *confestim* a *praelio,* "immediately *after* the battle." Cf. (*b*).

2. **Cum,** "with " (opposed to *sine*).

   (*a*) "In company with," tecum *Romam redii;* hence "having," " wearing," cum *gladio,* cum *sordida veste ;* even, cum *febri,* "suffering from ;" so, cum *imperio esse,* "to be invested with military power."

   (*b*) "With," of friendly, or unfriendly, relations : tecum *mihi amicitia, certamen,* etc., *est :* tecum (or *contra te*) *bellum gero ;* hoc mecum *communicavit,* "he imparted this *to* me."

   (*c*) Accompanying circumstances, or results : *maximo* cum *damno meo,* " *to* my great loss."

3. **De,** " down from."

   (*a*) De *moenibus deturbare,* "to drive in confusion *from* the walls ;" (*b*) de *spe dejicere,* "to disappoint ;" (*c*) "from," homo de *plebe,* "a man *of* (taken *from*) the people ;" (*d*) "concerning," etc., de te *actum est,* "it is *all over with* (concerning) you ;" (*e*) ("time," **328,** *c*), de *via languere,* "to be tired *after* a journey ;" (*f*) de *industria,* "on purpose ;" (*g*) bene *mereri* de ..., "to deserve well *of*," " to serve ;" (*h*) *poenas sumere* de ..., "to punish."

4. **Ex** (before all letters), **e** (only before consonants), "out of ;" many uses.

   Ex *equo pugnare,* "on horseback ;" e *rebus futuris pendere,* "to depend *upon* the future ;" ex *sententia,* "according to one's wish *or* views ;" e *republica* (opposed to *contra r. p.*), "in accordance with the constitution ;" ex *improviso,* "unexpectedly," etc.

5. **In**, "in," also "among," etc.

> (*a*) In *bonis ducere*, "to reckon *among* blessings ;" (*b*) (*time*),
> in *deliberando*, "whilst deliberating ;" (*c*) *quae* in *oculis
> sunt*, "*before* our eyes ;" (*d*) in *armis esse*, "*under* arms ;"
> (*e*) *quid* in *nobis fecit?* "*as concerns*, or, *with* us ;" (*f*) in
> *te nihil potestatis habet*, "no power *over* you ;" (*g*) *quantum*
> in *me est*, "to the utmost of my power ;" (*h*) (of circum-
> stances), *satis ut* in *re trepida impavidus*, "with fair courage
> *considering* the critical state of things ;" (*i*) "in spite of, in
> face of," in *tanto discrimine*. (See **273**, *Obs.*)

6. **Prae**, "in front of ;" commonest uses metaphorical.

> (*a*) Prae *se ferre*, "to *avow*," "make no secret of ;" (*b*) "as a
> *preventive* cause," prae *clamore vix audiri potuit*, he could
> scarcely be heard *for* the shouting = "his voice *was drowned
> in* the shouting."

7. **Pro**, also "in front of."

> (*a*) Pro *tribunali dicere*, "to speak (in front of) *from* the magi-
> strate's tribunal ;" (*b*) "in defence of," pro *aris et focis;*
> (*c*) "in place of," "as good as," *unus ille mihi* pro *exercitu
> est; (d)* "as," pro *certo habere*, "to feel sure of ;" (*e*) "in
> proportion to," pro *meritis ejus gratiam reddere; (f)* "in
> accordance with," pro *prudentiā tuā; (g)* "in virtue of,"
> pro *potestate; (h)* "in proportion to ;" with comparatives,
> *caedes minor quam* pro *tantā victoriā*, "small in *proportion
> to* the greatness of the victory."

8. **Sine**, "without," but not nearly so often used as the English
preposition. Its place is taken by many constructions.

> *Nullo negotio*, "*without* trouble ;" *re infecta*, "*without* result ;"
> *nullo repugnante*, "*without* resistance ;" *imprudens*, "*without*
> being aware." (See **425**.)

Compare also—

> *Stetit impavidus* neque *loco cessit*. He stood, etc., *without* yield-
> ing ground ;
> or—*Non potes mihi nocere* quin *tibi ipsi* noceas. You cannot hurt me
> *without* injuring yourself.

333. There is nothing difficult in the use of the other prepositions.

Tenus is used occasionally with the genitive, and follows its noun ;
it should be noticed in such forms as *hac*tenus, *aliqua*tenus, and
verbo tenus, "as far as words go."

Sub must never be used with the ablative after verbs of *motion
towards*; its metaphorical use, "under a leader *or* king," is rare in
Latin ; "*under* his guidance" is *eo duce*.

1. In the midst of this dire confusion and tumult, the emperor was seen with his staff on the left wing. He was now[1] free from care as to the enemy's cavalry, and his words of encouragement were drowned in shouts of joy and triumph. 2. I fear that[2] it is all over with our army: for[3] ten successive days there has been the greatest want of provisions; in front, in flank, in rear, enemies are threatening (them); all the neighbouring tribes are in arms: on no side is there any prospect of aid: yet, for myself,[4] in the face of these great dangers, I am unwilling wholly to despair. 3. Immediately after the battle they bring out[5] and slay the prisoners: they begin with the general; none[6] are spared; all are butchered to a man. 4. I will begin, then,[7] with you: you pretend that your countrymen are fighting for their homes and hearths; and yet[8] you avow that they have repeatedly made raids upon our territory, and wasted our land with fire and sword without provocation or resistance. 5. I have known this young man from a boy: both his father and he have again and again in your father's lifetime stayed under my roof; and I consider him wanting in nothing either in point of knowledge or natural powers. 6. In virtue of the power with which my countrymen have intrusted me, I intend to reward all who have deserved well of the nation: the rest I shall punish in proportion to their crimes. 7. I will aid you to the utmost[9] of my power; but I fear that it is all over with your hopes. 8. I should be sorry to disappoint you, but I fear that your brother has returned without result. 9. Considering the greatness of the danger, he showed great courage, and we ought all to show him gratitude in proportion to his many services to us and to the nation. 10. We should[10] all of us look at what is before our eyes; to depend on the future is useless.

---

[1] See **328**, *b*. [2] **138**. [3] Turn in two ways. (See **321**, *Obs.* 2.)
[4] **334**, i. [5] Accusative of passive participle. (See **15**.)
[6] Use *nemo ;* case? [7] Why not *tum ?* = "therefore." (Intr. **56**, *d*.)
[8] Use *idem*. (See **366**, ii.) [9] (See **332**, 5, *g*.) Tense? (See **190**, ii.)
[10] *Oportet*. (See **198**, ii.)

EXERCISES ON PRONOUNS.

₊ *The following Exercises—XLV. to XLVIII.—may either be done consecutively, in the order in which they stand, or any one of them may be taken singly at any time after the first twenty-four Exercises have been done.*

EXERCISE XLV.

PRONOUNS.

Personal and Demonstrative.

334. It has already been stated that the English pronouns, *I, you, he, we,* etc., when used as subjects to a verb, are, in the absence of any special emphasis, sufficiently expressed by the termination of the Latin verb. (See 11, *a, b*.)

But many causes will account for their insertion.

(i.) *Ego* often begins a sentence in which the speaker is giving an account of his own conduct or feelings.

> Ego *cum primum ad rempublicam accessi.* (*For myself*) when first I entered on political life.

(ii.) *Tu* (especially) is often used indignantly.

> *An* tu *Praetorem accusas?* Or is it that you (*one like you*) are bringing a charge against a Praetor?

(iii.) *Ego, tu,* and even *ille,* are often inserted without any special emphasis side by side with the oblique case of another pronoun. (Intr. 106.)

> *His ego periculis* me *objeci:* te ille *semper contempsit.* These were the dangers to which I exposed myself; he always had a contempt for you.

(iv.) They, especially *ille,* are often joined closely with *quidem,* and inserted in a clause where an admission is made in contrast with a statement which follows.

> *Vir optimus* ille *quidem, sed mediocri ingenio.* He was an excellent man, but of moderate abilities.

224

The following are the main uses of the **Demonstrative Pronouns**, those which **point out** (*demonstro*), without naming, the person or thing of which we are speaking.

Is, ille, hic, iste.

335. Latin has many words which answer to our " he," " she," " they," in addition to the termination of the third person. In "*he* says that *he* has not done wrong," the second " he " might be expressed in Latin by *negat* se, eum, hunc, istum, *or* illum *peccásse*, according to the precise meaning of *he* in the English sentence. The first " he " might be either unexpressed as above, or translated by *is, hic, iste, ille,* according to circumstances.

336. Is is the pronoun of **mere reference**. It is regularly used, especially in the oblique cases, for " he," " she," " him," " her," " it," as an unemphatic pronoun referring to some person or thing *already mentioned,* or *to be mentioned.*

Is is, in all cases, the regular pronoun corresponding to *qui.* The other demonstrative pronouns have each a special force of their own, in addition to that of mere reference to some person or thing indicated.

337. Hic is the demonstrative of the *first person.* " *This* " person, or thing, *near me* " (the speaker).

> *Haec patria,* this *our* country ; *haec vita,* this *present* life ; *haec omnia,* everything *around* us ; *piget haec perpeti,* it is painful to endure the *present state of things ; his sex diebus,* in *the* last six days ; *his cognitis,* after learning *this* (*which I have just related*).

338. Iste on the other hand is the demonstrative of the *second person* (the person addressed), " that *near you.*"

> *Cur* ista *quaeris ?* why do *you* put *that,* or *this,* question ? *opinio* ista, that belief *of yours ; Epicurus* iste, *your friend* Epicurus ; *casus* iste, *your present* disaster.

Obs. 1.—In the language of the law-court *hic* is often opposed to *iste.* *Hic* then means " the man near me," " my *client*[1] and friend here," and is opposed to *iste,* " the man near you," " my opponent," " the *defendant.*" " *Iste* " has this meaning because the jury are addressed, and the accused sat near the seats of the jury ; so *iste* has its proper meaning, " the man *beside you.*"

---

[1] *Cliens* is never used in this sense ; either *hic,* or, if more emphatic, *hic cujus causam suscepi,* hic *quem defendo,* etc.

Obs. 2.—This meaning "that of yours" often, but by no means always, gives *iste* a meaning of contempt: ista *novimus,* we know *that story; isti,* those *friends of yours* (whom *I* think lightly of).

339. Ille is the demonstrative of the *third person,* other than those present, or engaged in conversation: "that *yonder,*" "that *out there.*" Hence come various uses.

(i.) The remote in *time* as opposed to the present: "Illis *temporibus,* "in those days;" *antiquitas* illa, "the far-off past," "the good old times."

(ii.) The "distinguished," as opposed to the common: *Cato* ille, "the great Cato."

(iii.) The *emphatic* "he," the "he" of whom we are all thinking or speaking; whom we all know; *ille* is substituted for *is,* where a well-known person is meant, even with *qui;* illi *qui,* those (whom we all know) who, not merely "*men* who."

(iv.) So, "he" in the sense of "the other" of two parties; often substituted for a proper name in a narrative.

340. Hic and ille are often opposed to each other.

(i.) Of two persons or things already mentioned, *hic* relates to the *nearer,* the *latter; ille* to the *more remote,* the *former.*

> *Romulum Numa excepit;* hic *pace,* ille *bello melior fuit.* To Romulus succeeded Numa; the *latter* excelled in peace, the *former* in war.

(ii.) So, of persons or things already mentioned or implied.

> *Neque* hoc *neque* illud. Neither the *one* nor the *other.* *Et* hic *et* ille (= *uterque*). Both *one* and the *other.*

(iii.) Sometimes they answer to "some," "others."

> Hi *pacem, bellum* illi *volunt.*

341. *Illud* is often used to introduce an emphatic statement, or a quotation.

> Illud *vereor, ne fames in urbe sit.* My real fear is, *or,* what I fear is, lest there should be a famine in the city. *Notum* illud *Catonis.* The *saying* of Cato is well-known.

It will sometimes answer to the English "this," "the following."

> *Ne* illud *quidem intellegunt* . . . They do not even perceive *this,* that . . .

342. *Is,* as the **pronoun of reference,** is the regular correlative to *qui,* and is used with all three persons.

Read again **70-76**, and explain the following examples :—

(a.) Qui *hoc fecerint* (**190**, i.) *poenas dabunt.*
(b.) *De* eis qui *hoc fecerint, poenas sumam.*
(c.) *Qui olim terrarum orbi imperavimus*, ei (ii) *hodie servimus.*
(d.) *In* eos qui defecerant *sacritum est.*   The *rebels*[1] (**175**) were treated with severity.

343. For the difference between *cum eo res est, qui nos semper contempserit* (subjunctive), and the same sentence with *contempsit*, see **506**.
It will be enough to say here that
Is *sum qui* feci, is, " I am the man *who did* (it)."
Non is *sum qui* faciam, is, " I am not *such* a person *as to do it,*" "one to do it."

344. *Et is, isque, idque,* etc., are often added with some detail to which attention is drawn.

Decem capti sunt, et ii *Romani.*   Ten men have been taken, and *those too* Romans.
Litteris operam dedi, idque *a puero.*   I have been a student, and *that* from my boyhood.

345. The pronoun " that," " those," is most rarely used, as it is constantly in English, to represent with a genitive case a noun already mentioned.

" Our own children are dearer to us than *those* of our friends," is, *nostri nobis liberi cariores sunt quam* amicorum ; never, *ei* (*ii*) *amicorum.*

If the second substantive represented by " those " is in a different case it is repeated.

Liberi nostri amicorum liberis *cariores sunt.*

346. So also it must be again noticed (see **74**) that neither *is* nor *ille* can be used like the Greek article, or the English demonstrative, to define a participle, adjective, or phrase.

" He ordered *those* near him " is not eos *prope se,* but *eos* qui *prope se erant* or *stabant ;* " to *those* questioning him " is not iis *interrogantibus,* but either *interrogantibus,* or *eis* qui *interrogabant ;* " those like ourselves " is not *eos nostri similes,* but *nostri similes,* or *eos qui nostri sunt similes.*

---

[1] Observe that the Latin substantives in *-tor, -sor,* express a more permanent and inherent quality than the English in *-er : gubernator* is not the " steerer " of the moment, but the *professional pilot. Defector* is first used in Tacitus.

347. When *is, hic,* or *qui,* etc., stands as the *subject* of the verb " to be," or some link verb, the pronoun generally agrees with the predicate where we might have expected it to be *neuter.*   (See **83.**)

> Ea *demum est vera felicitas.*   This and this only is true good fortune.

N.B.—Felicitas never means " happiness" (see **98**, *b*), but " good luck" or " fortune ;" note also the use of *demum :* this " at length," " nothing *till we come to* this."

348. Both *ille* and *is* sometimes represent the English " article" *the,* itself a shortened demonstrative.

> I remember *the* day on which.   *Venit mihi in mentem diei* illius, *quo.*
> The friendship which existed between you and me.   Ea *quae mihi tecum erat amicitia.*

So " *the* saying of Cato ;" see above, **341.**

Exercise 45.

1. Those friends of yours are in the habit of finding fault with the men, the institutions, the manners, of the present[1] day, and of sighing for, and sounding the praises of, the good old times ; possibly you yourself have sometimes fallen into that mistake.   2. There is the greatest disagreement on[2] political matters in my house ; one party wishes everything changed, the other nothing.   For myself, I believe neither of the two parties to be in the right.   3. He[3] always showed himself proof against these perils, these bugbears ; do[4] not you then appear unworthy of your noble forefathers.   4. Of this at least I am convinced, that that belief of yours as to[2] the antiquity of this custom is groundless ; it is for you to consider[5] its origin.[6]   5. The saying of Caesar is pretty well known, that chance has the greatest influence in war.   6. When just on the point of pleading his cause, my client was

---

[1] See **337.**   Repeat the pronoun with each word.   (See **49.**)
[2] See **300.**   [3] **334**, iii.   [4] See **143.**
[5] See **146.**   [6] See **174**. *e.*

ready to be reconciled with the defendant, and this design [1]
he shortly accomplished against my will, and in the teeth
of all his friends. 7. To the question why he preferred
being an exile to living in his own home, the other replied
that he could not return yet without violating the law,
(and) must [2] wait for the king's death. 8. This only, it is
said,[3] is true wisdom : to command one's-self. 9. I value
my own reputation more highly than you (do) yours, but
I am ready to sacrifice my freedom to that of the nation.
10. I who [4] twenty years ago never quailed even before
the bravest foe, now in the face [5] of an inconsiderable
danger am alarmed for my own safety and that of my
children. 11. To those who asked why they refused to
comply with the royal caprice, they replied that they were
not men [6] to quail before pain or danger. 12. You have
been praised by an excellent man, it is true,[7] but by one
most unversed in these matters.

---

[1] *Id quod.* (See **67.**)   [2] **198**, iii.
[3] See **32** *b*, and **44.**   [4] See **75**, and **342**, *c.*
[5] **273**, *Obs.*   [6] See **343.**   [7] **334**, iv.

PRONOUNS—*Continued.*

Reflexive and Emphatic Pronouns—*Se, suus, ipse.*

349. Se, sese, sui, sibi, as also the possessive **suus,** are used where the person whom they denote is the same as the grammatical subject of the sentence in which they occur, *i.e.* as the nominative to the principal verb.

They are used of the **third person** only. In the first and second, *me* (*memet*), *te* (*temet*), are used with *ipse*. (See **356.**)

> *Brutus pugione se interfecit suo.* Brutus killed *himself* with *his* dagger.
> *An* temet ipse *contemnis?* Is it that you despise *yourself?*

Obs.—*Suus* is not expressed wherever we use *his, theirs, etc.,* but only for emphasis, or to avoid ambiguity.

> *Animum advertit,* " he turned *his* attention;" *filii mortem deplorabat,* " he was lamenting *his* son's death."

But it is often used emphatically, as opposed to *alienus; suo tempore,* "at the time that suited himself;" or in combination with *quisque, suam quisque virtutem laudant;* and always in the phrase *sua sponte. Sui* is often used for a man's "friends," "party," "followers," or even " countrymen :" *ad suos rediit.*

350. *Se* (*suus*), when used as the subject to a verb in the **infinitive,** refers to the *subject* of the verb on which the infinitive verb depends.

This use will cause no difficulty, though the English idiom is different.

> *Ait se hæc vidisse.* He says *he* saw this. (See **34.**)

Obs.—Where there is no danger of ambiguity, the *se* may refer to the *object* of the principal verb.

> *Reliquos sese convertere cogunt.* The rest they compel to turn.
> *Diffidentem rebus suis confirmavit.* He cheered him while distrusting (against his distrust of) his own position.

For the insertion of *se* after verbs of *promising,* etc., see **37.**

351. Sometimes, as with the English "one's self," "one's own," the subject must be supplied from the context ; Latin, like English, having no such indefinite word as the Greek τις, or the French *on*.

> *Alienis injuriis vehementius quam* suis *commoveri.* The being more deeply moved by other men's wrongs than by *one's own*.

So *sui poenitere, sibi placere,* " self-reproach," " self-satisfaction."

352. Very common uses of *se, suus,* are—*sua sponte,* of his own accord ; *secum habere,* to keep to one's-self ; *fiducia sui,* self-confidence ; *per se, propter se, pro se quisque* (" each in turn ") ; *sui compos,* master of himself, his reason ; *quantum* in se *fuit,* to the utmost of his power.

These phrases are freely used without any reference in the *se* to any other than the nearest word.

> *Tum illum vix jam* sui compotem *esse videt.* Then he sees that he (the other) is scarcely any longer master of himself.
>
> *Haec omnia* per se *ac* propter se *expetenda esse ait.* All these things are, he says, desirable *in themselves* and *for their own sake.*

Obs.—So *se, suus,* are constantly combined with *quisque,* either in a different case or with a different construction.

> *Milites* ad sua quemque *signa redire jussit . . .,* " to *their respective,* or *several,* standards."

353. In dependent clauses introduced by *qui* or a conjunction no precise or mechanical rule for the use of *se* (suus) can be given ; but

(i.) In **adjectival** clauses *se generally* refers to the subject of the verb in its own clause.

> *Milites,* qui se suaque *omnia nosti tradiderant, laudare noluit.* He objected to praise soldiers who had surrendered *themselves* and all that belonged to *them* to the enemy.

(ii.) In all other subordinate clauses *se generally* refers to the subject, not of its own, but of the principal clause.

> *Cicero effecerat,* ut *Q. Curius consilia Catilinae* sibi *proderet.* Cicero had contrived that Q. Curius should betray to *him* (Cicero) the designs of Catiline.

But neither rule is universal ; sometimes in subordinate clauses *ipse* represents the subject of the principal, *se, suus,* that of the dependent verbs ; the general rule is the opposite of this.

354. Sometimes, and constantly with *inter, se* supplies the place of the **reciprocal pronoun,** which is wanting in Latin.

> *Furtim* inter se *aspiciebant.* They would look stealthily at *each other.*

Otherwise *alius alium.* (See **371,** iv.)

355. Ipse can be used of any person (with *ego, tu*, etc.) and in any case; it may also emphasise *se* and *suus*, and is joined freely with substantives.

> *Quid* ipsi *sentiatis velim fateamini.* I would fain have you confess *your own* sentiments.

It answers to various English expressions.

> (*a.*) Ipsis *sub moenibus, close* beneath the walls (place).
> (*b.*) *Illo* ipso *die*, on that *very* day (time).
> (*c.*) *Adventu* ipso *hostes terruit*, "by his *mere* arrival."
> (*d.*) Ipse *hoc vidi*, "with my own eyes," or, as with *inveni*, "unaided," or "of my own accord;" sometimes "on my part."

Obs. 1.—*Ipse* is often inserted in Latin for the sake of clearness or contrast where we should hardly express it.

> *Dimissis suis* ipse *navem conscendit.* He dismissed his followers and embarked.

Obs. 2.—It very often denotes the leading person, the host as opposed to the guests, "the master" as opposed to "the disciples."

356. (i.) When used to emphasise *suus* ("own"), it is added to it in the possessive genitive, singular or plural as the sense requires.

> *Mea* ipsius *culpā, vestra* ipsorum *culpā.* Through *my* own, *or your* own, fault.

(ii.) When *ipse* emphasises the oblique case of *se* or a personal pronoun ("self," "selves"), it sometimes agrees with that case—

> *Nos* ipsos *omnes natura diligimus.* We all of us instinctively love ourselves;

but more commonly it is used in the nominative as subject to the verb—

> *Me*, or *memet*, ipse *consolor.* I console *myself.*
> *Virtus per se et propter se* ipsa *expetenda est.* Goodness is desirable in itself and for its own sake.

The most emphatic combination is *egomet* ipse, *temet*, or *semet*, ipse, *vosmet* ipsi, etc.

Exercise 46.

1. Many evils and troubles befall us through our own fault, and it[1] is often men's lot to atone for the offences of their boyhood in mature life. 2. Having thus spoken, he sent back the officers to their several regiments, and then, telling[2] the cavalry to wait for his arrival under shelter of the rising ground, he started at full gallop

---

[1] "It" emphatic. (**341**.)   [2] Why not present participle? (See **411**.)

and encouraged by voice and gesture the infantry, who
had retreated quite up to the camp, to turn back[1] and
follow him. 3. You are one whom your countrymen
will intrust[2] with office from the mere impression of
your goodness. 4. It is a king's duty (291) to have
regard not only to himself, but to his successors. 5. I
heard him with my own ears deploring the untimely
death of his son, a calamity which[3] you pretend that he
treated very lightly. 6. We ought, says he, to be scarcely
more touched by our own sorrows than by those of our
friends. 7. Having returned to his countrymen, he proceeded[4] to appeal to them not to surrender him at the
conqueror's bidding to men who were[5] his and their[6]
deadliest enemies, to his father's murderers and their[6]
betrayers, but rather to brave[1] the worst, and perish in
the field. 8. He intends, he says, to lead his men out to
fight[7] at his own time, not at that of the Germans.
9. Any one[8] may be dissatisfied with himself and his
own generation; but it requires[8] great wisdom to perceive how we can retrieve the evils of the past, and treat
with success the national wounds. 10. To those who
asked what advantage he had reaped from such numerous
friends, he replied that friendship was to be cultivated in
itself[9] and for its own sake. 11. Taking[10] his seat, he
sent[1] for the ambassadors of the allies, and asked them
why they were ready to desert him, and betray their own
liberties at such a crisis.

---

[1] Participle, see **15**, (for mood of "follow" and "perish" see **118**).
[2] Mood? (**343.**)　　　　　　　　　　[3] " Which calamity."
[4] See **184.**　　　　　　　　　　　　[5] Mood? (**77.**)
[6] Use *ipse* for "their" in both places.　[7] *Ad* with Gerund.
[8] See **292, 4,** and **291,** *Obs.* 4.　　[9] See **352**
[10] Use *consido.* Why not present participle? (See **411.**)

PRONOUNS—*Continued.*

Indefinite Pronouns—*Quisquam, aliquis, etc.*

THERE are many pronouns which may be called **indefinite demonstratives** in Latin; but their main distinctions are easily pointed out. We may divide them into (1) those that are of a **negative** as well as of an indefinite nature ("Any"), and (2) those that are mainly **affirmative** ("Some").

357. "**Any,**" after *si, nisi, num, ne, quo, quanto*, is the very indefinite **quis** (qui, when used as an adjective, *i.e.* as attached to a substantive).

> Si quis *ita fecerit, poenas dabit.* If *any* one does (191, i.) so, he will be punished.
> Num quis *irascitur infantibus?* Does *anybody* feel anger towards infants?
> Ne quis *aedes intret, januam claudimus.* We shut the door to prevent (101, ii.) *any one* from entering the house.
> Quo quis *versutior, eo suspectior.* The more shrewd a man (*any one*) is, the more is he suspected.

N.B.—*Quis* in this sense can never begin a sentence.

Obs.—In place of *quis,* in all but the last sentence, *quisquam* might be used. "Does any one *at all,* any *though it be but one,* feel anger?"

358. (i.) A more emphatic "**any**" is **quisquam** (subst.), (ullus, adj.). It is used after a negative **particle** (*nec, vix, etc.*), or a **verb** of denying, forbidding, preventing, or a

234

question implying a negative, or **si**, where the negative sense of "any" is emphasised.

> *Haec aio*, nec quisquam *negat*. This I say, *and no one* denies it.
>
> Negant *se* cujusquam *imperio esse obtemperaturos*. They refuse to (**136**, *a*) obey *any one's* command.
>
> *Et est* quisquam *?* And is there *any one?* (It is implied that there is no one.)
>
> *Vetat lex* ullam rem *esse* cujusquam, *qui legibus parere nolit.*[1] The law forbids that *anything* should belong to *any one* who refuses to obey the laws.

Obs.—Nec quisquam is always used (not *et nemo*) for "and no one." (See **110**.)

(ii.) As *quisquam* (*ullus*)=" any *at all*," it is naturally used in *comparisons*.

> *Fortior erat* quam *amicorum* quisquam. He was braver *than any* of his friends.
>
> *Solis candor illustrior est* quam ullius *ignis*. The brightness of the sun is more intense than that of *any* fire.

359. "**Any**," in the *affirmative* sense of "any one (or thing) *you please*," almost equivalent to "every," is **quivis** or **quilibet**.

> Quodlibet *pro patria, parentibus, amicis adire periculum oportet*. We ought to encounter *any* danger (*i.e. all* dangers) for our country, our parents, and our friends.
>
> *Mihi* quidvis *satis est*. *Anything* is enough for me.

Obs.—Quivis expresses a more deliberate, *quilibet* a more blind or capricious choice (*voluntas* compared with *libido*).

360. "**Some**" is *aliquis* (*-qui*), *quispiam, quidam, nescio quis*. We might say for "some one spoke," *locutus est* aliquis, quidam, nescio quis, according to our precise meaning.

(i.) **Aliquis** (-**qui**) is "some,"[2] "some one," as opposed to "none," "no one."

> *Dixerit* aliquis. *Some* one (no *definite person* thought of) will say (have said).
>
> *Senes quibus* aliquid *roboris supererat*. Old men who had still *some* strength remaining.

---

[1] For mood of *nolit* see **77** with *Obs.*

[2] Hence with *sine* in a negative sentence *aliqui*, "some," is used, just as with *sine* in a positive sentence *ullus*, "any:" *nemo est sine aliqua virtute*, there is no one without *some* virtue (or other): *homo est sine ulla virtute*, he is a man without *any* virtue.

(ii.) **Quispiam** is not so often used, and is vaguer.

Dicet quispiam.   *Some one* will say.

(iii.) "Some," when used in an emphatic and yet indefinite sense is often *sunt qui, erant qui*, with the **subjunctive.**

Sunt qui dicant. Some say. *Erant qui dicerent.* Some said.

(iv.) **Nonnulli** is "some few," "more than one," as opposed to "one" or "none."

Disertos *cognovi* nonnullos, *eloquentem* neminem. I have met with *several* clever speakers, but not a single man of eloquence.

361. Quidam is "a certain one," or simply "a." It expresses some **definite** person (and therefore differs from *aliquis*) sufficiently known to the speaker for the purpose in hand, but not further described.

Quidam *ex* (or *de*) *plebe orationem habuit.* *A* man of the commons made a speech.

Quodam *tempore.* At *a certain* time (I need not go on to give the date).

Civis quidam *Romanus.* A (certain) citizen of Rome.

Obs. 1.—*Quidam* also is very commonly used to qualify a strong expression, or to introduce some metaphorical language; it corresponds in use to *ut dicam*, "so to speak." (**100**, note [1].)

Erat in eo viro divina quaedam *ingenii* vis. There existed in that man *almost* a divine, or, *i. really* heroic, force of character.

Progreditur respublica naturali quodam *itinere et cursu.* The state advances *in a natural* path and progress.

Obs. 2.—As the English language **admits of the use of metaphorical expressions** much more readily than the Latin, the Latin *quidam*, or some qualifying phrase (*tanquam*, "as if," etc.), will often be used where no answering phrase is required in English.

362. Nescio quis (**qui**) is also used as a single word with the **indicative**, or even without a verb (*e.g. contra* nescio quem). (See **169**.) It does not merely decline to name, as *quidam* does, but asserts ignorance. When used of a person it is often therefore contemptuous.

Alcidamas quidam, "one Alcidamas," whom I *need not* stop to describe further.

But—*Alcidamas* nescio quis, "an *obscure person* called Alcidamas."

363. The phrases *nescio quid, nescio quo modo, quo pacto* (also *quodam modo*), are used where there is anything expressed that is not easily defined or accounted for.

> *Inest* nescio quid *in animo ac sensu meo.* There is something (*which I cannot define*) in my mind and feelings.
>
> *Boni sunt* nescio quomodo *tardiores.* Good people are *somehow or other* rather sluggish.
>
> Nescio quo pacto *evenit ut . . . . Somehow or other* it happened that . . . .

364. Quicunque, quisquis (substantive), "whoever," though occasionally used as indefinite demonstratives, as a rule are indefinite **relatives**, and as such are followed by a dependent verb in the **indicative**; by the subjunctive only when required on other grounds.

> *Cras tibi* quodcunque voles *dicere licebit.* To-morrow you may say *whatever you like.* (**190,** ii.)
>
> Quisquis *huc* venerit, *vapulabit. Whoever comes* (**190,** i.) here shall be beaten.

Caution.—Beware of thinking that *quicunque* governs a subjunctive. (**153.**)

Exercise 47.

1. Do not,[1] says he, be angry with any one, not to mention[2] your own brother, without adequate grounds. 2. Scarcely any one[3] can realise the extent and nature of this disaster, and perhaps[4] it can never be retrieved. 3. Your present disaster might have[5] befallen any one, but it seems to me that you have been somehow more unlucky than any of your contemporaries. 4. No one ever attained to any such goodness without, so[6] to speak, some divine inspiration, and no one ever sank to such a depth of wickedness without any consciousness of his own guilt. 5. Some believed that after the defeat of Cannae the very name of Rome[7] would disappear, and no one imagined

---

[1] Use *cave.* (**143.**)

[2] *Ne dicam* (the *dicam* does not govern the case of "brother"). (See **100,** note.)

[3] **291,** *Obs.* 4.   [4] = "which perhaps." (See **169.**)

[5] See **196.**   [6] **361,** *Obs.*   [7] Adjective. (**58** and **319.**)

that the nation would have[1] so soon recovered from so crushing a calamity.   6. It seems to me, to express[2] myself with more accuracy, that this nation has long been advancing in learning and civilisation, not of its own impulse, but by[3] what I may call an engrafted training. 7. Some one of his countrymen once said that my client was naturally disposed to laziness and timidity; to me it seems that he is daily becoming somehow braver, firmer, and more uncomplaining under any toil or danger. 8. In the[4] army that was investing Veii was a[5] Roman citizen who had been induced to have a conference with one or other of the townsmen.   He[6] warned him that such a terrible disaster was threatening the army and people of Rome, that scarcely a soul was likely to return home in safety.

---

[1] See **193**, v.   [2] See **100**, note.   [3] *Quidam.* (See **361**, *Obs.* i)
[4] See **348**.   [5] **361**.   [6] **339**, iv.

₌ *The next Exercise* (XLVIII.) *is on certain words nearly allied to Pronouns (sometimes called* **Pronominalia**)*, and is divided into two parts,* **A** *and* **B**.

EXERCISE XLVIII.

A

PRONOUNS.

Idem, alius, alter, ceteri.

365. Idem. It has been already said (84) that "the same *as*" is usually expressed in Latin by *idem qui,* occasionally by *idem atque,* or (before consonants only) *ac.* (90.)

> *Idem sum* qui *semper fui.* I am the same *as* (or *that*) I have always been.
> *Eadem vos* quae, *or* atque, *ego sentitis.* Your views are the same *as* mine.

366. *Idem* has two idiomatic uses.

(i.) It joins together two *similar* ideas in the sense of "also," "at the same time."

> *Quicquid honestum est,* idem *est utile.* Whatever is right, is *also* expedient.

It is sometimes repeated :—

> Idem *vir fortissimus,* idem *orator eloquentissimus. At once* a man of the highest courage and the most eloquent of speakers.

(ii.) It also unites two *contrasted* statements as regards a common subject.

> *Accusat me Antonius,* idem *laudat.* "Antonius accuses and *at the same time, or not the less, or in the same breath,* praises me."

367. Alius. To express "different *from,* or *to,*" *alius ac, atque,* is used. (91.)

> *Alio ac tu est ingenio.* He is of a different disposition to you.

So with the adverb *aliter;* so also with *pariter, juxta,* etc.

> *Aliter* atque *sentit loquitur.* His language is different to his (real) sentiments.

239

368. *Alius,* "other" (of any number), is opposed to **alter,** "other of two," or "second" or "one" of two, as opposed to the other.

> *Consulum* alter *domi,* alter *militiae, famam sibi paravit.* One of the consuls won glory at home, *the other* in war. (**312.**)
>
> *Duorum fratrum* alter *mortuus est.* One of the two brothers is dead.
>
> *Amicus est tanquam* alter *idem.* A friend is a *second* self. (**361,** *Obs.* 2.)
>
> *Dies unus,* alter, *plures intercesserant.* One. *two,* several, days had passed.

369. A repeated **alius** is used in *four* common constructions.

(i.) In a distributive sense, "some . . . some . . . others."

> *Tum* alii *Romam versus, in Etruriam* alii, alii *in Campaniam, domum reliqui dilabuntur.* Thereupon they disperse, some towards Rome, some, etc.

Of course, of *two* persons, *alter . . . alter,* or *unus . . . alter,* will be used for "one . . . the other," sometimes *hic . . . ille.* (See **340.**)

370. (ii.) When used as a predicate in separate clauses, a repeated *alius* marks an essential difference. (**92.**)

> Aliud *est maledicere, accusare* aliud. There is a vast difference between reviling (**94**) and accusing.
>
> Aliud *loquitur,* aliud *facit.* His language is irreconcilable with his actions.

371. (iii.) When *alius* is repeated *in different cases* in the same clause, it answers to a common use of the English " different," " various."

> *Hi omnes* alius aliā *ratione rempublicam auxerunt.* All of these by *different* methods promoted the interests of the nation.

So with **adverbs**: alii aliunde *congregantur; omnes* alius aliter *sentire videmini.* "They flock together from *various* quarters;" "all of you, it seems, have *different* views."

Obs.—The *singular* of the doubled *alius* is generally used in apposition with a *plural* subject.

Caution.—Avoid using *diversus* or *varius* in this sense. *Diversus* is rather " opposite ;" *varius,* " varying."

> Diversi fugiunt, is, speaking strictly, "fly in *opposite* directions."

(iv.) Sometimes a repeated *alius* (or of *two* persons *alter*) supplies the place of the **reciprocal** "each other." (354.)

> *Tum omnes* alius alium *intuebamur.* Thereupon all of us began to look at *each other.*
>
> *At fratres* alter alterum *adhortari.* . . . But the (two) brothers began to encourage *each other,* etc.

372. Ceteri is "the rest;" as is **reliqu-us, -i.**

Reliqui is opposed to "the mass," those who (or that which) *remain* after many have been deducted.

Ceteri, "the rest," as *contrasted* with some one or more already named, or indicated.

Thus either *ceteri* or *alter* will answer to our "others," "your neighbours," "fellow-creatures," as opposed to "yourself."

> *Qui* ceteros, *or* alterum, *odit, ipse eis,* or *ei, odio erit.* He who hates his neighbours will be hated by them.

Obs. 1.—*Ceteri* has no singular masculine nominative; in other forms it may be used in the singular, but only with collective nouns: *cetera multitudo.*

Obs. 2.—Note the phrase, *nec quidquam nobis Fortuna* reliqui fecit *nisi ut serviamus.* (All else is lost,) and Fate has left us nothing but slavery. (**298,** *b.*)

Exercise 48.

A.

1. Human beings pursue various objects; of these brothers, the one devoted himself to the same tastes and studies as his distinguished father, the other entered political life in quite early manhood. 2. Your judgment (**91**) in this matter has been quite different to mine. You might[1] have shown[2] yourself a true patriot, and lived in freedom in a free country; you preferred riches and pleasure[3] to the toil and danger which freedom involves.[4] 3. All of[4] these men in different modes did good service to the human race; all of them preferred being of use to their neighbours to studying their own interest. 4. We form different aims; some are devoted to wealth, others to pleasure; others place happiness in holding[5] office,[3] in

---

[1] **196.** [2] **241.**

[3] *Plural,* as also for "toil," "danger," "office;" why? Latin uses *abstract* terms much less than English. (See **174.**)

[4] **297.** [5] Gerundive. (**389.**)

power, in the administration of the state, others again[1]
in popularity, interest, influence.   5. Hearing this, the
soldiers began to look[2] at each other, and to wonder
silently what the general wished them to do, and why he
was angry with them rather than with himself.   6. You
pay me compliments in every other (377) word, at the
same time you tax me with the foulest treachery.   I would
have[3] you remember that speaking the truth is one thing,
speaking pleasantly another.   7. The enemy now fled[2] in
opposite directions; of the fugitives the greater part were
slain, the rest threw down their arms[4] and were taken[5]
prisoners to a man.   Few asked for quarter, none obtained
it.   8. We, most of us, came to a stand, looking silently
at each other, and wondering which of us would be[6] the
first to speak.   But Laelius and I held our peace, each
waiting for the other.   9. After raising[7] two armies, they
attack the enemies' camp with one, with the other they
guard the city.   The former (*pl.*) returned without success,
and a sudden panic attacked the latter; thus in both
directions the campaign was most disastrous.

---

[1] *Denique*=lastly, used often in enumerations.
[2] Historic inf.   (See 186.)   [3] 149, i.   [4] Abl. abs.   (See 15.)
[5] Present, 179.   [6] 173, iii. and 62.   [7] Abl. abs.

B

PRONOUNS—*Continued.*

Quisque, uterque, singuli, etc.

373. Quisque is "each," "any," or "every one," of a large number. It so far (in classical prose) resembles an *enclitic* (p. 27, *n.*) that it always comes *after* the word to which it most nearly belongs.

Such words are **relative, interrogative,** and **reflexive** pronouns, **superlatives, comparatives, ordinal** numerals, and **ut.**

It is very rarely used in the plural in prose, but often stands in the singular in apposition to a plural noun. (Cf. *alius* and *alter*, **371,** *Obs.,* and **371,** iv.).

Romani *domum, cum suā* quisque *praedā, redeunt.*

In the neuter, *quidque* is substantival, *quodque* adjectival.

It is sometimes emphasised by prefixing *unus : unus quisque,* "each and every one."

374. With **pronouns** its use is simple, if its proper place in the sentence is remembered.

Milites, quem quisque *viderat, trucidabant.* The soldiers would butcher whomever *any* of them saw. **(192.)**

Non meum est statuere quid cuique *debeas.* It is not for me **(291,** *Obs.* 2) to determine your debt to *each.*

Suum cuique *tribuito.* Give to *every one* his due.

Its other uses are more idiomatic.

375. It is used with **superlative** (most rarely with positive) adjectives, almost always in the *singular,*[1] to express "all," or "every."

Haec optimus[2] quisque *sentit.* These are the views of *all good men,* or, *of every good man.*

Beware of *bonus quisque,* or, *optimi quique.*

---

[1] In the *neuter* the plural is occasionally used, *fortissima quaeque consilia tutissima sunt ;* masculine and feminine most rarely.

[2] This phrase is generally used in a *political* sense,= all good patriots, all the "well-disposed."

376. (i.) If the superlative is *repeated*, we have one of the Latin modes of expressing *proportion*.

> Optimum *quidque* rarissimum *est*.   Things, or all things, are rare in *proportion to* their excellence.

(ii.) The same idea is sometimes expressed by *quisque* with *ut* and *ita*.

> Ut quisque *est* sollertissimus, ita *ferme laboris est* patientissimus. *In proportion to* a man's skill is, as a rule, his readiness to endure toil.

(iii.) Sometimes by *quisque* with *quo, eo, quanto, tanto,* and a **comparative**.

> Quo quisque *est* sollertior, eo *est laboris* patientior.

> *Quo*, "in proportion," *quanto*, "in *exact* proportion."

377. *Quisque* is also joined with **ordinal numerals** : *quinto quoque anno*, "every five years ;" *decimus quisque*, "every tenth man ;" *quotusquisque*, "how few" (lit. each, one only *of how large a number,* —"the thousandth," or "ten-thousandth," that you meet).

> *Primum quidque videamus.*   Let us look at each *in turn*, take each (in turn) as first.
> *Primo quoque tempore.*   At the earliest opportunity possible.

It is also joined with *ut* in a *frequentative* sense.

> Ut cujusque *sors exciderat, alacer arma capiebat.*   As each man's lot fell in turn, he took up arms with enthusiasm.   (See **192.**)

378. (i.) **Uterque** is "both," in the sense of " each *of two*," and denotes two things or persons as looked on *separately*.

> *Propter* utramque *causam.*   For *both* reasons, *i.e.* for *each of the two*.

Ambo is "both," but it is used of two individuals as forming *one whole;* " both together."

> *Qui* utrumque *probat,* ambobus *debet uti.*   He who approves of *each* of these (separately) is bound to use them *both* (together).

So *alter ambove,* "one or both."

(ii.) *Uterque* (like *nemo*) is used with the genitive of *pronouns.* but in apposition with *substantives.*

> Horum *utrumque,* "each of these ;" so vestrum *uterque,* but filius *uterque;* so horum *nemo,* but *nemo* pictor.

(iii.) *Uterque* is used in Latin after *interest inter,* where we should use " the two."

> *Quantum inter* rem utramque *intersit, vides.*   You see the great difference between the *two things.*

(iv.) *Uterque* can be used in the **plural** only where it denotes not two single things or persons, but each of two *parties* or *classes* already represented by a plural word.

> *Stabant instructi acie* Romani Samnitesque ; *par* utrisque *pugnandi studium* (each felt the same ardour for the fight).

379. As *uterque* unites two, and = *unus* et *alter*, so **utervis, uterlibet,** disjoin them, and = *unus* vel *alter*, "whichever of the two you "like," *i.e.* excluding the other. (See **359,** *Obs.*)

Uter is generally interrogative (occasionally a relative) ; it is often repeated.

> Uter utri *plus nocuerit, dubito.* I doubt which of the two injured the other most.

380. Singuli (-ae, -a) is **only used in the plural,** and has two main uses.

(*a*) A distributive numeral, "one apiece," "one each." (See **532.**)

> *Cum* singulis *vestimentis exeant.* Let them go out each with one set of garments.
> *Ejusmodi homines vix* singuli singulis *saeculis nascuntur.* Such men come into the world scarcely once in a century (*one in each* century).

(*b*) As opposed to **universi,** "the mass," "all," looked on as forming one class, *singuli* denotes "individuals ;" "one by one."

> *Romanos* singulos *diligimus,* universos *aversamur.* While we feel affection for *individual* Romans, we loathe the *nation,* or "them as a nation."
> *Nec vero* universo *solum hominum generi, sed etiam* singulis *provisum est.* Nor is it only mankind *in general* (as a whole), but the *individual* that has been cared for.

381. "A single person," where the *single* is emphatic, may be turned by *unus aliquis : ad* unum aliquem *regnum detulerunt,* "offered the crown to a single person ;" "not a single,"=an emphatic "no one," is *ne unus quidem.*

Obs.—*Singularis* is generally used of *qualities,* and denotes "rare," "remarkable."

Exercise 48.

B.

1. As a society we praise the poet whom as individuals we neglected.   2. All true patriots and wise men are on our side, and we would fain have those whom we love and admire hold the same sentiments as ourselves.   3. Men are valued by their countrymen in proportion[1] to their public usefulness; this man was at once a brave[2] soldier and a consummate statesman; for both reasons therefore he enjoyed the highest praise and distinction.   4. It is often the case that men are talkative and obstinate in exact[3] proportion to their folly and inexperience.   5. It is a hackneyed saying that all weak characters[4] crave for different things at different times.   6. It was now evident that the enemy intended[5] to attack our camp at the first possible opening, but that at the same time they would wait for a favourable opportunity.   7. We are one by one deserting and abandoning the man who saved us all.   8. All good patriots are, I believe,[6] convinced of this,[7] that it is quite impossible for us to effect anything by hesitation (**94, 99**), procrastination, and hanging back; so that I feel[8] sure that there is need of haste rather than of deliberation. 9. He found a difficulty in persuading his countrymen that[9] their enemies and allies were powerless separately, most powerful in combination.   10. Thereupon all, each in turn, answered his questions; this done,[10] the greater part besought the senate, appealing[11] to the whole body and to individuals, that one or both the consuls should at the earliest opportunity bring them relief.

---

[1] May be done in two ways. (See **376**, ii. and iii.)

[2] **57**, *a*.   [3] **376**, iii.

[4] "Characters" is of course not to be expressed literally in Latin, it = men. (See **174**, end.)   [5] **14**, *c*.

[6] **32**, *b*.   [7] **341**.   [8] Mood? (**106**.)

[9] See **122**, *b*.   [10] Abl. abs.   [11] Past participle of *obtestor*. (See **413**.)

₊ *The five next Exercises (XLIX.-LIII.) will be on the*
Gerund, Gerundive, Supines, *and* **Participles.**

These, like the infinitive mood (see **94**, and note), are all **verbal nouns** (Intr. 5). They are all derived directly from the verb ; but they are none of them true verbs, for they cannot by themselves make a statement or predication (Intr. 11). But they retain in other respects more or less of the nature of the verb from which they are formed, combined with that of either the **substantive** or the **adjective.**

EXERCISE XLIX.

GERUND AND GERUNDIVE.[1]

Nominative Case.

THE GERUND.

382. The **Gerund** is a verbal substantive in *-ndum*, formed from the present tense of the verb.[2]

It has no plural, but is declined throughout the singular like other neuter substantives in *-um*. Its cases are determined by the same rules as those of other substantives, and are often combined with prepositions : regnandi *studium,* "the desire of reigning ;" ad regnandum *natus,* "born to rule," *or* "a born ruler."

383. But it resembles a verb in so far as it is (*a*) qualified by adverbs, not by adjectives, and is (*b*) followed by the same case as the verb from which it is derived: *ad* bene *vivendum, parcendo* hostibus, orbem *terrarum subigendo.*

---

[1] These are names given by grammarians to a substantival and an adjectival form of what is often called the *participle in -dus,* sometimes the *future participle passive.* Their origin and precise nature are much disputed. Whether the Gerund arose out of the Gerundive, or *vice versa,* is a question which lies outside the scope of this work ; it will be taken for granted here that by the **Gerund** is meant the whole substantival declension, *including the nominative,* of the singular neuter form, *faciendum, -i, -o ;* by the **Gerundive** the whole adjectival declension, as seen in *facien-dus, -da, -dum* (when attached to, or predicated of, a noun), through all cases and genders, and in both numbers.

[2] The word Gerund is derived from this active sense, as expressing the *action* of the verb (*a gerendo, gerundo*), the verb *agere* being already appropriated to the term *active verb.* Most grammarians limit the term Gerund to the oblique cases ; it is perhaps more reasonable to include the nominative.

247

384. The **gerund** therefore, like the **infinitive** mood, corresponds to the English verbal substantive in *-ing*: "for *living* well," "by *sparing* the enemy," "by *subduing* the world," (see **94**); sometimes to the English infinitive in the form "*to do,*" "*to see,*" properly itself a gerundial infinitive.

But as the Latin infinitive is not used as a substantive in the genitive, dative, or ablative, or with prepositions, its place is taken by the gerund in *-ndi, -ndo, -ndum.* (See Examples in **99.**)

385. In the nominative (and accusative in *oratio obliqua*) the two verbal nouns, the **infinitive** and **gerund**, exist side by side, but their uses are quite different.

(*a*) The **nominative gerund** has *laid aside* its power [1] of governing an accusative of the nearer object, and has acquired **the sense of duty, necessity, obligation.**

(*b*) Thus *currere* = running, and we can say, currere *mihi jucundum est, running* is delightful to me; but we do not use *currendum* in the same sense; for *mihi* currendum *est* (*lit.* there is *a running* for me), is only used in the sense of "I *must* run."[2]

386. But this use of the *nominative* of the gerund is only found with **intransitive** verbs, or **transitive** verbs used **absolutely.** (Intr. 40.)

We cannot say, hostes *nobis vincendum est,* we must conquer *the enemy,* but must use the **gerundive,** *hostes . . .* vincendi sunt; but we can say, *vincendum est,* we must *win the day;* and we can say *hostibus parcendum est,* we ought to spare the enemy, or *occasione utendum fuit,* the opportunity should have been used, for *parco* and *utor* are *intransitive* verbs. (See **228,** *Obs.*)

387. The **person** on whom the duty lies is in the **dative.**

But with verbs which are combined with a *dative* as their object, the ablative with *a, ab,* should be substituted **to avoid ambiguity**: *civibus* a te *consulendum est,* you must consult the interests of your countrymen; *tibi* would leave the meaning doubtful; but, *suo* cuique *judicio utendum est,* each should follow his own judgment.

Obs.—The gerund therefore, though properly **active,** has sometimes the construction of **passive** verbs.

---

[1] There are still traces of this construction in classical Latin :—
     Aeternas poenas *in morte timendum est.*—LUCRETIUS.
     Quam (viam) *nobis quoque ingrediendum sit.*—CICERO.

[2] The reader may be referred to a very interesting discussion of the whole question in Mr. Roby's preface to the second volume of his *Latin Grammar.*

388. By the aid of the gerund and the verb *sum*, a whole conjugation can be formed to express the idea of what *is, was, will be,* etc., a duty or necessity.

Mihi, tibi, ei, etc., *scribendum* est, fuit, erit. I, you, he, etc., *must* write, *should have* written, *shall* or *will* have to write.

So also—Ne *nobis moriendum* sit. To prevent our *having to* die.

Or—*Dixit sibi scribendum* esse, fuisse. He said that he *had,* had *had,* to write.

Obs.—This is the commonest of all modes of expressing duty, obligation, etc., commoner even than *oportet, debeo,* or *necesse est.* (See **198**, iii.)

THE GERUNDIVE.

389. When we wish to use a transitive verb *with its direct object expressed,* we cannot use the gerund, but must have recourse to the **gerundive**.

The **gerundive** is a verbal *adjective* in *-ndus,* and as such is used in agreement with (Intr. 9) substantives and pronouns.

Though probably not originally passive, it has assumed a passive meaning; the object of the transitive verb will therefore, where a duty is asserted, be in the nominative, and the gerundive be used as a *predicative adjective.*

The person on whom the duty falls will still be in the *dative.*

Hostes tibi timendi *erant.* You *ought to have* feared the enemy.

390. In the **nominative** (and accusative of *oratio obliqua*), the gerundive, like the gerund, denotes *necessity* or *duty;* in **other cases** it, like the gerund, denotes merely the *action of the verb,* the English verbal in *-ing.*

Nom. Amici tibi consolandi sunt. You *ought to* console your friends.

Gen. Tui consolandi causā. For the sake of *consoling* you.

391. The use of the gerundive is confined to **transitive** verbs, including **deponents**.

N.B.—We cannot say *tu parcendus eras,* "you ought to have been spared," but we can say *gloria consequenda est.*

With verbs which govern any case but the accusative, the **gerund** must be used, not the **gerundive**.

Tibi parcendum[1] *erat, tibi persuadendi causā.*

---

[1] Such exceptional uses as haec *utenda, fruenda, pudenda,* etc., *sunt,* are to be accounted for by the fact that in older Latin these verbs were occasionally transitive, *i.e.* were used with the accusative; it is better to write, his rebus *utendum est.*

Obs.—The difference will be shown by the double use of *consulo.* Just as *consulo* Caium, means, "I ask Caius for advice," *consulo* Caio, "I consult the interests of Caius," so we must say—

Caius *consulendus est.*   Caius must be consulted.
But—Caio *consulendum est.*   The interests of Caius must be consulted.

So also tibi *credendum fuit;* haec *credenda sunt,* for, "you ought to have been believed (trusted);" "these (statements) ought to be believed." (See **248.**)

Compare the impersonal use of the passive voice of intransitive verbs. (217.)

392. As with the gerund, a whole conjugation may be formed by the *gerundive* and verb *sum.*

> *Hostes tum* debellandi fuere.   The enemy *should have been* conquered then.
> *Dixit rem* perficiendam fuisse.   He said that the matter *should* have (=ought to have) been finished.

393. The gerundive is sometimes used as an *attributive* adjective with a sense of *necessity, fitness,* etc., even in the *oblique cases.*

> *Cum haud* irridendo *hoste pugnavi.*   I have fought with no *despicable* foe (no fit object for ridicule).

394. Caution.—Neither gerund nor gerundive denotes **possibility**; our "is to be" requires caution, as it may mean either *possibility* or *duty.*

"Your son was not to be persuaded" is not *filio tuo non fuit* persuadendum (=your son *should* not have been persuaded), but, *filio tuo persuaderi* non potuit.

But sometimes with *a negative* word it approaches the idea of possibility.

> *Calamitas* vix toleranda.   A scarcely *endurable* calamity.

Exercise 49.

The Gerund and Gerundive to be used exclusively for "ought," "should," etc.

1. He ought voluntarily to have endured exile, or else died on the field of battle, or done anything[1] rather than this. 2. Ought we not to return thanks to men to whom we are under an obligation? 3. The soldiers should have been ordered[2] to cease from slaughter, and to slay no unarmed person; women at least and children ought to have been spared, to say nothing[3] of the sick and wounded. 4. I do not object to your exposing your own person to danger, but you ought in the present emergency to be careful for your soldiers' safety. 5. This is what one so sensible[4] as yourself should have done, and not left that undone. 6. Seeing[5] that he must either retreat, or come into collision on the morrow with a far from contemptible enemy, he decided on forming line and fighting at once. 7. Nor should we listen to men (72) who tell us that we ought to be angry with a friend who refuses[6] to flatter and fawn upon us. 8. Your son was unwise enough[7] not to be persuaded to confess that the matter should or could be forgotten. 9. We shall all have to die one day: when[8] and how each will have to meet the common and universal doom, is beyond[9] the power of the wisest of mankind to foresee or to foretell. 10. It seems that you have one and all come to me in[10] the king's palace from two motives, partly for the sake of consulting me, partly to clear yourselves;[11] you must therefore seize the opportunity, and plead your cause while the king is present (*abl. abs.*).

---

[1] **359.**   [2] Do in two ways, *i.e.* use both *jubeo* and *impero*. (See **120.**)
[3] Use *ne dicam* (**100**, note); it is used almost as an adverb, *i.e.* any case may be used by the side of the *dicam* (**364**, Ex. *note* [1]).
[4] **224,** *Obs.* 2.   [5] *Quum videret.* (See **429.**)
[6] Mood? (See **77.**)
[7] Turn "your son, being most unwise, was not," etc. (**224,** *Obs.* 1.)
[8] Not *quum.* (See **157,** ii.)
[9] "Not even the wisest of mankind can," etc.
[10] See **315.**   [11] See **399,** *Obs.* 1.

GERUND AND GERUNDIVE—*Continued.*

Oblique Cases.

395. In other cases than the nominative (and accusative of *oratio obliqua*) neither the Gerund nor (with few exceptions) the Gerundive conveys any sense of *duty, necessity,* etc.

They merely denote the **general action** of the verb, and correspond to the infinitive mood used as a noun, and to the English verbal substantive in -*ing.* (See **384, 390,** and **99.**)

When thus used, the **gerund** retains its proper verbal power of governing an accusative (**385**); we can say "patres vestros *videndi,*" of seeing your fathers; "vera *judicando,*" by forming a right decision; but oftener than not, and especially in the *accusative* and *dative,* it gives place to the **gerundive.** Thus—

> *Acc. Ad Gall*os *insequend*os is far more common than *ad Gall*os *insequend*um, which is scarcely ever used.
>
> *Dat.* Bello *gerendo* is always used, rather than, bellum *gerendo.*
>
> *Abl. Epistolā scribendā* is commoner than *epistola*m *scribend*o.
>
> *Gen. Epistol*ae *scribend*ae is commoner than *epistol*am *scribend*i.

Of course with **intransitive** verbs the **gerund** is invariably used. (**391.**)

> *Ad succurrend*um *miseris, parcendo feminis, hostibus persuadendi,* etc., never *ad miseros succurrend*os, *parcend*is *femin*is, etc. So, *miseris succurritur* not *miseri succurruntur,* etc.

396. The **accusative** of both the gerund and gerundive is used with *ad*, as a substitute for a separate **final** *clause*, with *ut, quo*, etc. (See 100.)

"To," "in order to," "for the purpose of," is constantly thus expressed; sometimes also by the **genitive** with *causā* or *gratiā*.

> *Gerund.*—Ad consultandum, or consultandi causa, *huc venimus*. We have come here *to deliberate*.
> *Gerundive.*—Ad pacem petendam, or, pacis petendae causā missi sumus. We have been sent for the purpose of asking for peace.

Sometimes we find the participle in -rus : *consultaturi adsumus*, we are here *to deliberate*.

Its use with other prepositions is rare : inter *ludendum*, ob *judicandum :* "in the midst of play," "for the sake of giving a verdict."

397. The **dative** of both forms is used after certain verbs and adjectives such as *praeficere, praeesse, dare operam, impar*, etc., and also in the sense of *aim* or *purpose*.

> *Gerund.*—Legendo dabat operam. He was giving his attention *to* reading.
> *Gerundive.*—Bello gerendo me praefecistis. You made me preside *over* the carrying on the war.
> *Gerundive.*—Comitia consulibus creandis. The meeting *for* the election of consuls.

Note also, solvendo *non esse*, not to be *able to* pay (one's debts). The **gerundive** is almost invariably preferred with transitive verbs.

398. The use of the **ablative** is mainly *instrumental* and *causal*.

With transitive verbs the **gerundive** is more common (except with neuter pronouns) than the **gerund;** aliquid *agendo* (by doing *something*); but, bello *trahendo vinces* (by prolonging the war).

Obs.—It is also occasionally used with the preposition *in ;* but it is *not* used with *pro* and *sine* to represent our "instead of," "without," followed by the verbal substantive ; you cannot say pro *sequendo*, sine *sequendo* for "instead of," *or* "without following." (See **332. 8.**)

399. The **genitive** of both gerund and gerundive is used in most of the senses of the genitive ; with transitive verbs the latter is to be preferred, unless **ambiguity,** or a recurrence of the same sound, would arise. Thus *discendi* aliquid (*alicujus* **would be ambiguous**); vera *judicandi;* patres vestros *videndi causā* (to avoid *vestrorum videndorum*).

Obs. 1.—The genitive *singular* of the gerundive is used with *sui,* even when it denotes a number of persons: *sui* purgandi *causā adsunt,* they are here to clear *themselves,* so *vestri, nostri.*

Obs. 2.—Notice such phrases as *respirandi spatium,* a breathing space ; *sui colligendi facultas,* an opportunity of rallying ; *pacis faciendae auctor et princeps fui,* I was the suggestor of, and the leader in making peace. The idiom *hoc conservandae libertatis est,* this *tends to* the preservation of freedom, has been noticed above. (**292,** *Obs.*)

400. The accusative of the gerundive is used **predicatively** (**239**) in a *final* sense in combination with certain verbs : *do,* I give, *curo,* I take care of, *suscipio,* I undertake, etc.

> *Obsides Aeduis* custodiendos *tradit.* He hands over the hostages to the Aedui, to keep in guard.
> *Agros eis* habitandos *dedit.* He gave them lands *to dwell in.*
> *Caesar pontem* faciendum *curavit.* Caesar *had a* bridge made.

It thus retains the idea of **obligation**, and often answers to the English infinitive (*to* keep, etc.), itself originally a dative of aim or purpose.

Exercise 50.

1. These men came, it is said, to our camp for the purpose of praising themselves[1] and accusing you (*pl.*); they are now intent on pacifying you, and clearing themselves of a most serious indictment.   2. The matter must on no account be postponed; you must on this very day come to a decision, as to whether it tends to the destruction or to the preservation of the constitution.   3. Such gentleness and clemency did he show in the very hour of triumph, that it may be questioned whether he won greater[2] popularity by pardoning his enemies or by relieving his friends.   4. There can be no question that

---

[1] **399,** *Obs.* 1.   [2] *Plus.* (See **294.**)

in point[1] of consulting his country's interests rather than his own, of sacrificing his own convenience (*pl.*) to that[2] of his friends, of keeping in check alike his temper and his tongue, this young man far outdid all[3] the old. 5. All the spoil which the defendant had obtained by sacking temples, by confiscating the property of individuals, and by levying contributions on so many communities, he secretly had[4] carried out of the country. 6. It was by venturing on something, he said, and by pressing on, not by delay and hanging back, nor by much[5] discussion and little action, that they had effected what they had hitherto achieved.[6] 7. It was I who suggested the following up the enemy (*sing.*), in order to leave[7] him no breathing space, no[8] opportunity of rallying, or of ascertaining the nature[9] or number of his assailants. ·

---

[1] Simply abl. of limitation, or reference. (**274.**)
[2] See **345.**
[3] Use *quisque.* (**375.**)
[4] *Curo.* (**400.**)
[5] "Much," "little," with gerund. (See **53.**)
[6] Repeat the same verb ; mood ? (See **77.**)
[7] Use the passive. (**216.**)
[8] Use *ullus* after *ne*, as more emphatic than *qui.* (See **357, 358.**)
[9] See **174.**

THE SUPINES.

401. The so-called **Supines** in -um and -u are the accusative and ablative cases of a **verbal substantive** of the fourth declension.

This substantive is formed in the same manner as the passive participle (*auditus, factus,* etc.), and the name *supine* is a Latin translation of the Greek ὔπτιος (on his back), which, by a metaphor borrowed from wrestlers, was fancifully applied to the passive as distinguished from the active voice. Neither, however, of the supines has a really passive signification.

402. The **Supine** in -um is used only in combination with *verbs of motion.* It expresses the purpose, design, or *final cause,* of the motion. It is thus included among the various Latin modes of expressing purpose or design mentioned in **100.**

It so far keeps its verbal nature as to govern the case of the verb from which it is formed.

> *Pacem nos* flagitatum *venerunt* (**230**). They have come to importune us for peace.
>
> *Pabulatum emisit milites.* He sent his soldiers out to forage, *or* "a foraging" (a = an, on).

Obs.—This *supine* is one of the few instances of *motion towards* being expressed by the accusative without a preposition. (See **235.**)

403. It is used with *ire* (to go) oftener than with any other verb, and forms with this sometimes a kind of additional tense, though rarely, if ever, in Caesar or Cicero : "I am on the way to," "I set about." It thus gives the action an intensive force, sometimes almost equal to our "goes out of his way to."

> *Video te patris tui injurias* ultum ire. I observe that you are *on the way to* avenge the wrongs done to your father.
>
> *Fortunas suas* perditum it. He is *on the way to* ruin his own fortunes.
>
> *Sibi* nocitum it. He is *on the way to* damage himself.

Obs.—Its use with the impersonal passive of *iri* to supply the place of the absent **passive infinitive future** has been noticed (**193, iv.**).

> *Injurias patris ultum iri dixit.* He said that the wrongs done to his father would be avenged.

404. The **Supine** in -u is the **ablative** of a similar verbal substantive. It is in fact an ablative of *limitation* (**274**). It is mostly confined to forms derived from verbs of **speaking** and of the **senses**, such as *dictu, memoratu, auditu, visu*, etc., but includes *factu* and *natu*.

It is only used with **adjectives** (mostly such as express *difficulty and ease, credibility and the reverse*), and a few **substantives** resembling adjectives, such as *fas, nefas, scelus*, and the **verb** *pudet*.

> Difficile *est* dictu *quanto simus in odio.* It is *hard to say* how hated we are.
>
> Nefas *est* dictu *talem senectutem miseram fuisse.* It is *sacrilege to say* that such an old age was wretched.

Note that the *supine* in *-u* does not, as that in *-um*, govern a case; but it may, as in these two examples, have either an interrogative clause (**165**), or an infinitive dependent upon it.

It may be compared with the Greek infinitive active καλός ἰδεῖν, or the English "fair *to see.*"

Exercise 51.

1. Ambassadors came from the Athenians to Philip at Olynthus[1] to complain of wrongs done to their countrymen. 2. He started to his father at Marseilles from his uncle at Narbonne to see the games, but within the last[2] few days was killed, either by an assassin, or by brigands, while[3] on his journey. 3. Do you (*pl.*) remain within the camp in order to take food and rest and all else that you require; let us, who are less exhausted with fighting—for did we not arrive fresh and untouched immediately after the contest?—go out to get food and forage. 4. We have come to deprecate your (*pl.*) anger, and to entreat for peace; we earnestly hope that we shall obtain what (*pl.*) we seek for. 5. He sent ambassadors to the senate to congratulate Rome[4] on her victory. 6. It sounds incredible how repeatedly and how urgently I have warned[5] you to place no reliance in that man. 7. It is not easy to say whether this man should be spared, and be[6] sent away with his companions, or whether he should at once be either slain or cast into prison.

---

[1] For this and the "*at's*" in the next sentence, see **315**.
[2] See **325**, *Obs.* [3] Either *dum* (see **180**), or present participle (**410**).
[4] Why not *Roma?* (See **319**.)
[5] Mood? (See **165, 166.**) [6] *ipse.* (See **355**, *Obs.* 1.)

R

PARTICIPLES.

General Remarks.

405. Participles are verbal adjectives, or rather **verbs used as adjectives.**[1]

Hence their name, *participia*, as sharing in (*participari*) the nature of two parts of speech. They differ from the Gerundive as they may govern all cases precisely as finite **verbs**, and also as representing more distinctly *tense* and *voice;* but they are inflected as **adjectives,** and, as adjectives, are both *attached to*, and, as in compound tenses, *predicated of*, substantives and pronouns. (See Intr. 8.)

> *Res* abstrusa *ac* recondita (attribute). A deep and mysterious question.
> *Multi* occisi *sunt* (predicate). Many were slain.

406. (i.) But their most characteristic use is that in which they stand in **apposition to the subject or object of a verb,** and form as in English, but to a still greater extent, a substitute for a *subordinate clause,* either adjectival or adverbial. (Intr. 81, 82.) Thus—

> *Caesar haec* veritus. Caesar fearing (= *who*, or *as he,* feared) this.
> *Haec* scribens *interpellatus sum.* I was interrupted *while*[2] *I was* writing this.
> *Urbem* oppugnaturus *constitit.* He halted *when*[2] *he was* on the point of assaulting the city.
> *Nobiles, imperio suo jamdiu* repugnantes, *uno praelio oppressit.* He crushed in a single battle the nobles, *who had* long been contesting his sovereignty.

---

[1] The **action or state** which the verb in its finite form (*i.e.* when used as a true verb) *predicates*, is looked on as a **quality** embodied in, and attached by language, or *attributed*, to some person or thing. "Caesar seeing this, etc.,"—we add to our general idea of Caesar the special quality of *seeing this.*

[2] In English the temporal conjunctions *when, while,* can *apparently* be closely connected with participles, "when coming," "while writing." These are really elliptical expressions, "when (he was) a (on) coming," "while (he was) a *writing;*" and the apparent *participle* was originally a verbal noun. In Latin such combinations as "*dum scribens,*" "*quum veniens,*" are of course absolutely inadmissible.

(ii.) Sometimes the Latin participle represents not a *sub-ordinate*, but a *co-ordinate*, clause. (Intr. 74, 75.)

> *Militem* arreptum *trahebat.* He *seized* the soldier, *and* began to·drag him off. (See 15.)
>
> *Patrem* secutus *ad Hispaniam navigavit.* He *followed* his father, *and* sailed to Spain.

407. Some participles are used precisely as **adjectives**, and as such admit of comparative and superlative degrees.

(i.) Such past participles as *doctus, eruditus, paratus, erectus,* etc., are constantly so used.

(ii.) So also such present participles as *abstinens, amans, appetens, fidens, florens, nocens,* etc. ; these when transitive are often joined with the genitive in place of the accusative : patriae *amantissimus.* (See **302**.)

(iii.) Some even, as adjectives, admit the negative prefix *in-*, which is never joined with the verb : in*nocens,* im*potens,* in*sipiens,* in*domitus,* in*victus,* in*tactus.*

Obs.—At the same time, though this use of the participle is common in both languages, we must be cautious in translating English *participial adjectives* literally : " a *threatening* letter," is " *literae* minaces ;" " a *moving* speech," " *oratio* flebilis ;" " a *smiling* landscape," " *aspectus* amoenus ;" " *burning* heat," " *aestus* fervidus."

408. Others, like adjectives, are used exactly as **substantives** : *adolescens, infans, senatus-consultum, candidatus, praefectus,* etc. (See 51.)

> Such are—*Institutum,* "fixed course," "principle" (sing.), "institutions" (pl.) ; *acta,* "measures," "proceedings ;" *facta,* "deeds ;" *merita (in),* "services" (towards) ; *peccatum, delictum,* "wrong-doing," "crime ;" the *future participle* is only so used in the word *futur-um* (-a, pl.).

Obs.—It has already been said that many of these still retain their true participial, *i.e. verbal,* construction : *multa* ab eo *praeclare facta.* (See **55**.) But we may also say *merita* ejus, *facta, acta, dicta, praecepta, delicta,* ejus, etc.

409. There are in Latin **three** participles, exclusive of the **gerundive**, which is not here included among the participles as it cannot govern a case.

> *Active* verbs have **two** : *Dicens* (pres.), *dicturus* (fut.).
>
> *Deponent* verbs have **three** : *Sequens* (pres.), *secutus* (past), *secuturus* (fut.).
>
> *Passive* verbs have **one** : *Dictus* (past).

Obs.—This last has occasionally a middle signification. (See **233** and **413**.)

Present Participle.

410. This participle is always **active**. When used as a participle (not as a mere adjective) it denotes **uncompleted action contemporaneous with** that of the verb to whose subject or object it is in apposition.

> *Haec dixit* moriens. He said this *while dying.*
>
> *Provincia* decedens[1] *Rhodum praetervectus sum. In the act of* (or, *while*) returning home from my province, I sailed past Rhodes.
>
> *Ad mortem* eunti *obviam factus sum.* I met him *as he was going to death.*

Obs.—Thus after "to hear," and "to see," the present participle is used when the actual presence of the hearer or seer is emphasised.

> I heard you say. *Audivi te* dicentem.[2]
>
> He saw the house blaze. *Aedes* flammantes *vidit.*

411. Hence (especially in the **nominative**) its meaning is far more limited than that of the English present participle, which is often used *vaguely,* as regards even time, and *widely* to represent other conjunctions than those of mere time. Thus—

> "*Mounting* (*i.e.* after mounting) his horse he galloped off to the camp;" "*arriving* (*i.e.* having arrived) in Italy he caught a fever;" "*hearing* this (*i.e.* in consequence of hearing), he ordered an inquiry;" "*throwing* themselves at his feet (*i.e.* having thrown) they made a long speech."

In all these cases the Latin present participle would be entirely wrong; *equum conscendens* would mean that he galloped to the camp while *in the act of* mounting; *in Italiam perveniens,* that the fever was caught at *the moment of reaching* Italy; *haec audiens,* that the inquiry was ordered *while he* was listening to a story; *se projicientes,* that they made a long speech *whilst* in the very act of falling prostrate; —all of which would of course be wrong or absurd.

In the first three instances *quum* should be used with the pluperfect subjunctive: quum *equum* conscendisset; quum pervenisset; quum *haec* audivisset (or *his auditis*); and in the last the passive, or rather *middle,* past participle,—*ad pedes ejus* projecti.

---

[1] *Decedere* is the technical word for *to return home* from holding the government of a province.

[2] Sometimes, *audivi te,* cum diceres. (See **429.**)

412. So too, when the English present participle, while expressing time **contemporaneous with a verb in the past,** implies also a *cause, quum* with the **imperfect subjunctive** should be used.

"Caesar, *hoping* soon to win the day, led out his men," should be, *Caesar,* quum *se brevi victurum esse* speraret, *suos eduxit;* not *Caesar sperans,* etc.

Though this rule should be strictly observed, it is not without exceptions, especially in Caesar.

Obs.—The present participle sometimes represents a *concessive* or *though*-clause. (Intr. 59, *g.*)

> *Re* consentientes, *verbis,* or *vocabulis, discrepamus. Though* we agree (*while* agreeing) in substance, we differ in words.

413. On the other hand, the **past participles of deponent** and **semi-deponent verbs** (Intr. 44), such as *veritus, ratus, ausus, confisus, diffisus, usus, progressus* (advancing), *aversatus* (expressing disgust at), *indignatus* (feeling indignation at), and those of passive verbs used in a *middle* or *reflexive* sense, as *conversus* (turning), *projectus* (throwing himself), *humi provolutus* (rolling on the ground), are used much in the same sense as the English participles "fearing," "thinking," "venturing," "trusting," "advancing."

"Caesar *fearing* this" should be either, *Caesar haec* veritus, or, *Caesar* quum *haec* timeret; "*turning* to his friends" should be either, quum *ad suos* se convertisset, or, *ad suos* conversus.

414. But the oblique cases, especially the **dative** and **genitive,** are used with greater freedom, and often take the place of an adjectival (or adverbial) clause, or of a substantive. (See **73.**)

> *Verum* (or *vera*) dicentibus *facile cedam.* I will always yield *to those who* speak the truth; or, to men *if* they speak the truth.
>
> Pugnantium *clamore perterritus.* Alarmed by the shouts of the *combatants,* or of those *who* were fighting.
>
> *Nescio quem prope* adstantem *interrogari.* I questioned some one *who* was standing by.

Obs.—Even here a relative clause is equally common, and in the **nominative,** "men doing this," or "those who do this," should be translated by *qui hoc faciunt; hoc* facientes *laudantur* would mean, not "*men who* do this are praised," but "*they* are praised *while doing* this," and ii *hoc facientes,* in imitation of "those doing this" (οἱ ταῦτα ποιοῦντες) is not Latin at all. (See **346.**)

415. These two oblique cases of the present participle very often take the place of an **English noun**.

> (*a.*) Interroganti *mihi respondit*. He replied to my *question*.
>
> So—*Haec* interroganti *hoc respondit*. To this *question* he made this *answer*.
>
> (*b.*) Lugentium *lacrimae*, tears of *mourning*. Gratulantium *clamores*, shouts of *congratulation*.
>
> (*c.*) Notice also, *vox ejus* morientis, his *dying* voice or words; adhortantis *verba*, his *cheering* words, or words of *encouragement*.

Caution.—Beware of such Latin as luctūs *lacrimae, voces* doloris, etc.

Past Participle.

416. The **past participle** belongs entirely, except in *deponent* verbs, to the **passive voice**. We cannot say *adventus*, "having arrived," *auditus*, "having heard," but must use *quum*. (See Elementary Rules, 14.)

The use of this participle to form the compound tenses of the passive is obvious; its use with *habeo* (*hoc* cognitum *habeo*) has been pointed out (**188**); also the phrases, *tibi* consultum *volo*, "I wish your interests consulted" (**240**, *Obs.*), and, properato, *or* consulto, *opus est*, "there is need of haste *or* deliberation." (**286**.)

417. (i.) The passive participle combined with a substantive often answers to an English verbal or abstract noun, connected with another noun by the preposition *of*, and used to denote a fact in the past.

> *Post* urbem conditam. After the *foundation of* the city.
> Violati foederis *poenas dabis*. You shall be punished for the *violation*, or breach, *of* the treaty.
> Nuntiata *clades*. The *news of* the disaster.

(ii.) Occasionally the **gerundive** is used in a similar way as almost the equivalent of a present passive participle.

> *Qui* violandis legatis *interfuere*. Those who took part in the *outrage on the* ambassadors.

Obs.—We have here (and in **415**) another instance of the comparative **poverty of Latin in substantives**, especially in those of an *abstract* and *generalising* nature. (See **54, 174**.)

Future Participles.

418. The **future participle** in *-rus* is always **active**; for its various meanings besides those of mere futurity, see **14, c.** It forms (with *sum*) a substitute for the **future subjunctive** (114) and for the **future infinitive** (193, iii.) The following examples will recall some of its more idiomatic uses.

(*a.*) *Hoc se unquam* facturum *fuisse negat.* He says he *would* never *have done* this. (**193, v.**)

(*b.*) *Nunquam* futurum fuisse *ut urbs caperetur respondit.* He replied that the city *would* never *have been* taken.

(*c.*) *Vereor ne domum nunquam* sis rediturus. I fear that you are never *destined to* return home. (**139.**)

(*d.*) *Plura* locuturos *dimisit.* He sent them away, as they were on *the point of* speaking further.

(*e.*) *Adeo territi sunt* ut *arma facile* tradituri fuerint. They were so terrified that they *would have* easily delivered up their arms. (**115.**)

(*f.*) *Hic* mansurus fui. Here I *intended*, or *was prepared*, to remain.

(*g.*) *Fiet, quod* futurum est. That which *is to be*, will be.

Exercise 52.

The asterisk* means that the participle is to take the place of the *relative* or *conjunction.*

1. Are we[1] then to spare those who* resist (us), and hurl darts at us? 2. Are we to spare these men even though* they resist us? 3. I heard you ask more than once whether we were going to return to[2] my home, or to go to your father in London. 4. I heard the whole city ring with the shouts of joy and triumph. 5. Returning in his old age from India, he died in his own house; his sons and grandsons stood round his sick-bed, gazed sadly (61) on his dying countenance, and retained in their memories his prophetic words. 6. To my complaint that he had broken his word, he said that he had done nothing of the kind, but was ready to pay the penalty of having caused[4] such a loss. 7. I saw the soldiers brandishing

---

[1] Gerund with *erit.* (See **388.**)
[2] **316, iii.**
[3] **415, c.**
[4] = of the causing of . . . (**417.**)

their weapons throughout the city; I heard the voices of joy and triumph; I recognised the clear proofs of the announcement of a victory.· 8. Throwing themselves at the king's[1] feet, they solemnly appealed to him not to give over to certain destruction men who* were not guilty up to that time, and who* were likely to be of the utmost value to the nation one day.   9. Embarking at Naples, and fearing for the safety of himself and his family,[2] he took refuge with my father at Marseilles.   10. His words alike of praise (415, *c*) and of rebuke were drowned in shouts of indignation, and in groans and outcries of disapproval. 11. Distrusting my own sense of hearing, I asked some[3] one who* was standing nearer you whether I had heard aright; he answered my question in the affirmative.[4] 12. Are you not ashamed[5] and sorry[5] for the abandonment of your undertaking, the desertion of your friend, and the violation of your word?

---

[1] See **257**.   [2] *Sui,* **349,** *Obs.*   [3] *Nescio quis,* **362.**
[4] See **162.**   [5] **202.**

THE ABLATIVE ABSOLUTE.

ONE of the commonest uses of the Latin participle is that called the **Ablative Absolute**.

419. A **participle** and **substantive** (or pronoun) joined together in the ablative, and standing by themselves, often in a Latin sentence form a substitute for a **subordinate clause.** *Caesar*, acceptis litteris, *proficisci constituit. Acceptis litteris* is here the exact equivalent of such a clause as *quum litteras accepisset.*

420. (i.) This ablative absolute is represented in English, sometimes by a participle in apposition, "receiving" or "having received;" sometimes by such phrases as "on," "after," "in consequence of," "in spite of," "without," "instead of," followed by a verbal substantive, as that in -*ing*; sometimes by a subordinate clause introduced by "after that," "when," "while," "because," "although," "if," etc., sometimes by a co-ordinate clause (**406,** ii.) ; **very rarely by the almost obsolete English absolute case,** once a dative, now a nominative : "this said," "this done."

Thus—(ii.) *His auditis,* having heard, or, hearing this; *te praesente,* in your presence; *me invito,* against my will; *hoc comperto scelere, in consequence of* discovering this crime ; *te repugnante, in spite* of, in the teeth of, your resistance ; *illo manente, as long* as he remains ; *Antonio oppresso, if* Antony is crushed ; *his dictis abiit, this said,* he went off; *patefacta porta erupit,* he had the gate opened *and* sallied forth.

421. The ablative, therefore, is occasionally that of mere *time,* as *regnante Tiberio,* "in the reign of Tiberius," but much oftener of *attendant circumstances* and *cause.*

Owing to the absence of a past participle active in Latin, the use of this idiom, as of the *quum* clause, is exceedingly frequent.

It is a good rule never to translate it into English by an absolute case, or by a clause beginning with "when."

422. Cautions.—The **ablative absolute**, however, is not always admissible.

(*a.*) It can of course only be used in the passive with *transitive* verbs (**416**). You cannot say *Caesare pervento* for "Caesar having arrived," or *Caesare persuaso* for "Caesar having been persuaded," but *Caesar* quum *pervenisset, Caesari* quum *persuasum esset.*

(*b.*) It must never be used if the person denoted by its substantive or pronoun is either the subject or object of the principal verb of the clause.

"Caesar having taken the *enemy* massacred *them*" is not captis hostibus *Caesar eos trucidavit*, but *Caesar* captos hostes *trucidavit*. "As I was reading this I saw you" is not, me *haec* legente *te vidi*, but *haec* legens *te vidi*.

423. (*c.*) It *need* not be used when a past participle active is supplied by a deponent verb.

Haec locutus is as good Latin as *his dictis*.

(*d.*) It is *rarely* used to represent more than a substantive and verb, or verb with its accusative : *haec me dicente;* but for so long a combination as *Caesare a militibus imperatore salutato*, a *quum*-clause should be substituted.

(*e.*) Its use with a **future** participle is very rare in the best *prose*. The phrase *Caesare venturo* is from Horace.

424. Sometimes (as the verb *sum* has no participle) the place of the participle is taken by an **adjective** or **substantive**, which is joined in a predicative sense with another substantive or pronoun.

> *Me* invito, against my will ; *te* duce, with you for leader (under your leadership (**333**)) ; *me* auctore, at my suggestion ; salvis *legibus*, without violating the law ; honestis *judicibus*, if the judges are honourable men.

Obs.—Sometimes the participle is used alone with a dependent clause.

> *Missis* qui rogarent. Having sent people to ask.
> *Comperto* eum aegrotare. Having ascertained that he was ill.

425. With a **negative** the ablative absolute often represents the English "without" joined to the verbal noun. (See 398, *Obs.*) Thus—

> *Te* non adjuvante, *without* your assistance ; nullo *expectato* duce, *without* waiting for any guide ; re infecta, *without* success ; nullo *respondente*, *without* receiving an answer from any one ; causā incognitā, *without* hearing the case ; indictā causā condemnatur, he is condemned *without* pleading his cause.

426. The proper place for the ablative absolute is early in, or quite at the beginning of, a sentence. (Intr. 104.) It is only when extremely emphatic that it comes last. (Intr. 92.)

Exercise 53.

N.B.—1. " And " enclosed in brackets is to be omitted and a participial construction substituted. (**406**, ii.)
    2. The asterisk* marks the use of the participle as in Ex. 52.

1. Thereupon, after saluting the enemies' general, he turned to his companions, (and) setting spurs to his horse, rode past the ranks of the Germans without either waiting for his staff or receiving an answer[1] from any one. 2. It was at my suggestion, to prevent your voice and strength failing you, that you suspended for a while the speech which* you had begun. 3. For myself, fearing that glory and the pursuit of honour had but little effect with you, I abandoned such topics[2] (and) tried to work upon your feelings by a different method. 4. All this he did at the instigation of your brother, without either receiving or hoping for any reward. 5. It was most fortunate for me that, fighting[3] as I did against your wishes and advice, not to say in spite of your opposition and resistance, I gained the victory without the loss of a single[4] soldier, and with few wounded. 6. After attacking the camp for several hours, the barbarians were so exhausted by the heat and with thirst and fatigue, that having lost more than 1200 men they abandoned[5] the attempt and returned[5] home without success. 7. It was at your suggestion, not only against my will, but in spite of my opposition, resist-ance, and appeals to heaven and earth, that your country-men were persuaded to condemn a whole people without a hearing. 8. This I am persuaded of, that you will not pass this law without violating the constitution. 9. As I was thus speaking, the news of the enemies' arrival, and the handing in of a despatch from the king, filled my

---

[1] = or any one replying.
[3] Present participle. (**412**, *Obs.*)
[5] Use different tenses. (See **113**.)

[2] Simply *ista*. (**54**.)
[4] See **381**.

audience[1] with mingled rage and panic; but some,[2] judging that haste was necessary, seized their arms (and) hastened to go down to meet the foe.   10. So long as you survive and are unharmed, I feel sure that my children will never be orphans.   11. Under your leadership I was prepared (418, *f*) to take up arms, but hearing[3] that you were ill, I resolved to remain behind at home without[4] taking part in that contest.

---

[1] " The minds (*animi*) of my audience." (See **17,** *Obs.*)
[2] Use *erant qui.* (**360,** iii.)   [3] **424,** *Obs.*
[4] Use " and not to," *neque.* (**332. S.**

TEMPORAL CLAUSES.

427. **Temporal** clauses are those which qualify the statement made by the verb in the main clause, in some particular as to **previous, contemporaneous,** or **subsequent time.** They are therefore *adverbial* clauses. (See Intr. 82.)

They are introduced in Latin and English by various temporal **conjunctions,** such as those given in Intr. 59, *c*, and others.

Obs.—Their place is often taken by the participial constructions given in the last two exercises, *e.g. haec locutus, his dictis* are exactly equivalent to *haec* quum *dixisset.*

428. Of those conjunctions which answer to the English "when," all but *quum* (*cum*) are as a rule used with the **indicative** mood, precisely as in English.

Thus in past time—

> *Quae postquam (postea quam), ubi, simul atque,*[1] audivit (or audiverat), *abiit.* "When he heard (or had heard) this he took his departure," or "*no sooner* had he heard this *than,*" etc.

Obs. 1.—This use of *audivit* (aor.) in place of the more strictly correct *audierat* is even more common in Latin than in English.

So also with **present** and **future** time—*Quae simul atque* audit, *abit ; quae postquam, ubi, quoties, simul atque,* audierit (190, i.) *abibit.*

Obs. 2.—Though the indicative is the rule with these conjunctions, the **subjunctive** must be used if the principal verb is in **oratio obliqua :** dicunt *eum, postquam haec* audiverit, abiisse. (**77.**)

---

[1] *Simul ac* only before consonants.

429. The exception to the rule is *quum*, or *cum*, the commonest of all these conjunctions. With the **imperfect** or **pluperfect** tenses *quum* is joined with the **subjunctive**.

> *Caesar*, quum *haec* videret, *milites impetum facere jussit.*
> Caesar, seeing this, ordered his troops to charge.
> *Legati*, quum *haec non* impetrassent, *domum redierunt.*
> The ambassadors having failed (*or* on failing) to obtain this. returned home.

The reason of this is that, while the other conjunctions express the relation of *time*, and time only, *quum* introduces the **circumstances** which **led up to**, or **accompanied**, the fact stated by the principal verb. These circumstances are looked on as not merely preceding, or accompanying, but as affecting and *accounting for* the fact, like our own participial construction : "*seeing that* I could be of no use, I went away."

Now whenever *quum* (conjunction formed from *qui*) implies in any way *cause* (or *contrast*) the tendency is to use the subjunctive, precisely as with the relative itself (see **501**). Hence in describing *past* events *quum* is habitually joined with the subjunctive mood, as the previous circumstance introduced is looked on as more or less influencing, or even causing, the main event which followed it, even when such causal relation is scarcely discernible ; hence such a sentence as—

> Quum *in portum* venisset, vitā *excessit.* He died *after* reaching the harbour.

430. Sometimes *quum* expresses more clearly still the idea of **cause**.

> *Quae* quum *ita se* habeant, *or* haberent. *Seeing that*, or *as* the case stands, or stood, thus ; *this being the case.*

In this purely causal sense it is regularly joined with the subjunctive mood in **all** tenses.

431. Sometimes also *quum*, without laying aside the idea of time, answers almost to "although," and points a **contrast**, *i.e.* is used as almost a *concessive* conjunction. (Intr. 59, *g.*) It is then also joined with the **subjunctive**.

> Quum *liber esse* posset, *servire maluit.* At a time when, or *although*, he might have been free, he preferred to be a slave.
> Quum *dicere* deberet, conticuit. At a time when, or *although*, he ought to have spoken, he held his peace.

Obs.—This is an obvious mode of turning the English "**instead of**" with the verbal noun in -*ing* (see **398**): "Instead of being free," "instead of speaking."

It can, however, only be used where the neglect of a *duty* or *opportunity* is implied, otherwise we may use *adeo non . . . ut*, or *non modo non . . . sed.* (See **124.**)

Quum *with the Indicative.*

432. *Quum* however is frequently used with the **indicative.** Thus, if simply temporal, it is regularly used with the indicative of the *present* or *future* tenses.

> Quum *in portum* dico, *in urbem dico.* When I say into the harbour, I say into the city; *or,* In saying into the harbour, I say into the city.
> *Poenam lues* quum venerit (**190,** i.) *solvendi dies.* You shall pay the penalty when the day of payment *comes.*

Obs.—So also *Decem sunt anni,* or *decimus hic est annus,* quum *haec* facis. You *have been* doing this (**181**) for the last ten years.

433. It is used also with the indicative even of **past** time in certain cases.

(*a*) When two clauses mark strictly *contemporaneous* events. This is often impressed on the reader by the presence of a *tum* in the principal clause.

> Quum *tu ibi* eras, tum *ego domi eram.* At the time, *or* at the moment, when you were there, I was at home.

As the cause must come *before* the effect, the presence of *tum* excludes from the *quum* any notion of *causal* circumstances, and fixes it down to a purely temporal meaning.

434. (*b*) In a **frequentative** sense, where a number of repeated acts are described, *quum* in the sense of "whenever," "as often as," is joined with the indicative.

If the principal verb is in past time, *quum* (*cum*) is used with the **pluperfect**; if in present time, with the **perfect.**

> Cum *rosam* viderat, *tum ver esse* arbitrabatur (**184**). *Whenever* he saw the rose in bloom (year after year), he judged that it was spring-time.
> Cum *ad villam* veni, *hoc ipsum nihil agere* me delectat. *As often as* I come to my country-house, this mere doing nothing (**94**) has a charm for me.

Obs.—The same construction is used with *si quando, ubi, ut quis-que,* and the *relative qui, quicunque.*

> Ut quisque *huc* venerat, *haec* loquebatur.   *Whenever* any one *came* here, he *would* use this language.
>
> Quos *cessare* viderat, *verbis* castigabat.   *Whomever* he *saw* hanging back he *made a point* of rebuking.

But in Livy often, in Tacitus regularly, the subjunctive is used, in accordance with the Greek use of the optative.

> *Id fetialis* ubi dixisset, *hastam* immittebat.   As soon as (*in every case*) the herald had uttered this, he would launch a spear, etc.

N.B.—*Quoties* is only used where the idea of "*every* time that" is strongly emphasised.

435. (*c*) The indicative is also used where, by an inverted construction, what would otherwise be the principal assertion is stated in a subordinate clause introduced by *quum*.

> *Jam ver appetebat,* quum *Hannibal ex hibernis* movit.[1]   Spring was already approaching, when Hannibal left his winter quarters.

This sentence would stand with the same sense almost more naturally—

> *Vere jam appetente Hannibal ex hibernis movit.*

The indicative is natural, for *quum* here = "and suddenly," "and at once," and may be compared with the co-ordinating use of *qui.* (See **78.**)

Exercise 54.

The asterisk * means that one of the various constructions of *quum* is to be used. Where "and" is in brackets use the participial construction (**406,** ii.).

1. This * being the case, he was reluctant to leave the city, and openly refused,[2] in the governor's presence, to do so.   2. As* I was wearied with my journey, I determined (**45**) on staying at home the whole day and doing nothing.   3. No sooner was he made aware, by the hoisting of a flag from the summit of the citadel, that the advanced guard of the enemy was approaching, than, taking advantage[3] of the darkness[4] of the night, he caused a gate to

---

[1] A military term : *castra* must be supplied.
[2] See **136.**   [3] *Utor* (**413.**)   [4] = night and darkness.

be thrown open (and) sallied out boldly into their midst.
4. No sooner had he heard of the landing of the enemies'
forces, than, instead of remaining quietly at home, he
determined on taking up arms and doing his utmost[1] to
repel the invasion.   5. Seeing* that his prayers and
entreaties were of no avail with the king, he brought his
speech to an end; no sooner was he (*qui*) silent, than the
door was opened (and) two soldiers were introduced each[2]
with a sword.   6. At the moment when* the enemy was
entering the gates of your crushed and ruined city, not
one of you so much as heaved a groan; when* even worse
than this (*pl.*) befalls you, who will[3] pity you? you will
bewail, I fear, your[4] destiny in vain.   7. Whenever* he
heard anything of this kind, he would instantly say that
the story was invented by some neighbour.   8. Whomever he saw applauding the conqueror he would blame,
and exhort not to congratulate their country's enemies.
9. For the last five years the enemy has been[5] sweeping
in triumph through the whole of Italy, slaughtering our
armies, destroying our strongholds, setting fire to our
towns, devastating and ravaging our fields, shaking the
allegiance of our allies, when* suddenly the aspect of
affairs is changed, (and) he sends ambassadors, and pretends to sigh for peace, tranquillity, and friendship with[6]
our nation.

---

[1] See **332. 5,** *g.*   [2] Why not *quisque?* (**378.**)   [3] **309.**
[4] *Iste.* (**338.**)   [5] **432,** *Obs.*   [6] Genitive. (**288.**)

TEMPORAL CLAUSES—*Continued.*

Dum, donec, priusquam, etc.

436. The other temporal conjunctions will cause little difficulty, if the remarks on Tenses are carefully read, especially those in 190.

The general rule is that **the indicative is used unless** (*a*) **the clause falls under oratio obliqua (77), or** (*b*) **some other idea than that of time** is introduced. Thus—

437. *Dum,* as also *donec, quamdiu, quoad* in the sense of "while," "as long as," where they connect together two periods of time *of equal length,* are used with the **indicative** in various tenses.

> *Haec feci,* dum licuit.   I did this as long as I was permitted.
>
> *Vivet ejus memoria,* dum erit *haec civitas.*   His memory will live as long as this country *exists.*

Obs.—*Quamdiu* implies a *long* period ; *donec* generally in prose "until," or "up to *the last moment* that ;" *quoad* also "to the last moment that," but not limited to *time: quoad potui,* " to the utmost extent of my power" = *quantum in me fuit.*   (**332.** 5.)

438. But *when* dum,[1] "while," denotes a longer period, **during part of which** something else has happened, it is joined with the **present indicative** (historic) even when past time is referred to (see 180), and even in *oratio obliqua.*

> *Allatum est praedatores,* dum *latius* vagantur, *ab hostibus interceptos fuisse.* News was brought that the plunderers, while they *were* wandering too far, had been cut off by the enemy.

---

[1] "While" is constantly used in English without any idea of *time,* simply to place two statements side by side, generally with the idea of *contrast,* "while you hate him, we love him." *Dum* is never used in this sense in Latin : we must write either, *tu* quidem *eum odisti, nos* vero amamus ; or simply, *tu eum odisti, nos amamus.* (See also **406**, *note* [2].)

439. When *dum* is used for "so long as," in the sense of "if," "provided that," it invariably takes the **subjunctive**, and with negative clauses is joined with *ne.*[1]

Veniant igitur, dum ne *nos* interpellent.   Let them come then, provided they don't interrupt us.

440. When *dum, donec, quoad* mean "until," their mood is determined by the rule in **436.**   If nothing more than **time** is indicated they take the **indicative** (except in *oratio obliqua*).

Mane hic, dum *ego* rediero, redibo, *or even* redeo.   Remain here till I return.   (**182** and **190.**)

In senatu fuit quoad (*or* donec) *senatus* dimissus est.   He was (as we should say) in the House, till the moment when it was adjourned.

441. But if some further idea of *expectation, purpose,* or *watching* is introduced, the **subjunctive** is used, as the mood proper to **final** clauses.

Num expectatis dum *testimonium* dicat?   Are you waiting till he gives his evidence?   *i.e. with a view* of hearing him.

Thus—*Epaminondas ferrum in corpore retinuit,* quoad *renuntiatum est vicisse Boeotios.*   Epaminondas retained the spear in his body, till it was reported to him that the Bœotians were victorious.

Here the two facts are related as connected together in time, but by nothing else.

Esset in place of *est* would imply that he retained the spear *with the purpose of* waiting till the news should be brought.

Differant, donec *ira* defervescat.   Let them put off till their anger cools ; *i.e.* let them put off with the *purpose* that their anger may cool, *till they feel* their anger cool.

Defervescet would mean simply till the *time when* their anger shall be cooling ; *deferbuerit,* "has cooled." (**190,** i. ii.)

442. *Antequam* and *priusquam* follow the same principle.   To denote simple *priority of time* the indicative is used.

Quarto ante *die* quam *huc* veni.   Four days (**323,** *n.*) before I came here.

---

[1] *Modo ne* is often used in the same sense ; literally "only let (them) not."

But when the idea of an *end in view, motive,* or *result prevented,* is added to that of time, the subjunctive of **final** and **consecutive** clauses (see 106) is invariably used.

> Priusquam *e pavore* reciperent *animos, impetum fecerunt hostes.* The enemy made a charge before they *could recover* from the panic, *i.e.* to *prevent them* from recovering (*end in view*).
> Priusquam pugnaretur *nox intervenit.* Before the fight *could begin* night interposed (*result prevented*).

The subjunctive is also used in general maxims, especially when the second person is used in an indefinite sense. (**141,** *Obs.*)

> Priusquam *incipias, consulto opus est.* Before *men* begin, they require deliberation.

Obs.—In these wider senses *priusquam* is more common than *antequam.*

443. *Priusquam* (as *antequam*) is properly a *phrase* of two words, which may be placed in separate clauses, especially in negative sentences.

(i.) So used, they are often equivalent to *not . . . until.*

> *Non* prius *respondebo* quam *tacueris.* I will *not* answer *until* you are silent.

(ii.) They may also sometimes translate *without.* (See **425.**)

> Prius *ire noluit* quam *judicum sententias audivisset.* He refused to go *without hearing* the verdict of the jury. (*Audivisset* is *virtual oratio obliqua,* "*said he* would not go." See **448.**)

Obs.—"Not until" is often expressed by *tum demum* (or *denique*).

> Tum demum *respondebo,* quum *tacueris.* I will *not* answer *till* you are silent.

Exercise 55.

The asterisk * means that *dum* is to be used in one of its various constructions. ** *Antequam* or *priusquam* is to be used.

1. I am ready to pay you the greatest possible honour, so* long as you are ready to estimate at its proper value all the slander and detraction of my rivals. 2. The[1] launching of this handful of cavalry against the enemies' left wing caused such universal panic that, while* the king was inquiring of his staff what was happening, even the centre began[2] to fall into confusion; before

---

[1] **417.**　　　[2] "Even in the centre confusion began." (See **219.**)

worse[1] befell us, night intervened, so that fighting ceased[2] on both sides. 3. And now before we could reap the fruit of a contest which had cost us so much bloodshed, a second army came on the scene, so that, while* our general was sleeping in his tent, the battle had to be[3] begun anew. 4. He will be dear to his countrymen as long* as this nation exists, nor will his memory die out of the hearts of men till** all things are (190) forgotten. 5. He did not enter political life till[4] by the death[5] of his father he was able, as[6] he had long desired, to join the ranks[7] of the aristocratic party. 6. Let them venture on anything,[8] provided * they do not injure the influence and authority of those with whom rests the administration of the nation. 7. As long[9] as I believed you to be studying these matters for their own sake, so long I honoured you highly; now I estimate you at your true value. 8. As long* as those who are to [10] command our armies are chosen either by chance, or on grounds of interest, the nation can never be served successfully.

---

[1] Neut. pl.   [2] Impersonal construction. **(219.)**
[3] Gerundive : tense of *sum* as in **115.**   [4] See **443,** *Obs.*
[5] Abl. abs. with *mortuus.*   [6] **67.**
[7] Why not *ordines?* (See **17.**)   [?] See **359.**
[9] *Quamdiu* (**437,** *Obs.*), *tamdiu.*   [10] **418.** *q.*

SUBORDINATE CLAUSES IN *ORATIO OBLIQUA.*

444. It has been already said (77) that **in all subor-dinate clauses in** *oratio obliqua*, **whether introduced by a** *relative* **or a** *conjunction,* **the subjunctive mood takes the place of the indicative.**

This usage is so unlike English that it is constantly overlooked by the young scholar.

In English, if we alter "the man who does this *is* foolish" into "*he says that* the man who does this is foolish ;" or, if to "as soon as they saw the enemy they *fled*," we prefix the words, "*they say that,*" no change takes place in the mood of either of the verbs.

In Latin not only does the principal verb, "*is,*" "*fled,*" pass in such cases into the *infinitive* mood, but it carries with it, so to speak, all verbs really subordinate to it into a fresh mood, the *subjunctive.*

Oratio recta.	*Oratio obliqua.*
Stultus est, *qui hoc* facit.	(Ait) *stultum* esse, *qui hoc* faciat.
Simul atque hostem viderunt, fugēre.	(Dicunt eos) *simul atque hostem* viderint, fugisse.
Qui hoc fecerint,[1] *poenas* dabunt.	(Dixit) *eos qui hoc* fecissent, *poenas* daturos esse.

445. The same rule applies to indirect or dependent *questions* and *commands* as much as to indirect *statements,* for the term *oratio obliqua* in its full sense includes all three kinds of such substantival sentences.   (Intr. 80.)

Oratio recta.	*Oratio obliqua.*
QUESTION.	
Cur priusquam vidistis *hostem, pedem retulistis ?*	(Rogavit) *cur priusquam* vidissent *hostem, pedem retulissent.*
COMMAND.	
Qui adsunt, *me sequantur.*	(Jussit) *eos qui* adessent, *se* sequi.

---

[1] For the tense of *fecerit* see **190,** ii.   This *future perfect* will be represented after a past verb of *saying* by the *pluperfect subjunctive.* (See **471,** *Obs.*)

446. It will be remembered therefore that rules as to *postquam, quod, quanquam,* etc., being joined with the indicative, do not apply to clauses that are dependent on any form of *oratio obliqua;* in such clauses the **indicative is inadmissible.**

447. The principle is the same throughout. Let A be the author of the book, or the speaker; B any one else *through* whom A makes any statement, or whom he mentions as asking or commanding something: no verb that forms any part of what B says will be in the indicative mood. In the examples (**444, 445**) *all* on the left hand, but on the right hand only *ait, dicunt, rogavit, jussit,* are A's words; the rest of each sentence expresses the ideas of the subject of each of those verbs, or of B, and the **indicative therefore is excluded.**

Obs.—Indeed, the *tendency* is to introduce the subjunctive into the subordinate clause when the principal verb is in the infinitive or subjunctive for *any* cause; and though such *assimilation* does not amount to a rule, it will sometimes help to account for unexpected subjunctives.

> *Hoc feci, ut eos qui me* sequerentur, *incolumes praestarem.* I did this to secure the safety of my followers.

Virtual *Oratio obliqua.*

448. The subjunctive also takes the place of the indicative, not only where the form of the sentence shows that the writer is reporting what *some one else* said, thought, asked, or ordered, but where in the absence of any verb *declarandi, sentiendi, rogandi,* or *praecipiendi* we have ourselves to supply the idea, "as he said," or even "as I thought."

It is a short mode of distinguishing what the writer or speaker (A) states on his own responsibility, from that for which he declines to be responsible, and which he tacitly shifts to B.

Thus in the fable, "The vulture invited the little birds to a feast which he was going to give them," "*quod illis daturus* erat" would mean that he really *was* going to give them the feast: but "*quod illis daturus* esset" would only mean that *he said* he was going to do so. So with the verbs of *accusing,* the charge often stands with *quod* in the *subjunctive,* because the *accusers are made to assert* that the crime has been committed; the *indicative* would make the historian or speaker assert, and be *responsible for,* the truth of the charge.

This has been happily named the subjunctive of *virtual oratio obliqua.*[1]

> *Socrates accusatus est quod* corrumperet *juventutem.*   Socrates was accused of corrupting the young men.

Quod corrumperet throws the responsibility of the charge on the accuser.   *Corrumpebat* would imply that the historian agreed with the charge

This construction is especially common with *quod*-clauses.   (See below, 484.)

EXCEPTIONS.

449. Sometimes the subordinate clause, though *grammatically* subordinate to a verb in *oratio obliqua*, is really an explanatory parenthesis inserted by the writer, and is therefore in the indicative.

> *Themistocles certiorem cum fecit, id agi, ut pons,* quem ille in Hellesponto fecerat, *dissolveretur.*   Themistocles sent him word that it was intended to break down the bridge, which he (Xerxes) had made over the Hellespont.

The words "*quem ille in Hellesponto* fecerat" are inserted by the historian, they do not belong to the words reported as used by Themistocles.   They belong to A, not to B.   (**447.**)

Similarly, in such a sentence as "he ordered him to send for the troops who were in the rear," the *who*-clause would be in the *subjunctive* if it were part of the order given, in the *indicative* if a mere definition of the troops were meant, and inserted as such by the *historian*.

Exercise 56.

1. Then turning to Cortes, he made a vehement attack upon the Spaniards, who, without any[2] adequate justification, were invading his territory, and were either inviting or compelling his subjects to rebel.   2. He gave orders not to spare a single (**358**) person who had been present at the massacre of the prisoners, or the outrage on the ambassadors.   3. Then the gallant and undaunted chief, though surrounded on all sides by armed men, turned to the

---

[1] Dr. Kennedy.   Such curious constructions as *quod religionibus impediri se* diceret, for *quod* impediretur, though by no means uncommon, will not be noticed here.

[2] See p. 235, *note* 2.

conqueror and denounced the cowardice of his countrymen, who by surrendering him to the Spaniards had flung away the priceless possessions[1] of freedom and of honour. 4. He promised not to leave the city till they had brought safely within the walls all who had survived from the massacre of yesterday. 5. He asked the many[2] bystanders whether those who wished for their king's safety were ready to follow him, and using[3] all speed to inflict chastisement on those who had violated their allegiance and their oath. 6. On reaching the summit of the mountain he called to him his staff, and pointed out the streams which (he said) flowed down towards Italy. 7. He said that he would not allow himself to put faith in men who had not only showed themselves cowardly and disloyal, but were still, in the face of such a political emergency, on the point[4] of sacrificing everything to their own comfort and interest.

---

[1] See **222**, *Obs.*   [2] See **69**.
[3] Abl. abs. of *adhibeor*.   [4] Either fut. in *-rus*, or *in eo esse ut*.

CONDITIONAL CLAUSES.

Rules for Mood and Tense after *si.*

450. Conditional clauses are those which are introduced by the Latin and English conjunctions *si*, "if," etc., enumerated in Intr. 59, *e.* Their *adverbial* relation to the principal clause is explained in Intr. 82.

The use of the right **mood** and right **tense** in such clauses will require some care, owing mainly to the almost entire obliteration in English of the *subjunctive mood*, and the want of a true future tense. (190.)

A. Mood after *si.*

451. The construction of such clauses, as regards the **mood** to be used after *si*, will be perfectly clear if the following **observations** and **rules** are borne in mind.

Obs.—In all conditional or hypothetical sentences, *i.e.* such compound *sentences* as contain an *if*-clause, or its equivalent, it is quite true that the *truth* of any assertion made in the principal clause depends upon that of the condition contained in the *if*-clause; as a matter of *reasoning* or *inference*, the principal clause, called also the *apodosis*, is dependent on the subordinate clause, or *protasis.*

Thus, in "*if* it has lightened there will be thunder," that "there will be thunder" is dependent, as an *inference*, on whether or no "it has lightened."

But *grammatically* "there will be thunder" is the principal clause, *qualified* by the secondary or subordinate clause, "if it has lightened." It is this *grammatical* relation, and this only, which we need consider in writing grammatically, and we shall find that in **conditional sentences the mood of the verb in the *si*-clause will depend, as a rule, on that of the verb in the main clause.**

The following two Rules must be carefully observed.

452. RULE I.—If the verb in the principal clause is in the **indicative** or **imperative** mood, the verb in the conditional clause will be in the **indicative**.

Si hoc dicis, erras ; *si abire* vis, abi. If you *say* this you *are* wrong; if you *wish* to depart, *depart.*

282

Obs. 1.—Dismiss all idea that *si* "governs a subjunctive" because it *suggests a doubt*, and the subjunctive mood implies a doubt. The word *si* ("if") in its very nature implies doubt ; but the mood with which it is joined depends upon the nature of the whole sentence, and this is decided by that of the *principal*, not of the subordinate, clause. If the principal verb is in the **indicative** or **imperative**, this shows that the whole sentence belongs to the sphere of **practical** and **real** life, and the indicative is the appropriate mood for the *qualifying si*-clause, as well as for the main clause.

Obs. 2.—Nor does the **mood** of the *si*-clause depend upon the *likelihood, unlikelihood, possibility*, or *the reverse*, of the supposition made ; but simply on *the mood* (that is to say, the general tone) *of the principal clause.* Cicero says, *excitate eum, si* potestis, *ab inferis;* he did not think it possible that they could raise a man from the dead ; yet he says *si potestis*, not *si possitis*.[1]

Caution.—Beware then of such Latin as—

> *Si hoc* dicas, *errabis.* If you *were to* say so, you *will* be
> wrong.

The Latin here is as unnatural as the English ; half the sentence belongs to one sphere of thought, the *practical*, "you *will*," etc., half to that of mere *conception*, "if you *were to*," etc. (But see **463,** *b.*)

453. RULE II.—If the verb in the principal clause is in the **subjunctive** mood, the verb in the *si*-clause will be also in the **subjunctive**.

> *Si hoc* dicas, erres. If you *were* to say this, or, *were* you
> to say this, you *would* be wrong.

Erres is in the subjunctive mood because it does not say "you *are* wrong," but only that you *would* be in certain imagined conditions, on a certain *hypothesis;* it shows that the whole sentence has left the sphere of *fact* and *practice* to which the **indicative** and **imperative** belong, and entered that of *conception* or *imagination.* The *si*-clause therefore will, as the subordinate clause, follow the mood of the

---

[1] Cicero says, Parcite *Lentuli dignitati,* si *ipse famae suae unquam* pepercit. This is in accordance with Rule I. Of course Cicero did not mean that Lentulus *had* shown tenderness to his own reputation, but the very reverse, yet he uses the indicative after *si.* So he says, *Si es Romae, vix enim puto,* sin es, . . . he uses the *indicative* because he goes on to make a *practical request.* The indicative mood is, so to speak, *colourless ;* it makes a statement (Intr. 11) : but colour may be given to the statement it makes by another word. Fortasse *hoc dicit ;* si *hoc dicit :* the *doubt* and *condition* are expressed by *fortasse* and *si,* the verb is left unaltered.

ruling or principal clause, and may be called a *hypothetical* as distinct from a *conditional* clause.[1]

> Si *hoc* dixisses, erravisses.   If you had said this, *or*, had you said
> this, you *would have* been wrong.

If these two RULES, I. and II., are observed, few mistakes will arise as to the **mood** of the Latin verb.

Exercise A (page 286) should now be done.

B. Tense after *si*.

454. Under RULE I. the main difficulty as regards **tense** will be in the use of the **future**.

(i.) Read carefully **190** and examples **5-10 in 194**, and you will see that the best mode of translating

> "If you *do* this you *will* be punished," is, *hoc si* feceris, *poenas
> dabis.*

Si facis would be "if you are now doing," *or*, "intending to do" (an *anticipative* use, **182**) ; *si facies,* "if you shall *be doing,*" *i.e.* at the time (**189**) ; but *si* facias **would be entirely wrong,** "if you *were* to do this, you *will* be punished."

(ii.) Remember also that, if a **command** regards the *future*, as most commands do, the **future** must be used with *si*.   "Come (to-morrow) if you *can*" will be, *veni (cras) si* poteris, because ."can" is really future time, and contemporaneous with the tense denoted by "come;" *potes* would mean, "if you can *now.*"

> *Obs.*—This future is especially common with *volo* and *possum.*
> *Cras veniant* (imperative) or *venient* (fut.), si *salvi esse* volent.
> Let them come, *or*, they will come, to-morrow if they (then)
> *wish* for safety.

455. Remember also the idiomatic use of the Latin **pluperfect indicative** with *si* to express *repetition* or *frequency ;* it corresponds with the **imperfect** in the principal clause.   (See **192** and **434.**)

> *Si quem cessare* viderat, *non verbis solum sed etiam verberibus*
> castigabat.   If he *saw* that any one was hanging back, he
> *would correct* him, not with words only, but with stripes.

---

[1] The word "*condition*" would be used in such practical matters as a *treaty* or *lease,* etc. ; "*hypothesis*" we apply to an assumption in science on the truth of which we base an unproved theory.   The *apodosis* to the *condition* is naturally in the **indicative,** to the *hypothesis* in the **subjunctive.**

456. Under RULE II., the only difficulty as regards Tenses will be in the use of the **imperfect subjunctive,** as distinct from that of the **pluperfect** and **present** of the same mood

(i.) The **imperfect** represents in the subjunctive, as in the indicative, *continuous action* in the past (**183**) ; the **pluperfect** simply past time.

> *Hoc si* dixisses, erravisses. *Had* you (*before* some past time) said this, you would *have been* wrong (once for all).
> But—*Hoc si* diceres, errares. Had you *been saying* this (*during* some past time), you would (*during that time*) *have been* in the wrong.

(ii.) But sometimes the imperfect subjunctive extends up to the *present* moment, and *hoc si diceres, errares,* means, "Had you been saying this *now*, you would have been *now* wrong."

The meaning of the imperfect subjunctive in a Latin sentence must therefore sometimes be decided by the **context.**

457. The more ordinary form in speaking *hypothetically* of the **present** is, *hoc si* dicas, erres ; but, especially when we wish strongly to imply that the supposition is false, we may use in Latin, as in English, a **past** form. But this use of the **imperfect** can never, either in suppositions or wishes, extend to the **future.**

> *Utinam* adsit. Would he *were* here (*now*, or *for the future*).
> *Utinam* adesset. Would he *had been* here (either *yesterday*, or even *to-day*).
> *Si* adsit. If he *were* here (*to-day*, or *in the future*).
> *Si* adesset. *Had* he *been* here, or *were* he but here (*previously*, or *to-day*).

458. The sense sometimes calls for a difference of *tense* in the two clauses.

> *Ego nisi* peperissem, *Roma non* oppugnaretur. Had I not become a mother, Rome would not now be under siege.

Peperissem, *merely past time,* oppugnaretur, a *continued* state, extending to the present moment.

Caution.—Remember that *si* is never used in Latin as an **interrogative** particle. "He asked him *if* he was well," is, *ex eo,* num *valeret, quaesivit.* (**167.**)

♦ *Obs.*—*Si* begins a sentence less commonly in Latin than in English. It often follows a name or pronoun : *Caesar* si, etc., *Ego* si, etc. Often *quod* is prefixed to connect it with the previous sentence : *quod si* = "*but if,*" sometimes "*and if,*" properly "*as to which,* if."

459. The following examples should be carefully studied.

RULE I.

Si quid habebat, dabat. If he (*during* a past time) had anything, he gave it, or *would give* it (habitually).

Si quid habuit, dedit. If he (*at* a past time) had anything, he gave it (aorist).

Si quem viderat, irascebatur. If he saw any one (*frequentative,* **434,** *Obs.*) he *would* get angry.

Si opus erit, *or* fuerit (see **190**), adero. I will be there if need *arises.*

RULE II.

Tum *si hoc* dixissem, *non* auditus fuissem. If I had said this then, I should not have found a hearing (aorist).

Tum *si hoc* dicerem, *non* audirer. If I had said (*i.e.* been saying, **183**), I should not have found (been *likely to* find) a hearing.

Si hoc dicam, *non* audiar. If I *were* to say this (*now,* or at any *future* time), I should not be listened to.

Si hoc dicerem *non* audirer. If I were to say (or *had been* saying) this *now,* I should not be (or *have been*) listened to (as I am).

Exercise 57.

A.

Mainly on the **Moods** to be used with *Si.*

1. If you love me, be sure to send a letter to me at Rome. 2. If you are at home—I am not yet sure whether[1] you have returned—I hope soon to receive a letter from you. 3. Were your country to use this language to[2] you, would she not have a claim to obtain her request? 4. If I am speaking falsely, Metellus, refute me; if I am speaking the truth, why do you hesitate[3] to put confidence in me? 5. Were virtue denied this reward, yet she would be satisfied with her own self.[4] 6. Time[5] would fail me were I to try to reckon up all his services to the nation. 7. If ever any[6] one was indifferent to empty fame and vulgar[7] gossip, it[8] is I. 8. If any one were to make this request of you, he would be justly ridiculed. 9. If you

---

[1] **167.** [2] " *With* you" (*tecum*). [3] **136,** *b.*

[4] See **356,** ii. [5] "The day," *dies.* [6] See **357.**

[7] Gen. of *vulgus.* (See **59.**) [8] "I am *he,*" *is.* (See **70.**)

are desirous to enter political life, do not[1] hesitate to count me among your friends. 10. Had he been a man of[2] courage, he would never have declined this contest. 11. If you have any regard, either for your own safety or your private property, do not[3] delay your reconciliation with the conqueror. 12. But if you are aiming at the crown, why do you use the language of a citizen,[4] and pretend[5] to sacrifice everything to the judgment and inclination of your countrymen?

B.

On the **Moods** and **Tenses** used with *Si*.

1. If the enemy had with a veteran army invaded our territory, and routed our army of recruits, no[6] German would have survived to-day. 2. If I either decline the contest, or show[7] myself a coward and a laggard, then you may[8] taunt me if you will, with my lowly birth, then call[9] me, if you choose, the basest and meanest of mankind. 3. If once[10] Napoleon throws his army across the Rhine, I am afraid that[11] no one will be able to stand in his way on this side the Vistula. 4. If we have had[12] enough of fighting to-day, let us recall the soldiers to their several (**352**, *Obs.*) standards, and hope for better things for[13] the morrow; if to-morrow resistance[14] is manifestly no longer possible, let us yield, however[15] reluctantly, to necessity, and bid each take care[16] of himself. 5. If, when you have got to Rome, you care[17] to receive a letter from me, mind you are the first[18] to write to me. 6. When once Italy is reached,[19] I will either lead you (*pl.*), said he, at once to Rome, if you wish, or having let you

---

[1] See **142**.   [2] **303**, ii.   [3] *Cave.* (**143**.)
[4] Adj. *civilis*. (See **58**.)   [5] **39**.   [6] See **223**.
[7] *Praebeo.* (**241**.)   [8] *Licet* with subj. (**197**.)
[9] Fut. imperat. of *dico* (p. 113, *n.*).
[10] Need not be expressed otherwise than by the right tense. (**190**, i.)
[11] *Ut quisquam.* (See **138**.)   [12] See **218**.
[13] *In.* (See **326**.)   [14] **219**.
[15] *Quamvis.* (**480**, *Obs.*)   [16] Use *consulo.* (**248**.)
[17] *Volo.*   [18] *Prior.* (See **62**.)   [19] **217**, *Obs.*

sack such[1] wealthy cities as Milan and Genoa, will send you home, if you prefer it, laden with plunder and spoil. 7. If they saw any of our soldiers running forward from (*ex*) the line of march, or left behind by his comrades, they would all hurl their darts at him.   8. It is haste,[2] said he, not deliberation, that we need ; had we used it[3] earlier, we should have had[4] no war to-day.   9. These men, had you permitted it, would have been alive to-day, and been maintaining with the sword the national cause. 10. Had you asked me yesterday if I feared so worthless a person as your brother, I should have answered no ; to-day the news of this defeat makes[5] me so anxious, that, were you to ask the same question, I should answer yes.

---

[1] Apposition, *urbs* used as *homo* in **224,** *Obs.* **2.**   (See **317.**)
[2] Use *properatum,* and see **286.**   [3] Relative.
[4] Use *sum.* (**251.**)   [5] See **240.**

CONDITIONAL CLAUSES—*Continued.*

Exceptional Constructions of *si.*

460. Exceptions will be found to Rules I. and II. as given above in **452** and **453**; these exceptions, however, are in many cases part of the regular construction of Latin, and are always easily accounted for.

461. Apparent Exceptions.—With the **modal verbs** *possum, debeo, oportet*, etc., and with **periphrastic tenses**, formed either by the *gerund* or *gerundive* (to express *duty*, etc.), or by the *future participle* (to express *intention*, etc.), with the verb *sum*, the **indicative** is regularly used in the *apodosis* or principal clause in place of the **subjunctive**. (153.)

The place of these modal verbs and participial phrases is taken in English by the auxiliary verbs *may, might, would, should, must, ought, am to, have to*, etc., which often form a substitute for our nearly obsolete subjunctive mood. Thus—

Quid, si hostes ad urbem veniant, *facturi* estis? In case the enemy *should* come to the city, what *would you* do?=what *do* you intend to do?

Hunc hominem, si ulla in te esset *pietas, colere* debebas. If you *had had* any natural affection (*as you had not*), you *ought to have* respected this man.

Deleri totus exercitus potuit, *si fugientes persecuti victores* essent. The whole army *might* have been destroyed, if the victors had pursued the fugitives (*which they did not*).

Hos nisi manu misisset, *tormentis etiam dedendi* fuerunt. If he had not set these men free, they *must have been* given up to torture.

Bonus vates poteras *esse, si* voluisses. You *might have been* a good prophet, had you cared to be one.

Aliter si fecisses, *idem* eventurum fuit. Had you acted otherwise, the result *would have been* the same.

These are exceptions to, but not real violations of, Rule I. Thus *facturi estis* is another form of expressing *faciatis, colere debebas* of *coluisses*. These *modal* verbs, and the other periphrastic forms, supply the Latin verb with, as it were, fresh *moods*, or *modes of*

T

statement. (See **42.**) They add an assertion of **intention, duty, probability**, etc., to the idea conveyed by the verb.

Thus in, *Si quis haec* loquatur, *vix* puto *cum impetraturum esse*, "if any one were to use this language, I scarcely think he would obtain his request," the *vix puto*, etc., is equivalent to a subjunctive mood, *vix impetret.*

So *facturus fui* is almost equivalent to *fecissem, culpari potui* to *culpatus fuissem.*

462. Nor is, *Si hoc* dixi, nolim *dictum*, "If I said this, I am sorry," a violation of Rule II., for *nolim* is only a polite form of the indicative. (See **149,** i.)

So, moriar, *nisi hoc verum* est (may I perish, if this is not true), is no real violation of Rule I., for *moriar* is practically an *imperative*, not "I should die," but "let me die;" nor is, *Si in hoc* erravi, *quis mihi* irascatur (if I have done wrong in this, who would be angry with me?) a violation of Rule II., for the question is a *virtual* negative, equivalent to *nemo mihi* irascetur. (See **150.**)

463. Real Exceptions.—Sometimes, however, Rules I. and II. are really violated.

(*a*) Perieram *nisi tu* accurrisses. I should have perished if you had not run to my assistance.

Compare the English *"I had perished had you not run up."* [1]

(*b*) *Si fractus* illabatur *orbis, impavidum* ferient *ruinae.* Were the globe to be rent and fall upon him, the fragments *will* strike but not dismay him.

In the first example (*a*) what is *unreal* (he had not perished) is stated *as though it were real*, for the sake of making the language more emphatic : "I all but perished."

The second (*b*) is from the *poet* Horace, who in *ferient* passes from the ordinary form of the conditional sentence to that of strong assertion or *prophecy*. These idioms, at all events the second, should never be imitated by the young composer.

Exercise 58 A should now be done (page 293).

Nisi, si non, sin, si minus ; sive, seu.

464. The rules for **mood** and **tense** are the same as those given for *si*.

---

* In using this pluperfect we are really, though unconsciously, using the now obsolete form of the English subjunctive.

Nisi, "if not," "unless," negatives a *whole clause;* with *si non* the negative applies to a *single word*.

> *Morietur*, nisi *medicum adhibuerit.* Unless he calls in, *or*, if he does not call in, a physician he will die.
>
> *Morietur*, si *medicum* non *adhibuerit.* He will die, if he *fails*-to-call-in a physician.

465. *Sin* (*si ne*, properly "if not")= "but if," and is used to introduce a fresh *si*-clause, *contrary* in sense to one already expressed or implied. If the fresh clause is *negative*, *si non* with a verb, or simply *si minus*, takes the place of *sin*.

> *Si luna clara est, domo exeunt*, sin *obscurior, domi manent.* If the moon is bright, they leave their houses, *but if* it is at all dim (**57**, *b*), they stay at home.
>
> *Si haec feceris, gaudebo,* $\begin{cases} \text{si non } feceris, \\ \text{si minus,} \end{cases}$ *aequo animo feram.* If he *does* this, I shall be glad; if he *does not* (or *if not*), I shall take it quietly.

466. *Si, nisi, si non, si minus*, are sometimes like some other conjunctions (Intr. 27) joined with single words in place of clauses.

> (*a*) *Juravit se*, nisi *victorem, nunquam rediturum.* He swore never to return, unless victorious.
>
> (*b*) *Nihil aliud discere est*, nisi recordari. Learning is nothing else than recollecting.
>
> (*c*) *Cum spe*, si non *optimā, at aliquā* tamen *vivere.* To live with some hopes, if not the highest. (Note *order of English.*)

Caution.—It is only in such phrases, where it emphasises a single word, that *at tamen* should be used; it should **never begin a sentence**, as it so often does in later Latin.

467. Sive, *seu*, though translated by "whether," "or," are never used as *interrogatives*, never, that is, as identical with *utrum, an.* (See **171.**) They introduce two or more alternative *conditions*, between which the speaker makes no choice; they affect the principal clause, or *apodosis*, equally.

> Sive *adhibueris medicum*, sive *non adhibueris*, convalesces.
> You will get well, *whether* you call in a physician *or* no, *i.e.* if you do, and if you do not.

The rules for the **mood** are the same as the two given for *si* (**452, 453**).

> *Seu* legit, *seu* scribit, *nihil temporis* terit. Whether he *reads* or *writes*, he *wastes* no time. (RULE I.)
>
> *Seu* legat, *seu* scribat. *nihil temporis* terat. Whether he *were to read*, or *were to write*, he *would waste* no time. (RULE II.)

Caution.—Great care must be taken to distinguish *sive
. . . sive, seu . . . seu,* from *utrum . . . an,* and *aut . . . aut.*

(*a*) *Sive . . . seu* introduce **adverbial** clauses (conditional).
(*b*) *Utrum . an* „ **substantival** clauses (interrogative).
(*c*) *Aut . . . aut* „ **co-ordinate** clauses.

(*a*) Seu *legit,* seu *scribit, nihil temporis terit.* *Whether* he reads
or writes, he wastes no time.
(*b*) Utrum *legat* an *scribat nescio.* I do not know *whether* he is
reading *or* writing.
(*c*) Aut *legit* aut *scribit.* He is *either* reading *or* writing.

The manner, therefore, in which " whether " and " or " are to be
translated into Latin depends entirely on the sense in which they are
used, that is, on the nature of the clause which they introduce. (See
171.)

468. *Dum, modo (dum modo), ita . . . ut* (consecutive),
when used in the sense of "provided that," "on the condition that," will cause no difficulty, as they are invariably
used with the **subjunctive**.

(*a*) *Oderint* dum *metuant;* (*b*) *maneat,* modo *taceat* (jussive) ;
(*c*) ita *maneat* ut[1] *mihi pareat, ut ne quid me invito faciat.*

(*a*) is " Let them hate me, so long as they fear me ;" (*b*) "let him
remain on condition of being silent ;" (*c*) "let him remain on condition that he obeys me, (and) does nothing against my will."
But *ita . . . ut* (comparative=as) is sometimes used in a similar
sense with the **indicative.**

Ita vivam ut te amo. May I die if I do not love you ; *lit.* may
I live *so far* (only) *as* I love you.

Exercise 58.

A.

Exceptional uses of the Mood with *Si.*

1. Had he listened to your warnings, had he endured
everything in silence, the result would have been the
same then as to-day. 2. Had you been in office during

---

[1] The *ut* here is of course consecutive, "so as to," and hence
equivalent to a *condition ;* but it approaches also a *final* sense " with
the intention of ;" hence the *ne* in the next clause. Cf. the Greek
ὥστε, ὥστε μή.

(in) the same year as my father, had you encountered the same political storms as he did, you would have shewn,[1] if not[2] as great self-control, yet as much good sense as he did. 3. Had I said this with the intention of being of use to, and of pleasing, him, yet I should have had to put up with his abuse and insults. 4. Had your father said this with the intention of displeasing you, yet you should have remembered that he was your father, and have endured his angry mood calmly and in silence. 5. This is the course, which, had I been born in the same position as you, I should have had to take; but happily I have never had to undertake such a task. 6. Had the son been of the same character as the father, I might have touched his heart by prayer[3] and entreaty; but in truth he is so inhuman, so cruel, that, had all mankind endeavoured to soften him, no one would[4] have prevailed. 7. If you wish to see me before I leave the city, I would have[5] you write to your father not[6] to summon me to the army till you have come to Rome. 8. If you have been persuaded[6] to pardon him his offences, and not to exact punishment for so many crimes, would any[7] one impute that to you as a fault, or taunt you with your clemency and gentleness? It might perhaps have been[8] better not to have listened to prayer; but error is one thing, wrong-doing another.

B.

Nisi, si non, sin; sive, seu.

1. If you fail to return at the end of a week, you will greatly injure your own[9] cause. 2. I should not have written thus[10] had not I been convinced that your father took the same view on this question as I. 3. He was a man of the highest ability, the highest character, of respectable, if humble origin. 4. If I obtain my request,

---

[1] Use *adhibeo*, I employ. call in.   [2] See **466**.   [3] Gerund.
[4] See **115**.   [5] **141**.   [6] **122**, *c, b.*   [7] **358**.   [8] **153**.
[9] See **356**, i.
[10] *Haec.* So *haec*, or *hoc, facere*, is "to act *thus*," never *ita agere.*

I shall be most grateful; if not, I will do my best[1] to bear it with resignation. 5. In the morning he[2] promised and bound himself by oath never to return from the field, unless victorious; yet[3] in the evening I saw him with my[4] own eyes walking in the park, with countenance unmoved and calm, if not cheerful. 6. Let him speak out his whole mind, his whole wishes; provided that he is silent for the future, it matters little what he says at present. 7. You shall obtain your request, but only on[5] condition that you depart at once, and never more return. 8. Whether you were absent intentionally, or by chance, concerns yourself, and is of no small importance to your own reputation; what[6] we have to decide is whether you were absent[7] or present; if you were absent[7] during[8] the battle, whether it happened by design or by mere chance, you will be condemned, and that[9] deservedly, by a unanimous verdict, for you ought never to have[10] left the camp. 9. Whether you will do me this favour or not, I do not yet know, but whether you consent to do it or no, I shall always be grateful to you for[11] your many kind deeds, and will show my gratitude if I can. 10. Whether this bill is constitutional or unconstitutional may be questioned; but whether it is constitutional or unconstitutional, I venture to say this, that if not indispensable, it is so beneficial, so useful to the nation in the face[12] of the present crisis, that it has been approved of by every patriot.

---

[1] See **332**, **5**, *g.* (p. 222).
[2] *Iste.* (See **338**, *Obs.* 2.)
[3] *Idem* for "yet him." (See **366**, ii.)
[4] *Ipse.* (**355**, *d.*)
[5] *Ita* . . *ut.* (**468**, *c.*)
[6] **341**.
[7,7] Tenses? one the mere fact, the other continuous time. (**173**.)
[8] "Then . . . when the fight was going on." (**218**.) Mood? (See **433**.)
[9] *Idque.* (See **344**.)
[10] Tense? (**198**, i., ii., *b.*)
[11] *Propter tot.*
[12] **273**. *Obs.*

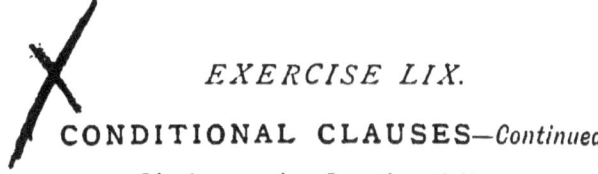

EXERCISE LIX.

CONDITIONAL CLAUSES—*Continued.*

Si-clause in Oratio obliqua.

469. If a verb of *saying* or *thinking* is inserted before the **principal** clause of a conditional sentence, the verb of that clause will of course pass from the **indicative** or **subjunctive** mood into the **infinitive** (**31**), which represents the English finite verb with "that" prefixed.

(i.) With the apodosis, or main clause, of sentences under Rule I., this will give no difficulty; in those that fall under Rule II., the subjunctive, answering to the English *would, would have,* will be (somewhat roughly) represented by the future in *-rus* with *esse* and *fuisse* respectively. (See **36.**)

Amem (I would love) will be represented by (*dico*) *me amaturum esse.*

Amarem and *amavissem* (I would have loved), by (*dico*) *me amaturum fuisse.*

(ii.) The verb in the *si*-clause will, in all such cases, be in the **subjunctive** mood; the indicative has no proper place in any clause dependent on a verb in *oratio obliqua.* (**444.**)

470. (i.) Thus with sentences under Rule I. (**452.**)

Oratio recta.		*Oratio obliqua.*
(*a*) Si *hoc* dico, erro,	will become	(*dicit*) me, *si hoc* dicam, errare.
(*b*) Si *hoc* dicebam, errabam	„	(*dicit*) me, *si hoc* dicerem, erravisse.
(*c*) Si *hoc* dixi erravi	„	(*dicit*) me, *si hoc dixerim,* erravisse.
(*d*) Si *hoc* dicam (fut.) errabo	„	(*dicit*) me, *si hoc* dicam, erraturum esse.

(ii.) If, as in narrative is more usual, the verb of saying is in a **historic** tense. (**177,** *b.*)

Oratio obliqua.

(*a*) and (*b*) will become (*dixit*) me, *si hoc* dicerem, errare.
(*c*)   „   (*dixit*) me, *si hoc* dixissem, erravisse (*or* dixerim).
(*d*)   „   (*dicit*) me, *si hoc* dicerem, erraturum esse.

471. But when, as is more usual, the **future perfect** is used in the protasis to a future clause, care must be taken.

Oratio recta.	*Oratio obliqua.*
Si hoc dixero, erràbo, will become	(dicit) *me, si hoc* dixerim, errà-turum esse, but
	(dixit) *me, si hoc* dixissem, *erra-turum esse.*

That is, after a past verb, expressed or implied, of *narrating*, the **future perfect** of *oratio recta* passes into the **pluperfect**, after a *present* verb into the **perfect**, subjunctive.

Obs.—The *future perfect* of the indicative of *oratio recta* has a **double** sense, *future* and *past* (*shall have*); both cannot be represented in the subjunctive; accordingly Latin represents only the **past** sense, English sometimes only the future, sometimes the past very vaguely.

Oratio recta.	*Oratio obliqua*
Eng. If [1]*once* he *does* this he *shall*, or *will*, die.	**He said that** if he *should* once do, or once *did*, this, he *should*, or *would*, die.
Lat. Si hoc fecerit, *morietur.*	*Eum si hoc* fecisset, *moriturum fore.*
Or *Ei, si ,, ,, moriendum erit.*	*Ei, si ,, ,, moriendum fore.*

472. With sentences under RULE II. (**453**) there will be no change in the mood of the *si*-clause; the tense will of course vary with that of the verb of *saying* or *thinking*.

Oratio recta.	*Oratio obliqua.*
Si hoc dicam, errem, will become	(dicit) *me, si hoc* dicam, erra-turum esse.
	(dixit) *me, si hoc* dicerem, erra-turum esse.

Si hoc dicerem, errarem ; $\left\{ \begin{array}{c} dicit \\ dixit \end{array} \right\}$ *me si hoc* dicerem, erraturum fuisse. If I had *been saying* this, I should have been in error.

Si hoc dixissem, erravissem ; $\left\{ \begin{array}{c} dicit \\ dixit \end{array} \right\}$ *me si hoc* dixissem, erratu-rum fuisse. If I *had said,* etc.

---

[1] Remember how often our "*if once*" is expressed by the Latin future perfect (*semel* need rarely be inserted), and this tense and its representatives in the subjunctive must always be used if the time indicated is. though still future, prior to that of the principal verb.

473. The periphrasis for the future, and contingent future, **passive** must not be forgotten. (**193**, iii. and v.)

(*a*) "He said that the city *would be taken*, if Caesar *did* not come to its aid." (*Dixit*) *urbem, nisi* subvenisset *Caesar*, captum iri, *or*, fore ut *urbs caperetur* (*captam fore* is found, but rarely).

(*Nisi subveniret* would mean, *were* coming, or *were ready* to come.)

(*b*) "He said that the city would *have been* taken if Caesar had not come to its aid," or "*but for* Caesar *having* come," etc. (Dixit) *Caesar nisi* subvenisset, futurum fuisse *ut urbs caperetur*.

In *oratio recta* we should have (*a*) *urbs, nisi* subvenerit *Caesar*, capietur, (*b*) *urbs* capta fuisset, or *capi* potuit (see **461**), *nisi* subvenisset *Caesar*.

474. Such apparent violations of RULE I. as (*a*) *mortem mihi* denuntiavit *pater, si* pugnassem, (*b*) expectabat *Caesar, si hostes* posset *opprimere*, are both instances of **virtual** *oratio obliqua*. (See **449**.)

(*a*) is "My father threatened me with death, *if I should fight*, or *fought;*" (*b*) "Caesar was waiting, *in hopes of being able* to crush the enemy."

In (*a*) *si pugnassem* is not really the *protasis* or adverbial clause to *denuntiavit*, which is quite unqualified : it belongs really to a suppressed clause contained in *mortem*, such as *fore ut perirem;* it is therefore a perfectly regular instance of a *si*-clause in *oratio obliqua :* "He *said* that I should die if I fought" (his words were "*si pugnaveris moriere*").

In (*b*) *si posset* does not qualify *expectabat*, which is quite unqualified. It is used in the sense "in hopes that," and it answers to a suppressed clause expressing what *was in Caesar's mind*, "intending to use the chance, in case," etc. It is therefore virtual *oratio obliqua*, and the mood is quite regular.

475. How to express "would have" in the **principal clause** of a conditional sentence after consecutive *ut*, or a dependent interrogation.

The **pluperfect subjunctive** is not used, but gives place to the **perfect subjunctive** of the modal verb *possum* or of the periphrasis formed by the future in *-rus*, or gerund or gerundive with *sum*. (**461**.)

Quid tu, *si tum adesses*, dixisses, will become *rogo, quid tu, si tum adesses*, dicturus fueris.

Si id fecissem, periissem, will become *ut* ("so that") *si id fecissem*, periturus fuerim, *or* pereundum *mihi* fuerit. (**115**.)

Some additional examples of more or less **exceptional** constructions are added for careful observation.

1. Debuisti *enim, etiam* si *falso in suspicionem* venisses, *mihi ignoscere.* You ought to *have* forgiven me, or it *would have* been your duty to forgive me, even if you had been falsely suspected. (**461.**)

2. *Atrox certamen* aderat, ni *Fabius rem* expedisset. A desperate contest was at hand (*would have* taken place) had not Fabius solved the difficulty. (**463.**)

3. *Ibi* erat *mansurus,* si *ire* perrexisset. It was there he *would have* stayed, had he continued his journey. (**461.**)

4. *Quid enim futurum* fuit, si *res agitari coepta* esset. For what *would have* happened, if once the question had begun to be discussed. (**461.**)

5. *Neque hostem sustinere* poterant, ni *cohortes illae* se objecissent. And they *could not have* maintained themselves against the enemy, but for those cohorts' exposure of themselves. (**461.**)

6. *Virgines* si effugissent, impleturae *urbem tumultu* erant. Had the maidens escaped, they *would have* spread disorder through the whole city. (**461.**)

7. *Praeclare* viceramus, nisi *fugientem Antonium* recepisset *Lepidus.* We *should have* won a splendid victory, had not Lepidus given a reception to Antony when in full flight. (**463.**)

8. Si *in hoc* erravi, *id mihi* velim *ignoscas.* If I have blundered in this, I beg you to forgive me. (**462.**)

9. *Circumfunduntur hostes,* si *quem aditum reperire* possent. The enemy swarm (historic pres.) round, *in hopes of* finding some means of approach (*with the view of breaking* in, if), etc. (**474.**)

10. *Praemium proposuit,* si *quis ducem interfecisset.* He offered a prize, *i.e. said that* he would give a prize, in case any one should kill the leader. (**474.**)

11. *Nuntium ad te misi,* si *forte non* audisses. I sent you a messenger, in case you had not heard. (We must supply *ut audires,* etc.) (**474.**)

12. *Non recusavit quo minus vel extremo spiritu,* si *quam opem reipublicae ferre* posset, *experiretur.* He did not flinch from trying even with his latest breath whether he could not give some aid to his country—*lit.* from making the experiment *in hopes that* he could ... (**474.**)

A.

1. Did you imagine that, if all the rest were cut off either by the sword or by famine, you alone would be saved? 2. He feared, he said, that unless he consented to do everything that the king should command, he would never be allowed to return to his native land. 3. He will bear, he says, cheerfully his own destitution and that [1] of his family, if once he be freed from this degrading suspicion. 4. He warned them of the extent [2] and suddenness [2] of the crisis, that they could win the day if they were ready to show themselves brave men and worthy of their forefathers, but that if they hesitated or hung back, all the neighbouring tribes would soon be in arms. 5. He felt convinced of this, that if once he crushed the barbarians who had long been [3] infesting the mountains, the way to Italy would be open to himself and his soldiers. 6. He said that he would never have imparted this story to you, had he not when [4] leaving home promised his father to conceal nothing from such dear friends as [5] yourselves. 7. He felt convinced, he said, that unless they had placed so experienced a general as yourself at the head of a veteran army, the city would have been stormed within a week. 8. He said he would never have pardoned you so monstrous a crime, had not your aged father thrown [6] himself at his feet and implored him to spare you.

B.

The following Exercise is recapitulatory; the sentences contain various kinds of *if*-clauses.

1. If you are at Rome, I scarcely imagine you are, but if you are, please write at once. 2. If the enemy reaches the city, there will be reason [7] to fear a dreadful massacre. 3. I sent you a letter of Caesar's, in case you wished to

---

[1] See **345**.   [2] See **174**, *b* and *e*.
[3] Tense? (See **181**.) Mood? (See **444, 449**.)   [4] See **406**, *note* [2].
[5] **224**, *Obs.* 2.   [6] See **257**. Use passive (or middle) participle.
[7] "must (*tense ?*) be feared."

read it.   4. He declared that it was absolutely impossible for the Germans to win the day, if they engaged in battle before the new moon.   5. If you are ready to make some exertion, you will take the city.   6. If you once exert yourselves, you will take the city.   7. He said that if they once exerted themselves, they would take the city.   8. As the neighbouring tribes were all jealous of his fame, he felt that if he and his people surrendered their arms, their doom[1] was certain.   9. If anything falls out amiss,[2] we shall make you responsible.   10. He threatened him with violence and every species[3] of punishment, if he entered the senate-house.   11. It was certainly[4] a wonderful speech; I could not imitate it if I would; perhaps I would not if I could.   12. The Dictator announced a heavy penalty in case any one should fight without his permission.   13. They feared that if they once departed without success, they would lose everything for the sake of which they had taken up arms.   14. They now at last perceived that if, at his suggestion, they had consented to abandon the popular party, and join the nobles, they would have lost all their privileges and their freedom, if not their lives.   15. If you do this, you will possibly incur some loss; if you do not you will undoubtedly have acted dishonourably; it is for[5] you to decide which of the two you prefer to do.   16. If any one evades military service, he shall be declared infamous; if any one has fears for his own safety, let him at once lay down his arms, and leave his native land safe and sound.

---

[1] " were doomed to certain destruction."

[2] *Secus*, otherwise than *well.*   [3] Simply *omnis.*

[4] *Sane*, " certainly," in the sense of making an *admission.*

[5] **291**, *Obs.* 2.

EXERCISE LX.

CONCESSIVE CLAUSES.

Quanquam, quamvis, etc.

476. By **concessive clauses** we mean such adverbial clauses as are introduced in English by "although" and the like, in Latin by the conjunctions *etsi* (*tametsi, etiam si*); *quanquam, quamvis, licet.* (See Intr. 59, *g.*)

Such clauses are called *concessive* because they admit or *concede* something, in spite of which the statement made in the main clause is true ; its truth is emphasised by the contrast.

477. Their syntax is not difficult.

RULE.—When the point conceded in the concessive clause is **admitted** as a **fact** the **indicative** is used ; otherwise, when only conceded **for the sake of argument**, the **subjunctive**.

The difference is still occasionally marked in English : "though he *is* guilty," "though he *be* guilty ;" "though he *was* guilty," "though he *were* guilty ;" but the nearly obsolete use of the English subjunctive is a precarious guide.

(*a*) In the sense of the Latin **indicative** we constantly use such phrases as, *in spite of*, or *notwithstanding*, his guilt, *or*, guilty *as* he is, etc.

(*b*) In that of the **subjunctive**, *whatever* his guilt=*however* guilty he is (be), *were* he guilty, etc.

478. *Etsi* (*tametsi*), when it contrasts one *fact* with another *fact*, is joined with the **indicative**.

> Etsi *mons Cevenna iter* impediebat, *tamen ad fines Arvernorum pervenit.* Although the Cevennes were in the way of his march (or *in spite of . . . being* in the way) he reached the territory of the Arverni.

But when both the concession and the other statement are purely **imaginary**, the **subjunctive** is used.

> *Ego* etsi abessem, *tamen cum ceteris me condemnasses?* Though I *had been absent* (*all the* time), *would* you yet *have* condemned me with all the rest ?

That is, the *etsi* clause follows the mood, as a rule, of the main clause, precisely as the *si*-clause, of which it is only another form.

479. *Quanquam* (a doubled *quam*), which contrasts one *fact* with another, naturally takes the **indicative.** It should never be joined with the subjunctive unless in **oratio obliqua**.

> *Romani* quanquam *itinere et aestu fessi* erant, *tamen obviam hostibus* procedunt. Though the Romans were fatigued with the march and the heat, yet they advanced (historic present) to meet the enemy.

Observe how often *tamen,* "yet," "still," is inserted in the main clause to mark the contrast; but *at tamen* should never be used except with single words. (See **466.**)

Obs.—Quanquam is often used *co-ordinately* [1] to introduce an entirely fresh sentence in contrast with what precedes it, and is then = "and yet;" cf. the co-ordinate use of *quum.* (**435.**)

480. (i.) *Quamvis,* on the other hand, **requires a subjunctive**.

> *Quamvis* sit *magna expectatio, tamen eam vinces.* Although expectations are (*or,* may be) great, you will surpass them (or, *however* great are (*be*) the expectations formed of you).

Quamvis=*quam vis,*[2] "as you will," must have a subjunctive from the nature of the case, as the above sentence would originally be, "*Let* expectations *be* as great *as you please,* you will surpass them."

Obs.—Quamvis, like *nisi* (**466**), is sometimes joined closely with a single word (*quamvis* audax, "however bold," "whatever his boldness"), without a verb.

(ii.) *Licet,* "although," is simply the impersonal **verb**, "it is granted" (**197**). It should therefore never be used with the indicative.

> Licet *undique pericula* impendeant, *tamen subibo. Though* dangers threaten me on every side, I will face them.

481. As in English, so in Latin, the same idea as is denoted by the concessive conjunctions "although" *quanquam,* etc., may be expressed in many other ways.

---

[1] Cf. the opening of the fine passage in Georgic I. 469—
        "Tempore *quanquam* illo," etc.

[2] *Quamvis* is properly a separate clause, "*as* you *choose,*" and the subjunctive is *jussive* (**144**); it is sometimes even inflected: *quam* volet *cunctetur,* (lit.) let him delay *as much as he chooses.* But in later Latin its origin, and that of *licet,* became obliterated, and they were used freely with the indicative, *quanquam* with the subjunctive.

Thus "Though he is an excellent man, he does wrong sometimes," may be translated not only by, Quanquam *homo optimus est,* tamen *interdum peccat,* but by (*a*) *Homo optimus* ille quidem, sed *interdum* peccat (**334,** iv.); or (*b*) Ut ("granted that") sit *homo ille optimus, tamen interdum peccat;* or (*c*) Ita *homo optimus est* ut *interdum* peccet, *i.e.* "*so far only,*" etc. (**111**); or (*d*) Sit (jussive) *homo ille optimus, tamen interdum peccat;* or (*e*) very commonly by the use of *sane* in one clause, followed by an *adversative conjunction* (Intr. 56, *c*) in the other,—*res* sane *difficilis, sed tamen investiganda,* "*though a* difficult question, *yet still* one that demands investigation ;" or (*f*) by the mere participle,—*hoc crimine* absolutus, *furti tamen condemnatus est,* "*though* acquitted on this charge he was found guilty of theft." (**406.**)

For the use of *qui*   for "although" see **509,** *b.*
        ,,   *quum*   ,,   **431.**
        ,,   *sicut . . . ita*   ,,   **492** (i.).

Exercise 60.

1. Though he feels neither remorse nor shame for this deed, yet he shall pay me the penalty of his crime. 2. Even though it were quite impossible to pardon his fault, yet you ought[1] to have taken into account his many services to the nation. 3. Whatever his guilt,[2] whatever his criminality, no one has a right to indict him in his absence and to condemn him unheard. 4. Entirely guilty as he is, and absolutely deserving of condign punishment, yet I cannot help comparing his present fallen and low condition with his former good fortune · and renown. 5. Miserable as it is for an innocent man to be suspected and charged, yet it is better for the innocent to be acquitted than for the guilty not to be accused. 6. However criminal he had been, however worthy of every kind of punishment, yet it would have[3] been better for ten guilty persons to be acquitted, than for one innocent to be found guilty. 7. In spite of his having had the sovereignty and supreme power offered and intrusted to him by the unanimous vote[4] of his countrymen, he long refused to take any part in politics, and was the only person in my day who attained to the highest distinctions

---

[1] Gerundive. (**389.**)   [2] Use adjective. (**477,** *b.*)
[3] Mood? (**153.**)   [4] Number?

against his will, and almost under compulsion. 8. Though[1] freed from this apprehension, I was soon suspected of a darker[2] crime, and perhaps but for your having come to my aid, might have fallen a victim[3] to the hatred and schemes of my enemies. 9. Many[4] as are the evils that you have endured, you will one day, I still believe,[5] not only enjoy good fortune, but a rarer gift,[6] happiness.

---

[1] **481,** *f.*   [2] Metaphor.   (See Vocab.)
[3] Metaphor; **(17)**="been crushed by."
[4] "Although . . . so many" (*tot*, **477,** *a*).   [5] **32,** *b.*
[6] "Gift," metaphor; "that which **(67)** more rarely falls to men's lot.

CAUSAL AND EXPLANATORY CLAUSES.

482. By these are meant such **subordinate**[1] adverbial clauses as give a **reason** or **explanation** of the statement, etc., made by the verb in the principal clause. They are introduced in English by " because," " inasmuch as," " seeing that," " whereas," " considering that," etc. (Intr. 59, *d.*)

483. The conjunctions *quod, quia,* "because," *quoniam* (i.e. *quum jam*), *quandoquidem*, " since," are followed by an **indicative** mood.

> *Vos, inquit,* quoniam *jam nox* est, *domum discedite.* Do you, says he, *since* it is now night, depart home.

Obs.—These conjunctions are all formed from the *relative*, and like the relative (**84**) often have a *demonstrative* particle or phrase corresponding to them in the other clause. Cf. *tamen* in concessive, *idcirco* in final, clauses, etc. (See **107.**)

> Idcirco, eo, hanc ob causam, etc., *ad te scribo* quod *me id facere jussisti.* The *reason* of my writing is *that* you told me to do so.
> *Nullam aliam* ob causam . . . *quam* quod, etc. The one and only *cause* or *motive* . . . is *that*, etc.

484. All of these conjunctions however may be joined with the **subjunctive**, on either of two grounds.

(*a*) The principal clause may be in *oratio obliqua.* (446.)

> *Jussit eos,* quoniam *nox* esset, *discedere.*

(*b*) The *quod*-clause may be in *virtual oratio obliqua.* (See 448.)

That is, we may supply in thought the words " as he (they) said," or " thought," after the causal conjunction ; or translate *quod* by " asserting that," " under the impression that," " in the belief that."

> *Abire voluit,* quoniam *nox* esset. Since it was, *as he said*, night.

---

[1] The connexion of cause and effect may be stated by a co-*ordinate* clause with causal or inferential conjunctions (Intr. 56, *d* and *e*): *Rediisti: gaudeo* igitur; or *gaudeo: rediisti* enim ; but the construction of such co-ordinate conjunctions presents no difficulty, as they have no effect on the mood of the verb.

π

Obs.—This use of the subjunctive in a *quod*-clause is exceedingly common after words of *praising, blaming, accusing, admiring, complaining, wondering.*

> *Rex civibus odio erat*, quod *leges* violasset.   The king was hated by his subjects, because (*they felt that*) he had broken the law, or, *as* having, *or*, for having (*as they thought*), broken the law.

Violarat would be a statement made and accredited by the historian. "for having (*as he had*) broken the law."

It is naturally most common after verbs of *complaining, blaming,* etc.

> *Mihi irascitur*, quod *eum* neglexerim.   Because (*as he says or fancies*) I have neglected him, *as* having neglected him.

The responsibility of the statement is shifted from the speaker or writer to the subject of the principal verb. (See 448.)

485. When a reason is mentioned only to be set aside, *non quo*, "not that," *non quin*, "not but what," are used, always with the **subjunctive**.

Sometimes the reason *accepted* follows, with *sed quod* and the **indicative**.

> Non quo *tui me* taedeat, or, non quin *me* ames, sed quod *abire* cupio.   *Not that* I am tired of you, or *not but what* you love me (or, *not that* you don't), *but because* I am anxious to depart.

Quum with the subjunctive is often causal (see **430**).   So also is *qui* (see **509**).

486. *Quod* ("that") often answers to the English "the fact *that*," or, "*of*," and is used to **explain** the object or subject of a verb, especially in apposition with a neuter pronoun.

> *Magnum est hoc*, quod *victor victis* pepercit.   This is no small thing, I mean *the fact of* his having spared the vanquished when victorious.
> *Omitto illud*, quod *regem patriamque* prodidit.[1]   I pass over *the fact of* his having betrayed his king and country; or simply, "his *betrayal of*," etc.

---

[1] Sometimes a kind of *virtual oratio obliqua* is used, where there is only a single speaker, who looks on himself as, so to speak, *two persons*: *Omitto . . . quod prodiderit,* I pass over *my belief that* he betrayed.

Obs.—This *quod* with the indicative (or subjunctive) will be found very useful in translating the English verbal **substantive** of the present or perfect tense, *e.g.* "your *saying* or *having said* this," and such **abstract nouns** as "circumstance," "fact," "reason," "reflexion."

Of course it cannot be used for "that" after verbs **sentiendi et declarandi**. (See 32, *a*.) *Illud* dico, quod *patriam prodidisti* would mean, not, "I *say that* you have betrayed your country," but, "I *mean the fact* of your having betrayed," etc.

487. Notice also the phrases—

(*a*) *Peropportune* accidit quod *venisti*. Your *coming* was *very* fortunate (only substituted for *ut* (**123**) when an *adverb* is joined with *accidit*).

(*b*) Accedit quod *domi non est*. There is the *additional reason* that he is not at home.

(*c*) Quod scribis *cum rediisse, num verum sit dubito*. *As to your writing* to say that he has returned, I doubt its truth.

Obs.—With verbs of **rejoicing**, etc., there is no perceptible difference between the infinitive (**41**, *b*) and the *quod*-clause : Te rediisse *gaudeo* =quod rediisti *gaudeo*. The latter emphasises the *fact* of the return.

Exercise 61.

1. The reason of my somewhat disliking in my youth one so attached to me as[1] your excellent relative, was my being unable to bear his want of steadiness and principle. 2. I am hated by every[2] bad citizen for having been the very last to uphold the national cause, and because I have constantly disdained to flatter the conqueror. 3. I received[3] the thanks of parliament and the nation for having been alone[4] in not despairing of the commonwealth. 4. It was scarcely possible[5] for you not to incur the hatred[6] of your countrymen,—not that you had been guilty of betraying your country, but because you had the courage to be the advocate of a burdensome and distasteful, however[7] necessary, peace. 5. All honoured your gallant father for having sacrificed the unanimous offer[8] of a throne to the true and more substantial glory of

---

[1] 224, and *Obs.* 2.　　　　　　　[2] 375.
[3] = "thanks were returned to me by . . .."　[4] See 62, and 484, *Obs.*
[5] 132, *e*.　　　[6] *Pl.*, why? Because "countrymen" is plural.
[7] Use either *ille quidem* (**481**, *a*) or *si . . . at tamen* (**466**, *c*) or *quamvis*. (**480**, *Obs.*)
[8] Same construction as that in **417**.

giving[1] freedom to his country.   6. Though the whole
world is angry with me for having pardoned (as they
say[2]) my father's murderers, yet I shall never be ashamed
of the reflexion[3] of having spared the vanquished in the
hour of victory.   7. As for your having still a grudge
against me, under the impression[2] that six years ago I
injured you in your absence, and sacrificed your interests
to my own gain (*pl.*), my only motive in wishing to
refute such a charge is because I count your friendship
worth seeking.   8. And now, in spite of his being incapable of any such baseness, he was the object of universal
unpopularity, as having[2] supplied the enemy with funds,
and treated the office with which the nation had intrusted
him as a source of disgraceful gain; though no one was
ever more incapable of so black a crime.

---

[1] Same construction as that in **417**.   [2] See **484**, *b*.
[3] **486**, *Obs.* and *note*.

EXERCISE LXII.

COMPARATIVE CLAUSES.

Proportion.

488. By **comparative clauses** we mean here such adverbial clauses (Intr. 82-84) as express *likeness, agreement,* or the *opposite,* with what is stated, asked, or ordered, in the principal clause.

He acted *as I had ordered him;* why was he treated worse *than he deserved?* Do as *I bid you;* he behaved *as though he were mad;* are instances of such clauses in English.

In Latin the number of **conjunctions** or **conjunctional phrases** used to introduce such clauses is very large ; *ut* (*sicut*), *quemadmodum, atque* (*ac*), *quam, quasi, velut* (si), *tanquam* (si), *quasi, ac si.* (Intr. 59, *f.*)

They correspond also to a number of **demonstrative adverbs** or phrases, which stand to them in the same relation as *is* to *qui, tantus* to *quantus, idcirco,* or *adeo,* to *ut, tamen* to *quanquam,* etc.

Such are *ita, sic, pro eo, perinde, pariter, potius, aliter, secus,* etc.

489. All such clauses, both in English and Latin, fall naturally into **two classes.**

Class I.—Those in which the **comparison** made in the subordinate clause is *stated,* or *predicated,* as something *real,* as for example :—

He was punished *as he deserved. Perinde ac meritus est, poenas persolvit.*

Class II.—Those in which such **comparison** is introduced as a mere *conception* of the mind, something *imaginary* or *unreal,* not stated as a *fact ;* as—

He was punished *as though he had deserved it. Perinde ac si,* or *ut si,* or *quasi, meritus esset, poenas persolvit.*

In CLASS I. the **indicative** is the rule (except in *oratio obliqua*), in CLASS II. the **subjunctive.**

Class I.—Comparative Clauses with the Indicative.

490. Observe that the ideas of *likeness, equality, difference,* etc., which are often expressed by *adverbial* or *conjunctional* clauses, may be otherwise expressed both in English and Latin.

(i.) In Latin the place of the **conjunction** is often taken by the **relative,** *i.e.* we have an adjectival (correlative) instead of an adverbial clause.

> Tanta *est tempestas* quantam *numquam antea vidi.* The storm is greater *than I ever saw before,* or, is unparalleled in my experience. (See **84, 85.**)

(ii.) In Latin, but to a far greater extent in English, the place of the adverbial **clause** of comparison is taken by an adverbial **phrase** included in a simple sentence. (Intr. 70.)

Thus in the compound sentence, "he was punished *as he deserved,*" the adverbial clause may in both languages be expressed in three different ways : (1) by an *adverbial* clause ; (2) by an *adjectival* clause ; (3) by an *adverbial phrase,* or an *adverb.*

> (1) *Perinde* ac meritus est *poenas persolvit.* He was punished *as he deserved.*
>
> (2) *Poenas* quas debuit *persolvit.* He paid the penalty *which he merited.*
>
> (3) Pro meritis, *or* merito, *or* pro scelere, *poenas persolvit.* He was punished *in accordance with his guilt,* or, *deservedly.*

In English one of the last of these modes, the *adverbial phrase,* is far commoner than in Latin, and must constantly be translated by a Latin *adverbial clause.*

General Rule.

491. In Class I.—To express (*a*) **likeness,** *ut* ("as") corresponds to *ita, sic,* sometimes to *perinde; atque (ac)* corresponds to *perinde, pariter, aeque, juxta, pro eo,* etc.

To express (*b*) **difference,** *atque (ac)* corresponds to *aliter, secus; ac* and *quam* to *contra; quam* to *potius,* and other *comparatives.*

> (*a*) Ut *sunt,* ita *nominantur senes.* Their title "old men" corresponds to the fact.
>
> Pro eo ac, *or* perinde ac, *debui, feci.* I have acted *in accordance with my duty.*
>
> (*b*) Aliter ac, *or* non perinde ac, *meriti sumus, laudamur.* We are not praised *in proportion to our deserts.*
>
> Contra quam *pollicitus es fecisti.* You have acted *in violation of your promises.*

Obs. 1.—Note the recurrence of the **indicative** mood, and the constant substitution of the English **adverbial** and other **phrases** for the Latin **adverbial clause.**

Obs. 2.—A very strong contrast may be marked by a double *aliter.*

Aliter *tum locutus es,* aliter *te geris hodie.* Your behaviour to-day is *most inconsistent with* your language at that time.

Special Idioms.

492. Ut as a comparative conjunction (="as") has many uses.

(i.) Sometimes with *ita, ut* (or *sicut*) marks a contrast, "as, or *while* (p. 274, *note*) one fact is true, so, *on the other hand,* is another," and is virtually *concessive.*

Ut *fortasse honestum est hoc,* sic *parum utile.* *Though* this is perhaps right, *yet* it is scarcely expedient.

(ii.) Sometimes, with *ita,* it is used in a *restrictive* sense, and is virtually *conditional.*

Ita *vivam* ut *te amo.* May I live *so far only* as I love you, *i.e.* May I die *if I do not love you.* (**468,** *ad fin.*)

(iii.) Without *ita,* it introduces a *general remark* in accordance with which a particular fact is noticed.

Tum *rex,* ut *erat natura benignus,* *omnibus veniam dedit.* Thereupon the king, *in accordance* [1] *with* the kindness of his nature, forgave them all.

(iv.) It introduces, as the English "as," parenthetic clauses : *ut fit,* "as (often) happens," *ut aiunt,* "as the proverb says."

But such parentheses as, *ut credo, ut arbitror, ut videtur,* are far rarer in Latin than in English, and are used in an *apologetic* and self-depreciatory sense, "*as at least* I think," or else are *ironical,* as is almost invariably the parenthetic *credo.*   (See **32,** *b.*)

(v.) It is used even *without any verb* in two senses.

(*a*) "As you would expect."

Magnus *pavor,* ut *in re improvisa, fuit.* The panic was great, *as was natural* in so unexpected an occurrence.

(*b*) In a *restrictive* sense, "*so far as* could be expected."

Satis *intrepide,* ut *in re improvisa, se gessit.* He showed considerable presence of mind, *considering* the unexpected nature of the occurrence.

---

[1] The same idea might be expressed by *quâ erat animi benignitate,* or *pro solitâ ejus benignitate,* or *homo natura benignissimus.* All these are substitutes for the much needed present participle of *esse.* (**224,** *Obs.* 1.)

493. Quam (see **275**) generally introduces a clause of the same construction as that of the main clause.

> *Nec ultra* saeviit *quam satis* erat.   Nor did he show more severity than was necessary,—any needless severity.
>
> *Nos potius hostem* aggrediamur quam *ipsi cum* propulsemus.   Let us take an aggressive, rather than a merely defensive, attitude.

But where **design** or **result** is indicated, a subjunctive is of course necessary.

> *Nihil ultra commotus est* quam ut *abire eos* juberet.   He was only so far moved as to bid them depart.

Obs. 1.—A **subjunctive** clause is used where a course is mentioned only to be rejected.

> *Omnia potius tentanda* quam hoc faciamus.   We ought to try any course *rather than* (allow ourselves to) *act thus.*

With *tam, quam* expresses equality [1] of *degree.*

> Tam *timidus hodie est* quam *tum fuit audax.*   He is as cowardly to-day as he was then over bold.

Obs. 2.—When two **adjectives** or **adverbs** are contrasted by the comparative degree followed by *quam,* Latin often uses the comparative degree with *both.*

> *Pestilentia minacior fuit quam* perniciosior.   The pestilence was more alarming than fatal.
>
> *Hoc bellum fortius quam felicius gessistis.*   You have carried on this war with more courage than good fortune.

494. Quum, tum. These are often used, in the sense of "whereas," "so especially," to unite two clauses, of which the *tum*-clause is always the most *emphatic in sense,* as well as the main clause in grammar.

> Quum *omnis servitus misera est,* tum *haec omnium est miserrima.*   *As* all slavery is wretched, *so* is this the most wretched of all, *or,* all slavery is wretched, *but* this, etc.

Obs.—The indicative is used with *quum* when the **time of the two verbs is the same**; but when the *quum*-clause denotes a time **prior to**

---

[1] In Livy the comparative clause is often introduced in a way impossible to imitate in English.

> *Cujus rei non* tam *ausim tantum virum insimulare . . .* quam *ea suspicio haud sane purgata est.*   *Though* I would not venture *. . . yet* that suspicion, etc.

that of the *tum*-clause the usual idiom is followed, and the subjunctive used even though a fact is asserted in the former. (See **429**.)

> *Cum te semper* amavi, *tum mei amantissimum* cognovi. Not only have I always felt affection for you, but I have found you most affectionate towards myself.

But—*Cum te semper* dilexerim, *tum hodie multo plus* diligo. I have always loved you, but I love you far more now.

Class II.—Comparative Clauses with the Subjunctive.

495. In comparisons made with an **unreal** or **imaginary** case, the adverbial clause is introduced by *velut, tanquam* (often with *si* added), *ut si, quasi, ac si.* The corresponding demonstratives are *sic, ita, perinde, proinde, non secus,* or such phrases as *similes sunt, similiter faciunt,* etc. The **subjunctive** is always used in the adverbial clause.

> Sic *eum ames velim* ut si *frater* esset *tuus.* I would have you love him *as if* he were your own brother.
> Ita *se gessit* quasi *consul* esset. He behaved as *though he* were consul.

496. These conjunctions are often used with a **single word** (substantive, adjective, or participle) or a **phrase**.

> *Eum* tanquam hostem, *or* tanquam patriae proditorem, *odi.*
> I hate him as (though he were) an enemy, *or,* a traitor.

They are constantly so used in Latin to **qualify a strong expression** or **metaphor**, and must often be inserted where there is nothing answering to them in English, where metaphors are much more freely used. (See **17**.)

> "The soul flies forth from the *prison-house* of the body."
> *E corpore,* velut e carcere, *evolat animus.*
> *Neve te obrui,* tanquam fluctu, sic *magnitudine negotii, sinas.*
> And do not suffer yourself to be overwhelmed by *the tide of business.*

In the same sense *quidam* (**361**, *Obs.* 1, 2), *quodammodo,* and *ut dicam* are often used.

497. Proportional clauses.—Such ideas as are expressed in English by a clause introduced by "in proportion as," or by the phrase "in proportion to," or by a double *the* with the comparative ("*the* more . . . *the* more"), may be best translated into Latin by one of two constructions.

(*a*) *Ut quisque* with a *superlative* in one clause may correspond to *ita* with a *superlative* in another (**376**), or (*b*) *Tanto,* or *eo,* the ablative of *measure of difference* (279), joined with a *comparative* adjective, or adverb, in one clause, may correspond to *quanto*, or *quo* with a *comparative* in another.

(a) Ut quisque *est vir* optimus, ita difficillime *alios esse improbos suspicatur*. *In proportion to* a man's excellence is his difficulty in suspecting others to be evil-minded, *or, the* better a man is, *the greater* his difficulty in, etc., *or,* those whose character is *the highest* will find *most difficulty,* etc.

(b) Quo *quisque est vir* melior, eo difficilius, etc.

The same constructions would express such a sentence as, "A man's readiness to suspect others is *in inverse proportion to* his own goodness."

Obs.—*Tanto . . . quanto* mark a more *precise* correspondence than *eo . . . quo.* The latter is identical with the English *the . . . the; "* the " is the old ablative of the *demonstrative* pronoun, which in the form *that* came into use as a relative earlier than the *interrogative* "who," "which."

Exercise 62.

The asterisk (*) indicates that the *Phrases* are to be translated by a Latin *clause.* (See 490, ii.)

1. The soldiers having now reached the summit of the mountain, and seeing a vast level plain, fertile territory, and rich cities, spread beneath their eyes, crowded round their leader, and as though they had already triumphed over every obstacle, congratulated him on the conquest[1] of Italy. 2. He behaved far differently to what I hoped and you expected. For in violation * of his repeated promises,[2] as though he made no account of the ancient tie which had long existed between his own father and mine, instead[3] of coming to my aid in my adversity, he has rejected up to this day my friendship, and has paid no attention to my more than once repeated and solemn appeals.[4] 3. May each and every one of you, when the hour of battle arrives, conduct himself in accordance * with his duty, and may each fare in accordance * with his deserts. 4. Let us endure everything rather than act in this matter contrary to * our promises. 5. We should[5] abide by the

---

[1] See 417, i.

[2] 491, *b ;* "repeated" will of course be turned by an *adverb.*

[3] See 398, *Obs.*, and use one of the constructions given in 124.

[4] *i.e.* "to me more than once solemnly *appealing.*" (415.)

[5] Gerund, and for second clause see 493, *Obs.* 1.

most oppressive conditions, rather than break our word
and brand our country with dishonour.   6. Then, with his
usual [1] passionateness and want of self-control, he orders
the ambassadors to be brought before him; as though their
mere sight had added fuel to his fury,[2] after roaring out that
their king had acted in defiance * of his promise and oath,
he ordered them to be dragged to prison.   The next day
he showed more gentleness than was consistent [3] with the
ferocity of his language of the day before, and, after apolo-
gising for his outrage on the rights of hospitality, invited
them to a banquet on [4] the next day as though he had done
nothing strange [5] or unusual.   Their answer showed [6]
more daring, considering the [7] perilous ground on which
they stood, than caution.   7. Then, putting spurs to his
horse, he dashed, with his usual [8] eagerness for battle, into
the thick of the contest, as though it were the part of a
good general to act with spirit [9] rather than with deliberation.   8. The longer the war is protracted, the more
oppressive will be the conditions of peace which will be
imposed upon us; do not wonder then at the reason [10] of
the truest patriots being the most ardent advocates of peace.
9. The more hidden a danger is, the greater will be the
difficulty [11] in avoiding it, and those [12] among our enemies
(*gen.*) are likely to be the most formidable who are readiest
in dissembling their ill-will.   10. And it seemed to me that,
considering the importance [13] of the matter, he spoke with
some want of energy, as though he were ashamed to speak
in the presence of the conqueror with greater warmth and
emotion than became [3] either his former rank or his recent
disaster.

---

[1] **492**, iii.   [2] Participle of *ardeo*. (**415**.)
[3] *Quam pro.* (See **332**, 7, *h.*)   [4] **326**.   [5] *Novus.* Case? (See **294**.)
[6] "Showed." Avoid *ostendit.* (See **241**.)   "They answered with more
daring (*adv.*) than caution." (**493**, *Obs.* 2.)
[7] "Ground," etc., a mere metaphor. (See **273**, *Obs.*, and **492**, v. *b.*)
[8] Use *ut* with *semper.* (**492**, iii.)
[9] Two comparative adverbs. (Intr. 19.)   [10] *Cur.* (See **174**, *a.*)
[11] Substitute *adverb.* "will be avoided *with greater difficulty.*"
[12] Use *ut quisque.* (**497**, *a.*)   [13] Simply *tanta res.*

Qui WITH THE SUBJUNCTIVE.

498. (i.) **Recapitulatory.**—It has been already said that qui, when used simply as the **relative** pronoun, to introduce what are called **adjectival** clauses (Intr. 81), is regularly followed by the **indicative** mood. (See **77.**)

> Qui *boni* sunt, *iidem sunt beati.* Those who are good are *also* happy. (**366, i.**)

Obs.—Here *qui* is used in its widest and most *indefinite* sense, =*quicunque*, but for all that is joined with the **indicative** in classical Latin, as is *quicunque*. (**364.**)

(ii.) It has been also pointed out, that if such adjectival clauses are subordinate to a verb in *oratio obliqua*, the mood must be the **subjunctive**. (**444.**)

> The same principle applies equally to **virtual** *oratio obliqua*. (**448.**)

> *Omnia, quae pater suus* reliquisset, *mihi legavit.* He bequeathed to me everything which his father *had left.*

Legavit is, " he bequeathed in the *terms of his* will," *quae reliquisset,* " which the will *spoke of* as left by his father."

But in such cases the subjunctive is used, not as *governed by qui,* but on the general principle that in *all* clauses subordinate to *oratio obliqua,* whether adjectival or adverbial, the **indicative** is **inadmissible.**

499. **Qui** also, in its **co-ordinating** use, when it stands in the place of an English *conjunction* and demonstrative *pronoun,* or even of the latter alone, can of course have no effect on the mood of the verb, which will depend entirely on the nature of the clause which it introduces.

> *Fratrem tuum, virum praeclarissimum, vidi,* qui *brevi consul* fiet, *or,* qui *utinam brevi consul* fiat, *or,* quem *brevi consulem* factum iri *spero.* (See **78.**)

500. But there are many cases in which *qui,* even in *oratio recta,* must be joined not with the indicative but with the **subjunctive.**

This is because *qui,* while in form a mere relative, yet in addition to referring to some antecedent word often conveys some additional idea of either *purpose, result, cause,* or *contrast.* It then takes the place

316

of such conjunctions as *ut, quia, quanquam,* and introduces clauses which, though in form **adjectival**, are **adverbial** in sense; and in proportion to its departure from its proper nature as a pure relative, is the urgency with which it calls for a **subjunctive** mood to mark the amount of that departure.

501. RULE.—Whenever *qui* is used in a **final** or consecutive sense, it is *invariably*, and whenever in a **causal** or **concessive** sense, it is *generally*, followed by the **subjunctive**.

Qui final.

502. (i.) *Qui* may express a **purpose**; it is then equivalent to *ut is*, and is always followed by a **subjunctive**.

Legatos misit, qui *pacem* peterent. He sent ambassadors *to sue* for peace (lit. *who were to sue* for peace; jussive, see 151).

Equites in castris reliquit, qui erumperent. He left cavalry behind in the camp, *to make* a charge.

With this compare *qui* with *indicative*.

Legatos misit, qui *pacem* petierunt. He sent ambassadors, *who sued* for peace.

Equites in castris reliquit, qui eruperunt. He left cavalry behind in the camp, *who made* a charge.

In these cases *qui* is equivalent to *et ii*, "and they," and therefore has no effect on the mood.

It will be seen at once that the difference of meaning between two such uses of *qui* is very great.

Qui consecutive.

503. (ii.) *Qui* may express a **consequence**, and *sometimes* even be translated by a *consecutive phrase* in English; but whenever the English "who" or "that" implies "*such as to*," "*of such a kind as to*," *qui* must be joined with the **subjunctive**.

Darius exercitum, quem *immensa planities vix caperet*, comparavit. "Which could not be contained," = "*such as was not to be* contained within," etc.

*** This use of *qui* extends very widely; the commonest of the less apparent examples of this meaning may be thus arranged.

504. The **subjunctive** is used after *sunt qui, erant qui* (="some") *reperiuntur qui, quotusquisque est qui,* and such **negative** and **interrogative** forms as *nemo est qui, quis est qui? neminem habeo qui,* etc. Thus—

> *Erant qui* putarent. Some fancied (there were people *of such a kind as to* fancy).
>
> *Nihil est quod dicere* velim. There is nothing that I care to say (*of such a kind as for me to,* etc.).
>
> *Quotusquisque est (invenitur) qui haec facere* audeat. How few there are (are met with) who venture to do this (one of how great a number ["one in a thousand," "*the thousandth*"] is he *who is such* as to, etc.).

Hence the use of the subjunctive after *quin* (=qui ne [non]).

> *Nemo est* quin *sciat.* All the world knows (**134**), *i.e.* there is no one *of such a kind as not* to know.

Obs.—When *est, sunt,* etc., are joined in an affirmative clause with a *numeral* or *plural* adjective of *number* the **indicative** is used.

> Multi, trecenti, duo, quidam, *sunt qui haec* dicunt. There are *many, three hundred, two, certain,* persons who say this.

Qui is here used in its proper relatival sense, "the people *who say this* are three hundred, etc."

But after *solus, unus,* used as predicates, with *sum* as link verb, the **subjunctive** is used.

> Solus *es* cui *omnes* pareamus. You are the only person whom all of us obey (somewhat more emphatic than, tibi soli *paremus omnes.*)

505. Qui is also used with the **subjunctive**—

(i.) After *dignus* or *indignus.*

> *Dignus est qui* ametur. He deserves to be loved (*lit.* He is worthy *that he should* be loved).
>
> *Indignus erat cui summus honos* tribueretur. He was not a proper person *to receive* the highest mark of distinction.

(ii.) After **comparatives** followed by *quam.*

> *Quae beneficia majora sunt quam quibus gratiam referre* possim. These favours are greater than I can requite (*too great for me to* requite).

(iii.) After **negative** and **interrogative** clauses, *qui* may take the place of *ut* in correspondence with *tam, sic, adeo,* and even *tantus.*

> Quis tam, or nemo tam, *ferreus est qui haec* faciat. Who is *or* no one is, *so* hard-hearted *as to do* this.
>
> Nulla *vis* tanta *est* quae *hoc* efficiat. No force is *so great as to* produce this result.

But you cannot say with an *affirmative* clause, *hic homo tam ferreus est qui . . .,* but must use *ut.*

506. Is is largely used (both affirmatively and negatively) with *qui* in a consecutive sense.

> *Non* is *sum* qui *haec* faciam. I am not the man *to do* this, *or*, I am not one *to do* this.
>
> Ea *est Romana gens* quae *victa quiescere* nesciat.[1] The race of Romans *is one* (of a kind) *that* knows not how to rest under defeat.

The difference between *is qui* with an **indicative** and *is qui* with a **subjunctive** must be carefully noticed, as it is one which is often not at all marked in English.

(*a*) When *is* and *qui* denote *identity*, the **indicative** is always used (in *oratio recta*).

> Is *sum* qui feci. I am the man who did this.
>
> *Cum* eo *hoste pugnamus* cui *nullo modo parcendum* est. We are fighting with an enemy who ought in no wise to be spared.

In both these cases *is* and *qui* are *co-extensive;* the *qui-* and *cui-* clauses apply to the person denoted by *is* and *eo*, and to *no one else.*

(*b*) But when the *qui*-clause is used *generically*, denotes a *larger class* to which we say that the *is* belongs, the **subjunctive** is used.

When we say, *non* is *sum* qui *haec* faciam, we mean, "I do not *belong to the larger* class (or *genus*) of men who do this."

By *cum* eo *pugnamus hoste* cui *nullo modo parcendum* sit, we mean, "we are fighting with a foe who is *one of those who* ought in nowise to be spared;" not a single person who *in himself* does not deserve quarter (**indicative**), but *one of those who do* not deserve quarter. In such sentences therefore we may use either mood according to the precise meaning of the English ; the **subjunctive** is far more common.

507. *Qui* also, like consecutive *ut*,[2] is used in a *corrective* or *limiting* sense.

> *Nemo*, quod sciam ; *nemo*, qui *quidem* paulo *prudentior* sit. No one *to my knowledge ;* no one, *at all events* no sensible man. (57, *b*.)

Obs.—But *quantum* scio, *quod* attinet *ad ;* because the word *quantum* and the phrase *quod attinet ad* express limitation by their own meaning, and do not need a change of mood.

508. All that has been said of the **final** and **consecutive** use of *qui* applies equally to relatival **adverbs**, *ubi, unde,*

---

[1] *Nesciat* is here a *modal verb* (42), equivalent to *non possit*, or *nequeat.* Compare the English "I can," properly "I know" (ken).

[2] Compare—Ita *sapiens est ut interdum erret.* He is wise *with this limitation, that* he sometimes makes a mistake ; and see 111.

cur, etc., when used as final or consecutive **conjunctions**.[1]

> *Massilium ivit* ubi *exularet*. He went   Marseilles *to live*
> in exile *there*.
>
> *Cupit habere* unde *solvat*. He wishes to have *means to pay*.
>
> *Nihil est* cur *irascare*. You have no *reason to be* angry

Exercise 63.

1. Caesar, seeing that the tide of battle[2] was turning,
and that he must take advantage of the critical[3] moment,
sent forward all his cavalry to attack the enemies' infantry in the rear; he himself, with the rest of his soldiers,
whom wounds, heat, and fatigue left[4] scarcely capable of
supporting their arms, hastened to charge them in front.
2. He was one who was worthy of every kind of distinction, for no one, within my knowledge, has governed the
nation in this generation, whose public services have been
equal to his, and who has been satisfied with so moderate
a reward of his exertions. How few there are who have
been, or will be, like him. 3. The chiefs of the enemy
easily perceived that in the recent rebellion and mutiny
their offences had been too great[5] to be pardoned; at the
same time (366, ii.). in spite of this great defeat, they
were too high-spirited to ask for mercy, and too powerful
to obtain it. 4. He is not, so far as I know, one who
hesitates to follow his own line in a discussion, or prefers
to bow to the opinion[6] of others. 5. Who is there in the
whole world so stony-hearted as not to be ashamed of
having, in order to please his worst enemies, abandoned
his friends, and of having betrayed his country to win the
favour of its most ancient foes ? 6. We have[7] to carry on
war with an enemy who has no respect for any treaty, or
armistice, or promise, or agreement; unless we conquer him
in the field, there will be nothing which can keep him back
from our shores, or repel him from our walls and homes.

---

[1] When used, that is, not to qualify the verb, or predicate, of a simple
sentence, but to connect together two clauses. (Intr. 16 and 25.) Mr.
Roby uses the term *connective adverbs*.

[2] Use the phrase *res inclinatur*. Why would the use of this English
metaphor be less admissible in Latin?

[3] Simply *tempus*.   [4] Use *possum* with *prae*. (332, 6, *b*.)

[5] Use *majora delinquere*, or *peccare*. (See **54**.)

[6] *Auctoritas*. As an opinion which claims to *have weight*.

[7] Gerundive.

Qui—CAUSAL AND CONCESSIVE.

509. **Qui** is also used both in a **causal** and a **concessive** sense; and in each of these is joined with the **subjunctive** on the principle stated in 500.

> (a) *Me miserum,* qui *haec non* viderim! Unhappy that I am (**239,** *note* [1]) *in not having seen this.*

Here *qui* is obviously **causal** = quod *haec non* vidi.

> (b) *Ego,* qui *serus* advenissem, *non tamen desperandum esse arbitratus sum.* For myself, *though I had arrived late* (or *in spite of my having,* etc.), yet I did not think I need despair.

Here *qui* is as obviously **concessive** = quanquam *serus* adveneram.

510. But in neither of these senses is the subjunctive (though it should be used by the young scholar) so invariable after *qui* as in its *consecutive* and *final* uses.

The writer sometimes prefers to emphasise the **reality** of the statement which *qui* introduces, and to leave the reader to infer the relation of **cause** or **contrast** in which it stands to the other clause.

Gratiam tibi habeo, qui *vitam meam* servasti, is as good Latin as, though less usual than, *gratiam . . .* servaveris, for, "I am grateful to you, *for* you have saved my life."

So, *Caesar fertur in caelum,* qui *contra te bellum* comparavit, "Caesar is extolled to the skies (by you), *although he* (or, *and yet he*) levied war against you:" *comparaverit* would be more usual, but the indicative **emphasises the fact,** and leaves the reader to draw the **contrast.**

511. An exceedingly common use of *qui* with the **subjunctive** in either its causal or concessive sense is to represent the **circumstances** *under,* or *in spite of,* which the action of the principal verb takes place.

It corresponds therefore exactly to the use of *quum* (**429**) or to the *abl. abs.* (**420**), or the *past participle of deponent* verbs (**413**), and to a common use of the English participle (**411**).

> *Tum Caesar,* qui *haec omnia explorata* haberet, *redire statuit.* Then (or thereupon) Caesar, *having* full knowledge of all this, etc.
> *Tum ille,* qui *homo* esset *justissimus,* etc. Then he (the other) *being* a just man, etc.

Obs.—Where a concessive sense, or *adversative* circumstances, are implied, this is generally made clear by a *tamen* in the main clause, cf. the use of *idcirco, adeo*, etc., to mark the precise sense of *ut*. (107.)

> *Tum Caesar, qui hoc intellegeret*, tamen *redire statuit.* Then Caesar, *in spite of his* being aware of this, yet, etc.

512. The **causal** force of *qui* is sometimes made more clear by prefixing *quippe*, sometimes *utpote*, or *ut*.

In Cicero *quippe qui* (=*for* or *because* he, etc.) is always followed by the subjunctive.

> *Eum semper pro amico habui*, quippe quem scirem *mei esse amantissimum.* I always looked on him as a friend, *for* I knew that he bore me the warmest affection.

In Sallust and Livy *quippe qui* is used with the indicative as though=*quod*, but *ut qui* with the subjunctive is very common in Livy.

> *Nec consul*, ut qui *id ipsum* quaesisset, *moram certamini fecit.* Nor did the Consul, *as* this was the very object at which he had aimed, delay the contest.

513. When *qui*, or *quicunque*, expresses an action **repeated in past time**, a difference of usage is found in the best Latin writers.

(1) In Cicero and Caesar it is followed by an **indicative** of the pluperfect.

(2) In Livy, by a **subjunctive**.

> *Quicunque* venerat, *damnabatur.*—(*Cicero* and *Caesar.*) Whoever came (*from time to time*), was condemned.
>
> *Quocunque eques impetum* tulisset, *Romani cedebant.*—(*Livy.*) Wherever the rider charged, the Romans yielded. Cicero or Caesar would have written *tulerat*.

This difference has been already noticed under Temporal Clauses (**434**). Nor in the best writers is *qui* used with a subjunctive, because it means "any[1] who," "all who," **498**, *Obs.;* this usage came in, as in the *frequentative* sense, under the influence of Greek.

Exercise 64.

The asterisk* indicates that *qui* causal or concessive is to be used.

1. Thereupon the messenger, seeing* that it was im-

---

[1] In Livy's description of Hannibal's character, *id quod gerendis rebus* superesset, *quieti datum* (Bk. xxi. 4), "*Any* time that remained (or *might* remain) after active work was done, was given to repose," the mood of *superesse* is no doubt due to Greek influence.

possible by fair[1] words to succeed in persuading the
Spaniards not to advance further, aimed at producing[2]
the same effect by menaces (*gerund*), and appeals to fear.
The forces, he said,[3] which were gathering and concealed
on the other side of the mountain, were too numerous
(505, ii.) to be counted, while[4] those who were already
assembled, and were visible close at hand, were veteran
soldiers, too brave and well trained to be routed, as[5] the
Spaniards seemed to hope, in the first onset of a single
fight. 2. Who is there of you, who in any way is
worthy of this assembly and this nation, that does not
cherish and value highly the memories[6] of the heroes[7]
of the past, even though he has never seen them.*
3. There are things which I fear still[8] more; in his
absence his brother, since* his influence with that faction
is unrivalled, will be still more formidable; as long as
he lives, will the party[9] of disorder, do you[3] suppose,
ever lack a standard round which to rally? 4. Thereupon he dismissed the council, and ordered the Indian[10]
chiefs to be brought before him; the unhappy men, as*
they had no suspicion or fear of his intentions,[11] hurry in
joyfully,[12] for there was none among[13] them who had
any fears either for[14] his freedom or his safety, or was
aware of the extent[15] of the danger which threatened
them, or of the[15] character of the host with whom he was
to have an interview. Even he, though* he blushed at no
treachery, and felt remorse for no crime, was, it seemed,
somewhat touched by the confidence and friendliness of
those whom he (felt[16] that he) was on the point of betraying.

---

[1] " By pleading gently." [2] *Idem efficere.* (See **54.**)
[3] Beware of this parenthesis. (**32,** *b.*)
[4] Why not *dum?* (**438,** note): *et* or *vero* would do.
[5] **67,** *Obs.* [6] *Memoria* is never used in the pl., cf. *spes.*
[7] Why not *heros?* a Greek word=demigod; say of "illustrious
men, and those (**344**) ancient (ones)." [8] Rarely expressed in Latin.
[9] Use *perditi*, or *improbi, cives;* the latter is Cicero's usual term as
opposed to the *boni*, or *optimus quisque.*
[10] "Of the Indians." [11] " As to what he would do." (**173, iii. ; 174.**)
[12] Adj. (**61.**) [13] Gen. or *ex.* (**296.**) [14] **248.**
[15] **174.** [16] See **448.**

REPORTED SPEECHES IN *ORATIO OBLIQUA*

Preliminary.

514. In reporting another person's language two methods may be used.

(i.) The historian may name the speaker, and give what purport to be the words he used in the precise form in which he spoke them, as (*e.g.*) in a play of Shakespeare,

> To this Caesar replied, " I will come if you are ready to follow."

In such professedly *verbatim* reports the whole speech may be spoken of as being in *oratio recta*, as coming, as it were, *directly* from the lips of the speaker.

(ii.) This method is used in Latin, sometimes in a formal report of **long speeches** in the senate or elsewhere, sometimes in reporting a **short saying**, if very memorable or striking. In the latter case it is marked, as by *inverted commas* in English, so by the insertion of *inquit* after the first or second word of the speech or saying. Such speeches should never be preceded, as in English, by verbs like *dixit, ait, respondit*, etc., which are as a rule reserved for the second and more usual mode of reporting, the *indirect* rather than the *direct*.

" I will come, he said," " I will come, he replied," must be translated either by " se venturum esse *dixit, respondit*," or by " veniam, *inquit*." (See **40.**)

515. But the more usual method in Latin, more common even than it is in English, is not to profess to give the speaker's words in the form in which they were spoken, but to insert (or imply) [1] a verb of *saying, asking*, etc., and then to report what was said, or its substance, in the third person, that is, in **oratio obliqua.** All the principal verbs will now be dependent on a verb of *saying*, expressed or understood. Thus, instead of Caesar's own words, " I will go, if you are ready to follow," we should have " Caesar replied that *he* would go, if *he* were ready to follow."

---

[1] The actual verb is often omitted, the infinitive or subjunctive moods being sufficient evidence of the construction.

> *Legatos ad Caesarem mittunt:* " *sese paratos esse portas aperire.*"
> They send ambassadors to Caesar : (*saying*), We are ready to open the gates.

> *Colonis triste responsum redditum est : facesserent propere ex urbe.*
> The colonists received a severe answer : " Begone at once from the city."

516. The great difference between the two methods will be seen at a glance.

Oratio recta.	*Oratio obliqua.*
Tum Caesar, ibo, inquit, *si* tu me *sequi* vis.	*Tum Caesar*, iturum se respondit si ille se *sequi* vellet.

Obs.—This method of reporting speeches, or even reflexions, in the third person is common in English (as for instance in reporting speeches in Parliament), but far more common in Latin, and should often be used in translating into Latin what in English is reported in the more *dramatic* form of *oratio recta*.

The following are the principal rules for the conversion of *oratio recta* into *oratio obliqua*.

Pronouns.

517. The **first** and **second** person will entirely disappear; both will be converted into the **third**.

(*a*) *Ego, meus, nos, noster*, will become *se,*[1] *suus* (in the nominative *ipse*).

(*b*) *Tu, vos, tuus, vester*, will become *ille, illi, illius, illorum, ipsius*, etc.

Tu Tarentum amisisti; ego recepi, will become, *respondit* illum *Tarentum amisisse*, se *recepisse;* or better (**216,** *Obs.*), ab illo *amissum esse Tarentum*, a se *receptum*.

Nostram patriam civitati vestrae anteponimus, will become, suam se[1] *patriam* illorum *civitati anteponere*.

So *hic* and *iste* will give place to *ille* and *is*.

Obs. 1.—Latin has here a great advantage over English; "I and you" have alike, in English *oratio obliqua*, to be expressed by *he;* hence constant obscurity. In Latin the "I" will become *se*, the "you" *ille*.

Obs. 2.—*Ille* will be in very constant use in place of *is*, as it is more distinctive, and opposes the *other party* to the speaker; sometimes as in English, a proper name will be introduced.

Adverbs.

518. As speeches are generally reported in *past* or *historic* time, **adverbs** of **present** time must be changed into those of **past** time. *Nunc, hodie*, will become *jam, tunc, illo die*, etc. So with **place**, *hic* will become *ibi*, etc.

---

[1] The insertion of the *se* will often be necessary where no pronoun is required in *oratio recta:* compare *tibi parco* with *dixit* se *ei parcere*.

But all these changes are common to Latin with English. "*I* say that *I* will speak to *you* now and *here*" would in English be converted into "*He* said that *he* would speak to *them* then and *there*."

The rules more peculiar to Latin are connected with the use of **Moods** in **principal** and **subordinate** clauses.

Principal Clauses.

519. In all these the **indicative** will entirely disappear.

Statements and **denials** made in Latin by a verb in the **indicative** will of course pass into the **infinitive**. *Nihil doleo,* "I feel no pain," will become, *nihil se dolere,* "he felt no pain;" *hoc faciam,* will become, *id se facturum esse,* etc.

Obs. 1.—This infinitive will even follow *qui* if strictly **co-ordinate**.

Adsunt *hostes,* instat Catilina, qui *brevi scelerum poenas* dabit.
Adesse *hostes,* instare Catilinam, quem *brevi scelerum poenas* daturum esse. **(499.)**

Obs. 2.—Statements (hypothetical) made in the **subjunctive,** because qualified by a *si*-clause, will pass from the

Present subjunctive into the future in *-rus* with *esse* or *fore.*
Imperfect or pluperfect subjunctive into the future in *-rus* with *fuisse.* (See **469,** i.)
Thus, *Rideat si adsit* into *risurum eum fore, si adesset.*
Rideret si adesset } into *risurum eum fuisse, si adesset,* or,
Risisset si adfuisset } *adfuisset.*

520. **Questions** asked by the speaker in the **indicative** mood will pass into the **subjunctive**; and if, as is usual, the narrative is in past time, from the **present** into the **imperfect** tense.

Nonne auditis ? will become, *nonne* audirent ?
Quid vultis ? *quid* optatis ? will become, *Quid* vellent ? *quid* optarent ?

Questions already in the **subjunctive (150)** will remain in the **subjunctive** ; the *tense* only being altered if, as is usual, it is necessary, and of course the *person.*

Quid faciam ? " what *am I* to do ?" will become, *quid* faceret ? " what *was he* to do ?"
Quo eamus ? " whither *are we* to go ?" will become, *quo* irent ? " whither *were they* to go ?"

521. But questions that do not expect an answer (**rhetorical** questions, 150), especially those in the **first** and **third persons**, will pass from the **indicative** or **subjunctive** to the **infinitive**, for such questions are really **denials** in disguise.

> Ecquis *unquam ejusmodi monstrum* vidit? "did any one ever see such a monster?" will become, Ecquem *unquam ejusmodi monstrum* vidisse?
>
> *Num* haec *tolerare* debemus? will become, *Num* illa se *tolerare* debere?
>
> So *quo* eamus? will often become, *quo* sibi eundum esse? for the meaning is often merely, "we have *no place* to go to."

522. Commands, prohibitions, and **wishes,** expressed by the **imperative** or **subjunctive,** will pass into the **subjunctive** with the necessary alteration of **tense** and **person.**

Oratio recta.	*Oratio obliqua.*
Festinate; utinam salvi sitis.	*Festinarent; utinam* salvi essent.
Nolite cunctari; ne despexeris.	*Ne cunctarentur; ne* despiceret.

Obs.—The **hortative** 1st person (and even other forms of command) will be easily converted into a statement by the aid of the **gerund** or **gerundive.**

> *Nihil temere* agamus. *Nihil* sibi *temere* agendum esse.

Subordinate Clauses.

523. Moods.—**The indicative will entirely disappear.**

Even the exceptional indicative after *qui* mentioned in **449** will hardly find place in the report of a speech of any length.

RULE.—**Subordinate** clauses, whether introduced by the **relative** (except where strictly **co-ordinate**) or by any subordinating **conjunction** (except occasionally *dum*), will always be in the **subjunctive.**

This has been fully explained before. (See **444.**)

524. Tenses.—As reported speeches are usually part of a narrative of **past** events, the most usual and regular tenses in subordinate clauses will be the **imperfect** and **pluperfect** subjunctive.

(i.) The **imperfect,** as the tense of *time contemporaneous with a date now past,* will take the place of the **present, imperfect,** and even the **future** i. of *oratio recta.*

> *Qui* adsunt, *fugiant,* will become *qui* adessent, *fugerent.*
> *Idcirco fugi, quod* timebam „ *fugisse se, quod* timeret.
> *Qui hoc* dicet, *errabit*   „   *qui id,* or *illud,* diceret, *erraturum esse.*

(ii.) But **future ii.** (future perfect) will be changed into the **pluperfect.** (See **471,** *Obs.*)

Qui hoc dixerit, *errabit* will become *qui illud* dixisset, *erraturum esse.*

(iii.) The **perfect** as well as the **pluperfect** will generally be represented by the **pluperfect** subjunctive.

Hic est locus quem ostendi.   *Illum esse locum quem* ostendisset.

525. But though the exclusive use of the **imperfect** and **pluperfect** subjunctive would be grammatically correct, yet the **present, perfect,** and **future perfect** are very often introduced into *oratio obliqua* (just as in *oratio recta* the *historic present* often takes the place of the [*aorist*] *perfect*), in order to give greater *liveliness* to the reported speech by representing parts of it in the actual tense used, as though the speaker were *in our presence.*

> *Indignum videri ab iis se obsideri quorum exercitus saepe* fuderint. They *said* that it *seemed* degrading to be besieged by men whose armies they had (lit. *have*) often routed.

In *oratio recta* the word used would have been *fudimus* —"*we have* routed."

There are few reported speeches in Caesar or Livy in which this rhetorical use of present for past, perfect for pluperfect, tenses will not be found.

526. The following examples should be carefully studied :—

1. "Your children have gone; when will they return? (rhetorical question), try to avenge them."[1]

Oratio recta.	*Oratio obliqua.*
Profecti sunt liberi vestri; quando redituri sunt? vos, quantum potestis, ultum ite.	Jam liberos illorum profectos esse; quando redituros fore? quantum possent ultum irent.

---

[1] In English *oratio obliqua* the passages would run thus :—

"*Their* children *had* gone; when *would* they return? *Let them* try to avenge them."

"Away then with such follies! *Did they* not see that *their* liberty and lives were *that* day at stake? Why *did they* obey a few centurions, still fewer tribunes, who *could* do nothing against *their* will? When *would they* dare to demand redress? It *was* of the utmost importance what *they did. Let them* awake at last and follow *him*, remembering the ancestors from whom *they were* sprung. If *they* let slip this opportunity, *they would* deservedly be slaves, and no one *would* give *them* a thought, or compassionate *their* present condition."

2. Away then with such follies! Do you not see that your liberty
and lives are at stake to-day? why do you obey a few centurions,
still fewer tribunes, who can do nothing against your will? When
will you dare to demand redress! It is of the utmost importance
what you do. Awake at last, and follow me! remember the ancestors
from whom you are sprung. If you let slip this opportunity, you will
deservedly be slaves, and no one will give you a thought, or compassionate your present condition.[1]

Oratio recta.	*Oratio obliqua.*
Pellantur igitur, inquit, *ineptiae istae ; nonne videtis de liber- tate, de vitis vestris, agi hodie? Cur paucis centurionibus, pau- cioribus tribunis, qui nihil invitis vobis facere possunt dicto audi- entes estis? quando remedia exposcere audebitis? Maximi quid faciatis refert. Exper- giscimini aliquando ; majorum quibus orti estis reminiscimini: me sequimini. Hanc occasionem si praetermiseritis, merito servi- bitis, nec quisquam vel rationem vestri habebit, vel istius fortunae miserebitur.*	Pellerentur *igitur ineptiae* illae ; nonne viderent *de libertate* ip- sorum, *de vitis,* eo die agi? Cur paucis centurionibus, paucioribus tribunis, qui invitis illis nihil facere possent, dicto audientes essent? quando remedia expos- cere ausuros? maximi referre quid facerent. Expergiscerentur aliquando, et se sequerentur. Majorum quibus orti essent re- miniscerentur. Eam occasionem si praetermisissent, merito servi- turos esse, nec quenquam vel rationem eorum habiturum fore, vel fortunae illius miseriturum.

Caesar and Livy will furnish abundant instances for practice, and
the learner should translate every "reported speech" in either, into
English oratio recta.

Exercise 65.

A.

The following sentences are all to be converted into *oratio obliqua ;*
the tenses to be altered throughout from *primary* to *historic.*
(See **177.**) It may be well to begin by converting the sentences
into *English oratio obliqua.*

1. Can any[2] one endure this? ought we to abandon
this great undertaking? it would have been better to
have fallen on the field with honour, than to submit to
such slavery. 2. Do not delay then; a few soldiers will
suffice; we have no other allies anywhere, no other hopes,
whither can we turn if you think of abandoning us? but
if you wish[3] for our safety, you must away[4] with all

---

niceties of argument;[1] it is haste, not deliberation, that is
needed.   3. What are you doing ? what are you wishing
for ? are you waiting till the enemy is at hand, till you
hear their shouts, till you see their standards?   Even
now[2] resistance is possible, provided you do not linger or
hesitate.   4. It is possible that I on my part[3] have made
the same mistake as you ; if the case is so, I pray, forget
the past,[4] and in union with your king consult the national
interests.   Is there any thing in the world which we
ought to value more highly ?   5. What am I to do?
whither to turn ? do you bid me to go to meet the enemy?
I would do so most gladly, if it could be done without
ruin to the nation.   But what could be more foolish, what
more fatal, than with[5] an army of recruits to engage in
conflict with veteran soldiers[6] trained in twenty years of
battle ?[7]   6. How many of you are there ? whence do
you come ? what do you demand or hope for ? when do
you expect to[8] be allowed to enjoy freedom, (and) to
return home ?   Possibly the time is even now at hand,
provided you do not let slip the opportunity, or injure
your cause by putting off the contest.   But if you refuse
to take up arms till[9] I assist you, you will ruin the
common cause, and sigh in vain for the[10] freedom which
brave men assert by arms.

B.

To be translated into *oratio obliqua :* a Spaniard speaks.

In vain therefore do you appeal to Spain ;[11] it makes no
difference whether you intend to make an alliance with
the rebels, or to threaten them with war.   I shall neither
rely on your friendship, nor do I dread your enmity.
For what could be more despicable than your policy
and schemes, seeing that within the last five years you

---

[1] Gerund. [2] See **518**. [3] See **355**, *d.*
[4] "What is past." [5] **270**, *note* [2]. [6] Sing.
[7] "Battles of twenty years." (See **303**, *Obs.* 1.)
[8] *Fore ut*, etc. (**193**, iii.) [9] *Prius . . . quam.* (**443**, i.)
[10] **348**. [11] **319**.

have thrice abandoned your allies, twice joined your enemies like[1] deserters, and have not now sent ambassadors to me to sue for a peace of which you are so unworthy, till[2] you had made sure that, unless with our[3] aid you can get over this danger, you are doomed to infallible destruction? Would any one have put trust in such allies? would any one in the future feel gratitude to such friends? If you wish to find a remedy and shelter against[4] your present[5] dangers, return home; lay down your arms; throw open the gates of your cities and strongholds, place yourselves entirely at the mercy of the sovereign against whom you have been so long waging an unnatural war. Possibly I may be touched by your prayers; I shall pay no attention to your envoys and orations.

---

[1] *Velut.*   [2] **443,** *Obs.*

[3] Use for clearness the proper noun and abl. abs., "The Spaniards helping." (**517,** *Obs.* 2.)

[4] See **300.**   [5] *Hic* in *oratio recta.* (**337.**)

NUMERALS.

Numerals form in Latin, as in English, a special class of **adjectives**; in certain cases, as in the plural of *mille* (*duo civium* milia,[1] cf. hundreds, thousands), they have a **substantival** character, and they are all accompanied by appropriate **adverbs**.

Their two main classes are, as in English, **Cardinal** and **Ordinal**.

527. Cardinal (*cardo*, hinge), or primary, numerals answer the question "how many?" *quot?*

Unus, duo, tres, quattuor; undecim, duodecim, tredecim (decem et tres); duodeviginti (decem et octo), undeviginti (decem et novem); viginti, unus et viginti (viginti unus), duodetriginta (28), quadra-ginta, nonaginta octo (octo et nonaginta), centum (et) unus (101); ducenti, -ae, -a, trecenti, -ae, -a, quadringenti, quingenti, ses-(sex-)centi, septingenti, octingenti, nongenti, mille (substantive), duo milia, unum et viginti milia, centum milia, quingenta milia, decies centena milia (1,000,000).

The full list will be found in any Grammar; those enumerated are examples given for special reasons, the alternative forms are added in brackets.

528. The **first three** are (as in many kindred languages) declinable; the rest, including *viginti*, are indeclinable up to *ducenti, -ae, -a*: this, and the series of hundreds, are plural declinable adjectives; *mille* is indeclinable in the singular, *exercitus* mille *militum*, "an army *of* 1000," but declined in the plural (*cum duobus* milibus) as a **substantive**.

As in English so in Latin, from 20 to 100 a compound number may be arranged in two ways, "one-and-twenty" or "twenty-one;" above 100 the higher number stands first; 28,455 is, *duodetriginta milia quadringenti quinquaginta (et) quinque* (*et* is rarely expressed).

---

[1] The second *l* is usually omitted in the plural, as coming before *i*.

Unus.

529. The English numeral "**one**" gave rise to the indefinite article *an*, *a*, (not probably to the indefinite "one" in "one knows," etc.) The uses of *unus* in Latin are very different; thus (*a*) our "none" is *ne* "not" and *unus* "one," but *non unus* is the very opposite of *nullus;* it means "*more than* one;" non uno *praelio devictus sum:* "not one" is *ne unus quidem*, or even *nemo unus*. So (*b*) *unus* is a strong form of *solus:* unus *hoc fecisti*, "you are the *only* one who has done this." (*c*) It is used to strengthen *quisque*, *unus quisque*, each one, "each and every" (**373**), and (*d*) to emphasise **superlatives** : the Latin superlative often not retaining its full force (**57**, *a*). Thus *Ducem praestantissimum amisimus*, "we have lost *one of our* best leaders, or *a distinguished* leader," but *Ducem* unum *praestantissimum*, "we have lost *the very best* of our leaders." (*e*) It often, however, represents the English "one of" (a class) without any stress on the numeral: unus *ex captivis*, "*one of* the prisoners." (*f*) In the predicate it often answers to our "belonging to the class of :" unus *ex fortunatis hominibus esse videtur*, "he seems to be one of (*i.e.* to belong to the number of) fortune's favourites." (*g*) "One, two, three, several," is in Latin, *unus*, *alter*, *tertius*, *plures*. "One or two" is *unus vel* (*aut*) *alter*, *unus alterve*.

Ordinal Numerals.

530. These answer to the question "in what order?" *quotus ?*

They are all *declinable adjectives;* only a few will be enumerated. *Primus (prior)* ; *secundus* or *alter; tertius decimus* (13th), *duodevicesimus (octavus decimus)* (18th), *unus (primus) et vicesimus* (21st), *alter (secundus) et tricesimus (tricesimus alter)* (32nd,) *undetricesimus* (29th), *quadragesimus* (40th), *quintus et nonagesimus (nonagesimus quintus)* (95th), *centesimus primus (primus et centesimus)* (101st), *millesimus*, *bis millesimus* (2000th), *decies millesimus* (10,000th), *semel et vicies millesimus* (21,000th), etc.

531. Notice that (*a*), as in English, the two first **ordinals** are not derived from the corresponding **cardinals** ; and that *alter*, as "other" in older English, is largely used for "second." *Secundus* is rather "following" next in *time* or in *rank*.

" *Alter idem* " is "a second self," *altero tanto*, " by as much again."

(*b*) *Unus* often takes the place of our "first" in enumerating.

> *Hujus rei tres sunt causae*, una, altera (or *alia*), tertia ; "*first, second, third.*"

(*c*) The **ordinal** is often used in reckoning time.

> Undevicesimum *jam annum bellum* gerebatur. The war had now gone on *for* 19 years. (See **321**, *Obs.* 2.)

(*d*) "After," "since," with an ordinal is expressed by *ab.*

> *Anno ab urbe condita millesimo.* In the 1000th year (or the year 1000) after the foundation of the city. (See **323**, *a.*)

(*e*) The ordinal is always used in giving *dates*, as in the last example.

532. Another class is the **Distributives**, answering to the question "how many at a time?" *quoteni?* or "how many each?" "*by twos*," "*two each*." Among these are—

> *Singuli, bini, seni* (6); *terni deni* (13); *viceni singuli* (21); *centeni, singula milia, centena milia.*

(*a*) *Ex* singulis, *or* binis, *familiis* singulos, binos, ternos, *obsides elegimus.* We selected *one, two,* or *three,* hostages from *each separate* household, or *each pair* of households.

(*b*) They are also used as **cardinal** numerals with names that have no singular, *uni, -ae, -a* taking the place of *singuli.*

> *In* unis *aedibus* binae *fuere nuptiae.* There were *two* weddings in *one* house.

(*c*) For the special uses of *singuli* as opposed to *universi* and *singularis* (*imperium singulare* is used for "a *personal* despotism)," see **380.**

Obs.—The distributive numerals are used with **multiplicatives.** (See below.)

533. The numeral **adverbs** are those that answer to the question "how often?" "how many times?" *quoties,* (*quotiens*)? Such are—

> *Semel, bis, ter, sexies, ter decies, vicies, bis et vicies, tricies,* etc.
> Once, twice,   13 times.   20 times.   30 times.

(*a*) These are both adverbs **of time,** and also simple *multiplicatives;* cf. the English six *times,* ten *times.*

> Sexies *consul factus est.* He was made consul *six times* (but *sextum, for* the *sixth time*).
> Quinquies *tantum quam quantum licuit civitatibus imperavit.* He ordered the states to furnish *five times as much as* was legal.

(*b*) They are coupled with *distributives* in the multiplication table.

> Bis bina *sunt quattuor.* Twice *two* is four.

(*c*) With *semel* as an adverb of *time, iterum* is used in place of *bis. Iterum* means *not* "again," but "for a second time;" *semel atque iterum* is not "once and again," in the sense of "frequently," but "once and even *twice*;" "once and again," "more than once," is *semel ac saepius*; "again and again," *saepissime.*

534. Ordinal adverbs of time are *primum, iterum, tertium,* etc.; these answer to the English "for the first, second, third, time," etc.

> Iterum, quartum, *Consul factus* est. He was made Consul for the second *or* fourth time.
>
> *Tum* primum *justo praelio interfuit.* That was the first occasion on which he took part in a regular engagement.

Obs.—"In the first place," "secondly," "lastly," is expressed in a narrative or argument, *primo (-um,, deinde (deinceps), tum,* or *post, denique, postremo, ad extremum; denique* is often inserted in an emphatic and final clause.

535. Fractions are expressed thus :—(*a*) One-half, *dimidium* or *dimidia pars.* (*b*) Others, where the *numerator* is 1, by ordinals with *pars :* ⅓, tertia pars, $\frac{1}{1000}$, *millesima pars;* "tithes," *decumae* (*sc.* partes). (*c*) ⅔, *duae partes;* ¾, *tres partes;* ⅗, *tres quintae* (*sc.* partes). (*d*) *Dimidio plures,* "half as many again;" *duplo plures,* "twice as many."

> Dimidium *exercitus* quam quod, *or* quantum *acceperat, reduxit.* He brought back half the army which he had received.

536. The following are the common modes of expressing numbers.

(*a*) *Nostrorum,* or, *e nostris, decem, triginta, ducenti, ad mille* ducenti (1200, *ad* is here *adverbial* and governs no case), *tria milia quingenti* (3500) *interfecti sunt.*

(*b*) *Nostrorum,* sometimes *nostri* (the numeral being occasionally used in *apposition*), duo milia *caesa,* or *caesi* (*milia* being treated sometimes as masculine where men are concerned), *aut desiderati sunt* (were missing).

(*c*) *Milites praemisit ducentos viginti; pedites ad mille ducentos cum amplius*[1] *mille equitum praemisit,* or *peditum tria milia ducentos,* etc.

Obs.—Large *indefinite* numbers are expressed by sex-(ses-)centi, -a, -ae : sexcenta *alia,* "a hundred other things ;" milies *mori praestat,* "'twere better to die a *thousand* deaths ;" *ne* millesimam *quidem partem intelligo,* "I don't understand a *particle* (of what he says)."

Exercise 66.

A.

1. In his ninety-second[2] year he was still[3] able to answer those who[4] asked his opinion. 2. I ask first

---

[1] Remember that with numbers *quam* is rarely expressed after *plus, amplius,* etc. (**318,** *Obs.*)

[2] Either *anno aetatis,* or as in **327.**

[3] "Still" need not be expressed.   [4] Part. pres. (**414.**)

whence you come, secondly, whither you are going,
thirdly, why you are armed, lastly, why you are in my
house.   3. The generals met at the river side, each with
an interpreter and ten soldiers.   4. One, two, three days
had now passed, yet[1] no agreement had been come to
as regards the conditions of peace.   5. In prosperity I
thought your father one of Fortune's favourites, in these
dark[2] days I see that he belongs, and always has
belonged, to the class of great men.[3]   6. He stayed at
Milan, one of the richest and most populous of cities,
one or two days; yet out of 100,000 citizens, not one
thanked him for the preservation[4] of the city and the
repulse of the enemy from its walls, and perhaps[5] not
one single soul felt the gratitude which he owed.   7.
There has been a disastrous[6] battle; 2,500[7] of our men
have been slain; it is said that half as many again are
taken prisoners, and that one or two[8] of the four generals
are missing.   8. We have lost an excellent man; if not
the very best of his class, yet at all events one of those
who come but once[9] in a generation.   9. I have received
two[10] letters from you to-day, one yesterday; the rest I
have looked for in vain; though I have waited for them
one or two days, and sent to inquire,[11] not once,[12] but
twice.   10. This is the nineteenth day from the commencement of the siege.   The commander of the garrison
is demanding two hostages from every[13] household, to
prevent[14] any rising on the part of the townspeople, who
are mostly[15] armed, and who outnumber his troops by
two to one.

---

[1] *Nec tamen quidquam.* (See 110.)   [2] Simply *tempora.*
[3] Use *vir* with *summus.* (See 224, note [3].)   [4] See 417, i.
[5] Use *haud scio an.* (169.)   [6] Impersonal, 218, *Obs.*
[7] 536, *a.*   [8] Ex, e. (296, *Obs.*)   [9] 380, *a.*
[10] 532, *b.*   [11] Supine of *sciscitari.* (402.)
[12] 533, *c.*   [13] 532, *a.*
[14] "That no (103) rising *of* . . . may take place."
[15] Use *plerique* in app., often so used where *the whole* and a *part* are
not contrasted. (297.)

Exercise 66.

B.

At the age of scarcely nineteen he had again and again taken part in regular engagements, and had more than once slain an enemy in single combat, and was now[1] on the point[2] of engaging an army half as large again as that which he[3] commanded. Yet in the face of such a crisis, he did not hesitate to detach more than 1600 infantry to defend[4] his allies against an irruption of the Indians, although two-thirds of his army consisted of recruits,[5] who[6] were now to fight their first battle. But he preferred to die a thousand[7] deaths, rather than turn his back on a barbarian foe, who if once he won[8] the day would, he well[9] knew, afflict his country with every kind of wrong.

---

[1] **328.** *b.*   [2] **418,** *d.*   [3] **355,** *Obs.* 1.

[4] " To repel (gerundive) from his allies."   [5] *Tiro miles,* sing. **(223.)**

[6] Part. in *-rus.* **(406.)**   [7] **536,** *Obs.*

[8] Mood and tense? **(471,** *Obs.)*   [9] **32,** *b.*

THE ROMAN CALENDAR.

537. The Roman months consisted (after the reform of the Calendar by Julius Caesar) of the same number of days as the English months; but the days were numbered quite differently.

538. The *first* day of the month was called *Kalendae* (the **Kalends**); the **Nones** (*Nonae*) fell on the *fifth* or *seventh*; the **Ides** (Id-us, -uum, f.) were always eight days after the **Nones**, that is, the *thirteenth* or *fifteenth*.

" In March, July, October, May,
The Nones were on the seventh day."
(The **Ides** therefore on the 15th.)

To these names of days, the names of the month were attached as *adjectives :*[1] *ad Kalendas* Maias, "*by* the 1st *of May*" (326); *In Nonas* Junias, "*for* the 5th *of June ;*" *Idus* Martiae, "the 15th *of March.*"

539. From these three fixed points the other days of the month were reckoned *backwards*, and *inclusively, i.e.* both days were counted in.

Days between the Kalends and the Nones were reckoned by their distance from the **Nones**; those between the Nones and the Ides by their distance from the **Ides**; those after the Ides by their distance from the **Kalends** of the *following month*.

To suit this Roman way of reckoning, we must subtract the given day from the *number of the day* on which the Nones or Ides fall *increased by one*. If the day be one

---

[1] These forms are, Januarius, Februarius, Martius, Aprilis, Maius, Junius, Quintilis (*or* Julius), Sextilis (*or* Augustus), Septem-, Octo-, Novem-, Decem-, bris.

The months of July and August were called *Quintilis, Sextilis,* respectively (= the *fifth* and *sixth* month, reckoning from *March,* the old beginning of the year), till those names were exchanged for *Julius* and *Augustus* in honour of the two first Caesars.

before the Kalends, we must subtract from *the last day* of the month *increased by two*, as the Kalends fall within the next month.

Thus take the 3rd, 9th, 23rd of June :—

(1) In June the Nones are on the *fifth;* therefore three must be subtracted from $(5+1=)$ *six;* and the remainder being 3, the day is "the *third* day before the *Nones* of June."

(2) In June the Nones being on the fifth, the Ides are on the *thirteenth*, and the subtraction must be from *fourteen*. Hence subtract 9 from 14; the remainder being 5, the day is the *fifth* day before the Ides of June.

(3) Since June has *thirty* days, we must subtract from thirty-two. Hence subtract 23 from 32; the remainder being 9, the day is the *ninth* day before the *Kalends of July.*

So December 30th is not the *second*, but the *third* day before the Kalends of January.

540. The names for days are thus expressed in Latin.

"On the third before the Kalends of March" is by rule " *die tertio* ante Kalendas Martias," which was shortened by the omission of *die* and *ante* into " *tertio Kalendas Martias*," or iii. *Kal. Mart.*

But another form is used (almost exclusively) by *Cicero* and *Livy;* this form is " *ante diem tertium Kalendas Martias*," shortened into " a. d. iii.[1] *Kal. Mart.*"

This *ante-diem* came to be treated as an indeclinable substantive, and the prepositions *ad, in, ex* were prefixed to it, as to other substantives of time.

The last day of the month is *pridie Kalendarum* or *pridie Kalendas.*

The following are examples.

1. *Natus est Augustus* ix. Kal. Oct. (nono Kalendas Octobres), *i.e. on the 23rd of September.*
2. Kalendis Augustis *natus est Claudius*, iii. Id. Oct. (tertio Idus Octobres) *excessit.* (1st of August and October 13th.)
3. *Meministi me* a. d. xii. Kal. Nov. *sententiam dicere in Senatu ?* Do you remember my speaking in the Senate *on the 21st of October ?*

---

[1] For an explanation of this form see ROBY, *L. G.* vol. i. p. 454.

4. *Quattuor dierum supplicatio indicta est* ex a. d. v. Id. Oct. A four days' public thanksgiving has been proclaimed *from the 11th of October.*

5. *Consul comitia* in a. d. iii. Non. Sext. *edixit.* The Consul fixed *the 3rd of August* for the elections.

6. In ante dies octavum et septimum Kalendas Octobres *comitiis dicta dies.* The date fixed for the elections is *the 24th and 25th of September.*

Exercise 67.

1. We have been looking for you day [1] after day from the third of March to the tenth of April : your father and I [2] begin to fear that something has happened amiss. 2. Your father parted from us at [3] Rhodes on the 14th of July : he seemed to be suffering seriously both from sea-sickness and home-sickness; we have not [4] yet received any letter from him, but we hope that he will reach home safe and sound by [5] the twelfth of August. The day after [6] he left us we heard that he ought [7] to have started three days earlier [8] if he wished [9] to be at home in good time. 3. You promised six months ago to stay in my house [10] from the 3rd to the 21st of April. I hope that you will do your utmost to keep your word ; you have been looked for now these ten [11] days. 4. Instead [12] of keeping his word by starting to his father at Rome on the last day of August, he preferred to linger in the fair city [13] of Naples for over twenty days. He scarcely reached home by the 25th of September; a circumstance [14] of which, as [15] it was fatal also to his own prospects and his father's good name, he repented, I believe, from that day [16] to the latest day of his life.

---

[1] **328,** *c.*   [2] See **26,** *note.*   [3] See **315.**
[4] *Nullus adhuc.* (See **328,** *d.*)   [5] *Ad.* (**326.**)
[6] **323,** *b.*   [7] Gerund. (**388.**)   [8] *Ante* with abl. (**322,** *a.*)
[9] Mood ? (**444.**)   [10] **316,** iii.   [11] **321,** *Obs.* 2.
[12] **431,** *Obs.*   [13] **317.**   [14] *Quae res.* (**67.**)
[15] *Quum.* (**430.**)   [16] **326.**

SUPPLEMENTARY EXERCISES.

541. The following Supplementary Exercises are added, partly for the purpose of enlarging the range of practice in applying the rules and remarks contained in the earlier portion of the book, partly also with a view of introducing a few specimens of continuous passages adapted to at least the standard of an ordinary Entrance or "Pass" Examination at the Universities or elsewhere.

The last Exercise (No. 15) is recapitulatory, and consists of a hundred short sentences bearing mainly on the same portion of the work (Exercises i.-xxiii.). Reference here and in other Exercises is frequently made to later sections. The sentences, though necessarily limited in their range, will be found to illustrate a large number of the most fundamental points of difference between the Latin and English languages.

Obs.—In attempting any more continuous passage it should be borne in mind that the connexion in thought between each fresh sentence and that which precedes it is much oftener indicated by some word or phrase in Latin than it is in English. Hence in writing Latin we must often insert some **co-ordinating conjunction** (Intr. 56), answering to "moreover," "but," "for," "therefore," etc., which is wanting in the English, or change "**not**" into "**nor**," or the **demonstrative** into the **relative**. (See **78**.)

No. 1.

To follow Exercises 1 and 2.

1. Not even[1] the vilest of mankind would have envied his own father.   2. Yesterday he returned from Naples, to-morrow he is to[2] set out from Italy to Spain.   3. No one in the world is more secure against[3] violence, for no one[4] ever consulted to such[5] a degree the interests of the country.   4. Having obtained the throne by violence, he yet became before long[6] most dear to the whole nation, for no one ever less consulted his own interests.   5. On the fourth day after his father's death he ascended the throne, on the fifth he was saluted Emperor by the soldiers, on the sixth, having led his army into the enemies' country, he was wounded by his own sword while he was mounting[7] his horse.   6. No one was ever more famous, and no one ever attained to higher (*greater*) rank, or acquired such (87) wealth ; yet he was dear to few, hated by many, and no one ever did his country greater harm.   7. You are obeyed by no one, yet your father was the ruler[8] of a mighty nation.   8. That[9] deed of yours will never be pardoned by your countrymen.

[1] Intr. 90.   [2] Fut. in -*rus.* 14, *c.*   [3] *a, ab.*
[4] *neque enim quisquam* (see 110); *non* is but rarely used before *enim.*
[5] *tantum,* adv.   [6] ="soon."   [7] Tense? See 180. Cf. 411.
[8] *impero, -are.* See 25.   [9] *iste.* 11, *d.*

No. 2.

To follow Exercise 3.

1. For three days[1] we waited for you (*pl.*) and hoped in vain for your arrival : on the fourth day the Indians, who were blockading our camp, dispersed and[2] took their departure; a[3] circumstance which gave us freedom from long-continued fear and anxiety.   2. You (*pl.*) crave for freedom, and are going[4] to fight for[5] your native land, for your altars and hearths ; these (men) pray for peace, and are afraid of the hardships and toils of war.   You I honour, them[6] I despise.
3. Your riches increase daily, but they neither increase your leisure, nor bring you (243) either happiness or peace of mind.   4. Your native land, which was once the ruler of many nations, is now most cruelly oppressed by the vilest enemy, whom lately she both despised and hated.   5. I am waiting here in vain for the arrival of the soldiers whom I sent for yesterday, the enemies' forces are increasing daily, and we shall soon despair of peace.   6. By a bloody and long-continued war we have freed our country, and repelled from our walls a haughty foe ; we now pray for peace.   7. Having[7] advanced into the thick[8] of the battle he received a mortal wound ; while[9] dying, he foretold the ruin of his nation and the triumph of the enemy.

[1] 9, *a.*   [2] 15.   [3] See 67.   [4] 14, *c.*
[5] *pro.*   Se 6.   [6] *ille.* 11. *d.*   [7] 14, *a.*   [8] "midst of."   See 60.
[9] See 406, *note* 2.

No. 3.

To follow Exercise 4.

1. Both your brother and you were at that time in exile; my father and I were at home, exposed to the fury and cruelty of our deadliest[1] enemies. We had provoked no one either by words or acts, yet we endured much, and long and sorely[2] sighed in vain for freedom and safety; now you and I are secure and free from care, and no[3] one will any longer[4] inflict on us injury or wrong. 2. Freed from the barbarous tyranny of an alien race, we have spared those[5] who had most cruelly oppressed our country, (and) we have pardoned those who in the face[6] of national ruin had neglected[7] the welfare of the nation, and were consulting merely their own interests; but neither you nor I will any longer[8] consent to forgive the offences of these[9] men, or to listen to those who, having obtained rank and riches by the vilest arts, are now urging upon us a dishonourable peace.

1 55.	2 *multum diuque.*	3 110.	4 *jam.* See 328, *a.*
5 *is.* 70.	6 *in* (abl.). 273, *Obs.*	7 Abl. abs. 14, *b.*	
8 *diutius.* See 328, *a.*		9 *iste,* contemptuous. See 338, *Obs.* 2.	

No. 4.

To follow Exercises 5 and 6.

1. You and I were, he replied, in the country with[1] your brother, but would return to Naples on the first[2] of August; I believe that he made[3] a great mistake, and that[4] not designedly but by pure[5] accident, for I do not imagine that he would have endeavoured to deceive a friend and guest; but we shall, it is plain, be looked for in vain both by your father and my relations. 2. He ascertained that the weather had changed,[6] and that the crowd, which had gathered together in the morning, would soon disperse; he hoped therefore before night to be able to leave his house, and reach our camp in safety; having arrived there[7] he wished to have an interview with Caesar, whom he had long been pretending to wish to join, and from whom he was anxious to obtain[8] safety and assistance. For he hoped by his[9] aid to attain to the highest rank and office in his[9] own nation.

1 *i.e.* "in the house of," *apud.* 331, 4 *a.*	2 *Kalendis Sextilibus.* See 538.
3 Use *multum* or *vehementer* with a verb. 25.	4 *neque id.* Cf. 344.
5 Use two adverbs with *ac.* See Vocab., under *chance.*	
6 Abl. abs. 14 and 15.	7 "Whither when he had arrived." 14, *a.*
8 *i.e.* "by asking." See Vocab.	9 See 11, *d* and *e*; "aid" is *opera.*

No. 5.

To follow Exercise 7.

1. News was now brought to me that my brother, having been struck by a javelin, and exhausted by many [1] serious wounds, was no longer able either to keep[2] the saddle, or lead his men[3] against the enemy. Having[4] heard this, I was much affected, for I could neither hurry to him as[5] I wished to do, nor did I hope that he would be able any longer to keep the enemy in check. It seemed moreover, that the soldiers who were with[6] me were losing heart, and it was said that the enemy was expecting large reinforcements before night, and would soon take the aggressive. I resolved therefore to try to finish the matter by a single charge. 2. Your brother was, he said, a man of[7] a kindly heart, and abounded[8] in wealth and resources, and he was sure that he would never desert his friends, nor wish such a blow to be inflicted on his own relations. 3. It seems that he had resolved to become consul in that year, but that he pretended to be craving for repose and quiet. 4. He was unwilling, he replied, to despair, but would rather be in exile than be a slave.

---

[1] See below, 56. [2] *in equo haerere*. [3] *sui*. [4] Intr. 58.
[5] 67. [6] 8, *Obs*. [7] Abl. 271. [8] *circumfluo*. 284.

No. 6.

To follow Exercises 7 and 8.

1. He talked very little about the past; about the future his hopes were high, but he perceived that he was at variance on this question[1] with many excellent men, and he preferred being[2] silent to disagreeing[2] with these, and agreeing[2] with his own enemies, and his country's foes; neither you nor I can think that he was mistaken, for we know that his good sense, honesty, and courage were worthy of all praise. 2. He promised to send me[3] a letter on the 15th of March,[4] and made many other fine pretences,[5] but he has neither kept his promises, nor does he any longer venture to make a secret of having purposely broken his word. 3. He threatens, they say, to take from me all the distinctions which I have obtained from the Senate and people of Rome; for myself,[6] I hardly think he will succeed in this[7] design. 4. He would rather, he replied, obey the most unjust laws, than be at variance with true patriots, and disagree with every sensible[8] man. 5. We scarcely dare to hope that your brother will return to Rome and imitate the noble acts of his forefathers, but all his contemporaries can guarantee[9] that he will never desert his friends, or break his word, or join the enemies of his native land.

---

[1] *in hac causa*, lit. "in this *suit*." [2] Infinitive in each case. See 94, and 42.
[3] *ad me*. See 6. [4] See 538. [5] See 54.
[6] *ego* or *equidem*, 11, *a*. [7] *qui* (see Intr. 58), early in the clause.
[8] Superlative with *quisque*. 375. [9] Use *spondeo*.

To follow Exercise 9.

1. You (*pl.*) have come here[1] manifestly with reluctance, and you say that you will not[2] wait any longer for the arrival of your friends, who will, you think,[3] be far from[4] secure in our camp. For myself, I have promised you again and again to say nothing about the past, and I have resolved both to pardon you, and to spare them. But you apparently expect that in the hour of triumph, I shall break my word, and act[5] towards[6] you and them with the height of treachery. I know that you can scarcely believe that I am speaking the truth, and that you are silently despairing both of your own and your children's safety. What falsehood[7] have I ever told? When have I ever broken my word? 2. It is said that the king himself was the only one of[8] the whole of his army to ride in safety past the fatal marsh (*pl.*), and the first to reach the foot of the mountains, whence on the next day he mournfully and reluctantly led back his troops and never[9] again ventured to form such high hopes or embark[10] on such great enterprises. It seemed that as[11] he had been the first to hope for the best,[12] so he was the first to abandon his undertaking; he preferred to appear fickle and cowardly rather than to bring ruin and destruction on his country.

[1] Why not *hic? huc* after verbs of motion. [2] 33. [3] 32, *b*.
[4] *parum,* "but little." [5] *utor,* "employ treachery" (with abl.).
[6] *in vobis,* "in your case." [7] See 54. [8] *e, ex,* "out of."
[9] *nec unquam postea.* Never join *et* with *nunquam,* or any negative word. 110.
[10] Metaphor. Use *moliri,* and see 54. [11] *sicut ... ita,* or *et ... et.* [12] Neut. pl.

To follow Exercises 10 and 11.

1. As[1] I was making my way through the lowest part of the valley, I fell unawares into an ambush of brigands. My captors[2] had, it seemed, been long expecting my arrival, and having seized[3] and made[3] me fast with chains, and dragged me from the road[4] into the neighbouring forest, they again and again threatened me with (247) torture and death. At last, when I promised to send a large amount[5] of gold within four days, my chains[6] were struck off and I was set at liberty, and in company[7] with two armed guards, returned to the place[8] whence I had set out. 2. He had now, he said, ceased to hope for much, for he had lost (he said) the best friends he had,[9] and was going to live with men who had always been his deadly enemies, by whom he had been both accused and condemned in his absence, and who had reluctantly spared his life. 3. Your accusers[10] will, I expect, reach the city to-morrow; I hope that you will be (193, iv.) unanimously acquitted. 4. You[11] who once set at nought bodily (59) pain (*pl.*), are now apparently dismayed by it. It is[12] with reluctance that I say this of (*de*) the son of so great a man. 5. You obviously treat lightly the affairs of others; I hope that you will value highly the good opinion of your countrymen.

[1] *dum* with pres. See 180. [2] 76. [3] Acc. of participle pass. 15.
[4] *de via.* [5] *pondus, n.* [6] Abl. abs.
[7] 8, *b.* [8] *eo, unde.* See 89. [9] Mood? See 77.
[10] 14, *c.* Not *accusator.* See 76. [11] See 75. [12] See 82.

To follow Exercises 12 and 13.

1. It is generally[1] agreed among historians that this king, trained by toil (*pl.*) and accustomed to bear with patience the frowns[2] of fortune, showed[3] in the midst of disaster (*pl.*) and ruin the same character as in prosperity. As he had been the first to help his country in its hour[4] of distress, so he was the last to despair of it (when) conquered and downtrodden. But he preferred being an exile in his old age to living in safety at home, and obeying one whom the rest of the world, almost without exception, believed to be likely to keep his word. 2. There is all the difference between returning thanks and showing gratitude. As I was the last to believe that you would have set at nought honour, honesty, and the good opinion of your countrymen, so to-day I refuse to think that you have proved[6] to be of such a character as the rest of the world represent[7] you to be ; and it is with reluctance that I yield to those who deny that you are the same man as I once fancied you to be

---

[1] *satis* or *fere*.   [2] Metaphor, "adverse fortune."
[3] See 241.   [4] Simply part.pres. of *laboro, -are.*
[5] See 14, c.   [6] Use *existo.* See 241.   [7] "assert."

To follow Exercises 14 and 15.

On the next day the king, to avoid wearying by a long march his soldiers (who were) exhausted with a long and indecisive battle, kept his men within their lines. Meantime the enemy having sent for reinforcements were waiting for an attack (on the part) of our men, so that they seemed by no means desirous of fighting. After noonday the king, seeing[1] that the strength and spirits of his men were now so much restored, that they were likely to shrink from no danger, and stood (up) prepared for fighting,[2] threw open[3] two gates, and having made a sudden[4] sally surprised the enemy (who were taken) unawares and looking for nothing of the[5] kind. Great numbers they surround[6] and slay, and so great was the slaughter that out of (*ex*) more than[7] 3000 soldiers scarcely 500 escaped unwounded, and that, had[8] not night interposed, not even these would have survived. So (entirely) in short did fortune change (sides), that those who quite lately[9] were on the point of winning the day, were now stealing away and praying for night and darkness, and those who but lately[10] were despairing of their safety, and looking for death or slavery, were exulting in victory and freedom.

---

[1] See 412.   [2] 99.   [3] Abl. abs.   [4] Use adverb.   [5] 87.
[6] 14, c.   [7] 318, *Obs.*   [8] *nisi* with pl.-perf. subj.   [9] *paulo ante.*   [10] *modo.*

To follow Exercise 16.

Thereupon, he sent[1] for their chief men, and exhorted them not to be disheartened on account of such a serious disaster. He had warned them, he said,[2] that the enemy was at hand, but it had been impossible to persuade them not to put faith in idle rumours and fictitious messages. The Indians earnestly implored him to forgive them[3] for this great error; they succeeded at last by their prayers or tears in persuading him that they would never again[4] allow themselves to be so easily overreached and entrapped (*caught*). While[5] they were thus[6] conversing, it happened that a[7] prisoner was brought to Cortes, who professed to be one[8] of the king's[9] bodyguard. The general ordered his[10] fetters to be struck off and himself to be set at liberty, and sent him back with a letter to the king. He did this with the intention of appearing to be anxious for a truce; but so far was he from wishing for anything[11] of the kind that he was ready to reject any[12] conditions, and preferred to put the fortune of war a second time to the test (rather) than to accept from the king even the most honourable peace.

---

1 Acc. part. pass. 15.   2 Avoid parenthesis. 32.   3 Pronoun? See 353, ii. and 247.
4 *postea*.   5 *dum :* tense? 180.   6 *haec*.   7 *quidam*. 361.
8 *unus e.*   See 529, e.   9 Adj. 58.   10 Relative. 78.
11 *quisquam*. 358.   12 359.

To follow Exercises 17 and 18.

I am afraid that this letter will not reach you across the enemies' lines. We have now been[1] invested here for a whole month (321), and[2] I cannot help beginning to despair of the whole state[3] of affairs. The numbers[4] of the enemy are such as we had never dreamed of,[5] and as[6] all the roads are closed, no supplies can be brought up; scarcely any letters reach us, so that it is impossible to doubt that we are involved in very serious danger. Do you therefore not hesitate to write to the general to hasten to bring us assistance, and do not allow yourself to think that I am writing thus with the intention of calling[7] him away from his great designs and bringing him here for the sake of our safety. I fear that the enemy (if once) victorious here, will soon become formidable to him also, and I do not think that we can be crushed without[8] drawing others into the same ruin.

---

1 Tense? 181.   2 *neque*, etc. ; cf. 110.   3 *summa res*.
4 *multitudo* (sing.).   5 Metaphor, "fancied would come together."
6 Abl. abs. 420.   7 Part. pass. 15.   8 See 111.

No. 13.

To follow Exercises 19 and 20.

Are we to say that Caesar was foully[1] murdered or that he was rightfully[2] slain? That either one[3] or the other is true is most certain. Do you (*sing.*) then choose whichever[4] you like; but do not say now this, now that, and[5] do not to-day look on Brutus as a patriot, to-morrow as an assassin. Did Caesar pay the penalty of his crimes? You answer "No;" then let his slayers be either banished or put[6] to death as traitors. Or[7] did Brutus speak the truth,[8] when (while) raising aloft the bloody dagger, he exclaimed that the nation's freedom was recovered? "Yes," you reply. Then why do you heap abuse on one to whom alone[9] you are indebted for your freedom? Or[7] do you think that what Brutus did was in[10] itself right and a benefit[11] to the nation, but that he himself acted criminally, and should be punished[12] with banishment, or imprisonment, or death? For myself I decline to meddle with so nice[13] a question : I leave it to philosophers (146).

---

[1] "criminally."
[2] "*jure caesus,*" a legal phrase answering to our "justifiable homicide."
[3] *hic, ille.* See 340, ii.   [4] *utervis.* 379.   [5] 145.
[6] "He is put to death, etc.," *more majorum in eum animadvertitur*, a *euphemism* for scourging and beheading.   [7] *An.* 161.   [8] *tum . . . quum.* 433, a.   [9] *unus.* 529, b.
[10] *per se.*   [11] Use *utilis,* avoid *beneficium* in this sense.
[12] Gerundive of *multo, -are,* with abl.   [13] *subtilis,* or *difficilis.*

No. 14.

To follow Exercises 21 and 22.

The king summoned his staff and set before them the nature and extent of the danger, the numbers of the enemy, the magnitude of their resources, their aims,[1] designs,[1] and hopes. For my part, said he, I will utter my real sentiments and will not hide the fact[2] that I have no doubt that both all (of) you and I myself are to-day involved in the greatest danger. I know that it is difficult to say[3] whether the reinforcements which we look for will ever reach us, or whether we shall perish first[4] overwhelmed by the weapons of this enormous[5] host. But whether we are[6] to live or die, I venture to feel sure of this at least, that no one of us will allow himself to think it a light[7] matter, whether our countrymen are to be grateful to us in our graves[8] or to scorn (despise) us in our lives; so that we need only deliberate on one single question, by what[9] course of action or of endurance we shall best serve (332, 3, *g*) our common country. Possibly we can consult our own safety by remaining here, sheltered and preserved by these walls; and perhaps this[10] is the safer plan; but it sometimes happens that the most daring[11] course is the safest; and I hope to persuade you that it will so turn out to-day.

---

[1] 174. Use the verbs *peto,* and *mol-ior, -iri.*   [2] *illud.* 341.   [3] Supine in *-u.* 404.
[4] *prius.*   [5] Simply *tantus.* 88.   [6] Fut. in *-rus.*   [7] *parvi facere.* 305, i.
[8] Metaphor, use *mortuus.* 61.   [9] "By doing what, enduring what." 398.
[10] Relative.   [11] See 375, *note* [1].

The following Exercise is mainly recapitulatory; it, or any part of it, may follow Sections 1-194.

1. The whole world knows why you are envied. 2. He asked if you had ever spared a single enemy. 3. He hoped, he said, that the matter would turn out contrary to his expectations.[1] 4. Have you not come from the same place[2] as I? 5. He was the first to reach the summit of the mountain, the last to descend. 6. He was revolving many thoughts (64) in silence. 7. He said that he was no longer[3] such as he had once been. 8. There had been, he replied, as many opinions as there were men standing by. 9. It seems that you were the first within human memory to venture on this enterprise. 10. Having promised to settle these matters, he held his peace. 11. In my youth I travelled over many lands and seas, in my old age I remain at home. 12. He came home with a weapon intending[4] to kill your father; fortunately[5] no one was at home. 13. It seemed that he was returning thanks unwillingly; but it is most certain that he feels grateful. 14. All the world knows that you are under an obligation to me, no one believes that you will show gratitude. 15. I who was once your advocate am to-day your accuser. 16. So alarmed was he by the shouts of the bystanders that he could scarcely answer his questioners.[6] 17. Both you and I have lost an excellent friend, whom we are never likely to see again in this world. 18. Neither you nor I are likely to believe that the world was made by chance. 19. I know not whether you wish to be a friend[7] to me or an enemy. 20. I did this with the intention of pleasing you; I earnestly beg you therefore not to be angry. 21. He wrote me word[8] not to leave the city; I happened by chance to have[9] already set out. 22. I know not whether I am likely to deter him from[10] injuring his friends. 23. I fear that we have lost the city; it remains to see if we can retake it. 24. Three months[11] ago the city[12] of Veii was invested by the troops of Rome; it has now been (181) long blockaded, it will soon be assaulted, and there is danger,[13] they say, of its being stormed. 25. The weather was now changing, and the sailors were dreading the violence of the winds. 26. I have silently resolved to be at leisure to-morrow, but perhaps this is[14] impossible. 27. I asked him first (534, *Obs.*) if he had committed that monstrous crime; he answered "Yes;" secondly, why he had acted so; next, when; lastly, with what weapon. 28. He turned to his companions[15] and asked them when they intended to return home. 29. That your friend is fortunate is indisputable (64); I

---

1 See 91. Mood, 77, *Obs.*	2 89.	3 *jam.* 328, *a.*
4 14, c.	5 64.	6 73.
7 46, d.	8 122, c.	9 123.
10 137, ii.	11 324.	12 222.
13 138.	14 169.	15 349. *Obs.*

entirely disagree with those who say that he is happy ; happiness [1] is
one thing, prosperity another.   30. Having started with his followers
(**349**, *Obs.*) the next day, he fell unawares into an ambush ; most
fortunately [2] I came to his assistance, and attacked the enemy from [3]
behind.   31. Both he and you, it is plain, were persuaded to believe
men who were deceiving you.   32. I fear that in his old age he no
longer has the same views as in his youth.   33. You ask me if [4] he
is of the same character as his brother, I unwillingly answer " No." [5]
34. I earnestly implored him to warn his father not to put confidence
in that man.   35. Perceiving (*quum*, **412**) that he was unwilling to
trust me, I ceased to urge him to go with me.   36. Be sure you come
to me at Rome (**315**) that we may both [6] have an interview with
Caesar.   37. So cowardly and mean-spirited was he, that I think I
have never seen any one like him.[7]   38. I have stayed here so long
that I begin to believe I shall never go away.   39. So dear was he to
his friends that they never ceased to sigh for him in his absence, to
admire him when present.   40. What was I to do ? whither to turn ?
I could have wished you had stood by me ; but both my friends and
you were absent.   41. It would be tedious to tell all this [8] story,
but I cannot help praising one of (*ex*) his exploits.   42. Do not believe, judges, that I am of the character [9] which this man attributes [10]
to me.   43. It is of great consequence whether (**166**) you inflict punishment on men who deserve punishment, or on the innocent.   44.
Whether you have devoted me to death or [11] not, I know not, nor does
it matter much.   45. Do you not perceive that it is absolutely impossible for the privileges and liberty of the nation to be outraged by you
with impunity.   46. I asked him if he wished to make me responsible
for a brother's [12] crime.   He answered in the affirmative.   47. He
asked if I was willing to aid men who were aiming at giving freedom
to their oppressed and down-trodden country.   48. A (*is*) massacre
followed, the like of which [13] I had never seen ; of such an extent
and character that I can hardly dare to recall to mind the scene.[14]   49. I
have spoken thus with the intention of persuading him to pardon you :
whether he will do so or not is uncertain.   50. He succeeded [15] in
persuading the king to forgive [16] him this great error.   51. It has
repeatedly fallen to my lot to be suspected of many crimes ; I have
never before been condemned in my absence and unheard.   52. Possibly your countrymen, freed from an alien despotism, are going
to offer you the supreme power ; what they doubt is (**341**) whether
you will accept it.   53. He said that he had never taken any part [17]
in politics, or made it his aim (**118**) to attain to any distinctions, or to
acquire rank or riches.   54. You are, I see, victorious and most fortunate ;
that you enjoy happiness I do not allow.   55. I might have [18] said

---

[1] 98, *a, b.*	[2] 64.	[3] 61.
[4] 167.	[5] 162.	[6] *ambo.* 378,
[7] 255.	[8] 54.	[9] *talis.* 84.
[10] "pretends (*fingit*) that I am."	[11] 168, *Obs.*	[12] Adj. 58.
[13] "(one) like which." 255.	[14] " The things which I saw." 176.	
[15] 125, *j.*	[16] 247.	
[17] Use either *versari in republica* or *rempublicam attingere.*		[18] 196, *b.*

much more on (*de*) the vileness of these men ; but I do not wish to be either tedious or burdensome to you. 56. More than once (**533**, *c*) he took advantage of my gentleness and clemency; in my absence, he loaded me with abuse and insults. 57. I fear that our soldiers have been incapable of sustaining the onset of such[1] a well-trained host. 58. Thrice with his army of recruits[2] he advanced against the enemy; thrice he retreated : at last his soldiers dispersed, and fled in opposite directions. 59. He was at last persuaded to spare the innocent (*pl.*) and unarmed ; but he long refused to do so. 60. As a young man, he attained to the height of fame, in his old age he was undeservedly disgraced. 61. Overreached and deceived by men[3] who pretended to be his friends, he could no longer put confidence in those who wished his interest consulted (**240**, *Obs*. 1). 62. It is almost incredible (**166**) how seldom it has been my lot to see so famous a person. 63. Do not object[4] to be free. Let cowards act so, and those who dread death. 64. The manner[5] of his death I have never heard, all the world knows that he is dead. 65. Having returned home in his old age, he became dear to many excellent members of the state. 66. So far from hating him, I am anxious to defend him against[6] his deadliest enemies. 67. I could never see your brother without[7] calling to mind his dead father's countenance. 68. I cannot help wondering at the reason[8] of your having come here. 69. He swore (**37**) to confess to no one the motive[8] of his having told these falsehoods. 70. It is almost incredible (**166**) how often he has been warned against[9] doing anything of this kind (**87**). 71. I was so foolish as to be almost persuaded (**5**) to turn back[10] to the place from whence (**89**) I had set out. 72. No one in the world (**16**, *b*) could have spoken with more prudence,[11] or more candour. 73. What you have done is possibly (**64**) in accordance[12] with law, I greatly doubt[13] whether it is constitutional.[14] 74. Do you think that such a man as this[15] can be restrained from[16] using violence? 75. I know that this is right and honourable, whether it is expedient or no I leave[17] to wiser men to decide. 76. You pretend to be a citizen of Rome ; for myself I cannot help[18] suspecting that you are not only a foreigner, but one of the soldiers of Carthage. 77. It is impossible to doubt (**200**, *Obs.*) that he has injured the nation ; whether he has done this accidentally or designedly, I leave to himself to decide. 78. I was the last to perceive what you were aiming at ; I shall be the first to oppose you in that aim[19] (**415**). 79. He bade the soldiers drag their own (**356**, i.) general to execution ; reluctantly and mournfully they obeyed his orders (**415**, *a*). 80. Do you go to meet the enemy in front (**61**), I will charge him from behind, and off his guard. 81. The whole world knows now-a-days that the earth moves round the sun ; it is (**82**) into the nature,[20] properties, and

---

[1] **88.**　[2] See **223.**　[3] **72.**
[4] *recuso* with inf. **136.**　[5] **174,** *c.*　[6] *ab.*
[7] **132,** *b.*　[8] **174,** *a.*　[9] **118.**
[10] *revertor,* "I turn back," return without completing my intended journey.
[11] Adv. *prudenter.* **64.**　[12] **331,** 21.　[13] *vehementer.*
[14] **332,** 4.　[15] **87.**　[16] **131.**
[17] **146.**　[18] **137,** *j.*　[19] "aiming at that." **415**
[20] See **174.** Use *quid, quale,* etc.

magnitude of the sun that philosophers are inquiring. 82. I never feared that you were not (138) going to consult my interest; the real[1] danger was that fortune would change. 83. So changed was your brother's face and features that I hardly knew that he was the same person that I knew in my youth. 84. To-morrow we are to fight; be sure to (141) take part in the contest, if you can (190, ii.). 85. What was I to do (150)? what to say? whither to turn? no one was coming to my aid; it seemed that the whole world thought me out of my mind. 86. He was unanimously (59) acquitted, but at the same time (366, ii.) universally condemned. 87. Your father refused to leave his own house; would he had been here (152) to-day. 88. The weather, I fancy, will change to-morrow; be sure, therefore, to cross the channel to-day. 89. Let us no longer obey a master of this kind, it would be better to die a thousand[2] deaths than endure such disgrace. 90. The whole of the city echoed with voices of weeping[3] and mourning; you would have thought[4] that there was no one but had lost a parent or children. 91. So earnestly did he implore me to spare the unarmed that I could no longer withstand his entreaties.[5] 92. Having communicated[6] this matter to me, he warned me to be on my guard[7] against an[8] enemy of my brother. 93. To this advice[5] of his I replied that I had no fears for myself, but was anxious to provide[7] for the safety of my friends. 94. I have been informed, said he, by[9] my scouts that you have long been (181) supplying[10] the enemy with corn. 95. It seems that you are threatening[10] us with imprisonment and death; perhaps[11] it would have been better (153) to provide for your own safety. 96. It is said that he intrusted[10] you with the whole of this matter; perhaps he relied[12] on you too much. 97. Three days[13] ago, I asked when you were to come here; it seemed that no one knew. 98. Your father happened[14] that day to be absent; he hoped to return within a[15] week. 99. In the study of nature your son has made great progress; in everything that relates to literature I incline to think that many of his contemporaries have outstripped him. 100. It is uncertain whether at that[16] time he preferred to be a politician or a student (175).

---

[1] 341.
[2] 536, *Obs.*
[3] 415, *b.*
[4] 149, ii.
[5] 415.
[6] 253, iv.
[7] 248 (for this and next sentence).
[8] 361.
[9] *Per.* 267, *Obs.*
[10] 247.
[11] *haud scio an.* 170.
[12] 244, c.
[13] 324
[14] 123.
[15] "the seventh day." 325.
[16] *tum temporis.* 294, *Obs.*

GENERAL VOCABULARY.

Caution.—It should be understood that the Latin words given in this Vocabulary are not necessarily equivalent to the English when the latter are used with a meaning and context different to that in which they occur in the Exercises. (See 17-19.)

Figures refer to sections, except where p. (= page) or Ex. (= Exercise) is prefixed.

abandon, I (a person), deser-o,[1] ĕre, -ui, -tum; de-sum, esse, -fui (*dat.*, **251**); destitu-o, ĕre, -i; de-scisco, ĕre, scivi, ab *or* abl. (*fall off from a party*).

abandon, I (a thing or work), o-mitto, ĕre, -misi, -missum (see note under *undone, I leave*); de-sisto, ĕre, -stiti, ab, *or* abl.

abandoned (wicked), perditus.

abandonment of, the, use o-mitto, ĕre, etc. (**417**, i.)

abide by, I, sto, are (*abl.*).

ability, or abilities, ingenium, *n.* (*sing.*).

able, I am, possum, posse, potui.

abound in, I, circum-fluo, ĕre, -fluxi. (**284**.)

about (adv.), circa, circiter; fere, ferme.

about (prep.), de. (**332**, 3, *d.*)

absence, in my. (**61**, and **420**, ii.)

absent, I am, absum, esse; *from*, a, ab.

absolutely, plane; *or superl. of adj.*

absolutely impossible. (**125**, *f.*)

abstain from, I. (**264**.)

abundance of, plurimum. (**294**.)

abuse, maledicta, *n. pl.* (**51**, *b.*)

accept, I, ac-cipio, ĕre, -cepi, -ceptum.

acceptable to, gratus. (See note under *delightful*.)

accident, cas-us, -ūs, *m.*

accident, by, casu; fortuito. (**268**.)

accomplish, I, ef- *or* con-ficio, ĕre, etc.

accordance with, in, perinde ac, etc. (**491**, *a*); pro (**332**, 7, *f*).

account of, on, propter (*acc.*).

account, on no, nullo modo; minime.

account, I take into, rationem habeo (*gen.*).

accuracy, with more, verius. (Intr. **52**.)

accuse, I, accuso, are.

accuser, = he who accuses. (**76**.)

accustomed, I am, soleo, ĕre, solitus.

achievements, res gestae.

achievements, I perform, res gero, ĕre, gessi, gestum.

acquire, I, ad-ipiscor, i, -eptus. (See **19**.)

acquit, I, absol-vo, ĕre, -vi, -utum. (**306**.)

across, trans (*acc.*).

act, I (behave), me gero, ĕre.

act rightly, I, recte facio.

act thus, I, haec facio.

action, by, agendo, aliquid (**398**); nom. agere (**95**, **99**).

acts, facta, *n. pl.* (**51**, *b.*)

address (= speech), orati-o, -onis, *f.*

address (the people), I, verba (apud populum) facio.

adequate, justus.

---

[1] *Relinquo*, I abandon, in neutral and general sense of "leaving;" *desero*, I quit a place or person where or with whom duty bids me stay; *destituo*, I leave "in the lurch" one who without me will be unaided; *desum*, I fail to be present where my presence is desirable or right; *deficio(ab* or acc.), "I fail" or "fall off from," those whom I have hitherto stood by.

Z

administering the government, rei publicae procurati-o, -onis, *f.* ; rempublicam gubernare.

administration, procurati-o, -onis,*f.*

admire, *I*, admiror, ari.

advance, *I*, pro-cedo, ĕre, -cessi, -cessum ; pro-gredior, i, -gressus.

advance in learning, *I*, doctior fio.

advanced (*age*), provecta (aetas). (See 303, *Obs.* 1.)

advanced in life or years. (303, *Obs.* 1.)

advanced guard, primum agm-en, -inis, *n.*

advantage, emolumentum, *n.*

advantage, to your. (269, *Obs.*)

advantage, what? quid emolumenti? (294.)

adverse, adversus (*adj.*).

adversity, res adversae.

advice, against your, turn by pres. part. of dissuadeo, ēre. (See 420, ii.)

advise, *I*, moneo.

advocate of (*peace*), auctor.

advocate of, I am an, suadeo, ēre, *with acc. of thing.* (See 247.)

advocate, *I am your*, te defendo, ĕre.

affair, res, rei, *f.*

affected (*agitated*), *I am*, com-move-or, ēri, -motus.

affirmative, to reply in the. (162.)

afflict with, *I*, afficio, ĕre. (283.)

afraid, I am, timeo.

afraid of, I am, = *I fear* (25), per-timesco, ēre, -timui (*acc., or* ne, ut, 138).

after (*prep.*), post (*acc.*). (See 322, 323.)

after (*with verbal subst.*), *use* quum. (429.)

again, rursus. (328, *f.*)

again (*with neg.*), posthac ; postea.

again and again, saepe, saepissime. (57, *a* ; see also 533, *c.*)

against, contra (*acc.*).

against (*my wishes*) = "*in spite of.*" (420, ii.)

age (*time of life*), aet-as, -atis, *f.*

age (*of things*), vetust-as, -atis, *f.*

age, old, senect-us, -utis, *f.*

age, of that. (238, iii.)

age, those of his own, aequales. (51, *a.*)

age of, at the. (327.)

aged, exactae aetatis. (303, *Obs.* 1.)

aggressive, I take the, ultro arma or bellum, infero.

agitation, there is, trepidatur. (218.)

ago. (324.)

agree with, I do not, parum (*but little*) consen-tio, ire, -si (cum).

agreed by (*all*), *it is*, constat inter (*acc.*).

agreed on by, it is, con-vĕnit, -vēnit, inter.

agreement, an, pactum, *n.*

agreement is come to, an, convēnit (*impers.*).

agreement with, I am in, consen-tio, īre, -si, -sum, cum (*abl.*).

aid, auxilium, *n.*

aid, I, opem fero (*dat.*).

aid, I come to your, tibi subvenio.

aid or assistance, I come to your (Ex. 32). (260, 1.)

aid, by your, operā tuā.

aim at, I, or I form aims, pet-o, ĕre, -ivi, -ii (-isti), -ītum ; ap-peto, ĕre, etc. (*trans.*).

aim at (*doing, etc.*), *I, or I make it my aim*, id ago, ēgi, ut. (118.)

alarmed, I am, timeo, ēre.

alarmed (*anxious*) *for, I am*, metuo (*with dat.*, 248).

Alexander, Alexan-der, -dri.

alien (*adj.*), externus.

alien (*subst.*), peregrin-us, -i, *m.*

alike (*adv.*), juxta, pariter.

alike . . . and ; or . . . as, sicut . . . ita ; vel . . . vel (p. 14, *n.*).

alive, I am, vivo, ĕre.

all, omnis, *also* cunctus, universus.[1]

all (*things*), *n. pl. of* omn-is, -e.

all is lost, de summa re actum est.

allegiance, fid-es, -ei, *f.*

---

[1] *Universi*, all as a body, opposed to *singuli* ; *omnes*, all without exception, opposed to *nemo* or to *unus* ; *cuncti*, a stronger *omnes*, "all together ;" *omnis* (sing.), every kind of ; *cunctus* (sing.), all as a whole, nearly = *totus*, the whole as opposed to a part.

alliance with, I make, societatem
ineo ire, -ivi. -ii, cum.

allow, I (let), per-mitto, ĕre, -misi,
-missum *(dat.,* **128,** *end).*

allow, I (grant), concedo, ĕre.

allow, I (confess, admit), fateor,
ēri, fassus ; cou-cedo, ĕre, -cessi.

allow myself to, I will not, ñon
committam ut. (**125,** *i.*)

allowed, I am, licet mihi. (**197.**)

*allowed, it is, admitted, or agreed
on,* constat *(impers.);* allowed *by,*
constat inter *(acc.).* (**46,** *c.*)

ally, an, soci-us, -i, *m.*

almost, fere,[1] paene, prope.

aloft, alte.

alone in doing this, I am, solus *or*
unus (**529,** *b*), hoc facio. (**62.**)

along. (**331,** 5 *and* 21.)

already, jam.

also, quoque (Intr. 9S) ; *or (sometimes),* idem, idemque. (**366,** i.)

altars and hearths, arae atque foci.

altering, I am (intrans.), mutor,
ari. (**21,** *a.*)

always, semper.

ambassador, legat-us, -i, *m.*

ambush, ambuscade, insidiae, *f. pl.*

amiss, secus.

among, inter *(acc.).*

ancestors, major-es, -um. (**51,***a,n.*5.)

ancient, pristinus,[2] vet-us, -eris ;
vetustus, a, um, *superl.* vetus-
tissimus ; antiquus. (See *note.*)

and, et, -que, atque, ac (p. 14,
note ; see also **110**).

anew, de integro. (**328,***f.*)

anger, ira, *f. ; I cherish,* suc-censeo,
ĕre, -censui, -censum *(dat.).*

angry with, I am, ira-scor, i, -tus
(dat.).

angry mood, iracundia, *f.*

angry outcries. (See *outcries.*)

annihilate, I, del-eo, ĕre, -ēvi,
-ētum.

announcement, of, use nuntio, are.
(**417,** i.)

another (a second), alt-er, *gen.*
-erius. (**368.**)

answer, I, respon-deo, ēre, -di,
-sum.

*answer, I make no, = I answer
nothing.* (**54** and **237.**)

answer to, in. (**331,** 1, *b,* and 2, *c.*)

antiquity (of a thing existing), vetust-
as, -atis, *f.*

anxiety, sollicitud-o, -inis, *f.*

anxiety, free from, securus.

anxious for, I feel, dif-fido, ĕre,
-fisus *(dat.).*

anxious to, I am, cupio, ĕre *(inf.).*

any (after negat.), any one, anything,
quisquam, quidquam, ullus. (See
358.)

any? (impassioned interrogative),
ecqui, ecquis.

any longer, ultra. (See also **328,** *a.*)

any man may, cujusvis est. (**292,**
4.)

any one (in final and consec. clauses).
(**109.**)

anything (you please), quidvis, *gen.*
cujusvis. (**359.**)

anywhere (after negat.), usquam.

Apiolae, Apiolae, arum.

apologise for, I, veniam peto, *with*
quod *or gen. of participle.*

apparently. (**64.**)

appeal to, I, obtestor, ari *(acc.);
to you, not to,* te obtestor, ari, ne.
(See **118.**)

appeal to you, I solemnly, fidem
tuam imploro, are, ut *or* ne.

appeal to fear, to, deterr-eo, ēre,
-ui. (**25.**)

appear (seem), I, videor, ēri, visus.
(**43.**)

applaud, I, plau-do, ĕre, -si, -sum
(dat.).

apprehension, met-us, -ūs, *m.*

---

[1] *Fere (ferme* in Livy) is "more or less." "about ;" *pacne, prope,* less than but bor-
dering on. Hence *quod fere fit,* as *generally* happens ; but, *prope divinus, all but* divine,
"heroic."

[2] *Antiquus,* old and no longer existing ; *vetus* (fem. and neut., often borrowed from
vetustus), old and still existing. Thus *domus antiqua,* "what was long ago my home ;"
domus (vetus or) *vetusta,* "what has long been my home ;" *mos antiquus,* an old custom
now obsolete ; *veteri more,* in accordance with long-established custom. *Antiquus =*
"of the good old times," often used in praise. *Priscus =* "old-fashioned," "rarely
seen now ;" *pristinus,* simply " arlier," as opposed to "the present."

approach, I, advento, are.

approval for this, I get your, hoc tibi probo. (247.)

approved of (by you), it is, (tibi) probatur. (258, ii.)

apt to, I am, = I am wont, soleo.

ardently, vehement-er, -ius, -issime.

ardour for, studium, n. (with gen.). (300.)

argue, I, dis-sero, ĕre, -serui.

aright, recte

aristocratic party, the, optimat-es, -um or -ium, m. pl. (See 51, a, and note.)

arm (one), bracchium, n. (alter-um, 368).

armed, armatus.

arms, arma, n. pl.

armistice, an, indutiae, f. pl.

army, exercit-us, -ūs, m.

arrival, advent-us, -ūs, m.

arrive (at), I, per-vĕnio, ire, -vēni, -ventum (ad with acc.).

arrow, sagitta, f.

art, ars, artis, f.

as, or as . . . so, sicut (with ita in main clause); et . . . et.

as (as though), tanquam. (496.)

as (= while), dum. (180.)

as often as, quoties; cum. (See 192, 434.)

as regards, or as to (= about), de (abl.). (332, 3.)

as to (free from care as to), ab (332, 1, e); (from the side of, as regards), ibid.

as to (inf.) (See 108.)

ascend the throne, I (see 17), rex fio, or regnum accipio.

ascertain, I, cog-nosco, ĕre, -novi, -nitum; certior fio.

ascribe to you, I, tibi acceptum refero. (See indebted to you.)

ask (you), I (a question), te rogo, interrogo; ex, abs, te quae-ro, ĕre, -sivi. (See p. 157, note.)

ask (you), I (request, beg), te rogo, oro, are; abs te pet-o, ĕre, -ivi, -ii, -itum (ut). (See 127, c.)

ask for, I, posco, ĕre, poposci.

ask your opinion, I, te consul-o, ĕre, -ui, -tum. (248.)

aspect of affairs, the, rerum faci-es, -ei, f.

assailants, = those who assail (ag-gredior). (See 175.)

assassin, sicari-us, -i, m.

assault, I. (See attack.)

assemble, to (intrans.), convenire.

assembly, convent-us, -ūs, m.

assert, I (pretend), dictito, are.

assert, I (as a fact), affirmo, are.

assert, I would. (149, i.)

assert, I (maintain), vindico, are.

assert my country's freedom, I, patriam in libertatem vindico.

assertors of (freedom), = those who have asserted, etc. (175.)

assist, I, adjuvo, are. (245.)

assistance, I bring you, tibi opem fero.

assistance, I come to his, subvenio, ire, etc. (dat.).

assured, I am. (240.)

Athenians, Atheniens-es, -ium.

atone for, I, luo, ĕre; poenas do (gen.).

attached to me, mei amantissimus. (302.)

attack, I (general sense), ag-gredior, -i, -gressus (acc.); (a city or place), oppugno, are (see 24); (suddenly), ad-orior, iri, -ortus.

attack, I (in words), in-vehor, i, -vectus, in (acc.).

attack, to (of a pestilence, panic), inva-dĕre, -si, -sum.

attain to, I (= arrive at), pervenio ad. (19.)

attain to, I (= obtain), adipiscor. (19.)

attempt, I, conor, ari; id ago ut.

attempt (subst.), inceptum, n.; conat-us, -ūs, m.

authority, potest-as, -atis. (See influence, note.)

avail myself of, I, utor, i, usus (abl.).

avail with, I am of no, nihil valeo apud. (331, 4, d.)

avarice, avaritia, f.

avert from, I, prohib-eo, ĕre, -ui, -itum, ab.

avoid, I (a burden, etc.), de-fugio, ĕre, -fūgi.

avoid, I (a danger), vito, are.
avoid, to (= *in order not to, etc.*).
  (**101,** ii. ; cf. **109.**)
avow, I, prae me fero.
aware of, I am, or *become,* sen-tio,
  ire, -si, -sum.

backs, they turn their, terga dant,
  dĕderunt.
band, man-us, -ūs, *f.*
banish, I, civitate pello, expello ;
  in exilium pello, ĕre, pepuli,
  pulsum, *or* exigo, ĕre, exēgi, ex-
  actum : *banishment,* exilium, *n.*
bank, ripa, *f.*
banquet, a, epul-ae, -arum, *f.*
barbarian, a, barbar-us, -i, *m.*
barbarous, superl. of crudelis.
  (**57,** *a.*)
base (adj.), turpis.
baseness, turpitud-o,-inis, *f.* ; *the
  baseness of,* = *how base it is.*
  (**174,** *e.*)
battle, proelium, *n.*
battle, in, in acie.
bear, I, fero, ferre, tuli, latum.
beautiful, pul-cher,-chrior,-cherri-
  mus. (See Voc. 9, *n.*)
because, quia, quod, etc. (Intr.
  59, *d.*)
become, I, fio, fieri, factus.
becomes (*us*), *it,* (nos) decet (**234**) ;
  or gen. with est. (**291,** *Obs.* 4.)
befall, to, accĭ-dĕre, -di (*dat.*).
before (adv.), antea ; antehac ;
  ante (**322**) ; (*prep.*), ante (*acc.*).
before long, = *soon* or *shortly.*
beg, I, rogo, oro, etc. (See *ask.*)
begin, I, in-cipio, ĕre, -cēpi, -cep-
  tum ; coepi (*I begin*) (*mostly
  modal*), coeptum est (**219**) ; *often
  expressed by imperf. tense* (**184**) ;
  begin anew, redintegro, are
  (*acc.*) ; *begin with.* (**332.** 1, *f.*)
beginning, the, initium, *n.*
behalf of, on, pro (*abl.*).
behave, I, me gero, ĕre, gessi, gestum (*with adv.*). (See **241.**)
behold, I, a-spicio, ĕre,-spexi,-spec-
  tum.
belief, a, opini-o, -onis, *f.*

believe, I, cred-o, ĕre, -idi, -itum :
  with dat. = *I trust.* (**248.**)
belong to the class of, I, unus sum
  ex. (**529,** *f.*)
beneficial, salutaris ; utilis.
benefit you, I, tibi prosum, pro-
  desse, profui.
beseech, I, oro, are. (**118.**)
besiege, I (*blockade*), ob-sideo, ēre,
  -sedi, sessum ; (*by actual attack*),
  oppugno, are.
best, the very. (**529,** *d.*)
bestow (*these things on you*), *I,* haec
  tibi larg-ior, īri, -itus.
betake myself to, I, me confero ad.
betray, I, pro-do, ĕre, -didi,
  -ditum ; *betrayers,* = *those who
  had betrayed.* (See **175.**)
better, for the, in melius.
better, it would have been, satius,
  melius fuit. (**153.**)
between. (**331,** 10.)
bewail, I, comploro, are.
bid, I, ju-beo, ēre, -ssi, -ssum.
  (**120.**)
bidding, at the, jussu. (**269,** *Obs.*)
Bill, a, rogati-o,-onis, *f.*
bind myself, I, me obstrin-go, ĕre,
  -xi.
black (metaph. of crime), simply
  tantus ; *or* tam atrox.
blame, culpa, *f.*
blame, I, vitupero, are ; reprehen-
  do, ĕre, -di, -sum.
blessing, a, bonum, *n.* (**51,** *c.*)
blind, caecus.
blockade, I. (See *besiege.*)
blood, sangui-s, -nis, *m.* ; cru-or,
  ōris, *m.* ; *so much.* (**295,** *c.*)
bloodshed, caed-es, -is, *f.*
bloody, cruentus.
blow, a (metaph.), calamit-as, -atis, *f.*
blunder, err-or, -oris, *m.*
blush at, or *for, I,* me pudet, *with
  inf.* (**202**) *or gen.* (**309**).
boast, I make a, glorior, ari.
body, the whole, universi. (**380,** *b.*)
  (See note under *all.*)
body-guard, a, satell-es, -itis, *m.*
boldly, audacter ; ferociter ; *often
  adj.* (**61**), ferox.[1]

---

[1] *Ferox* is not used in the sense of "ferocious ;" it denotes "high spirit" carried to
excess.

book, a, lib-er, -ri, m.
born, natus (nascor).
born and brought up, natus educa-
tusque.
both, uterque ; ambo. (See 378.)
both . . . and, et . . . et, vel . . .
vel (p. 14, n.).
bound, I am (in duty) (p. 143,
note).
bow to, I (metaph.), obsequor, i
(dat.).
boy, pu-er, -eri.
boy, from a, or from boyhood, a
puero ; when used of more than
one, a pueris.
boyhood, in. (63.)
brand (you) with dishonour, I,
ignominiae notam (tibi) in-uro,
ĕre, -ussi, -ustum.
brandish, I, jacto, are.
brave (adj.), fort-is, -e ; adv. fortiter.
brave the worst, I, ultima ex-perior,
iri, -pertus.
break, I (metaph.), violo, are.
break my word, I, fidem fallo, ĕre,
fefelli, falsum.
break up, I (trans.), dissipo, are.
break up, I (intrans.), dissipor,
ari.
breathing space. (399. Obs. 2.)
bribery, ambit-us, -ūs,¹ m.
brigand, a, latr-o, -onis, m.
bring, I, duco, ĕre, duxi, ductum.
bring (you this), I, hoc tibi af-fero,
ferre, attuli, allatum.
bring back word, I, renuntio, are.
bring (a person) before you, I, ad
te ad-duco, ĕre, etc.
bring credit to, = be creditable to.
(260, 3.)
bring forward, I (a law), fero,
ferre, tuli.
bring help, I, opem fero, ferre,
etc.
bring loss on you, I, tibi damnum
in-fero, ferre, -tuli, illatum.
bring out (persons), I, pro-duco,
ĕre.
bring (cause) punishment to. (260,
3.)

bring (my speech) to an end, I,
finem facio with gen. of gerund.
bring under, I, facio, with gen. of
jus (juris), or arbitrium. (See
290, Obs.)
bring up, I (of supplies, etc.), sub-
ve-ho, ĕre, -xi, -ctum ; sup-
porto, are ; of soldiers, adduco,
ĕre.
bringer of a message, I am the,
nuntio, are.
broad, latus.
brother, frat-er, -ris.
brought up (= bred), educatus
(educo, are).
bugbears, terrores, m. pl. ; terri-
cula, n. pl. (Livy).
burden (of administering), use res
laboriosissima in appos. (222,
Obs.)
burdensome, molestus ; gravis.
business, the, res, rei, f.
but, sed ; verum (emphatic).
butcher, I, trucido, are.
bystander, bystanders, use adsto or
circumsto. (See 71, 73, 175.)

calamity, calamit-as, -atis, f.
call away, I, avoco, are
call to me, I, ad me voco, convoco,
are ; call to mind, see recall.
called, I am, vocor, ari. (7.)
calm (adj.), tranquillus.
calmly, acquo animo.
camp, castr-a, -orum, n. pl.
campaign, = year, ann-us, -i, m.
campaign was disastrous, was
prosperous, res infeliciter (-is-
sime), prospere, gesta est.
can, I, possum, posse, potui.
candid, liber.
candidate for, I am a, pet-o, ĕre,
-ivi, -ii, -itum. (22, 23.)
Cannae, of, Cannensis. (58.)
cannot, I, nequ-eo, ire, -ivi, -ii.
caprice, libid-o, -inis, f.
care, cura, f.
care, free from, securus.
care to, I, volo, velle, volui.
careful for (your safety), I am,
tibi caveo. (248.)

¹ Ambio, lit. "I go round," or "I canvass;" hence for illegal canvassing or bribery.

carry across, *I*, transporto, are. (**229**, *Obs.*)

carry on, *I*, = *I wage*, gero, ĕre, gessi, gestum.

carry out, *I*, exsequor ; conficio.

carry out of the country, *I*, exporto, are.

Carthage, C[K]arthag-o, *loc.* -ini.

case, in our, in nobis ("*in us*").

case, it is the, fit ut. (**123.**)

cast, *I*, conjicio, ĕre, etc.

catch, *I*, capio.

cause, a, causa, *f.*

cause (*loss*), *I*, infero, ferre, etc.

cause (*panic*), *I*, injicio, ĕre, etc., *with acc. and dat.*

cause of, *I am the*, per me fit ut, stat quominus. (**131.**)

cause to be thrown open, *I*. (See *I open*.)

caution, want of, temeritas, -atis, *f.*

caution, with, caut-e, -ius.

cavalry, equit-es, -um, *m. pl.*

cease, *I*, de-sino, ĕre, -ivi, -ii, -itum ; or de-sisto, ĕre, -stiti.

certain, certus.

certain (*victory*), exploratus.

certain, as, pro certo. (**240**, *Obs.*)

certain, I am, certo (*adv.*) scio, -ire.

certainly (= *I grant that*), sane.

centre of, the. (**60.**)

centre (*of army*), media (**60**) aci-es, -ei.

centurion, centuri-o, -onis, *m.*

chain (*general term*), vinculum, *n.*, and see *fetters*.

Chance (*personified*), Fortuna, *f.*

chance, by mere, forte ac casu. (**268.**)

change, *I* (*trans.*), muto, commuto, are (see **20, 21**) ; (*intrans.*), mutor, ari.

change of purpose, inconstantia, *f.*

change of sides, transIti-o, -onis, *f.*

channel, fretum, *n.*

character, often turned (*as in Ex.* 22) *by a dependent clause*. (See **174.**)

character (*natural*), ingenium,[1] *n.*

character (*good*), virt-us, -utis, *f.* (See *note*.)

character (*mode of life*), mor-es, -um, *m.* (See *note*.)

character, highest, optimi mores ; virtus summa.

character, of the same, as, talis, . . . qualis. (See **84**.)

characteristic of, it is the. (**291**, *Obs.* **4**.)

charge, a (*of troops*), impet-us, ūs, *m.*

charge, I make a, inva-do, ĕre, -si, -sum (in) ; impetum facio (in).

charged, I am (*with*), in crimen venio (*gen.*).

charm (*subst.*), dulced-o, -inis, *f.*

chastisement on, I inflict, animadvert-o, ĕre, -i, in (*acc.*).

check, I keep in (*temper, etc.*), moderor, ari (**249**) ; (*troops*), continue-o, ĕre, -ui.

cheer, a, clam-or, -oris, *m.*

cheer, I am of good. (**303**, *Obs.* **2**.)

cheer on, *I*, hortor, ari ; adhortor.

cheerful, hilaris.

cheerfully, facile.

cherish, *I*, tueor, ēri.

choose to, *I* (*or like*), mihi libet. (**246.**)

choose (*for*), *I*, e-ligo, ĕre, -legi, -lectum. (See **259**, *note*.)

chief, a (*chieftain*), regul-us, -i.

chief (*chief man*), *a*, prin-ceps, -cipis.

child, a, pu-er, -eri.

children (*offspring*), liber-i, -orum.

circumstance, res, rei, *f.*

circumstances (*I yield to*), temp-us, -oris, *n.* (**292, 7.**)

citadel, arx, arcis, *f.*

city, urb-s, -is, *f.*

civilisation, I advance in, humani- or fio.

---

[1] *Ingenium* (*ingigno*), "natural gifts," mostly used of *intellectual* as *indoles* of natural moral gifts : *ingenium moresque* sometimes expresses the whole idea of "character" as natural and acquired by habit. *Ingenium* often = "abilities," "genius," as distinct from *indoles* or *virtus*. It is never used in the plural of a single person : once Cicero joins the two words, *summa ingenii indoles*, "the highest natural gifts." When "character"=good character, *virtus* should be used.

claim, I have a, debeo.

clamour for, I, flagito, are (*acc.*).

class, gen-us, -ĕris, *n. ; of his class,* sui generis.

clear, certus ; manifestus.

clear as, as, clari-or, -us. (276.)

clear, it is, appar-et, ēre, -uit (see 46, *c*); *or* manifestum est.

clear (myself) of, I, (me) purgo, are, de (306, *Obs.*), *or with abl. simply.*

clemency, clementia, *f. ; adj.* clemens.

client, my, hic. (338, *Obs.* 1.) *Clitus,* Clit-us, -i.

close (friend), superl. of amicus. (55.)

close, I (shut up), interclu-do, ĕre, -si, -sum.

close at hand, prope ; haud procul.

close to. (331, 13 *or* 19.)

closely resembling, use superl. of similis.

clothing, vestīt-us, ūs, *m.*

coast along, I, (nave) praeter-vehor, i, -vectus (*acc.*). *With* praetervehor, nave *and* equo *are often omitted.*

cold (subst.), frig-us, -oris, *n.*

colleague, collēga, -ae, *m.*

collision (with), I come into, con-fligo, ĕre, -flixi, -flictum (cum).

colony, colonia, *f.*

combination, in, conjuncti.

comfort, commoda, *n. pl.*

command (an army), I, praesum (*dat.*, 251) ; duco.

command myself, I, mihi impero, are.

commander (of garrison, etc.), praelectus. (408.)

commanders (general sense), = *those who lead* (duco).

commencement of, initium, *n. or part. pass. of* incipio. (See 417, 1.)

commit, I (a crime), com-mitto, ĕre, etc. ; facio.

commit a fault, I, pecco, are. (25.)

common (belonging to many), communis ; *common to you and me,* communis tibi mecum.

commonwealth, respublica.

communicate to, I (=*I impart to*), communico, are, cum. (253, iv.)

community (civil), civit-as, -atis, *f.*

companions, his, sui. (349, *Obs.*)

compare, I, con-fero, ferre (cum).

compassion, misericordia, *f.*

compel, I, cogo, ĕre, coēgi, coactum.

competent, I am, = *I am able.*

competition for, contenti-o, -onis, *f.* (*with gen.*, 300).

complain, make complaints, I, queror, i, questus ; conqueror.

compliments to, I pay, collaudo. (25.)

comply with, I, ob-sequor (*dat.*). (See 253, i.)

compulsion, under, coactus (cogo).

comrades, his. (See *companions.*)

conceal, I, celo, are. (See 230.)

concerning (prep.), de (*abl.*).

concerns, it, pertinet (253, iv.) ad ; *used with inf.*

condemn, I, condemno, are. (306, 307.)

condemnation, condemnati-o, -onis, *f.*

condign (punishment), gravissimus.

condition (lot), fortuna, *f.; (term),* conditi-o, -onis, *f.; condition of slavery.* (58.)

conduct myself (of soldiers), I, rem gero.

conference (with), I have a, col-loquor, i, -locutus, (cum).

confess, I, fateor, ēri, fassus : confiteor, ēri, -fessus.

confidence, fiducia, *f.; I put confidence in,* con-fido, ĕre, -fisus (282, *Obs.*) ; fidem (tibi) habeo.

confiscate, I, publico, are.

confusion, trepidati-o, -onis, *f.*

confusion reigns, etc. ; use impers. pass. of trepido, are. (See 218.)

congratulate you on this, I, hoc (*acc.*), hanc rem, *or* ob nanc rem, *or* de hac re, tibi gratulor, ari.

conquer, I, vinco, ĕre, vici, victum.

conqueror, the, vict-or, -oris.

conscience, with a good. (See 64.)

consciousness, sens-us, -ūs, *m.*

consent (subst.), consens-us, -ūs, *m.*

consent to, I (modal verb), volo.

consider, I, arbitror, ari. (See note under *fancy.*)

considerations, all, = everything.
(53, 54.)

considering, ut in (492, v. b);
considering the greatness of, ut in
with tantus. (332, 5, h.)

consist of, I, consto, are, e, ex.

consolation, is a great, magno est
solatio (dat.). (260, 3.)

conspire, I (against), conjuro, are
(contra) (acc.).

conspirator, turn by qui with verb.
(175.)

Constantinople, Constantinopolis,
acc. -im, loc. -i.

constantly, semper or nunquam non.

constitution, the, respublica. (See
292, Obs. and note.)

constitutional ; unconstitutional, e
republica (332, 4) ; contra rempublicam.

consul, cons-ul, -ulis.

consulship, consulat-us, -ūs, m.

consult, I (= I ask the opinion of),
consul-o, ĕre, -ui, -tum (with acc.).

consult the good or interest of, I,
consulo, with dat. (See 248.)

consummate. (See statesman.)

contemporary, a, aequalis. (51, a.)

contempt for, contemptus, -ūs, m.
(with gen., 300.)

contemptible, far from, haud (169,
n.) contemnendus (393).

content with, I am, contentus sum
(abl.).

contest, a, certam-en, inis, n. ; or
use impers. pass. of certo, are.
(218.)

continent, the, continen-s, -tis (sc.
terra).

contrary (adj.), contrarius.

contrary to, contra quam. (491, b.)

convenience, commoda, n. pl.

conversation, I have, col-loquor, i,
-locutus.

converse (with), I, colloquor, i (cum)
(of two or more, inter se, 354).

convinced, I am, = I am persuaded.
(See 122, b.)

convinced of this, I am, or feel, hoc
mihi persuasum habeo. (240.)

corn, frumentum, n.

Cortes, Cortesi-us, -i.

cost, I, consto (280, Obs.); costs too
much, it, nimio constat.

council, a, consilium, n.

count, I (number), numero, are.

count, I (= I hold), habeo ; duco.

count among, I. (240, Obs. 2.)

countenance, vult-us, ūs, m.

country (one's), patria, f. (see 16,
a) ; (the), respublica.

country (territory), fin-es, -ium, m.
(See 16, a.)

country (as distinct from the town),
rus, ruris, n. (see 16, a) ; in the
country, ruri.

countryman, civ-is, -is.

courage, virt-us, -utis, f. ; constantia, f. ; fortitud-o, -inis, f.

courage, a man of. (58, Obs.)

courage, I show. (241.)

courage to, I have the, = I venture (25) ; audeo, ere, ausus.

course, I take this, haec facio ; hanc
rationem ineo.

course which, a, id quod. (67.)

court, the, judicium, n.

cover, I (with armies or fleets), infestum habeo. (240.)

coward, timidus, ignavus ; cowards,
ignavi.

cowardice, ignavia, f. ; timidit-as,
-atis, f.

cowardly, ignavus ; timidus.

crave for, I, desidero, are (acc.)
(mostly for what I have had and
have lost) ; in Ex. 48 B use
appeto, ĕre.

craving (partic.) for, appetens (with
gen.). (302.)

credible, it is scarcely, vix credi
potest. (200, Obs.)

credit, a, or creditable, it is. (260, 3.)

crime, a, facin-us, -oris, n. ; flagitium, n. ; scelus,[1] -eris, n. ; delictum, n. (See note.)

---

[1] *Scelus*, a crime ; offence against a fellow-creature, ἀδίκημα ; also the guilt which causes overt crimes, ἀδικία ; *vitium*, a fault, that which marks imperfection ; *peccatum*, a sin or offence which deserves blame or punishment ; *delictum*, an omission, or con-travention, of some duty ; *flagitium*, a crime as a breach of duty towards oneself ; *facinus*, an act of heinous crime (sometimes a great exploit) ; *nequitia*, wickedness in the sense of " worthlessness.'

criminal, sceleratus.
criminally, nefarie.
crisis, a, discrim-en, -inis, n. ;
  temp-us, oris, n.
critical moment (such a), use simply
  tempus, or occasio.
cross, I, trajicio, ĕre.
crowd, a, multitud-o, -inis, f.
crowd, to (intrans.), congregari.
crowds, in. (61.)
crown (kingly), regnum, n. (See 17.)
crown (circlet), corona, f.
cruel, crudelis, e.
cruelly, crudel-iter, -ius, -issime.
cruelty, crudelit-as, -atis, f.; I show,
  saev-io, ire, -ii, itum.
crush, I, op-primo, ĕre, -pressi,
  -pressum ; crushed (pass. part.),
  oppressus.
crushing (calamity), use tantus or
  tantus tamque gravis.
cry, I raise a, conclamo, are.
cultivated, to be (= sought for),
  expetendus.
custom, a, mos, moris, m.
cut off, I (destroy), ab-sumo, ĕre, etc.
cut off (destroyed), I am, intereo, ire.

dagger, pugi-o, -onis, m.
daily, quotidie ; with comparatives
  and certain verbs, in dies. (See
  328, c.)
danger, periculum, n.
danger was (of), the. (138.)
dangerous, periculosus.
Danube, the, Danubius, m.
dare, see venture: daring (adj.),
  audax.
daringly, audacit(act)-er, -ius.
dark (metaph. applied to crime),
  atrox.
dark, I keep you in the, te celo, are
  (acc., 230, or de ; 231).
darkness, tenebrae, f. pl.
dart, a, jaculum, n. ; telum, n.
dash (of), a, non nihil. (294.)
dash into, I, me im-mitto, ĕre, -misi, in.
dash over, I (intrans., see 20, 21),
  in-fundor, i, -fusus (dat.).
date, temp-us, -oris, n.

day, di-es, -ei, m.
day after day. (328, c.)
day before, the, pridie.
day before, of the, hesternus.
day, for the, in diem.
day, in my, = in my time (pl.).
daybreak, prima lux (lucis).
deadly (hostile), infensus.
deadly (enemy). (See 55.)
dear, car-us, -ior, -issimus.
dear friends, homines amicissimi.
  (224, Obs. 2.)
death, mor-s, -tis, f.; after his. (61.)
debt, aes alienum ; gen. aeris
  alieni, n.
deceive, I, decipio, ĕre.
decide (resolve), to, or on, I, statuo ;
  constituo. (45.)
decide (pass judgment), I, or I
  decide on (a fact), judico, are.
decide (let others, etc.) (146.)
decision, I come to a, decerno, ĕre.
decision, depends on my. (292, 9.)
declare (war), I, indi-co, ĕre, -xi,
  -ctum. (253, ii.)
decline, I (trans.), detrecto, are.
decline (to), I (modal), nolo.
decree, I, de-cerno, ĕre, -crēvi,
  -cretum.
decree, a, decretum, n. (See 51, b.)
deed. (See 51, b.)
deep (of feelings), gravis.
deeper (impression). See impression.
defeat, clad-es, -is, f. ; of Cannae,
  Cannensis (adj., 58).
defend, I, defen-do, ĕre, -di, -sum.
defendant, the, iste. (338, Obs.)
defiance of, in, contra, contra quam.
  (491, b.)
defile, a, salt-us, -ûs, m.
degrading, indignus (unmerited) ;
  humilis (abject).
delay (to), I, cunctor, ari.
delay, by, gerund of cunctor. (99.)
delay, without, confestim.
deliberate, I, delibero, are.
deliberation, need of. (286.)
deliberation, with, consult-o, -ius
  (adv.).
delightful, jucundus.[1]

---

[1] Jucundus (juvicundus), that which causes joy or delight ; gratus, what s acceptable, deserves gratitude ; ista veritas etiamsi jucunda non est, mihi tamen grata est. —
(Cicero.)

demand, *I*, postulo,[1] are. (127, *c*.)
demand (*exact*) *this from you*, *I*,
hoc tibi impero, are.
demeanour, habit-us, -ūs, *m*. (*sc*.
corporis).
denied this, I am, hoc (*abl*.) carco, ēre.
denounce, *I* (*upbraid*), in-crepo, are,
-crepui.
deny, *I*, nego, are.
depart, *I* (= *go away*), ab-eo, ire,
-ii ; dis-cedo, ĕre, -cessi.
departure, *I take my*. (25.)
depend on, *I*, pendeo, ēre, e, ex.
depends on you, *this*. (331, 15.)
deplore, *I*, deploro, are.
deprecate, *I*, deprecor, ari.
deprive of, *I*, privo, are (264) ; ad-
imo, ĕre, -emi, -emptum (243).
depth of, *of the*, *use gen*. (318, *end*.)
depth of, *such a*, *use* tantus ; *or eo*
with gen. (294, *Obs*.)
descend, *I*, descend-o, ĕre, -i.
desert, *I*, deser-o, ĕre, -ui, -tum ;
destitu-o, ĕre, -i. (See note
under *abandon*.)
deserter, transfŭg-a, ae, *m*.
desertion, *use* desero, ĕre. (417, i.)
deserts, *in accordance with his*.
(490, ii. 3.)
deserve, *I*, mereor, meritus ; *also*
mere-o, ēre, -ui.
deserve well of, *I*. (332, 3, *g*.)
deservedly, merito.
deserving of, dignus. (285.)
design (*subst*.), consilium, *n*. ; *by*
design, *or designedly* (*abl*.) (268) ;
consulto (*adv*.).
desire, *I*, *am desirous to*, cupio, ĕre,
ivi (ii) ; studeo, ēre (*inf*.).
desire (*subst*.), = *that which* (*you*)
desire. (76.)
desire for, *with little*, parum appetens (*with gen*., 302).
despair, *I*, despero, are ; *of*, de (*abl*.).
despatch, *a*, litterae, *f. pl*.
desperately, atro-citer, -cius.
despicable. (See 276.)
despise, *I*, contem-no, ĕre, -psi,
-ptum ; de-spicio, ĕre, -spexi,
-spectum. (See Voc. 10, *note*.)

despot, domin-us, -i.
despotism, dominium, *n*.
destitution, egest-as, -atis, *f*.
destined, fatalis, e (see Voc. 3.
n.) ; *for or to*, ad. (331, 1, *e*.)
destiny, fatum, *n*.
destroy, *I*, exsci-ndo, ĕre, -di,
-ssum.
destruction (*general sense*), exitium,
n. ; pernici-es, -ei, *f*.; (*massacre*),
interneci-o,- onis, *f*.
destruction of (*tends to the*). (See
. 292, *Obs*.)
detach (*troops*), *I*, = *I send*.
detain, *I*, re-tineo, ēre, -tinui.
determine on, I, decerno, ĕre (*inf*., 45).
detraction, obtrectati-o. -onis, *f*.
detrimental, *it is*. (260, 3.)
devastate, *I*, vasto, are.
devote myself to, I, operam do (*dat*.);
or (*stronger*), in-cumbo, ĕre,
-cubui, in. (253, iv.)
devoted to, studiosus (*gen*., 301, ii.).
dictate terms to you, *I*, leges tibi
impono.
dictator, dictat-or, -oris.
die, *I*, mor-ior, -i (-tuus est), vitā
excessit. (See Voc. 7, *note*.)
die out of, *to* (*metaphor*), ex-cīdĕre,
-cīdi, e, ex.
difference between, *there is this* (331.
10); *there is all the*. (92.)
difference, *it makes no*, nihil interest
(166); *to us*, nostrā (310, i.).
different, alius ; *to*, ac. (91 ; see
also 92, and 370, 371.)
different times, *at*, alius alio tempore. (371.)
differently to, aliter ac. (491, *b*.)
difficult, difficilis.
difficulty in persuading, *I find a*,
= *I persuade this* (illud) *with*
difficulty (aegre).
difficulty, *with*, aegre ; vix ; diffi-
culter, *comp*. difficilius.
din, strepit-us, -ūs, *m*.
dire, *use* tantus.
directions, *in both*, utrimque ; *in*
different, opposite, diversi. (61 ;
and see also 371, and *caution*.)

---

1 *Posco*, I " call for," make a sharp, peremptory demand ; often used of what is unjust
postulo, I claim in accordance with, or as though in accordance with, what is right.

disaffected, I am, male seutio.

disagree with, I, dissen-tio, irc, -si ab or cum.

disagreement on, dissensi-o, -onis, *f.* (*with gen.*, **300**).

disappear, I (=*I am destroyed*), ex-tinguor, i, -tinctus.

disappoint, I. (**332, 3**, *b.*)

disapproval (*expressed by clamour*), acclamo,[1] are. (**415**, *b.*)

disaster, cas-us,[2] -us, *m.*; calamit-as, -atis, *f.*

disastrous, most, use the adv., infeliciter, -issime. (**218**, *Obs.*)

discharge the duties of, I, fung-or, i, -ctus. (**281**.)

discipline, disciplina, *f.*

discontinue, I, inter-mitto, ĕre, misi. (See note under *undone, I leave.*)

discussion, by, in, gerund of dissero, ĕre. (**99**.)

disdain to, I, dedignor, ari.

disease, a, morbus, i, *m.*

disembark, I. (**331, 24**, *a.*)

disgrace, ignominia, *f.*

disgraceful, turpis, e. (See **57**.)

disgraceful, it is. (**260, 3**, and *Obs.* 1.)

disheartened, I am. (See **118**, *example.*)

dishonour (*subst.*), ignominia, *f.*

dishonourable, inhonest-us; *adv.*, -e.

dishonourable, it is. (**260, 3**.)

dislike, I somewhat, haud multum amo.

disloyal, infidus.

dismayed, I am, perterreor, ēri.

dismiss, I, dimitto, ere.

dispense with, I, careo, ĕre (**284**); or carere volo.

disperse, to (*intrans.*), di-labi, -lapsus. (See **20**.)

displease, I, displiceo, ēre (*dat.*).

disposed to (*a quality*), *use comparative of adj.* (**57**, *b.*)

dissatisfied with oneself, one is, sui poenitet.

dissemble, I (=*I hide*), dissimulo, are.

distance, from a, e longinquo.

distance from, I am at a, absum. (**318**.)

distant, longinquus.

distasteful, ingratus.

distinction (*mark of difference*), discrim-en, -inis, *n.*

distinction (*honourable*), hon-os, -oris, *m.*

distinguished (*adj.*), praeclarus (*sup.*, **224**).

district, ag-er, -ri, *m.*

distrust, I, dif-fido, ĕre, -fisus. (**244**, *c.*)

ditch, fossa, *f.*

divine, divinus.

do, I, facio, ĕre, feci, factum.

doer, the, = *he who committed*, facio, committo.

doom, fatum, *n.*

doomed to, I am, destīnor, ari, *with dat. or ad.*

doors, for-es, -um, *f.*

Doria, Doria, *f.*

doubt, I am in (=*I doubt*), dubito, are.

down from, de (*abl.*).

down-trodden, afflictus.

drag (*to prison*), *I*, tra-ho, ĕre, -xi, -ctum, in.

draw, I (=*I drag*), traho, ĕre.

draw up, I (*a law*), scribo.

draw up, I (*soldiers*), instru-o, ĕre, -xi, -ctum.

dread, I, reformido, are.

dreadful, atrox.

dress, vest-is, -is, *f.* (**303**, *Obs.* 2.)

drive from, I, ex-igo, ĕre, -ēgi, -actum; pello, ĕre, pepuli, pulsum.

drive on shore, to, ejicĕre, ejēci, ejectum.

drowned (*metaph. of words*). (**332, 6**, *b.*)

dull, I, hebĕto, are; afficio.

duration (*its future*). = *how lasting* (diuturnus) *it will*, or *would, be.* (**174**.)

duty, it is my, debeo. (**198**.)

duty of, it is the, use gen. (**291**.)

---

[1] *Acclamo* always in Cicero of disapproval; in later writers, of approval.

[2] *Casus*, properly an accident, that which *falls* out, is mostly used in a bad sense, as misfortune or disaster; but is not so strong a word as *calamitas*.

duty (*as opposed to expediency*), honest-as, -atis, *f.* ; *or* honesta, *n. pl.* (51, *c*)

dwelling, domicilium, *n.*

each and every, unus quisque. (529, *c.*)

each other, one another, alius alium; *of two*, alter alterum (see 371, iv.); inter se (354).

eager for, cupidus (*gen.*, 301, i.).

eager to, I am, gest-io, ire, -ii.

early manhood. (See *manhood*.)

earlier (*adv.*), maturius.

earlier than (=*before*), ante. (331, 3.)

earliest, =*first.*

earnestly, magnopere.

earnestly implore, I, oro atque obsecro (127, *a*). *Notice double phrase equivalent to English adverb.*

ears, with my own. (355, *d.*)

earth, the, tell-us, -uris, *f.*

easy, facilis.

easily (*readily*), facile ; nullo negotio (*without effort*).

echo with, to, person-are, -ui (*abl.*).

effect, I, efficio, ěre.

effect on, I have but little, parum valeo apud.

eight, octo (*indecl.*).

eighteenth. (530.)

either . . . or, aut . . . aut ; vel . . . vel (p. 14, *note*).

elected, I am, fi-o, -ěri, factus.

eloquence, eloquentia, *f.*

else, or, aut (p. 14, *n.*).

embark, I (*intrans.*), navem conscend-o, ěre, -i.

emergency, temp-us, -oris, *n.; in the present*, see, for *in*, 273, *Obs.*, and for *present*, 337.

emotion, with, commot-e, -ius.

Emperor, Imperat-or, -oris.

empire, imperium, *n.*

empty, inanis.

enacted, I get (*a law*), per-fero, -ferre, -tuli.

encamp, I, castra pono, ěre.

encourage, I, co-, *or* ad-hortor, ari (*acc. and* ut, 118).

encouragement, words of, adhortantis vox. (415, *c.*)

encounter, I (*death*), oppeto, ere, -ii, -ivi, -itum ; *evil*, exper-ior, iri, -tus.

end, fin-is, -is, *m.* (*rarely f.*).

endanger, I, periclitor, ari (*dep.*).

endeavour, I, conor, ari.

endure, I, per-fero, ferre, -tuli.

enemy (*private*), inimicus.

enemy (*public*), host-is, -is.

energy, with some want of, paulo (279) remissius.

engage (*an enemy*), *I*, con-gredior, i, -gressus, cum.

engage in, I (= *I take part in*), intersum 251); *in battle*, praelium committo, ěre ; *in conflict*, manus conser-o, ěre, -ui, -tum.

England (*the people*), Angli. (See 319.)

engrafted, insitivus.

enjoy, I, fru-or, i, -ctus (281); *the friendship of*, amico utor (282); *praise, etc.*, flor-eo, ěre, -ui (*abl.*).

enjoy happiness, I, beatus sum.

enmity, inimicitia, *f.*

enormity, flagitium, *n.* (See note under *crime*.)

enormous, such, tantus.

enough and to spare, satis superque (*with gen.*, 294).

entail this upon you, I, hoc tibi in-*or* af-fero. (252.)

enter, I, in-gredior, i, -gressus ; venio, ire, in.

enter political life, I. (See *political life*.)

enterprise. (See 54.)

enthusiasm, alacrit-as, atis, *f.*

entire innocence. (See *innocence*.)

entirely, totus (*with verbs*, 61) ; *for adjs.*, *use superl.*

entreat, I, oro, are. (127, *a.*)

entreat for, earnestly, I, flagito, are. (127, *d.*)

entreaty, obsecrati-o, -onis, *f.*

entrust, I. (See *intrust.*)

enumerate, I, enumero, are.

envoy (*embassy*), legati-o, -onis, *f.*

envy, I, in-video, ěre, -vidi, -visum (*dat.*). (See 5.)

equal to, use tantus . . . quantus. (490, i.)

err, I, erro, errare.

error, err-or, -oris, *m. ; or* errare.[1]
(**94, 99**.)

escape, *I*, ef-fugio, ĕre, -fūgi.

establish, *I*, stabil-io, ire, -ivi.

estimate, *I*, aestimo, are. (**305.**)

eternal, sempiternus.

evade (*shirk*), *I*, subterfugio, ĕre
(*acc.*) ; *a law*, legi fraudem facio.

even, etiam ; quoque (*enclitic*) ;
before adj., vel ; *not even*, ne . . .
quidem. (Intr. **99**.)

even now (*i.e. at the present time*),
hodie.

evening, in the, vesperi.

events, at all, certe. (See note
under *least, at.*)

ever (*always*), semper ; *with negat.*
(= *at any time*), unquam.

every (= *all, pl.*), omnis ; *everything*, omnia, *n. pl.* (**53.**)

evident, it was, (satis) apparebat.
(**46,** *c.*)

evil, an, incommodum, *n.* ; malum,
n. (**51,** *b*

exact from, *I* (*make requisition of*),
impero, are. (**247.**)

exact (*punishment*), *I*, sum-o, ĕre,
-psi, ab, de *or* ex.

exasperate, I, irrīto, are.

excellent, optimus, a, um (see **57,**
a) ; *for use with proper noun or
person see* **224.**

except to, nisi ut.

exception, without, = *all.*

excessive, nimius.

exchange for, *I*, muto, are ; per-
muto, are. (See **280.**)

exclaim, I, ex- *or* con-clamo, are.

execrable (*by*), *considered*, execra-
bilis (*with dat.*).

execution (*punishment*), supplicium,
n.

exertion, I make (*some*), (paulum)
ad-nitor, i, -nisus.

exertions, = *toils.*

exhausted, fatigatus ; confectus ; *I
am, or become*, fatigor, ari.

exhort, I, hortor, ari. (**118.**)

exile, an, ex-ul, -ulis.

exile, I am driven into, in exilium
pellor. (See *banish.*)

exile, I am in, or I endure, exŭlo,
are.

exist, I, sum, esse, fui. (Intr. 49, *Obs.*)

existence, use sum (*no Latin subst.*) ;
est Deus = *God exists.*

expect, I, expecto, are.

expedient, utilis.

expediency, utilit-as, -atis, *f.*

experience, I, exper-ior, iri, -tus.

experience of life, rerum peritia, *f.*

experienced (*adj.*), (rerum) peritus.
(**301**, ii.)

explain, I, expono, ĕre, etc.

exploit, res gesta.

expose, I (*to danger, etc.*), ob-jicio,
ĕre. (**253,** ii.)

expose, I (*confute*), coargu-o, ĕre, -i.

express myself, to, ut dicam. (**100,**
note.)

extent. (**174,** *b.*)

extortion, res repetundae, *f. pl.*

extreme, extremus.

extremely, use superl. of adj.

extremity of, extremus (*adj.*). (**60.**)

exult in, I, exulto, are (*abl.*).

eye, ocul-us, -i, *m.*

eyes, with my own, ipse (**355,** *d*) ;
before our (**332,** 5, *c*).

face, I (*meet*), obviam eo, ire
(*dat.*).

face, I (*put to the proof*), ex-perior,
iri, -pertus.

face, faci-es, ei, *f.* ; *in the face of,*
in (*with abl.*, **273,** *Obs.*)

fact, a, res, rei, *f.*

faction, a, facti-o, -onis, *f.*

fail, I (*am wanting to*), deficio, ĕre
(*used absolutely or with acc.*) ;
desum (*dat.*, **251**). (See note
under *abandon.*)

fain, I would; or I would fain have
(*done*), velim, vellem. (See **149,** i.)

fair (*adj.*), pulcher ; amoenus.
(Voc. **9,** *note.*)

fair (= *fair amount of*), satis.
(**294.**)

faith, good, fid-es, -ei, *f.*

faith in you, I put, fidem tibi
habeo.

faithful, fidelis, e.

---

[1] *Errare*, error generally, in the abstract ; *error*, an error or blunder.

fall, I (*in battle*), pereo, ire, ii.

fall into, I, in-cido, ĕre, -cidi, in (*acc.*) ; *or* praecipito, are (*fall headlong*) ; *into ruin,* corru-o, ĕre, -i.

fallen, afflictus.

falls out, it, accidit ut.

falls to (*my*) *lot.* (See *lot.*)

false (*of persons*), mend-ax, -acis ; (*of things*), falsus ; fictus.

false to, I am, de-sum (*dat.,* 251). (See note under *abandon.*)

falsehood, a, mendacium, *n.*

falsehood (*abstract*), mentiri. (98, *a.*)

falsehood, I tell a ; I speak falsely, ment-ior, iri, -itus. (54.)

fame, gloria, *f.*

family, familia, *f. ; his family,* sui. (349, *Obs.*)

family (*adj.*), domesticus.

famine, fam-es, -is, *f.*

famous, praeclarus. (19.)

fancy, I, puto,[1] are ; opinor, ari.

far, by, multo. (279.)

far from (*adv.*), parum.

far removed from, alienus (*superl.*) ab.

fare (*subst.*), vict-us, -ūs, *m.*

fare, I, mihi evĕnit (*impers.*).

farmhouse, villa, *f.*

fatal, pernicios-us, -issimus ; funestus. (Voc. 3, *note.*)

Fate, Fortuna (*personified*).

father, pat-er, -ris.

fatigue, lassitud-o, -inis, *f.*

fault, culpa, *f.*

fault, I commit a, pecco, are. (25.)

favour (*kindness*), *a,* beneficium, *n.*

favour, I, făveo, ĕre, făvi, fautum (*dat.,* 5).

favour, I do you this, hoc (*acc.,* 237) tibi gratificor, ari.

favour, I win your, apud te gratiam ineo, ire.

favourable (*suitable*), idoneus.

fawn upon, I, adulor, ari. (253, iii.)

fear, met-us, -ūs, *m.* ; tim-or, -oris, *m.*

fear, I,[2] metu-o, ĕre, -i ; vereor, ĕri, verĭtus (see 138, 139) ; *I fear,* or *have fears, for,* metuo *with dat.* (248).

fear for my safety, I, saluti meae dif-fido, ĕre, -fisus.

feasting (*subst.*), epulae, *f. pl.*

features, vult-us, -ūs (*sing.*).

feel, I, sen-tio, ire, -si, -sum.

feelings, anim-us, -i, *m.*

fellow-subject, civ-is, -is, *m.*

ferocity (*of an act*), atrocit-as, -atis, *f.*

fertile, fertilis, e.

fetters, catenae, *f. pl.*

few, pauci, ae, a ; perpauci (*very few*).

fickle, lĕvis.

fictitious, fictus.

field of battle, aci-es,[3] -ei, *f.*

field, in the (*in war*), militiae, *opposed to* domi. (312.)

fiercely (*boldly*), ferociter ; acriter.

fifth, quintus.

fight, I, pugno, are ; *a battle,* praelium com-mitto, ĕre, -misi, -missum.

fill with (*panic*), *I,* in-cutio, ĕre, -cussi, -cussum. (Ex. 53, note.)

find, I, reper-io, ire, -i, -tum (*by search*) ; in-venio, ire, -vĕni, -ventum (*by chance*).

find fault with, I, vitupero, are.

fine, pulcher. (Voc. 9, *note.*)

finish, I, con-ficio, ĕre, -feci, -fectum.

fire and sword, ferrum et ign-is (*abl.* -i). (See Voc. 1, *note.*)

firm, constans.

first (*adv.*) ; *first . . . then ; first . . . secondly, etc.* (534, and *Obs.*)

---

[1] *Puto,* "I incline to think," "I fancy," "I suspect," I think without having as yet any full clearly reasoned grounds for thinking ; *opinor,* "I conjecture," with still less clear grounds ; *reor,* rather "I calculate," "I come to a conclusion ; " *arbitror,* I form my own personal judgment ; *censeo,* I form and express a clear view or judgment.

[2] *Timere,* the feeling of fear, causing a wish to fly ; *metuere,* the sense of danger, causing us to take precautions ; *vereri,* often, to look on with respect or awe.

[3] *Acies,* the *edge* or *line* of battle, often answers to the English "field," or even "battle."

first of June, the, kalendae Juniae (538) ; *by the* (326).

first to, first who. (62.)

five, quinque.

fix (my eyes) on, I, defi-go, ĕre, -xi, -xum, in (acc.).

flag, signum, *n.*

flank, a, lat-us, -ĕris, *n. ; in.* (332, i, c.)

flatter, I, assentor, ari. (253, i.)

fleet, a, class-is, -is, *f.*

flight, fuga, *f.*

fling away, I, pro- or ab-jicio, ĕre, -jeci, -jectum.

flock (subst.), grex, gregis, *m*

flock together, to, congregari.

flourishing, opulentus (*use superl.,* 57, *a*).

flow down, I, de-fluo, ĕre, -fluxi.

fly, I, fugio, ĕre, fūgi.

foe, host-is, -is, *m.*

follow, I, sequor, i, secutus ; *follow up,* insector, ari (acc.).

follow that, it does not, non idcirco.

folly, stultitia, *f. ; or use adj.* stultus. (376.)

food, vict-us, ūs, *m.*

food, I get (of soldiers), frumentor, ari.

food, I take, cibum capio.

food, want of, inedia, *f.*

foolish, insipiens ; *it is foolish.* (291, Obs. 1.)

foot of (a mountain) īmus. (60.)

foot-soldier, ped-es, itis.

for (prep.), pro. (See 6 and 332, 7, b.)

for (conj.), nam ; enim (Intr. 98) ; quippe. (See also Intr. 56, e.)

for some time (past), jamdudum. (181.)

forage, I get, pabulor, ari.

force, vis, *f.* (abl. vi).

force of arms, by, vi et armis.

force from, I, deturbo, are, de (abl.); *force out of* (=*wrench from*), extor-queo, ĕre, -si, -tum. (257.)

forces (troops), copiae, *f. pl.*

forefathers, major-es, -um. (See Voc. 2, *n.,* and p. 63, *note* 5.)

foreign, externus.

foreigner, a (opposed to civis), peregrin-us, -i, *m*

foremost, primus.

foresee, I, praesentio ; pro-spicio, ĕre, -spexi, -spectum, pro-video, -vidi, -visum. (248.)

forest, a, silva, *f.*

foretell, I, praedī-co, ĕre, -xi, -ctum ; praesagio, ire.

forget, I, obliviscor, i, oblītus (gen., 308).

forgive, I, ignosco, ĕre, -novi, -notum (dat., see 5) ; veniam do (dat. of person, gen. of thing) ; or condono, are (dat. of person, acc. of thing).

forgotten, I become, or *I am,* in oblivionem vĕnio, ire, vēni.

form line (of battle), I, aciem instruo, ĕre, -xi, -ctum.

former, pristinus (see note under *ancient*), *often joined with* ille. (339, i.)

formidable, formidandus (393) ; *comp.* magis formidandus.

fortress, arx, arcis, *f.*

fortunate, fel-ix, -īcis.

fortunate, it was most, peroppor-tune accidit ut. (123.)

fortune, fortuna, *f. ; fortunes,* fortunae, *pl.*

fortune, good, felicit-as, -atis, *f.*

Fortune's favourites. (529, *f.*)

foul, foedus.

foully, nefarie.

found, I (a colony), de-duco, ĕre, -duxi, -ductum.

fourteen, quattuordecim.

fourth, quartus.

free (adj.), liber, a, um ; *free from,* vacuus (265) ; *free from blame,* extra culpam (331, 9) ; *free from care,* securus (19).

free, I ; I give freedom to ; or *I set at liberty (from),* libero, are, ab or abl. (264); *freed from, I am,* liberor, ari, etc.

freedom, libert-as, -atis, *f.*

freedom, in, liber. (61.)

fresh, recens.

friend, amic-us, -i (51 a, and 55, 256); *close friend,* amicissimus.

friend here, my ; your friend there. (338, Obs. 1 and 2.)

friend, I make my, amicorum in numero habeo. (240, Obs. 2.)

friendliness, benevolentia, *f.*

friendship, amicitia, *f.* ; *friendship of, I enjoy the,* amico utor. (282.)

from, a, ab (*abl.*). (332, I.)

front, in, a fronte (332, I, c); adversus, *adj* (see 61) ; *in the front of* (=*before*), ante (331, 3).

fuel, I add (*metaph.*), faces subjicio, ĕre (*dat.*)

fugitives, use pres. part. of fugio.

full (= *the whole of*), totus. (60.)

full of, plenus (*abl.*).

funds, pecuniae, *f. pl.*

funeral, fun-us, -eris, *n.*

further, ultra.

fury, ira, *f., not* furor. (Voc. 6, *note ;* see also Ex. 62, *note.*)

fury, with the utmost, vehementissime.

future, the, futura, *n. pl.* (52, 408.)

future, in, or *for, the,* in futurum ; in posterum. (331, 24, *b.*)

gain, emolumentum, *n.* ; utilit-as, -atis, *f.; (for) a source of gain,* quaestui. (260, 3.)

gain by, I, = *it is profitable to me.* (260, 3.)

gained, partus (pario, peperi, *I produce*).

gallant, fortis (*superl.*) ; *for usage with proper noun* or *word denoting a person, see* 224.

gallantly, fortiter.

gallop, at full, equo concitato.

games, the, ludi, *m. pl.*

garrison, praesidium, *n.*

gate, porta, *f.*

gather (together), to (*intrans.*), convĕnire, -vēni, -ventum ; congregari. (20.)

Gauls, the, Gall-i, -orum.

gaze on, I, intu-eor, -ēri.

general, a, dux, ducis.

general (*adj.*), = *of all.* (59.)

generally (believed), = *by most men.*

generation, a, aet-as, -atis, *f.*

Genoa, Genua, *f.*

gentle, mitis ; mitissimi ingenii (303, i.); *so gentle as* (224, *Obs.* 2).

gentlemen of the jury, judices.

gentleness, lenit-as, -atis, *f.; I show*

gentleness (241) ; *such,* tam *or* adeo mitis, etc.

gently, leniter.

German, a, German-us, -i.

Germany, Germania, *f.*

gesture, gest-us, -ūs, *m.*

get over (danger), I, fungor, i, -ctus, *or* defungor. (281.)

get ready for, I, me paro, are, *ad with gerund.* (396.)

get to, I. (See *I reach.*)

give, I, do, dăre, dĕdi, dătum ; *a verdict,* sententiam dico, ĕre : *a name,* nomen in-do, ere, -didi, -ditum ; *my word (formally),* fidem interpono, ĕre.

gladly, libenter ; or *use adj.,* libens. (61.)

globe, the, orbis terrarum, *m.*

glorious, praeclarus.

glory, gloria, *f.*

gluttony, gula, *f.* (*lit. the gullet*).

go away, I, ab-eo, ire, -ii, -iturus.

go down to meet, I, obviam (*dat.*) descend-o, ĕre, -i.

go out, I, ex-cedo, ĕre, -cessi ; exeo, ire, -ivi, -ii (*abl. with* or *without,* e, ex).

God, De-us, -i, *nom. pl.* Di.

gold, of, aureus.

good fortune, I enjoy, felix sum.

good name, existimati-o, -onis, *f.;* fama, *f.*

good old times. (339, i.)

good sense, prudentia, *f.*

good-will, benevolentia, *f.*

goodness, virt-us, -utis, *f.*

gossip, rumusculi, *m. pl.* (*diminutive of contempt*).

govern, I, praesum. (251.)

government, the. (175.)

governor (of city), praefect-us. -i.

gradually, paulatim.

grandfather, av-us, -i.

grandson, nepo-s, -tis.

gratitude, I show, gratiam re-fero, -ttuli ; *I feel,* habeo. (98. *b.*)

grateful, gratus ; *I am most grateful,* maximam habeo gratiam. (98, *b.*)

great, magnus, *comp.* major, *superl.* maximus ; *great men,* summi viri ; viri praestantissimi.

greater (= *more of*), plus. (294.)

greatly, magnopere; vehementer; maxime; *with comparatives*, multo. (279.)

greatness of (your) debt = *how much (you) owe* (debeo). (174.)

Greeks, the, Graec-i, -orum.

greet, I, saluto, are.

groans (*angry*), convīcium, n. (*sing.*).

ground, on the, humi. (312.)

ground, perilous, on which they stood, tale tempus; tantum periculum. (See Ex. 62, *note*.)

groundless, falsus.

grounds (= *reason*), causa, f.; *on grounds of*, propter. (331, 19, b.)

grow, I, = *become*.

grudge against you, I have a, tibi succens-eo, ēre, -ui.

guard, a, custo-s, -dis, m.

guard, off his, incautus. (61.)

guard, I, custod-io, ire, -ivi, -ii, -itum; *guard against*, caveo, ēre, cavi, cautum. (248.)

guest, a, hosp-es, -itis.

guide, dux, ducis.

guilt, scel-us, -eris, n. (See note under *crime*.)

guilty, nocen-s, -tis.

guilty deed, a, facin-us, -oris, n. (See note under *crime*.)

guilty, I find, condemno, are; *I am found*, condemnor.

guilty of, I am (*not*), (non) id committo ut.

habit of, I am in the, soleo, ēre, solitus (*inf.*).

hackneyed, tritus, *lit. "well worn"* (tero).

hair, white, cani capilli (*pl.*).

half as many, large, again. (535, d.)

halt, I, or come to a halt, con sisto, ēre, -stiti.

hand, a, man-us, -ūs, f.

hand, I am at, ad-sum, -esse, -fui.

hand in, I, af-fero, ferre.

hand over to, I, per-mitto, ēre, -misi. (128.)

handful of = *so small a band of*.

hang back, I, cesso,[1] are.

happens, it, accidit, ēre. (123.)

happily (see 64), deorum beneficio or peropportune accidit.

happiness, vita beata; beate vivere; beatum esse (98, b); *I enjoy* beatus sum.

happy, beatus.

hard pressed, I am, premor, i.

hard to say, difficile dictu. (404.)

hardly, vix.

hardship, incommodum, n.; *hardships*, molestiae, pl.

harm, I do. (See *injure*.)

harsh, asper, asperior, asperrimus.

harvest, mess-is, -is, f.

haste (*subs.*), celerit-as, -atis, f.; *there is need of haste*, properato opus est. (See 286 and 416.)

hasten, I, propero, are; *absolutely or with inf.*; contend-o, ēre.

hate, I, od-i, -isse, -eram (*perf. with pres. meaning*); *am hated*, odio sum. (260, *Obs.* 2.)

hatred, odium, n.

haughty, superbus. (57, a.)

have you, I would. (149, i.)

he himself, ipse (355); *he* (11, a, d; see Ex. 45).

head, cap-ut, -itis, n.

head of, I am the, prae-sum. (251.)

headlong, prae-ceps, -cipitis (*adj.*).

health, I am in good, valeo, ēre, -ui.

heap (*abuse*) *on you, I*, te (maledictis) onero, are.

hear, I, or hear of, aud-io, ire, -ivi, -ītum; accipio, ēre.

heard of by, have been. (258, ii.)

hearing, in my, use abl. abs., pres. partic. (420, ii.); *without a hearing* (425).

hearing, sense of, aur-es, -ium, f. pl.

heart (*affections, spirit*), anim-us, -i, m.; (*disposition*), ingenium, n.

heat, aest-us, -ūs, m.

heave a groan, I, ingem-isco, ēre, -ui.

Heaven (*metaph.*), Di immortales. (See 17.)

---

[1] *Cesso*, I hang back from something which I have begun or have to do; *differo*, I put off action, adjourn it to another time; *cunctor*, I delay from caution or indecision.

heaven and earth, I appeal to, deorum hominumque fidem imploro.

heavy, gravis ; *or, in metaphorical sense only,* laboriosus (*use superl.,* **57, a**).

height of, summus. (**60.**)

heir, the, haer-es, -edis.

help, I can (*not*). (**137, 1, j.**)

help you, I, auxilio tibi sum. (**259, 260, 1**) ; tibi opem fero.

helplessness, in, in-ops, -opis (*adj.*). (See **61.**)

henceforth, jam.

herdsman, bubulc-us, -i, *m.*

here, hic.

here, I am, ad-sum, -esse, -fui.

hesitate to, I, dubito, are, *inf.* (**136, b.**)

hidden, occultus.

hide, I (*by silence*), dissimulo, are (p. 55, *note*).

high, altus ; *high hopes.* (See **54.**)

high-spirited, ferox. (See note under *boldly.*)

highest, summus.

highly (*I honour*). (See *I honour.*)

hill, coll-is, -is, *m.*

himself, ipse, a, um. (**355.**)

his, ejus ; illius ; suus. (See **11, c, d** and **e**, and Pronouns I.)

his own (*enemy*), sibi, *or* sui (**55**), ipse (inimicus).

historian, rerum script-or, -oris.

hoist (*a flag*), *I,* e-do, ĕre, -didi, -ditum.

hold, I, obtin-eo, ēre, -ui (**19**) ; habeo.

hold, I (*think*), duco, ĕre, duxi, ductum ; *hold* (*count*) as, habeo (**240**) ; habeo pro (**240,** *Obs.* 2).

hold my peace, I, contic-esco, ĕre, -ui. (See **17,** *Obs.*)

home, at, domi (**312**) ; *at his own home* (**316,** iii.) ; *from home* (*with verb of motion*), domo (**9,** *b*) ; *home* (*I return*), domum (**9,** *b*).

home-sickness, suorum desiderium.

homes and hearths, for, pro aris et focis.

honest, probus.

honesty, probit-as,[1] -atis, *f.*

honour (*good faith*), fid-es, -ei, *f.*

honour (*distinction*), hon-os, -oris, *m.*

honour (*self-respect*), dignit-as, -atis, *f.*

honour (*as opposed to expediency*), honest-as, -atis, *f.* (**51, c ;** see note under *honesty.*)

honour, I pay (*you*), *or I honour* (*you*), honorem (tibi) habeo ; *te in honore habeo ; honour highly,* in summo honore habeo.

honour (*with*) *I* (*publicly*), orno, are (*abl.*) ; *or* pro-sequor, i, -secutus.

honourable, honestus ; *to be honourable* (*creditable to*), honori esse. (**260,** 3.)

hope for, I, spero, are. (**23.**)

hopes, spes,[2] spei, *f.* ; *I form hopes,* spero. (**54.**)

horrified at, I am, per-horresco, ĕre, -horrui.

hospitality, rights of, jus hospitii.

host, a (opp. to *guest*), hosp-es, -itis, *m.*

host, a, multitud-o, -inis, *f.*

hostage, obs-es, -idis.

hour, hora, *f.* ; *of victory.* (**63.**)

house, in my, apud me (**331, 4, a**) ; domi meae (**316,** iii.).

household, a, familia, *f.*

how. (See **157,** ii.)

how (*disgraceful, etc.*) (**260,** *Obs.* 1.)

how much (*adv.*), quantum.

how much (*with comparat.*), quanto.

how often, quoties. (**157,** ii.)

human, humanus ; *or gen. pl. of* homo. (**59.**)

human beings, homines.

humble means, tenuis fortuna.

humble origin, of, humili loco natus.

humour, I, gratificor, ari (*dat.*).

hundred thousand, a. (**527.**)

---

[1] *Honestas* is not "honesty," but the *abstract term* for what is honourable (*honestum*) in a general sense.

[2] *Spes* is one of the few words in which Latin goes further in forming an abstract noun than English : it is rarely used in the plural of the "hopes" of a single person, or even of many. Cf. *ingenium, memoria.*

hurl, *I*, con-jicio, ĕre, -jēci, -jec-
tum ; *at*, in (*acc.*).
hurry away from, *I*, avolo, are.
hurry to, *I*, conten-do, ĕre, -di
(ad) ; festino, are.
husband, vir, viri.

I, ego.   (See **11**, *a* and *b ;* also
334.)
idle (*vain*), vanus.
if, si. (See Conditional Clauses and
171.)
if not . . . *yet.* (**466**, *c.*)
ignorant of, *I am*, ignoro,[1] are
(*trans.*) ; nescio, ire. (**174**, *e.*)
ill, *I am*, aegroto, are.
ill-starred, infelix, *comp.* infelicior.
(**57**, *b.*)
illustrious,   praeclarus   (*superl.*) ;
praestans (*superl.*).   (**57**, *a.*)
ill-will, malevolentia, *f.*
imagine, *I* (*think*), puto, are.   (See
note under *fancy.*).
imagine, *I* (*conceive*), animo concipio, ĕre.
imitate, *I*, imitor, ari.
immediately after.   (**332**, **1**, *g*, *or*
331, **21**, *c.*)
immensely, quam plurimum.
impart (*to*), *I*, communico, are
(cum).   (**253**, iv.)
impiety, impiet-as, -atis, *f.*
implore, *I*, obsecro, are.
importance of the matter, the, tanta
res.
importance to me, it is of, meā
interest (**310**) ; *of the utmost importance to* (= *with reference to*).
(**310**, iii. and iv.)
important, gravis.
impose upon you (*conditions*), *I*, tibi
impono, ĕre.
impossible, it is, or *it is quite.* (**125**, *f.*)
impress (*affect*) *you*, *I ; make an
impression on you*, te, *or oftener*
animum tuum, moveo *or* com-
moveo, ēre, -mōvi, -mōtum ;
*where more than one person is
implied*, *pl.* animos.

impression (*of*), opini-o, -onis, *f.*
imprisonment, vincula, *n. pl.*
improvident, improvidus.
impulse, of its own, sua sponte.
(See note under *voluntarily.*)
impunity, with, impune (*adv.*).
impute this to you as a fault, *I*,
hoc tibi vitio ver-to, ĕre, -ti,
-sum ; culpae do, dăre, dedi,
datum. (**260**, 2.)
in ; in a time of, in (*abl.*).   (See
332, **5** ; **273**, *Obs.*)
incapable of, *I am* (*morally*), ab-
horreo, ēre, ab ; alienissimus
sum ab. (See *unable.*)
inclination, volunt-as, -atis, *f.*
incline to think that, *I.*   (**169**.)
incompetence (*ignorance*), inscītia, *f.*
inconsiderable (*of danger*), parum
gravis.
inconsistent with, alienus ab.
incorruptibility, integrit-as, -atis, *f.*
increase, *I* (*trans.*), au-geo, ēre, -xi,
-ctum.
increase, *I* (*intrans.*), cresco, ĕre,
crevi.
incur, *I*, incurro, ĕre, in (*acc.*) ;
incur loss, damnum capio, ĕre,
cēpi.
indebted to you for this, *I am*, hoc
tibi acceptum re-fero, -ferre,
-ttuli (*metaph. from account-book*).
indecisive, an-ceps, -cipitis.
India, India, *f.*; *an Indian*, Ind-us, i.
indict, *I*, reum facio ; accuso.
(**306**.)
indictment, crim-en, -inis, *n.*
indifferent to, neglegens (*with gen.*,
301) ; *I am indifferent to*, parvi
or nihili (**305**) facio.
indignation, use indignor, ari. (**415**,
b.)
indispensable, necessarius.
individuals ; as individuals, singuli.
(**380**, *b.*)
induced, *I am*, mihi persuadetur.
(**244**, *Obs.*)
indulge, *I*, indul-geo, ēre, -si (*dat.*).
indulgence (*forgiveness*), venia, *f.*

---

[1] *Nescio*, "I am absolutely ignorant of," opposed to *scio ; ignoro*, "I have not made
myself acquainted with," opposed to *novi : illum ignoro* (not *nescio*), I do not know
him.

inexperience, use adj., imperitus. (376, iii.).

infallible, certissimus.

infamous, I am declared, ignominiā notor, ari.

infant, infan-s, -tis.

infantry, pedit-es, -um.

inferior to. (278.)

infest, I, infestum habeo. (240.)

inflict (loss) on (you), I (damno te) afficio, ĕre. (283.)

inflict death on you (judicially), I, morte te multo, are.

inflict punishment on, I, poenas sum-o, ĕre, -psi, -ptum, de (*abl.*).

influence, auctorit-as,[1] -atis, *f.*

influence with, I have (much, etc.), possum apud. (331, 4, *d.*)

information, I give, doceo. (231.)

inhuman, inhumanus.

injure, I, noc-eo, ĕre, -ui, -itum (*dat.*).

injury (harm), damnum, *n.* (See note under *wrong*.)

innocence, entire, use superl. of innocens, and see 224, *Obs.* 1.

innocent, I am, extra culpam sum. (331, 9.)

innocent, the, innocentes. (50.)

inquire, I, quaero, ĕre, a *or* ex; (te) rogo, inter-rogo, are (231, *note*); percunctor, ari (*acc.*).

inspiration, afflat-us, -ūs, *m.*

instantly, continuo.

instead of (doing, etc.), adeo non . . . ut; non modo . . . sed; tantum abfuit ut . . . ut (124); *or* quum posset, deberet (431, *Obs.*).

instigation, use auctor (424), *or* suadeo, moneo (420, ii.).

institution, an, institutum. (51, *b.*)

instrumentality, by your. (267, *Obs.*)

insult, an, contumelia, *f.*

intellect, men-s, -tis, *f.*

intend to, I, use fut. in -rus. (See 14, *c.*)

intent on, I am, do operam. (397.)

intention of, with the. (107.)

intentionally, consulto; consilio. (268.)

interest, gratia, *f.* (See note under *influence*.)

interest (advantage), utilit-as, -atis, *f.* (51, *c.*)

interest or interests of, I consult, consulo, ĕre *with dat.* (See 248.)

interest of, in the, causā. (290, *Obs.*)

interfere with, I, inter-venio, ire, vēni (*dat.*).

interpose, I (intrans.), = interfere.

interposition, miraculous. (64.)

interpreter, interpr-es, -etis.

intervene, I, inter-venio, ire, -vēni.

interview with, I have an, con-venio, ire, -vēni (*trans.*, 24 and 229); col-loquor, i, -locutus (cum).

intimate terms with, I live on. (282.)

into, in. (331, 24.)

intolerable (to), almost, vix ferendus. (394 and 258, i.)

intrust, I, per-mitto, ĕre, -misi, -missum; mando, are. (See 247 and 128.)

invade, I, bellum, *or* arma, in-fero, ferre, -tuli, illatum, in (*acc.*, 331, 24, *c*).

invasion, use bellum infero (*pass. part.*, 417, i.).

invest (a city), I, circum-sedeo, ēre (*trans.*, 229).

inveigh against, I. (331, 24, *c.*)

invent, I (fabricate), fingo, ĕre, finxi, fictum.

inventor, invent-or, -oris : *fem. form* inventr-ix, -icis.

invite, I, invito, are. (331, 24, *b.*)

involved in, I am, versor, ari, in (*abl.*).

involves, it (implies), habet.

irruption, an, incursi-o, -onis, *f.*

island, insula, *f.*

issue, the, event-us, -ūs, *m.* ; but see 174, *d.*

---

[1] *Auctoritas*, moral influence as distinct from authority in the sense of *power; potestas*, legal or legitimate authority or power; *imperium*, military authority or power; *potentia*, "power," "might," in a more general sense; *regnum*, kingly or despotic power; *gratia*, "interest" with the powerful; *favor*, "popularity" with the masses.

Isthmus, the, Isthm-us, -i, *f.*

Italy, Italia, *f.*

itself, ipse, a, um. (355.)

January, Januarius. (See Voc. 1, *note.*)

javelin (*Roman soldiers'*), pilum, *n.*

jealous of you, I am, tibi in-video, ēre, -vīdi.

jewel (*metaph.*), res sufficient. (222, *Obs.*)

join (*you*), *I* (*intrans.*), me (tibi, *or* ad te), adjun-go, ēre, -xi, -ctum ; *the ranks of,* ad.

journey, a, it-er, -ineris, *n. ; I am on a journey,* iter facio.

joy, laetitia, *f. ; shouts of joy,* lae-tantium (laetor) clamor. (See 415, *b,* and the *caution.*)

joyful, laetus.

judge, I (*think*), reor, ratus sum. (See note under *fancy.*)

judgment (*decision*), judicium, *n.*

judgment (*will*), arbitrium, *n.*

judgment (*good*), consilium, *n.*

judgment is different, my, aliter judico. (54.)

June (*month of*), (mensis) Junius : *first of,* kalendae Juniae. (538.)

juniors, juniores ; natu minores.

jury (*judges*), judices. (Voc. 7, *note* 2.)

just (*adj.*), justus

just (*lately*), nuperrime (nuper).

just (*then*), jam tum.

justification, causa, *f.*

justly, jure. (See note under *rightly.*)

keenness, aci-es, -ei, *f.* (*lit. edge*).

keep, I (*promises*), sto, stare, stĕti (*abl.*).

keep (*within*), *I,* contin-eo, ēre, -ui (intra).

keep anxious about, I, sollicitum habeo de. (240.)

keep back from, I, prohibeo, ēre ; arceo, ēre (*abl.*).

keep in the dark, or secret, I, celo. (230, 231.)

keep my word, I, fidem prae-sto, are, -stiti.

kill, I, inter-ficio,[1] ĕre, -feci, -fectum ; occī-do, ĕre, -di, -sum.

kind deed, a, beneficium, *n. ;* officium, *n.*

kind of, every, omnis, e.

kind of man, the, use qualis. (174, *c.*)

kind, of this, hujusmodi ;[2] *of the, of that kind ; that kind of,* ejusmodi.[2] (See 87.)

kindly (*adj.*), benignus ; humanus.

kindly disposed to, bene-volus, -vol-entior, in. (255, *Obs.*)

kindness, bonit-as, -atis, *f.; (act of),* beneficium, *n. ; I return* (see *gratitude*).

king, rex, regis ; *king's,* regius (*adj.,* 58).

know, I, scio, irs (*a fact*) ; nōvi, nŏsse, nōveram (nōram) (*a person*) ; notum habeo (188).

knowledge (*learning*), doctrina, *f.*

knowledge, to, or within, my. (507.)

lack, I, mihi deest. (251.)

laden, onustus.

laggard, a, ignavus.

lamentations, I make, lamentor, ari.

land, terra, *f. ;* ag-er, ri, *m.*

land, our (*territory*), agri nostri. (See *country* and 16, *a.*)

land on, I (*trans.*), ex-pono, ĕre, -posui, -positum, in (*abl.*).

landing of, the, partic. of expono. (417, i.)

language (*conversation*), serm-o, onis, *m.*

language, I use this, haec loquor, i. (See 25 and 54.)

large. (See *great.*)

last (*to*), *the,* ultimus. (62.)

last (*of past time*), proximus *; for,* *or within, the last* (*days, etc.*) (325, *Obs.*)

last, at, tandem ; demum.

lasting, diuturnus.

late (*recent*), recen-s, -tis.

---

[1] *Interficere,* general word for to kill : *occidere,* to kill with a weapon, as in war : *necare,* to put to death cruelly ; *trucidare,* to murder inhumanly, to "butcher."

[2] *Hujusmodi, ejusmodi.* etc.; are constantly used contemptuously ; *talis* rarely so. (Ex. 33 B, *n.* 4.)

late in life, jam senex (63) ; provecta jam aetate (*abl. abs.*).

late, too (*adv.*), sero.

lately, nuper, *superl.,* nuperrime ; *but lately,* paulo ante. (279, *caution.*)

launch against, I, im-mitto, ĕre, in (*acc.*).

law, a, lex, legis, *f.* (Ex. 9, *n.* 2.)

lawful, legitimus.

lay before, I, defero, ferre, ad.

lay down my arms, I (*disband or surrender*), ab armis dis-cedo, ĕre, -cessi.

lay violent hands on myself, I. (253, ii.)

lay waste, I. (See *waste.*)

lazy, ignavus.

lead, I, duco, ĕre, duxi, ductum.

lead a life, I. (237.)

lead across, or through, I, transduco, ĕre, -duxi. (229, *Obs.*)

lead back, I, reduco, ĕre.

lead out, I, educo, ĕre.

leadership. (424.)

learn, I, disco, ĕre, didici.

learn fresh (*additional*), *I,* ad-disco, ĕre, -didici.

learning, doctrina. f. ; but *I advance in learning,* doctior fio ; and see 279 for *superior in learning.*

least, at, saltem ; *I at least,* ego certe.[1]

leave, I, or leave behind, re-linquo, ĕre, -liqui, -lictum (see note under *abandon*); (*a place*), excedo, ĕre, *abl.* or ex: proficiscor, i, -fectus (*abl.,* see 314); *leave my country* (264).

leave you (*free*) *to, I.* (197, *Obs.* 2.)

leave alone, I, missum, am, um, facio. (240.)

leave nothing, I (298, *b*); *leave nothing undone* (137, *i.*).

leave, you have my. (331, 16, *c.*)

left (*adj.*), sinist-er, -ra, -rum.

legion, a, legi-o, -onis, *f.*   •

leisure, otium, *n. ; at leisure,* otiosus (*adj.*).

Lemnos, Lemn-os, *gen.* -i.

less (*adv.*) minus ; *less than* (*with numerals*). (318, *Obs.*)

let (*you*), *I,* (tibi) tra-do, ĕre, -didi, ditum *with gerundive.* (400.)

let slip, I (*an opportunity*), desum. (251.)

letter, a, litter-ae, -arum, *f. ; from,* a, ab.

level plain, planiti-es, -ei, *f.*

levy (*subst.*), delect-us, -ūs, *m. ; I hold a levy,* delectum habeo.

levy contributions on you, I, pecunias tibi impero, are.

liar, a, mend-ax, -acis (*adj.*).

liberties, libert-as, -atis, *f.* (sing.) ; =*exemptions,* immunitat-es, -um, *f. pl.*

life, vita, *f.*

lifetime, in his (61); *in your father's,* =*your father being alive* (rivus), *abl. abs.* (424).

like (*adj.*), similis. (254, 255.)

likely to, use partic. in -rus. (14, *c.*)

line (*of battle*), aci-es, -ei, *f.* (see note under *field*); *line of march,* agm-en, -inis, *n. ; lines* (*fortified*), munimenta, *n. pl. ; line* (*metaph.* for " *opinion* "), judicium, *n.*

linger, I, cunctor, ari.

list of, I write a, per-scribo, ĕre (*trans.*).

listen to, I, audio, ire. (23.)

listen to, I (*comply with* or *obey*), obtempero, are. (See *obey,* note) ; *listen to prayer,* exoror.

literature, litterae, *f. pl.*

little (see 53); *little of,* parum (294).

live, I, vivo, ĕre, vixi, victum.

load, I, onero, are.

load, a, ŏn-us, -eris, *n.*

locality, loc-a, -orum, *n.*

lofty, praealtus.

London, Londinium, *n.*

long (*in distance*), longus ; *in time,* diutinus,[2] diuturnus.

long (*adv.*), diu, *or* jam diu ; *long ago,* jam pridem ; *long continued,* diutinus ; *long tried,* spectatus. (57, *a.*)

---

[1] *Certe,* when it follows a word, means "at least," and is equivalent to *saltem,* more emphatic than *quidem.*

[2] *Diuturnus,* long, lasting, of long standing: *diutinus* long continued, in a bad sense, "wearisome."

longer (adv.), diutius ; *no longer*, or *any longer (after a negative)*, jam or diutius (**328**, *a*); *how much longer ?* quousque, or quousque tandem (**157**, *Obs.*)

look at, I, specto, are (see note under *see*) ; intueor, ēri (*perf. rare*).

look down on, I, de-spicio, ĕre, -spexi, -spectum (*trans.*).

look for, I, (wait for), expecto, are. (**23**.)

look for (in vain), I, desidero, are.

look forward to, I, provideo, ēre (*acc.*).

look round for, I, circum-spicio, ĕre, -spexi. (**22, 23**.)

look up at, I, suspicio, ŏre.

looked for, than I had, spe, or expectatione, meā. (**277**.)

lose, I, a-mitto, ĕre, -misi, -missum.

lose, I (opportunity), de-sum, esse. (**251**.)

lose heart, I, animo deficio, ĕre ; *of more than one person*, animis.

lose my labour I (= I effect nothing), nihil ago.

lose time, I, tempus tero, ĕre, trivi, tritum.

lose the day, I (= I am conquered), vincor, i, victus.

loss, damnum, *n.* ; detrimentum, *n.*

loss of, without the, use a-mitto, ĕre. (**425**.)

loss what to do, I am at a. (**172**.)

lost, all is, de summa re actum est.

lot (metaph.), lot in life, fortuna, *f.*

lot, it falls to (my), (mihi) contingit :[1] *it is men's lot to*, hominibus . . . ut. (**123**.)

love, I, di-ligo, ĕre, -lexi, -lectum ; amo,[2] are.

lovely, pulcherrimus.

low, abjectus ; *very low*, infimus. (**57**, *a*.)

low, or lowly, birth, ignobilitas, -atis, *f.*

lowest part of, Imus. (**60**.)

loyal, fidelis.

loyalty, fid-es, -ei, *f.*

luxury, luxuria, *f.*

mad, I am (quite), furo, ĕre. (See Voc. 6, *n.*)

made, I am being, fio, fieri, factus.

magnificent, praeclarissimus.

magnitude, use quantus. (**174**, *a*.)

mainly, potissimum.

maintain, I, sustin-eo, ēre, -ui.

make, I, facio, ĕre, feci, factum , *make war*, infero, ferre (**253**, ii.); *make my way*, iter facio.

make fast (bind), I, constri-ngo, ĕre, -nxi, -ctus.

malice, malitia ;[3] malevolentia.

Malta, Melita, *f.*

man, vir, viri ; hom-o, -inis (for the difference see p. 153, *note*, 3); *to a man* (**331**, i., *f.*).

management, procuratio, -onis, *f.*

manhood, in quite early, admodum adolescens. (**63**, and p. 63, *note* 3.)

manifestly, = obviously. (**64**.)

mankind, homines ; *or* genus humanum.

manliness, with, viril-iter, -ius.

manner, in this. (**268** and *Obs.*)

manner of life. (**174**, *c.*)

manners, mor-es, -um, *m. pl.*

many, mult-i, -ae, -a.

marble (adj.), marmoreus.

march, a, it-er, -ineris, *n.*

march, I, iter facio.

Marseilles, Massilia, *f.*

marsh, pal-us, -udis, *f.*

mass, a, mol-es, -is, *f.*

mass (of the people), vulg-us, -i, *n.*; *for dat. in* vulgus, 254, *note.*

massacre, caed-es, -is, *f.; I am present at the, use gerundive.* (**417**, ii.)

---

[1] *Contingit*, "happens" by a natural process ; oftener, but not always, of what is desirable : *accidit*, "happens," "falls out," by chance, often, but not always, of what is undesirable : *usu venit*, "falls within my experience :" *evenit*, "happens," "turns out," as the result of previous circumstances.

[2] *Amare* expresses greater warmth of feeling than *diligere : it is* "to love passionately." "to be enamoured of."

[3] *Malevolentia*, ill-will; *malitia*, the same feeling shown in underhand attacks or schemes ; *malignitas*, ill-will shown in a desire to defraud, "niggardliness."

massacre, I, trucĭdo, are. (See *kill.*)
master, a, domin-us, -i, *m.*
matter, a, res, rei,*f.*
matters little, it, parvi rēfert (310 *at
  end*); *it matters not,* nihil refert
  (*ibid.*).
mature life, in, jam adultus. (63.)
May (month of), (mensis) Maius.
  (538, *n.*)
may, I. (197 and *Obs.*)
mean (adj.), sordidus ; abjectus.
*mean, what I, you, etc. ; or what
  is the meaning* (174) *of,* quid mihi
  velim, tibi velis, ?tc. (163).
means, by no, nequaquam ; haudquaquam ; nullo modo ; minime.
means, by this. (263.)
means, humble, tenuis fortuna.
meantime, interea.
meddle with, I, at-tingo, ĕre -tigi,
  -tactus.
Medes, the, Medi, -orum.
meditate on, I, cogito, are de (*abl.*).
meet, I, obviam fio (*dat.*);*I come, go,
  go down, to meet,* obviam venio,
  ire ; eo, ire ; descendo, ĕre.
meet, I (endure), ex-perior, iri,
  -pertus.
meet (doom), I, ob-eo, ire, -ii (*acc.*).
meet (together) at, to, convĕnire ad.
  (331, i. c.)
member of the nation, or state, civ-is,
  -is, *m.*
memory, memoria,*f.*
menace (with), I, denuntio, are
  (*acc. of thing, dat. of person*) ;
  for menaces use gerund. (99.)
mention, I, mentionem facio (*gen.*).
mention, not to, ne dicam. (100,
  note.)
merchant vessel, navis oneraria.
mercy, misericordia, *f.* ; *I place
  myself entirely at your,* totum
  me tibi trado ac permitto.
mere (from the), ipse (*use abl. of
  cause, or* propter: see also 355,
  c): *merely, = only:* "*mere*" *and
  "merely" are often expressed by
  emphatic order simply.*
message, a, nuntium, *n.*
messenger, nunti-us, -i, *m.*
method, rati-o, -onis,*f.*
mid-day, meridi-es, -ei, *m.*

middle of, midst of. (60.)
midst of, in the. (332, 5, *h.*)
mighty, superl. of magnus.
Milan, Mediolanum, *n.*
mile, a, mille, *pl.* milia, *sc.* passuum (1000 *paces of 5 feet*).
mind, animus, -i, *m.* ; (= *intellect*),
  men-s, -tis, *f. ; his whole mind,
  = all that he thinks* (sentio, ire).
mind (verb imperat.), fac, cura, ut.
  (141.)
mind, I am out of my, insan-io,
  ire, -ivi, -ii. (See 25.)
mind, I am of one (with), consentio, ire, -sensi (cum).
mingle with, I (intrans.), im-misceor,
  (20), ūri, -mixtus (*dat.*).
mingled . . . and, et . . . et.
miraculous interposition, by a.
  (64.)
miserable, mis-er, -era, -erum.
mislead, I, decipio, ĕre, etc.
missile, a, telum, *n.*
missing, I am, desideror, ari.
mistake, a, err-or, -oris, *m.* ; *in,
  gen.* (300.)
mistake, I make a ; am mistaken,
  erro, are.
Mithridates, Mithridat-es, -is.
mob, multitud-o, -inis, *f.*
mode, rati-o, -onis,*f.*
moderate (not too great), modicus ;
  mediocris ("*middling*").
moment when, at the. (433.)
money, pecunia,*f.*
monstrous (wicked), nefarius.
monument, monumentum, *n.*
moon, luna,*f.*
morals, mor-es, -um, *m.*
more (adv.), plus ; magis : *as subst.*
  (294), plus, *n. pl.* (54) plura ;
  more than (= rather than), magis
  quam ; *more than once,* see once.
more (never), posthac.
moreover, praeterea.
morning, in the, mūne (*adv.*).
morrow, the (still in future), dies
  crastinus ; *on the morrow (of a
  past date*), die postero.
mortal (wound), morti-fer, -fera,
  -ferum. (18, 19.)
*most (used loosely in comparing two
  only),* plus. (See *more.*)

most men, plerique.

motive, from, or *with*, *a, use* ob (331, 14) *and* causa, *f. ; my only motive is* (483, *Obs.*). (See also 107.)

mount up, *I*, ascend-o, ĕre, -i.

mountain, mon-s, -tis, *m.*

mournfully, maestus. (61.)

mouth, in every one's. (257.)

move, I (*intrans.*), moveor, ēri, motus. (20.)

much, multus, a, um ; *as subst.* (see 53) ; = *much of* (294) ; *with com-parat.*, multo (279).

multitude, multitud-o, -inis, *f.*

murder, a, caed-es, -is, *f.*

murder, I, neco, are.

murderer. (See 175.)

must be, use part. in -dus. (198, iii.)

mutiny, sediti-o, -onis, *f.*

my, meus. (See 11, *c.*)

myself (*emphatic*), ipse (355, *d*) ; (*reflexive*), me, me ipsum (356, ii.); *for myself*, ego, *or* equidem (11, *a*, and 334, i.).

name, a, nom-en, -inis, *n. ; in name* (*nominally*). (274.)

name, good, fama, *f.*

Naples, Neapol-is, -is, *loc.* -i.

Narbonne, Narbo, -onis, *m.*

nation, popul-us, -i, *m.* ; civit-as, -atis, *f.. or* civ-es, -ium ; respub-lica. (See 19, and Voc. 2, *n.*)

national, communis ; *or gen. of* respublica. (58.)

national cause, the, respublica ; communis rei p. causa.

natural powers, natura, *f.*, and see note under *character.*

naturally (*by nature*), naturā.

nature, use qualis *or* quis. (174, *b.*)

native land, or *country* (see 16, *a*) ; *I leave my*, patriā cedo (264).

nearly, prope, paene. (See note under *almost.*)

necessary, necessarius ; *is necessary.* (See 286.)

necessaries (*of life*). (286.)

necessity (=*emergency*), temp-us, -oris, *n.*

need of ; is needed, etc., opus. (286.)

needs must, necesse est. (201, and p. 144, *note.*)

neglect, I, negle-go, ĕre, -xi, -ctum.

neighbour (*actual*), vicin-us, -i ; *in sense of "fellow man," or "men,"* alter ; ceteri. (372.)

neighbouring, finitimus.

neither . . . nor, neque . . . neque.

neither of the two. (340, ii.)

never, nunquam ; *and never*, nec unquam. (110.)

new, novus.

news of, the, use nuntio, are (417 i.) ; *news has been brought* (46, *a*).

next, the, proximus ; insequen-s, -tis ; *next* (*day*), posterus ; *or* (*on the*), postridie (*adv.*).

next to (*prep.*). (331, 21, *c.*)

niceties (*of argument*), argutiae, *f. pl.*

night, nox, noctis, *f.*

nineteen, undeviginti. (527.)

ninety-second. (See 530 and 531.)

no (162) ; *I say* or *answer "no,"* nego, are.

no, none (*adj.*), nullus.

no (*not*) *more* (*adv.*) *than*, nihilo magis quam.

no one, none, nemo, *gen.* nullius (see 223, *note*) ; *and no one, none*, nec quisquam (110).

no sooner . . . than, ubi primum ; simul atque. (428.)

noble (*morally*), praeclarus (p. 63, *note* 4) ; pulcherrimus (57, *a*) ; *for usage with proper nouns and persons see* 224.

nobles. (51, *a*, and *note.*)

noon, noon-day. (See *mid-day.*)

nor, neque ; *in final clauses*, neu.

not yet, nondum.

nothing, nihil.

now, jam (=*by this time, can be used of the past*) ; nunc (*at the present, at the moment of speak-ing*) ; hodie (*to-day*).

now . . . long, jamdiu ; jampridem. (181.)

now . . . now, modo . . . modo.

number (*proportion or part*), par-s, -tis, *f.*

number of, the (*interrog.*). (174, *a.*)

numbers, great, multi ; complures ; *superior*, multitud-o. -inis, *f.*

numerous, more, plures; *such numerous,* tot.

oath, jusjurandum, jurisjurandi, *n.*

obedient to, I am, = obey.

obey, I, par-eo,[1] ēre, -ui (*dat.*, 5) ; obtempero, are (*dat.*) ; *the orders of,* dicto audiens sum (*dat.*).

object, I, recuso, are (136, *a*); I do not (131).

object (*subst.*), objects, (see 54) ; object of unpopularity with you, I am, invidiā flagro, are, apud vos.

obligation, I am under, gratiam debeo. (98, *b.*)

obstacle, (id) quod obstat.

obstinate, pertin-ax, *comp.* -acior.

obtain, I, adipiscor,[2] i, adeptus ; con-sequor, ī, -secutus (18, 19) ; a request, impetro, are.

obviously. (64.)

occasion, on that, tum. (Intr. 19.)

occupy, I (*hold*), ten-eo, ēre, -ui.

ocean, ocean-us, -i, *m.*

off (*at a distance of*), I am, absum. (318.)

offence, an, peccatum, *n.* (408.)

offend, I (*annoy*), offen-do, ěre, -di, -sum. (245.)

offer, I, de-fero, -ferre, -tuli, -latum ; offer (*terms*), fero.

office, magistrat-us, -ūs (18, 19) ; I am in, in magistratu sum ; I hold, m. habeo ; obtineo.

officers, the (*military*), tribuni (militum) centurionesque.

often, saepe ; so often, toties.

old. (See *ancient,* and note.)

old age, senect-us, -utis, *f.* ; in my. (63.)

old man, sen-ex, -is.

old-world, old-fashioned, priscus ; antiquus. (See note under *ancient.*)

oldest, natu maximus.

once, semel ; often exp. by tense of verb (471, note); more than once, semel ac saepius. (533, *c.*)

once (*formerly*), quondam : olim.[3]

once, at (*immediately*), statim.

once, at (*at the same time*), use idem. (366, i.)

one (*numeral*), unus ; of, ex '529, *e*) ; one of the best (529, *d*) one or two; one, two, several. (529, *g.*)

one (*indefinite*), one who (see 72) ; one so (224, Obs. 2).

one, not, nemo (223, note), ne unus quidem (529, *a*).

one, . . . the other. (368.)

one and all, cuncti (see under *all*) ; omnes (*placed last*).

one by one, singuli. (380, *b.*)

one day (= at some time or other), aliquando. (See note under *once.*)

one thing . . . another, it is. (92.)

only, solum, modo, tantum (*placed after the word qualified*) ; this and only this (347, example) ; not only, non solum, non modo.

onset, impet-us, -ūs, *m.*

open, I ; throw open ; open wide ; cause to be opened, pate-facio, ěre, -feci, -factum.

open, to be, patēre (no fut. in -rus 192, iii.).

open to question, is, = can be doubted, dubitari potest.

opening, first possible. (377.)

openly, palam.

opinion, good, existimati-o, -onis, *f.*

opinion on, your, = what you think of (censeo, ēre, de).

opponent, I am an. See I oppose.

opportunity, occasi-o, -onis, *f.* ; facult-as, -atis, *f.* ; first possible. (377.)

---

[1] Pareo, the general word for "I obey," applied often to habitual obedience of any kind : obtempero, I obey as from a sense of reason and right : oboedio, I obey a single command ; obsequor, "I comply with," "I suit myself to ;" dicto audiens sum, I render implicit obedience, as that of a soldier.

[2] Nanciscor, I obtain, often without effort, by circumstances or chance : consequor, I obtain a thing which I follow after as a good ; adipiscor. I obtain after effort : impetro, by entreaty.

[3] Olim (ille, olle), at a distant point, in the past or (sometimes) in the future ; quondam (quidam), only of the past, and generally during some space of time in the past ; aliquando, at some time or other, past, present or future, opposed to "never."

oppose, I, adversor, ari (*dat.*, **244**, *b*); ob-sto, are, -stiti (**253**, i.).

opposite to. (**331**, 2.)

opposition, in spite of your, use partic. of adversor, ari. (**420**, ii.)

oppress, I, vexo, are. (**19.**)

oppressive, iniquus.

or, aut, vel (see p. 14, *note*); *in final and consec. clauses,* 103, 110; *interrog.,* 159, 160; 168, *and Obs.*

orator, orat-or, -oris.

order, I, jubeo, ēre, jussi, jussum. (**120, 128.**)

orders, jussa, *n. pl.* (**51**, *b.*)

orders, I give, impero, are; edico, ēre, etc. (**127**, *b,* and **128.**)

origin (extraction), gen-us, -eris, *n.*; *of humble origin,* humili loco natus.

originally (sprung). (See *sprung.*)

orphan, orbus, a, um.

other, the (of two), ille (**339**, iv.); alter (**368**); *others,* alii, *or* (= *other men, the rest*) ceteri (**372**); *it is for, use gen.* (**291**, *Obs.* 4).

other men's, or persons', alienus (*adj.*, **58**).

ought, I. (**198.**)

our, nost-er, -ra, -rum.

our men, nostri. (**50.**)

out of, e, ex (**332**, 5), *or* de (*abl.*).

outcries, angry, maledicta, *n. pl.* (**408.**)

outdo, I (far), (facile) vinco, -ēre, supero, are.

outnumber, we, plures sumus quam.

outrage on, the, use gerundive or partic. of violo. (**417**, ii. *or* i.)

outside (the city). (**311**, *Obs.*)

outstrip, I, = *outdo.*

over (more than), plus. (**318**, *Obs.*).

over with, all. (**332**, 3, *d.*)

over-reach, I, circum-venio, ire, -vēni. (**229.**)

overwhelm, I, obru-o, ēre, -i, -tum; op-primo, ēre, -pressi, -pressum.

owe, I, debeo, ēre.

owing to, propter (*acc.,* **331**, 20, *b*).

own, his, suus (**11**, *c*); *my own,* meus.

pacify, I, placo, are.

pain, dol-or, -oris, *m.*

painful, is. (**260**, 3.)

palace, dom-us, -ūs, *f.; the king's,* domus regia. (**58.**)

panic, pav-or, -oris, *m.*

pardon, I, ig-nosco, ēre, -novi, -notum (*dat.,* **5**); *pardon (you) for (this),* hoc tibi condono, are (**247**); *I wish you pardoned;* tibi ignotum volo (**240**, *Obs.* 1); *by pardoning, gerund of* ignosco (**99**).

parent, paren-s, -tis.

park (pleasure grounds), horti, *m. pl.*

Parliament = *Senate.*

part, for my, equidem. (See also **334**, i.)

part, it is our. (**291**, *Obs.* 2.)

part, the greater, plerique.

part from, I, discedo, ēre, ab.

part in, I take, me im-misceo, ēre, -miscui, -mixtum (*dat.*); *a battle,* intersum (*dat.*); *politics,* attingo.

part in, without, exper-s, -tis (*gen.,* **301**, ii.).

partly, partim.

party, the (popular), pars, -tis, *and* see *popular* and *aristocratic.*

party, one . . . the other. (**340**, iii.)

pass (a law), I, perfero, ferre.

pass (time), I, dēgo, ēre, dēgi; ago, ēre.

pass, to (intrans., of intervals of time), inter-cedēre, -cessit.

pass by, I, praeter-eo, ire, -ii.

passion (anger), ira, *f.*

passionate, iracundus.

passionateness, iracundia, *f.*

past (adj.), praeteritus; *the past,* praeterita (**52**); tempus praeteritum.

pathless, invius.

patience, with, aequo animo, *or* patienter.

patriot, true patriot, bonus civis; civis optimus; *patriots, every patriot, all true patriots;* optimus quisque (**375**, *and note*); *best patriot,* optimus civis.

pay attention to, I, rationem habeo (*with gen.*); *pay (you) honour;* honorem (tibi) habeo; *pay my respects to,* saluto, are (*acc.*); *pay the penalty* (**243**, *and* see *penalty*).

peace, pax, pacis, *f.*
peace (of mind), securit-as, -atis, *f.*
peculiarity, special, proprium, *n.* (**255.**)
penalty, poena, *f.;* supplicium, *n.; I pay the penalty of,* poenas do (*gen.*). (See note under *punishment.*)
people (=*men*), homines; *a people* (=*nation*), pŏpul-us, -i, *m.*
perceive, I, intel·lego, ĕre, -lexi, ·lectum. (**19.**)
perhaps, nescio an (see **169**), *or* haud scio an (*the latter should always be used before an adj. when no verb is expressed*); fortasse; forsitan (**170**).
perilous, periculosus. (**57,** *a.*)
period, at that. (**294,** *Obs.*)
perish, I, pereo, ire.
permission, with your kind; without his. (**269,** *Obs.*)
permit, I, per me licet (**331,** 15, *c*); *I am permitted,* mihi licet (**197**).
perpetrate, I, com·, *or* ad·, mitto, ĕre; facio, ĕre.
perpetrator (of), =*he who perpetrated.* (**175.**)
persecute, I, insector, ari (*dep.*).
persevere or *persist, I,* persevero. are.
person, a, homo, -inis. (**224,** *Obs.* 2 and note,* and Ex. 39, *note.*)
person, a single (*after a negat.*), quisquam. (**358,** i.)
person (*your own*), caput, *n.*
personal appearance, corporis (**59**) habit-us, -ûs.
persuade, I, persua-deo, ĕre, -si, ·sum (**5**); *I cannot be persuaded,* persuaderi mihi non potest. (**219,** see also **122,** *b.*)
pestilence, pestilentia, *f.*
philosopher, philosoph-us, -i.
philosophy, philosophia, *f.*
pierce, I, con-fodio, ĕre, -fōdi, -fossum.
pitch of, to such a, eo (*gen.*, **294,** *Obs.*).
pity for, I feel, me miseret (*gen.*, **309**).
place, loc-us, -i, *m.; in the place* (*where*), ibi; *to the* (. . . *whence*), eo. (**89.**)

place, I, pono, ĕre.
plain, camp-us, -i, *m.*
plain (*adj.*), manifestus; *as plain as,* manifestior. (**276.**)
plan, consilium, *n.*
plead (*as excuse*), *I,* excuso, are; =*negotiate,* ago, ere; *my cause,* causam oro, arc, dico, ĕre.
pleasantly (*I speak*), jucunda, *n. pl.*
please, I (*you*), plac-eo, ĕre, -ui, ·itum (*dat.*, **5**).
please, I (= *it pleases me*), mihi libet, libuit *or* libitum est (**246**); *if you please,* si libet.
pleasing to, gratus (*dat.*).
pleasure, volupt-as, -atis, *f.* (*often in pl., when used for pleasure in the abstract*).
pledge myself, I, spondeo, ĕre, spopondi.
plunder, praeda, *f.*
poet, poeta, *m.*
point (*in every*), res (*pl.*).
point of, in. (**332,** 1, *e.*)
point of, on the, use fut. in -rus (**189,** iii.); *when on the, partic. in* -rus (**418,** *d*).
point (*whence*), *to the,* eo. (**89.**)
point out, I, monstro, are; ostend-o, ĕre, -i.
poison, venenum, *n.*
policy, consilia, *n. pl.*
political, gen. of res publica (see **59**); *for political storms,* in republica.
political life, res publica; *I enter political life; ad* rem p. me confero, ferre; *or* ac-cedo, ĕre, -cessi.
politicians. (**175.**)
politics, respublica (*never pl.*).
poor, paup·er, -eris; *the poor,* pauper·es, -um. (**51,** *a.*)
popular (*party*), popularis; *or the popular party,* popular·es, -ium, *m. pl.* (p. 63, *note* 4).
popularity, fav·or, -oris, *m.* (See note under *influence.*)
populous, frequen-s, -tissimus.
position, loc-us, -i, *m.*
possible (*with superlatives*), vel.
possible, it is. (**125,** *e.*)
possibly, use potest fieri ut. (**64** and **125,** *e.*)

post up, I, figo, ĕre, fixi, fixum.

posterity. (See **51,** *a, and note.*)

postpone, I, differo, ferre. (See note under *hang back.*)

poverty, paupert-as, -atis, *f.*

power, potentia, *f.* ; potest-as, -atis, *f.* (See note under *influence.*)

power, under his own, gen. of ditio sua, arbitrium suum. (**290,** *Obs.*)

powerful, potens ; *the powerful,* potentissimus quisque (*sing.,* **375**) ; *I am most powerful,* plurimum possum.

powerless, I am, nihil possum.

praise (*subst.*), lau-s, -dis, *f.*

praise, I, laudo, are.

praised, to be (*adj.*), laudandus.

praiseworthy, laudabilis.

pray for, I (*I desire much*), opto, are (*acc.*) ; *I make one prayer,* unum opto.

prayers, prec-es, -um, *f.*

preceding, proximus.

precious, pretiosus (*superl.,* **57,** *a*).

predecessors. (**175.**)

prefer, I (*modal verb*), malo, malle, malui. (**42,** i. *d,* and ii.)

prefer (*him to you*), *I,* (eum tibi) prae-, *or* ante-pono, ĕre, -posui, -positum (**253,** ii.) ; *or* prae-fero, ferre, -tuli.

preparations, I make, paro, are. (**54.**)

prepare (*trans.*), *I* (*for* .*or against you*), (tibi) in-tendo, ĕre, -tendi.

preparing to, use partic. in -rus. (**14,** *c.*)

presence, in his, my, etc., praesens. (**61,** *or* **420,** ii.)

presence of, in the (*prep.*), in (**273,** *Obs.*) ; coram (*abl. of persons*).

present (*adj.*), hic (**337**) ; but *your present,* iste (**338**).

present, I am, ad-sum, -esse, -fui ; *present at,* intersum. (**251.**)

present, at, or *for the,* in praesens. (**331,** 2+, *b.*)

present, as a. (**260, 3.**)

present you with this, I, hoc (*abl.*) te (*acc.*) dono, are.

presently, mox ; brevi.

preservation of, the, use conservo, are. (**399,** *Obs.* 2 ; **292,** *Obs.*)

preserve, I, servo, are ; conservo, are.

press on, I, insto, are ; *by pressing on, gerund* (**99.**)

pretend, I, simulo, are (**39**) ; dictito,[1] are (*assert*) ; fingo, ĕre, finxi, fictum.

pretty (*adv.*) ; *pretty well,* satis.

prevail by prayer, I, impetro, are, *upon,* ab. (**127,** *c.*)

prevent, I (*from*), ob-sto, -stare, -stiti (*dat.*), quominus. (**137,** ii.)

prevent, to (*in order that . . . not*), ne. (**101,** ii.)

priceless, pretiosissimus.

prince, rex, regis.

principle, want of, levit-as, -atis, *f.*

prison, vincula, *n. pl.*

prisoner, captiv-us, -i, *m.* ; *I am being taken,* capior, i, captus.

private (*person*), privatus ; *private property,* res familiaris.

privilege, a, jus, juris, *n.*

procrastinate, I, differo, ferre, distuli. (See note under *hang back.*)

procrastination, cunctati-o, -onis, *f.* ; *or use verb,* cunctor. (**98,** *a.*)

profess, I, pro-fiteor, ēri, -fessus.

progress in, I make (*much, more*), (multum, plus) proficio, ĕre, in (*abl.*).

project (*subst.*), consilium, *n.*

prolonged, diutinus.

promise, I, pollic-eor, ēri, -itus ; promitto, ĕre, -misi, -missum. (**37.**) (Voc. 6, *n.*)

promise, a, promissum, *n.* (**51,** *b*) ; *of good, or the highest* (**303,** *Obs.* 2) ; *I make promises,* polliceor (**54**).

proof, indicium, *n.* ; *is a proof.* (**260, 3.**)

proof against, invictus ab, *or* adversus (*acc.*).

---

[1] For *simulo* see p. 55, *note.* When the pretence is applied to words rather than to conduct, *dictito* (a frequentative form of *dico*) is common in the sense of "I assert, allege." *Fingo,* and still more *mentior,* emphasises the falsehood of the allegation.

proper, suus, a, um.
property, bona, *n. pl.* (51, *b*) ; fortunae, *f. pl.* ; res, rei, *f.*
prophet, vat-es, -is, m.
prophetic, = *of him foretelling the future.*
proportion to, in (332, 7, *h* ; 376) : *exact proportion to* (*with verbs of valuing*), tanti . . . quanti.
prosecuted for, I am, reus fio ; accusor. (306.)
prospect, or prospects, spes, spei, *f.* (*sing.*) (See note under *hope.*)
prosperity, res prosperae, *or* secundae.
protect your interests, I, tibi (248) caveo, ēre, cavi, cautum, wish . . . protected (240, *Obs.* 1).
protest against, I. (136, *a.*)
protract, I (*war*), traho, ĕre.
proud, superbus.
proud of, I am, glorior, ari. (281 *and* 282, *Obs.*)
prove, I (*intrans.*). (259, *Obs.*)
provide against, I, caveo, ēre, cāvi, cautum, ne, *or, with subst., acc.*
provide for, I, pro-video, ēre, -vīdi, -visum. (248.)
provided that, modo, modo ne. (468.)
provision, I make no, nihil provideo ; for. (331, 24, *b.*)
provisions (for army), frumentum, *n.* ; res frumentaria.
provocation, without, = no one provoking, abl. abs. (See 332, 8, *and* 425.)
provoke, I, lacess-o, ĕre, -ivi, or -i, -itum ; irrīto, are.
prudence, prudentia, *f.*
prudence, want of, imprudentia, *f.*
public (services), = to the people ; public interest, respublica ; public life, see political life.
punish, I, poenas sumo, ĕre, de (332, 3, *h*) ; am punished for, poenas do, dăre, with gen. of the crime.
punishment, poena,[1] *f.* ; supplicium, *n.* (heavy) ; to bring punishment, fraudi esse. (260, 3.)

purpose, a, propositum, *n.* (51, *b*) ; consilium, *n.*
purposely, consulto.
pursue, I, sequor, i, secutus.
pursuit, studium, *n.*
put off, I, differo, ferre, distuli.
put to death, I, caedo, ĕre, cecīdi, caesum: (See also under *kill.*)
put to the test, I, periclitor, ari (dep.).
put up with, I, tolero, are (*acc.*).
Pyrrhus, Pyrrh-us, -i.

quail before, I, pertim-esco, ĕre, -ui (*acc.*).
qualities, good, virtut-es, -um, *f. pl.*
quantity, vis, acc. vim. (See also 174.)
quarter, I ask for, ut mihi parcatur precor, -ari ; mortem *or* victoris iram deprecor ; I obtain, ut mihi parcatur impetro, are ; *or* mihi parcitur.
question, I (ask), interrogo, are (231, *note*) ; it is questioned (doubted), dubitatur : may be, dubitari potest.
question, my, his, the ; to my, etc., pres. part. of interrogo (415, a, and 346) ; the real question (see *real*).
question, a (matter), res, rei, *f.*
quiet (subst.), tranquillit-as, atis, *f.*
quietly, use adj. (61), securus.
quit, I, exce-do, ĕre, -ssi, -ssum (with or without e, ex, 314).
quite, not, parum ; vix.
quite up to, ad with ipse. (Cf. 355, *a.*)

race (nation), gen-s, -tis *f. ; the human race,* hominum (59), *or* humanum, gen-us, -eris, *n.*
rage, ira, *f.*
raid upon, I make a, incursionem facio in (*acc.*).
raise, I, tollo, ĕre, sustuli, sublatum; (an army) (exercitum) comparo, are ; (a cheer) (clamorem) tollo.
raise up, I, attollo, ĕre, sustuli, sublatum.

---

[1] *Poena,* "requital ;" *supplicium* is used mainly of the punishment of death.

rally, *I* (*intrans.*), me col-ligo, ĕre, -lēgi ; *to rally* (*of a number*), concurrĕre.

rank (*position*), stat-us, -ūs, *m.* ; (*of army*), ord-o, -inis, *m.* ; *ranks* (*metaph. of a party*), part-es, -ium, *f. pl.* ; *high rank*, dignit-as, -atis, *f.*

rare (*remarkable*), singularis.

rarely, raro, *comp.* rarius.

rash, temerarius.

rashness, temerit-as, -atis, *f.*

rather (*adv.*), potius.

rather, *I had*, or *I would*, malo, malle, malui.

ravage, *I*, populor, ari (*dep.*).

reach, *I*, pervĕnio ad (**253**, iv.) ; *reach such a pitch of*, eo (**294**, *Obs.*) procedo, ĕre ; *to reach* (*of letters*), perferri ad.

reach (*of darts*), *the*, jact-us, -ūs, *m.*

read through, or *of*, *I*, per-lego, ĕre, -lēgi, -lectum.

ready to, *I am*, volo, velle, volui (*modal*) ; or *use fut. in* -rus. (**14**, *c.*)

real (*question*) *is*, *the*, illud (**341**) quaeritur (**218**).

realise, *I* (*conceive*), animo, or mente, concipio, ĕre.

reality, *in* ; *really*, re ; re ipsā ; re verā. (**274**.)

reap (*gain*), *I*, per-cipio, ĕre ; *the fruit of*, fructum percipio (*gen.*).

rear, tergum, *n.* ; *in the*, a tergo (**332**, **1**, *c*), *or* aversus (See **61**.)

reason, *a*, causa, *f.* ; *for* (*both*) *reasons* (**378**, i.) ; *what reason?* (**137**, **1**, *l*) ; *the reason* (*of*) ; quas ob causas *or* cur (**174**, *a*) ; *the reason* (*of*) . . . *was* (**483**, *Obs.*).

rebel [1] *a*, qui contra regem arma sumpsit. (**175**.)

rebel to (*I invite*), = *to rebellion.*

rebellion (*renewal of war after submission*), rebelli-o, -onis, *f.* ; (*revolt*), defecti-o, -onis, *f.*

rebuke (*subs.*), *use* increpo, are. (**415**, *b* and *c*.)

recall (*to*), *I*, revoco, are (ad) ; *to mind*, in animum.

receive, *I*, ac-cipio, ĕre, -cēpi, -ceptum (**19**) ; *without receiving* (**425**, **420**, i.).

recent, recens.

reckon up, *I*, enumero, are.

recognise, *I*, cognosco, ĕre.

reconciled with you, *I am*, tecum in gratiam red-eo, ire, ii.

reconciliation (*you delay your*), = *to be reconciled with.*

recover, *I* (*trans.*), recupero, are ; recipio, ĕre ; *recover myself*, me recipio ; *recover* (*intrans.*) *from*, emer-go, ĕre, -si, -surus, e, ex.

recruit, *a*, tir-o, -onis ; *army of recruits.* (**223**.)

reflect on, *I*, recordor, ari.

refrain from, *I*. (**137**, **1**, *f.*)

refuge with, *I take*, con-fugio, ĕre, -fūgi, ad.

refuse, *I*, nolo. (**136**, *a.*)

refute, *I* (*an opponent*), redarguo, ĕre ; *a charge*, diluo, ĕre ; *a me removeo*, ĕre.

regard for or *to*, *I have*, rationem habeo (*gen.*).

regiment, *use* cohor-s, -tis, *f.*

regret, *I*, me pud-et, ĕre, -uit. (**309**.)

regular engagement, *a*, justum praelium.

reign, *I*, regno, are.

reinforcements, subsidia, *n. pl.*

reject, *I*, repudio, are.

rejoice, *I*, gaudeo, ēre, gavisus. (Intr. **44**.)

rejoicing (*subst.*), laetitia, *f.*

relates to, spectat ad.

relation, *a*, propinqu-us, -i. *m.* (**256**.)

reliance on (*you*), *I place*, fidem (tibi) habeo.

relief, *I bring you*, tibi succurr-o, ĕre, -i.

relieve, *I*, sublevo, are (*acc.*) ; *relieve of*, levo, are (*abl. of thing*).

relinquish, *I*, o-mitto, ere, -misi, -missum. (See note under *un done*, *I leave.*)

reluctant, *I am*, nolo, nolle.

reluctantly ; *with reluctance.* (**61**.)

rely on, *I*, con-fido, ĕre, -fisus (**282**, *Obs.*, **244**, *c*) ; fidem habeo (*dat.*).

---

[1] A "rebel" might also be "*qui a fide descivit* or *defecit;*" or *rem publicam* might be substituted for *regem.*

relying on (*adj.*), fretus. (**285.**)

remain behind, I, re-maneo, ēre, -mansi.

remain firm, I, permaneo, ēre.

remains, it, restat ut. (See **125**, *g.*)

remarkable, singularis.

remember, I, memin-i, -isse (*imperative* memento ; *for pres. subj.* meminerim).

Remi, the, Rem-i, -orum.

remorse for, I feel, me (**234**) poenit-et, ēre, -uit (*gen.*, **309**).

remove (*my home*), *I*, commigro, are (*intrans.*).

removed from, I am far. (**264.**)

renown, gloria, *f.*

repeatedly, saepe; saepissime (**57**, *a*); persaepe.

repel, I, propulso, are ; *from*, ab.

repent of, I, me poenit-et, -ēre, -uit. (**309.**)

reply, I, respond-eo, ēre, -i.

repose, otium, *n.*; *I enjoy*, otiosus sum.

reproach, it is a. (**260**, 3.)

reputation, existimati-o, -onis, *f.* ; fama, *f.* ; *reputation for*, lau-s, -dis, *f.* (*gen.*).

request, I make a, peto, ēre (**127**, *c*), posco, ēre, poposci (**231.**) (See note under *demand*) ; *I make this*, hoc (*acc.*) peto ; *my request*, quae peto. (**175.**)

require, I, *use* opus. (**286.**)

resemble (*closely*), *I*, similis (*superl.*) sum. (**255.**)

resentment, dol-or, -oris, *m.*

resident, I am, domicilium habeo ; *at.* (**312.**)

resignation, with, aequo animo.

resist, I, repugno, are. (*dat.*)

resistance, use inf. pass. of resisto, ēre (**219**), *in spite of resistance*, resisto *or* repugno (**420**, ii.).

resolution (*design*), consilium, *n.*

resolution, I pass a, decerno, ēre.

resolve, I, statu-o, ēre, -i ; decerno, ēre, -crevi, -cretum. (**45.**)

resources, op-es, -um, *f.*

respect, observantia, *f.*

respectable, honestus.

responsible (*for*), *I make you*, rationem a te reposco, ēre (*with gen.*)

rest, qui-es, -ētis, *f.*

rest (*of*), *the*, ceteri ; *or* (**372**) reliqu-us, -i (*in agreement*, **60**, *or with gen.*) ; *rest of the world*. (See *world*.)

rest on, I, ni-tor, i, -sus (*abl.*, **282**, *Obs.*).

rest with, to, penes (**331**, 15) esse.

restore, I (*strength, etc.*), redintegro, are.

restrained from, to be. (**137**, 1, *k.*)

result, res, rei, *f.*; (*of toil*), fruct-us, -ūs, *m.* ; *the result is, was, etc.*, evĕnit, evēnit, eventurum ; *without result*. (**332**, **8.**)

retain, I, re-tineo, ēre, -tinui.

retake, I, re-cipio, ēre, -cepi, -ceptum.

retire from, I, abeo, ire. (**264.**)

retreat, I, me recipio, ēre ; *pedem* refero, ferre.

retrieve, I, sano, are.

return (*subst.*), redit-us, -ūs, *m.*

return, I (*intrans.*), red-eo, ire, -ii, -iturus.

return kindness, I, gratiam refero. (**98**, *b.*)

revolt, a, defecti-o, -onis, *f.*

reward, praemium, *n.* (*prize*); merc-es, -ēdis, *f.* ; fruct-us, -us, *m.* (*fruit*).

reward, I, praemiis afficio.

rich (*of persons*), div-es, -itis, divit- (dit-)ior, -issimus; *of cities*, opulentus ; *the rich* (**51**, *a*).

riches, diviti-ae, -arum.

ride past, I, (equo) praeter-vehor, i, -vectus (*trans.*, **24**); cf. *coast along*.

ridge, jugum, *n.*

ridiculed, I am, irrideor, ēri. (**253**, iii.)

right (*subst.*), jus, juris, *n.* ; *I have a right*, debeo, ēre : *I am in the right*, vere, recte, sentio, ire.

right hand, dextra, *f.*

rightly, rightfully, jure.[1] (**268.**)

rigour, severit-as, -atis, *f.*

ring with, to (*echo with*), person-are, -ui (*abl.*).

---

[1] *Jure* is "rightly" in the sense of "rightfully," "deservedly :" *recte*, "correctly," "accurately ;" *rite*, in accordance with religious usage or ceremonial.

rising, a, sediti-o, -onis, *f.*

rising ground, tumul-us, -i, *m.* (*use pl.*).

rival, invid-us, -i, *m.*

river, flum-en, -inis, *n.* ; fluvi-us, -i, *m.*

road, a, via,

roar out, I, vociferor, ari ; magnā voce conclamo, are.

rock, saxum, *n.*

roll, I (*intrans.*), volvor, i, volutus. (21, *a.*)

Rome (*the city*), Roma, *f.* ; (*the nation*) populus Romanus. (319.)

roof, under my. (331, 4, *a.*)

round (*prep.*), circa or circum (*acc.*, 331, 5) ; *round which* (*standard*), quo (508).

rout, I, fundo, ěre, fudi, fusum.

royal, regius.

ruin, interit[1]-us, -ūs, *m.* ; exitium, *n.;* pernici-es, -ei,*f.;* clad-es, -is, *f.* ; calamit-as, -atis, *f.* ; *without ruin to, use* salvus (*abl. abs.*, 424).

ruin, I, pessum do, dare (Sallust) ; *ruined,* afflictus (affligo).

ruler of, I am, impero, are (*dat.*).

rumour, rum-or, -oris, *m.*

run forward, I, pro-curro, ěre, -curri.

run into, I, incurro, ěre (in, *acc.*).

rural, rusticus.

rustic (*adj.*), agrestis.

sack (*a city*) *I,* di-ripio, ěre, -ripui, -reptum.

sacrifice to (*metaph.*), *I = I place behind,* post-habeo. (253, ii.)

sad, maestus.

safe, tutus ; incolumis (*safe and sound*) ; salvus (*of things as well as persons*). For *adv. use* tutus or incolumis. (61.)

safety, sal-us, -utis, *f.* ; *in safety,* tuto (*adv.*); incolumis (*adj.*, 61) ; *I wish for your safety,* te salvum volo. (240, *Obs.* 1.)

sail, I, navigo, are ; *sail round,* circumnavigo, are (*trans.*)

sailor, naut-a, -ae, *m.*

sake of, for the, causā, or gratiā, *with gen. or pronominal adj.* (289); *or with gerund* (396) ; *for its own sake,* propter se (331, 20, *b*).

sally, a, erupti-o, -onis, *f.* ; *I make a,* eruptionem facio, ěre.

sally out, I, e-rumpo, ěre, -rupi.

salute, I, saluto, are.

same as, the. (84, 365.)

satisfactory. (See Voc. 6.)

satisfied with, contentus (*abl.*, 285).

save you, I, tibi salutem affero, ferre.

say, I, dico, ěre, dixi, dictum ; *said he* (*parenthetic*) (40) ; *it is said* (44). (See also under *speak.*)

saying, a, dictum (see 51, *b,* 55); *the saying,* illud (341).

scale, I, conscen-do, ěre, -di.

scanty, exiguus.

scarcely, vix.

scatter, to, (*intrans.*), dissipari. (20, 21, *a.*)

scene, I come on the, intervenio, ire.

scenes (*places*), loc-i, -orum, *m.*

schemes, insidiae, *f.*; art-es, -ium, *f.*

science of war, res militaris.

scout, a, explorat-or, -oris.

sea, mar-e, -is, *n.* ; *by sea and land,* terra marique (*note the order*).

sea-sickness, nausea, *f.*

second, alter (531, *a*) ; (*for*) *a second time,* iterum (533, *c*) ; *secondly,* deinde (534, *Obs.*).

secret from, I keep, celo, are (230) ; *I make a secret of,* dissimulo, are (*with constr. of* simulo, 39).

secretly, secreto (*adv.*)

secure (*safe*), tutus. (19.)

secure, I (*make secure*), confirmo, are.

see, I, video,[2] ěre, vīdi, visum ; (*as a spectator*) specto, are; (*in sense of perceive*), intel-lego, ěre, -lexi, -lectum ; *I am seen,* con-spicior, i, -spectus.

---

[1] *Ruina* is the fall (literal) of a building, etc., and is only occasionally used in a metaphorical sense. (See 17-19.)

[2] *Videre,* the general word, to see ; *spectare,* to look long at, to watch as a spectacle ; *cernere,* to see clearly, to discern ; *conspicere,* to get sight of ; *aspicere,* to turn the eye towards ; *intueri,* to gaze at earnestly or steadfastly.

seek for, I, pet-o, ĕre, -ii, -ivi, -ĭtum.

seem, I, videor, ēri, visus (43); it seems as though (149, ii.).

seize, I, comprehen-do, ĕre, -di, -sum ; (an opportunity), utor, i, usus. (281.)

seldom, raro.

self-confidence, sui fiducia, f. (300.)

self-control, ´modestia ; (animi) moderati-o, -onis, f.

self-control, want of, impotentia, f.; adj. impotens, adv. impotenter.

Senate, the, Senat-us, -ūs, m.

Senate House, the, Curia, f.

send, I, mitto, ĕre, misi, missum ; to, ad (6); send back (to), remitto, ĕre (ad); send for, arcess-o, ĕre, -ivi, -ītum (acc.).

sense, good, prudentia, f.

sensible, or of sense, pruden-s, -tior, -tissimus ; one so sensible as (224, Obs. 2) ; adv., prudenter.

sentenced to, I am, multor, ari. (307.)

sentiments, I hold the same, eadem (365) sentio (54).

separately, singuli. (380, b.)

serious, grav-is, -ior, -issimus.

serpent, serpen-s, -tis, f.

served, the nation is, respublica geritur, gesta est.

service, military, militia, f.

service to, I do (good, the best, such good), (bene, optime, tam bene) mereor, ēri, meritus, de (332, 3, g); but services to, merita (51, b) in (331, 24, d).

set (spurs), I, subdo, ĕre (dat.).

set at liberty, I, libero, are.

set at naught, I, con-temno, ĕre, -tempsi, -temptum (see Voc. 10, n.); parvi, minimi, nihili, facio or habeo (305).

set before (you), I, (tibi) expo-no, ĕre, -sui, -situm.

set fire to, I, incen-do, ĕre, -di, -sum (acc.).

set out, I, pro-ficiscor, i, -fectus.

settle, I, constit-uo, ĕre, -ui (trans.).

several (= some), aliquot (indecl.) ; =respective, suus with quisque. (352, Obs.)

severe, gravis.

sex, sex-us, -ūs, m.

shake, I (trans.), labefacto, are.

shamelessness, impudentia, f.

share (with), I, communico, are (cum, 253, iv.).

shatter, I, quasso, are.

shelter, I, tego, ĕre, texi, tectum.

shelter, perfugium, n.; under shelter of, tectus (abl.).

shew, I. (See show.)

shield, scutum, n.

ship of war, a, navis longa ; merchant ship, navis oneraria.

short, in, denique.

short-lived (panic) = of the shortest time. (303, Obs. 1.)

shortly, brevi.

shout, a, clam-or, -oris, m.

show, I (point out), monstro, are ; I show (display) clemency, etc., or, I show myself (prove) (see 241) ; I show such cruelty to, adeo saevio, ire, in (abl.) ; show gratitude (98, b).

shrewd, acutus (superl. 57, a.).

shrink from, I, detrecto, are (acc.).

sick, aeg-er, -ra, -rum ; I am sick, aegroto, are ; his sick-bed, = him whilst sick and failing.

side (of a river), ripa, f.

side, I am by your, tibi praesto (adv.) sum ; on your, a te sto, are, stĕti. (332, i., d.)

side, on no, nusquam ; nec usquam ; on this side (of), prep., cis (331, 6) ; on the other, ultra (331, 23) ; on all sides, undique.

sigh for, I (metaph.), desidero, are (trans., 22, 23).

signal, a, signum, n.

silence, in. (61.)

silent, I am, taceo, ĕre.

since, (adv.), postea ; as prep., = from. (326.)

single combat, in, comminus.

single, a, unus ; not a single ; not one ; ne unus quidem. (529, a.)

sink, I (trans.), demer-go, ĕre, -si, -sum ; intrans. (metaph.), descend-o, ĕre, -i : I am sinking (fainting) under, exanimor, ari (abl., 267).

sister, sor-or, -oris.

sit, I, sĕdeo, ĕre, sēdi ; *sit down,* con-sido, ĕre, -sēdi.

situation, sit-us, -ūs, *m.*

six, sex ; *sixth,* sextus.

size, magnitud-o, -inis, *f. ;* and see **174.**

slander, maledicta, *n. pl.* **(51,** *b.***)**

slaughter, I, *use* occidione oc-cīdo, ĕre, -cīdi, -cīsum.

slave, serv-us, -i, *m.; I am a slave,* serv-io, ire, -ii, -ītum.

slavery, servīt-us, -utis, *f.*

slay, I. (See *kill.*)

sleep, I, dorm-io, ire, -ivi, -ii, -itum; *in his sleep, use pres. partic.*

sleep, somn-us, -i, *m.*

sleep, want of, vigiliae, *f. pl.*

slingstone, a, glan-s, -dis, *f.*

so, ita : *with verbs,* adeo; *so little,* adeo non : *with adjs. and advs. only,* tam : *so = accordingly,* itaque : *so great, so many* (**84**) : *so small,* tantulus: *so far from,* tantum abest ut (**124**): *so, or as, long as, abl. abs.* (**420,** ii.) (See also **224,** *Obs.* 2.)

society, as a. (**380,** *b.***)**

soften (metaph.), I, exoro, are.

solemnly appeal, I. (See *appeal.*)

soldier, mil-es, -itis.

solitude (of a place), infrequentia, *f.*

Solon, Sol-on, -onis.

some (some one), aliquis (**360**); nescio quis (**362**); *some . . others,* alii . . . alii (**369**).

some (amount of), aliquantum (*gen.,* **294**) ; *for some time,* aliquantum temporis.

somehow. (**363.**)

something (opposed to nothing), aliquid (**360**).

sometimes, nonnunquam ;[1] interdum.

son, fili-us, -i.

soon, mox ; brevi ; jam (**328,** *b*) ; *sooner than he had hoped=quicker* (celerius) *than his own hope* (**277**).

sore (of famine), gravis.

sorrows, incommoda, *n. pl.,* aerumnae (*stronger*).

sorry, I should be, nolim. (**231,** *example.*)

soul, (not) a, quisquam (**358,** i.); *in Livy* unus *is sometimes added;* ne unus quidem. (**529,** *a.*)

sound your praises, I, laudibus te fero, ferre.

sounds incredible, it, incredibile dictu est. (**404.**)

source of (metaph.), the, use unde (**174,** *e*); *a source of (gain)* (**260,** 3).

sovereign (king), rex.

sovereignty, principat-us, -ūs, *m.*

Spaniard, a, Hispan-us, -i ; *Spain* (= *the nation*), Hispani. (**319.**)

spare, I, parco, ĕre, peperci (*dat.,* **5**) ; *for perf. pass.* temperatum est (**249**).

speak, I, loquor,[2] i, locutus ; dico, ĕre ; *I speak out,* eloquor, i ; *in speaking, abl. of gerund.*

special peculiarity of. (See *peculiarity.*)

speech, a, orati-o, -onis, *f.*; *if to soldiers or multitude,* conti-o, -onis, *f.; my speech is over; I have done my speech,* dixi. (**187.**)

speed, celerit-as, -atis, *f.*

spirit, anim-us, -i, *m.; of more than one person,* animi ; *with spirit,* ferociter. (See note under *boldly.*)

spite of, in, in (**273,** *Obs.*) ; *of your resistance, etc.*), *abl. abs.* (**420,** ii.); *in spite of his innocence* (**224,** *Obs.* 1).

spoil, praeda, *f.*

spotless, integer, integerrimus ; innocen-s, -tior, -tissimus.

---

[1] *Nonnunquam,* "fairly often ;" approaches *saepius. Interdum,* "now and then," more rarely than *nonnunquam. Aliquando,* "on certain occasions," opposed to "never," almost = *raro.*

[2] *Dico,* I "speak" or "say," *i.e.* I give expression to thoughts or views which I have formed : *loquor,* I "speak," use the organs of speech to utter articulate words. Hence *dico* = I make a formal speech *loquor* = I utter informal or casual words.

spread beneath, I (*trans.*), sub-jicio, ĕre, -jeci, -jectum; *intrans.*, sub-jicior, ì. **(20.)**

spring, the, vcr, vēris, *n.*

spring, I (*am sprung*), orior, īri, ortus; *sprung from*, ortus (*abl.*); *originally sprung from*, oriundus ab.

spur, calc-ar, -aris, *n.* ; *I put spurs to*, calcaria subdo, ĕre (*dat.*).

spy, a, speculat-or, -oris, *m.*

staff (*military*), legati, *m. pl.*

stand, I, sto, stare, stĕti; *stand by*, ad-sto, -stare, -stiti (*dat.*); *stand round*, circum-sto, are, -steti (*acc.*).

stand for, I, (*am a candidate for*), peto, ĕre (*acc.*).

stand in need of, I, indigeo, ĕre. **(284.)**

stand in your way, I, tibi obsto, are. **(253, i.)**

standard, a, signum, *n.*; vexillum,*n.*

start (*set out*), *I*, pro-ficiscor, i, -fectus, -fecturus.

state (*condition*), stat-us, -ūs, *m.*

state (*adj.*), publicus.

statesman, a consummate, reipublicae gubernandae peritissimus. **(301, ii.)**

stay with, I (*I visit*), commoror, ari apud **(331, 4, *a*)**; deverto, ĕre (*reflexive*), apud; *I stay at home*, domi maneo, ēre.

steadily, turn by *did not cease to* (desisto, ĕre, -stiti).

steadiness, want of, inconstantia, *f.*

steal away, I (*intrans.*), di-labor, i, lapsus.

stern, severus.

sternly, I act, saevio, irc. **(25.)**

still (*adv.*), adhuc; etiam nunc (*of the present*); etiam tum (*past or fut.*).

stony-hearted, ferreus.

storm, tempest-as, -atis, *f.*

storm, I (*take by storm*), expugno, are.

story, a, res, rei, *f.*; and see **54**; *there is a story*, ferunt **(44).**

strangely, nescio quo pacto. (See **169.**)

stream, riv-us, -i, *m.* ; see *river*.

strength, vir-cs, -ium, *f. pl.; strength of mind*, constantia, *f.*

stretch forth, I, por-rigo, ĕre, -rexi, -rectum.

strike off, I, excu-tio, ĕre, -ssi, -ssum.

strikingly, graviter.

strive, I (*to*), conor, ari (*modal*).

stronghold, arx, arcis, *f.*

struck (*partic.*), ictus (ico, ĕre); *I am struck*, per-cutior, i, -cussus.

study, a, ar-s, -tis, *f.* ; *study* (*of*), cogniti-o, -onis, *f.*

study, I, operam do (*dat.*) ; *study my own interest*, mihi **(248)** con-sulo, ĕre.

subject, a, civ-is, -is, *m.*

submit to, I, per-fero, -ferre (*acc.*).

substantial, solidus, *comp.* magis solidus.

succeed in, I (*a design, etc.*), per-ficio, ĕre (*trans.*); efficio *with* ut. **(125, j.)**

succeed to, I (*the throne*), (regnum) ex-cipio, ĕre, -cēpi, -ceptum **(17)**; *I succeed you*, tibi suc-cedo, ĕre, -cessi, -cessum.

success **(98, *a*)** ; *without success*, in-fecta re **(332, 8 ; 425).**

successfully, prospere.

successive, continuus.

successors (*his*), =*those who reigned after* (*him*) ; *or those who are to* (*fut. in* -rus) *succeed* (*him*). (Scc **175, 342, *n*.**)

succour, I, subvenio, ire (*dat.*).

such (=*of such a kind*), talis ; (=*so great*), tantus ; *as*, qualis *or* quantus (see **86**) : *such . . . as this*, hujusmodi **(87)**, *or* hic talis, hic tantus **(88, *Obs.*)**: *such as to*, *of such a kind that* **(108)** : *such* (*adv.*), *such a* (*with adj.*), tam ; talis (*or tantus*) tamque **(88)** : *where English subst. is expressed by Latin verb*, use adeo ; *I show such cruelty*, adeo saevio.

sudden, subitus; repentinus (*unexpected*).

suddenly, subĭto.

suddenness of, the, =*how sudden it was.* **(174, e.)**

suffer from, I, laboro, are (*abl.*).

suffering (*adj.*), afflictus (affligo).

sufficient, justus ; satis, *with gen.*

suffices, it, satis est.

suggest, I, auctor sum (**399**, *Obs.* 2) ; admoneo, ĕre (**127**, *a*).

suggestion, at (*my*), (me) auctore (*abl. abs.*, **424**).

suicide, I commit, mortem mihi con-scisco, ĕre, -scivi. (**253**, ii.)

summer, aest-as, -atis, *f.*

summit. (**60.**)

summon, I, voco, are ; *to,* ad.

sun, sol, solis, *m.*

sunlight, lux, lucis, *f.* (solis *may be added*).

superior to, I am, = *I surpass ;* (*in courage, etc.*), *use comparat. of adj.* (**278**, **279**); *superior numbers* (*see numbers*).

superstition, superstiti-o, -onis, *f.*

supper, caena, *f. ; to,* ad (**331**, 24, *b, example*).

supplies, commeat-us, -ūs, *m.* (*sing. and pl.*)

supply with, I, suppedito, are. (**247.**)

support (*subst.*), subsidium, *n.*

support (*my*) *arms, I,* arma fero, ferre.

suppose, I, puto, are. (See note under *fancy.*)

supreme power, imperium, *n.*

sure, I am or feel, certo scio ; pro certo habeo ; *I have made sure of,* compertum habeo (**188**) : *be sure to,* fac, cura (ut). (See **141.**)

surpass, I, supero, are.

surprise (*as a foe*), *I,* opprimo, ĕre.

surrender, I (*trans.*), de-do, ĕre, -didi, -dītum ; (*intrans.*), me dedo (see **21**, *b*); *I surrender my arms,* arma trado, ĕre.

surround, to, circumvĕnire (*trans.*); *surrounded, use pres. partic. of* circumsto, are (*abl. abs.*, **420**, ii.); *surrounded* (*by defences*), cinctus (cingo) : *to be surrounded* (*as by water*), circum-fundi, -fusus.

survive, I, supersum ; *from,* e, ex : *so long as you survive,* te super-stite (*abl. abs.*, **424**).

suspect, I, suspicor, ari ; = *I think,* puto, are (see note under *fancy*); *I am* (*become*) *suspected of,* in sus-picionem vĕnio, ire (*gen.*).

suspend, I, inter-mitto, ĕre. (See note under *undone, I leave.*)

suspicion, suspici-o, -onis, *f. ; I have no,* = *I suspect nothing.* (**54.**)

sustain (*onset*), *I,* sustineo, ĕre.

swallow, a, hirund-o, -inis, *f.*

swarm out of, to, ef-fundi, -fusus (*abl.*).

swear, I, juro, are.

sweep, I (*metaph.*), volito, are.

sword, gladius, -i, *m. ; in meta-phorical sense,* arma, *n. pl.* ; fer-rum, *n. ; with fire and sword,* ferro et igni ; *by sword and violence,* vi et armis : *note the order.*

Syracuse, Syracusae, *f.*

take, I (*a city*), capio, ĕre ; *by as-sault,* expugno, are.

take advantage of, I, utor, i, usus. (**281.**)

take care that, I, facio ut. (**118.**)

take from you, I, tibi ad-imo, ĕre, -ēmi, -emptum. (**243.**)

take part in, I. (See *part in.*)

take place, to, fieri.

take prisoner, I, capio, ĕre.

take the same view, I. (See *view.*)

take up, I (*arms*), sum-o, ĕre, -psi, -ptum, = *I spend,* consumo, ĕre.

talk, I, loquor, i, locutus.

talkative, loqu-ax, -acior.

tall, procērus.

task, op-us, -ĕris, *n.*

taste, a, studium, *n.*

taunt you with, I, tibi ob-jicio, ĕre, -jeci. (**247.**)

tax with, I, incuso,[1] are , insimulo, are (*acc. of person, gen. of thing*).

teacher, magist-er, -ri : *fem. form,* magistra.

teaching, the, praecepta, *pl.*

tear, a, lacrima, *f.*

tedious, longus.

teeth of, in the. (**420**, ii.)

tell, I (*bid*), jubeo, ēre. (**120.**)

---

1 *Incuso,* "I tax with," "charge with," but informally, not as *accuso* with gen. "bring a charge in court." *Insimulo,* "I hint charges without proof." *Arguo,* "I try to prove guilty."

tell (*a story*), *I*, narro, are.
temper, anim-us, i, *m.*
temperament, indol-es, -is, *f.* (See note under *character.*)
temple, templum, *n.*
ten, decem ; (*a-piece*), deni. (532.)
tenacious of, tenax. (301, i.)
tends to, use gen. with est. (292, *Obs.*)
tent, tabernaculum, *n.*
terms, condition-es, -um, *f. pl.*
terrible, so, tantus.
territory, fin-es, -ium, *m.*
terror, I am in such, adeo pertimesco, ĕre, -ui.
testify, I (*show*), declaro, are.
than, quam ; *or abl.* (275, 493.)
thank you (*for*), *I*, gratias (tibi) ago, ob *or* pro.
thanks, I return, gratias ago (98, *b*) ; "*thanks to*", propter (331, 20, *b*).
that(*demonstrative*), ille, a, ud (339).
that, after verbs of saying (see Oratio Obliqua) : =*in order that,* (*so*) *that* (see Final, Consecutive, Clauses).
themselves (*reflexive*), se (ipsos) (356, ii.) ; *emphatic*, ipsi (355).
then, tum, tunc ; *then and there,* illico. (See also *therefore.*)
thence, inde.
there, ibi ; illic ; *after verb of motion*, eo, illuc.
therefore, igitur ; *in narrative*, itaque.
thereupon, tum.
thick of, the, = *the midst of.* (60.)
think, I (*reflect*), cogito, are.
third, tertius (*adj.*).
thirst, sit-is, -is, *f.*, *abl.* siti.
thirty, triginta (*indecl.*).
this, hic, haec, hoc. (337.)
thoroughly (*with adj.*), *use superl.*
though, use pres. part. (412, *Obs.*)
thousand (*subst.*), mille, *pl.* milia ; *to die a thousand deaths,* = *a thousand times*, milies (*adv.*).
threaten, I, insto, are ; *of things,* immineo, ĕre ; impend-eo, ēre, -i (253, i.) ; *I threaten with,* minor, ari, minitor, ari, denuntio, are (247) ; *threaten, to,* minor, ari. (See 37.)

threats, minae, *f. pl.* ; *I make threats*, =*I threaten* (minor).
three, tres, tria ; *three days* (*space of*), triduum, *n.* ; *three years,* triennium, *n.*
thrice, ter.
throne, regnum, *n.*, *or* imperium, *n.* ; *I am on the throne*, regno, are. (See 17.)
throng, multitud-o, -inis, *f.*
throughout, per (*acc.*) ; *throughout* (*the city*), = *in the whole* (*abl.*).
throw, I, conjicio, ĕre, -jeci, -jectum ; *into*, in (*acc.*) ; *myself* (*at the feet of*), me projicio, ĕre (257) ; *throw across*, trajicio, ĕre ; *throw away*, projicio, ĕre ; *throw down* (*arms*), abjicio, ĕre.
tie (*subst.*), necessitud-o, -inis, *f.*
till, I, col-o, ĕre, -ui, cultum.
till (440, 441) ; *not till* (443, *Obs.*).
time, temp-us, -oris, *n.* ; *at that time*, tum ; *eā tempestate* ; tum temporis (294, *Obs.*) ; *at his own time* (349, *Obs.*) ; *in good time*, ad tempus (326).
timid, timidus.
to, ad (331, 1) ; *in* (331, 24). (See 6.)
to-day, hodie.
toil, lab-or, -oris, *m.*
toilsome, = *of such toil.* (303, i.)
tomb, sepulcrum, *n.*
to-morrow, cras.
tongue, lingua, *f.*
too (*also*), quoque. (Intr. 9S.)
too, with adjectives. (See 57, *b.*)
too little (*of*), parum. (294.)
too much, 294 ; *it costs*, nimio (280, *Obs.*).
torture, cruciat-us, -ūs, *m.*
touch (*his heart*), *I*, (animum ejus) flecto, ĕre ; *I am touched by,* moveor, ēri (*abl.*).
towards, ad (331, 1, 22) ; *with countries, towns, and* domum.
town, oppidum, *n.*
townsman, oppidan-us, -i.
traditions, I hand down, trado, ĕre ; *there is a tradition.* (44.)
train, I, exerc-eo, ēre, -ui, -itum : exercito, are ; *trained in*, exercitatus (*abl.*).
training, disciplina, *f.*

traitors, cives impii.

transact, I, ago, ĕre, ēgi, actum.

tranquillity, otium, *n.*

transported, I am (metaph.), exardesco, ĕre, -si (*lit. I become hot*).

travel, I, iter facio ; = *go abroad,* peregrinor, ari ; *travel over,* perlustro, are (*acc.*).

treachery, perfidia, *f.*

treat as a source of gain, I. (260, 3.)

treat lightly, I, parvi facio. (305.)

treat with success (heal), I, medeor, ēri (*dat.*).

treaty, a, foed-us, -ĕris, *n.*

tree, a, arb-or, -ŏris, *f.*

tribe, a, nati-o, -ŏnis, *f.* ; gen-s, -tis, *f.* (Voc. 2, *note.*)

trifling, (adj.), levissimus (57, *a*) ; inconstan-s, -tissimus. (See 224.)

triumph (success), victoria, *f.* ; (*a Roman general's*), triumph-us, -i (see note under *I triumph*) ; *in triumph,* victor (63) ; *in the very hour of,* in ipsā victoriā ; *shouts of triumph,* exultantium clamor (415, *b*).

triumph, I (metaph.), exulto,[1] are ; *triumph over,* supero, are (*acc.*).

troops, copiae, *f.* ; milit-es, -um, *m.*

trouble, without, nullo negotio (269, *Obs.*) ; *troubles,* molestiae, *f. pl.* ; *troublesome,* molestus.

truce, a, indutiae, *f. pl.*

true, verus ; *it is true, use* ille (334, iv.) ; *truest patriot* (see *patriot*).

trust (that), I, con-fido, ĕre, -fisus ; *trust your word,* fidem tibi habeo.

truth, the, vera, *n. pl.* (53) ; *but in truth (opposed to a supposition),* nunc vero.

try (to), I, conor, ari.

trying, (adj.), difficilis. (57, *a.*)

tumult, tumult-us, -ūs, *m.*

turn, I (trans.), vert-o, ĕre, -i ; *my back on you,* tergum tibi verto.

turn, I (intrans.), vertor, i, versus ; convertor, i (20) ; *to,* ad ; *turn back,* re-vertor, i.

turn, each in, pro se quisque. (352.)

turn out, I (prove), eva-do, ĕre, -si (Intr. 50) ; *it turns out,* evĕnit ; nsu vĕnit (see note under *lot*) ; *turns out so,* eo evadit.

twelve hundred, mille ducenti. (527, 528.)

twentieth, vicesimus.

twenty, viginti (*indecl.*).

twice over, semel atque iterum ; *twice two,* bis bina.

two, du-o, -ae, -o ; *two a-piece,* bini (532, *a*) ; *two-thirds,* duae partes (535, *c*) ; *two years (space of),* biennium, *n.*

tyrant, tyrann-us, -i.

tyranny, dominati-o, onis, *f.*

unable to, I am, nequ-eo, -ivi, -ii ; non possum.

unanimous; unanimously, use omnis. (59.)

unarmed, inermis.

unawares, imprudens (*adj.,* 61).

uncertain, it is, incertum est. (166.)

uncle, avuncul-us, -i.

uncomplaining under, patiens (57, *a*), *with gen.* (302).

unconstitutional, unconstitutionally, contra rempublicam. (331, 7.)

uncultivated, rudis.

undaunted, intrepidus (*for usage with proper nouns and persons, see* 224.)

under (disgrace), cum. (269.)

understand, I, intel-lego, ĕre, -lexi, -lectum.

undertake, I, suscipio, ĕre.

undertaking, an, inceptum, *n.* (51, *b.*)

undeserved, immeritus.

undiminished, = *the same as before.* (84.)

undone, I leave, o-mitto,[2] ĕre, -misi, -missum.

undoubtedly, = *indisputably.* (64.)

unequalled, tantus . . . quantus (*followed by* nemo etc.). (See 490, i.)

unhappy, mis-er, -era, -erum.

---

[1] *Triumpho* is rarely used metaphorically, or in any other sense than that of celebrating a *triumphus, i.e.* of a general entering the city in triumphal procession.

[2] *Omitto* is I give up, or do not begin, something, *designedly; intermitto,* I leave alone *for a time; praetermitto,* I pass by, omit, *undesignedly.*

unharmed, incolumis.
unhealthy, pestilentus.
unheard, indictā causā (*abl. abs.*).
union, in, conjuncti.
universal, use omnis. (**59.**)
unjust, iniquus.
unlucky, infel-ix, -icior.
unmoved, immotus.
unnatural, nefarius.
unpatriotic, the, mali, *or* improbi, cives. (**50,** *note.*)
unpopularity, invidia, *f. ; object of* (*see object*).
unprincipled, nequ-am, -ior, -issi-mus (*lit. worthless*) : *see* 224.
unquestionable, it is, = *it cannot be doubted.* (See **137.**)
unrivalled. (**358,** ii., *or* **490,** i.'
until. (See *till.*)
untimely, immaturus.
untouched, integ-er, -ra, -rum.
unusual, inusitatus.
unversed in, imperitus (*gen.*, **301,** ii.).
unwilling, I am, nolo, nolle, nolui.
unwillingly. (**61.**)
unwise, insipiens.
unwounded, integer.
up to, ad ; *up to this day,* ad hunc usque diem.
uphold, I, sus-tineo, ēre, -tinui.
uproar, tumult-us, -ūs, *m.*
urge, I (*to do*), sua-deo, ēre, -si ; insto, are (*both with dat. and* ut *or* ne) : *urge to* (*crime*), ad (scelus) impello, ēre, -puli : *urge this upon you,* hoc tibi suadeo ; hujus rei auctor tibi ac suasor sum.
urgently, vehementer.
use of, I make, utor, i, usus. (**282.**)
use to, I am of, prosum. (**251.**)
usefulness, public, use verb (**376,** ii. iii.), reipublicae (plus, maxime) prosum.
useless, is, nihil prodest.
utmost (*to*), *I will do my,* quantum in me est *or* erit (**333,** 5, *g*), *with fut.*
utmost value. (See *value.*)

vain, in, frustra,[1] nequidquam.

valley, a, vall-is, -is, *f.*
value (*to*), *I am of* (*the utmost*), (maxime) prosum. (**251.**)
value highly, more highly, I, magni, pluris, aestimo, are ; facio, ěre : *I am valued,* fio, fieri ; *by,* apud : *I estimate you at your proper value,* tanti te quanti debeo facio (see **305**) : *I value above,* = *prefer to* (**253,** i.).
vanquish, I, vinco, ěre, vīci, vic-tum.
variance with, to be at, pugnare cum (*abl.*).
various. (**371.**)
vast, maximus ; ingen-s, -tis. (See Voc. 3, *n.*)
vehement, use adv. vehement-er, -issime.
Veii, Veii, *m. pl.*
venture, I, audeo, ēre, ausus ; *by venturing on something,* audendo aliquid. (**99,** 360, i.)
verdict, sententia, *f.* (*use pl.* : see Voc. 7, *n.* 2) ; *I give my,* dico, ēre.
versed in, peritus (*gen.*, **301,** ii.).
very, this, hic ipse (see **355,** *b*) : *for very, with adjs. see* **57,** *a.*
veteran (*adj.*), veteranus.
victorious, when he was, victor (*subst.*, **63**).
victory, victoria, *f.* ; vincěre. (**98,** *a.*)
view (*opinion*), sententia, *f.*
view, I take the same, idem, eadem, sentio, quod, quae, *or* ac (**365**) ; *a different,* aliter sentio ac (**367.**)
vigour (*spirit*), ferocia, *f.* ; (*force*), vis, *acc.* vim, *f.*
vile, turpis, e. (**19.**)
vileness, turpitud-o, -inis, *f.*
violating, without, use salvus (**424.**)
violation of, partic. of violo, are (**417,** i.) : *in violation of,* contra quam (**491,** *b*).
violence, vis, *abl.* vi, *f.*
virtue, virt-us, -utis, *f.* ; *in virtue of,* pro (**332,** 7, *g.*)
virtuously, honeste.
visible, I am, appareo, ēre,
visit, I, vis-o, ēre, -i.

---

[1] *Frustra,* "in vain," of the *person* who fails in his object ; *nequidquam,* "in vain," of the *attempt* which has produced no result.

voice, vox, vocis, *f.*
voluntarily, ultro.[1]
vote (of elector), suffragium, *n.* ; *(of judge or senator)*, sententia, *f.*
voyage, navigati-o, -onis, *f.* ; *I have, or make, a*, navigo, are.

wage, I, gero, ĕre, gessi, gestum ; *with*, cum *or* contra.
wailing, plorat-us, -ûs, *m.*
wait (for), I, expecto, are *(acc., 22)*; *wait to see* (174, *d* ; 474 *b.*)
walk (take a walk) in, I, inambulo, are *(abl.).*
wall (general term), mur-us, -i, *m.* ; *walls (of city or fortress)*, moenia, *n. pl.*, *3rd decl.*
want (of), there has been the greatest, maxime laboratum est (ab, 332, I, *e*) : *want of caution, etc.*, see *caution, etc.*
want (to), I, volo, velle, volui.
wanting to, I am (I fail), de-sum, esse, -fui (251) : *wanting in (nothing)*, (nihil) mihi deest.
war, bellum, *n.* ; *I make war against*, bellum, *or* arma, infero, ferre (253, ii.) ; *I declare*, indico, ĕre *(ibid.)*: *ship of war* (see *ship*).
warfare, militia, *f.*
warmth, with, vehementer.
warn, I, mon-eo, ēre, -ui, -itum ; admoneo, ĕre (127, *a*): *warnings*, (415, *a*).
waste, I lay, populor, ari ; vasto, are ; *waste (time)*, tero, ĕre.
wave, a, fluct-us, -ûs, *m.*
way, via, *f.*
weak (morally), levis; *weak characters* (375).
weakness, infirmit-as, -atis, *f.* ; *in his weakness*, imbecillus *(adj.*, 61).
wealth, divitiae, *f. pl.*
wealthy (of cities), opulentus.
weapon, a, telum, *n.*
weariness, lassitud-o, -inis, *f.* ; *I feel weariness of*, = am weary of.
weary, I (trans.), fatigo, are : *I am wearied with*, langueo, ĕre de (332, 3, *e*), *or* e, ex.

weary of, I am, me taedet, ēre, pertaesum est. (309.)
weather, the, tempest-as, -atis, *f.*
week, substitute approximate number of days ; at the end of a, within a, = *after, before, the 7th day.*
weep over, I, illacrimo, are *(dat.).*
weight, I have great, no, multum, nihil, valeo (apud.) (331, 4, *d.*)
welfare, sal-us, -utis, *f.*
well (adv.), bene; *well enough*, satis : *I know well*, certo scio ; *well known*, satis notus.
well-disposed to, bene-volus, -volentior in *or* erga. (255, *Obs.*)
well-earned, meritus.
well-trained, exercitatus.
well-wishers. (175.)
what. (157 ; and see *who.*)
when (interrogat.), quando (157, ii.): *conj.*, cum (quum). (See Temporal Clauses, I.)
whence, unde; *interrogat.* (157, ii.); *correlat.* (89).
whenever. (434, and *Obs.*)
where, ubi ; *where . . . from* (= *whence*), unde ; = *whither*, quo ; *where in the world?* ubi gentium. (294, *Obs.*)
whether . . . or. (168 ; see also 171, *c, d*, and 467.)
which (see *who*): *which of two*, uter (157, i.).
while (conj.), dum. (180.) See also Temporal Clauses, II.
while, for a, paulisper.
whither, quo. (157, ii.)
who, which (that), what (relat.), qui, quae, quod. (See Relative.)
who, which, what (interrogat.), quis, quae, quid *(subst.)* ; qui, quae, quod *(adj.).* (See 157, i.)
whoever, quicunque : *often exp. by tense of verb.* (434, *Obs.*)
whole, totus, a, um ; *whole of.* (60.)
wholly (61): *(to despair)*, de summa re, *i.e. of our most important interests.*
why, cur, quamobrem (157, ii.). (See also 174, *a*, and *note.*)

---

[1] *Ultro*, before receiving, without waiting for, provocation, solicitation, etc : *sua, mea*, etc., *sponte*, of one's own impulse, without external pressure or advice.

wicked, the, improbi. **(50,** and *note.)*
wickedness, nequitia, *f.* (See note under *crime.*)
widow, vidua.
will, against my, me invito, *abl. abs.* **(420,** ii.)
willing, I am, volo, velle, volui.
win, I (obtain), consequor, i ; *win the day, I,* vinco, ĕre. (Intr. 40.)
wind, vent-us, -i, *m.*
wing (of army), cornu, *n.; on the,* **332, I, c.**)
winter (adj.), hibernus.
winter, I (pass the winter), hiemo, are.
wisdom, sapientia, *f.*
wise, sapien-s, -tior, -tissimus ; *all the wisest men.* **(375.)**
wish, I, volo, velle, volui : *could have wished* **(149,** i.): *I do not wish,* nolo, nolle nolui.
wish for this, I, hoc opto, are : volo, velle.
wishes (against your), = will. **(424.)**
with, (See S, and **332, 2 ;**) *weight with* (see *weight*).
withdraw-from, I, me recipio, ĕre, e, ex.
within, intra **(331, 12);** *of time,* **325;** *within memory,* post **(331, 17,** *b*): *I am within a little of* **(137, I,** *h*).
without (prep.), sine : *more often exp. by abl. abs.* **(332, 8,** and **425);** ita ut **(111)** ; quin **(132,** *b*); *without any* **(360,** *note*).
withstand, I, ob-sto, are, -stiti *(dat.,* **244,** *b*).
woman, a, muli-er, -eris.
wonder, I, miror, ari.
wonderful, mirificus.
word, a, verbum, *n.* ; *words,* dicta. **(55.)**
word (of honour), fid-es, ei, *f.*
work, a, op-us, -eris, *n.*
work upon (your feelings), I, flecto, ĕre, flexi, flexum.
world (see **16,** *b*) : *all the world,* nemo est quin **(80);** *in the, in the whole, world,* usquam : *the rest of*

the, ceteri homines ; ceterae gentes.
worse, pej-or, -us ; deteri-or, -us ; *for the,* in.
worst foe, enemy, superl. of inimicus. **(256.)**
worth seeking, gerundive of appeto, ĕre. **(393.)**
worthless, nequ-am, -ior, -issimus ; *see* **224.**
worthy of, dignus. **(285.)**
would that. **(152.)**
wound, vuln-us, -eris, *n.; national,* reipublicae. **(58.)**
wound, I, vulnero, are ; *wounded,* saucius *(adj.)* ; *I am wounded,* vulneror, ari ; *saucior,* ari *(severely).*
wrench from (you), I, (tibi) extorqueo, ĕre, -torsi, -tortum. **(257.)**
write, I, scri-bo, ĕre, -psi, -ptum ; *write you word,* ad te scribo.
wrong, a, injuria,[1] *f.; I do wrong,* pecco, are ; *wrong-doing,* peccare **(98,** *a*).

year, ann-us, -i, *m.; (space of) two, three, years.* (See *two, three.*)
yes (see **162**) ; *I say yes,* aio, *pres. part.,* aien-s, -tis.
yesterday, heri ; *of yesterday,* hesternus *(adj.).*
yet (nevertheless), tamen ; vero *(emphatic).*
yet, not, nondum.
yield (to), I, cedo, ĕre, cessi *(dat.).*
you, tu, *pl.* vos. (See **11,** *a, b ;* **334,** i.-iii.)
young, juvenis, junior. **(51,** *a, note.*)
your, your own (sing.), tuus : *(pl.),* vester (see **11,** *c*) ; *that of yours,* iste **(338).**
yourself (emphatic), ipse **(355)** ; *(reflexive),* te, vos **(356,** ii.).
youth (time of), adolescentia, *f.; in my* **(63.)** (See also **51** *a, note.*)

zeal, studium, *n.*

---

[1] *Injuria* is never used for "injury" in the sense of mere *harm* or *damage;* this must be expressed by *damnum.*

INDEX OF SUBJECTS.

LATIN INDEX.[1]

a, ab, 8, *a*; 264-7; 314; 326; 330; 332, 1; 387.
abhinc, 324.
absolvo, 306.
absum, 251, *Obs.*; *impers.*, 132, *a.*
accidit, 123, *and Obs.*; 246; 487, *a*; p. 376, *n.*
acclamo, p. 364, *n.*
acies, p. 367, *n.*
acta, 19; 408.
accuso, 306; p. 390, *n.*
ad, 252; 311, *Obs.*; 313; 326; 330, 331, 1.
adeo, 107; 124.
adhortor, 127, *a.*
adimo, 243, *and note*; 247.
adipiscor, p. 379, *n.*
admoneo, 127, *a*; 308, *a.*
adolescens, 51, *a, and note*; 55; 63; 408.
adsum, 251, *and note.*
adversus (*adj.*), 61.
adversus (*prep.*), 330; 331, 2.
aequalis, 51, *a*; 256.
affinis, 256; 301, ii.
ait, 162.
aliquando, p. 379, *n.*; p. 388, *n.*
aliquis, 360, i.; 381.
aliter, 91; lxii.; 491, *Obs.* 2.
alius, 91; 92; 367-71.
alter, 368-9; 372; 531.
ambio, p. 358, *n.*
ambo, 378, i.
amicus, 51, *a*; 55; 256.
amo, p. 376, *n.*
amoenus, Voc. 9, *n.*
amplius, 318, *Obs*
an, 155; 159-61; 168-9; 171.
ante, 252; 322; 330; 331, 3.
ante diem, 540.
antequam, 442-3.
antiquus, p. 355, *n*
apparet, 46, *c.*
aptus, 255, *Obs.*
apud, 330, 331, 4.
arbitror, p. 367, *n.*
arguo, 306; p. 390, *n.*
aspernor, Voc. 10, *n.*
aspicio, p. 386, *n.*

assuetus, assuefactus, 255, *Obs.*
atque, p. 14, *n.*; 90, 91; lxii.
auctoritas, p. 373, *n.*
audio, 23; 410, *Obs.*
aut, p. 14, *n.*; 29; 171; 467, *caution.*
autem, Intr. 98.
auxilio, 260, 1.
aversus, 61.
avi, 51, *a, note.*

beate vivere, beatum esse, 98, *a.*
bene, 252.
benevolus, 255, *Obs.*
boni, 50, *n.*; bona, 51,

calamitas, p. 364, *n.*
candidatus, 51, *a*; 408.
capax, 301, i.
careo, 284.
casus, p. 364, *n.*
causa (*abl.*), 289; 329, *Obs.*
caveo, 248.
celo, 230-1.
censeo, p. 367, *n.*
cerno, p. 386, *n.*
certe, p. 375, *n.*
certiorem facio, 301, *Obs.*
cesso, p. 370, *n.*
ceteri, 372.
circum; circa, 330; 331, 5.
circumdo, 250.
circumfluo, 284.
cis, citra, 330; 331, 6.
coepi, 42, i. *b*; 216; coeptum est, 219.
commonefacio, 308.
compleo, 284.
condemno, 306-7.
condono, 247.
confido, 244, *c*; 253, i.; 282, *Obs.*
conor, 120.
consequor, p. 379, *n.*
conspicio, p. 386, *n.*
constat, 46, *c.*
consto, 280, *Obs.*
constituo, 45.
consulo, 248; 391, *Obs.*

contemno, Voc. 10, *n.*
contentus, 285.
contingit, 246; p. 376, *n.*
contra, 91; 330; 331, 7; 491, *b.*
corona, 17.
credo, 32, *b*; 217, *and note*; 248; 391, *Obs.*
culpae do, 260, 2.
cum, 8, *b, and Obs.*; 252; 269 *and Obs.*; 270; 330; 332, 2.
cunctor, p. 370, *n.*
cunctus, p. 354, *n.*
cupio, 41, *a*; 42, i. *d*; 120.
cur, 157, ii.; 174, *and note.*
curo, 121; 400.

damno, 307.
de, 296; 306, *Obs.*; 330; 332, 3.
de integro, 328, *f.*
debeo, 42, i. *c*; 153; 198, i., *and note.*
decedo, 410, *n.*
decet, dedecet, 234.
deficio, p. 353, *n.*
delictum, 408; p. 361, *n.*
demum, 347; 443, *Obs.*
denique, 443, *Obs.*; 534, *Obs.*
desero, p. 353, *n.*
desitum est, 219.
despicio, Voc. 10, *n.*
destituo, p. 353, *n.*
desum, 251; p. 353, *n.*
dico, 32, *b*; 44; p. 388, *n.*; dicor, 43.
dictito, p. 382, *n.*
dicto audiens sum, p. 379, *n.*
dies, 328, *c*; Voc. 1, *n.*
differo, p. 370, *n.*
dignor, 281.
dignus, 285.
diligo, p. 376, *n.*
dissensio, 300.
dissimulo, 39, *note.*
diu, 181.
diurnus, 328, *c.*
diutinus, diuturnus, p. 375, *n.*
diversus, 61; 371, *caution.*
divites, 51, *a, and note.*
do, 259; 400.

---

1 This Index is chiefly limited to words specially noticed. Many, therefore, which occur merely as examples, or in the Vocabulary will not be contained in it.

velim, 126 ; 141.
velut, lxii.
vereor, 138, 139 ; p. 367, *n.*
vero, Intr. 98.
versus, p. 216, *n.* ; 330, 331, 22.
verto, 250.
vendo, 280 ; 305.
vēnire, 280, *Obs.*
venum dare, 235.

vescor, 281.
vesperi, 312.
veto, 120 ; 245 ; 127, *a* ; 137, ii.
vetus, vetustus, p. 355, *n.*
vicem, 238, iii.
vicinus, 256.
video, 118 ; 410, *Obs.* ; p. 386, *n.* : videor, 43: videtur, 46, *b* ; 202 : videro, 146.

vilis, 19.
vir, 224 *and note*; Ex. 39, *n.* 6.
vitium, p. 361, *n.* : **vitio** verto, 260, 2.
vix, 130.
vixi, 187.
volo, 41, *a* ; 42, i. *d* ; 46, *d* ; 120 ; 240.
vulgus, 254, *and note.*